A COURT OF THORNS AND ROSES

"Simply dazzles." —*Booklist*, starred review

"Passionate, violent, sexy and daring. . . . A true page-turner." —*USA Today*

"Suspense, romance, intrigue and action. This is not a book to be missed!" —HuffPost

"Vicious and intoxicating. . . . A dazzling world, complex characters and sizzling romance." —*RT Book Reviews*, Top Pick

"A sexy, action-packed fairytale." —Bustle

A COURT OF MIST AND FURY

"Fiercely romantic, irresistibly sexy and hypnotically magical. A veritable feast for the senses." —*USA Today*

"Hits the spot for fans of dark, lush, sexy fantasy." —*Kirkus Reviews*

"An immersive, satisfying read." —*Publishers Weekly*

"Darkly sexy and thrilling." —Bustle

A COURT OF WINGS AND RUIN

"Fast-paced and explosively action-packed." —*Booklist*

"The plot manages to seduce you with its alluring characters, irresistible world and never-ending action, leaving you craving more." —*RT Book Reviews*

BOOKS BY SARAH J. MAAS

THE COURT OF THORNS AND ROSES SERIES

A Court of Thorns and Roses

A Court of Mist and Fury

A Court of Wings and Ruin

A Court of Frost and Starlight

A Court of Silver Flames

A Court of Thorns and Roses Colouring Book

THE CRESCENT CITY SERIES

House of Earth and Blood

House of Sky and Breath

THE THRONE OF GLASS SERIES

The Assassin's Blade

Throne of Glass

Crown of Midnight

Heir of Fire

Queen of Shadows

Empire of Storms

Tower of Dawn

Kingdom of Ash

The Throne of Glass Colouring Book

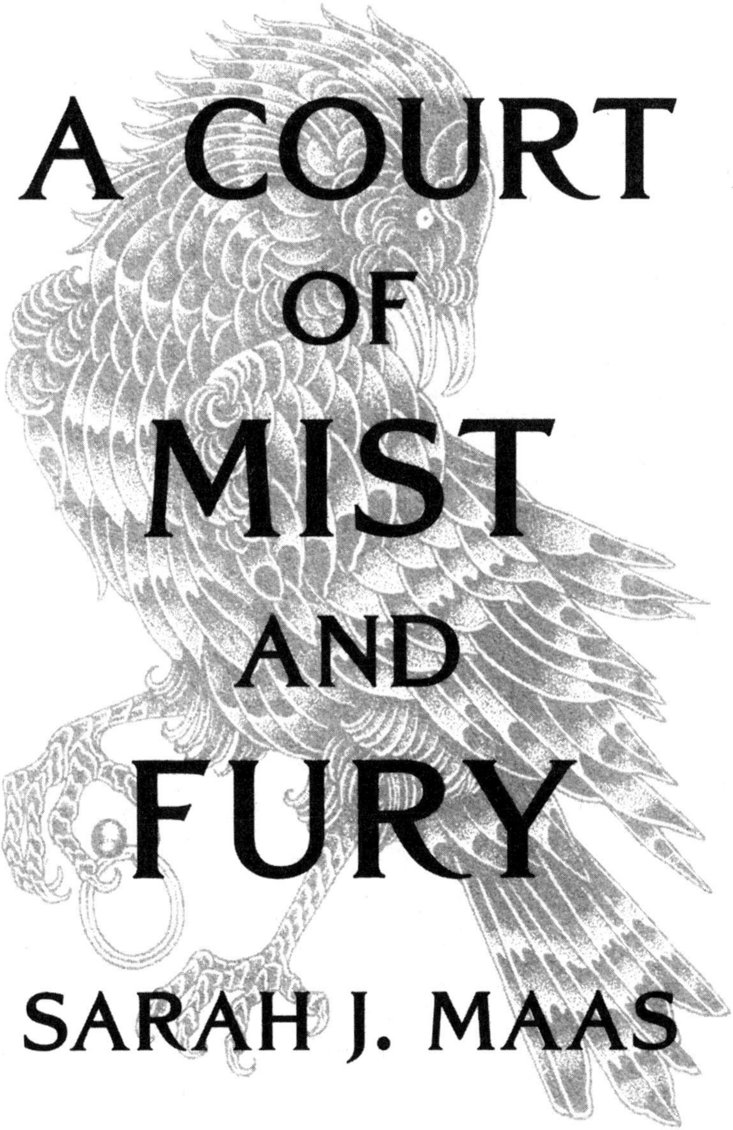

A COURT OF MIST AND FURY

SARAH J. MAAS

B L O O M S B U R Y P U B L I S H I N G
LONDON • OXFORD • NEW YORK • NEW DELHI • SYDNEY

BLOOMSBURY PUBLISHING
Bloomsbury Publishing Plc
50 Bedford Square, London, WC1B 3DP, UK
29 Earlsfort Terrace, Dublin 2, Ireland

BLOOMSBURY, BLOOMSBURY PUBLISHING and the Diana logo are trademarks of Bloomsbury Publishing Plc

First published in Great Britain 2016
This paperback edition published 2021

A catalogue record for this book is available from the British Library

ISBN: PB: 978-1-5266-4114-4

5 7 9 10 8 6

Typeset by Westchester Publishing Services
Printed and bound in India by Thomson Press India Ltd

FSC www.fsc.org
MIX
Paper from responsible sources
FSC® C010615

To find out more about our authors and books visit www.bloomsbury.com and sign up for our newsletters, including news about Sarah J. Maas.

For sale in the Indian subcontinent only

For Josh and Annie—
my own Court of Dreams

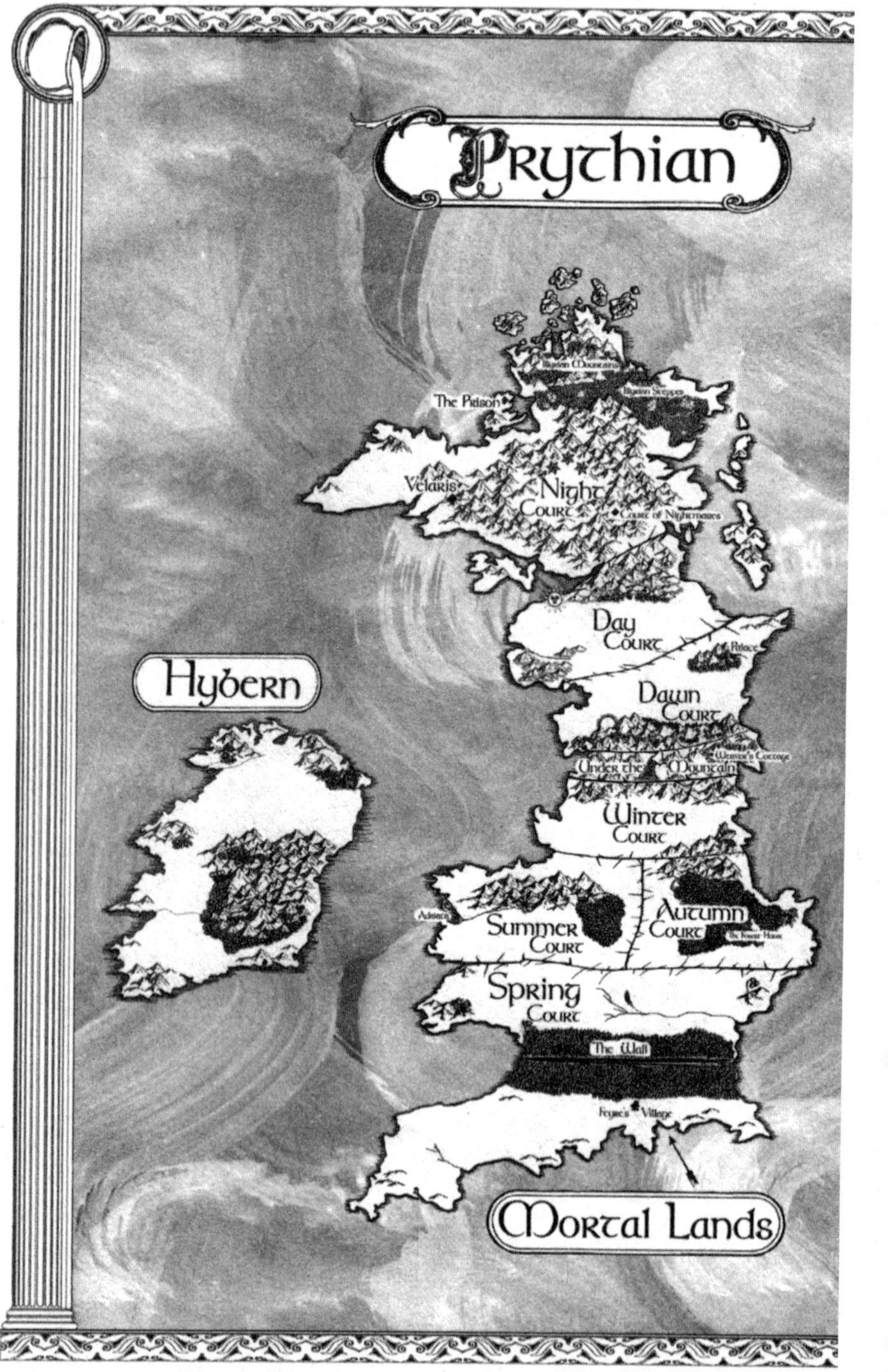
Prythian
The Prison
Velaris
Night Court
Court of Nightmares
Day Court
Palace
Hybern
Dawn Court
Under the Mountain
Winter Court
Summer Court
Autumn Court
Spring Court
The Wall
Mortal Lands

Vallahan
Montesere
Rask
Faerie Realms
North to Faerie Realms
The Wall
Scythia
South to Mortal Lands
Mortal Lands

Maybe I'd always been broken and dark inside.

Maybe someone who'd been born whole and good would have put down the ash dagger and embraced death rather than what lay before me.

There was blood everywhere.

It was an effort to keep a grip on the dagger as my blood-soaked hand trembled. As I fractured bit by bit while the sprawled corpse of the High Fae youth cooled on the marble floor.

I couldn't let go of the blade, couldn't move from my place before him.

"Good," Amarantha purred from her throne. "Again."

There was another ash dagger waiting, and another Fae kneeling. Female.

I knew the words she'd say. The prayer she'd recite.

I knew I'd slaughter her, as I'd slaughtered the youth before me.

To free them all, to free Tamlin, I would do it.

I was the butcher of innocents, and the savior of a land.

"Whenever you're ready, lovely Feyre," Amarantha drawled, her deep red hair as bright as the blood on my hands. On the marble.

Murderer. Butcher. Monster. Liar. Deceiver.

I didn't know who I meant. The lines between me and the queen had long since blurred.

My fingers loosened on the dagger, and it clattered to the ground, splattering the spreading pool of blood. Flecks splashed onto my worn boots—remnants of a mortal life so far behind me it might as well have been one of my fever-dreams these few last months.

I faced the female waiting for death, that hood sagging over her head, her lithe body steady. Braced for the end I was to give her, the sacrifice she was to become.

I reached for the second ash dagger atop a black velvet pillow, its hilt icy in my warm, damp hand. The guards yanked off her hood.

I knew the face that stared up at me.

Knew the blue-gray eyes, the brown-gold hair, the full mouth and sharp cheekbones. Knew the ears that had now become delicately arched, the limbs that had been streamlined, limned with power, any human imperfections smoothed into a subtle immortal glow.

Knew the hollowness, the despair, the corruption that leaked from that face.

My hands didn't tremble as I angled the dagger.

As I gripped the fine-boned shoulder, and gazed into that hated face—*my* face.

And plunged the ash dagger into my awaiting heart.

PART ONE

THE HOUSE OF BEASTS

CHAPTER 1

I vomited into the toilet, hugging the cool sides, trying to contain the sounds of my retching.

Moonlight leaked into the massive marble bathing room, providing the only illumination as I was quietly, thoroughly sick.

Tamlin hadn't stirred as I'd jolted awake. And when I hadn't been able to tell the darkness of my chamber from the endless night of Amarantha's dungeons, when the cold sweat coating me felt like the blood of those faeries, I'd hurtled for the bathing room.

I'd been here for fifteen minutes now, waiting for the retching to subside, for the lingering tremors to spread apart and fade, like ripples in a pool.

Panting, I braced myself over the bowl, counting each breath.

Only a nightmare. One of many, asleep and waking, that haunted me these days.

It had been three months since Under the Mountain. Three months of adjusting to my immortal body, to a world struggling to piece itself together after Amarantha had fractured it apart.

I focused on my breathing—in through my nose, out through my mouth. Over and over.

When it seemed like I was done heaving, I eased from the toilet—but didn't go far. Just to the adjacent wall, near the cracked window, where I could see the night sky, where the breeze could caress my sticky face. I leaned my head against the wall, flattening my hands against the chill marble floor. Real.

This was real. I had survived; I'd made it out.

Unless it was a dream—just a fever-dream in Amarantha's dungeons, and I'd awaken back in that cell, and—

I curled my knees to my chest. Real. *Real.*

I mouthed the words.

I kept mouthing them until I could loosen my grip on my legs and lift my head. Pain splintered through my hands—

I'd somehow curled them into fists so tight my nails were close to puncturing my skin.

Immortal strength—more a curse than a gift. I'd dented and folded every piece of silverware I'd touched for three days upon returning here, had tripped over my longer, faster legs so often that Alis had removed any irreplaceable valuables from my rooms (she'd been particularly grumpy about me knocking over a table with an eight-hundred-year-old vase), and had shattered not one, not two, but *five* glass doors merely by accidentally closing them too hard.

Sighing through my nose, I unfolded my fingers.

My right hand was plain, smooth. Perfectly Fae.

I tilted my left hand over, the whorls of dark ink coating my fingers, my wrist, my forearm all the way to the elbow, soaking up the darkness of the room. The eye etched into the center of my palm seemed to watch me, calm and cunning as a cat, its slitted pupil wider than it'd been earlier that day. As if it adjusted to the light, as any ordinary eye would.

I scowled at it.

At whoever might be watching through that tattoo.

I hadn't heard from Rhys in the three months I'd been here. Not a whisper. I hadn't dared ask Tamlin, or Lucien, or anyone—lest it'd somehow summon the High Lord of the Night Court, somehow remind him of the fool's bargain I'd struck Under the Mountain: one week with him every month in exchange for his saving me from the brink of death.

But even if Rhys had miraculously forgotten, I never could. Nor could Tamlin, Lucien, or anyone else. Not with the tattoo.

Even if Rhys, at the end . . . even if he hadn't been exactly an enemy.

To Tamlin, yes. To every other court out there, yes. So few went over the borders of the Night Court and lived to tell. No one really knew what *existed* in the northernmost part of Prythian.

Mountains and darkness and stars and death.

But I hadn't felt like Rhysand's enemy the last time I'd spoken to him, in the hours after Amarantha's defeat. I'd told no one about that meeting, what he'd said to me, what I'd confessed to him.

Be glad of your human heart, Feyre. Pity those who don't feel anything at all.

I squeezed my fingers into a fist, blocking out that eye, the tattoo. I uncoiled to my feet, and flushed the toilet before padding to the sink to rinse out my mouth, then wash my face.

I wished I felt nothing.

I wished my human heart had been changed with the rest of me, made into immortal marble. Instead of the shredded bit of blackness that it now was, leaking its ichor into me.

Tamlin remained asleep as I crept back into my darkened bedroom, his naked body sprawled across the mattress. For a moment, I just admired the powerful muscles of his back, so lovingly traced by the moonlight, his golden hair, mussed with sleep and the fingers I'd run through it while we made love earlier.

For him, I had done this—for him, I'd gladly wrecked myself and my immortal soul.

And now I had eternity to live with it.

I continued to the bed, each step heavier, harder. The sheets were now cool and dry, and I slipped in, curling my back to him, wrapping my arms around myself. His breathing was deep—even. But with my Fae ears . . . sometimes I wondered if I heard his breath catch, only for a heartbeat. I never had the nerve to ask if he was awake.

He never woke when the nightmares dragged me from sleep; never woke when I vomited my guts up night after night. If he knew or heard, he said nothing about it.

I knew similar dreams chased him from his slumber as often as I fled from mine. The first time it had happened, I'd awoken—tried to speak to him. But he'd shaken off my touch, his skin clammy, and had shifted into that beast of fur and claws and horns and fangs. He'd spent the rest of the night sprawled across the foot of the bed, monitoring the door, the wall of windows.

He'd since spent many nights like that.

Curled in the bed, I pulled the blanket higher, craving its warmth against the chill night. It had become our unspoken agreement—not to let Amarantha win by acknowledging that she still tormented us in our dreams and waking hours.

It was easier to not have to explain, anyway. To not have to tell him that though I'd freed him, saved his people and all of Prythian from Amarantha . . . I'd broken myself apart.

And I didn't think even eternity would be long enough to fix me.

CHAPTER 2

"I want to go."

"No."

I crossed my arms, tucking my tattooed hand under my right bicep, and spread my feet slightly further apart on the dirt floor of the stables. "It's been three months. Nothing's happened, and the village isn't even five miles—"

"No." The midmorning sun streaming through the stable doors burnished Tamlin's golden hair as he finished buckling the bandolier of daggers across his chest. His face—ruggedly handsome, exactly as I'd dreamed it during those long months he'd worn a mask—was set, his lips a thin line.

Behind him, already atop his dapple-gray horse, along with three other Fae lord-sentries, Lucien silently shook his head in warning, his metal eye narrowing. *Don't push him*, he seemed to say.

But as Tamlin strode toward where his black stallion had already been saddled, I gritted my teeth and stormed after him. "The village needs all the help it can get."

"And we're still hunting down Amarantha's beasts," he said,

mounting his horse in one fluid motion. Sometimes, I wondered if the horses were just to maintain an appearance of civility—of normalcy. To pretend that he couldn't run faster than them, didn't live with one foot in the forest. His green eyes were like chips of ice as the stallion started into a walk. "I don't have the sentries to spare to escort you."

I lunged for the bridle. "I don't need an escort." My grip tightened on the leather as I tugged the horse to a stop, and the golden ring on my finger—along with the square-cut emerald glittering atop it—flashed in the sun.

It had been two months since Tamlin had proposed—two months of enduring presentations about flowers and clothes and seating arrangements and food. I'd had a small reprieve a week ago, thanks to the Winter Solstice, though I'd traded contemplating lace and silk for selecting evergreen wreaths and garlands. But at least it had been a break.

Three days of feasting and drinking and exchanging small presents, culminating in a long, rather odious ceremony atop the foothills on the longest night to escort us from one year to another as the sun died and was born anew. Or something like that. Celebrating a winter holiday in a place that was permanently entrenched in spring hadn't done much to improve my general lack of festive cheer.

I hadn't particularly listened to the explanations of its origins—and the Fae themselves debated whether it had emerged from the Winter Court or Day Court. Both now claimed it as their holiest holiday. All I really knew was that I'd had to endure two ceremonies: one at sunset to begin that endless night of presents and dancing and drinking in honor of the old sun's death; and one at the following dawn, bleary-eyed and feet aching, to welcome the sun's rebirth.

It was bad enough that I'd been required to stand before the gathered courtiers and lesser faeries while Tamlin made his many toasts and salutes. Mentioning that my birthday had also fallen on that longest night of the year was a fact I'd conveniently forgotten to tell anyone. I'd received enough presents, anyway—and would no doubt receive many, many more on my wedding day. I had little use for so many *things*.

Now, only two weeks stood between me and the ceremony. If I didn't get out of the manor, if I didn't have a day to do *something* other than spend Tamlin's money and be groveled to—

"Please. The recovery efforts are so slow. I could hunt for the villagers, get them food—"

"It's not safe," Tamlin said, again nudging his stallion into a walk. The horse's coat shone like a dark mirror, even in the shade of the stables. "Especially not for you."

He'd said that every time we had this argument; every time I begged him to let me go to the nearby village of High Fae to help rebuild what Amarantha had burned years ago.

I followed him into the bright, cloudless day beyond the stables, the grasses coating the nearby foothills undulating in the soft breeze. "People want to come back, they want a place to *live*—"

"Those same people see you as a blessing—a marker of stability. If something happened to you . . . " He cut himself off as he halted his horse at the edge of the dirt path that would take him toward the eastern woods, Lucien now waiting a few yards down it. "There's no point in rebuilding anything if Amarantha's creatures tear through the lands and destroy it again."

"The wards are up—"

"Some slipped in before the wards were repaired. Lucien hunted down five naga yesterday."

I whipped my head toward Lucien, who winced. He hadn't told me that at dinner last night. He'd *lied* when I'd asked him why he was limping. My stomach turned over—not just at the lie, but . . . naga. Sometimes I dreamed of their blood showering me as I killed them, of their leering serpentine faces while they tried to fillet me in the woods.

Tamlin said softly, "I can't do what I need to if I'm worrying about whether you're safe."

"Of course I'll be safe." As a High Fae, with my strength and speed, I'd stand a good chance of getting away if something happened.

"Please—please just do this for me," Tamlin said, stroking his stallion's thick neck as the beast nickered with impatience. The others had already moved their horses into easy canters, the first of them nearly within the shade of the woods. Tamlin jerked his chin toward the alabaster estate looming behind me. "I'm sure there are things to help with around the house. Or you could paint. Try out that new set I gave you for Winter Solstice."

There was nothing but wedding planning waiting for me in the house, since Alis refused to let me lift a finger to do anything. Not because of who I was to Tamlin, what I was about to become to Tamlin, but . . . because of what I'd done for her, for her boys, for Prythian. All the servants were the same; some still cried with gratitude when they passed me in the halls. And as for painting . . .

"Fine," I breathed. I made myself look him in the eye, made myself smile. "Be careful," I said, and meant it. The thought of him going out there, hunting the monsters that had once served Amarantha . . .

"I love you," Tamlin said quietly.

I nodded, murmuring it back as he trotted to where Lucien still waited, the emissary now frowning slightly. I didn't watch them go.

I took my time retreating through the hedges of the gardens, the spring birds chirping merrily, gravel crunching under my flimsy shoes.

I hated the bright dresses that had become my daily uniform, but didn't have the heart to tell Tamlin—not when he'd bought so many, not when he looked so happy to see me wear them. Not when his words weren't far from the truth. The day I put on my pants and tunics, the day I strapped weapons to myself like fine jewelry, it would send a message far and clear across the lands. So I wore the gowns, and let Alis arrange my hair—if only so it would buy these people a measure of peace and comfort.

At least Tamlin didn't object to the dagger I kept at my side, hanging from a jeweled belt. Lucien had gifted both to me—the dagger during the months before Amarantha, the belt in the weeks after her downfall, when I'd carried the dagger, along with many others, everywhere I went. *You might as well look good if you're going to arm yourself to the teeth*, he'd said.

But even if stability reigned for a hundred years, I doubted I'd ever awaken one morning and not put on the knife.

A hundred years.

I had that—I had centuries ahead of me. Centuries with Tamlin, centuries in this beautiful, quiet place. Perhaps I'd sort myself out sometime along the way. Perhaps not.

I paused before the stairs leading up into the rose-and-ivy-covered house, and peeked toward the right—toward the formal rose garden and the windows just beyond it.

I'd only set foot in that room—my old painting studio—once, when I'd first returned.

And all those paintings, all the supplies, all that blank canvas waiting for me to pour out stories and feelings and dreams . . . I'd hated it.

I'd walked out moments later and hadn't returned since.

I'd stopped cataloging color and feeling and texture, stopped noticing it. I could barely look at the paintings hanging inside the manor.

A sweet, female voice trilled my name from inside the open doors of the manor, and the tightness in my shoulders eased a bit.

Ianthe. The High Priestess, as well as a High Fae noble and childhood friend of Tamlin's, who had taken it upon herself to help plan the wedding festivities.

And who had taken it upon herself to worship me and Tamlin as if we were newly minted gods, blessed and chosen by the Cauldron itself.

But I didn't complain—not when Ianthe knew everyone in the court and outside of it. She'd linger by my side at events and dinners, feeding me details about those in attendance, and was the main reason why I'd survived the merry whirlwind of Winter Solstice. She'd been the one presiding over the various ceremonies, after all—and I'd been more than happy to let her choose what manner of wreaths and garlands should adorn the manor and grounds, what silverware complemented each meal.

Beyond that . . . while Tamlin was the one who paid for my everyday clothes, it was Ianthe's eye that selected them. She was the heart of her people, ordained by the Hand of the Goddess to lead them from despair and darkness.

I was in no position to doubt. She hadn't led me astray yet—and I'd learned to dread the days when she was busy at her own temple on the grounds, overseeing pilgrims and her acolytes. Today, though—yes, spending time with Ianthe was better than the alternative.

I bunched the gauzy skirts of my dawn-pink gown in a hand and ascended the marble steps into the house.

Next time, I promised myself. Next time, I'd convince Tamlin to let me go to the village.

"Oh, we can't let *her* sit next to him. They'd rip each other to shreds, and then we'd have blood ruining the table linens." Beneath her pale, blue-gray hood, Ianthe furrowed her brow, crinkling the tattoo of the various stages of a moon's cycle stamped across it. She scribbled out the name she'd dashed onto one of the seating charts moments before.

The day had turned warm, the room a bit stuffy even with the breeze through the open windows. And yet the heavy hooded robe remained on.

All the High Priestesses wore the billowing, artfully twisted and layered robes—though they certainly were far from matronly. Ianthe's slim waist was on display with a fine belt of sky-blue, limpid stones, each perfectly oval and held in shining silver. And atop her hood sat a matching circlet—a delicate band of silver, with a large stone at its center. A panel of cloth had been folded up beneath the circlet, a built-in swath meant to be pulled over the brow and eyes when she needed to pray, beseech the Cauldron and Mother, or just think.

Ianthe had shown me once what the panel looked like when down: only her nose and full, sensuous mouth visible. The Voice of the Cauldron. I'd found the image unsettling—that merely covering the upper part of her face had somehow turned the bright, cunning female into an effigy, into something Other. Mercifully, she kept it folded back most of the time. Occasionally, she even took the hood off entirely to let the sun play in her long, gently curling golden hair.

Ianthe's silver rings gleamed atop her manicured fingers as she wrote another name down. "It's like a game," she said, sighing through her pert nose. "All these pieces, vying for power or dominance, willing to shed blood, if need be. It must be a strange adjustment for you."

Such elegance and wealth—yet the savagery remained. The High Fae weren't the tittering nobility of the mortal world. No, if they feuded, it *would* end with someone being ripped to bloody ribbons. Literally.

Once, I'd trembled to share breathing space with them.

I flexed my fingers, stretching and contorting the tattoos etched into my skin.

Now I could fight alongside them, against them. Not that I'd tried.

I was too watched—too monitored and judged. Why should the bride of the High Lord learn to fight if peace had returned? That had been Ianthe's reasoning when I'd made the mistake of mentioning it at dinner. Tamlin, to his credit, had seen both sides: I'd learn to protect myself . . . but the rumors would spread.

"Humans aren't much better," I told her at last. And because Ianthe was about the only one of my new companions who didn't look particularly stunned or frightened by me, I tried to make conversation and said, "My sister Nesta would likely fit right in."

Ianthe cocked her head, the sunlight setting the blue stone atop her hood glimmering. "*Will* your mortal kin be joining us?"

"No." I hadn't thought to invite them—hadn't wanted to expose them to Prythian. Or to what I'd become.

She tapped a long, slender finger on the table. "But they live so close to the wall, don't they? If it was important for you to have them here, Tamlin and I could ensure their safe journey." In the hours we'd spent together, I'd told her about the village, and the house my sisters now lived in, about Isaac Hale and Tomas Mandray. I hadn't been able to mention Clare Beddor—or what had happened to her family.

"For all that she'd hold her own," I said, fighting past the memory of that human girl, and what had been done to her, "my sister Nesta detests your kind."

"*Our* kind," Ianthe corrected quietly. "We've discussed this."

I just nodded.

But she went on, "We are old, and cunning, and enjoy using words like blades and claws. Every word from your mouth, every turn of phrase, will be judged—and possibly used against you." As if to soften the warning, she added, "Be on your guard, Lady."

Lady. A nonsense name. No one knew what to call me. I wasn't born High Fae.

I'd been Made—resurrected and given this new body by the seven High Lords of Prythian. I wasn't Tamlin's mate, as far as I knew. There was no mating bond between us—yet.

Honestly . . . Honestly, Ianthe, with her bright gold hair, those teal eyes, elegant features, and supple body, looked more like Tamlin's mate. His equal. A union with Tamlin—a High Lord and a High Priestess—would send a clear message of strength to any possible threats to our lands. And secure the power Ianthe was no doubt keen on building for herself.

Among the High Fae, the priestesses oversaw their ceremonies and rituals, recorded their histories and legends, and advised their lords and ladies in matters great and trivial. I hadn't witnessed any magic from her, but when I'd asked Lucien, he'd frowned and said their magic was drawn from their ceremonies, and could be utterly lethal should they choose it. I'd watched her on the Winter Solstice for any signs of it, marking the way she'd positioned herself so that the rising sun filled her uplifted arms, but there had been no ripple or thrum of power. From her, or the earth beneath us.

I didn't know what I'd really expected from Ianthe—one of the twelve High Priestesses who together governed their sisters across every territory in Prythian. Ancient, celibate, and quiet had been the extent of my expectations, thanks to those whispered mortal legends, when Tamlin had announced that an old friend was soon to occupy and renovate the crumbling temple complex on our lands. But Ianthe had breezed into our house the next morning and those expectations had immediately been trampled. Especially the celibate part.

Priestesses could marry, bear children, and dally as they would. It would dishonor the Cauldron's gift of fertility to lock up their instincts, their inherent female magic in bearing life, Ianthe had once told me.

So while the seven High Lords ruled Prythian from thrones, the twelve High Priestesses reigned from the altars, their children as powerful and respected as any lord's offspring. And Ianthe, the youngest High Priestess in three centuries, remained unmarried, childless, and keen to *enjoy the finest males the land has to offer.*

I often wondered what it was like to be that free and so settled within yourself.

When I didn't respond to her gentle reprimand, she said, "Have you given any thought to what color roses? White? Pink? Yellow? Red—"

"Not red."

I hated that color. More than anything. Amarantha's hair, all that blood, the welts on Clare Beddor's broken body, spiked to the walls of Under the Mountain—

"Russet could be pretty, with all the green . . . But maybe that's too Autumn Court." Again, that finger tapped on the table.

"Whatever color you want." If I were being blunt with myself, I'd admit that Ianthe had become a crutch. But she seemed willing to do it—caring when I couldn't bring myself to.

Yet Ianthe's brows lifted slightly.

Despite being a High Priestess, she and her family had escaped the horrors of Under the Mountain by running. Her father, one of Tamlin's strongest allies amongst the Spring Court and a captain in his forces, had sensed trouble coming and packed off Ianthe, her mother, and two younger sisters to Vallahan, one of the countless faerie territories across the ocean. For fifty years, they'd lived in the foreign court, biding their time while their people were butchered and enslaved.

She hadn't once mentioned it. I knew better than to ask.

"Every element of this wedding sends a message to not only Prythian, but the world beyond," she said. I stifled a sigh. I knew—she'd told me this before. "I know you are not fond of the dress—"

Understatement. I hated the monstrosity of tulle she'd selected. Tamlin had, too—though he'd laughed himself hoarse when I showed him in the privacy of my room. But he'd promised me that though the dress was absurd, the priestess knew what she was doing. I'd wanted to push back about it, hating that though he agreed with me, he had sided with her, but . . . it took more energy than it was worth.

Ianthe went on, "But it makes the right statement. I've spent time amongst enough courts to know how they operate. Trust me in this."

"I do trust you," I said, and waved a hand toward the papers before us. "You know how to do these things. I don't."

Silver tinkled at Ianthe's wrists, so like the bracelets the Children of the Blessed wore on the other side of the wall. I sometimes wondered if those foolish humans had stolen the idea from the High Priestesses of Prythian—if it had been a priestess like Ianthe who had spread such nonsense among humans.

"It's an important moment for me as well," Ianthe said carefully, adjusting the circlet atop her hood. Teal eyes met mine. "You and I are so alike—young, untested amongst these . . . wolves. I am grateful to you, and to Tamlin, to allow me to preside over the ceremony, to be invited to work with this court, be a part of this court. The other High Priestesses do not particularly care for me, nor I for them, but . . . " She shook her head, the hood swaying with her. "Together," she murmured, "the three of us make a formidable unit. Four, if you count Lucien." She snorted. "Not that he particularly wants anything to do with me."

A leading statement.

She often found ways to bring him up, to corner him at events, to touch his elbow or shoulder. He ignored it all. Last week, I'd finally asked him if she'd set her sights on him, and Lucien had merely given me a look, snarling softly, before stalking off. I took that as a yes.

But a match with Lucien would be nearly as beneficial as one with Tamlin: the right hand of a High Lord *and* another High Lord's son . . . Any offspring would be powerful, coveted.

"You know it's . . . hard for him, where females are involved," I said neutrally.

"He has been with *many* females since the death of his lover."

"Perhaps it's different with you—perhaps it'd mean something he's not ready for." I shrugged, searching for the right words. "Perhaps he stays away because of it."

She considered, and I prayed she bought my half lie. Ianthe was ambitious, clever, beautiful, and bold—but I did not think Lucien forgave her, or would ever forgive her, for fleeing during Amarantha's reign. Sometimes I honestly wondered if my friend might rip her throat out for it.

Ianthe nodded at last. "Are you at least excited for the wedding?"

I fiddled with my emerald ring. "It'll be the happiest day of my life."

The day Tamlin had asked me to marry him, I'd certainly felt that way. I'd wept with joy as I told him yes, yes, a thousand times yes, and made love to him in the field of wildflowers where he'd brought me for the occasion.

Ianthe nodded. "The union is Cauldron-blessed. Your survival of the horrors Under the Mountain only proves it."

I caught her glance then—toward my left hand, the tattoos.

It was an effort not to tuck my hand beneath the table.

The tattoo on her brow was of midnight-blue ink—but somehow still fit, still accented the feminine dresses, the bright silver jewelry. Unlike the elegant brutality of mine.

"We could get you gloves," she offered casually.

And that would send another message—perhaps to the person I so desperately hoped had forgotten I existed.

"I'll consider it," I said with a bland smile.

It was all I could do to keep from bolting before the hour was up and Ianthe floated to her own personal prayer room—a gift from Tamlin upon her return—to offer midday thanks to the Cauldron for our land's liberation, my triumph, and Tamlin's ensured dominance over this land.

I sometimes debated asking her to pray for me as well.

To pray that I'd one day learn to love the dresses, and the parties, and my role as a blushing, pretty bride.

I was already in bed when Tamlin entered my room, silent as a stag through a wood. I lifted my head, going for the dagger I kept on the nightstand, but relaxed at the broad shoulders, at the hallway candle-light gilding his tan skin and veiling his face in shadow.

"You're awake?" he murmured. I could hear the frown in his voice. He'd been in his study since dinner, sorting through the pile of paper-work Lucien had dumped on his desk.

"I couldn't sleep," I said, watching his muscles shift as he moved to the bathing room to wash up. I'd been trying to sleep for an hour now—but each time I closed my eyes, my body locked up, the walls of the room pushed in. I'd gone so far as to throw open the windows, but . . . It was going to be a long night.

I lay back on the pillows, listening to the steady, efficient sounds of him preparing for bed. He kept his own quarters, deeming it vital for me to have my own space.

But he slept in here every night. I'd yet to visit his bed, though I wondered if our wedding night would change that. I prayed I wouldn't thrash awake and vomit on the sheets when I didn't recognize where I was, when I didn't know if the darkness was permanent.

Maybe that was why he hadn't pushed the issue yet.

He emerged from the bathing room, slinging off his tunic and shirt, and I propped myself on my elbows to watch as he paused at the edge of the bed.

My attention went right to the strong, clever fingers that unfastened his pants.

Tamlin let out a low snarl of approval, and I bit my bottom lip as he removed his pants, along with his undergarments, revealing the proud, thick length of him. My mouth went dry, and I dragged my gaze up his muscled torso, over the panes of his chest, and then—

"Come here," he growled, so roughly the words were barely discernable.

I pushed back the blankets, revealing my already naked body, and he hissed.

His features turned ravenous while I crawled across the bed and rose up on my knees. I took his face in my hands, the golden skin framed on either side by fingers of ivory and of swirling black, and kissed him.

He held my gaze through the kiss, even as I pushed myself closer, biting back a small noise when he brushed against my stomach.

His callused hands grazed my hips, my waist, then held me there as he lowered his head, seizing the kiss. A brush of his tongue against the seam of my lips had me opening fully for him, and he swept in, claiming me, branding me.

I moaned then, tilting my head back to give him better access. His hands clamped on my waist, then moved—one going to cup my rear, the other sliding between us.

This—this moment, when it was him and me and nothing between our bodies . . .

His tongue scraped the roof of my mouth as he dragged a finger down the center of me, and I gasped, my back arching. "Feyre," he said against my lips, my name like a prayer more devout than any Ianthe had offered up to the Cauldron on that dark solstice morning.

His tongue swept my mouth again, in time to the finger that he slipped inside of me. My hips undulated, demanding more, craving the fullness of him, and his growl reverberated in my chest as he added another finger.

I moved on him. Lightning lashed through my veins, and my focus narrowed to his fingers, his mouth, his body on mine. His palm pushed against the bundle of nerves at the apex of my thighs, and I groaned his name as I shattered.

My head thrown back, I gulped down night-cool air, and then I was being lowered to the bed, gently, delicately, lovingly.

He stretched out above me, his head lowering to my breast, and all it took was one press of his teeth against my nipple before I was clawing at his back, before I hooked my legs around him and he settled between them. This—I needed *this*.

He paused, arms trembling as he held himself over me.

"Please," I gasped out.

He just brushed his lips against my jaw, my neck, my mouth.

"Tamlin," I begged. He palmed my breast, his thumb flicking over my nipple. I cried out, and he buried himself in me with a mighty stroke.

For a moment, I was nothing, no one.

Then we were fused, two hearts beating as one, and I promised myself it always would be that way as he pulled out a few inches, the muscles of his back flexing beneath my hands, and then slammed back into me. Again and again.

I broke and broke against him as he moved, as he murmured my name and told me he loved me. And when that lightning once more filled my veins, my head, when I gasped out his name, his own release found him. I gripped him through each shuddering wave, savoring the weight of him, the feel of his skin, his strength.

For a while, only the rasp of our breathing filled the room.

I frowned as he withdrew at last—but he didn't go far. He stretched out on his side, head propped on a fist, and traced idle circles on my stomach, along my breasts.

"I'm sorry about earlier," he murmured.

"It's fine," I breathed. "I understand."

Not a lie, but not quite true.

His fingers grazed lower, circling my belly button. "You are—you're everything to me," he said thickly. "I need . . . I need you to be all right. To know they can't get to you—can't hurt you anymore."

"I know." Those fingers drifted lower. I swallowed hard and said again, "I know." I brushed his hair back from his face. "But what about you? Who gets to keep you safe?"

His mouth tightened. With his powers returned, he didn't need anyone to protect him, shield him. I could almost see invisible hackles raising—not at me, but at the thought of what he'd been mere months ago: prone to Amarantha's whims, his power barely a trickle compared to the cascade now coursing through him. He took a steadying breath, and leaned to kiss my heart, right between my breasts. It was answer enough.

"Soon," he murmured, and those fingers traveled back to my waist. I almost groaned. "Soon you'll be my wife, and it'll be fine. We'll leave all this behind us."

I arched my back, urging his hand lower, and he chuckled roughly. I didn't quite hear myself speak as I focused on the fingers that obeyed my silent command. "What will everyone call me, then?" He grazed my belly button as he leaned down, sucking the tip of my breast into his mouth.

"Hmm?" he said, and the rumble against my nipple made me writhe.

"Is everyone just going to call me 'Tamlin's wife'? Do I get a . . . title?"

He lifted his head long enough to look at me. "Do you want a title?"

Before I could answer, he nipped at my breast, then licked over the small hurt—licked as his fingers at last dipped between my legs. He stroked lazy, taunting circles. "No," I gasped out. "But I don't want people . . . " Cauldron boil me, his damned *fingers*— "I don't know if I can handle them calling me High Lady."

His fingers slid into me again, and he growled in approval at the wetness between my thighs, both from me and him. "They won't," he said against my skin, positioning himself over me again and sliding down my body, trailing kisses as he went. "There is no such thing as a High Lady."

He gripped my thighs to spread my legs wide, lowering his mouth, and—

"What do you mean, there's no such thing as a High Lady?"

The heat, his touch—all of it stopped.

He looked up from between my legs, and I almost climaxed at the sight of it. But what he said, what he'd implied . . . He kissed the inside of my thigh. "High Lords only take wives. Consorts. There has never been a High Lady."

"But Lucien's mother—"

"She's Lady of the Autumn Court. Not High Lady. Just as you will be Lady of the Spring Court. They will address you as they address her. They will respect you as they respect her." He lowered his gaze back to what was inches away from his mouth.

"So Lucien's—"

"I don't want to hear another male's name on your lips right now," he growled, and lowered his mouth to me.

At the first stroke of his tongue, I stopped arguing.

CHAPTER
3

Tamlin's guilt must have hit him hard, because although he was gone the next day, Lucien was waiting with an offer to inspect the progress on the nearby village.

I hadn't visited in well over a month—I couldn't remember the last time I'd even left the grounds. A few of the villagers had been invited to our Winter Solstice celebrations, but I'd barely managed to do more than greet them, thanks to the size of the crowd.

The horses were already saddled outside the front doors of the stables, and I counted the sentries by the distant gates (four), on either side of the house (two at each corner), and the ones now by the garden through which I'd just exited (two). Though none spoke, their eyes pressed on me.

Lucien made to mount his dapple-gray mare but I cut off his path. "A tumble off your damned horse?" I hissed, shoving his shoulder.

Lucien actually staggered back, the mare nickering in alarm, and I blinked at my outstretched hand. I didn't let myself contemplate what the guards made of it. Before he could say anything, I demanded, "Why did you lie about the naga?"

Lucien crossed his arms, his metal eye narrowing, and shook the red hair from his face.

I had to look away for a moment.

Amarantha's hair had been darker—and her face a creamy white, not at all like the sun-kissed gold of Lucien's skin.

I studied the stables behind him instead. At least it was big, open, the stable hands now off in another wing. I usually had little issue with being inside, which was mostly whenever I was bored enough to visit the horses housed within. Plenty of space to move, to escape. The walls didn't feel too . . . permanent.

Not like the kitchens, which were too low, the walls too thick, the windows not big enough to climb through. Not like the study, with not enough natural light or easy exits. I had a long list in my head of what places I could and couldn't endure at the manor, ranked by precisely how much they made my body lock up and sweat.

"I didn't *lie*," Lucien said tightly. "I technically *did* fall off my horse." He patted his mount's flank. "After one of them tackled me off her."

Such a faerie way of thinking, of lying. "Why?"

Lucien clamped his mouth shut.

"*Why?*"

He just twisted back to the patient mare. But I caught the expression on his face—the . . . *pity* in his eye.

I blurted, "Can we walk instead?"

He slowly turned. "It's three miles."

"And you could run that in a few minutes. I'd like to see if I can keep up."

His metal eye whirred, and I knew what he'd say before he opened his mouth.

"Never mind," I said, heading for my white mare, a sweet-tempered beast, if not a bit lazy and spoiled. Lucien didn't try to convince me otherwise, and kept quiet as we rode from the estate and onto the forest road. Spring, as always, was in full bloom, the breeze laden with lilac, the brush flanking the path rustling with life. No hint of the Bogge, of the naga, of any of the creatures who had once cast such stillness over the wood.

I said to him at last, "I don't want your damn pity."

"It's not pity. Tamlin said I shouldn't tell you—" He winced a bit.

"I'm not made of glass. If the naga attacked you, I *deserve* to know—"

"Tamlin is my High Lord. He gives an order, I follow it."

"You didn't have that mentality when you worked around his commands to send me to see the Suriel." And I'd nearly died.

"I was desperate then. We all were. But now—now we need order, Feyre. We need rules, and rankings, and *order*, if we're going to stand a chance of rebuilding. So what he says goes. I am the *first* one the others look to—I set the example. Don't ask me to risk the stability of this court by pushing back. Not right now. He's giving you as much free rein as he can."

I forced a steady breath to fill my too-tight lungs. "For all that you refuse to interact with Ianthe, you certainly sound a great deal like her."

He hissed, "You have *no idea* how hard it is for him to even let you off the estate grounds. He's under more pressure than you realize."

"I know exactly how much pressure he endures. And I didn't realize I'd become a prisoner."

"You're not—" He clenched his jaw. "That's not how it is and you know it."

"He didn't have any trouble letting me hunt and wander on my own when I was a mere human. When the borders were far less safe."

"He didn't care for you the way he does now. And after what happened Under the Mountain . . . " The words clanged in my head, along my too-tense muscles. "He's terrified. *Terrified* of seeing you in his enemies' hands. And they know it, too—they know all they have to do to own him would be to get ahold of you."

"You think I don't know that? But does he honestly expect me to spend the rest of my life in that manor, overseeing servants and wearing pretty clothes?"

Lucien watched the ever-young forest. "Isn't that what all human women wish for? A handsome faerie lord to wed and shower them with riches for the rest of their lives?"

I gripped the reins of my horse hard enough that she tossed her head. "Good to know you're still a prick, Lucien."

His metal eye narrowed. "Tamlin is a High Lord. You will be his wife. There are traditions and expectations you must uphold. *We* must uphold, in order to present a solid front that is healed from Amarantha and willing to destroy any foes who try to take what is ours again." Ianthe had given me almost the same speech yesterday. "The Tithe is happening soon," he continued, shaking his head, "the first he's called in since . . . her curse." His cringe was barely perceptible. "He gave our people three months to get their affairs in order, and he wanted to wait until the new year had started, but next month, he will demand the Tithe. Ianthe told him it's time—that the people are ready."

He waited, and I wanted to spit at him, because he knew—he *knew* that I didn't know what it was, and wanted me to admit to it. "Tell me," I said flatly.

"Twice a year, usually around the Summer and Winter Solstices, each member of the Spring Court, whether they're High Fae or lesser faerie, must pay a Tithe, dependent on their income and status. It's how we keep the estate running, how we pay for things like sentries and food and servants. In exchange, Tamlin protects them, rules them, helps them when he can. It's a give or take. This year, he pushed the Tithe back by a month—just to grant them that extra time to gather funds, to celebrate. But soon, emissaries from every group, village, or clan will be arriving to pay their Tithes. As Tamlin's wife, you will be expected to sit with him. And if they can't pay . . . You will be expected to sit there while he metes out judgment. It can get ugly. I'll be keeping track of who does and doesn't show up, who doesn't pay. And afterward, if they fail to pay their Tithe within the three days' grace he will officially offer them, he'll be expected to hunt them down. The High Priestesses themselves—Ianthe—grant him sacred hunting rights for this."

Horrible—brutal. I wanted to say it, but the look Lucien was giving me . . . I'd had enough of people judging me.

"So give him time, Feyre," Lucien said. "Let's get through the wedding, then the Tithe next month, and then . . . then we can see about the rest."

"I've given him time," I said. "I can't stay cooped up in the house forever."

"He knows that—he doesn't say it, but he knows it. Trust me. You will forgive him if his family's own slaughter keeps him from being so . . . liberal with your safety. He's lost those he cares for too many times. We all have."

Every word was like fuel added to the simmering pit in my gut. "I don't want to marry a High Lord. I just want to marry *him*."

"One doesn't exist without the other. He is what he is. He will always, *always* seek to protect you, whether you like it or not. Talk to him about it—really talk to him, Feyre. You'll figure it out." Our gazes met. A muscle feathered in Lucien's jaw. "Don't ask me to pick."

"But you're deliberately *not* telling me things."

"He is my High Lord. His word is *law*. We have this one chance, Feyre, to rebuild and make the world as it should be. I will not begin that new world by breaking his trust. Even if you . . ."

"Even if I what?"

His face paled, and he stroked a hand down the mare's cobweb-colored mane. "I was forced to watch as my father butchered the female I loved. My brothers *forced me* to watch."

My heart tightened for him—for the pain that haunted him.

"There was no magic spell, no miracle to bring her back. There were no gathered High Lords to resurrect her. I watched, and she died, and I will *never* forget that moment when I *heard* her heart stop beating."

My eyes burned.

"Tamlin got what I didn't," Lucien said softly, his breathing ragged. "We all heard your neck break. But you got to come back. And I doubt that he will ever forget that sound, either. And he will do everything in his power to protect you from that danger again, even if it means keeping secrets, even if it means sticking to rules you don't like. In this, he will not bend. So don't ask him to—not yet."

I had no words in my head, my heart. Giving Tamlin time, letting him adjust . . . It was the least I could do.

The clamor of construction overtook the chittering of forest birds long before we set foot in the village: hammers on nails, people barking orders, livestock braying.

We cleared the woods to find a village halfway toward being built: pretty little buildings of stone and wood, makeshift structures over the supplies and livestock . . . The only things that seemed absolutely finished were the large well in the center of the town and what looked to be a tavern.

Sometimes, the normalcy of Prythian, the utter similarities between it and the mortal lands, still surprised me. I might as well have been in my own village back home. A much nicer, newer village, but the layout, the focal points . . . All the same.

And I felt like just as much an outsider when Lucien and I rode into the heart of the chaos and everyone paused their laboring or selling or milling about to look at us.

At me.

Like a ripple of silence, the sounds of activity died in even the farthest reaches of the village.

"Feyre Cursebreaker," someone whispered.

Well, that was a new name.

I was grateful for the long sleeves of my riding habit, and the matching gloves I'd tugged on before we'd entered the village border.

Lucien pulled up his mare to a High Fae male who looked like he was in charge of building a house bordering the well fountain. "We came to see if any help was needed," he said, loud enough for everyone to hear. "Our services are yours for the day."

The male blanched. "Gratitude, my lord, but none is needed." His eyes gobbled me up, widening. "The debt is paid."

The sweat on my palms felt thicker, warmer. My mare stomped a hoof on the ruddy dirt street.

"Please," Lucien said, bowing his head gracefully. "The effort to rebuild is our burden to share. It would be our honor."

The male shook his head. "The debt is paid."

And so it went at every place we stopped in the village: Lucien dismounting, asking to help, and polite, reverent rejections.

Within twenty minutes, we were already riding back into the shadows and rustle of the woods.

"Did he let you take me today," I said hoarsely, "so that I'd stop asking to help rebuild?"

"No. I decided to take you myself. For that exact reason. They don't want or need your help. Your presence is a distraction and a reminder of what they went through."

I flinched. "They weren't Under the Mountain, though. I recognized none of them."

Lucien shuddered. "No. Amarantha had . . . camps for them. The nobles and favored faeries were allowed to dwell Under the Mountain. But if the people of a court weren't working to bring in goods and food, they were locked in camps in a network of tunnels beneath the Mountain. Thousands of them, crammed into chambers and tunnels with no light, no air. For fifty years."

"No one ever said—"

"It was forbidden to speak of it. Some of them went mad, started preying on the others when Amarantha forgot to order her guards to feed them. Some formed bands that prowled the camps and did—" He rubbed his brows with a thumb and forefinger. "They did horrible things. Right now, they're trying to remember what it is to be normal—how to *live*."

Bile burned my throat. But this wedding . . . yes, perhaps it would be the start of that healing.

Still, a blanket seemed to smother my senses, drowning out sound, taste, feeling.

"I know you wanted to help," Lucien offered. "I'm sorry."

So was I.

The vastness of my now-unending existence yawned open before me.

I let it swallow me whole.

CHAPTER 4

A few days before the wedding ceremony, guests began arriving, and I was grateful that I'd never be High Lady, never be Tamlin's equal in responsibility and power.

A small, forgotten part of me roared and screamed at that, but . . .

Dinner after dinner, luncheons and picnics and hunts.

I was introduced and passed around, and my face hurt from the smile I kept plastered there day and night. I began looking forward to the wedding just knowing that once it was over, I wouldn't have to be pleasant or talk to anyone or *do* anything for a week. A month. A year.

Tamlin endured it all—in that quiet, near-feral way of his—and told me again and again that the parties were a way to introduce me to his court, to give his people something to celebrate. He assured me that he hated the gatherings as much as I did, and that Lucien was the only one who really enjoyed himself, but . . . I caught Tamlin grinning sometimes. And truthfully, he deserved it, had earned it. And these people deserved it, too.

So I weathered it, clinging to Ianthe when Tamlin wasn't at my side, or, if they were together, letting the two of them lead conversations while I counted down the hours until everyone would leave.

"You should head to bed," Ianthe said, both of us watching the assembled revelers packing the great hall. I'd spotted her by the open doors thirty minutes ago, and was grateful for the excuse to leave the gaggle of Tamlin's friends I'd been stuck talking to. Or *not* talking to. Either they outright stared at me, or they tried so damn hard to come up with common topics. Hunting, mostly. Conversation usually stalled after three minutes.

"I've another hour before I need to sleep," I said. Ianthe was in her usual pale robe, hood up and that circlet of silver with its blue stone atop it.

High Fae males eyed her as they meandered past where we stood by the wood-paneled wall near the main doors, either from awe or lust or perhaps both, their gazes occasionally snagging on me. I knew the wide eyes had nothing to do with my bright green gown or pretty face (fairly bland compared to Ianthe's). I tried to ignore them.

"Are you ready for tomorrow? Is there anything I can do for you?" Ianthe sipped from her glass of sparkling wine. The gown I wore tonight was a gift from her, actually—Spring Court green, she'd called it. Alis had merely lingered while I dressed, unnervingly silent, letting Ianthe claim her usual duties.

"I'm fine." I'd already contemplated how pathetic it would be if I asked her to permanently stay after the wedding. If I revealed that I dreaded her leaving me to this court, these people, until Nynsar—a minor spring holiday to celebrate the end of seeding the fields and to pass out the first flower clippings of the season. Months and months from now. Even having her live at her own temple felt too removed.

Two males that had circled past twice already finally worked up the courage to approach us—her.

I leaned against the wall, the wood digging into my back, as they flanked Ianthe. Handsome, in the way that most of them were handsome, armed with weapons that marked them as two of the High Fae who guarded Tamlin's lands. Perhaps they even worked under Ianthe's father. "Priestess," one said, bowing deep.

By now, I'd become accustomed to people kissing her silver rings and beseeching her for prayers for themselves, their families, or their lovers. Ianthe received it all without that beautiful face shifting in the slightest.

"Bron," she said to the one on her left, brown-haired and tall. "And Hart," she said to the one on her right, black-haired and built a bit more powerfully than his friend. She gave a coy, pretty tilt of her lips that I'd learned meant she was now on the hunt for nighttime companionship. "I haven't seen you two troublemakers in a while."

They parried with flirtatious comments, until the two males began glancing my way.

"Oh," Ianthe said, hood shifting as she turned. "Allow me to introduce Lady Feyre." She lowered her eyes, angling her head in a deep nod. "Savior of Prythian."

"We know," Hart said quietly, bowing with his friend at the waist. "We were Under the Mountain with you."

I managed to incline my head a bit as they straightened. "Congratulations on tomorrow," Bron said, grinning. "A fitting end, eh?"

A fitting end would have been me in a grave, burning in hell.

"The Cauldron," Ianthe said, "has blessed all of us with such a union." The males murmured their agreement, bowing their heads again. I ignored it.

"I have to say," Bron went on, "that trial—with the Middengard Wyrm? Brilliant. One of the most brilliant things I ever saw."

It was an effort not to push myself wholly flat against the wall, not to think about the reek of that mud, the gnashing of those flesh-shredding teeth bearing down upon me. "Thank you."

"Oh, it sounded terrible," Ianthe said, stepping closer as she noted I was no longer wearing that bland smile. She put a hand on my arm. "Such bravery is awe-inspiring."

I was grateful, so pathetically grateful, for the steadying touch. For the squeeze. I knew then that she'd inspire hordes of young Fae females to join her order—not for worshipping their Mother and Cauldron, but to learn how she *lived*, how she could shine so brightly and love herself, move from male to male as if they were dishes at a banquet.

"We missed the hunt the other day," Hart said casually, "so we haven't had a chance to see your talents up close, but I think the High Lord will be stationing us near the estate next month—it'd be an honor to ride with you."

Tamlin wouldn't allow me out with them in a thousand years. And I had no desire to tell them that I had no interest in ever using a bow and arrow again, or hunting anything at all. The hunt I'd been dragged on two days ago had almost been too much. Even with everyone watching me, I hadn't drawn an arrow.

They were still waiting for a reply, so I said, "The honor would be mine."

"Does my father have you two on duty tomorrow, or will you be attending the ceremony?" Ianthe said, putting a distracting hand on Bron's arm. Precisely why I sought her out at events.

Bron answered her, but Hart's eyes lingered on me—on my crossed arms. On my tattooed fingers. He said, "Have you heard from the High Lord at all?"

Ianthe stiffened, and Bron immediately cut his gaze toward my inked flesh.

"No," I said, holding Hart's gaze.

"He's probably running scared now that Tamlin's got his powers back."

"Then you don't know Rhysand very well at all."

Hart blinked, and even Ianthe kept silent. It was probably the most assertive thing I'd said to anyone during these parties.

"Well, we'll take care of him if need be," Hart said, shifting on his feet as I continued to hold his gaze, not bothering to soften my expression.

Ianthe said to him, to me, "The High Priestesses are taking care of it. We will not allow our savior to be treated so ill."

I schooled my face into neutrality. Was *that* why Tamlin had initially sought out Ianthe? To make an alliance? My chest tightened a bit. I turned to her. "I'm going up. Tell Tamlin I'll see him tomorrow."

Tomorrow, because tonight, Ianthe had told me, we'd spend apart. As dictated by their long-held traditions.

Ianthe kissed my cheek, her hood shielding me from the room for a heartbeat. "I'm at your disposal, Lady. Send word if you need anything."

I wouldn't, but I nodded.

As I slipped from the room, I peered toward the front—where Tamlin and Lucien were surrounded by a circle of High Fae males and females. Perhaps not as refined as some of the others, but . . . They had the look of people who had been together a long time, fought at each other's sides. Tamlin's friends. He'd introduced me to them, and I'd immediately forgotten their names. I hadn't tried to learn them again.

Tamlin tipped his head back and laughed, the others howling with him.

I left before he could spot me, easing through the crowded halls until I was in the dim, empty upstairs of the residential wing.

Alone in my bedroom, I realized I couldn't remember the last time I'd truly laughed.

The ceiling pushed down, the large, blunt spikes so hot I could see the heat rippling off them even from where I was chained to the floor. Chained, because I was illiterate and couldn't read the riddle written on the wall, and Amarantha was glad to let me be impaled.

Closer and closer. There was no one coming to save me from this horrible death.

It'd hurt. It'd hurt and be slow, and I'd cry—I might even cry for my mother, who had never cared for me, anyway. I might beg her to save me—

✠

My limbs flailed as I shot upright in bed, yanking against invisible chains.

I would have lurched for the bathing room had my legs and arms not shook so badly, had I been able to breathe, breathe, *breathe*—

I scanned the bedroom, shuddering. Real—this was real. The horrors, those were nightmares. I was out; I was alive; I was safe.

A night breeze floated through the open windows, ruffling my hair, drying the cold sweat on me. The dark sky beckoned, the stars so dim and small, like speckles of frost.

Bron had sounded as if watching my encounter with the Middengard Wyrm was a sporting match. As if I hadn't been one mistake away from being devoured whole and my bones spat out.

Savior and jester, apparently.

I stumbled to the open window, and pushed it wider, clearing my view of the star-flecked darkness.

I rested my head against the wall, savoring the cool stones.

In a few hours, I'd be married. I'd have my happy ending, whether I deserved it or not. But this land, these people—*they* would have their happy ending, too. The first few steps toward healing. Toward peace. And then things would be fine.

Then I'd be fine.

✠

I really, truly hated my wedding gown.

It was a monstrosity of tulle and chiffon and gossamer, so unlike the loose gowns I usually wore: the bodice fitted, the neckline curved to plump my breasts, and the skirts . . . The skirts were a sparkling tent, practically floating in the balmy spring air.

No wonder Tamlin had laughed. Even Alis, as she'd dressed me, had hummed to herself, but said nothing. Most likely because Ianthe had personally selected the gown to complement whatever tale she'd weave today—the legend she'd proclaim to the world.

I might have dealt with it all if it weren't for the puffy capped sleeves, so big I could almost see them glinting from the periphery of my vision. My hair had been curled, half up, half down, entwined with pearls and jewels and the Cauldron knew what, and it had taken all my self-control to keep from cringing at the mirror before descending the sweeping stairs into the main hall. My dress hissed and swished with each step.

Beyond the shut patio doors where I paused, the garden had been bedecked in ribbons and lanterns in shades of cream, blush, and sky blue. Three hundred chairs were assembled in the largest courtyard, each seat occupied by Tamlin's court. I'd make my way down the main aisle, enduring their stares, before I reached the dais at the other end—where Tamlin would be waiting.

Then Ianthe would sanction and bless our union right before sundown, as a representative of *all* twelve High Priestesses. She'd hinted that they'd pushed to be present—but through whatever cunning, she'd managed to keep the other eleven away. Either to claim the attention for herself, or to spare me from being hounded by the pack of them. I couldn't tell. Perhaps both.

My mouth went paper-dry as Alis fluffed out the sparkling train of my gown in the shadow of the garden doors. Silk and gossamer rustled and sighed, and I gripped the pale bouquet in my gloved hands, nearly snapping the stems.

Elbow-length silk gloves—to hide the markings. Ianthe had delivered them herself this morning in a velvet-lined box.

"Don't be nervous," Alis clucked, her tree-bark skin rich and flushed in the honey-gold evening light.

"I'm not," I rasped.

"You're fidgeting like my youngest nephew during a haircut." She finished fussing over my dress, shooing away some servants who'd come to spy on me before the ceremony. I pretended I didn't see them, or the glittering, sunset-gilded crowd seated in the courtyard ahead, and toyed with some invisible fleck of dust on my skirts.

"You look beautiful," Alis said quietly. I was fairly certain her thoughts on the dress were the same as my own, but I believed her.

"Thank you."

"And you sound like you're going to your funeral."

I plastered a grin on my face. Alis rolled her eyes. But she nudged me toward the doors as they opened on some immortal wind, lilting music streaming in. "It'll be over faster than you can blink," she promised, and gently pushed me into the last of the sunlight.

Three hundred people rose to their feet and pivoted toward me.

Not since my last trial had so many gathered to watch me, judge me. All in finery so similar to what they'd worn Under the Mountain. Their faces blurred, melded.

Alis coughed from the shadows of the house, and I remembered to start walking, to look toward the dais—

At Tamlin.

The breath knocked from me, and it was an effort to keep going down the stairs, to keep my knees from buckling. He was resplendent in a tunic of green and gold, a crown of burnished laurel leaves gleaming on his head. He'd loosened the grip on his glamour, letting that immortal light and beauty shine through—for me.

My vision narrowed on him, on my High Lord, his wide eyes glistening as I stepped onto the soft grass, white rose petals scattered down it—

And red ones.

Like drops of blood amongst the white, red petals had been sprayed across the path ahead.

I forced my gaze up, to Tamlin, his shoulders back, head high.

So unaware of the true extent of how broken and dark I was inside. How unfit I was to be clothed in white when my hands were so filthy.

Everyone else was thinking it. They had to be.

Every step was too fast, propelling me toward the dais and Tamlin. And toward Ianthe, clothed in dark blue robes tonight, beaming beneath that hood and silver crown.

As if I were good—as if I hadn't murdered two of their kind.

I was a murderer and a liar.

A cluster of red petals loomed ahead—just like that Fae youth's blood had pooled at my feet.

Ten steps from the dais, at the edge of that splatter of red, I slowed.

Then stopped.

Everyone was watching, exactly as they had when I'd nearly died, spectators to my torment.

Tamlin extended a broad hand, brows narrowing slightly. My heart beat so fast, too fast.

I was going to vomit.

Right over those rose petals; right over the grass and ribbons trailing into the aisle from the chairs flanking it.

And between my skin and bones, something thrummed and pounded, rising and pushing, lashing through my blood—

So many eyes, too many eyes, pressed on me, witnesses to every crime I'd committed, every humiliation—

I don't know why I'd even bothered to wear gloves, why I'd let Ianthe convince me.

The fading sun was too hot, the garden too hedged in. As inescapable as the vow I was about to make, binding me to him forever, shackling him to my broken and weary soul. The thing inside me was roiling now, my body shaking with the building force of it as it hunted for a way out—

Forever—I would never get better, never get free of myself, of that dungeon where I'd spent three months—

"Feyre," Tamlin said, his hand steady as he continued to reach for mine. The sun sank past the lip of the western garden wall; shadows pooled, chilling the air.

If I turned away, they'd start talking, but I couldn't make the last few steps, couldn't, couldn't, couldn't—

I was going to fall apart, right there, right then—and they'd see precisely how ruined I was.

Help me, help me, help me, I begged someone, anyone. Begged Lucien, standing in the front row, his metal eye fixed on me. Begged Ianthe, face serene and patient and lovely within that hood. *Save me—please, save me. Get me out. End this.*

Tamlin took a step toward me—concern shading those eyes.

I retreated a step. *No.*

Tamlin's mouth tightened. The crowd murmured. Silk streamers laden with globes of gold faelight twinkled into life above and around us.

Ianthe said smoothly, "Come, Bride, and be joined with your true love. Come, Bride, and let good triumph at last."

Good. I was not good. I was *nothing*, and my soul, my eternal soul, was damned—

I tried to get my traitorous lungs to draw air so I could voice the word. *No—no.*

But I didn't have to say it.

Thunder cracked behind me, as if two boulders had been hurled against each other.

People screamed, falling back, a few vanishing outright as darkness erupted.

I whirled, and through the night drifting away like smoke on a wind, I found Rhysand straightening the lapels of his black jacket.

"Hello, Feyre darling," he purred.

CHAPTER 5

I shouldn't have been surprised. Not when Rhysand liked to make a spectacle of everything. And found pissing off Tamlin to be an art form.

But there he was.

Rhysand, High Lord of the Night Court, now stood beside me, darkness leaking from him like ink in water.

He angled his head, his blue-black hair shifting with the movement. Those violet eyes sparkled in the golden faelight as they fixed on Tamlin, as he held up a hand to where Tamlin and Lucien and their sentries had their swords half-drawn, sizing up how to get me out of the way, how to bring him down—

But at the lift of that hand, they froze.

Ianthe, however, was backing away slowly, face drained of color.

"What a pretty little wedding," Rhysand said, stuffing his hands into his pockets as those many swords remained in their sheaths. The remaining crowd was pressing back, some climbing over seats to get away.

Rhys looked me over slowly, and clicked his tongue at my silk gloves. Whatever had been building beneath my skin went still and cold.

"Get the hell out," growled Tamlin, stalking toward us. Claws ripped from his knuckles.

Rhys clicked his tongue again. "Oh, I don't think so. Not when I need to call in my bargain with Feyre darling."

My stomach hollowed out. No—no, not now.

"You try to break the bargain, and you know what will happen," Rhys went on, chuckling a bit at the crowd still falling over themselves to get away from him. He jerked his chin toward me. "I gave you three months of freedom. You could at least look happy to see me."

I was shaking too badly to say anything. Rhys's eyes flickered with distaste.

The expression was gone when he faced Tamlin again. "I'll be taking her now."

"Don't you dare," Tamlin snarled. Behind him, the dais was empty; Ianthe had vanished entirely. Along with most of those in attendance.

"Was I interrupting? I thought it was over." Rhys gave me a smile dripping with venom. He knew—through that bond, through whatever magic was between us, he'd known I was about to say no. "At least, Feyre seemed to think so."

Tamlin snarled, "Let us finish the ceremony—"

"Your High Priestess," Rhys said, "seems to think it's over, too."

Tamlin stiffened as he looked over a shoulder to find the altar empty. When he faced us again, the claws had eased halfway back into his hands. "Rhysand—"

"I'm in no mood to bargain," Rhys said, "even though I could work it to my advantage, I'm sure." I jolted at the caress of his hand on my elbow. "Let's go."

I didn't move.

"Tamlin," I breathed.

Tamlin took a single step toward me, his golden face turning sallow, but remained focused on Rhys. "Name your price."

“Don’t bother,” Rhys crooned, linking elbows with me. Every spot of contact was abhorrent, unbearable.

He’d take me back to the Night Court, the place Amarantha had supposedly modeled Under the Mountain after, full of depravity and torture and death—

“Tamlin, please.”

“Such dramatics,” Rhysand said, tugging me closer.

But Tamlin didn’t move—and those claws were wholly replaced by smooth skin. He fixed his gaze on Rhys, his lips pulling back in a snarl. “If you hurt her—”

“I know, I know,” Rhysand drawled. “I’ll return her in a week.”

No—no, Tamlin couldn’t be making those kinds of threats, not when they meant he was letting me go. Even Lucien was gaping at Tamlin, his face white with fury and shock.

Rhys released my elbow only to slip a hand around my waist, pressing me into his side as he whispered in my ear, “Hold on.”

Then darkness roared, a wind tearing me this way and that, the ground falling away beneath me, the world gone around me. Only Rhys remained, and I hated him as I clung to him, I hated him with my entire heart—

Then the darkness vanished.

I smelled jasmine first—then saw stars. A sea of stars flickering beyond glowing pillars of moonstone that framed the sweeping view of endless snowcapped mountains.

“Welcome to the Night Court,” was all Rhys said.

It was the most beautiful place I’d ever seen.

Whatever building we were in had been perched atop one of the gray-stoned mountains. The hall around us was open to the elements, no windows to be found, just towering pillars and gossamer curtains, swaying in that jasmine-scented breeze.

It must be some magic, to keep the air warm in the dead of winter. Not to mention the altitude, or the snow coating the mountains, mighty winds sending veils of it drifting off the peaks like wandering mist.

Little seating, dining, and work areas dotted the hall, sectioned off with those curtains or lush plants or thick rugs scattered over the moonstone floor. A few balls of light bobbed on the breeze, along with colored-glass lanterns dangling from the arches of the ceiling.

Not a scream, not a shout, not a plea to be heard.

Behind me, a wall of white marble arose, broken occasionally by open doorways leading into dim stairwells. The rest of the Night Court had to be through there. No wonder I couldn't hear anyone screaming, if they were all inside.

"This is my private residence," Rhys said casually. His skin was darker than I'd remembered—golden now, rather than pale.

Pale, from being locked Under the Mountain for fifty years. I scanned him, searching for any sign of the massive, membranous wings—the ones he'd admitted he loved flying with. But there was none. Just the male, smirking at me.

And that too-familiar expression— "How *dare* you—"

Rhys snorted. "I certainly missed *that* look on your face." He stalked closer, his movements feline, those violet eyes turning subdued—lethal. "You're welcome, you know."

"For *what?*"

Rhys paused less than a foot away, sliding his hands into his pockets. The night didn't seem to ripple from him here—and he appeared, despite his perfection, almost normal. "For saving you when asked."

I stiffened. "I didn't ask for anything."

His stare dipped to my left hand.

Rhys gave no warning as he gripped my arm, snarling softly, and tore off the glove. His touch was like a brand, and I flinched, yielding a step, but he held firm until he'd gotten both gloves off. "I heard you begging someone, *anyone*, to rescue you, to get you out. I heard you say *no*."

"I didn't say anything."

He turned my bare hand over, his hold tightening as he examined the eye he'd tattooed. He tapped the pupil. Once. Twice. "I heard it loud and clear."

I wrenched my hand away. "Take me back. *Now.* I didn't want to be stolen away."

He shrugged. "What better time to take you here? Maybe Tamlin didn't notice you were about to reject him in front of his entire court—maybe you can now simply blame it on me."

"You're a bastard. You made it clear enough that I had . . . reservations."

"Such gratitude, as always."

I struggled to get down a single, deep breath. "What do you want from me?"

"*Want*? I want you to say thank you, first of all. Then I want you to take off that hideous dress. You look . . . " His mouth cut a cruel line. "You look exactly like the doe-eyed damsel he and that simpering priestess want you to be."

"You don't know anything about me. Or us."

Rhys gave me a knowing smile. "Does Tamlin? Does he ever ask you why you hurl your guts up every night, or why you can't go into certain rooms or see certain colors?"

I froze. He might as well have stripped me naked. "Get the hell out of my head."

Tamlin had horrors of his own to endure, to face down.

"Likewise." He stalked a few steps away. "You think I enjoy being awoken every night by visions of you puking? You send everything right down that bond, and I don't appreciate having a front-row seat when I'm trying to sleep."

"Prick."

Another chuckle. But I wouldn't ask about what he meant—about the bond between us. I wouldn't give him the satisfaction of looking curious. "As for what else I want from you . . . " He gestured to the house behind us. "I'll tell you tomorrow at breakfast. For now, clean yourself up. Rest." That rage flickered in his eyes again at the dress, the hair. "Take the stairs on the right, one level down. Your room is the first door."

"Not a dungeon cell?" Perhaps it was foolish to reveal that fear, to suggest it to him.

But Rhys half turned, brows lifting. "You are not a prisoner, Feyre. You made a bargain, and I am calling it in. You will be my guest here, with the privileges of a member of my household. None of my subjects are going to touch you, hurt you, or so much as think ill of you here."

My tongue was dry and heavy as I said, "And where might those subjects be?"

"Some dwell here—in the mountain beneath us." He angled his head. "They're forbidden to set foot in this residence. They know they'd be signing their death warrant." His eyes met mine, stark and clear, as if he could sense the panic, the shadows creeping in. "Amarantha wasn't very creative," he said with quiet wrath. "My court beneath this mountain has long been feared, and she chose to replicate it by violating the space of Prythian's sacred mountain. So, yes: there's a court beneath this mountain—the court your Tamlin now expects me to be subjecting you to. I preside over it every now and then, but it mostly rules itself."

"When—when are you taking me there?" If I had to go underground, had to see those kinds of horrors again . . . I'd beg him—*beg* him not to take me. I didn't care how pathetic it made me. I'd lost any sort of qualms about what lines I'd cross to survive.

"I'm not." He rolled his shoulders. "This is my home, and the court beneath it is my . . . occupation, as you mortals call it. I do not like for the two to overlap very often."

My brows rose slightly. "'You mortals'?"

Starlight danced along the planes of his face. "Should I consider you something different?"

A challenge. I shoved away my irritation at the amusement again tugging at the corners of his lips, and instead said, "And the other denizens of your court?" The Night Court territory was enormous—bigger than any other in Prythian. And all around us were those empty, snow-blasted mountains. No sign of towns, cities, or anything.

"Scattered throughout, dwelling as they wish. Just as *you* are now free to roam where you wish."

"I wish to roam home."

Rhys laughed, finally sauntering toward the other end of the hall, which ended in a veranda open to the stars. "I'm willing to accept your thanks at any time, you know," he called to me without looking back.

Red exploded in my vision, and I couldn't breathe fast enough, couldn't *think* above the roar in my head. One heartbeat, I was staring after him—the next, I had my shoe in a hand.

I hurled it at him with all my strength.

All my considerable, immortal strength.

I barely saw my silk slipper as it flew through the air, fast as a shooting star, so fast that even a High Lord couldn't detect it as it neared—

And slammed into his head.

Rhys whirled, a hand rising to the back of his head, his eyes wide.

I already had the other shoe in my hand.

Rhys's lip pulled back from his teeth. "*I dare you.*" Temper—he had to be in some mood today to let his temper show this much.

Good. That made two of us.

I flung my other shoe right at his head, as swift and hard as the first one.

His hand snatched up, grabbing the shoe mere inches from his face.

Rhys hissed and lowered the shoe, his eyes meeting mine as the silk dissolved to glittering black dust in his fist. His fingers unfurled, the last of the sparkling ashes blowing into oblivion, and he surveyed my hand, my body, my face.

"Interesting," he murmured, and continued on his way.

I debated tackling him and pummeling that face with my fists, but I wasn't stupid. I was in his home, on top of a mountain in the middle of absolutely nowhere, it seemed. No one would be coming to rescue me—no one was even here to witness my screaming.

So I turned toward the doorway he'd indicated, heading for the dim stairwell beyond.

I'd nearly reached it, not daring to breathe too loudly, when a bright, amused female voice said behind me—far away, from wherever Rhys had gone to at the opposite end of the hall, "So, *that* went well."

Rhys's answering snarl sent my footsteps hurrying.

My room was . . . a dream.

After scouring it for any sign of danger, after learning every exit and entrance and hiding place, I paused in the center to contemplate where, exactly, I'd be staying for the next week.

Like the upstairs living area, its windows were open to the brutal world beyond—no glass, no shutters—and sheer amethyst curtains fluttered in that unnatural, soft breeze. The large bed was a creamy white-and-ivory concoction, with pillows and blankets and throws for days, made more inviting by the twin golden lamps beside it. An armoire and dressing table occupied a wall, framed by those glass-less windows. Across the room, a chamber with a porcelain sink and toilet lay behind an arched wooden door, but the bath . . .

The bath.

Occupying the other half of the bedroom, my bathtub was actually a pool, hanging right off the mountain itself. A pool for soaking or enjoying myself. Its far edge seemed to disappear into nothing, the water flowing silently off the side and into the night beyond. A narrow ledge on the adjacent wall was lined with fat, guttering candles whose glow gilded the dark, glassy surface and wafting tendrils of steam.

Open, airy, plush, and . . . calm.

This room was fit for an empress. With the marble floors, silks, velvets, and elegant details, only an empress could have afforded it. I tried not to think what Rhys's chamber was like, if this was how he treated his guests.

Guest—not prisoner.

Well . . . the room proved it.

I didn't bother barricading the door. Rhys could likely fly in if he felt like it. And I'd seen him shatter a faerie's mind without so much as blinking. I doubted a bit of wood would keep out that horrible power.

I again surveyed the room, my wedding gown hissing on the warm marble floors.

I peered down at myself.

You look ridiculous.

Heat itched along my cheeks and neck.

It didn't excuse what he'd done. Even if he'd . . . saved me—I choked on the word—from having to refuse Tamlin. Having to explain.

Slowly, I tugged the pins and baubles from my curled hair, piling them onto the dressing table. The sight was enough for me to grit my teeth, and I swept them into an empty drawer instead, slamming it shut so hard the mirror above the table rattled. I rubbed at my scalp, aching from the weight of the curls and prodding pins. This afternoon, I'd imagined Tamlin pulling them each from my hair, a kiss for every pin, but now—

I swallowed against the burning in my throat.

Rhys was the least of my concerns. Tamlin had seen the hesitation, but had he understood that I was about to say no? Had Ianthe? I had to tell him. Had to explain that there couldn't be a wedding, not for a while yet. Maybe I'd wait until the mating bond snapped into place, until I knew for sure it couldn't be some mistake, that . . . that I was worthy of him.

Maybe wait until he, too, had faced the nightmares stalking him. Relaxed his grip on things a bit. On me. Even if I understood his need to protect, that fear of losing me . . . Perhaps I should explain everything when I returned.

But—so many people had seen it, seen *me* hesitate—

My lower lip trembled, and I began unbuttoning my gown, then tugged it off my shoulders.

I let it slide to the ground in a sigh of silk and tulle and beading, a deflated soufflé on the marble floor, and took a large step out of it. Even my undergarments were ridiculous: frothy scraps of lace, intended solely for Tamlin to admire—and then tear into ribbons.

I snatched up the gown, storming to the armoire and shoving it inside. Then I stripped off the undergarments and chucked them in as well.

My tattoo was stark against the pile of white silk and lace. My breath came faster and faster. I didn't realize I was weeping until I grabbed the first bit of fabric within the armoire I could find—a set of turquoise nightclothes—and shoved my feet into the ankle-length pants, then pulled the short-sleeved matching shirt over my head, the hem grazing the top of my navel. I didn't care that it had to be some Night Court fashion, didn't care that they were soft and warm.

I climbed into that big, fluffy bed, the sheets smooth and welcoming, and could barely draw a breath steady enough to blow out the lamps on either side.

But as soon as darkness enveloped the room, my sobs hit in full—great, gasping pants that shuddered through me, flowing out the open windows, and into the starry, snow-kissed night.

Rhys hadn't been lying when he said I was to join him for breakfast.

My old handmaidens from Under the Mountain appeared at my door just past dawn, and I might not have recognized the pretty, dark-haired twins had they not acted like they knew me. I had never seen them as anything but shadows, their faces always concealed in impenetrable night. But here—or perhaps without Amarantha—they were fully corporeal.

Nuala and Cerridwen were their names, and I wondered if they'd ever told me. If I had been too far gone Under the Mountain to even care.

Their gentle knock hurled me awake—not that I'd slept much during the night. For a heartbeat, I wondered why my bed felt so much softer, why mountains flowed into the distance and not spring grasses and hills . . . and then it all poured back in. Along with a throbbing, relentless headache.

After the second, patient knock, followed by a muffled explanation through the door of who they were, I scrambled out of bed to let them in. And after a miserably awkward greeting, they informed me that breakfast would be served in thirty minutes, and I was to bathe and dress.

I didn't bother to ask if Rhys was behind that last order, or if it was their recommendation based on how grim I no doubt looked, but they laid out some clothes on the bed before leaving me to wash in private.

I was tempted to linger in the luxurious heat of the bathtub for the rest of the day, but a faint, endlessly amused *tug* cleaved through my headache. I knew that tug—had been called by it once before, in those hours after Amarantha's downfall.

I ducked to my neck in the water, scanning the clear winter sky, the fierce wind whipping the snow off those nearby peaks . . . No sign of him, no pound of beating wings. But the tug yanked again in my mind, my gut—a summoning. Like some servant's bell.

Cursing him soundly, I scrubbed myself down and dressed in the clothes they'd left.

And now, striding across the sunny upper level as I blindly followed the source of that insufferable tug, my magenta silk shoes near-silent on the moonstone floors, I wanted to shred the clothes off me, if only for the fact that they belonged to this place, to *him*.

My high-waisted peach pants were loose and billowing, gathered at the ankles with velvet cuffs of bright gold. The long sleeves of the matching top were made of gossamer, also gathered at the wrists, and the top itself hung just to my navel, revealing a sliver of skin as I walked.

Comfortable, easy to move in—to run. Feminine. Exotic. Thin enough that, unless Rhysand planned to torment me by casting me into the winter wasteland around us, I could assume I wasn't leaving the borders of whatever warming magic kept the palace so balmy.

At least the tattoo, visible through the sheer sleeve, wouldn't be out of place here. But—the clothes were still a part of this court.

And no doubt part of some game he intended to play with me.

At the very end of the upper level, a small glass table gleamed like quicksilver in the heart of a stone veranda, set with three chairs and laden with fruits, juices, pastries, and breakfast meats. And in one of those chairs . . . Though Rhys stared out at the sweeping view, the snowy mountains near-blinding in the sunlight, I knew he'd sensed my arrival from the moment I cleared the stairwell at the other side of the hall. Maybe since I'd awoken, if that tug was any indication.

I paused between the last two pillars, studying the High Lord lounging at the breakfast table and the view he surveyed.

"I'm not a dog to be summoned," I said by way of greeting.

Slowly, Rhys looked over his shoulder. Those violet eyes were vibrant in the light, and I curled my fingers into fists as they swept from my head to my toes and back up again. He frowned at whatever he found lacking. "I didn't want you to get lost," he said blandly.

My head throbbed, and I eyed the silver teapot steaming in the center of the table. A cup of tea . . . "I thought it'd always be dark here," I said, if only to not look quite as desperate for that life-giving tea so early in the morning.

"We're one of the three Solar Courts," he said, motioning for me to sit with a graceful twist of his wrist. "Our nights are far more beautiful, and our sunsets and dawns are exquisite, but we do adhere to the laws of nature."

I slid into the upholstered chair across from him. His tunic was unbuttoned at the neck, revealing a hint of the tanned chest beneath. "And do the other courts choose not to?"

"The nature of the Seasonal Courts," he said, "is linked to their High Lords, whose magic and will keeps them in eternal spring, or winter, or fall, or summer. It has always been like that—some sort of strange stagnation. But the Solar Courts—Day, Dawn, and Night—are of a more . . . symbolic nature. We might be powerful, but even we cannot alter the sun's path or strength. Tea?"

The sunlight danced along the curve of the silver teapot. I kept my eager nod to a restrained dip of my chin. "But you will find," Rhysand went on, pouring a cup for me, "that our nights are more spectacular—so spectacular that some in my territory even awaken at sunset and go to bed at dawn, just to live under the starlight."

I splashed some milk in the tea, watching the light and dark eddy together. "Why is it so warm in here, when winter is in full blast out there?"

"Magic."

"Obviously." I set down my teaspoon and sipped, nearly sighing at the rush of heat and smoky, rich flavor. "But *why*?"

Rhys scanned the wind tearing through the peaks. "You heat a house in the winter—why shouldn't I heat this place as well? I'll admit I don't know *why* my predecessors built a palace fit for the Summer Court in the middle of a mountain range that's mildly warm at best, but who am I to question?"

I took a few more sips, that headache already lessening, and dared to scoop some fruit onto my plate from a glass bowl nearby.

He watched every movement. Then he said quietly, "You've lost weight."

"You're prone to digging through my head whenever you please," I said, stabbing a piece of melon with my fork. "I don't see why you're surprised by it."

His gaze didn't lighten, though that smile again played about his sensuous mouth, no doubt his favorite mask. "Only occasionally will I do that. And I can't help it if *you* send things down the bond."

I contemplated refusing to ask as I had done last night, but . . . "How does it work—this *bond* that allows you to see into my head?"

He sipped from his own tea. "Think of the bargain's bond as a bridge between us—and at either end is a door to our respective minds. A shield. My innate talents allow me to slip through the mental shields of anyone I wish, with or without that bridge—unless they're very, very strong, or have trained extensively to keep those shields tight. As a human, the gates to your mind were flung open for me to stroll through. As Fae . . . " A little shrug. "Sometimes, you unwittingly have a shield up—sometimes, when emotion seems to be running strong, that shield vanishes. And sometimes, when those shields are open, you might as well be standing at the gates to your mind, shouting your thoughts across the bridge to me. Sometimes I hear them; sometimes I don't."

I scowled, clenching my fork harder. "And how often do you just rifle through my mind when my shields are down?"

All amusement faded from his face. "When I can't tell if your nightmares are real threats or imagined. When you're about to be married and you silently beg anyone to help you. Only when you drop your mental shields and unknowingly blast those things down the bridge. And to answer your question before you ask, yes. Even with your shields up, I could get through them if I wished. You could train, though—learn how to shield against someone like me, even with the bond bridging our minds and my own abilities."

I ignored the offer. Agreeing to do anything with him felt too permanent, too accepting of the bargain between us. "What do you want with me? You said you'd tell me here. So tell me."

Rhys leaned back in his chair, folding powerful arms that even the fine clothes couldn't hide. "For this week? I want you to learn how to read."

CHAPTER 6

Rhysand had mocked me about it once—had asked me while we were Under the Mountain if forcing me to learn how to read would be my personal idea of torture.

"No, thank you," I said, gripping my fork to keep from chucking it at his head.

"You're going to be a High Lord's wife," Rhys said. "You'll be expected to maintain your own correspondences, perhaps even give a speech or two. And the Cauldron knows what else he and Ianthe will deem appropriate for you. Make menus for dinner parties, write thank-you letters for all those wedding gifts, embroider sweet phrases on pillows . . . It's a necessary skill. And, you know what? Why don't we throw in shielding while we're at it. Reading and shielding—fortunately, you can practice them together."

"They are *both* necessary skills," I said through my teeth, "but *you* are not going to teach me."

"What else are you going to do with yourself? Paint? How's that going these days, Feyre?"

"What the hell does it even matter to you?"

"It serves various purposes of mine, of course."

"What. Purposes."

"You'll have to agree to work with me to find out, I'm afraid."

Something sharp poked into my hand.

I'd folded the fork into a tangle of metal.

When I set it down on the table, Rhys chuckled. "Interesting."

"You said that last night."

"Am I not allowed to say it twice?"

"That's not what I was implying and you know it."

His gaze raked over me again, as if he could see beneath the peach fabric, through the skin, to the shredded soul beneath. Then it drifted to the mangled fork. "Has anyone ever told you that you're rather strong for a High Fae?"

"Am I?"

"I'll take that as a no." He popped a piece of melon into his mouth. "Have you tested yourself against anyone?"

"Why would I?" I was enough of a wreck as it was.

"Because you were resurrected and reborn by the combined powers of the seven High Lords. If I were you, I'd be curious to see if anything else transferred to me during that process."

My blood chilled. "Nothing else *transferred* to me."

"It'd just be rather . . . interesting," he smirked at the word, "if it did."

"It didn't, and I'm not going to learn to read or shield with you."

"Why? From spite? I thought you and I got past that Under the Mountain."

"Don't get me started on what you did to me Under the Mountain."

Rhys went still.

As still as I'd ever seen him, as still as the death now beckoning in those eyes. Then his chest began to move, faster and faster.

Across the pillars towering behind him, I could have sworn the shadow of great wings spread.

He opened his mouth, leaning forward, and then stopped. Instantly, the shadows, the ragged breathing, the intensity were gone, the lazy grin returning. "We have company. We'll discuss this later."

"No, we won't." But quick, light footsteps sounded down the hall, and then she appeared.

If Rhysand was the most beautiful male I'd ever seen, she was his female equivalent.

Her bright, golden hair was tied back in a casual braid, and the turquoise of her clothes—fashioned like my own—offset her sun-kissed skin, making her practically glow in the morning light.

"Hello, hello," she chirped, her full lips parting in a dazzling smile as her rich brown eyes fixed on me.

"Feyre," Rhys said smoothly, "meet my cousin, Morrigan. Mor, meet the lovely, charming, and open-minded Feyre."

I debated splashing my tea in his face, but Mor strode toward me. Each step was assured and steady, graceful, and . . . grounded. Merry but alert. Someone who didn't need weapons—or at least bother to sheath them at her side. "I've heard so much about you," she said, and I got to my feet, awkwardly jutting out my hand.

She ignored it and grabbed me into a bone-crushing hug. She smelled like citrus and cinnamon. I tried to relax my taut muscles as she pulled away and grinned rather fiendishly. "You look like you were getting under Rhys's skin," she said, strutting to her seat between us. "Good thing I came along. Though I'd enjoy seeing Rhys's balls nailed to the wall."

Rhys slid incredulous eyes at her, his brows lifting.

I hid the smile that tugged on my lips. "It's—nice to meet you."

"Liar," Mor said, pouring herself some tea and loading her plate. "You want nothing to do with us, do you? And wicked Rhys is making you sit here."

"You're . . . perky today, Mor," Rhys said.

Mor's stunning eyes lifted to her cousin's face. "Forgive me for being excited about having company *for once*."

"You could be attending your own duties," he said testily. I clamped my lips tighter together. I'd never seen Rhys . . . irked.

"I needed a break, and you told me to come here whenever I liked, so what better time than now, when you brought my new friend to finally meet me?"

I blinked, realizing two things at once: one, she actually meant what she said; two, hers was the female voice I'd heard speak last night, mocking Rhys for our squabble. *So,* that *went well*, she'd teased. As if there were any other alternative, any chance of pleasantness, where he and I were concerned.

A new fork had appeared beside my plate, and I picked it up, only to spear a piece of melon. "You two look nothing alike," I said at last.

"Mor is my cousin in the *loosest* definition," he said. She grinned at him, devouring slices of tomato and pale cheese. "But we were raised together. She's my only surviving family."

I didn't have the nerve to ask what happened to everyone else. Or remind myself whose father was responsible for the lack of family at my own court.

"And as my only remaining relative," Rhys went on, "Mor believes she is entitled to breeze in and out of my life as she sees fit."

"So grumpy this morning," Mor said, plopping two muffins onto her plate.

"I didn't see you Under the Mountain," I found myself saying, hating those last three words more than anything.

"Oh, I wasn't there," she said. "I was in—"

"Enough, Mor," he said, his voice laced with quiet thunder.

It was a trial in itself not to sit up at the interruption, not to study them too closely.

Rhysand set his napkin on the table and rose. "Mor will be here for the rest of the week, but by all means, do not feel that you have to oblige her with your presence." Mor stuck out her tongue at him. He rolled his eyes, the most human gesture I'd ever seen him make. He examined my plate. "Did you eat enough?" I nodded. "Good. Then let's go." He inclined his head toward the pillars and swaying curtains behind him. "Your first lesson awaits."

Mor sliced one of the muffins in two in a steady sweep of her knife. The angle of her fingers, her wrist, indeed confirmed my suspicions that weapons weren't at all foreign to her. "If he pisses you off, Feyre, feel free to shove him over the rail of the nearest balcony."

Rhys gave her a smooth, filthy gesture as he strode down the hall.

I eased to my feet when he was a good distance ahead. "Enjoy your breakfast."

"Whenever you want company," she said as I edged around the table, "give a shout." She probably meant that literally.

I merely nodded and trailed after the High Lord.

I agreed to sit at the long, wooden table in a curtained-off alcove only because he had a point. Not being able to read had almost cost me my life Under the Mountain. I'd be damned if I let it become a weakness again, his personal agenda or no. And as for shielding . . . I'd be a damned fool not to take up the offer to learn from him. The thought of anyone, especially Rhys, sifting through the mess in my mind, taking information about the Spring Court, about the people I loved . . . I'd never allow it. Not willingly.

But it didn't make it any easier to endure Rhysand's presence at the wooden table. Or the stack of books piled atop it.

"I know my alphabet," I said sharply as he laid a piece of paper in front of me. "I'm not that stupid." I twisted my fingers in my lap, then pinned my restless hands under my thighs.

"I didn't say you were stupid," he said. "I'm just trying to determine where we should begin." I leaned back in the cushioned seat. "Since you've refused to tell me a thing about how much you know."

My face warmed. "Can't you hire a tutor?"

He lifted a brow. "Is it that hard for you to even try in front of me?"

"You're a High Lord—don't you have better things to do?"

"Of course. But none as enjoyable as seeing you squirm."

"You're a real bastard, you know that?"

Rhys huffed a laugh. "I've been called worse. In fact, I think you've called me worse." He tapped the paper in front of him. "Read that."

A blur of letters. My throat tightened. "I can't."

"Try."

The sentence had been written in elegant, concise print. His writing, no doubt. I tried to open my mouth, but my spine locked up. "What, *exactly*, is your stake in all this? You said you'd tell me if I worked with you."

"I didn't specify *when* I'd tell you." I peeled back from him as my lip curled. He shrugged. "Maybe I resent the idea of you letting those sycophants and war-mongering fools in the Spring Court make you feel inadequate. Maybe I indeed enjoy seeing you squirm. Or maybe—"

"I get it."

Rhys snorted. "Try to read it, Feyre."

Prick. I snatched the paper to me, nearly ripping it in half in the process. I looked at the first word, sounding it out in my head. "Y-you . . . " The next I figured out with a combination of my silent pronunciation and logic. "Look . . . "

"Good," he murmured.

"I didn't ask for your approval."

Rhys chuckled.

"Ab . . . Absolutely." It took me longer than I wanted to admit to figure that out. The next word was even worse. "De . . . Del . . . "

I deigned to glance at him, brows raised.

"Delicious," he purred.

My brows now knotted. I read the next two words, then whipped my face toward him. "*You look absolutely delicious today, Feyre*?! That's what you wrote?"

He leaned back in his seat. As our eyes met, sharp claws caressed my mind and his voice whispered inside my head: *It's true, isn't it?*

I jolted back, my chair groaning. "*Stop that*!"

But those claws now dug in—and my entire body, my heart, my lungs, my *blood* yielded to his grip, utterly at his command as he said, *The fashion of the Night Court suits you.*

I couldn't move in my seat, couldn't even blink.

This is what happens when you leave your mental shields down. Someone with my sort of powers could slip inside, see what they want, and take your mind for themselves. Or they could shatter it. I'm currently standing on the threshold of your mind . . . but if I were to go deeper, all it would take would be half a thought from me and who you are, your very self, would be wiped away.

Distantly, sweat slid down my temple.

You should be afraid. You should be afraid of this, and you should be thanking the gods-damned Cauldron that in the past three months, no one with my sorts of gifts has run into you. Now shove me out.

I couldn't. Those claws were everywhere—digging into every thought, every piece of self. He pushed a little harder.

Shove. Me. Out.

I didn't know where to begin. I blindly pushed and slammed myself into him, into those claws that were everywhere, as if I were a top loosed in a circle of mirrors.

His laughter, low and soft, filled my mind, my ears. *That way, Feyre.*

In answer, a little open path gleamed inside my mind. The road out.

It'd take me forever to unhook each claw and shove the mass of his presence out that narrow opening. If I could wash it away—

A wave. A wave of self, of *me*, to sweep all of him out—

I didn't let him see the plan take form as I rallied myself into a cresting wave and struck.

The claws loosened—reluctantly. As if letting me win this round. He merely said, "Good."

My bones, my breath and blood, they were mine again. I slumped in my seat.

"Not yet," he said. "Shield. Block me out so I can't get back in."

I already wanted to go somewhere quiet and sleep for a while—

Claws at that outer layer of my mind, stroking—

I imagined a wall of adamant snapping down, black as night and a foot thick. The claws retracted a breath before the wall sliced them in two.

Rhys was grinning. "Very nice. Blunt, but nice."

I couldn't help myself. I grabbed the piece of paper and shredded it in two, then four. "You're a pig."

"Oh, most definitely. But look at you—you read that whole sentence, kicked me out of your mind, *and* shielded. Excellent work."

"Don't condescend to me."

"I'm not. You're reading at a level far higher than I anticipated."

That burning returned to my cheeks. "But mostly illiterate."

"At this point, it's about practice, spelling, and more practice. You could be reading novels by Nynsar. And if you keep adding to those shields, you might very well keep me out entirely by then, too."

Nynsar. It'd be the first Tamlin and his court would celebrate in nearly fifty years. Amarantha had banned it on a whim, along with a few other small, but beloved Fae holidays that she had deemed *unnecessary*. But Nynsar was months from now. "Is it even possible—to truly keep you out?"

"Not likely, but who knows how deep that power goes? Keep practicing and we'll see what happens."

"And will I still be bound by this bargain at Nynsar, too?"

Silence.

I pushed, "After—after what happened—" I couldn't mention specifics on what had occurred Under the Mountain, what he'd done for me during that fight with Amarantha, what he'd done after— "I think we can agree that I owe you nothing, and you owe *me* nothing."

His gaze was unflinching.

I blazed on, "Isn't it enough that we're all free?" I splayed my tattooed hand on the table. "By the end, I thought you were different, thought that it was all a mask, but taking me away, *keeping* me here . . . " I shook my head, unable to find the words vicious enough, clever enough to convince him to end this bargain.

His eyes darkened. "I'm not your enemy, Feyre."

"Tamlin says you are." I curled the fingers of my tattooed hand into a fist. "Everyone else says you are."

"And what do *you* think?" He leaned back in his chair again, but his face was grave.

"You're doing a damned good job of making me agree with them."

"Liar," he purred. "Did you even tell your friends about *what I did to you* Under the Mountain?"

So that comment at breakfast *had* gotten under his skin. "I don't want to talk about anything related to that. With you or them."

"No, because it's so much easier to pretend it never happened and let them coddle you."

"I don't *let* them coddle me—"

"They had you wrapped up like a present yesterday. Like you were *his* reward."

"So?"

"So?" A flicker of rage, then it was gone.

"I'm ready to be taken home," I merely said.

"Where you'll be cloistered for the rest of your life, especially once you start punching out heirs. I can't wait to see what Ianthe does when she gets her hands on *them*."

"You don't seem to have a particularly high opinion of her."

Something cold and predatory crept into his eyes. "No, I can't say that I do." He pointed to a blank piece of paper. "Start copying the alphabet. Until your letters are perfect. And every time you get through a round, lower and raise your shield. Until *that* is second nature. I'll be back in an hour."

"What?"

"Copy. The. Alphabet. Until—"

"I heard what you said." Prick. Prick, prick, *prick*.

"Then get to work." Rhys uncoiled to his feet. "And at least have the decency to only call me a prick when your shields are back up."

He vanished into a ripple of darkness before I realized that I'd let the wall of adamant fade again.

By the time Rhys returned, my mind felt like a mud puddle.

I spent the entire hour doing as I'd been ordered, though I'd flinched at every sound from the nearby stairwell: quiet steps of servants, the flapping of sheets being changed, someone humming a beautiful and winding melody. And beyond that, the chatter of birds that dwelled in the unnatural warmth of the mountain or in the many potted citrus trees. No sign of my impending torment. No sentries, even, to monitor me. I might as well have had the entire place to myself.

Which was good, as my attempts to lower and raise that mental shield often resulted in my face being twisted or strained or pinched.

"Not bad," Rhys said, peering over my shoulder.

He'd appeared moments before, a healthy distance away, and if I hadn't known better, I might have thought it was because he didn't want to startle me. As if he'd known about the time Tamlin had crept up behind me, and panic had hit me so hard I'd knocked him on his ass with a punch to his stomach. I'd blocked it out—the shock on Tam's face, how *easy* it had been to take him off his feet, the humiliation of having my stupid terror so out in the open . . .

Rhys scanned the pages I'd scribbled on, sorting through them, tracking my progress.

Then, a scrape of claws inside my mind—that only sliced against black, glittering adamant.

I threw my lingering will into that wall as the claws pushed, testing for weak spots . . .

"Well, well," Rhysand purred, those mental claws withdrawing. "Hopefully I'll be getting a good night's rest at last, if you can manage to keep the wall up while you sleep."

I dropped the shield, sent a word blasting down that mental bridge between us, and hauled the walls back up. Behind it, my mind wobbled like jelly. I needed a nap. Desperately.

"Prick I might be, but look at you. Maybe we'll get to have some fun with our lessons after all."

I was still scowling at Rhys's muscled back as I kept a healthy ten steps behind him while he led me through the halls of the main building, the sweeping mountains and blisteringly blue sky the only witnesses to our silent trek.

I was too drained to demand where we were now going, and he didn't bother explaining as he led me up, up—until we entered a round chamber at the top of a tower.

A circular table of black stone occupied the center, while the largest stretch of uninterrupted gray stone wall was covered in a massive map of our world. It had been marked and flagged and pinned, for whatever reasons I couldn't tell, but my gaze drifted to the windows throughout the room—so many that it felt utterly exposed, breathable. The perfect home, I supposed, for a High Lord blessed with wings.

Rhys stalked to the table, where there was another map spread, figurines dotting its surface. A map of Prythian—and Hybern.

Every court in our land had been marked, along with villages and cities and rivers and mountain passes. Every court . . . but the Night Court.

The vast, northern territory was utterly blank. Not even a mountain range had been etched in. Strange, likely part of some strategy I didn't understand.

I found Rhysand watching me—his raised brows enough to make me shut my mouth against the forming question.

"Nothing to ask?"

"No."

A feline smirk danced on his lips, but Rhys jerked his chin toward the map on the wall. "What do you see?"

"Is this some sort of way of convincing me to embrace my reading lessons?" Indeed, I couldn't decipher any of the writing, only the shapes of things. Like the wall, its massive line bisecting our world.

"Tell me what you see."

"A world divided in two."

"And do you think it should remain that way?"

I whipped my head toward him. "My family—" I halted on the word. I should have known better than to admit to having a family, that I cared for them—

"Your human family," Rhys finished, "would be deeply impacted if the wall came down, wouldn't they? So close to its border . . . If they're lucky, they'll flee across the ocean before it happens."

"*Will* it happen?"

Rhysand didn't break my stare. "Maybe."

"Why?"

"Because war is coming, Feyre."

CHAPTER 7

War.

The word clanged through me, freezing my veins.

"Don't invade," I breathed. I'd get on my knees for this. I'd crawl if I had to. "Don't invade—please."

Rhys cocked his head, his mouth tightening. "You truly think I'm a monster, even after everything."

"Please," I gasped out. "They're defenseless, they won't stand a chance—"

"I'm not going to invade the mortal lands," he said too quietly.

I waited for him to go on, glad for the spacious room, the bright air, as the ground started to slide out from beneath me.

"Put your damn shield up," he growled.

I looked inward, finding that invisible wall had dropped again. But I was so tired, and if war was coming, if my family—

"Shield. *Now*."

The raw command in his voice—the voice of the High Lord of the Night Court—had me acting on instinct, my exhausted mind building the wall brick by brick. Only when it'd ensconced my mind once more did he speak, his eyes softening almost imperceptibly. "Did you think it would end with Amarantha?"

"Tamlin hasn't said . . . " And why would he tell me? But there were so many patrols, so many meetings I wasn't allowed to attend, such . . . tension. He had to know. I needed to ask him—demand why he hadn't told me—

"The King of Hybern has been planning his campaign to reclaim the world south of the wall for over a hundred years," Rhys said. "Amarantha was an experiment—a forty-nine-year test, to see how easily and how long a territory might fall and be controlled by one of his commanders."

For an immortal, forty-nine years was nothing. I wouldn't have been surprised to hear he'd been planning this for far longer than a century. "Will he attack Prythian first?"

"Prythian," Rhys said, pointing to the map of our massive island on the table, "is all that stands between the King of Hybern and the continent. He wants to reclaim the human lands there—perhaps seize the faerie lands, too. If anyone is to intercept his conquering fleet before it reaches the continent, it would be us."

I slid into one of the chairs, my knees wobbling so badly I could hardly keep upright.

"He will seek to remove Prythian from his way swiftly and thoroughly," Rhys continued. "And shatter the wall at some point in the process. There are already holes in it, though mercifully small enough to make it difficult to swiftly pass his armies through. He'll want to bring the whole thing down—and likely use the ensuing panic to his advantage."

Each breath was like swallowing glass. "When—when is he going to attack?" The wall had held steady for five centuries, and even then, those damned holes had allowed the foulest, hungriest Fae beasts to sneak through and prey on humans. Without that wall, if Hybern was indeed to launch an assault on the human world . . . I wished I hadn't eaten such a large breakfast.

"That is the question," he said. "And why I brought you here."

I lifted my head to meet his stare. His face was drawn, but calm.

"I don't know when or where he plans to attack Prythian," Rhys went on. "I don't know who his allies here might be."

"He'd have allies here?"

A slow nod. "Cowards who would bow and join him, rather than fight his armies again."

I could have sworn a whisper of darkness spread along the floor behind him. "Did . . . did you fight in the War?"

For a moment, I thought he wouldn't answer. But then Rhys nodded. "I was young—by our standards, at least. But my father had sent aid to the mortal-faerie alliance on the continent, and I convinced him to let me take a legion of our soldiers." He sat in the chair beside mine, gazing vacantly at the map. "I was stationed in the south, right where the fighting was thickest. The slaughter was . . . " He chewed on the inside of his cheek. "I have no interest in ever seeing full-scale slaughter like that again."

He blinked, as if clearing the horrors from his mind. "But I don't think the King of Hybern will strike that way—not at first. He's too smart to waste his forces here, to give the continent time to rally while we fight him. If he makes his move to destroy Prythian and the wall, it'll be through stealth and trickery. To weaken us. Amarantha was the first part of that plan. We now have several untested High Lords, broken courts with High Priestesses angling for control like wolves around a carcass, and a people who have realized how powerless they might truly be."

"Why are you telling me this?" I said, my voice thin, scratchy. It made no sense—none—that he would reveal his suspicions, his fears.

And Ianthe—she might be ambitious, but she was Tamlin's friend. *My* friend, of sorts. Perhaps the only ally we'd have against the other High Priestesses, Rhys's personal dislike for her or no . . .

"I am telling you for two reasons," he said, his face so cold, so calm, that it unnerved me as much as the news he was delivering. "One, you're . . . close to Tamlin. He has men—but he also has long-existing ties to Hybern—"

"He'd *never* help the king—"

Rhys held up a hand. "I want to know if Tamlin is willing to fight with us. If he can use those connections to our advantage. As he and I have strained relations, you have the pleasure of being the go-between."

"He doesn't inform me of those things."

"Perhaps it's time he did. Perhaps it's time you insisted." He examined the map, and I followed where his gaze landed. On the wall within Prythian—on the small, vulnerable mortal territory. My mouth went dry.

"What is your other reason?"

Rhys looked me up and down, assessing, weighing. "You have a skill set that I need. Rumor has it you caught a Suriel."

"It wasn't that hard."

"I've tried and failed. Twice. But that's a discussion for another day. I saw you trap the Middengard Wyrm like a rabbit." His eyes twinkled. "I need you to help me. To use those skills of yours to track down what I need."

"What *do* you need? Whatever was tied to my reading and shielding, I'm guessing?"

"You'll learn of that later."

I didn't know why I'd even bothered to ask. "There have to be at least a dozen other hunters more experienced and skilled—"

"Maybe there are. But you're the only one I trust."

I blinked. "I could betray you whenever I feel like it."

"You could. But you won't." I gritted my teeth, and was about to say something vicious when he added, "And then there's the matter of your powers."

"I don't have any powers." It came out so fast that there was no chance of it sounding like anything but denial.

Rhys crossed his legs. "Don't you? The strength, the speed . . . If I didn't know better, I'd say you and Tamlin were doing a very good job of pretending you're normal. That the powers you're displaying aren't usually the first indications among our kind that a High Lord's son might become his Heir."

"I'm not a High Lord."

"No, but you were given life by all seven of us. Your very essence is tied to us, born of us. What if we gave you more than we expected?" Again, that gaze raked over me. "What if you could stand against us—hold your own, a High Lady?"

"There are no High Ladies."

His brows furrowed, but he shook his head. "We'll talk about *that* later, too. But yes, Feyre—there *can* be High Ladies. And perhaps you aren't one of them, but . . . what if you were something similar? What if you were able to wield the power of seven High Lords at once? What if you could blend into darkness, or shape-shift, or freeze over an entire room—an entire army?"

The winter wind on the nearby peaks seemed to howl in answer. That thing I'd felt under my skin . . .

"Do you understand what that might mean in an oncoming war? Do you understand how it might destroy you if you don't learn to control it?"

"One, stop asking so many rhetorical questions. Two, we don't know if I *do* have these powers—"

"You do. But you need to start mastering them. To learn what you inherited from us."

"And I suppose you're the one to teach me, too? Reading and shielding aren't enough?"

"While you hunt with me for what I need, yes."

I began shaking my head. "Tamlin won't allow it."

"Tamlin isn't your keeper, and you know it."

"I'm his subject, and he is my High Lord—"

"You are *no one's subject.*"

I went rigid at the flash of teeth, the smoke-like wings that flared out.

"I will say this once—and only once," Rhysand purred, stalking to the map on the wall. "You can be a pawn, be someone's reward, and spend the rest of your immortal life bowing and scraping and pretending you're less than him, than Ianthe, than any of us. If you want to pick that road, then fine. A shame, but it's your choice." The shadow of wings rippled again. "But I know you—more than you realize, I think—and I don't believe for one damn minute that you're remotely fine with being a pretty trophy for someone who sat on his ass for nearly fifty years, then sat on his ass while you were shredded apart—"

"Stop it—"

"Or," he plowed ahead, "you've got another choice. You can master whatever powers we gave to you, and make it count. You can play a role in this war. Because war is coming one way or another, and do not try to delude yourself that any of the Fae will give a shit about your family across the wall when our whole territory is likely to become a charnel house."

I stared at the map—at Prythian, and that sliver of land at its southern base.

"You want to save the mortal realm?" he asked. "Then become someone Prythian listens to. Become vital. Become a weapon. Because there might be a day, Feyre, when only you stand between the King of Hybern and your human family. And you do not want to be unprepared."

I lifted my gaze to him, my breath tight, aching.

As if he hadn't just knocked the world from beneath my feet, Rhysand said, "Think it over. Take the week. Ask Tamlin, if it'll make you sleep better. See what charming Ianthe says about it. But it's your choice to make—no one else's."

I didn't see Rhysand for the rest of the week. Or Mor.

The only people I encountered were Nuala and Cerridwen, who delivered my meals, made my bed, and occasionally asked how I was faring.

The only evidence I had at all that Rhys remained on the premises were the blank copies of the alphabet, along with several sentences I was to write every day, swapping out words, each one more obnoxious than the last:

Rhysand is the most handsome High Lord.
Rhysand is the most delightful High Lord.
Rhysand is the most cunning High Lord.

Every day, one miserable sentence—with one changing word of varying arrogance and vanity. And every day, another simple set of instructions: shield up, shield down; shield up, shield down. Over and over and over.

How he knew if I obeyed or not, I didn't care—but I threw myself into my lessons, I raised and lowered and thickened those mental shields. If only because it was all I had to do.

My nightmares left me groggy, sweaty—but the room was so open, the starlight so bright that when I'd jerk awake, I didn't rush to the toilet. No walls pushing in around me, no inky darkness. I knew where I was. Even if I resented being there.

The day before our week finally finished, I was trudging to my usual little table, already grimacing at what delightful sentences I'd find waiting and all the mental acrobatics ahead, when Rhys's and Mor's voices floated toward me.

It was a public space, so I didn't bother masking my footsteps as I neared where they spoke in one of the sitting areas, Rhys pacing before the open plunge off the mountain, Mor lounging in a cream-colored armchair.

"Azriel would want to know that," Mor was saying.

"Azriel can go to hell," Rhys sniped back. "He likely already knows, anyway."

"We played games the last time," Mor said with a seriousness that made me pause a healthy distance away, "and we lost. Badly. We're not going to do that again."

"You should be working," was Rhysand's only response. "I gave you control for a reason, you know."

Mor's jaw tightened, and she at last faced me. She gave me a smile that was more of a cringe.

Rhys turned, frowning at me. "Say what it is you came here to say, Mor," he said tightly, resuming his pacing.

Mor rolled her eyes for my benefit, but her face turned solemn as she said, "There was another attack—at a temple in Cesere. Almost every priestess slain, the trove looted."

Rhys halted. And I didn't know what to process: her news, or the utter rage conveyed in one word as Rhys said, "Who."

"We don't know," Mor said. "Same tracks as last time: small group, bodies that showed signs of wounds from large blades, and no trace of where they came from and how they disappeared. No survivors. The bodies weren't even found until a day later, when a group of pilgrims came by."

By the Cauldron. I must have made some tiny noise, because Mor gave me a strained, but sympathetic look.

Rhys, though . . . First the shadows started—plumes of them from his back.

And then, as if his rage had loosened his grip on that beast he'd once told me he hated to yield to, those wings became flesh.

Great, beautiful, brutal wings, membranous and clawed like a bat's, dark as night and strong as hell. Even the way he stood seemed altered—steadier, grounded. Like some final piece of him had clicked into place. But Rhysand's voice was still midnight-soft and he said, "What did Azriel have to say about it?"

Again, that glance from Mor, as if unsure I should be present for whatever this conversation was. "He's pissed. Cassian even more so—he's convinced it must be one of the rogue Illyrian war-bands, intent on winning new territory."

"It's something to consider," Rhys mused. "Some of the Illyrian clans gleefully bowed to Amarantha during those years. Trying to expand their borders could be their way of seeing how far they can push me and get away with it." I hated the sound of her name, focused on it more than the information he was allowing me to glean.

"Cassian and Az are waiting—" She cut herself off and gave me an apologetic wince. "They're waiting in the usual spot for your orders."

Fine—that was fine. I'd seen that blank map on the wall. I was an enemy's bride. Even mentioning where his forces were stationed, what they were up to, might be dangerous. I had no idea where Cesere even *was*—what it was, actually.

Rhys studied the open air again, the howling wind that shoved dark, roiling clouds over the distant peaks. Good weather, I realized, for flying.

"Winnowing in would be easier," Mor said, following the High Lord's gaze.

"Tell the pricks I'll be there in a few hours," he merely said.

Mor gave me a wary grin, and vanished.

I studied the empty space where she'd been, not a trace of her left behind.

"How does that . . . vanishing work?" I said softly. I'd seen only a few High Fae do it—and no one had ever explained.

Rhys didn't look at me, but he said, "Winnowing? Think of it as . . . two different points on a piece of cloth. One point is your current place in the world. The other one across the cloth is where you want to go. Winnowing . . . it's like folding that cloth so the two spots align.

The magic does the folding—and all we do is take a step to get from one place to another. Sometimes it's a long step, and you can feel the dark fabric of the world as you pass through it. A shorter step, let's say from one end of the room to the other, would barely register. It's a rare gift, and a helpful one. Though only the stronger Fae can do it. The more powerful you are, the farther you can jump between places in one go."

I knew the explanation was as much for my benefit as it was to distract himself. But I found myself saying, "I'm sorry about the temple—and the priestesses."

The wrath still glimmered in those eyes as he at last turned to me. "Plenty more people are going to die soon enough, anyway."

Maybe that was why he'd allowed me to get close, to overhear this conversation. To remind me of what might very well happen with Hybern.

"What are . . . ," I tried. "What are Illyrian war-bands?"

"Arrogant bastards, that's what," he muttered.

I crossed my arms, waiting.

Rhys stretched his wings, the sunlight setting the leathery texture glowing with subtle color. "They're a warrior-race within my lands. And general pains in my ass."

"Some of them supported Amarantha?"

Darkness danced in the hall as that distant storm grew close enough to smother the sun. "Some. But me and mine have enjoyed ourselves hunting them down these past few months. And ending them."

Slowly was the word he didn't need to add.

"That's why you stayed away—you were busy with that?"

"I was busy with many things."

Not an answer. But it seemed he was done talking to me, and whoever Cassian and Azriel were, meeting with them was far more important.

So Rhys didn't as much as say good-bye before he simply walked off the edge of the veranda—into thin air.

My heart stopped dead, but before I could cry out, he swept past, swift as the wicked wind between the peaks. A few booming wing beats had him vanishing into the storm clouds.

"Good-bye to you, too," I grumbled, giving him a vulgar gesture, and started my work for the day, with only the storm raging beyond the house's shield for company.

Even as snow lashed the protective magic of the hall, even as I toiled over the sentences—*Rhysand is interesting; Rhysand is gorgeous; Rhysand is flawless*—and raised and lowered my mental shield until my mind was limping, I thought of what I'd heard, what they'd said.

I wondered what Ianthe would know about the murders, if she knew any of the victims. Knew what Cesere was. If temples were being targeted, she should know. Tamlin should know.

That final night, I could barely sleep—half from relief, half from terror that perhaps Rhysand really did have some final, nasty surprise in store. But the night and the storm passed, and when dawn broke, I was dressed before the sun had fully risen.

I'd taken to eating in my rooms, but I swept up the stairs, heading across that massive open area, to the table at the far veranda.

Sprawled in his usual chair, Rhys was in the same clothes as yesterday, the collar of his black jacket unbuttoned, the shirt as rumpled as his hair. No wings, fortunately. I wondered if he'd just returned from wherever he'd met Mor and the others. Wondered what he'd learned.

"It's been a week," I said by way of greeting. "Take me home."

Rhys took a long sip of whatever was in his cup. It didn't look like tea. "Good morning, Feyre."

"Take me home."

He studied my teal and gold clothes, a variation of my daily attire. If I had to admit, I didn't mind them. "That color suits you."

"Do you want me to say please? Is that it?"

"I want you to talk to me like a person. Start with 'good morning' and let's see where it gets us."

"Good morning."

A faint smile. Bastard. "Are you ready to face the consequences of your departure?"

I straightened. I hadn't thought about the wedding. All week, yes, but today . . . today I'd only thought of Tamlin, of wanting to see him, hold him, ask him about everything Rhys had claimed. During the past several days, I hadn't shown any signs of the power Rhysand believed I had, hadn't *felt* anything stirring beneath my skin—and thank the Cauldron.

"It's none of your business."

"Right. You'll probably ignore it, anyway. Sweep it under the rug, like everything else."

"No one asked for your opinion, Rhysand."

"Rhysand?" He chuckled, low and soft. "I give you a week of luxury and you call me Rhysand?"

"I didn't ask to be here, or be given that week."

"And yet look at you. Your face has some color—and those marks under your eyes are almost gone. Your mental shield is stellar, by the way."

"Please take me home."

He shrugged and rose. "I'll tell Mor you said good-bye."

"I barely saw her all week." Just that first meeting—then that conversation yesterday. When we hadn't exchanged two words.

"She was waiting for an invitation—she didn't want to pester you. I wish she extended me the same courtesy."

"No one told me." I didn't particularly care. No doubt she had better things to do, anyway.

"You didn't ask. And why bother? Better to be miserable and alone." He approached, each step smooth, graceful. His hair was definitely ruffled, as if he'd been dragging his hands through it. Or just flying for hours to whatever secret spot. "Have you thought about my offer?"

"I'll let you know next month."

He stopped a hand's breadth away, his golden face tight. "I told you once, and I'll tell you again," he said. "I am not your enemy."

"And I told you once, so I'll tell you again. You're *Tamlin*'s enemy. So I suppose that makes you mine."

"Does it?"

"Free me from my bargain and let's find out."

"I can't do that."

"Can't, or won't?"

He just extended his hand. "Shall we go?"

I nearly lunged for it. His fingers were cool, sturdy—callused from weapons I'd never seen on him.

Darkness gobbled us up, and it was instinct to grab him as the world vanished from beneath my feet. Winnowing indeed. Wind tore at me, and his arm was a warm, heavy weight across my back while we tumbled through realms, Rhys snickering at my terror.

But then solid ground—flagstones—were under me, then blinding sunshine above, greenery, little birds chirping—

I shoved away from him, blinking at the brightness, at the massive oak hunched over us. An oak at the edge of the formal gardens—of *home*.

I made to bolt for the manor house, but Rhys gripped my wrist. His eyes flashed between me and the manor. "Good luck," he crooned.

"Get your hand off me."

He chuckled, letting go.

"I'll see you next month," he said, and before I could spit on him, he vanished.

✠

I found Tamlin in his study, Lucien and two other sentries standing around the map-covered worktable.

Lucien was the first to turn to where I lurked in the doorway, falling silent mid-sentence. But then Tamlin's head snapped up, and he was racing across the room, so fast that I hardly had time to draw breath before he was crushing me against him.

I murmured his name as my throat burned, and then—

Then he was holding me at arm's length, scanning me from head to toe. "Are you all right? Are you hurt?"

"I'm fine," I said, noticing the exact moment when he realized the Night Court clothes I was wearing, the strip of bare skin exposed at my midriff. "No one touched me."

But he kept scouring my face, my neck. And then he rotated me, examining my back, as if he could discern through the clothes. I tore out of his grip. "I said no one touched me."

He was breathing hard, his eyes wild. "You're all right," he said. And then said it again. And again.

My heart cracked, and I reached to cup his cheek. "Tamlin," I murmured. Lucien and the other sentries, wisely, made their exit. My friend caught my gaze as he left, giving me a relieved smile.

"He can harm you in other ways," Tamlin croaked, closing his eyes against my touch.

"I know—but I'm all right. I truly am," I said as gently as I could. And then noticed the study walls—the claw marks raked down them. All over them. And the table they'd been using . . . that was new. "You trashed the study."

"I trashed half the house," he said, leaning forward to press his brow to mine. "He took you away, he stole you—"

"And left me alone."

Tamlin pulled back, growling. "Probably to get you to drop your guard. You have no idea what games he plays, what he's capable of doing—"

"I know," I said, even as it tasted like ash on my tongue. "And the next time, I'll be careful—"

"There won't be a next time."

I blinked. "You found a way out?" Or perhaps Ianthe had.

"I'm not letting you go."

"He said there were consequences for breaking a magical bargain."

"Damn the consequences." But I heard it for the empty threat it was—and how much it destroyed him. That was who he was, what he was: protector, defender. I couldn't ask him to stop being that way—to stop worrying about me.

I rose onto my toes and kissed him. There was so much I wanted to ask him, but—later. "Let's go upstairs," I said onto his lips, and he slid his arms around me.

"I missed you," he said between kisses. "I went out of my mind."

That was all I needed to hear. Until—

"I need to ask you some questions."

I let out a low sound of affirmation, but angled my head further. "Later." His body was so warm, so hard against mine, his scent so familiar—

Tamlin gripped my waist, pressing his brow to my own. "No—now," he said, but groaned softly as I slid my tongue against his teeth. "While . . . " He pulled back, ripping his mouth from mine. "While it's all fresh in your mind."

I froze, one hand tangled in his hair, the other gripping the back of his tunic. "What?"

Tamlin stepped back, shaking his head as if to clear the desire addling his senses. We hadn't been apart for so long since Amarantha, and he wanted to press me for information about the Night Court? "Tamlin."

But he held up a hand, his eyes locked on mine as he called for Lucien.

In the moments that it took for his emissary to appear, I straightened my clothes—the top that had ridden up my torso—and finger-combed my hair. Tamlin just strode to his desk and plopped down, motioning for me to take a seat in front of it. "I'm sorry," he said quietly, as Lucien's strolling footsteps neared again. "This is for our own good. Our safety."

I took in the shredded walls, the scuffed and chipped furniture. What nightmares had he suffered, waking and asleep, while I was away? What had it been like, to imagine me in his enemy's hands, after seeing what Amarantha had done to me?

"I know," I murmured at last. "I know, Tamlin." Or I was trying to know.

I'd just slid into the low-backed chair when Lucien strode in, shutting the door behind him. "Glad to see you in one piece, Feyre," he said, claiming the seat beside me. "I could do without the Night Court attire, though."

Tamlin gave a low growl of agreement. I said nothing. Yet I understood—I really did—why it'd be an affront to them.

Tamlin and Lucien exchanged glances, speaking without uttering a word in that way only people who had been partners for centuries could do. Lucien gave a slight nod and leaned back in his chair—to listen, to observe.

"We need you to tell us everything," Tamlin said. "The layout of the Night Court, who you saw, what weapons and powers they bore, what Rhys did, who he spoke to, any and every detail you can recall."

"I didn't realize I was a spy."

Lucien shifted in his seat, but Tamlin said, "As much as I hate your bargain, you've been granted access into the Night Court. Outsiders rarely get to go in—and if they do, they rarely come out in one piece. And if they can function, their memories are usually . . . scrambled. Whatever Rhysand is hiding in there, he doesn't want us knowing about it."

A chill slithered down my spine. "Why do you want to know? What are you going to do?"

"Knowing my enemy's plans, his lifestyle, is vital. As for what we're going to do . . . That's neither here nor there." His green eyes pinned me. "Start with the layout of the court. Is it true it's under a mountain?"

"This feels an awful lot like an interrogation."

Lucien sucked in a breath, but remained silent.

Tamlin spread his hands on the desk. "We need to know these things, Feyre. Or—or can you not remember?" Claws glinted at his knuckles.

"I can remember everything," I said. "He didn't damage my mind." And before he could question me further, I began to speak of all that I had seen.

Because I trust you, Rhysand had said. And maybe—maybe he had scrambled my mind, even with the lessons in shielding, because describing the layout of his home, his court, the mountains around them, felt like bathing in oil and mud. He *was* my enemy, he was holding me to a bargain I'd made from pure desperation—

I kept talking, describing that tower room. Tamlin grilled me on the figures on the maps, making me turn over every word Rhysand had uttered, until I mentioned what had weighed on me the most this past week: the powers Rhys believed I now possessed . . . and Hybern's plans. I told him about that conversation with Mor—about that temple being sacked (Cesere, Tamlin explained, was a northern outpost in the Night Court, and one of the few known towns), and Rhysand mentioning two people named Cassian and Azriel. Both of their faces had tightened at that, but they didn't mention if they knew them, or of them. So I told him about whatever the Illyrians were—and how Rhys had hunted down and killed the traitors amongst them. When I finished, Tamlin was silent, Lucien practically buzzing with whatever repressed words he was dying to spew.

"Do you think I might have those abilities?" I said, willing myself to hold his gaze.

"It's possible," Tamlin said with equal quiet. "And if it's true . . . "

Lucien said at last, "It's a power other High Lords might kill for." It was an effort not to fidget while his metal eye whirred, as if detecting whatever power ran through my blood. "My father, for one, would not be pleased to learn a drop of his power is missing—or that Tamlin's bride now has it. He'd do anything to make sure you *don't* possess it—including kill you. There are other High Lords who would agree."

That *thing* beneath my skin began roiling. "I'd never use it against anyone—"

"It's not about using it against them; it's about having an edge when you shouldn't," Tamlin said. "And the moment word gets out about it, you will have a target on your back."

"Did you know?" I demanded. Lucien wouldn't meet my eyes. "Did you suspect?"

"I'd hoped it wasn't true," Tamlin said carefully. "And now that Rhys suspects, there's no telling what he'll do with the information—"

"He wants me to train." I wasn't stupid enough to mention the mental shield training—not right now.

"Training would draw too much attention," Tamlin said. "You don't *need* to train. I can guard you from whatever comes our way."

For there had been a time when he could not. When he had been vulnerable, and when he had watched me be tortured to death. And could do nothing to stop Amarantha from—

I would not allow another Amarantha. I would not allow the King of Hybern to bring his beasts and minions here to hurt more people. To hurt me and mine. And bring down that wall to hurt countless others across it. "I could use my powers against Hybern."

"That's out of the question," Tamlin said, "especially as there will be no war against Hybern."

"Rhys says war is inevitable, and we'll be hit hard."

Lucien said drily, "And Rhys knows everything?"

"No—but . . . He was concerned. He thinks I can make a difference in any upcoming conflict."

Tamlin flexed his fingers—keeping those claws contained. "You have no training in battle or weaponry. And even if I started training you today, it'd be years before you could hold your own on an immortal battlefield." He took a tight breath. "So despite what he thinks you might be able to do, Feyre, I'm not going to have you anywhere *near* a battlefield. Especially if it means revealing whatever powers you have to our enemies. You'd be fighting Hybern at your front, and have foes with friendly faces at your back."

"I don't care—"

"*I* care," Tamlin snarled. Lucien whooshed out a breath. "*I* care if you die, if you're hurt, if you will be in danger every moment for the rest of our lives. So there will be no training, and we're going to keep this between us."

"But Hybern—"

Lucien intervened calmly, "I already have my sources looking into it."

I gave him a beseeching look.

Lucien sighed a bit and said to Tamlin, "If we perhaps trained her in secret—"

"Too many risks, too many variables," Tamlin countered. "And there will be no conflict with Hybern, no war."

I snapped, "That's wishful thinking."

Lucien muttered something that sounded like a plea to the Cauldron.

Tamlin stiffened. "Describe his map room for me again," was his only response.

End of discussion. No room for debate.

We stared each other down for a moment, and my stomach twisted further.

He was the High Lord—*my* High Lord. He was the shield and defender of his people. Of me. And if keeping me safe meant that his people could continue to hope, to build a new life, that he could do the same . . . I could bow to him on this one thing.

I could do it.

You are no one's subject.

Maybe Rhysand *had* altered my mind, shields or no.

The thought alone was enough for me to begin feeding Tamlin details once more.

CHAPTER 8

A week later, the Tithe arrived.

I'd had all of one day with Tamlin—one day spent wandering the grounds, making love in the high grasses of a sunny field, and a quiet, private dinner—before he was called to the border. He didn't tell me why or where. Only that I was to keep to the grounds, and that I'd have sentries guarding me at all times.

So I spent the week alone, waking in the middle of the night to hurl up my guts, to sob through the nightmares. Ianthe, if she'd learned of her sisters' massacre in the north, said nothing about it the few times I saw her. And given how little *I* liked to be pushed into talking about the things that plagued me, I opted not to bring it up during the hours she spent visiting, helping select my clothes, my hair, my jewelry, for the Tithe.

When I'd asked her to explain what to anticipate, she merely said that Tamlin would take care of everything. I should watch from his side, and observe.

Easy enough—and perhaps a relief, to not be expected to speak or act.

But it had been an effort not to look at the eye tattooed into my palm—to remember what Rhys had snarled at me.

Tamlin had only returned the night before to oversee today's Tithe. I tried not to take it personally, not when he had so much on his shoulders. Even if he wouldn't tell me much about it beyond what Ianthe had mentioned.

Seated beside Tamlin atop a dais in the manor's great hall of marble and gold, I endured the endless stream of eyes, of tears, of gratitude and blessings for what I'd done.

In her usual pale blue hooded robe, Ianthe was stationed near the doors, offering benedictions to those that departed, comforting words to those who fell apart entirely in my presence, promises that the world was better now, that good had won out over evil.

After twenty minutes, I was near fidgeting. After four hours, I stopped hearing entirely.

They kept coming, the emissaries representing every town and people in the Spring Court, bearing their payments in the form of gold or jewels or chickens or crops or clothes. It didn't matter what it was, so long as it equated to what they owed. Lucien stood at the foot of the dais, tallying every amount, armed to the teeth like the ten other sentries stationed through the hall. The receiving room, Lucien had called it, but it felt a hell of a lot like a throne room to me. I wondered if he'd called it that because the other words . . .

I'd spent too much time in another throne room. So had Tamlin.

And I hadn't been seated on a dais like him, but kneeling before it. Approaching it like the slender, gray-skinned faerie slinking from the front of the endless line full of lesser and High Fae.

She wore no clothes. Her long, dark hair hung limp over her high, firm breasts—and her massive eyes were wholly black. Like a stagnant pond. And as she moved, the afternoon light shimmered on her iridescent skin.

Lucien's face tightened with disapproval, but he made no comment as the lesser faerie lowered her delicate, pointed face, and clasped her spindly, webbed fingers over her breasts.

"On behalf of the water-wraiths, I greet thee, High Lord," she said, her voice strange and hissing, her full, sensuous lips revealing teeth as sharp and jagged as a pike's. The sharp angles of her face accentuated those coal-black eyes.

I'd seen her kind before. In the pond just past the edge of the manor. There were five of them who lived amongst the reeds and lilypads. I'd rarely glimpsed more than their shining heads peeking through the glassy surface—had never known how horrific they were up close. Thank the Cauldron I'd never gone swimming in that pond. I had a feeling she'd grab me with those webbed fingers—those jagged nails digging in deep—and drag me beneath the surface before I could scream.

"Welcome," Tamlin said. Five hours in, and he looked as fresh as he'd been that morning.

I supposed that with his powers returned, few things tired him now.

The water-wraith stepped closer, her webbed, clawed foot a mottled gray. Lucien took a casual step between us.

That was why he'd been stationed on my side of the dais.

I gritted my teeth. Who did they think would attack us in our own home, on our own land, if they weren't convinced Hybern might be launching an assault? Even Ianthe had paused her quiet murmurings in the back of the hall to monitor the encounter.

Apparently, this conversation was not the same as all the others.

"Please, High Lord," the faerie was saying, bowing so low that her inky hair grazed the marble. "There are no fish left in the lake."

Tamlin's face was like granite. "Regardless, you are expected to pay." The crown atop his head gleamed in the afternoon light. Crafted with emeralds, sapphires, and amethyst, the gold had been molded into a wreath of spring's first flowers. One of five crowns belonging to his bloodline.

The faerie exposed her palms, but Tamlin interrupted her. "There are no exceptions. You have three days to present what is owed—or offer double next Tithe."

It was an effort to keep from gaping at the immovable face, and the pitiless words. In the back, Ianthe gave a nod of confirmation to no one in particular.

The water-wraith had nothing to eat—how could he expect her to give *him* food?

"Please," she whispered through her pointed teeth, her silvery, mottled skin glistening as she began trembling. "There is nothing left in the lake."

Tamlin's face didn't change. "You have three days—"

"But we have no gold!"

"Do *not* interrupt me," he said. I looked away, unable to stomach that merciless face.

She ducked her head even lower. "Apologies, my lord."

"You have three days to pay, or bring double next month," he repeated. "If you fail to do so, you know the consequences." Tamlin waved a hand in dismissal. Conversation over.

After a final, hopeless look at Tamlin, she walked from the chamber. As the next faerie—a goat-legged fawn bearing what looked to be a basket of mushrooms—patiently waited to be invited to approach the dais, I twisted to Tamlin.

"We don't need a basket of fish," I murmured. "Why make her suffer like that?"

He flicked his eyes to where Ianthe had stepped aside to let the creature pass, a hand on the jewels of her belt. As if the female would snatch them right off her to use as payment. Tamlin frowned. "I cannot make exceptions. Once you do, everyone will demand the same treatment."

I clutched the arms of my chair, a small seat of oak beside his giant throne of carved roses. "But we don't *need* these things. Why do we need a golden fleece, or a jar of jam? If she has no fish left, three days won't make a difference. Why make her starve? Why not help her replenish the pond?" I'd spent enough years with an aching belly to not be able to drop it, to want to scream at the unfairness of it.

His emerald eyes softened as if he read each thought on my face, but he said: "Because that's the way it is. That's the way my father did it, and his father, and the way my son shall do it." He offered a smile, and reached for my hand. "Someday."

Someday. If we ever got married. If I ever became less of a burden, and we both escaped the shadows haunting us. We hadn't broached the subject at all. Ianthe, mercifully, had not said anything, either. "We could still help her—find some way to keep that pond stocked."

"We have enough to deal with as it is. Giving handouts won't help her in the long run."

I opened my mouth, but shut it. Now wasn't the time for debate.

So I pulled my hand from his as he motioned the goat-legged fawn to approach at last. "I need some fresh air," I said, and slid from my chair. I didn't give Tamlin a chance to object before I stalked off the dais. I tried not to notice the three sentries Tamlin sent after me, or the line of emissaries who gaped and whispered as I crossed the hall.

Ianthe tried to catch me as I stormed by, but I ignored her.

I cleared the front doors and walked as fast as I dared past the gathered line snaking down the steps and onto the gravel of the main drive. Through the latticework of various bodies, High Fae and lesser faeries alike, I spotted the retreating form of the wraith heading around the corner of our house—toward the pond beyond the grounds. She trudged along, wiping at her eyes.

"Excuse me," I called, catching up to her, the sentries on my trail keeping a respectful distance behind.

She paused at the edge of the house, whirling with preternatural smoothness. I avoided the urge to take a step back as those unearthly features devoured me. Keeping only a few paces away, the guards monitored us with hands on their blades.

Her nose was little more than two slits, and delicate gills flared beneath her ears.

She inclined her head slightly. Not a full bow—because I was no one, but recognition that I was the High Lord's plaything.

"Yes?" she hissed, her pike's teeth gleaming.

"How much is your Tithe?"

My heart beat faster as I beheld the webbed fingers and razor-sharp teeth. Tamlin had once told me that the water-wraiths ate anything. And if there were no fish left . . . "How much gold does he want—what is your fish worth in gold?"

"Far more than you have in your pocket."

"Then here," I said, unfastening a ruby-studded gold bracelet from my wrist, one Ianthe had told me better suited my coloring than the silver I'd almost worn. I offered it to her. "Take this." Before she could grasp it, I ripped the gold necklace from my throat, and the diamond teardrops from my ears. "And these." I extended my hands, glittering with gold and jewels. "Give him what you owe, then buy yourself some food," I said, swallowing as her eyes widened. The nearby village had a small market every week—a fledgling gathering of vendors for now, and one I'd hoped to help thrive. Somehow.

"And what payment do you require?"

"Nothing. It's—it's not a bargain. Just take it." I extended my hands further. "Please."

She frowned at the jewels draping from my hands. "You desire nothing in return?"

"Nothing." The faeries in the line were now staring unabashedly. "Please, just take them."

With a final assessing look, her cold, clammy fingers brushed mine, gathering up the jewelry. It glimmered like light on water in her webbed hands.

"Thank you," she said, and bowed deeply this time. "I will not forget this kindness." Her voice slithered over the words, and I shivered again as her black eyes threatened to swallow me whole. "Nor will any of my sisters."

She stalked back toward the manor, the faces of my three sentries tight with reproach.

I sat at the dinner table with Lucien and Tamlin. Neither of them spoke, but Lucien's gaze kept bouncing from me, to Tamlin, then to his plate.

After ten minutes of silence, I set down my fork and said to Tamlin, "What is it?"

Tamlin didn't hesitate. "You know what it is."

I didn't reply.

"You gave that water-wraith your jewelry. Jewelry *I* gave you."

"We have a damned house full of gold and jewels."

Lucien took a deep breath that sounded a lot like: "Here we go."

"Why shouldn't I give them to her?" I demanded. "Those things don't mean anything to me. I've never worn the same piece of jewelry twice! Who cares about any of it?"

Tamlin's lips thinned. "Because you *undermine* the laws of this court when you behave like that. Because this is how things are *done* here, and when you hand that gluttonous faerie the money she needs, it makes me—it makes this entire court—look *weak*."

"Don't you talk to me like that," I said, baring my teeth. He slammed his hand on the table, claws poking through his flesh, but I leaned forward, bracing my own hands on the wood. "You still have no idea what it was like for me—to be on the verge of starvation for months at a time. And you can call her a glutton all you like, but I have sisters, too, and I remember what it felt like to return home without any food." I calmed my heaving chest, and that force beneath my skin stirred, undulating along my bones. "So maybe she'll spend all that money on stupid things—maybe she and her sisters have no self-control. But I'm not going to take that chance and let them starve, because of some *ridiculous* rule that your ancestors invented."

Lucien cleared his throat. "She meant no harm, Tam."

"I know she meant no harm," he snapped.

Lucien held his gaze. "Worse things have happened, worse things *can* happen. Just relax."

Tamlin's emerald eyes were feral as he snarled at Lucien, "Did I ask for your opinion?"

Those words, the *look* he gave Lucien and the way Lucien lowered his head—my temper was a burning river in my veins. *Look up*, I silently beseeched him. *Push back. He's wrong, and we're right*. Lucien's jaw tightened. That force thrummed in me again, seeping out, spearing for Lucien. *Do* not *back down*—

Then I was gone.

Still there, still seeing through my eyes, but also half looking through another angle in the room, another person's vantage point—

Thoughts slammed into me, images and memories, a pattern of thinking and feeling that was old, and clever, and sad, so endlessly sad and guilt-ridden, hopeless—

Then I was back, blinking, no more than a heartbeat passing as I gaped at Lucien.

His head. I had been *inside* his head, had slid through his mental walls—

I stood, chucking my napkin on the table with hands that were unnervingly steady.

I knew who *that* gift had come from. My dinner rose in my throat, but I willed it down.

"We're not finished with this meal," Tamlin growled.

"Oh, get over yourself," I barked, and left.

I could have sworn I beheld two burned handprints on the wood, peeking out from beneath my napkin. I prayed neither of them noticed.

And that Lucien remained ignorant to the violation I'd just committed.

CHAPTER 9

I paced my room for a good while. Maybe I'd been mistaken when I'd spotted those burns—maybe they'd been there before. Maybe I hadn't somehow summoned heat and branded the wood. Maybe I hadn't slid into Lucien's mind as if I were moving from one room to another.

Just as she always did, Alis appeared to help me change for bed. As I sat before the vanity, letting her comb my hair, I cringed at my reflection. The purple beneath my eyes seemed permanent now—my face wan. Even my lips were a bit pale, and I sighed as I closed my eyes.

"You gave your jewels to a water-wraith," Alis mused, and I found her reflection in the mirror. Her brown skin looked like crushed leather, and her dark eyes gleamed for a moment before she focused on my hair. "They're a slippery sort."

"She said they were starving—that they had no food," I murmured.

Alis gently coaxed out a tangle. "Not one faerie in that line today would have given her the money. Not one would have dared. Too many have gone to a watery grave because of their hunger. Insatiable appetite—it is their curse. Your jewels won't last her a week."

I tapped a foot on the floor.

"But," Alis went on, setting down the brush to braid my hair into a single plait. Her long, spindly fingers scratched against my scalp. "She will never forget it. So long as she lives, no matter what you said, she is in your debt." Alis finished the braid and patted my shoulder. "Too many faeries have tasted hunger these past fifty years. Don't think word of this won't spread."

I was afraid of that perhaps more than anything.

✢

It was after midnight when I gave up waiting, walked down the dark, silent corridors, and found him in his study, alone for once.

A wooden box wrapped with a fat pink bow sat on the small table between the twin armchairs. "I was just about to come up," he said, lifting his head to do a quick scan over my body to make sure all was right, all was fine. "You should be asleep."

I shut the door behind me. I knew I wouldn't be able to sleep—not with the words we'd shouted ringing in my ears. "So should you," I said, my voice as tenuous as the peace between us. "You work too hard." I crossed the room to lean against the armchair, eyeing the present as Tamlin had eyed me.

"Why do you think I had such little interest in being High Lord?" he said, rising from his seat to round the desk. He kissed my brow, the tip of my nose, my mouth. "So much paperwork," he grumbled onto my lips. I chuckled, but he pressed his mouth to the bare spot between my neck and shoulder. "I'm sorry," he murmured, and my spine tingled. He kissed my neck again. "I'm sorry."

I ran a hand down his arm. "Tamlin," I started.

"I shouldn't have said those things," he breathed onto my skin. "To you or Lucien. I didn't mean any of them."

"I know," I said, and his body relaxed against mine. "I'm sorry I snapped at you."

"You had every right," he said, though I technically didn't. "I was wrong."

What he said had been true—if he made exceptions, then other faeries would demand the same treatment. And what I had done *could* be construed as undermining. "Maybe I was—"

"No. You were right. I don't understand what it's like to be starving—or any of it."

I pulled back a bit to incline my head toward the present waiting there, more than willing to let this be the last of it. I gave a small, wry smile. "For you?"

He nipped at my ear in answer. "For you. From me." An apology.

Feeling lighter than I had in days, I tugged the ribbon loose, and examined the pale wood box beneath. It was perhaps two feet high and three feet wide, a solid iron handle anchored in the top—no crest or lettering to indicate what might be within. Certainly not a dress, but . . .

Please not a crown.

Though surely, a crown or diadem would be in something less . . . rudimentary.

I unlatched the small brass lock and flipped open the broad lid.

It was worse than a crown, actually.

Built into the box were compartments and sleeves and holders, all full of brushes and paints and charcoal and sheets of paper. A traveling painting kit.

Red—the red paint inside the glass vial was so bright, the blue as stunning as the eyes of that faerie woman I'd slaughtered—

"I thought you might want it to take around the grounds with you. Rather than lug all those bags like you always do."

The brushes were fresh, gleaming—the bristles soft and clean.

Looking at that box, at what was inside, felt like examining a crow-picked corpse.

I tried to smile. Tried to will some brightness to my eyes.

He said, "You don't like it."

"No," I managed to say. "No—it's wonderful." And it was. It really was.

"I thought if you started painting again . . . " I waited for him to finish.

He didn't.

My face heated.

"And what about you?" I asked quietly. "Will the paperwork help with anything at all?"

I dared meet his eyes. Temper flared in them. But he said, "We're not talking about me. We're talking—about you."

I studied the box and its contents again. "Will I even be allowed to roam where I wish to paint? Or will there be an escort, too?"

Silence.

A no—and a yes, then.

I began shaking, but for me, for *us*, I made myself say, "Tamlin—Tamlin, I can't . . . I can't live my life with guards around me day and night. I can't live with that . . . suffocation. Just let me help you—let me work with you."

"You've given enough, Feyre."

"I know. But . . . " I faced him. Met his stare—the full power of the High Lord of the Spring Court. "I'm harder to kill now. I'm faster, stronger—"

"My family was faster and stronger than you. And they were murdered quite easily."

"*Then marry someone who can put up with this.*"

He blinked. Slowly. Then he said with terrible softness, "Do you not want to marry me, then?"

I tried not to look at the ring on my finger, at that emerald. "Of course I do. *Of course I do.*" My voice broke. "But you . . . Tamlin . . . " The walls pushed in on me. The quiet, the guards, the stares. What I'd seen at the Tithe today. "I'm drowning," I managed to say. "I am *drowning*. And the more you do this, the more guards . . . You might as well be shoving my head under the water."

Nothing in those eyes, that face.

But then—

I cried out, instinct taking over as his power blasted through the room.

The windows shattered.

The furniture splintered.

And that box of paints and brushes and paper . . .

It exploded into dust and glass and wood.

CHAPTER 10

One breath, the study was intact.

The next, it was shards of nothing, a shell of a room.

None of it had touched me from where I had dropped to the floor, my hands over my head.

Tamlin was panting, the ragged breaths almost like sobs.

I was shaking—shaking so hard I thought my bones would splinter as the furniture had—but I made myself lower my arms and look at him.

There was devastation on that face. And pain. And fear. And grief.

Around me, no debris had fallen—as if he had shielded me.

Tamlin took a step toward me, over that invisible demarcation.

He recoiled as if he'd hit something solid.

"Feyre," he rasped.

He stepped again—and that line held.

"Feyre, please," he breathed.

And I realized that the line, that bubble of protection . . .

It was from me.

A shield. Not just a mental one—but a physical one, too.

I didn't know what High Lord it had come from, who controlled air or wind or any of that. Perhaps one of the Solar Courts. I didn't care.

"Feyre," Tamlin groaned a third time, pushing a hand against what indeed looked like an invisible, curved wall of hardened air. "*Please. Please.*"

Those words cracked something in me. Cracked me open.

Perhaps they cracked that shield of solid wind as well, for his hand shot through it.

Then he stepped over that line between chaos and order, danger and safety.

He dropped to his knees, taking my face in his hands. "I'm sorry, I'm sorry."

I couldn't stop trembling.

"I'll try," he breathed. "I'll try to be better. I don't . . . I can't control it sometimes. The rage. Today was just . . . today was bad. With the Tithe, with all of it. Today—let's forget it, let's just move past it. Please."

I didn't fight as he slid his arms around me, tucking me in tightly enough that his warmth soaked through me. He buried his face in my neck and said onto my nape, as if the words would be absorbed by my body, as if he could only say it the way we'd always been good at communicating—skin to skin, "I couldn't save you before. I couldn't protect you from them. And when you said that, about . . . about me drowning you . . . Am I any better than they were?"

I should have told him it wasn't true, but . . . I had spoken with my heart. Or what was left of it.

"I'll try to be better," he said again. "Please—give me more time. Let me . . . let me get through this. Please."

Get through what? I wanted to ask. But words had abandoned me. I realized I hadn't spoken yet.

Realized he was waiting for an answer—and that I didn't have one.

So I put my arms around him, because body to body was the only way I could speak, too.

It was answer enough. "I'm sorry," he said again. He didn't stop murmuring it for minutes.

You've given enough, Feyre.

Perhaps he was right. And perhaps I didn't have anything left to give, anyway.

I looked over his shoulder as I held him.

The red paint had splattered on the wall behind us. And as I watched it slide down the cracked wood paneling, I thought it looked like blood.

✢

Tamlin didn't stop apologizing for days. He made love to me, morning and night. He worshipped my body with his hands, his tongue, his teeth. But that had never been the hard part. We just got tripped up with the rest.

But he was good for his word.

There were fewer guards as I walked the grounds. Some remained, but no one haunted my steps. I even went on a ride through the wood without an escort.

Though I knew the stable hands had reported to Tamlin the moment I'd left—and returned.

Tamlin never mentioned that shield of solid wind I'd used against him. And things were good enough that I didn't dare bring it up, either.

✢

The days passed in a blur. Tamlin was away more often than not, and whenever he returned, he didn't tell me anything. I'd long since stopped pestering him for answers. A protector—that's who he was, and would always be. What *I* had wanted when I was cold and hard and joyless; what *I* had needed to melt the ice of bitter years on the cusp of starvation.

I didn't have the nerve to wonder what I wanted or needed now. Who I had become.

So with idleness my only option, I spent my days in the library.

Practicing my reading and writing. Adding to that mental shield, brick by brick, layer by layer. Sometimes seeing if I could summon that physical wall of solid air, too. Savoring the silence, even as it crept into my veins, my head.

Some days, I didn't speak to anyone at all. Even Alis.

I awoke each night, shaking and panting. And became glad when Tamlin wasn't there to witness it. When I, too, didn't witness him being yanked from his dreams, cold sweat coating his body. Or shifting into that beast and staying awake until dawn, monitoring the estate for threats. What could I say to calm those fears, when I was the source of so many of them?

But he returned for an extended stay about two weeks after the Tithe—and I'd decided to try to talk, to interact. I owed it to him to try. Owed it to myself.

He seemed to have the same idea. And the first time in a while . . . things felt normal. Or as normal as they could be.

I awoke one morning to the sound of low, deep voices in the hallway outside my bedroom. Closing my eyes, I nestled into the pillow and pulled the blankets higher. Despite our morning roll in the sheets, I'd been rising later every day—sometimes not bothering to get out of bed until lunch.

A growl cut through the walls, and I opened my eyes again.

"Get out," Tamlin warned.

There was a quiet response—too soft for me to make out beyond basic mumbling.

"I'll say it one last time—"

He was interrupted by that voice, and the hair on my arms rose. I studied the tattoo on my forearm as I did a tally. No—no, today couldn't have come so quickly.

Kicking back the covers, I rushed to the door, realizing halfway there that I was naked. Thanks to Tamlin, my clothes had been shredded and flung across the other side of the room, and I had no robe in sight. I grabbed a blanket from a nearby chair and wrapped it around me before opening the door a crack.

Sure enough, Tamlin and Rhysand stood in the hallway. Upon hearing the door open, Rhys turned toward me. The grin that had been on his face faltered.

"Feyre." Rhys's eyes lingered, taking in every detail. "Are you running low on food here?"

"What?" Tamlin demanded.

Those violet eyes had gone cold. Rhys extended a hand toward me. "Let's go."

Tamlin was in Rhysand's face in an instant, and I flinched. "*Get out.*" He pointed toward the staircase. "She'll come to you when she's ready."

Rhysand just brushed an invisible fleck of dust off Tamlin's sleeve. Part of me admired the sheer nerve it must have taken. Had Tamlin's teeth been inches from my throat, I would have bleated in panic.

Rhys cut a glance at me. "No, you wouldn't have. As far as your memory serves me, the last time Tamlin's teeth were near your throat, you slapped him across the face." I snapped up my forgotten shields, scowling.

"*Shut your mouth*," Tamlin said, stepping further between us. "*And get out.*"

The High Lord conceded a step toward the stairs and slid his hands into his pockets. "You really should have your wards inspected. Cauldron knows what other sort of riffraff might stroll in here as easily as I did." Again, Rhys assessed me, his gaze hard. "Put some clothes on."

I bared my teeth at him as I stepped back into my room. Tamlin followed after me, slamming the door hard enough that the chandeliers shuddered, sending shards of light shivering over the walls.

I dropped the blanket and strode for the armoire across the room, the mattress groaning behind me as Tamlin sank onto the bed. "How did he get in here?" I asked, throwing open the doors and rifling through the clothes until I found the turquoise Night Court attire I'd asked Alis to keep. I knew she'd wanted to burn them, but I told her I'd wind up coming home with another set anyway.

"I don't know," Tamlin said. I slipped on my pants, twisting to find him running a hand through his hair. I felt the lie beneath his words. "He just—it's just part of whatever game he's playing."

I tugged the short shirt over my head. "If war is coming, maybe we'd be better served trying to mend things." We hadn't spoken of that subject since my first day back. I dug through the bottom of the armoire for the matching silk shoes, and turned to him as I slid them on.

"I'll start mending things the day he releases you from your bargain."

"Maybe he's keeping the bargain so that you'll attempt to listen to him." I strode to where he sat on the bed, my pants a bit looser around the waist than last month.

"Feyre," he said, reaching for me, but I stepped out of range. "Why do you need to know these things? Is it not enough for you to recover in peace? You earned that for yourself. You *earned* it. I relaxed the number of sentries here; I've been trying . . . trying to be better about it. So leave the rest of it—" He took a steadying breath. "This isn't the time for this conversation."

It was never the time for *this* conversation, or *that* conversation. But I didn't say it. I didn't have the energy to say it, and all the words dried up and blew away. So I memorized the lines of Tamlin's face, and didn't fight him as he pulled me to his chest and held me tightly.

Someone coughed from the hall, and Tamlin's body seized up around me.

But I'd had enough fighting, and snarling, and going back to that open, serene place atop that mountain . . . It seemed better than hiding in the library.

I pulled away, and Tamlin lingered as I walked back into the hall.

Rhys frowned at me. I debated barking something nasty at him, but it would have required more fire than I had—and would have required caring what he thought.

Rhys's face became unreadable as he extended a hand.

Only for Tamlin to appear behind me, and shove that hand down. "You end her bargain right here, right now, and I'll give you anything you want. Anything."

My heart stopped dead. "Are you out of your mind?"

Tamlin didn't so much as blink in my direction.

Rhysand merely raised a brow. "I already have everything I want." He stepped around Tamlin as if he were a piece of furniture and took my hand. Before I could say good-bye, a black wind gathered us up, and we were gone.

CHAPTER 11

"What the hell happened to you?" Rhysand said before the Night Court had fully appeared around us.

"Why don't you just look inside my head?" Even as I said it, the words had no bite. I didn't bother to shove him as I stepped out of his hold.

He gave me a wink. "Where's the fun in that?"

I didn't smile.

"No shoe throwing this time?" I could almost see the other words in his eyes. *Come on. Play with me.*

I headed for the stairs that would take me to my room.

"Eat breakfast with me," he said.

There was a note in those words that made me pause. A note of what I could have sworn was desperation. Worry.

I twisted, my loose clothes sliding over my shoulders, my waist. I hadn't realized how much weight I'd lost. Despite things creeping back to normal.

I said, "Don't you have other things to deal with?"

"Of course I do," he said, shrugging. "I have so many things to deal with that I'm sometimes tempted to unleash my power across the world and wipe the board clean. Just to buy me some damned peace." He grinned, bowing at the waist. Even that casual mention of his power failed to chill me, awe me. "But I'll always make time for you."

I was hungry—I hadn't yet eaten. And that was indeed worry glimmering behind the cocky, insufferable grin.

So I motioned him to lead the way to that familiar glass table at the end of the hall.

We walked a casual distance apart. Tired. I was so—tired.

When we were almost to the table, Rhys said, "I felt a spike of fear this month through our lovely bond. Anything exciting happen at the wondrous Spring Court?"

"It was nothing," I said. Because it was. And it was none of his business.

I glanced sidelong at him—and rage, not worry—flickered in those eyes.

I could have sworn the mountain beneath us trembled in response.

"If you know," I said coldly, "why even ask about it?" I dropped into my chair as he slid into his.

He said quietly, "Because these days, all I hear through that bond is nothing. Silence. Even with your shields up rather impressively most of the time, I should be able to *feel* you. And yet I don't. Sometimes I'll tug on the bond only to make sure you're still alive." Darkness guttered. "And then one day, I'm in the middle of an important meeting when terror blasts through the bond. All I get are glimpses of you and him—and then nothing. Back to silence. I'd like to know what caused such a disruption."

I served myself from the platters of food, barely caring what had been laid on the table. "It was an argument, and the rest is none of your concern."

"Is it why you look like your grief and guilt and rage are eating you alive, bit by bit?"

I didn't want to talk about it. "Get out of my head."

"Make me. *Push* me out. You dropped your shield this morning—anyone could have walked right in."

I held his stare. Another challenge. And I just . . . I didn't care. I didn't care about whatever smoldered in my body, about how I'd slipped into Lucien's head as easily as Rhys could slip into mine, shield or no shield. "Where's Mor?" I asked instead.

He tensed, and I braced myself for him to push, to provoke, but he said, "Away. She has duties to attend to." Shadows swirled around him again and I dug into my food. "Is the wedding on hold, then?"

I paused eating barely long enough to mumble, "Yes."

"I expected an answer more along the lines of, '*Don't ask stupid questions you already know the answer to*,' or my timeless favorite, '*Go to hell.*'"

I only reached for a platter of tartlets. His hands were flat on the table—and a whisper of black smoke curled over his fingers. Like talons.

He said, "Did you give my offer any thought?"

I didn't answer until my plate was empty and I was heaping more food onto it. "I'm not going to work with you."

I almost felt the dark calm that settled over him. "And why, Feyre, are you refusing me?"

I pushed around the fruit on my plate. "I'm not going to be a part of this war you think is coming. You say I should be a weapon, not a pawn—they seem like the same to me. The only difference is who's wielding it."

"I want your help, not to manipulate you," he snapped.

His flare of temper made me at last lift my head. "You want my help because it'll piss off Tamlin."

Shadows danced around his shoulders—as if the wings were trying to take form.

"Fine," he breathed. "I dug that grave myself, with all I did Under the Mountain. But I need your help."

Again, I could feel the other unspoken words: *Ask me why; push me about it.*

And again, I didn't want to. Didn't have the energy to.

Rhys said quietly, "I was a prisoner in her court for nearly fifty years. I was tortured and beaten and fucked until only telling myself who I was, what I had to protect, kept me from trying to find a way to end it. Please—help me keep that from happening again. To Prythian."

Some distant part of my heart ached and bled at the words, at what he'd laid bare.

But Tamlin had made exceptions—he'd lightened the guards' presence, allowed me to roam a bit more freely. He was trying. We were trying. I wouldn't jeopardize that.

So I went back to eating.

Rhys didn't say another word.

✠

I didn't join him for dinner.

I didn't rise in time for breakfast, either.

But when I emerged at noon, he was waiting upstairs, that faint, amused smile on his face. He nudged me toward the table he'd arranged with books and paper and ink.

"Copy these sentences," he drawled from across the table, handing me a piece of paper.

I looked at them and read perfectly:

"*Rhysand is a spectacular person. Rhysand is the center of my world. Rhysand is the best lover a female can ever dream of.*" I set down the paper, wrote out the three sentences, and handed it to him.

The claws slammed into my mind a moment later.

And bounced harmlessly off a black, glimmering shield of adamant.

He blinked. "You practiced."

I rose from the table and walked away. "I had nothing better to do."

✣

That night, he left a pile of books by my door with a note.

I have business elsewhere. The house is yours. Send word if you need me.

Days passed—and I didn't.

✣

Rhys returned at the end of the week. I'd taken to situating myself in one of the little lounges overlooking the mountains, and had almost read an entire book in the deep-cushioned armchair, going slowly as I learned new words. But it had filled my time—given me quiet, steadfast company with those characters, who did not exist and never would, but somehow made me feel less . . . alone.

The woman who'd hurled a bone-spear at Amarantha . . . I didn't know where she was anymore. Perhaps she'd vanished that day her neck had snapped and faerie immortality had filled her veins.

I was just finishing up a particularly good chapter—the second-to-last in the book—a shaft of buttery afternoon sunlight warming my feet, when Rhysand slid between two of the oversized armchairs, twin plates of food in his hands, and set them on the low-lying table before me. "Since you seem hell-bent on a sedentary lifestyle," he said, "I thought I'd go one step further and bring your food to you."

My stomach was already twisting with hunger, and I lowered the book into my lap. "Thank you."

A short laugh. "*Thank you*? Not '*High lord and servant?*' Or: '*Whatever it is you want, you can go shove it up your ass, Rhysand.*'?" He clicked his tongue. "How disappointing."

I set down the book and extended a hand for the plate. He could listen to himself talk all day if he wished, but I wanted to eat. Now.

My fingers had almost grazed the rim of the plate when it just *slid* away.

I reached again. Once more, a tendril of his power yanked the plate further back.

"Tell me what to do," he said. "Tell me what to do to help you."

Rhys kept the plate beyond reach. He spoke again, and as if the words tumbling out loosened his grip on his power, talons of smoke curled over his fingers and great wings of shadow spread from his back. "Months and months, and you're still a ghost. Does no one there ask what the hell is happening? Does your High Lord simply not care?"

He did care. Tamlin *did* care. Perhaps too much. "He's giving me space to sort it out," I said, with enough of a bite that I barely recognized my voice.

"Let me help you," Rhys said. "We went through enough Under the Mountain—"

I flinched.

"She wins," Rhys breathed. "That bitch wins if you let yourself fall apart."

I wondered if he'd been telling himself that for months now, wondered if he, too, had moments when his own memories sometimes suffocated him deep in the night.

But I lifted the book, firing two words down the bond between us before I blasted my shields up again.

Conversation over.

"Like hell it is," he snarled. A thrum of power caressed my fingers, and then the book sealed shut between my hands. My nails dug into the leather and paper—to no avail.

Bastard. Arrogant, presuming *bastard.*

Slowly, I lifted my eyes to him. And I felt . . . not hot temper—but icy, glittering rage.

I could almost *feel* that ice at my fingertips, kissing my palms. And I swore there was frost coating the book before I hurled it at his head.

He shielded fast enough that it bounced away and slid across the marble floor behind us.

"Good," he said, his breathing a bit uneven. "What else do you have, Feyre?"

Ice melted to flame, and my fingers curled into fists.

And the High Lord of the Night Court honestly looked relieved at the sight of it—of that wrath that made me want to rage and burn.

A feeling, for once. Not like that hollow cold and silence.

And the thought of returning to that manor with the sentries and the patrols and the secrets . . . I sank back into my chair. Frozen once more.

"Any time you need someone to play with," Rhys said, pushing the plate toward me on a star-flecked wind, "whether it's during our marvelous week together or otherwise, you let me know."

I couldn't muster up a response, exhausted from the bit of temper I'd shown.

And I realized I was in a free fall with no end. I had been for a while. From the moment I'd stabbed that Fae youth in the heart.

I didn't look up at him again as I devoured the food.

The next morning, Tamlin was waiting in the shade of the gnarled, mighty oak tree in the garden.

A murderous expression twisted his face, directed solely at Rhys. Yet there was nothing amused in Rhys's smile as he stepped back from me—only a cold, cunning predator gazing out.

Tamlin growled at me, "Get inside."

I looked between the two High Lords. And seeing that fury in Tamlin's face . . . I knew there would be no more solitary rides or walks through the grounds.

Rhys just said to me, "Fight it."

And then he was gone.

"I'm fine," I said to Tamlin, as his shoulders slumped, his head bowing.

"I will find a way to end this," he swore.

I wanted to believe him. I knew he'd do anything to achieve it.

He made me again walk through every detail I had learned at Rhys's home. Every conversation, however brief. I told him everything, each word quieter than the last.

Protect, protect, protect—I could see the word in his eyes, feel it in every thrust he made into my body that night. I had been taken from him once in the most permanent of ways, but never again.

The sentries returned in full force the next morning.

CHAPTER 12

During that first week back, I wasn't allowed out of sight of the house.

Some nameless threat had broken onto the lands, and Tamlin and Lucien were called away to deal with it. I asked my friend to tell me what it was, yet . . . Lucien had that look he always did when he wanted to, but his loyalty to Tamlin got in the way. So I didn't ask again.

While they were gone, Ianthe returned—to keep me company, protect me, I don't know.

She was the only one allowed in. The semi-permanent gaggle of Spring Court lords and ladies at the manor had been dismissed, along with their personal servants. I was grateful for it, that I no longer would run into them while walking the halls of the manor, or the gardens, and have to dredge up a memory of their names, personal histories, no longer have to endure them trying not to stare at the tattoo, but . . . I knew Tamlin had liked having them around. Knew some of them were indeed old friends, knew he liked the manor being full of sound and laughter and chatter. Yet I'd found they all talked to each other like they were sparring partners. Pretty words masking sharp-edged insults.

I was glad for the silence—even as it became a weight on me, even as it filled my head until there was nothing inside of it beyond . . . emptiness.

Eternity. Was this to be my eternity?

I was burning through books every day—stories about people and places I'd never heard of. They were perhaps the only thing that kept me from teetering into utter despair.

Tamlin returned eight days later, brushing a kiss over my brow and looking me over, and then headed into the study. Where Ianthe had news for him.

That I was also not to hear.

Alone in the hall, watching as the hooded priestess led him toward the double doors at its other end, a glimmer of red—

My body tensed, instinct roaring through me as I whirled—

Not Amarantha.

Lucien.

The red hair was his, not hers. I was here, not in that dungeon—

My friend's eyes—both metal and flesh—were fixed on my hands.

Where my nails were growing, curving. Not into talons of shadow, but claws that had shredded through my undergarments time and again—

Stop stop stop stop stop—

It did.

Like blowing out a candle, the claws vanished into a wisp of shadow.

Lucien's gaze slid to Tamlin and Ianthe, unaware of what had happened, and then he silently inclined his head, motioning for me to follow.

We took the sweeping stairs to the second level, the halls deserted. I didn't look at the paintings flanking either side. Didn't look beyond the towering windows to the bright gardens.

We passed my bedroom door, passed his own—until we entered a small study on the second level, mostly left unused.

He shut the door after I'd entered the room, and leaned against the wood panel.

"How long have the claws been appearing?" he said softly.

"That was the first time." My voice rang hollow and dull in my ears.

Lucien surveyed me—the vibrant fuchsia gown Ianthe had selected that morning, the face I didn't bother to set into a pleasant expression . . .

"There's only so much I can do," he said hoarsely. "But I'll ask him tonight. About the training. The powers will manifest whether we train you or not, no matter who is around. I'll ask him tonight," he repeated.

I already knew what the answer would be, though.

Lucien didn't stop me as I opened the door he'd been leaning against and left without another word. I slept until dinner, roused myself enough to eat—and when I went downstairs, the raised voices of Tamlin, Lucien, and Ianthe sent me right back to the steps.

They will hunt her, and kill her, Ianthe had hissed at Lucien.

Lucien had growled back, *They'll do it anyway, so what's the difference?*

The difference, Ianthe had seethed, *lies in us having the advantage of this knowledge—it won't be Feyre alone who is targeted for the gifts stolen from those High Lords. Your children*, she then said to Tamlin, *will also have such power. Other High Lords will know that. And if they do not kill Feyre outright, then they might realize what* they *stand to gain if gifted with offspring from her, too.*

My stomach had turned over at the implication. That I might be stolen—and kept—for . . . breeding. Surely . . . surely no High Lord would go so far.

If they were to do that, Lucien had countered, *none of the other High Lords would stand with them. They would face the wrath of six courts bearing down on them. No one is that stupid.*

Rhysand is that stupid, Ianthe had spat. *And with that power of his, he could potentially withstand it. Imagine*, she said, voice softening as she had no doubt turned to Tamlin, *a day might come when he does not return her. You hear the poisoned lies he whispers in her ear. There are other ways around it*, she had added with such quiet venom. *We might not be able to deal with him, but there are some friends that I made across the sea . . .*

We are not assassins, Lucien had cut in. *Rhys is what he is, but who would take his place—*

My blood went cold, and I could have sworn ice frosted my fingertips.

Lucien had gone on, his tone pleading, *Tamlin. Tam. Just let her train, let her master this—if the other High Lords* do *come for her, let her stand a chance . . .*

Silence fell as they let Tamlin consider.

My feet began moving the moment I heard the first word out of his mouth, barely more than a growl. *No.*

With each step up the stairs, I heard the rest.

We give them no reason to suspect she might have any abilities, which training will surely do. Don't give me that look, Lucien.

Silence again.

Then a vicious snarl, and a shudder of magic rocked the house.

Tamlin's voice had been low, deadly. *Do not push me on this.*

I didn't want to know what was happening in that room, what he'd done to Lucien, what Lucien had even looked like to cause that pulse of power.

I locked the door to my bedroom and did not bother to eat dinner at all.

Tamlin didn't seek me out that night. I wondered if he, Ianthe, and Lucien were still debating my future and the threats against me.

There were sentries outside of my bedroom the following afternoon—when I finally dragged myself from bed.

According to them, Tamlin and Lucien were already holed up in his study. Without Tamlin's courtiers poking around, the manor was again silent as I, without anything else to do, headed to walk the garden paths I'd followed so many times I was surprised the pale dirt wasn't permanently etched with my footprints.

Only my steps sounded in the shining halls as I passed guard after guard, armed to the teeth and trying their best not to gawk at me. Not one spoke to me. Even the servants had taken to keeping to their quarters unless absolutely necessary.

Maybe I'd become too slothful; maybe my lazing about made me more prone to these outbursts. *Anyone* might have seen me yesterday. And though we'd never spoken of it . . . Ianthe knew. About the powers. How long had she been aware? The thought of Tamlin telling her . . .

My silk slippers scuffed on the marble stairs, the chiffon trail of my green gown slithering behind me.

Such silence. Too much silence.

I needed to get out of this house. Needed to *do* something. If the villagers didn't want my help, then fine. I could do other things. Whatever they were.

I was about to turn down the hall that led to the study, determined to ask Tamlin if there was *any* task that I might perform, ready to beg him, when the study doors flung open and Tamlin and Lucien emerged, both heavily armed. No sign of Ianthe.

"You're going so soon?" I said, waiting for them to reach the foyer.

Tamlin's face was a grim mask as they approached. "There's activity on the western sea border. I have to go." The one closest to Hybern.

"Can I come with you?" I'd never asked it outright, but—

Tamlin paused. Lucien continued past, through the open front doors of the house, barely able to hide his wince. "I'm sorry," Tamlin said, reaching for me. I stepped out of his grip. "It's too dangerous."

"I know how to remain hidden. Just—take me with you."

"I won't risk our enemies getting their hands on you." *What enemies? Tell me—tell me* something.

I stared over his shoulder, toward where Lucien lingered in the gravel beyond the house entrance. No horses. I supposed they weren't necessary this time, when they were faster without them. But maybe I could keep up. Maybe I'd wait until they left and—

"Don't even think about it," Tamlin warned.

My attention snapped to his face.

He growled, "Don't even try to come after us."

"I can fight," I tried again. A half-truth. A knack for survival wasn't the same as trained skill. "Please."

I'd never hated a word more.

He shook his head, crossing the foyer to the front doors.

I followed him, blurting, "There will *always* be some threat. There will always be some conflict or enemy or *something* that keeps me in here."

He slowed to a stop just inside the towering oak doors, so lovingly restored after Amarantha's cronies had trashed them. "You can barely sleep through the night," he said carefully.

I retorted, "Neither can you."

But he just plowed ahead, "You can barely handle being around other people—"

"You *promised*." My voice cracked. And I didn't care that I was begging. "I need to get out of this house."

"Have Bron take you and Ianthe on a ride—"

"I don't want to go for a ride!" I splayed my arms. "I don't want to go for a ride, or a picnic, or pick wildflowers. I want to *do* something. So take me with you."

That girl who had needed to be protected, who had craved stability and comfort . . . she had died Under the Mountain. *I* had died, and there had been no one to protect me from those horrors before my neck snapped. So I had done it myself. And I would not, *could not*, yield that part of me that had awoken and transformed Under the Mountain. Tamlin had gotten his powers back, had become whole again—become that protector and provider he wished to be.

I was not the human girl who needed coddling and pampering, who wanted luxury and easiness. I didn't know how to go back to craving those things. To being docile.

Tamlin's claws punched out. "Even if I risked it, your untrained abilities render your presence more of a liability than anything."

It was like being hit with stones—so hard I could feel myself cracking. But I lifted my chin and said, "I'm coming along whether you want me to or not."

"No, you aren't." He strode right through the door, his claws slashing the air at his sides, and was halfway down the steps before I reached the threshold.

Where I slammed into an invisible wall.

I staggered back, trying to reorder my mind around the impossibility of it. It was identical to the one I'd built that day in the study, and I searched inside the shards of my soul, my heart, for a tether to that shield, wondering if I'd blocked *myself*, but—there was no power emanating from me.

I reached a hand to the open air of the doorway. And met solid resistance.

"Tamlin," I rasped.

But he was already down the front drive, walking toward the looming iron gates. Lucien remained at the foot of the stairs, his face so, so pale.

"*Tamlin*," I said again, pushing against the wall.

He didn't turn.

I slammed my hand into the invisible barrier. No movement—nothing but hardened air. And I had not learned about my own powers enough to try to push through, to shatter it . . . I had *let* him convince me not to learn those things for *his* sake—

"Don't bother trying," Lucien said softly, as Tamlin cleared the gates and vanished—winnowed. "He shielded the entire house around you. Others can go in and out, but you can't. Not until he lifts the shield."

He'd locked me in here.

I hit the shield again. Again.

Nothing.

"Just—be patient, Feyre," Lucien tried, wincing as he followed after Tamlin. "Please. I'll see what I can do. I'll try again."

I barely heard him over the roar in my ears. Didn't wait to see him pass the gates and winnow, too.

He'd locked me in. He'd sealed me inside this house.

I hurtled for the nearest window in the foyer and shoved it open. A cool spring breeze rushed in—and I shoved my hand through it—only for my fingers to bounce off an invisible wall. Smooth, hard air pushed against my skin.

Breathing became difficult.

I was trapped.

I was trapped inside this house. I might as well have been Under the Mountain; I might as well have been inside that cell again—

I backed away, my steps too light, too fast, and slammed into the oak table in the center of the foyer. None of the nearby sentries came to investigate.

He'd trapped me in here; he'd *locked me up*.

I stopped seeing the marble floor, or the paintings on the walls, or the sweeping staircase looming behind me. I stopped hearing the chirping of the spring birds, or the sighing of the breeze through the curtains.

And then crushing black pounded down and rose up from beneath, devouring and roaring and shredding.

It was all I could do to keep from screaming, to keep from shattering into ten thousand pieces as I sank onto the marble floor, bowing over my knees, and wrapped my arms around myself.

He'd trapped me; he'd trapped me; he'd trapped me—

I had to get *out*, because I'd barely escaped from another prison once before, and this time, this time—

Winnowing. I could vanish into nothing but air and appear somewhere else, somewhere open and free. I fumbled for my power, for anything, *something* that might show me the way to do it, the way out. Nothing. There was nothing and I had become *nothing*, and I couldn't ever get out—

Someone was shouting my name from far away.

Alis—Alis.

But I was ensconced in a cocoon of darkness and fire and ice and wind, a cocoon that melted the ring off my finger until the golden ore dripped away into the void, the emerald tumbling after it. I wrapped that raging force around myself as if it could keep the walls from crushing me entirely, and maybe, maybe buy me the tiniest sip of air—

I couldn't get out; I couldn't get out; I couldn't get out—

Slender, strong hands gripped me under the shoulders.

I didn't have the strength to fight them off.

One of those hands moved to my knees, the other to my back, and then I was being lifted, held against what was unmistakably a female body.

I couldn't see her, didn't want to see her.

Amarantha.

Come to take me away again; come to kill me at last.

There were words being spoken around me. Two women.

Neither of them . . . neither of them was Amarantha.

"Please—please take care of her." Alis.

From right by my ear, the other replied, "Consider yourselves very, very lucky that your High Lord was not here when we arrived. Your guards will have one hell of a headache when they wake up, but they're alive. Be grateful." Mor.

Mor held me—carried me.

The darkness guttered long enough that I could draw breath, that I could see the garden door she walked toward. I opened my mouth, but she peered down at me and said, "Did you think his shield would keep us from you? Rhys shattered it with half a thought."

But I didn't spy Rhys anywhere—not as the darkness swirled back in. I clung to her, trying to breathe, to think.

"You're free," Mor said tightly. "You're free."

Not safe. Not protected.

Free.

She carried me beyond the garden, into the fields, up a hill, down it, and into—into a cave—

I must have started bucking and thrashing in her arms, because she said, "You're out; you're *free*," again and again and again as true darkness swallowed us.

Half a heartbeat later, she emerged into sunlight—bright, strawberry-and-grass-scented sunlight. I had a thought that this might be Summer, then—

Then a low, vicious growl split the air before us, cleaving even my darkness.

"I did everything by the book," Mor said to the owner of that growl.

I was passed from her arms to someone else's, and I struggled to breathe, fought for any trickle of air down my lungs. Until Rhysand said, "Then we're done here."

Wind tore at me, along with ancient darkness.

But a sweeter, softer shade of night caressed me, stroking my nerves, my lungs, until I could at last get air inside, until it seduced me into sleep.

CHAPTER 13

I woke to sunlight, and open space—nothing but clear sky and snow-capped mountains around me.

And Rhysand lounging in an armchair across from the couch where I was sprawled, gazing at the mountains, his face uncharacteristically solemn.

I swallowed, and his head whipped toward me.

No kindness in his eyes. Nothing but unending, icy rage.

But he blinked, and it was gone. Replaced by perhaps relief. Exhaustion.

And the pale sunlight warming the moonstone floors . . . dawn. It was dawn. I didn't want to think about how long I'd been unconscious.

"What happened?" I said. My voice was hoarse. As if I'd been screaming.

"You *were* screaming," he said. I didn't care if my mental shield was up or down or completely shattered. "You also managed to scare the shit out of every servant and sentry in Tamlin's manor when you wrapped yourself in darkness and they couldn't see you."

My stomach hollowed out. "Did I hurt any—"

"No. Whatever you did, it was contained to you."

"You weren't—"

"By law and protocol," he said, stretching out his long legs, "things would have become very complicated and very messy if I had been the one to walk into that house and take you. Smashing that shield was fine, but Mor had to go in on her own two feet, render the sentries unconscious through her own power, and carry you over the border to another court before I could bring you here. Or else Tamlin would have free rein to march his forces into my lands to reclaim you. And as I have no interest in an internal war, we had to do everything by the book."

That's what Mor had said—that she did everything by the book.

But— "When I go back . . ."

"As your presence here isn't part of our monthly requirement, you are under no obligation to go back." He rubbed at his temple. "Unless you wish to."

The question settled in me like a stone sinking to the bottom of a pool. There was such quiet in me, such . . . nothingness.

"He locked me in that house," I managed to say.

A shadow of mighty wings spread behind Rhys's chair. But his face was calm as he said, "I know. I felt you. Even with your shields up—for once."

I made myself meet his stare. "I have nowhere else to go."

It was both a question and a plea.

He waved a hand, the wings fading. "Stay here for however long you want. Stay here forever, if you feel like it."

"I—I need to go back at some point."

"Say the word, and it's done." He meant it, too. Even if I could tell from the ire in his eyes that he didn't like it. He'd bring me back to the Spring Court the moment I asked.

Bring me back to silence, and those sentries, and a life of doing nothing but dressing and dining and planning parties.

He crossed his ankle over a knee. "I made you an offer when you first came here: help me, and food, shelter, clothing . . . All of it is yours."

I'd been a beggar in the past. The thought of doing it now . . .

"Work for me," Rhysand said. "I owe you, anyway. And we'll figure out the rest day by day, if need be."

I looked toward the mountains, as if I could see all the way to the Spring Court in the south. Tamlin would be furious. He'd shred the manor apart.

But he'd . . . he'd locked me up. Either he so deeply misunderstood me or he'd been so broken by what went on Under the Mountain, but . . . he'd locked me up.

"I'm not going back." The words rang in me like a death knell. "Not—not until I figure things out." I shoved against the wall of anger and sorrow and outright despair as my thumb brushed over the vacant band of skin where that ring had once sat.

One day at a time. Maybe—maybe Tamlin would come around. Heal himself, that jagged wound of festering fear. Maybe I'd sort myself out. I didn't know.

But I did know that if I stayed in that manor, if I was locked up one more time . . . It might finish the breaking that Amarantha had started.

Rhysand summoned a mug of hot tea from nowhere and handed it to me. "Drink it."

I took the mug, letting its warmth soak into my stiff fingers. He watched me until I took a sip, and then went back to monitoring the mountains. I took another sip—peppermint and . . . licorice and another herb or spice.

I wasn't going back. Maybe I'd never even . . . gotten to come back. Not from Under the Mountain.

When the mug was half-finished, I fished for something, anything, to say to keep the crushing silence at bay. "The darkness—is that . . . part of the power *you* gave me?"

"One would assume so."

I drained the rest of the mug. "No wings?"

"If you inherited some of Tamlin's shape-shifting, perhaps you can make wings of your own."

A shiver went down my spine at the thought, at the claws I'd grown that day with Lucien. "And the other High Lords? Ice—that's Winter. That shield I once made of hardened wind—who did that come from? What might the others have given me? Is—is winnowing tied to any one of you in particular?"

He considered. "Wind? The Day Court, likely. And winnowing—it's not confined to any court. It's wholly dependent on your own reserve of power—and training." I didn't feel like mentioning how spectacularly I'd failed to even move an inch. "And as for the gifts you got from everyone else . . . That's for you to find out, I suppose."

"I should have known your goodwill would wear off after a minute."

Rhys let out a low chuckle and got to his feet, stretching his muscled arms over his head and rolling his neck. As if he'd been sitting there for a long, long while. For the entirety of the night. "Rest a day or two, Feyre," he said. "Then take on the task of figuring out everything else. I have business in another part of my lands; I'll be back by the end of the week."

Despite how long I'd slept, I was so tired—tired in my bones, in my crumpled heart. When I didn't reply, Rhys strode off between the moonstone pillars.

And I saw how I would spend the next few days: in solitude, with nothing to do and only my own, horrible thoughts for company. I began speaking before I could reconsider. "Take me with you."

Rhys halted as he pushed through two purple gossamer curtains. And slowly, he turned back. "You should rest."

"I've rested enough," I said, setting down the empty mug and standing. My head spun slightly. When had I last eaten? "Wherever you're going, whatever you're doing—take me along. I'll stay out of trouble. Just . . . Please." I hated the last word; choked on it. It hadn't done anything to sway Tamlin.

For a long moment, Rhys said nothing. Then he prowled toward me, his long stride eating up the distance and his face set like stone. "If you come with me, there is no going back. You will not be allowed to speak of what you see to anyone outside of my court. Because if you do, people will die—*my* people will die. So if you come, you will have to lie about it forever; if you return to the Spring Court, you *cannot* tell anyone there what you see, and who you meet, and what you will witness. If you would rather not have that between you and—your friends, then stay here."

Stay here, stay locked up in the Spring Court . . . My chest was a gaping, open wound. I wondered if I'd bleed out from it—if a spirit could bleed out and die. Maybe that had already happened. "Take me with you," I breathed. "I won't tell anyone what I see. Even—them." I couldn't bear to say his name.

Rhys studied me for a few heartbeats. And finally he gave me a half smile. "We leave in ten minutes. If you want to freshen up, go ahead."

An unusually polite reminder that I probably looked like the dead. I felt like it. But I said, "Where are we going?"

Rhys's smile widened into a grin. "To Velaris—the City of Starlight."

The moment I entered my room, the hollow quiet returned, washing away with it any questions I might have had about—about a city.

Everything had been destroyed by Amarantha. If there were a city in Prythian, I would no doubt be visiting a ruin.

I jumped into the bath, scrubbing down as swiftly as I could, then hurried into the Night Court clothes that had been left for me. My motions were mindless, each one some feeble attempt to keep from thinking about what had happened, what—what Tamlin had tried to do and had done, what *I* had done—

By the time I returned to the main atrium, Rhys was leaning against a moonstone pillar, picking at his nails. He merely said, "That was fifteen minutes," before extending his hand.

I had no glimmering ember to even try to look like I cared about his taunting before we were swallowed by the roaring darkness.

Wind and night and stars wheeled by as he winnowed us through the world, and the calluses of his hand scratched against my own fading ones before—

Before sunlight, not starlight, greeted me. Squinting at the brightness, I found myself standing in what was unmistakably a foyer of someone's house.

The ornate red carpet cushioned the one step I staggered away from him as I surveyed the warm, wood-paneled walls, the artwork, the straight, wide oak staircase ahead.

Flanking us were two rooms: on my left, a sitting room with a black marble fireplace, lots of comfortable, elegant, but worn furniture, and bookshelves built into every wall. On my right: a dining room with a long, cherrywood table big enough for ten people—small, compared to the dining room at the manor. Down the slender hallway ahead were a few more doors, ending in one that I assumed would lead to a kitchen. A town house.

I'd visited one once, when I was a child and my father had brought me along to the largest town in our territory: it'd belonged to a fantastically wealthy client, and had smelled like coffee and mothballs. A pretty place, but stuffy—formal.

This house . . . this house was a *home* that had been lived in and enjoyed and cherished.

And it was in a city.

PART TWO

THE HOUSE OF WIND

CHAPTER 14

"Welcome to my home," Rhysand said.

A city—a world lay out there.

Morning sunlight streamed through the windows lining the front of the town house. The ornately carved wood door before me was inset with fogged glass that peeked into a small antechamber and the actual front door beyond it, shut and solid against whatever city lurked beyond.

And the thought of setting foot out into it, into the leering crowds, seeing the destruction Amarantha had likely wreaked upon them . . . A heavy weight pressed into my chest.

I hadn't dredged up the focus to ask until now, hadn't given an ounce of room to consider that this might be a mistake, but . . . "What is this place?"

Rhys leaned a broad shoulder against the carved oak threshold that led into the sitting room and crossed his arms. "This is my house. Well, I have two homes in the city. One is for more . . . official business, but this is only for me and my family."

I listened for any servants but heard none. Good—maybe that was good, rather than have people weeping and gawking.

"Nuala and Cerridwen are here," he said, reading my glance down the hall behind us. "But other than that, it'll just be the two of us."

I tensed. It wasn't that things had been any different at the Night Court itself, but—this house was much, much smaller. There would be no escaping him. Save for the city outside.

There were no cities left in our mortal territory. Though some had sprung up on the main continent, full of art and learning and trade. Elain had once wanted to go with me. I didn't suppose I'd ever get that chance now.

Rhysand opened his mouth, but then the silhouettes of two tall, powerful bodies appeared on the other side of the front door's fogged glass. One of them banged on it with a fist.

"Hurry up, you lazy ass," a deep male voice drawled from the antechamber beyond. Exhaustion drugged me so heavily that I didn't particularly care that there were wings peeking over their two shadowy forms.

Rhys didn't so much as blink toward the door. "Two things, Feyre darling."

The pounding continued, followed by the second male murmuring to his companion, "If you're going to pick a fight with him, do it after breakfast." That voice—like shadows given form, dark and smooth and . . . cold.

"*I* wasn't the one who hauled me out of bed just now to fly down here," the first one said. Then added, "Busybody."

I could have sworn a smile tugged on Rhys's lips as he went on, "One, no one—*no one*—but Mor and I are able to winnow directly inside this house. It is warded, shielded, and then warded some more. Only those I wish—and *you* wish—may enter. You are safe here; and safe anywhere in this city, for that matter. Velaris's walls are well protected and have not been breached in five thousand years. No one with ill intent enters this city unless I allow it. So go where you wish, do what you wish, and see who you wish. Those two in the antechamber," he added, eyes sparkling, "might not be on that list of people you should bother knowing, if they keep banging on the door like children."

Another pound, emphasized by the first male voice saying, "You know we can hear you, prick."

"*Secondly*," Rhys went on, "in regard to the two bastards at my door, it's up to you whether you want to meet them now, or head upstairs like a wise person, take a nap since you're still looking a little peaky, and then change into city-appropriate clothing while I beat the hell out of one of them for talking to his High Lord like that."

There was such light in his eyes. It made him look . . . younger, somehow. More mortal. So at odds with the icy rage I'd seen earlier when I'd awoken . . .

Awoken on that couch, and then decided I wasn't returning home.

Decided that, perhaps, the Spring Court might not be my home.

I was drowning in that old heaviness, clawing my way up to a surface that might not ever exist. I'd slept for the Mother knew how long, and yet . . . "Just come get me when they're gone."

That joy dimmed, and Rhys looked like he might say something else, but a female voice—crisp and edged—now sounded behind the two males in the antechamber. "You Illyrians are worse than cats yowling to be let in the back door." The knob jangled. She sighed sharply. "Really, Rhysand? You locked us out?"

Fighting to keep that immense heaviness at bay a bit longer, I made for the stairs—at the top of which now stood Nuala and Cerridwen, wincing at the front door. I could have sworn Cerridwen subtly gestured me to hurry up. And I might have kissed both twins for that bit of normalcy.

I might have kissed Rhys, too, for waiting to open the front door until I was halfway down the cerulean-blue hallway on the second level.

All I heard was that first male voice declare, "Welcome home, bastard," followed by the shadowy male voice saying, "I sensed you were back. Mor filled me in, but I—"

That strange female voice cut him off. "Send your dogs out in the yard to play, Rhysand. You and I have matters to discuss."

That midnight voice said with quiet cold that licked down my spine, "As do I."

Then the cocky one drawled to her, "We were here first. Wait your turn, Tiny Ancient One."

On either side of me, Nuala and Cerridwen flinched, either from holding in laughter or some vestige of fear, or perhaps both. Definitely both as a feminine snarl sliced through the house—albeit a bit halfheartedly.

The upstairs hall was punctuated with chandeliers of swirled, colored glass, illuminating the few polished doors on either side. I wondered which belonged to Rhysand—and then wondered which one belonged to Mor as I heard her yawn amid the fray below:

"Why is everyone here so *early*? I thought we were meeting tonight at the House."

Below, Rhysand grumbled—*grumbled*—"Trust me, there's no party. Only a massacre, if Cassian doesn't shut his mouth."

"We're hungry," that first male—Cassian—complained. "Feed us. *Someone* told me there'd be breakfast."

"Pathetic," that strange female voice quipped. "You idiots are pathetic."

Mor said, "We know that's true. But *is* there food?"

I heard the words—heard and processed them. And then they floated into the blackness of my mind.

Nuala and Cerridwen opened a door, leading to a fire-warmed, sunlit room. It faced a walled, winter-kissed garden in the back of the town house, the large windows peering over the sleeping stone fountain in its center, drained for the season. Everything in the bedroom itself was of rich wood and soft white, with touches of subtle sage. It felt, strangely enough, almost human.

And the bed—massive, plush, adorned in quilts and duvets of cream and ivory to keep out the winter chill—that looked the most welcoming of all.

But I wasn't so far gone that I couldn't ask a few basic questions—to at least give myself the illusion of caring a bit about my own welfare.

"Who was that?" I managed to say as they shut the door behind us.

Nuala headed for the small attached bathing room—white marble, a claw-foot tub, more sunny windows that overlooked the garden wall and the thick line of cypress trees that stood watch behind it. Cerridwen, already stalking for the armoire, cringed a bit and said over a shoulder, "They're Rhysand's Inner Circle."

The ones I'd heard mentioned that day at the Night Court—who Rhys kept going to meet. "I wasn't aware that High Lords kept things so casual," I admitted.

"They don't," Nuala said, returning from the bathing room with a brush. "But Rhysand does."

Apparently, my hair was a mess, because Nuala brushed it as Cerridwen pulled out some ivory sleeping clothes—a warm and soft lace-trimmed top and pants.

I took in the clothes, then the room, then the winter garden and the slumbering fountain beyond, and Rhysand's earlier words clicked into place.

The walls of this city have not been breached for five thousand years.

Meaning Amarantha . . .

"How is this city here?" I met Nuala's gaze in the mirror. "How—how did it survive?"

Nuala's face tightened, and her dark eyes flicked to her twin, who slowly rose from a dresser drawer, fleece-lined slippers for me in hand. Cerridwen's throat bobbed as she swallowed.

"The High Lord is very powerful," Cerridwen said—carefully. "And was devoted to his people long before his father's mantle passed to him."

"*How* did it survive?" I pushed. A city—a lovely one, if the sounds from my window, the garden beyond it, were any indication—lay all around me. Untouched, whole. Safe. While the rest of the world had been left to ruin.

The twins exchanged looks again, some silent language they'd learned in the womb passing between them. Nuala set down the brush on the vanity. "It is not for us to tell."

"He *asked* you not to—"

"No," Cerridwen interrupted, folding back the covers of the bed. "The High Lord made no such demand. But what he did to shield this city is his story to tell, not ours. We would be more comfortable if he told you, lest we get any of it wrong."

I glared between them. Fine. Fair enough.

Cerridwen moved to shut the curtains, sealing the room in darkness.

My heart stumbled, taking my anger with it, and I blurted, "Leave them open."

I couldn't be sealed up and shut in darkness—not yet.

Cerridwen nodded and left the curtains open, both of the twins telling me to send word if I needed anything before they departed.

Alone, I slid into the bed, hardly feeling the softness, the smoothness of the sheets.

I listened to the crackling fire, the chirp of birds in the garden's potted evergreens—so different from the spring-sweet melodies I was used to. That I might never hear or be able to endure again.

Maybe Amarantha had won after all.

And some strange, new part of me wondered if my never returning might be a fitting punishment for him. For what *he* had done to me.

Sleep claimed me, swift and brutal and deep.

CHAPTER 15

I awoke four hours later.

It took me minutes to remember where I was, what had happened. And each tick of the little clock on the rosewood writing desk was a shove back-back-back into that heavy dark. But at least I wasn't tired. Weary, but no longer on the cusp of feeling like sleeping forever.

I'd think about what happened at the Spring Court later. Tomorrow. Never.

Mercifully, Rhysand's Inner Circle left before I'd finished dressing.

Rhys was waiting at the front door—which was open to the small wood-and-marble antechamber, which in turn was open to the street beyond. He ran an eye over me, from the suede navy shoes—practical and comfortably made—to the knee-length sky-blue overcoat, to the braid that began on one side of my head and curved around the back. Beneath the coat, my usual flimsy attire had been replaced by thicker, warmer brown pants, and a pretty cream sweater that was so soft I could have slept in it. Knitted gloves that matched my shoes had already been stuffed into the coat's deep pockets.

"Those two certainly like to fuss," Rhysand said, though something about it was strained as we headed out the front door.

Each step toward that bright threshold was both an eternity and an invitation.

For a moment, the weight in me vanished as I gobbled down the details of the emerging city:

Buttery sunlight that softened the already mild winter day, a small, manicured front lawn—its dried grass near-white—bordered with a waist-high wrought iron fence and empty flower beds, all leading toward a clean street of pale cobblestones. High Fae in various forms of dress meandered by: some in coats like mine to ward against the crisp air, some wearing mortal fashions with layers and poofy skirts and lace, some in riding leathers—all unhurried as they breathed in the salt-and-lemon-verbena breeze that even winter couldn't chase away. Not one of them looked toward the house. As if they either didn't know or weren't worried that their own High Lord dwelled in one of the many marble town houses lining either side of the street, each capped with a green copper roof and pale chimneys that puffed tendrils of smoke into the brisk sky.

In the distance, children shrieked with laughter.

I staggered to the front gate, unlatching it with fumbling fingers that hardly registered the ice-cold metal, and took all of three steps into the street before I halted at the sight at the other end.

The street sloped down, revealing more pretty town houses and puffing chimneys, more well-fed, unconcerned people. And at the very bottom of the hill curved a broad, winding river, sparkling like deepest sapphire, snaking toward a vast expanse of water beyond.

The sea.

The city had been built like a crust atop the rolling, steep hills that flanked the river, the buildings crafted from white marble or warm sandstone. Ships with sails of varying shapes loitered in the river, the white wings of birds shining brightly above them in the midday sun.

No monsters. No darkness. Not a hint of fear, of despair.

Untouched.

The city has not been breached in five thousand years.

Even during the height of her dominance over Prythian, whatever Rhys had done, whatever he'd sold or bartered . . . Amarantha truly had not touched this place.

The rest of Prythian had been shredded, then left to bleed out over the course of fifty years, yet Velaris . . . My fingers curled into fists.

I sensed something looming and gazed down the other end of the street.

There, like eternal guardians of the city, towered a wall of flat-topped mountains of red stone—the same stone that had been used to build some of the structures. They curved around the northern edge of Velaris, to where the river bent toward them and flowed into their shadow. To the north, different mountains surrounded the city across the river—a range of sharp peaks like fish's teeth cleaved the city's merry hills from the sea beyond. But these mountains behind me . . . They were sleeping giants. Somehow alive, awake.

As if in answer, that undulating, slithering power slid along my bones, like a cat brushing against my legs for attention. I ignored it.

"The middle peak," Rhys said from behind me, and I whirled, remembering he was there. He just pointed toward the largest of the plateaus. Holes and—*windows* seemed to have been built into the uppermost part of it. And flying toward it, borne on large, dark wings, were two figures. "That's my other home in this city. The House of Wind."

Sure enough, the flying figures swerved on what looked to be a wicked, fast current.

"We'll be dining there tonight," he added, and I couldn't tell if he sounded irritated or resigned about it.

And I didn't quite care. I turned toward the city again and said, "How?"

He understood what I meant. "Luck."

"Luck? Yes, how lucky for you," I said quietly, but not weakly, "that the rest of Prythian was ravaged while your people, your city, remained safe."

The wind ruffled Rhys's dark hair, his face unreadable.

"Did you even think for one moment," I said, my voice like gravel, "to extend that *luck* to anywhere else? Anyone else?"

"Other cities," he said calmly, "are known to the world. Velaris has remained secret beyond the borders of these lands for millennia. Amarantha did not touch it, because she did not know it existed. None of her beasts did. No one in the other courts knows of its existence, either."

"*How?*"

"Spells and wards and my ruthless, ruthless ancestors, who were willing to do anything to preserve a piece of goodness in our wretched world."

"And when Amarantha came," I said, nearly spitting her name, "you didn't *think* to open this place as a refuge?"

"When Amarantha came," he said, his temper slipping the leash a bit as his eyes flashed, "I had to make some very hard choices, very quickly."

I rolled my eyes, twisting away to scan the rolling, steep hills, the sea far beyond. "I'm assuming you *won't* tell me about it." But I had to know—how he'd managed to save this slice of peace and beauty.

"Now's not the time for that conversation."

Fine. I'd heard that sort of thing a thousand times before at the Spring Court, anyway. It wasn't worth dredging up the effort to push about it.

But I wouldn't sit in my room, *couldn't* allow myself to mourn and mope and weep and sleep. So I would venture out, even if it was an agony, even if the size of this place . . . Cauldron, it was enormous. I jerked my chin toward the city sloping down toward the river. "So what is there that was worth saving at the cost of everyone else?"

When I faced him, his blue eyes were as ruthless as the churning winter sea in the distance. "Everything," he said.

Rhysand wasn't exaggerating.

There was everything to see in Velaris: tea shops with delicate tables and chairs scattered outside their cheery fronts, surely heated by some warming spell, all full of chattering, laughing High Fae—and a few strange, beautiful faeries. There were four main market squares; Palaces, they were called: two on this side—the southern side—of the Sidra River, two on the northern.

In the hours that we wandered, I only made it to two of them: great, white-stoned squares flanked by the pillars supporting the carved and painted buildings that watched over them and provided a covered walkway beneath for the shops built into the street level.

The first market we entered, the Palace of Thread and Jewels, sold clothes, shoes, supplies for making both, and jewelry—endless, sparkling jeweler's shops. Yet nothing inside me stirred at the glimmer of sunlight on the undoubtedly rare fabrics swaying in the chill river breeze, at the clothes displayed in the broad glass windows, or the luster of gold and ruby and emerald and pearl nestled on velvet beds. I didn't dare glance at the now-empty finger on my left hand.

Rhys entered a few of the jewelry shops, looking for a present for a friend, he said. I chose to wait outside each time, hiding in the shadows beneath the Palace buildings. Walking around today was enough. Introducing myself, enduring the gawking and tears and judgment . . . If I had to deal with that, I might very well climb into bed and never get out.

But no one on the streets looked twice at me, even at Rhysand's side. Perhaps they had no idea who I was—perhaps city-dwellers didn't care who was in their midst.

The second market, the Palace of Bone and Salt, was one of the Twin Squares: one on this side of the river, the other one—the Palace of Hoof and Leaf—across it, both crammed with vendors selling meat, produce, prepared foods, livestock, confections, spices . . . So many spices, scents familiar and forgotten from those precious years when I had known the comfort of an invincible father and bottomless wealth.

Rhysand kept a few steps away, hands in his pockets as he offered bits of information every now and then. Yes, he told me, many stores and homes used magic to warm them, especially popular outdoor spaces. I didn't inquire further about it.

No one avoided him—no one whispered about him or spat on him or stroked him as they had Under the Mountain.

Rather, the people that spotted him offered warm, broad smiles. Some approached, gripping his hand to welcome him back. He knew each of them by name—and they addressed him by his.

But Rhys grew ever quieter as the afternoon pressed on. We paused at the edge of a brightly painted pocket of the city, built atop one of the hills that flowed right to the river's edge. I took one look at the first storefront and my bones turned brittle.

The cheery door was cracked open to reveal art and paints and brushes and little sculptures.

Rhys said, "This is what Velaris is known for: the artists' quarter. You'll find a hundred galleries, supply stores, potters' compounds, sculpture gardens, and anything in between. They call it the Rainbow of Velaris. The performing artists—the musicians, the dancers, the actors—dwell on that hill right across the Sidra. You see the bit of gold glinting near the top? That's one of the main theaters. There are five notable ones in the city, but that's the most famous. And then there are the smaller theaters, and the amphitheater on the sea cliffs . . . " He trailed off as he noticed my gaze drifting back to the assortment of bright buildings ahead.

High Fae and various lesser faeries I'd never encountered and didn't know the names of wandered the streets. It was the latter that I noticed more than the others: some long-limbed, hairless, and glowing as if an inner moon dwelled beneath their night-dark skin, some covered in opalescent scales that shifted color with each graceful step of their clawed, webbed feet, some elegant, wild puzzles of horns and hooves and striped fur. Some were bundled in heavy overcoats, scarves, and mittens—others strode about in nothing but their scales and fur and talons and didn't seem to think twice about it. Neither did anyone else. All of them, however, were preoccupied with taking in the sights, some shopping, some splattered with clay and dust and—and paint.

Artists. I'd never called myself an artist, never thought that far or that grandly, but . . .

Where all that color and light and texture had once dwelled, there was only a filthy prison cell. "I'm tired," I managed to say.

I could feel Rhys's gaze, didn't care if my shield was up or down to ward against him reading my thoughts. But he only said, "We can come back another day. It's almost time for dinner, anyway."

Indeed, the sun was sinking toward where the river met the sea beyond the hills, staining the city pink and gold.

I didn't feel like painting that, either. Even as people stopped to admire the approaching sunset—as if the residents of this place, this court, had the freedom, the safety of enjoying the sights whenever they wished. And had never known otherwise.

I wanted to scream at them, wanted to pick up a loose piece of cobblestone and shatter the nearest window, wanted to unleash that power again boiling beneath my skin and tell them, *show* them, what had been done to me, to the rest of the world, while they admired sunsets and painted and drank tea by the river.

"Easy," Rhys murmured.

I whipped my head to him, my breathing a bit jagged.

His face had again become unreadable. "My people are blameless."

That easily, my rage vanished, as if it had slipped a rung of the ladder it had been steadily climbing inside me and splattered on the pale stone street.

Yes—yes, of course they were blameless. But I didn't feel like thinking more on it. On anything. I said again, "I'm tired."

His throat bobbed, but he nodded, turning from the Rainbow. "Tomorrow night, we'll go for a walk. Velaris is lovely in the day, but it was built to be viewed after dark."

I'd expect nothing less from the City of Starlight, but words had again become difficult.

But—dinner. With him. At that House of Wind. I mustered enough focus to say, "Who, exactly, is going to be at this dinner?"

Rhys led us up a steep street, my thighs burning with the movement. Had I become so out of shape, so weakened? "My Inner Circle," he said. "I want you to meet them before you decide if this is a place you'd like to stay. If you'd like to work with me, and thus work with them. Mor, you've met, but the three others—"

"The ones who came this afternoon."

A nod. "Cassian, Azriel, and Amren."

"Who are they?" He'd said something about Illyrians, but Amren—the female voice I'd heard—hadn't possessed wings. At least ones I'd glimpsed through the fogged glass.

"There are tiers," he said neutrally, "within our circle. Amren is my Second in command."

A female? The surprise must have been written on my face because Rhys said, "Yes. And Mor is my Third. Only a fool would think my Illyrian warriors were the apex predators in our circle." Irreverent, cheerful Mor—was Third to the High Lord of the Night Court. Rhys went on, "You'll see what I mean when you meet Amren. She looks High Fae, but something different prowls beneath her skin." Rhys nodded to a passing couple, who bowed their heads in merry greeting. "She might be older than this city, but she's vain, and likes to hoard her baubles and belongings like a firedrake in a cave. So . . . be on your guard. You both have tempers when provoked, and I don't want you to have any surprises tonight."

Some part of me didn't want to know what manner of creature, exactly, she was. "So if we get into a brawl and I rip off her necklace, she'll roast and eat me?"

He chuckled. "No—Amren would do far, far worse things than that. The last time Amren and Mor got into it, they left my favorite mountain retreat in cinders." He lifted a brow. "For what it's worth, I'm the most powerful High Lord in Prythian's history, and merely interrupting Amren is something *I've* only done once in the past century."

The most powerful High Lord in history.

In the countless millennia they had existed here in Prythian, Rhys—*Rhys* with his smirking and sarcasm and bedroom eyes . . .

And Amren was worse. And older than *five thousand years*.

I waited for the fear to hit; waited for my body to shriek to find a way to get out of this dinner, but . . . nothing. Maybe it'd be a mercy to be ended—

A broad hand gripped my face—gently enough not to hurt, but hard enough to make me look at him. "Don't you *ever* think that," Rhysand hissed, his eyes livid. "*Not for one damned moment.*"

That bond between us went taut, and my lingering mental shields collapsed. And for a heartbeat, just as it had happened Under the Mountain, I flashed from my body to his—from my eyes to his own.

I had not realized . . . how I looked . . .

My face was gaunt, my cheekbones sharp, my blue-gray eyes dull and smudged with purple beneath. The full lips—my father's mouth—were wan, and my collarbones jutted above the thick wool neckline of my sweater. I looked as if . . . as if rage and grief and despair had eaten me alive, as if I was again starved. Not for food, but . . . but for joy and life—

Then I was back in my body, seething at him. "Was that a trick?"

His voice was hoarse as he lowered his hand from my face. "No." He angled his head to the side. "How did you get through it? My shield."

I didn't know what he was talking about. I hadn't *done* anything. Just . . . slipped. And I didn't want to talk about it, not here, not with him. I stormed into a walk, my legs—so damn thin, so *useless*—burning with every step up the steep hill.

He gripped my elbow, again with that considerate gentleness, but strong enough to make me pause. "How many other minds have you accidentally slipped into?"

Lucien—

"*Lucien?*" A short laugh. "What a miserable place to be."

A low snarl rippled from me. "*Do not* go into my head."

"Your shield is down." I hauled it back up. "You might as well have been shouting his name at me." Again, that contemplative angling of his head. "Perhaps you having my power . . . " He chewed on his bottom lip, then snorted. "It'd make sense, of course, if the power came from *me*—if my own shield sometimes mistook *you* for me and let you slip past. Fascinating."

I debated spitting on his boots. "Take your power back. I don't want it."

A sly smile. "It doesn't work that way. The power is bound to your life. The only way to get it back would be to kill you. And since I like your company, I'll pass on the offer." We walked a few steps before he said, "You need to be vigilant about keeping your mental wards up. Especially now that you've seen Velaris. If you ever go somewhere else, beyond these lands, and someone slipped into your mind and saw this place . . ." A muscle quivered in his jaw. "We're called daemati—those of us who can walk into another person's mind as if we were going from one room to another. We're rare, and the trait appears as the Mother wills it, but there are enough of us scattered throughout the world that many—mostly those in positions of influence—extensively train against our skill set. If you were to ever encounter a daemati without those shields up, Feyre, they'd take whatever they wanted. A more powerful one could make you their unwitting slave, make you do whatever they wanted and you'd never know it. My lands remain mystery enough to outsiders that some would find you, among other things, a highly valuable source of information."

Daemati—was I now one if I, too, could do such things? Yet another damned title for people to whisper as I passed. "I take it that in a potential war with Hybern, the king's armies wouldn't even know to strike here?" I waved a hand to the city around us. "So, what—your pampered people . . . those who can't shield their minds—they get your protection *and* don't have to fight while the rest of us will bleed?"

I didn't let him answer, and just increased my pace. A cheap shot, and childish, but . . . Inside, inside I had become like that distant sea, relentlessly churning, tossed about by squalls that tore away any sense of where the surface might be.

Rhys kept a step behind for the rest of the walk to the town house.

Some small part of me whispered that I could survive Amarantha; I could survive leaving Tamlin; I could survive transitioning into this new, strange body . . . But that empty, cold hole in my chest . . . I wasn't sure I could survive that.

Even in the years I'd been one bad week away from starvation, that part of me had been full of color, of light. Maybe becoming a faerie had broken it. Maybe Amarantha had broken it.

Or maybe I had broken it, when I shoved that dagger into the hearts of two innocent faeries and their blood had warmed my hands.

"Absolutely not," I said atop the town house's small rooftop garden, my hands shoved deep into the pockets of my overcoat to warm them against the bite in the night air. There was room enough for a few boxed shrubs and a round iron table with two chairs—and me and Rhysand.

Around us, the city twinkled, the stars themselves seeming to hang lower, pulsing with ruby and amethyst and pearl. Above, the full moon set the marble of the buildings and bridges glowing as if they were all lit from within. Music played, strings and gentle drums, and on either side of the Sidra, golden lights bobbed over riverside walkways dotted with cafés and shops, all open for the night, already packed.

Life—so full of life. I could nearly taste it crackling on my tongue.

Clothed in black accented with silver thread, Rhysand crossed his arms. And rustled his massive wings as I said, "No."

"The House of Wind is warded against people winnowing inside—exactly like this house. Even against High Lords. Don't ask me why, or who did it. But the option is either walk up the ten thousand steps, which I *really* do not feel like doing, Feyre, or fly in." Moonlight glazed the talon at the apex of each wing. He gave me a slow grin that I hadn't seen all afternoon. "I promise I won't drop you."

I frowned at the midnight-blue dress I'd selected—even with the long sleeves and heavy, luxurious fabric, the plunging vee of the neckline did nothing against the cold. I'd debated wearing the sweater and thicker pants, but had opted for finery over comfort. I already regretted it, even with the coat. But if his Inner Circle was anything like Tamlin's court . . . better to wear the more formal attire. I winced at the swath of night between the roof and the mountain-residence. "The wind will rip the gown right off."

His grin became feline.

"I'll take the stairs," I seethed, the anger welcome from the past few hours of numbness as I headed for the door at the end of the roof.

Rhys snapped out a wing, blocking my path.

Smooth membrane—flecked with a hint of iridescence. I peeled back. "Nuala spent an hour on my hair."

An exaggeration, but she had fussed while I'd sat there in hollow silence, letting her tease the ends into soft curls and pin a section along the top of my head with pretty gold barrettes. But maybe staying inside tonight, alone and quiet . . . maybe it'd be better than facing these people. Than interacting.

Rhys's wing curved around me, herding me closer to where I could nearly feel the heat of his powerful body. "I promise I won't let the wind destroy your hair." He lifted a hand as if he might tug on one of those loose curls, then lowered it.

"If I'm to decide whether I want to work against Hybern with you—with your Inner Circle, can't we just . . . meet here?"

"They're all up there already. And besides, the House of Wind has enough space that I won't feel like chucking them all off the mountain."

I swallowed. Sure enough, curving along the top of the center mountain behind us, floors of lights glinted, as if the mountain had been crowned in gold. And between me and that crown of light was a long, *long* stretch of open air. "You mean," I said, because it might have been the only weapon in my arsenal, "that this town house is too small, and their personalities are too big, and you're worried I might lose it again."

His wing pushed me closer, a whisper of warmth on my shoulder. "So what if I am?"

"I'm not some broken doll." Even if this afternoon, that conversation we'd had, what I'd glimpsed through his eyes, said otherwise. But I yielded another step.

"I know you're not. But that doesn't mean I'll throw you to the wolves. If you meant what you said about wanting to work with me to keep Hybern from these lands, keep the wall intact, I want you to meet my friends first. Decide on your own if it's something you can handle. And I want this meeting to be on *my* terms, not whenever they decide to ambush this house again."

"I didn't know you even had friends." Yes—anger, sharpness . . . It felt good. Better than feeling nothing.

A cold smile. "You didn't ask."

Rhysand was close enough now that he slid a hand around my waist, both of his wings encircling me. My spine locked up. A cage—

The wings swept back.

But he tightened his arm. Bracing me for takeoff. Mother save me. "You say the word tonight, and we come back here, no questions asked. And if you can't stomach working with me, with them, then no questions asked on that, either. We can find some other way for you to live here, be fulfilled, regardless of what I need. It's your choice, Feyre."

I debated pushing him on it—on insisting I stay. But stay for what? To sleep? To avoid a meeting I should most certainly have before deciding *what* I wanted to do with myself? And to fly . . .

I studied the wings, the arm around my waist. "Please don't drop me. And please don't—"

We shot into the sky, fast as a shooting star.

Before my yelp finished echoing, the city had yawned wide beneath us. Rhys's hand slid under my knees while the other wrapped around my back and ribs, and we flapped up, up, up into the star-freckled night, into the liquid dark and singing wind.

The city lights dropped away until Velaris was a rippling velvet blanket littered with jewels, until the music no longer reached even our pointed ears. The air was chill, but no wind other than a gentle breeze brushed my face—even as we soared with magnificent precision for the House of Wind.

Rhys's body was hard and warm against mine, a solid force of nature crafted and honed for this. Even the smell of him reminded me of the wind—rain and salt and something citrus-y I couldn't name.

We swerved into an updraft, rising so fast it was instinct to clutch his black tunic as my stomach clenched. I scowled at the soft laugh that tickled my ear. "I expected more screaming from you. I must not be trying hard enough."

"*Do not*," I hissed, focusing on the approaching tiara of lights in the eternal wall of the mountain.

With the sky wheeling overhead and the lights shooting past below, up and down became mirrors—until we were sailing through a sea of stars. Something tight in my chest eased a fraction of its grip.

"When I was a boy," Rhys said in my ear, "I'd sneak out of the House of Wind by leaping out my window—and I'd fly and fly all night, just making loops around the city, the river, the sea. Sometimes I still do."

"Your parents must have been thrilled."

"My father never knew—and my mother . . ." A pause. "She was Illyrian. Some nights, when she caught me right as I leaped out the window, she'd scold me . . . and then jump out herself to fly with me until dawn."

"She sounds lovely," I admitted.

"She was," he said. And those two words told me enough about his past that I didn't pry.

A maneuver had us rising higher, until we were in direct line with a broad balcony, gilded by the light of golden lanterns. At the far end, built into the red mountain itself, two glass doors were already open, revealing a large, but surprisingly casual dining room carved from the stone, and accented with rich wood. Each chair fashioned, I noted, to accommodate wings.

Rhys's landing was as smooth as his takeoff, though he kept an arm beneath my shoulders as my knees buckled at the adjustment. I shook off his touch, and faced the city behind us.

I'd spent so much time squatting in trees that heights had lost their primal terror long ago. But the sprawl of the city . . . worse, the vast expanse of dark beyond—the sea . . . Maybe I remained a human fool to feel that way, but I had not realized the size of the world. The size of Prythian, if a city this large could remain hidden from Amarantha, from the other courts.

Rhysand was silent beside me. Yet after a moment, he said, "Out with it."

I lifted a brow.

"You say what's on your mind—one thing. And I'll say one, too."

I shook my head and turned back to the city.

But Rhys said, "I'm thinking that I spent fifty years locked Under the Mountain, and I'd sometimes let myself dream of this place, but I never expected to see it again. I'm thinking that I wish I had been the one who slaughtered her. I'm thinking that if war comes, it might be a long while yet before I get to have a night like this."

He slid his eyes to me, expectant.

I didn't bother asking again how he'd kept this place from her, not when he was likely to refuse to answer. So I said, "Do you think war will be here that soon?"

"This was a no-questions-asked invitation. I told you . . . three things. Tell me one."

I stared toward the open world, the city and the restless sea and the dry winter night.

Maybe it was some shred of courage, or recklessness, or I was so high above everything that no one save Rhys and the wind could hear, but I said, "I'm thinking that I must have been a fool in love to allow myself to be shown so little of the Spring Court. I'm thinking there's a great deal of that territory I was never allowed to see or hear about and maybe I would have lived in ignorance forever like some pet. I'm thinking . . . " The words became choked. I shook my head as if I could clear the remaining ones away. But I still spoke them. "I'm thinking that I was a lonely, hopeless person, and I might have fallen in love with the first thing that showed me a hint of kindness and safety. And I'm thinking maybe he knew that—maybe not actively, but maybe *he* wanted to be that person for someone. And maybe that worked for who I was before. Maybe it doesn't work for who—what I am now."

There.

The words, hateful and selfish and ungrateful. For all Tamlin had done—

The thought of his name clanged through me. Only yesterday afternoon, I had been there. No—no, I wouldn't think about it. Not yet.

Rhysand said, "That was five. Looks like I owe you two thoughts." He glanced behind us. "Later."

Because the two winged males from earlier were standing in the doorway.

Grinning.

CHAPTER 16

Rhys sauntered toward the two males standing by the dining room doors, giving me the option to stay or join.

One word, he'd promised, and we could go.

Both of them were tall, their wings tucked in tight to powerful, muscled bodies covered in plated, dark leather that reminded me of the worn scales of some serpentine beast. Identical long swords were each strapped down the column of their spines—the blades beautiful in their simplicity. Perhaps I needn't have bothered with the fine clothes after all.

The slightly larger of the two, his face masked in shadow, chuckled and said, "Come on, Feyre. We don't bite. Unless you ask us to."

Surprise sparked through me, setting my feet moving.

Rhys slid his hands into his pockets. "The last I heard, Cassian, no one has ever taken you up on that offer."

The second one snorted, the faces of both males at last illuminated as they turned toward the golden light of the dining room, and I honestly wondered why no one hadn't: if Rhysand's mother had also been Illyrian, then its people were blessed with unnatural good looks.

Like their High Lord, the males—warriors—were dark-haired, tan-skinned. But unlike Rhys, their eyes were hazel and fixed on me as I at last stepped close—to the waiting House of Wind behind them.

That was where any similarities between the three of them halted.

Cassian surveyed Rhys from head to foot, his shoulder-length black hair shifting with the movement. "So fancy tonight, brother. And you made poor Feyre dress up, too." He winked at me. There was something rough-hewn about his features—like he'd been made of wind and earth and flame and all these civilized trappings were little more than an inconvenience.

But the second male, the more classically beautiful of the two . . . Even the light shied from the elegant planes of his face. With good reason. Beautiful, but near-unreadable. He'd be the one to look out for—the knife in the dark. Indeed, an obsidian-hilted hunting knife was sheathed at his thigh, its dark scabbard embossed with a line of silver runes I'd never seen before.

Rhys said, "This is Azriel—my spymaster." Not surprising. Some buried instinct had me checking that my mental shields were intact. Just in case.

"Welcome," was all Azriel said, his voice low, almost flat, as he extended a brutally scarred hand to me. The shape of it was normal—but the skin . . . It looked like it had been swirled and smudged and rippled. Burns. They must have been horrific if even their immortal blood had not been able to heal them.

The leather plates of his light armor flowed over most of it, held by a loop around his middle finger. Not to conceal, I realized as his hand breached the chill night air between us. No, it was to hold in place the large, depthless cobalt stone that graced the back of the gauntlet. A matching one lay atop his left hand; and twin red stones adorned Cassian's gauntlets, their color like the slumbering heart of a flame.

I took Azriel's hand, and his rough fingers squeezed mine. His skin was as cold as his face.

But the word Cassian had used a moment ago snagged my attention as I released his hand and tried not to look too eager to step back to Rhys's side. "You're brothers?" The Illyrians looked similar, but only in the way that people who had come from the same place did.

Rhysand clarified, "Brothers in the sense that all bastards are brothers of a sort."

I'd never thought of it that way. "And—you?" I asked Cassian.

Cassian shrugged, wings tucking in tighter. "I command Rhys's armies."

As if such a position were something that one shrugged off. And—armies. Rhys had armies. I shifted on my feet. Cassian's hazel eyes tracked the movement, his mouth twitching to the side, and I honestly thought he was about to give me his professional opinion on how doing so would make me unsteady against an opponent when Azriel clarified, "Cassian also excels at pissing everyone off. Especially amongst our friends. So, as a friend of Rhysand . . . good luck."

A friend of Rhysand—not savior of their land, not murderer, not human-faerie-*thing*. Maybe they didn't know—

But Cassian nudged his bastard-brother-whatever out of the way, Azriel's mighty wings flaring slightly as he balanced himself. "How the hell did you make that bone ladder in the Middengard Wyrm's lair when you look like your own bones can snap at any moment?"

Well, that settled that. And the question of whether he'd been Under the Mountain. But where he'd been instead . . . Another mystery. Perhaps here—with these people. Safe and coddled.

I met Cassian's gaze, if only because having Rhysand defend me might very well make me crumble a bit more. And maybe it made me as mean as an adder, maybe I relished being one, but I said, "How the hell did *you* manage to survive this long without anyone killing you?"

Cassian tipped back his head and laughed, a full, rich sound that bounced off the ruddy stones of the House. Azriel's brows flicked up with approval as the shadows seemed to wrap tighter around him. As if he were the dark hive from which they flew and returned.

I tried not to shudder and faced Rhys, hoping for an explanation about his spymaster's dark gifts.

Rhys's face was blank, but his eyes were wary. Assessing. I almost demanded what the hell he was looking at, until Mor breezed onto the balcony with, "If Cassian's howling, I hope it means Feyre told him to shut his fat mouth."

Both Illyrians turned toward her, Cassian bracing his feet slightly farther apart on the floor in a fighting stance I knew all too well.

It was almost enough to distract me from noticing Azriel as those shadows lightened, and his gaze slid over Mor's body: a red, flowing gown of chiffon accented with gold cuffs, and combs fashioned like gilded leaves swept back the waves of her unbound hair.

A wisp of shadow curled around Azriel's ear, and his eyes snapped to mine. I schooled my face into bland innocence.

"I don't know why I ever forget you two are related," Cassian told Mor, jerking his chin at Rhys, who rolled his eyes. "You two and your clothes."

Mor sketched a bow to Cassian. Indeed, I tried not to slump with relief at the sight of the fine clothes. At least I wouldn't look overdressed now. "I wanted to impress Feyre. You could have at least bothered to comb your hair."

"Unlike some people," Cassian said, proving my suspicions correct about that fighting stance, "I have better things to do with my time than sit in front of the mirror for hours."

"Yes," Mor said, tossing her long hair over a shoulder, "since swaggering around Velaris—"

"We have company," was Azriel's soft warning, wings again spreading a bit as he herded them through the open balcony doors to the dining room. I could have sworn tendrils of darkness swirled in their wake.

Mor patted Azriel on the shoulder as she dodged his outstretched wing. "Relax, Az—no fighting tonight. We promised Rhys."

The lurking shadows vanished entirely as Azriel's head dipped a bit—his night-dark hair sliding over his handsome face as if to shield him from that mercilessly beautiful grin.

Mor gave no indication that she noticed and curved her fingers toward me. "Come sit with me while they drink." I had enough dignity remaining not to look to Rhys for confirmation it was safe. So I obeyed, falling into step beside her as the two Illyrians drifted back to walk the few steps with their High Lord. "Unless you'd rather drink," Mor offered as we entered the warmth and red stone of the dining room. "But I want you to myself before Amren hogs you—"

The interior dining room doors opened on a whispering wind, revealing the shadowed, crimson halls of the mountain beyond.

And maybe part of me remained mortal, because even though the short, delicate woman *looked* like High Fae . . . as Rhys had warned me, every instinct was roaring to run. To hide.

She was several inches shorter than me, her chin-length black hair glossy and straight, her skin tan and smooth, and her face—pretty, bordering on plain—was bored, if not mildly irritated. But Amren's eyes . . .

Her silver eyes were unlike anything I'd ever seen; a glimpse into the creature that I knew in my bones wasn't High Fae. Or hadn't been born that way.

The silver in Amren's eyes seemed to swirl like smoke under glass.

She wore pants and a top like those I'd worn at the other mountain-palace, both in shades of pewter and storm cloud, and pearls—white and gray and black—adorned her ears, fingers, and wrists. Even the High Lord at my side felt like a wisp of shadow compared to the power thrumming from her.

Mor groaned, slumping into a chair near the end of the table, and poured herself a glass of wine. Cassian took a seat across from her, wiggling his fingers for the wine bottle. But Rhysand and Azriel just stood there, watching—maybe monitoring—as the female approached me, then halted three feet away.

"Your taste remains excellent, High Lord. Thank you." Her voice was soft—but honed sharper than any blade I'd encountered. Her slim, small fingers grazed a delicate silver-and-pearl brooch pinned above her right breast.

So that's who he'd bought the jewelry for. The jewelry I was to never, under any circumstances, try to steal.

I studied Rhys and Amren, as if I might be able to read what further bond lay between them, but Rhysand waved a hand and bowed his head. "It suits you, Amren."

"Everything suits me," she said, and those horrible, enchanting eyes again met my own. Like leashed lightning.

She took a step closer, sniffing delicately, and though I stood half a foot taller, I'd never felt meeker. But I held my chin up. I didn't know why, but I did.

Amren said, "So there are two of us now."

My brows nudged toward each other.

Amren's lips were a slash of red. "We who were born something else—and found ourselves trapped in new, strange bodies."

I decided I *really* didn't want to know what she'd been before.

Amren jerked her chin at me to sit in the empty chair beside Mor, her hair shifting like molten night. She claimed the seat across from me, Azriel on her other side as Rhys took the one across from him—on my right.

No one at the head of the table.

"Though there *is* a third," Amren said, now looking at Rhysand. "I don't think you've heard from Miryam in . . . centuries. Interesting."

Cassian rolled his eyes. "Please just get to the point, Amren. I'm hungry."

Mor choked on her wine. Amren slid her attention to the warrior to her right. Azriel, on her other side, monitored the two of them very, very carefully. "No one warming your bed right now, Cassian? It must be *so* hard to be an Illyrian and have no thoughts in your head save for those about your favorite part."

"You know I'm always happy to tangle in the sheets with you, Amren," Cassian said, utterly unfazed by the silver eyes, the power radiating from her every pore. "I know how much you enjoy Illyrian—"

"Miryam," Rhysand said, as Amren's smile became serpentine, "and Drakon are doing well, as far as I've heard. And what, exactly, is interesting?"

Amren's head tilted to the side as she studied me. I tried not to shrink from it. "Only once before was a human Made into an immortal. Interesting that it should happen again right as all the ancient players have returned. But Miryam was gifted long life—not a new body. And you, girl . . ." She sniffed again, and I'd never felt so laid bare. Surprise lit Amren's eyes. Rhys just nodded. Whatever that meant. I was tired already. Tired of being assessed and evaluated. "Your very blood, your veins, your bones were Made. A mortal soul in an immortal body."

"I'm hungry," Mor said nudging me with a thigh. She snapped a finger, and plates piled high with roast chicken, greens, and bread appeared. Simple, but . . . elegant. Not formal at all. Perhaps the sweater and pants wouldn't have been out of place for such a meal. "Amren and Rhys can talk all night and bore us to tears, so don't bother waiting for them to dig in." She picked up her fork, clicking her tongue. "I asked Rhys if *I* could take you to dinner, just the two of us, and he said you wouldn't want to. But honestly—would you rather spend time with those two ancient bores, or me?"

"For someone who is the same age as me," Rhys drawled, "you seem to forget—"

"Everyone wants to talk-talk-talk," Mor said, giving a warning glare at Cassian, who had indeed opened his mouth. "Can't we eat-eat-eat, and *then* talk?"

An interesting balance between Rhys's terrifying Second and his disarmingly chipper Third. If Mor's rank was higher than that of the two warriors at this table, then there had to be some other reason beyond that irreverent charm. Some power to allow her to get into the fight with Amren that Rhys had mentioned—and walk away from it.

Azriel chuckled softly at Mor, but picked up his fork. I followed suit, waiting until he'd taken a bite before doing so. Just in case—

Good. So good. And the wine—

I hadn't even realized Mor had poured me a glass until I finished my first sip, and she clinked her own against mine. "Don't let these old busybodies boss you around."

Cassian said, "Pot. Kettle. Black." Then he frowned at Amren, who had hardly touched her plate. "I always forget how bizarre that is." He unceremoniously took her plate, dumping half the contents on his own before passing the rest to Azriel.

Azriel said to Amren as he slid the food onto his plate, "I keep telling him to ask before he does that."

Amren flicked her fingers and the empty plate vanished from Azriel's scarred hands. "If you haven't been able to train him after all these centuries, boy, I don't think you'll make any progress now." She straightened the silverware on the vacant place setting before her.

"You don't—eat?" I said to her. The first words I'd spoken since sitting.

Amren's teeth were unnervingly white. "Not this sort of food."

"Cauldron boil me," Mor said, gulping from her wine. "Can we *not*?"

I decided I didn't want to know what Amren ate, either.

Rhys chuckled from my other side. "Remind me to have family dinners more often."

Family dinners—not official court gatherings. And tonight . . . either they didn't know that I was here to decide if I truly wished to work with Rhys, or they didn't feel like pretending to be anything but what they were. They'd no doubt worn whatever they felt like—I had the rising feeling that I could have shown up in my nightgown and they wouldn't have cared. A unique group indeed. And against Hybern . . . who would they be, what could they do, as allies or opponents?

Across from me, a cocoon of silence seemed to pulse around Azriel, even as the others dug into their food. I again peered at that oval of blue stone on his gauntlet as he sipped from his glass of wine. Azriel noted the look, swift as it had been—as I had a feeling he'd been noticing and cataloging all of my movements, words, and breaths. He held up his hands, the backs to me so both jewels were on full display. "They're called Siphons. They concentrate and focus our power in battle."

Only he and Cassian wore them.

Rhys set down his fork, and clarified for me, "The power of stronger Illyrians tends toward 'incinerate now, ask questions later.' They have little magical gifts beyond that—the killing power."

"The gift of a violent, warmongering people," Amren added. Azriel nodded, shadows wreathing his neck, his wrists. Cassian gave him a sharp look, face tightening, but Azriel ignored him.

Rhys went on, though I knew he was aware of every glance between the spymaster and army commander, "The Illyrians bred the power to give them advantage in battle, yes. The Siphons filter that raw power and allow Cassian and Azriel to transform it into something more subtle and varied—into shields and weapons, arrows and spears. Imagine the difference between hurling a bucket of paint against the wall and using a brush. The Siphons allow for the magic to be nimble, precise on the battlefield—when its natural state lends itself toward something far messier and unrefined, and potentially dangerous when you're fighting in tight quarters."

I wondered how much of that any of them had needed to do. If those scars on Azriel's hands had come from it.

Cassian flexed his fingers, admiring the clear red stones adorning the backs of his own broad hands. "Doesn't hurt that they also look damn good."

Amren muttered, "Illyrians."

Cassian bared his teeth in feral amusement, and took a drink of his wine.

Get to know them, try to envision how I might work with them, rely on them, if this conflict with Hybern exploded . . . I scrambled for something to ask and said to Azriel, those shadows gone again, "How did you—I mean, how do you and Lord Cassian—"

Cassian spewed his wine across the table, causing Mor to leap up, swearing at him as she used a napkin to mop her dress.

But Cassian was howling, and Azriel had a faint, wary smile on his face as Mor waved a hand at her dress and the spots of wine appeared on Cassian's fighting—or perhaps flying, I realized—leathers. My cheeks heated. Some court protocol that I'd unknowingly broken and—

"Cassian," Rhys drawled, "is not a lord. Though I'm sure he appreciates you thinking he is." He surveyed his Inner Circle. "While we're on the subject, neither is Azriel. Nor Amren. Mor, believe it or not, is the only pure-blooded, titled person in this room." Not him? Rhys must have seen the question on my face because he said, "I'm half-Illyrian. As good as a bastard where the thoroughbred High Fae are concerned."

"So you—you three aren't High Fae?" I said to him and the two males.

Cassian finished his laughing. "Illyrians are certainly not High Fae. And glad of it." He hooked his black hair behind an ear—rounded; as mine had once been. "And we're not lesser faeries, though some try to call us that. We're just—Illyrians. Considered expendable aerial cavalry for the Night Court at the best of times, mindless soldier grunts at the worst."

"Which is most of the time," Azriel clarified. I didn't dare ask if those shadows were a part of being Illyrian, too.

"I didn't see you Under the Mountain," I said instead. I had to know without a doubt—if they were there, if they'd seen me, if it'd impact how I interacted while working with—

Silence fell. None of them, even Amren, looked at Rhysand.

It was Mor who said, "Because none of us were."

Rhys's face was a mask of cold. "Amarantha didn't know they existed. And when someone tried to tell her, they usually found themselves without the mind to do so."

A shudder went down my spine. Not at the cold killer, but—but . . . "You truly kept this city, and all these people, hidden from her for fifty years?"

Cassian was staring hard at his plate, as if he might burst out of his skin.

Amren said, "We will continue to keep this city and these people hidden from our enemies for a great many more."

Not an answer.

Rhys hadn't expected to see them again when he'd been dragged Under the Mountain. Yet he had kept them safe, somehow.

And it killed them—the four people at this table. It killed them all that he'd done it, however he'd done it. Even Amren.

Perhaps not only for the fact that Rhys had endured Amarantha while they had been here. Perhaps it was also for those left outside of the city, too. Perhaps picking one city, one place, to shield was better than nothing. Perhaps . . . perhaps it was a comforting thing, to have a spot in Prythian that remained untouched. Unsullied.

Mor's voice was a bit raw as she explained to me, her golden combs glinting in the light, "There is not one person in this city who is unaware of what went on outside these borders. Or of the cost."

I didn't want to ask what price had been demanded. The pain that laced the heavy silence told me enough.

Yet if they might all live through their pain, might still laugh . . . I cleared my throat, straightening, and said to Azriel, who, shadows or no, seemed the safest and therefore was probably the least so, "How did you meet?" A harmless question to feel them out, learn who they were. Wasn't it?

Azriel merely turned to Cassian, who was staring at Rhys with guilt and love on his face, so deep and agonized that some now-splintered instinct had me almost reaching across the table to grip his hand.

But Cassian seemed to process what I'd asked and his friend's silent request that he tell the story instead, and a grin ghosted across his face. "We all hated each other at first."

Beside me, the light had winked out of Rhys's eyes. What I'd asked about Amarantha, what horrors I'd made him remember . . .

A confession for a confession—I thought he'd done it for my sake. Maybe he had things he needed to voice, *couldn't* voice to these people, not without causing them more pain and guilt.

Cassian went on, drawing my attention from the silent High Lord at my right, "We *are* bastards, you know. Az and I. The Illyrians . . . We love our people, and our traditions, but they dwell in clans and camps deep in the mountains of the North, and do not like outsiders. Especially High Fae who try to tell them what to do. But they're just as obsessed with lineage, and have their own princes and lords among them. Az," he said, pointing a thumb in his direction, his red Siphon catching the light, "was the bastard of one of the local lords. And if you think the bastard son of a lord is hated, then you can't imagine how hated the bastard is of a war-camp laundress and a warrior she couldn't or wouldn't remember." His casual shrug didn't match the vicious glint in his hazel eyes. "Az's father sent him to our camp for training once he and his charming wife realized he was a shadowsinger."

Shadowsinger. Yes—the title, whatever it meant, seemed to fit.

"Like the daemati," Rhys said to me, "shadowsingers are rare—coveted by courts and territories across the world for their stealth and predisposition to hear and feel things others can't."

Perhaps those shadows were indeed whispering to him, then. Azriel's cold face yielded nothing.

Cassian said, "The camp lord practically shit himself with excitement the day Az was dumped in our camp. But me . . . once my mother weaned me and I was able to walk, they flew me to a distant camp, and chucked me into the mud to see if I would live or die."

"They would have been smarter throwing you off a cliff," Mor said, snorting.

"Oh, definitely," Cassian said, that grin going razor-sharp. "Especially because when I was old and strong enough to go back to the camp I'd been born in, I learned those pricks worked my mother until she died."

Again that silence fell—different this time. The tension and simmering anger of a unit who had endured so much, survived so much . . . and felt each other's pain keenly.

"The Illyrians," Rhys smoothly cut in, that light finally returning to his gaze, "are unparalleled warriors, and are rich with stories and traditions. But they are also brutal and backward, particularly in regard to how they treat their females."

Azriel's eyes had gone near-vacant as he stared at the wall of windows behind me.

"They're barbarians," Amren said, and neither Illyrian male objected. Mor nodded emphatically, even as she noted Azriel's posture and bit her lip. "They cripple their females so they can keep them for breeding more flawless warriors."

Rhys cringed. "My mother was low-born," he told me, "and worked as a seamstress in one of their many mountain war-camps. When females come of age in the camps—when they have their first bleeding—their wings are . . . clipped. Just an incision in the right place, left to improperly heal, can cripple you forever. And my mother—she was gentle and wild and loved to fly. So she did everything in her power to keep herself from maturing. She starved herself, gathered illegal herbs—anything to halt the natural course of her body. She turned eighteen and hadn't yet bled, to the mortification of her parents. But her bleeding finally arrived, and all it took was for her to be in the wrong place, at the wrong time, before a male scented it on her and told the camp's lord. She tried to flee—took right to the skies. But she was young, and the warriors were faster, and they dragged her back. They were about to tie her to the posts in the center of camp when my father winnowed in for a meeting with the camp's lord about readying for the War. He saw my mother thrashing and fighting like a wildcat, and . . ." He swallowed. "The mating bond between them clicked into place. One look at her, and he knew what she was. He misted the guards holding her."

My brows narrowed. "Misted?"

Cassian let out a wicked chuckle as Rhys floated a lemon wedge that had been garnishing his chicken into the air above the table. With a flick of his finger, it turned to citrus-scented mist.

"Through the blood-rain," Rhys went on as I shut out the image of what it'd do to a body, what *he* could do, "my mother looked at him. And the bond fell into place for her. My father took her back to the Night Court that evening and made her his bride. She loved her people, and missed them, but never forgot what they had tried to do to her—what they did to the females among them. She tried for decades to get my father to ban it, but the War was coming, and he wouldn't risk isolating the Illyrians when he needed them to lead his armies. And to die for him."

"A real prize, your father," Mor grumbled.

"At least he liked you," Rhys countered, then clarified for me, "my father and mother, despite being mates, were wrong for each other. My father was cold and calculating, and could be vicious, as he had been trained to be since birth. My mother was soft and fiery and beloved by everyone she met. She hated him after a time—but never stopped being grateful that he had saved her wings, that he allowed her to fly whenever and wherever she wished. And when I was born, and could summon the Illyrian wings as I pleased . . . She wanted me to know her people's culture."

"She wanted to keep you out of your father's claws," Mor said, swirling her wine, her shoulders loosening as Azriel at last blinked, and seemed to shake off whatever memory had frozen him.

"That, too," Rhys added drily. "When I turned eight, my mother brought me to one of the Illyrian war-camps. To be trained, as all Illyrian males were trained. And like all Illyrian mothers, she shoved me toward the sparring ring on the first day, and walked away without looking back."

"She abandoned you?" I found myself saying.

"No—never," Rhys said with a ferocity I'd heard only a few times, one of them being this afternoon. "She was staying at the camp as well. But it is considered an embarrassment for a mother to coddle her son when he goes to train."

My brows lifted and Cassian laughed. "Backward, like he said," the warrior told me.

"I was scared out of my mind," Rhys admitted, not a shade of shame to be found. "I'd been learning to wield my powers, but Illyrian magic was a mere fraction of it. And it's rare amongst them—usually possessed only by the most powerful, pure-bred warriors." Again, I looked at the slumbering Siphons atop the warriors' hands. "I tried to use a Siphon during those years," Rhys said. "And shattered about a dozen before I realized it wasn't compatible—the stones couldn't hold it. My power flows and is honed in other ways."

"So difficult, being such a powerful High Lord," Mor teased.

Rhys rolled his eyes. "The camp-lord banned me from using my magic. For all our sakes. But I had no idea how to fight when I set foot into that training ring that day. The other boys in my age group knew it, too. Especially one in particular, who took a look at me, and beat me into a bloody mess."

"You were so *clean*," Cassian said, shaking his head. "The pretty half-breed son of the High Lord—how fancy you were in your new training clothes."

"Cassian," Azriel told me with that voice like darkness given sound, "resorted to getting new clothes over the years by challenging other boys to fights, with the prize being the clothes off their backs." There was no pride in the words—not for his people's brutality. I didn't blame the shadowsinger, though. To treat *anyone* that way . . .

Cassian, however, chuckled. But I was now taking in the broad, strong shoulders, the light in his eyes.

I'd never met anyone else in Prythian who had ever been hungry, desperate—not like I'd been.

Cassian blinked, and the way he looked at me shifted—more assessing, more . . . sincere. I could have sworn I saw the words in his eyes: *You know what it is like. You know the mark it leaves.*

"I'd beaten every boy in our age group twice over already," Cassian went on. "But then Rhys arrived, in his clean clothes, and he smelled . . . different. Like a true opponent. So I attacked. We both got three lashings apiece for the fight."

I flinched. Hitting children—

"They do worse, girl," Amren cut in, "in those camps. Three lashings is practically an encouragement to fight again. When they do something truly bad, bones are broken. Repeatedly. Over weeks."

I said to Rhys, "Your mother willingly sent you into that?" Soft fire indeed.

"My mother didn't want me to rely on my power," Rhysand said. "She knew from the moment she conceived me that I'd be hunted my entire life. Where one strength failed, she wanted others to save me.

"My education was another weapon—which was why she went with me: to tutor me after lessons were done for the day. And when she took me home that first night to our new house at the edge of the camp, she made me read by the window. It was there that I saw Cassian trudging through the mud—toward the few ramshackle tents outside of the camp. I asked her where he was going, and she told me that bastards are given nothing: they find their own shelter, own food. If they survive and get picked to be in a war-band, they'll be bottom-ranking forever, but receive their own tents and supplies. But until then, he'd stay in the cold."

"Those mountains," Azriel added, his face hard as ice, "offer some of the harshest conditions you can imagine."

I'd spent enough time in frozen woods to get it.

"After my lessons," Rhys went on, "my mother cleaned my lashings, and as she did, I realized for the first time what it was to be warm, and safe, and cared for. And it didn't sit well."

"Apparently not," Cassian said. "Because in the dead of night, that little prick woke me up in my piss-poor tent and told me to keep my mouth shut and come with him. And maybe the cold made me stupid, but I did. His mother was *livid*. But I'll never forget the look on her beautiful face when she saw me and said, 'There is a bathtub with hot running water. Get in it or you can go back into the cold.' Being a smart lad, I obeyed. When I got out, she had clean nightclothes and ordered me into bed. I'd spent my life sleeping on the ground—and when I balked, she said she understood because she had felt the same once, and that it would feel as if I was being swallowed up, but the bed was mine for as long as I wanted it."

"And you were friends after that?"

"No—Cauldron no," Rhysand said. "We hated each other, and only behaved because if one of us got into trouble or provoked the other, then neither of us ate that night. My mother started tutoring Cassian, but it wasn't until Azriel arrived a year later that we decided to be allies."

Cassian's grin grew as he reached around Amren to clap his friend on the shoulder. Azriel sighed—the sound of the long-suffering. The warmest expression I'd seen him make. "A new bastard in the camp—and an untrained shadowsinger to boot. Not to mention he couldn't even *fly* thanks to—"

Mor cut in lazily, "Stay on track, Cassian."

Indeed, any warmth had vanished from Azriel's face. But I quieted my own curiosity as Cassian again shrugged, not even bothering to take note of the silence that seemed to leak from the shadowsinger. Mor saw, though—even if Azriel didn't bother to acknowledge her concerned stare, the hand that she kept looking at as if she'd touch, but thought better of it.

Cassian went on, "Rhys and I made his life a living hell, shadowsinger or no. But Rhys's mother had known Az's mother, and took him in. As we grew older, and the other males around us did, too, we realized everyone else hated us enough that we had better odds of survival sticking together."

"Do you have any gifts?" I asked him. "Like—them?" I jerked my chin to Azriel and Rhys.

"A volatile temper doesn't count," Mor said as Cassian opened his mouth.

He gave her that grin I realized likely meant trouble was coming, but said to me, "No. I don't—not beyond a heaping pile of the killing power. Bastard-born nobody, through and through." Rhys sat forward like he'd object, but Cassian forged ahead, "Even so, the other males knew that we were different. And not because we were two bastards and a half-breed. We were stronger, faster—like the Cauldron knew we'd been set apart and wanted us to find each other. Rhys's mother saw it, too. Especially as we reached the age of maturity, and all we wanted to do was fuck and fight."

"Males are horrible creatures, aren't they?" Amren said.

"Repulsive," Mor said, clicking her tongue

Some surviving, small part of my heart wanted to . . . laugh at that.

Cassian shrugged. "Rhys's power grew every day—and everyone, even the camp-lords, knew he could mist *everyone* if he felt like it. And the two of us . . . we weren't far behind." He tapped his crimson Siphon with a finger. "A bastard Illyrian had never received one of these. Ever. For Az and me to both be appointed them, albeit begrudgingly, had every warrior in every camp across those mountains sizing us up. Only pure-blood pricks get Siphons—born and bred *for* the killing power. It still keeps them up at night, puzzling over where the hell we got it from."

"Then the War came," Azriel took over. Just the way he said the words made me sit up. Listen. "And Rhys's father visited our camp to see how his son had fared after twenty years."

"My father," Rhys said, swirling his wine once—twice, "saw that his son had not only started to rival him for power, but had allied himself with perhaps the two deadliest Illyrians in history. He got it into his head that if we were given a legion in the War, we might very well turn it against him when we returned."

Cassian snickered. "So the prick separated us. He gave Rhys command of a legion of Illyrians who hated him for being a half-breed, and threw me into a different legion to be a common foot soldier, even when my power outranked any of the war-leaders. Az, he kept for himself as his personal shadowsinger—mostly for spying and his dirty work. We only saw each other on battlefields for the seven years the War raged. They'd send around casualty lists amongst the Illyrians, and I read each one, wondering if I'd see their names on it. But then Rhys was captured—"

"*That* is a story for another time," Rhys said, sharply enough that Cassian lifted his brows, but nodded. Rhys's violet eyes met mine, and I wondered if it was true starlight that flickered so intensely in them as he spoke. "Once I became High Lord, I appointed these four to my Inner Circle, and told the rest of my father's old court that if they had a problem with my friends, they could leave. They all did. Turns out, having a half-breed High Lord was made worse by his appointment of two females and two Illyrian bastards."

As bad as humans, in some ways. "What—what happened to them, then?"

Rhys shrugged, those great wings shifting with the movement. "The nobility of the Night Court fall into one of three categories: those who hated me enough that when Amarantha took over, they joined her court and later found themselves dead; those who hated me enough to try to overthrow me and faced the consequences; and those who hated me, but not enough to be stupid and have since tolerated a half-breed's rule, especially when it so rarely interferes with their miserable lives."

"Are they—are they the ones who live beneath the mountain?"

A nod. "In the Hewn City, yes. I gave it to them, for not being fools. They're happy to stay there, rarely leaving, ruling themselves and being as wicked as they please, for all eternity."

That was the court he must have shown Amarantha when she first arrived—and its wickedness must have pleased her enough that she modeled her own after it.

"The Court of Nightmares," Mor said, sucking on a tooth.

"And what is this court?" I asked, gesturing to them. The most important question.

It was Cassian, eyes clear and bright as his Siphon, who said, "The Court of Dreams."

The Court of Dreams—the dreams of a half-breed High Lord, two bastard warriors, and . . . the two females. "And you?" I said to Mor and Amren.

Amren merely said, "Rhys offered to make me his Second. No one had ever asked me before, so I said yes, to see what it might be like. I found I enjoyed it."

Mor leaned back in her seat, Azriel now watching every movement she made with subtle, relentless focus.

"I was a dreamer born into the Court of Nightmares," Mor said. She twirled a curl around a finger, and I wondered if her story might be the worst of all of them as she said simply, "So I got out."

"What's your story, then?" Cassian said to me with a jerk of his chin.

I'd assumed Rhysand had told them everything. Rhys merely shrugged at me.

So I straightened. "I was born to a wealthy merchant family, with two older sisters and parents who only cared about their money and social standing. My mother died when I was eight; my father lost his fortune three years later. He sold everything to pay off his debts, moved us into a hovel, and didn't bother to find work while he let us slowly starve for years. I was fourteen when the last of the money ran out, along with the food. He wouldn't work—couldn't, because the debtors came and shattered his leg in front of us. So I went into the forest and taught myself to hunt. And I kept us all alive, if not near starvation at times, for five years. Until . . . everything happened."

They fell quiet again, Azriel's gaze now considering. He hadn't told his story. Did it ever come up? Or did they never discuss those burns on his hands? And what did the shadows whisper to him—did they speak in a language at all?

But Cassian said, "You taught yourself to hunt. What about to fight?" I shook my head. Cassian braced his arms on the table. "Lucky for you, you've just found yourself a teacher."

I opened my mouth, protesting, but— Rhysand's mother had given him an arsenal of weapons to use if the other failed. What did I have in my own beyond a good shot with a bow and brute stubbornness? And if I had this new power—these *other* powers . . .

I would not be weak again. I would not be dependent on anyone else. I would never have to endure the touch of the Attor as it dragged me because I was too helpless to know where and how to hit. Never again.

But what Ianthe and Tamlin had said . . . "You don't think it sends a bad message if people see me learning to fight—using weapons?"

The moment the words were out, I realized the stupidity of them. The stupidity of—of what had been shoved down my throat these past few months.

Silence. Then Mor said with a soft venom that made me understand the High Lord's Third had received training of her own in that Court of Nightmares, "Let me tell you two things. As someone who has perhaps been in your shoes before." Again, that shared bond of anger, of pain throbbed between them all, save for Amren, who was giving me a look dripping with distaste. "One," Mor said, "you have left the Spring Court." I tried not to let the full weight of those words sink in. "If that does not send a message, for good or bad, then your training will not, either. Two," she continued, laying her palm flat on the table, "I once lived in a place where the opinion of others mattered. It suffocated me, nearly broke me. So you'll understand me, Feyre, when I say that I know what you feel, and I know what they tried to do to you, and that with enough courage, you can say to hell with a reputation." Her voice gentled, and the tension between them all faded with it. "You do what you love, what *you* need."

Mor would not tell me what to wear or not wear. She would not allow me to step aside while she spoke for me. She would not . . . would not do any of the things that I had so willingly, desperately, allowed Ianthe to do.

I had never had a female friend before. Ianthe . . . she had not been one. Not in the way that mattered, I realized. And Nesta and Elain, in those few weeks I'd been at home before Amarantha, had started to fill that role, but . . . but looking at Mor, I couldn't explain it, couldn't understand it, but . . . I felt it. Like I could indeed go to dinner with her. Talk to her.

Not that I had much of anything to offer her in return.

But what she'd said . . . what they'd all said . . . Yes, Rhys had been wise to bring me here. To let me decide if I could handle them—the teasing and intensity and power. If I *wanted* to be a part of a group who would likely push me, and overwhelm me, and maybe frighten me, but . . . If they were willing to stand against Hybern, after already fighting them five hundred years ago . . .

I met Cassian's gaze. And though his eyes danced, there was nothing amused in them. "I'll think about it."

Through the bond in my hand, I could have sworn I felt a glimmer of pleased surprise. I checked my mental shields—but they were intact. And Rhysand's calm face revealed no hint of its origin.

So I said clearly, steadily to him, "I accept your offer—to work with you. To earn my keep. And help with Hybern in whatever way I can."

"Good," Rhys merely replied. Even as the others raised their brows. Yes, they'd obviously *not* been told this was an interview of sorts. "Because we start tomorrow."

"Where? And what?" I sputtered.

Rhys interlaced his fingers and rested them on the table, and I realized there was another point to this dinner beyond my decision as he announced to all of us, "Because the King of Hybern is indeed about to launch a war, and he wants to resurrect Jurian to do it."

Jurian—the ancient warrior whose soul Amarantha had imprisoned within that hideous ring as punishment for killing her sister. The ring that contained his eye . . .

"Bullshit," Cassian spat. "There's no way to do that."

Amren had gone still, and it was she whom Azriel was observing, marking.

Amarantha was just the beginning, Rhys had once told me. Had he known this even then? Had those months Under the Mountain merely been a prelude to whatever hell was about to be unleashed? Resurrecting the dead. What sort of unholy power—

Mor groaned, "Why would the king want to resurrect *Jurian*? He was so odious. All he liked to do was talk about himself."

The age of these people hit me like a brick, despite all they'd told me minutes earlier. The War—they had all . . . they had all fought *in* the War five hundred years ago.

"That's what I want to find out," Rhysand said. "And how the king plans to do it."

Amren at last said, "Word will have reached him about Feyre's Making. He knows it's possible for the dead to be remade."

I shifted in my seat. I'd expected brute armies, pure bloodshed. But this—

"All seven High Lords would have to agree to that," Mor countered.

"There's not a chance it happens. He'll take another route." Her eyes narrowed to slits as she faced Rhys. "All the slaughtering—the massacres at temples. You think it's tied to this?"

"I know it's tied to this. I didn't want to tell you until I knew for certain. But Azriel confirmed that they'd raided the memorial in Sangravah three days ago. They're looking for something—or found it." Azriel nodded in confirmation, even as Mor cast a surprised look in his direction. Azriel gave her an apologetic shrug back.

I breathed, "That—that's why the ring and the finger bone vanished after Amarantha died. For this. But who . . ." My mouth went dry. "They never caught the Attor, did they?"

Rhys said too quietly, "No. No, they didn't." The food in my stomach turned leaden. He said to Amren, "How does one take an eye and a finger bone and make it into a man again? And how do we stop it?"

Amren frowned at her untouched wine. "You already know how to find the answer. Go to the Prison. Talk to the Bone Carver."

"Shit," Mor and Cassian both said.

Rhys said calmly, "Perhaps you would be more effective, Amren."

I was grateful for the table separating us as Amren hissed, "I will not set foot in the Prison, Rhysand, and you know it. So go yourself, or send one of these dogs to do it for you."

Cassian grinned, showing his white, straight teeth—perfect for biting. Amren snapped hers once in return.

Azriel just shook his head. "I'll go. The Prison sentries know me—what I am."

I wondered if the shadowsinger was usually the first to throw himself into danger. Mor's fingers stilled on the stem of her wineglass, her eyes narrowing on Amren. The jewels, the red gown—all perhaps a way to downplay whatever dark power roiled in her veins—

"If anyone's going to the Prison," Rhys said before Mor opened her mouth, "it's me. And Feyre."

"What?" Mor demanded, palms now flat on the table.

"He won't talk to Rhys," Amren said to the others, "or to Azriel. Or to any of us. We've got nothing to offer him. But an immortal with a mortal soul . . ." She stared at my chest as if she could see the heart pounding beneath . . . And I contemplated yet again what she ate. "The Bone Carver might be willing indeed to talk to her."

They stared at me. As if waiting for me to beg not to go, to curl up and cower. Their quick, brutal interview to see if they wanted to work with *me*, I supposed.

But the Bone Carver, the naga, the Attor, the Suriel, the Bogge, the Middengard Wyrm . . . Maybe they'd broken whatever part of me truly feared. Or maybe fear was only something I now felt in my dreams.

"Your choice, Feyre," Rhys said casually.

To shirk and mourn or face some unknown horror—the choice was easy. "How bad can it be?" was my response.

"Bad," Cassian said. None of them bothered to contradict him.

CHAPTER 17

Jurian.

The name clanged through me, even after we finished dinner, even after Mor and Cassian and Azriel and Amren had stopped debating and snarling about who would do what and be where while Rhys and I went to the Prison—whatever that was—tomorrow.

Rhys flew me back over the city, plunging into the lights and darkness. I quickly found I much preferred ascending, and couldn't bring myself to watch for too long without feeling my dinner rise up. Not fear—just some reaction of my body.

We flew in silence, the whistling winter wind the only sound, despite his cocoon of warmth blocking it from freezing me entirely. Only when the music of the streets welcomed us did I peer into his face, his features unreadable as he focused on flying. "Tonight—I felt you again. Through the bond. Did I get past your shields?"

"No," he said, scanning the cobblestone streets below. "This bond is . . . a living thing. An open channel between us, shaped by my powers, shaped . . . by what you needed when we made the bargain."

"I needed not to be dead when I agreed."

"You needed not to be alone."

Our eyes met. It was too dark to read whatever was in his gaze. I was the one who looked away first.

"I'm still learning how and why we can sometimes feel things the other doesn't want known," he admitted. "So I don't have an explanation for what you felt tonight."

You needed not to be alone. . . .

But what about him? Fifty years he'd been separated from his friends, his family . . .

I said, "You let Amarantha and the entire world think you rule and delight in a Court of Nightmares. It's all a front—to keep what matters most safe."

The city lights gilded his face. "I love my people, and my family. Do not think I wouldn't become a monster to keep them protected."

"You already did that Under the Mountain." The words were out before I could stop them.

The wind rustled his hair. "And I suspect I'll have to do it again soon enough."

"What was the cost?" I dared ask. "Of keeping this place secret and free?"

He shot straight down, wings beating to keep us smooth as we landed on the roof of the town house. I made to step away, but he gripped my chin. "You know the cost already."

Amarantha's whore.

He nodded, and I think I might have said the two vile words aloud.

"When she tricked me out of my powers and left the scraps, it was still more than the others. And I decided to use it to tap into the mind of every Night Court citizen she captured, and anyone who might know the truth. I made a web between all of them, actively controlling their minds every second of every day, every decade, to forget about Velaris, to forget about Mor, and Amren, and Cassian, and Azriel. Amarantha wanted to know who was close to me—who to kill and torture. But my true court was here, ruling this city and the others. And I used the remainder of my power to shield them all from sight and sound. I had only enough for one city—one place. I chose the one that had been hidden from history already. *I* chose, and now must live with the consequences of knowing there were more left outside who suffered. But for those here . . . anyone flying or traveling near Velaris would see nothing but barren rock, and if they tried to walk through it, they'd find themselves suddenly deciding otherwise. Sea travel and merchant trading were halted—sailors became farmers, working the earth around Velaris instead. And because my powers were focused on shielding them all, Feyre, I had very little to use against Amarantha. So I decided that to keep her from asking questions about the people who mattered, I would be her whore."

He'd done all of that, had done such horrible things . . . done *everything* for his people, his friends. And the only piece of himself that he'd hidden and managed to keep her from tainting, destroying, even if it meant fifty years trapped in a cage of rock . . .

Those wings now flared wide. How many knew about those wings outside of Velaris or the Illyrian war-camps? Or had he wiped all memory of them from Prythian long before Amarantha?

Rhys released my chin. But as he lowered his hand, I gripped his wrist, feeling the solid strength. "It's a shame," I said, the words nearly gobbled up by the sound of the city music. "That others in Prythian don't know. A shame that you let them think the worst."

He took a step back, his wings beating the air like mighty drums. "As long as the people who matter most know the truth, I don't care about the rest. Get some sleep."

Then he shot into the sky, and was swallowed by the darkness between the stars.

I tumbled into a sleep so heavy my dreams were an undertow that dragged me down, down, down until I couldn't escape them.

I lay naked and prone on a familiar red marble floor while Amarantha slid a knife along my bare ribs, the steel scraping softly against my skin. "Lying, traitorous human," she purred, "with your filthy, lying heart."

The knife scratched, a cool caress. I struggled to get up, but my body wouldn't work.

She pressed a kiss to the hollow of my throat. "You're as much a monster as me." She curved the knife over my breast, angling it toward my peaked nipple, as if she could see the heart beating beneath. I started sobbing. "Don't waste your tears."

Someone far away was roaring my name; begging for me.

"I'm going to make eternity a hell for you," she promised, the tip of the dagger piercing the sensitive flesh beneath my breast, her lips hovering a breath above mine as she pushed—

Hands—there were hands on my shoulders, shaking me, squeezing me. I thrashed against them, screaming, screaming—

"*FEYRE.*"

The voice was at once the night and the dawn and the stars and the earth, and every inch of my body calmed at the primal dominance in it.

"Open your eyes," the voice ordered.

I did.

My throat was raw, my mouth full of ash, my face soaked and sticky, and Rhysand—Rhysand was hovering above me, his eyes wide.

"It was a dream," he said, his breathing as hard as mine.

The moonlight trickling through the windows illuminated the dark lines of swirling tattoos down his arm, his shoulders, across his sculpted chest. Like the ones I bore on my arm. He scanned my face. "A dream," he said again.

Velaris. I was in Velaris, at his house. And I had—my dream—

The sheets, the blankets were ripped. Shredded. But not with a knife. And that ashy, smoky taste coating my mouth . . .

My hand was unnervingly steady as I lifted it to find my fingers ending in simmering embers. Living claws of flame that had sliced through my bed linens like they were cauterizing wounds—

I shoved him off with a hard shoulder, falling out of bed and slamming into a small chest before I hurtled into the bathing room, fell to my knees before the toilet, and was sick to my stomach. Again. Again. My fingertips hissed against the cool porcelain.

Large, warm hands pulled my hair back a moment later.

"Breathe," Rhys said. "Imagine them winking out like candles, one by one."

I heaved into the toilet again, shuddering as light and heat crested and rushed out of me, and savored the empty, cool dark that pooled in their wake.

"Well, that's one way to do it," he said.

When I dared to look at my hands, braced on the bowl, the embers had been extinguished. Even that power in my veins, along my bones, slumbered once more.

"I have this dream," Rhys said as I retched again, holding my hair. "Where it's not me stuck under her, but Cassian or Azriel. And she's pinned their wings to the bed with spikes, and there's nothing I can do to stop it. She's commanded me to watch, and I have no choice but to see how I failed them."

I clung to the toilet, spitting once, and reached up to flush. I watched the water swirl away entirely before I twisted my head to look at him.

His fingers were gentle, but firm where he'd fisted them in my hair. "You never failed them," I rasped.

"I did . . . horrible things to ensure that." Those violet eyes near-glowed in the dim light.

"So did I." My sweat clung like blood—the blood of those two faeries—

I pivoted, barely turning in time. His other hand stroked long, soothing lines down the curve of my back, as over and over I yielded my dinner. When the latest wave had ebbed, I breathed, "The flames?"

"Autumn Court."

I couldn't muster a response. At some point, I leaned against the coolness of the nearby bathtub and closed my eyes.

When I awoke, sun streamed through the windows, and I was in my bed—tucked in tightly to the fresh, clean sheets.

I stared up at the sharp grassy slope of the small mountain, shivering at the veils of mist that wafted past. Behind us, the land swept away to brutal cliffs and a violent pewter sea. Ahead, nothing but a wide, flat-topped mountain of gray stone and moss.

Rhys stood at my side, a double-edged sword sheathed down his spine, knives strapped to his legs, clothed in what I could only assume were Illyrian fighting leathers, based on what Cassian and Azriel had worn the night before. The dark pants were tight, the scale-like plates of leather worn and scarred, and sculpted to legs I hadn't noticed were quite that muscled. His close-fitting jacket had been built around the wings that were now fully out, bits of dark, scratched armor added at the shoulders and forearms.

If his attire hadn't told me enough about what we might be facing today—if my *own*, similar attire hadn't told me enough—all I needed was to take one look at the rock before us and know it wouldn't be pleasant. I'd been so distracted in the study an hour ago by what Rhys had been writing as he drafted a careful request to visit the Summer Court that I hadn't thought to ask what to expect *here*. Not that Rhys had really bothered explaining why he wanted to visit the Summer Court beyond "improving diplomatic relations."

"Where are we?" I said, our first words since winnowing in a moment ago. Velaris had been brisk, sunny. This place, wherever it was, was freezing, deserted, barren. Only rock and grass and mist and sea.

"On an island in the heart of the Western Isles," Rhysand said, staring up at the mammoth mountain. "And that," he said, pointing to it, "is the Prison."

There was nothing—no one around.

"I don't see anything."

"The rock is the Prison. And inside it are the foulest, most dangerous creatures and criminals you can imagine."

Go inside—inside the stone, under another mountain—

"This place," he said, "was made before High Lords existed. Before Prythian was Prythian. Some of the inmates remember those days. Remember a time when it was Mor's family, not mine, that ruled the North."

"Why won't Amren go in here?"

"Because she was once a prisoner."

"Not in that body, I take it."

A cruel smile. "No. Not at all."

I shivered.

"The hike will get your blood warming," Rhys said. "Since we can't winnow inside or fly to the entrance—the wards demand that visitors walk in. The long way."

I didn't move. "I—" The word lodged in my throat. Go under another mountain—

"It helps the panic," he said quietly, "to remind myself that I got out. That we all got out."

"Barely." I tried to breathe. I couldn't, I couldn't—

"We got out. And it might happen again if we don't go inside."

The chill mist bit at my face. And I tried—I did—to take a step toward it.

My body refused to obey.

I tried to take a step again; I tried for Elain and Nesta and the human world that might be wrecked, but . . . I couldn't.

"Please," I whispered. I didn't care if it meant that I'd failed my first day of work.

Rhysand, as promised, didn't ask any questions as he gripped my hand and brought us back to the winter sun and rich colors of Velaris.

✢

I didn't get out of bed for the rest of the day.

CHAPTER 18

Amren was standing at the foot of my bed.

I jolted back, slamming into the headboard, blinded by the morning light blazing in, fumbling for a weapon, anything to use—

"No wonder you're so thin if you vomit up your guts every night." She sniffed, her lip curling. "You reek of it."

The bedroom door was shut. Rhys had said no one entered without his permission, but—

She chucked something onto the bed. A little gold amulet of pearl and cloudy blue stone. "This got me out of the Prison. Wear it in, and they can never keep you."

I didn't touch the amulet.

"Allow me to make one thing clear," Amren said, bracing both hands on the carved wooden footboard. "I do not give that amulet lightly. But you may borrow it, while you do what needs to be done, and return it to me when you are finished. If you keep it, I will find you, and the results won't be pleasant. But it is yours to use in the Prison."

By the time my fingers brushed the cool metal and stone, she'd walked out the door.

Rhys hadn't been wrong about the firedrake comparison.

Rhys kept frowning at the amulet as we hiked the slope of the Prison, so steep that at times we had to crawl on our hands and knees. Higher and higher we climbed, and I drank from the countless little streams that gurgled through the bumps and hollows in the moss-and-grass slopes. All around the mist drifted by, whipped by the wind, whose hollow moaning drowned out our crunching footsteps.

When I caught Rhys looking at the necklace for the tenth time, I said, "What?"

"She gave you that."

Not a question.

"It must be serious, then," I said. "The risk with—"

"Don't say anything you don't want others hearing." He pointed to the stone beneath us. "The inmates have nothing better to do than to listen through the earth and rock for gossip. They'll sell any bit of information for food, sex, maybe a breath of air."

I could do this; I could master this fear.

Amren had gotten out. And stayed out. And the amulet—it'd keep me free, too.

"I'm sorry," I said. "About yesterday." I'd stayed in bed for hours, unable to move or think.

Rhys held out a hand to help me climb a particularly steep rock, easily hauling me up to where he perched at its top. It had been so long—too long—since I'd been outdoors, using my body, relying on it. My breathing was ragged, even with my new immortality. "You've got nothing to be sorry for," he said. "You're here now." But enough of a coward that I never would have gone without that amulet. He added with a wink, "I won't dock your pay."

I was too winded to even scowl. We climbed until the upper face of the mountain became a wall before us, nothing but grassy slopes sweeping behind, far below, to where they flowed to the restless gray sea. Rhys drew the sword from his back in a swift movement.

"Don't look so surprised," he said.

"I've—never seen you with a weapon." Aside from the dagger he'd grabbed to slit Amarantha's throat at the end—to spare me from agony.

"Cassian would laugh himself hoarse hearing that. And then make me go into the sparring ring with him."

"Can he beat you?"

"Hand-to-hand combat? Yes. He'd have to earn it for a change, but he'd win." No arrogance, no pride. "Cassian is the best warrior I've encountered in any court, any land. He leads my armies because of it."

I didn't doubt his claim. And the other Illyrian . . . "Azriel—his hands. The scars, I mean," I said. "Where did they come from?"

Rhys was quiet a moment. Then he said too softly, "His father had two legitimate sons, both older than Azriel. Both cruel and spoiled. They learned it from their mother, the lord's wife. For the eleven years that Azriel lived in his father's keep, she saw to it he was kept in a cell with no window, no light. They let him out for an hour every day—let him see his mother for an hour once a week. He wasn't permitted to train, or fly, or any of the things his Illyrian instincts roared at him to do. When he was eight, his brothers decided it'd be fun to see what happened when you mixed an Illyrian's quick healing gifts with oil—and fire. The warriors heard Azriel's screaming. But not quick enough to save his hands."

Nausea swamped me. But that still left him with three more years living with them. What other horrors had he endured before he was sent to that mountain-camp? "Were—were his brothers punished?"

Rhys's face was as unfeeling as the rock and wind and sea around us as he said with lethal quiet, "Eventually."

There was enough rawness in the words that I instead asked, "And Mor—what does she do for you?"

"Mor is who I'll call in when the armies fail and Cassian and Azriel are both dead."

My blood chilled. "So she's supposed to wait until then?"

"No. As my Third, Mor is my . . . court overseer. She looks after the dynamics between the Court of Nightmares and the Court of Dreams, and runs both Velaris and the Hewn City. I suppose in the mortal realm, she might be considered a queen."

"And Amren?"

"Her duties as my Second make her my political adviser, walking library, and doer of my dirty work. I appointed her upon gaining my throne. But she was my ally, maybe my friend, long before that."

"I mean—in that war where your armies fail and Cassian and Azriel are dead, and even Mor is gone." Each word was like ice on my tongue.

Rhys paused his reach for the bald rock face before us. "If that day comes, I'll find a way to break the spell on Amren and unleash her on the world. And ask her to end me first."

By the Mother. "What *is* she?" After our chat this morning, perhaps it was stupid to ask.

"Something else. Something worse than us. And if she ever finds a way to shed her prison of flesh and bone . . . Cauldron save us all."

I shivered again and stared up at the sheer stone wall. "I can't climb bare rock like that."

"You don't need to," Rhys said, laying a hand flat on the stone. Like a mirage, it vanished in a ripple of light.

Pale, carved gates stood in its place, so high their tops were lost to the mist.

Gates of bone.

✢

The bone-gates swung open silently, revealing a cavern of black so inky I had never seen its like, even Under the Mountain.

I gripped the amulet at my throat, the metal warm under my palm. Amren got out. I would walk out, too.

Rhys put a warm hand on my back and guided me inside, three balls of moonlight bobbing before us.

No—no, no, no, no—

"Breathe," he said in my ear. "One breath."

"Where are the guards?" I managed to get out past the tightness in my lungs.

"They dwell within the rock of the mountain," he murmured, his hand finding mine and wrapping around it as he tugged me into the immortal gloom. "They only emerge at feeding time, or to deal with restless prisoners. They are nothing but shadows of thought and an ancient spell."

With the small lights floating ahead, I tried not to look too long at the gray walls. Especially when they were so rough-hewn that the jagged bits could have been a nose, or a craggy brow, or a set of sneering lips.

The dry ground was clear of anything but pebbles. And there was silence. Utter silence as we rounded a bend, and the last of the light from the misty world faded into inky black.

I focused on my breathing. I couldn't be trapped here; I couldn't be locked in this horrible, dead place.

The path plunged deep into the belly of the mountain, and I clutched Rhys's fingers to keep from losing my footing. He still had his sword gripped in his other hand.

"Do all the High Lords have access?" My words were so soft they were devoured by the dark. Even that thrumming power in my veins had vanished, burrowing somewhere in my bones.

"No. The Prison is law unto itself; the island may be even an eighth court. But it falls under my jurisdiction, and my blood is keyed to the gates."

"Could you free the inmates?"

"No. Once the sentence is given and a prisoner passes those gates . . . They belong to the Prison. It will never let them out. I take sentencing people here very, very seriously."

"Have you ever—"

"Yes. And now is not the time to speak of it." He squeezed my hand in emphasis.

We wound down through the gloom.

There were no doors. No lights.

No sounds. Not even a trickle of water.

But I could feel them.

I could feel them sleeping, pacing, running hands and claws over the other side of the walls.

They were ancient, and cruel in a way I had never known, not even with Amarantha. They were infinite, and patient, and had learned the language of darkness, of stone.

"How long," I breathed. "How long was she in here?" I didn't dare say her name.

"Azriel looked once. Into archives in our oldest temples and libraries. All he found was a vague mention that she went in before Prythian was split into the courts—and emerged once they had been established. Her imprisonment predates our written word. I don't know how long she was in here—a few millennia seems like a fair guess."

Horror roiled in my gut. "You never asked?"

"Why bother? She'll tell me when it's necessary."

"Where did she come from?" The brooch he'd given her—such a small gift, for a monster who had once dwelled here.

"I don't know. Though there are legends that claim when the world was born, there were . . . rips in the fabric of the realms. That in the chaos of Forming, creatures from other worlds could walk through one of those rips and enter another world. But the rips closed at will, and the creatures could become trapped, with no way home."

It was more horrifying than I could fathom—both that monsters had walked between worlds, and the terror of being trapped in another realm. "You think she was one of them?"

"I think that she is the only one of her kind, and there is no record of others ever having existed. Even the Suriel have numbers, however small. But she—and some of those in the Prison . . . I think they came from somewhere else. And they have been looking for a way home for a long, long time."

I was shivering beneath the fur-lined leather, my breath clouding in front of me.

Down and down we went, and time lost its grip. It could have been hours or days, and we paused only when my useless, wasted body demanded water. Even while I drank, he didn't let go of my hand. As if the rock would swallow me up forever. I made sure those breaks were swift and rare.

And still we went onward, deeper. Only the lights and his hand kept me from feeling as if I were about to free-fall into darkness. For a heartbeat, the reek of my own dungeon cell cloyed in my nose, and the crunch of moldy hay tickled my cheek—

Rhys's hand tightened on my own. "Just a bit farther."

"We must be near the bottom by now."

"Past it. The Bone Carver is caged beneath the roots of the mountain."

"Who is he? What is he?" I'd only been briefed in what I was to say—nothing of what to expect. No doubt to keep me from panicking too thoroughly.

"No one knows. He'll appear as he wants to appear."

"Shape-shifter?"

"Yes and no. He'll appear to you as one thing, and I might be standing right beside you and see another."

I tried not to start bleating like cattle. "And the bone carving?"

"You'll see." Rhys stopped before a smooth slab of stone. The hall continued down—down into the ageless dark. The air here was tight, compact. Even my puffs of breath on the chill air seemed short-lived.

Rhysand at last released my hand, only to lay his once more on the bare stone. It rippled beneath his palm, forming—a door.

Like the gates above, it was of ivory—bone. And in its surface were etched countless images: flora and fauna, seas and clouds, stars and moons, infants and skeletons, creatures fair and foul—

It swung away. The cell was pitch-black, hardly distinguishable from the hall—

"I have carved the doors for every prisoner in this place," said a small voice within, "but my own remains my favorite."

"I'd have to agree," Rhysand said. He stepped inside, the light bobbing ahead to illuminate a dark-haired boy sitting against the far wall, eyes of crushing blue taking in Rhysand, then sliding to where I lurked in the doorway.

Rhys reached into a bag I hadn't realized he'd been carrying—no, one he'd summoned from whatever pocket between realms he used for storage. He chucked an object toward the boy, who looked no more than eight. White gleamed as it clacked on the rough stone floor. Another bone, long and sturdy—and jagged on one end.

"The calf-bone that made the final kill when Feyre slew the Middengard Wyrm," Rhys said.

My very blood stilled. There had been many bones that I'd laid in my trap—I hadn't noticed which had ended the Wyrm. Or thought anyone would.

"Come inside," was all the Bone Carver said, and there was no innocence, no kindness in that child's voice.

I took one step in and no more.

"It has been an age," the boy said, gobbling down the sight of me, "since something new came into this world."

"Hello," I breathed.

The boy's smile was a mockery of innocence. "Are you frightened?"

"Yes," I said. *Never lie*—that had been Rhys's first command.

The boy stood, but kept to the other side of the cell. "Feyre," he murmured, cocking his head. The orb of faelight glazed the inky hair in silver. "Fay-ruh," he said again, drawing out the syllables as if he could taste them. At last, he straightened his head. "Where did you go when you died?"

"A question for a question," I replied, as I'd been instructed over breakfast.

The Bone Carver inclined his head to Rhysand. "You were always smarter than your forefathers." But those eyes alighted on me. "Tell me where you went, what you saw—and I will answer your question."

Rhys gave me a subtle nod, but his eyes were wary. Because what the boy had asked . . .

I had to calm my breathing to think—to remember.

But there was blood and death and pain and screaming—and she was breaking me, killing me so slowly, and Rhys was there, roaring in fury as I died, Tamlin begging for my life on his knees before her throne . . . But there was so much agony, and I wanted it to be over, wanted it all to stop—

Rhys had gone rigid while he monitored the Bone Carver, as if those memories were freely flowing past the mental shields I'd made sure were intact this morning. And I wondered if he thought I'd give up then and there.

I bunched my hands into fists.

I had lived; I had gotten out. I would get out today.

"I heard the crack," I said. Rhys's head whipped toward me. "I heard the crack when she broke my neck. It was in my ears, but also inside my skull. I was gone before I felt anything more than the first lash of pain."

The Bone Carver's violet eyes seemed to glow brighter.

"And then it was dark. A different sort of dark than this place. But there was a . . . thread," I said. "A tether. And I yanked on it—and suddenly I could see. Not through my eyes, but—but his," I said, inclining my head toward Rhys. I uncurled the fingers of my tattooed hand. "And I knew I was dead, and this tiny scrap of spirit was all that was left of me, clinging to the thread of our bargain."

"But was there anyone there—were you seeing anything beyond?"

"There was only that bond in the darkness."

Rhysand's face had gone pale, his mouth a tight line. "And when I was Made anew," I said, "I followed that bond back—to me. I knew that home was on the other end of it. There was light then. Like swimming up through sparkling wine—"

"Were you afraid?"

"All I wanted was to return to—to the people around me. I wanted it badly enough I didn't have room for fear. The worst had happened, and the darkness was calm and quiet. It did not seem like a bad thing to fade into. But I wanted to go home. So I followed the bond home."

"There was no other world," the Bone Carver pushed.

"If there was or is, I did not see it."

"No light, no portal?"

Where is it that you want to go? The question almost leaped off my tongue. "It was only peace and darkness."

"Did you have a body?"

"No."

"Did—"

"That's enough from you," Rhysand purred—the sound like velvet over sharpest steel. "You said a question for a question. Now you've asked . . . " He did a tally on his fingers. "Six."

The Bone Carver leaned back against the wall and slid to a sitting position. "It is a rare day when I meet someone who comes back from true death. Forgive me for wanting to peer behind the curtain." He waved a delicate hand in my direction. "Ask it, girl."

"If there was no body—nothing but perhaps a bit of bone," I said as solidly as I could, "would there be a way to resurrect that person? To grow them a new body, put their soul into it."

Those eyes flashed. "Was the soul somehow preserved? Contained?"

I tried not to think about the eye ring Amarantha had worn, the soul she'd trapped inside to witness her every horror and depravity. "Yes."

"There is no way."

I almost sighed in relief.

"Unless . . . " The boy bounced each finger off his thumb, his hand like some pale, twitchy insect. "Long ago, before the High Fae, before man, there was a Cauldron . . . They say all the magic was contained inside it, that the world was born in it. But it fell into the wrong hands. And great and horrible things were done with it. Things were *forged* with it. Such wicked things that the Cauldron was eventually stolen back at great cost. It could not be destroyed, for it had Made all things, and if it were broken, then life would cease to be. So it was hidden. And forgotten. Only with that Cauldron could something that is dead be reforged like that."

Rhysand's face was again a mask of calm. "Where did they hide it?"

"Tell me a secret no one knows, Lord of Night, and I'll tell you mine."

I braced myself for whatever horrible truth was about to come my way. But Rhysand said, "My right knee gets a twinge of pain when it rains. I wrecked it during the War, and it's hurt ever since."

The Bone Carver bit out a harsh laugh, even as I gaped at Rhys. "You always were my favorite," he said, giving a smile I would never for a moment think was childlike. "Very well. The Cauldron was hidden at the bottom of a frozen lake in Lapplund—" Rhys began to turn for me, as if he'd head there right now, but the Bone Carver added, "And vanished a long, long time ago." Rhys halted. "I don't know where it went to—or where it is now. Millennia before you were born, the three feet on which it stands were successfully cleaved from its base in an attempt to fracture *some* of its power. It worked—barely. Removing the feet was like cutting off the first knuckle of a finger. Irksome, but you could still use the rest with some difficulty. The feet were hidden at three different temples—Cesere, Sangravah, and Itica. If *they* have gone missing, it is likely the Cauldron is active once more—and that the wielder wants it at full power and not a wisp of it missing."

That was why the temples had been ransacked. To get the feet on which the Cauldron stood and restore it to its full power. Rhys merely said, "I don't suppose you know *who* now has the Cauldron."

The Bone Carver pointed a small finger at me. "Promise that you'll give me her bones when she dies and I'll think about it." I stiffened, but the boy laughed. "No—I don't think even you would promise that, Rhysand."

I might have called the look on Rhys's face a warning. "Thank you for your help," he said, placing a hand on my back to guide me out.

But if he knew . . . I turned again to the boy-creature. "There was a choice—in Death," I said.

Those eyes guttered with cobalt fire.

Rhys's hand contracted on my back, but remained. Warm, steady. And I wondered if the touch was more to reassure him that I was there, still breathing.

"I knew," I went on, "that I could drift away into the dark. And I chose to fight—to hold on for a bit longer. Yet I knew if I wanted, I could have faded. And maybe it would be a new world, a realm of rest and peace. But I wasn't ready for it—not to go there alone. I knew there was something else waiting beyond that dark. Something good."

For a moment, those blue eyes flared brighter. Then the boy said, "You know who has the Cauldron, Rhysand. Who has been pillaging the temples. You only came here to confirm what you have long guessed."

"The King of Hybern."

Dread sluiced through my veins and pooled in my stomach. I shouldn't have been surprised, should have known, but . . .

The Carver said nothing more. Waiting for another truth.

So I offered up another shattered piece of me. "When Amarantha made me kill those two faeries, if the third hadn't been Tamlin, I would have put the dagger in my own heart at the end."

Rhys went still.

"I knew there was no coming back from what I'd done," I said, wondering if the blue flame in the Carver's eyes might burn my ruined soul to ash. "And once I broke their curse, once I knew I'd saved them, I just wanted enough time to turn that dagger on myself. I only decided I wanted to live when she killed me, and I knew I had not finished whatever . . . whatever it was I'd been born to do."

I dared a glance at Rhys, and there was something like devastation on his beautiful face. It was gone in a blink.

Even the Bone Carver said gently, "With the Cauldron, you could do other things than raise the dead. You could shatter the wall."

The only thing keeping human lands—my family—safe from not just Hybern, but any other faeries.

"It is likely that Hybern has been quiet for so many years because he was hunting the Cauldron, learning its secrets. Resurrection of a specific individual might very well have been his first test once the feet were reunited—and now he finds that the Cauldron is pure energy, pure power. And like any magic, it can be depleted. So he will let it rest, let it gather strength—learn its secrets to feed it more energy, more power."

"Is there a way to stop it," I breathed.

Silence. Expectant, waiting silence.

Rhys's voice was hoarse as he said, "Don't offer him one more—"

"When the Cauldron was made," the Carver interrupted, "its dark maker used the last of the molten ore to forge a book. The Book of Breathings. In it, written between the carved words, are the spells to negate the Cauldron's power—or control it wholly. But after the War, it was split into two pieces. One went to the Fae, one to the six human queens. It was part of the Treaty, purely symbolic, as the Cauldron had been lost for millennia and considered mere myth. The Book was believed harmless, because like calls to like—and only that which was Made can speak those spells and summon its power. No creature born of the earth may wield it, so the High Lords and humans dismissed it as little more than a historical heirloom, but if the Book were in the hands of something reforged . . . You would have to test such a theory, of course—but . . . it might be possible." His eyes narrowed to amused slits as I realized . . . realized . . .

"So now the High Lord of Summer possesses our piece, and the reigning mortal queens have the other entombed in their shining palace by the sea. Prythian's half is guarded, protected with blood-spells keyed to Summer himself. The one belonging to the mortal queens . . . They were crafty, when they received their gift. They used our own kind to spell the Book, to bind it—so that if it were ever stolen, if, let's say, a High Lord were to winnow into their castle to steal it . . . the Book would melt into ore and be lost. It must be freely given by a mortal queen, with no trickery, no magic involved." A little laugh. "Such clever, lovely creatures, humans."

The Carver seemed lost in ancient memory—then shook his head. "Reunite both halves of the Book of Breathings and you will be able to nullify the powers of the Cauldron. Hopefully before it returns to full strength and shatters that wall."

I didn't bother saying thank you. Not with the information he'd told us. Not when I'd been forced to say those things—and could still feel Rhys's lingering attention. As if he'd suspected, but never believed just how badly I'd broken in that moment with Amarantha.

We turned away, his hand sliding from my back to grip my hand.

The touch was light—gentle. And I suddenly had no strength to even grip it back.

The Carver picked up the bone Rhysand had brought him and weighed it in those child's hands. "I shall carve your death in here, Feyre."

Up and up into the darkness we walked, through the sleeping stone and the monsters who dwelled within it. At last I said to Rhys, "What did you see?"

"You first."

"A boy—around eight; dark-haired and blue-eyed."

Rhys shuddered—the most human gesture I'd seen him make.

"What did you see?" I pushed.

"Jurian," Rhys said. "He appeared exactly as Jurian looked the last time I saw him: facing Amarantha when they fought to the death."

I didn't want to learn how the Bone Carver knew who we'd come to ask about.

CHAPTER 19

"Amren's right," Rhys drawled, leaning against the threshold of the town house sitting room. "You *are* like dogs, waiting for me to come home. Maybe I should buy treats."

Cassian gave him a vulgar gesture from where he lounged on the couch before the hearth, an arm slung over the back behind Mor. Though everything about his powerful, muscled body suggested someone at ease, there was a tightness in his jaw, a coiled-up energy that told me they'd been waiting here for a while.

Azriel lingered by the window, comfortably ensconced in shadows, a light flurry of snow dusting the lawn and street behind him. And Amren . . .

Nowhere to be seen. I couldn't tell if I was relieved or not. I'd have to hunt her down to give her back the necklace soon—if Rhys's warnings and her own words were to be believed.

Damp and cold from the mist and wind that chased us down from the Prison, I strode for the armchair across from the couch, which had been shaped, like so much of the furniture here, to accommodate Illyrian wings. I stretched my stiff limbs toward the fire, and stifled a groan at the delicious heat.

"How'd it go?" Mor said, straightening beside Cassian. No gown today—just practical black pants and a thick blue sweater.

"The Bone Carver," Rhys said, "is a busybody gossip who likes to pry into other people's business far too much."

"But?" Cassian demanded, bracing his arms on his knees, wings tucked in tight.

"But," Rhys said, "he can also be helpful, when he chooses. And it seems we need to start doing what we do best."

I flexed my numbed fingers, content to let them discuss, needing a moment to reel myself back in, to shut out what I'd revealed to the Bone Carver.

And what the Bone Carver suggested I might actually be asked to do with that book. The abilities I might have.

So Rhys told them of the Cauldron, and the reason behind the temple pillagings, to no shortage of swearing and questions—and revealed nothing of what I had admitted in exchange for the information. Azriel emerged from his wreathing shadows to ask the most questions; his face and voice remained unreadable. Cassian, surprisingly, kept quiet—as if the general understood that the shadowsinger would know what information was necessary, and was busy assessing it for his own forces.

When Rhys was done, his spymaster said, "I'll contact my sources in the Summer Court about where the half of the Book of Breathings is hidden. I can fly into the human world myself to figure out where they're keeping their part of the Book before we ask them for it."

"No need," Rhys said. "And I don't trust this information, even with your sources, with anyone outside of this room. Save for Amren."

"They can be trusted," Azriel said with quiet steel, his scarred hands clenching at his leather-clad sides.

"We're not taking risks where this is concerned," Rhys merely said. He held Azriel's stare, and I could almost hear the silent words Rhys added, *It is no judgment or reflection on you, Az. Not at all.*

But Azriel yielded no tinge of emotion as he nodded, his hands unfurling.

"So what *do* you have planned?" Mor cut in—perhaps for Az's sake.

Rhys picked an invisible piece of dirt off his fighting leathers. When he lifted his head, those violet eyes were glacial. "The King of Hybern sacked one of our temples to get a missing piece of the Cauldron. As far as I'm concerned, it's an act of war—an indication that His Majesty has no interest in wooing me."

"He likely remembers our allegiance to the humans in the War, anyway," Cassian said. "He wouldn't jeopardize revealing his plans while trying to sway you, and I bet some of Amarantha's cronies reported to him about Under the Mountain. About how it all ended, I mean." Cassian's throat bobbed.

When Rhys had tried to kill her. I lowered my hands from the fire.

Rhys said, "Indeed. But this means Hybern's forces have already successfully infiltrated our lands—without detection. I plan to return the favor."

Mother above. Cassian and Mor just grinned with feral delight. "How?" Mor asked.

Rhys crossed his arms. "It will require careful planning. But if the Cauldron is in Hybern, then to Hybern we must go. Either to take it back . . . or use the Book to nullify it."

Some cowardly, pathetic part of me was already trembling.

"Hybern likely has as many wards and shields around it as we have here," Azriel countered. "We'd need to find a way to get through them undetected first."

A slight nod. "Which is why we start now. While we hunt for the Book. So when we get both halves, we can move swiftly—before word can spread that we even possess it."

Cassian nodded, but asked, "How are you going to retrieve the Book, then?"

I braced myself as Rhys said, "Since these objects are spelled to the individual High Lords, and can only be found by them—through their power . . . Then, in addition to her uses regarding the handling of the Book of Breathings itself, it seems we possibly have our own detector."

Now they all looked at me.

I cringed. "*Perhaps* was what the Bone Carver said in regard to me being able to track things. You don't know . . . " My words faded as Rhys smirked.

"You have a kernel of all our power—like having seven thumbprints. If we've hidden something, if we've made or protected it with our power, no matter where it has been concealed, you will be able to track it through that very magic."

"You can't know that for sure," I tried again.

"No—but there is a way to test it." Rhys was still smiling.

"Here we go," Cassian grumbled. Mor gave Azriel a warning glare to tell him *not* to volunteer this time. The spymaster just gave her an incredulous look in return.

I might have lounged in my chair to watch their battle of wills had Rhys not said, "With your abilities, Feyre, you might be able to find the half of the Book at the Summer Court—and break the wards around it. But I'm not going to take the Carver's word for it, or bring you there without testing you first. To make sure that when it counts, when we need to get that book, you—*we* do not fail. So we're going on another little trip. To see if you can find a valuable object of mine that I've been missing for a considerably long time."

"Shit," Mor said, plunging her hands into the thick folds of her sweater.

"Where?" I managed to say.

It was Azriel who answered. "To the Weaver."

Rhys held up a hand as Cassian opened his mouth. "The test," he said, "will be to see if Feyre can identify the object of mine in the Weaver's trove. When we get to the Summer Court, Tarquin might have spelled his half of the Book to look different, feel different."

"By the Cauldron, Rhys," Mor snapped, setting both feet on the carpet. "Are you out of your—"

"Who is the Weaver?" I pushed.

"An ancient, wicked creature," Azriel said, and I surveyed the faint scars on his wings, his neck, and wondered how many such things he'd encountered in his immortal life. If they were any worse than the people who shared blood ties with him. "Who should remain unbothered," he added in Rhys's direction. "Find another way to test her abilities."

Rhys merely shrugged and looked to me. To let me choose. Always—it was always my choice with him these days. Yet he hadn't let me go back to the Spring Court during those two visits—because he knew how badly I needed to get away from it?

I gnawed on my lower lip, weighing the risks, waiting to feel any kernel of fear, of emotion. But this afternoon had drained any reserve of such things. "The Bone Carver, the Weaver . . . Can't you ever just call someone by a given name?"

Cassian chuckled, and Mor settled back in the sofa cushions.

Only Rhys, it seemed, understood that it hadn't entirely been a joke. His face was tight. Like he knew precisely how tired I was—how I knew I should be quaking at the thought of this Weaver, but after the Bone Carver, what I'd revealed to it . . . I could feel nothing at all.

Rhys said to me, "What about adding one more name to that list?"

I didn't particularly like the sound of that. Mor said as much.

"Emissary," Rhysand said, ignoring his cousin. "Emissary to the Night Court—for the human realm."

Azriel said, "There hasn't been one for five hundred years, Rhys."

"There also hasn't been a human-turned-immortal since then, either." Rhys met my gaze. "The human world must be as prepared as we are—especially if the King of Hybern plans to shatter the wall and unleash his forces upon them. We need the other half of the Book from those mortal queens—and if we can't use magic to influence them, then they're going to have to bring it to us."

More silence. On the street beyond the bay of windows, wisps of snow brushed past, dusting the cobblestones.

Rhys jerked his chin at me. "You are an immortal faerie—with a human heart. Even as such, you might very well set foot on the continent and be . . . hunted for it. So we set up a base in neutral territory. In a place where humans trust us—trust *you*, Feyre. And where other humans might risk going to meet with you. To hear the voice of Prythian after five centuries."

"My family's estate," I said.

"Mother's tits, Rhys," Cassian cut in, wings flaring wide enough to nearly knock over the ceramic vase on the side table next to him. "You think we can just take over her family's house, demand that of them?"

Nesta hadn't wanted any dealings with the Fae, and Elain was so gentle, so sweet . . . how could I bring them into this?

"The land," Mor said, reaching over to return the vase to its place, "will run red with blood, Cassian, regardless of what we do with her family. It is now a matter of where that blood will flow—and how much will spill. How much human blood we can save."

And maybe it made me a cowardly fool, but I said, "The Spring Court borders the wall—"

"The wall stretches across the sea. We'll fly in offshore," Rhys said without so much as a blink. "I won't risk discovery from any court, though word might spread quickly enough once we're there. I know it won't be easy, Feyre, but if there's any way you could convince those queens—"

"I'll do it." I said. Clare Beddor's broken and nailed body flashed in my vision. Amarantha had been one of his commanders. Just one—of many. The King of Hybern had to be horrible beyond reckoning to be her master. If these people got their hands on my sisters . . . "They might not be happy about it, but I'll make Elain and Nesta do it."

I didn't have the nerve to ask Rhys if he could simply force my family to agree to help us if they refused. I wondered if his powers would work on Nesta when even Tamlin's glamour had failed against her steel mind.

"Then it's settled," Rhys said. None of them looked particularly happy. "Once Feyre darling returns from the Weaver, we'll bring Hybern to its knees."

✢

Rhys and the others were gone that night—where, no one told me. But after the events of the day, I barely finished devouring the food Nuala and Cerridwen brought to my room before I tumbled into sleep.

I dreamed of a long, white bone, carved with horrifying accuracy: my face, twisted in agony and despair; the ash knife in my hand; a pool of blood leaking away from two corpses—

But I awoke to the watery light of winter dawn—my stomach full from the night before.

A mere minute after I'd risen to consciousness, Rhys knocked on my door. I'd barely granted him permission to enter before he stalked inside like a midnight wind, and chucked a belt hung with knives onto the foot of the bed.

"Hurry," he said, flinging open the doors of the armoire and yanking out my fighting leathers. He tossed them onto the bed, too. "I want to be gone before the sun is fully up."

"Why?" I said, pushing back the covers. No wings today.

"Because time is of the essence." He dug out my socks and boots. "Once the King of Hybern realizes that someone is searching for the Book of Breathings to nullify the powers of the Cauldron, then his agents will begin hunting for it, too."

"You suspected this for a while, though." I hadn't had the chance to discuss it with him last night. "The Cauldron, the king, the Book . . . You wanted it confirmed, but you were waiting for me."

"Had you agreed to work with me two months ago, I would have taken you right to the Bone Carver to see if he confirmed my suspicions about your talents. But things didn't go as planned."

No, they most certainly hadn't.

"The reading," I said, sliding my feet into fleece-lined, thick-soled slippers. "That's why you insisted on the lessons. So if your suspicions were true and I could harness the Book . . . I could actually read it—or any translation of whatever is inside." A book that old might very well be written in an entirely different language. A different alphabet.

"Again," he said, now striding for the dresser, "had you started to work with me, I would have told you why. I couldn't risk discovery otherwise." He paused with a hand on the knob. "You should have learned to read no matter what. But yes, when I told you it served my own purposes—it was because of this. Do you blame me for it?"

"No," I said, and meant it. "But I'd prefer to be notified of any future schemes."

"Duly noted." Rhys yanked open the drawers and pulled out my undergarments. He dangled the bits of midnight lace and chuckled. "I'm surprised you didn't demand Nuala and Cerridwen buy you something else."

I stalked to him, snatching the lace away. "You're drooling on the carpet." I slammed the bathing room door before he could respond.

He was waiting as I emerged, already warm within the fur-lined leather. He held up the belt of knives, and I studied the loops and straps. "No swords, no bow or arrows," he said. He'd worn his own Illyrian fighting leathers—that simple, brutal sword strapped down his spine.

"But knives are fine?"

Rhys knelt and spread wide the web of leather and steel, beckoning for me to stick a leg through one loop.

I did as instructed, ignoring the brush of his steady hands on my thighs as I stepped through the other loop, and he began tightening and buckling things. "She will not notice a knife, as she has knives in her cottage for eating and her work. But things that are out of place—objects that have not been there . . . A sword, a bow and arrow . . . She might sense those things."

"What about me?"

He tightened a strap. Strong, capable hands—so at odds with the finery he usually wore to dazzle the rest of the world into thinking he was something else entirely. "Do not make a sound, do not touch *anything* but the object she took from me."

Rhys looked up, hands braced on my thighs.

Bow, he'd once ordered Tamlin. And now here he was, on his knees before me. His eyes glinted as if he remembered it, too. Had that been a part of his game—that façade? Or had it been vengeance for the horrible blood feud between them?

"If we're correct about your powers," he said, "if the Bone Carver wasn't lying to us, then you and the object will have the same . . . imprint, thanks to the preserving spells I placed on it long ago. You are one and the same. She will not notice your presence so long as you touch *only* it. You will be invisible to her."

"She's blind?"

A nod. "But her other senses are lethal. So be quick, and quiet. Find the object and run out, Feyre." His hands lingered on my legs, wrapping around the back of them.

"And if she notices me?"

His hands tightened slightly. "Then we'll learn precisely how skilled you are."

Cruel, conniving bastard. I glared at him.

Rhys shrugged. "Would you rather I locked you in the House of Wind and stuffed you with food and made you wear fine clothes and plan my parties?"

"Go to hell. Why not get this object yourself, if it's so important?"

"Because the Weaver knows me—and if I am caught, there would be a steep price. High Lords are not to interfere with her, no matter the direness of the situation. There are many treasures in her hoard, some she has kept for millennia. Most will never be retrieved—because the High Lords do not dare be caught, thanks to the laws that protect her, thanks to her wrath. Any thieves on their behalf . . . Either they do not return, or they are never sent, for fear of it leading back to their High Lord. But you . . . She does not know you. You belong to every court."

"So I'm your huntress and thief?"

His hands slid down to cup the backs of my knees as he said with a roguish grin, "You are my salvation, Feyre."

CHAPTER 20

Rhysand winnowed us into a wood that was older, more aware, than any place I'd been.

The gnarled beech trees were tightly woven together, splattered and draped so thoroughly with moss and lichen that it was nearly impossible to see the bark beneath.

"Where are we?" I breathed, hardly daring to whisper.

Rhys kept his hands within casual reach of his weapons. "In the heart of Prythian, there is a large, empty territory that divides the North and South. At the center of it is our sacred mountain."

My heart stumbled, and I focused on my steps through the ferns and moss and roots. "This forest," Rhys went on, "is on the eastern edge of that neutral territory. Here, there is no High Lord. Here, the law is made by who is strongest, meanest, most cunning. And the Weaver of the Wood is at the top of their food chain."

The trees groaned—though there was no breeze to shift them. No, the air here was tight and stale. "Amarantha didn't wipe them out?"

"Amarantha was no fool," Rhys said, his face dark. "She did not touch these creatures or disturb the wood. For years, I tried to find ways to manipulate her to make that foolish mistake, but she never bought it."

"And now we're disturbing her—for a mere test."

He chuckled, the sound bouncing off the gray stones strewn across the forest floor like scattered marbles. "Cassian tried to convince me last night not to take you. I thought he might even punch me."

"Why?" I barely knew him.

"Who knows? With Cassian, he's probably more interested in fucking you than protecting you."

"You're a pig."

"You could, you know," Rhys said, holding up the branch of a scrawny beech for me to slip under. "If you needed to move on in a physical sense, I'm sure Cassian would be more than happy to oblige."

It felt like a test in itself. And it pissed me off enough that I crooned, "Then tell him to come to my room tonight."

"If you survive this test."

I paused atop a little lichen-crusted rock. "You seem pleased by the idea that I won't."

"Quite the opposite, Feyre." He prowled to where I stood on the stone. I was almost eye level with him. The forest went even quieter—the trees seeming to lean closer, as if to catch every word. "I'll let Cassian know you're . . . open to his advances."

"Good," I said. A bit of hollowed-out air pushed against me, like a flicker of night. That power along my bones and blood stirred in answer.

I made to jump off the stone, but he gripped my chin, the movement too fast to detect. His words were a lethal caress as he said, "Did you enjoy the sight of me kneeling before you?"

I knew he could hear my heart as it ratcheted into a thunderous beat. I gave him a hateful little smirk, anyway, yanking my chin out of his touch and leaping off the stone. I might have aimed for his feet. And he might have shifted out of the way just enough to avoid it. "Isn't that all you males are good for, anyway?" But the words were tight, near-breathless.

His answering smile evoked silken sheets and jasmine-scented breezes at midnight.

A dangerous line—one Rhys was forcing me to walk to keep me from thinking about what I was about to face, about what a wreck I was inside.

Anger, this . . . flirtation, annoyance . . . He knew those were my crutches.

What I was about to encounter, then, must be truly harrowing if he wanted me going in there mad—thinking about sex, about anything but the Weaver of the Wood.

"Nice try," I said hoarsely. Rhysand just shrugged and swaggered off into the trees ahead.

Bastard. Yes, it had been to distract me, but—

I stormed after him as silently as I could, intent on tackling him and slamming my fist into his spine, but he held up a hand as he stopped before a clearing.

A small, whitewashed cottage with a thatched roof and half-crumbling chimney sat in the center. Ordinary—almost mortal. There was even a well, its bucket perched on the stone lip, and a wood pile beneath one of the round windows of the cottage. No sound or light within—not even smoke puffed from the chimney.

The few birds in the forest fell quiet. Not entirely, but to keep their chatter to a minimum. And—there.

Faint, coming from inside the cottage, was a pretty, steady humming.

It might have been the sort of place I would have stopped if I were thirsty, or hungry, or in need of shelter for the night.

Maybe that was the trap.

The trees around the clearing, so close that their branches nearly clawed at the thatched roof, might very well have been the bars of a cage.

Rhys inclined his head toward the cottage, bowing with dramatic grace.

In, out—don't make a sound. Find whatever object it was and snatch it from beneath a blind person's nose.

And then run like hell.

Mossy earth paved the way to the front door, already cracked slightly. A bit of cheese. And I was the foolish mouse about to fall for it.

Eyes twinkling, Rhys mouthed, *Good luck*.

I gave him a vulgar gesture and slowly, silently made my way toward the front door.

The woods seemed to monitor each of my steps. When I glanced behind, Rhys was gone.

He hadn't said if he'd interfere if I were in mortal peril. I probably should have asked.

I avoided any leaves and stones, falling into a pattern of movement that some part of my body—some part that was not born of the High Lords—remembered.

Like waking up. That's what it felt like.

I passed the well. Not a speck of dirt, not a stone out of place. A perfect, pretty trap, that mortal part of me warned. A trap designed from a time when humans were prey; now laid for a smarter, immortal sort of game.

I was not prey any longer, I decided as I eased up to that door.

And I was not a mouse.

I was a wolf.

I listened on the threshold, the rock worn as if many, many boots had passed through—and perhaps never passed back over again. The words of her song became clear now, her voice sweet and beautiful, like sunlight on a stream:

"There were two sisters, they went playing,
To see their father's ships come sailing . . .
And when they came unto the sea-brim
The elder did push the younger in."

A honeyed voice, for an ancient, horrible song. I'd heard it before—slightly different, but sung by humans who had no idea that it had come from faerie throats.

I listened for another moment, trying to hear anyone else. But there was only a clatter and thrum of some sort of device, and the Weaver's song.

"Sometimes she sank, and sometimes she swam,
'Til her corpse came to the miller's dam."

My breath was tight in my chest, but I kept it even—directing it through my mouth in silent breaths. I eased open the front door, just an inch.

No squeak—no whine of rusty hinges. Another piece of the pretty trap: practically inviting thieves in. I peered inside when the door had opened wide enough.

A large main room, with a small, shut door in the back. Floor-to-ceiling shelves lined the walls, crammed with bric-a-brac: books, shells, dolls, herbs, pottery, shoes, crystals, more books, jewels . . . From the ceiling and wood rafters hung all manner of chains, dead birds, dresses, ribbons, gnarled bits of wood, strands of pearls . . .

A junk shop—of some immortal hoarder.

And that hoarder . . .

In the gloom of the cottage, there sat a large spinning wheel, cracked and dulled with age.

And before that ancient spinning wheel, her back to me, sat the Weaver.

Her thick hair was of richest onyx, tumbling down to her slender waist as she worked the wheel, snow-white hands feeding and pulling the thread around a thorn-sharp spindle.

She looked young—her gray gown simple but elegant, sparkling faintly in the dim forest light through the windows as she sang in a voice of glittering gold:

"But what did he do with her breastbone?
He made him a viol to play on.
What'd he do with her fingers so small?
He made pegs to his viol withall."

The fiber she fed into the wheel was white—soft. Like wool, but . . . I knew, in that lingering human part of me, it was not wool. I knew that I did not want to learn what creature it had come from, *who* she was spinning into thread.

Because on the shelf directly beyond her were cones upon cones of threads—of every color and texture. And on the shelf adjacent to her were swaths and yards of that woven thread—woven, I realized, on the massive loom nearly hidden in the darkness near the hearth. The Weaver's loom.

I had come on spinning day—would she have been singing if I had come on weaving day instead? From the strange, fear-drenched scent that came from those bolts of fabric, I already knew the answer.

A wolf. I was a wolf.

I stepped into the cottage, careful of the scattered debris on the earthen floor. She kept working, the wheel clattering so merrily, so at odds with her horrible song:

"And what did he do with her nose-ridge?
Unto his viol he made a bridge.
What did he do with her veins so blue?
He made strings to his viol thereto."

I scanned the room, trying not to listen to the lyrics.

Nothing. I felt . . . nothing that might pull me toward one object in particular. Perhaps it would be a blessing if I were indeed *not* the one to track the Book—if today was not the start of what was sure to be a slew of miseries.

The Weaver perched there, working.

I scanned the shelves, the ceiling. Borrowed time. I was on borrowed time, and I was almost out of it.

Had Rhys sent me on a fool's errand? Maybe there was nothing here. Maybe this *object* had been taken. It would be just like him to do that. To tease me in the woods, to see what sort of things might make my body react.

And maybe I resented Tamlin enough in that moment to enjoy that deadly bit of flirtation. Maybe I was as much a monster as the female spinning before me.

But if I was a monster, then I supposed Rhys was as well.

Rhys and I were one in the same—beyond the power that he'd given me. It'd be fitting if Tamlin hated me, too, once he realized I'd truly left.

I felt it, then—like a tap on my shoulder.

I pivoted, keeping one eye on the Weaver and the other on the room as I wove through the maze of tables and junk. Like a beacon, a bit of light laced with his half smile, it tugged me.

Hello, it seemed to say. *Have you come to claim me at last?*

Yes—yes, I wanted to say. Even as part of me wished it were otherwise.

The Weaver sang behind me,

"What did he do with her eyes so bright?
On his viol he set at first light.
What did he do with her tongue so rough?
'Twas the new till and it spoke enough."

I followed that pulse—toward the shelf lining the wall beside the hearth. Nothing. And nothing on the second. But the third, right above my eyeline . . . There.

I could almost smell his salt-and-citrus scent. The Bone Carver had been correct.

I rose on my toes to examine the shelf. An old letter knife, books in leather that I did not want to touch or smell; a handful of acorns, a tarnished crown of ruby and jasper, and—

A ring.

A ring of twisted strands of gold and silver, flecked with pearl, and set with a stone of deepest, solid blue. Sapphire—but different. I'd never seen a sapphire like that, even at my father's offices. This one . . . I could have sworn that in the pale light, the lines of a six-pointed star radiated across the round, opaque surface.

Rhys—this had Rhys written all over it.

He'd sent me here for a *ring*?

The Weaver sang,

"Then bespake the treble string,
'O yonder is my father the king.'"

I watched her for another heartbeat, gauging the distance between the shelf and the open door. Grab the ring, and I could be gone in a heartbeat. Quick, quiet, calm.

"Then bespake the second string,
'O yonder sits my mother the queen.'"

I dropped a hand toward one of the knives strapped to my thighs. When I got back to Rhys, maybe I'd stab him in the gut.

That fast, the memory of phantom blood covered my hands. I knew how it'd feel to slide my dagger through his skin and bones and flesh. Knew how the blood would dribble out, how he'd groan in pain—

I shut out the thought, even as I could feel the blood of those faeries soaking that human part of me that hadn't died and belonged to no one but my miserable self.

"Then bespake the strings all three,
'Yonder is my sister that drowned me.'"

My hand was quiet as a final, dying breath as I plucked the ring from the shelf.

The Weaver stopped singing.

CHAPTER 21

I froze, the ring now in the pocket of my jacket. She'd finished the last song—maybe she'd start another.

Maybe.

The spinning wheel slowed.

I backed a step toward the door. Then another.

Slower and slower, each rotation of the ancient wheel longer than the last.

Only ten steps to the door.

Five.

The wheel went round, one last time, so slow I could see each of the spokes.

Two.

I turned for the door as she lashed out with a white hand, gripping the wheel and stopping it wholly.

The door before me snicked shut.

I lunged for the handle, but there was none.

Window. Get to the window—

"Who is in my house?" she said softly.

Fear—undiluted, unbroken fear—slammed into me, and I remembered. I remembered what it was to be human and helpless and weak. I remembered what it was to want to *fight* to live, to be willing to do anything to stay breathing—

I reached the window beside the door. Sealed. No latch, no opening. Just glass that was not glass. Solid and impenetrable.

The Weaver turned her face toward me.

Wolf or mouse, it made no difference, because I became no more than an animal, sizing up my chance of survival.

Above her young, supple body, beneath her black, beautiful hair, her skin was gray—wrinkled and sagging and dry. And where eyes should have gleamed instead lay rotting black pits. Her lips had withered to nothing but deep, dark lines around a hole full of jagged stumps of teeth—like she had gnawed on too many bones.

And I knew she would be gnawing on my bones soon if I did not get out.

Her nose—perhaps once pert and pretty, now half-caved in—flared as she sniffed in my direction.

"What are you?" she said in a voice that was so young and lovely.

Out—out, I had to get *out*—

There was another way.

One suicidal, reckless way.

I did not want to die.

I did not want to be eaten.

I did not want to go into that sweet darkness.

The Weaver rose from her little stool.

And I knew my borrowed time had run out.

"What is like all," she mused, taking one graceful step toward me, "but unlike all?"

I *was* a wolf.

And I bit when cornered.

I lunged for the sole candle burning on the table in the center of the room. And hurled it against the wall of woven thread—against all those miserable, dark bolts of fabric. Woven bodies, skins, lives. Let them be free.

Fire erupted, and the Weaver's shriek was so piercing I thought my head might shatter; thought my blood might boil in its veins.

She dashed for the flames, as if she'd put them out with those flawless white hands, her mouth of rotted teeth open and screaming like there was nothing but black hell inside her.

I hurtled for the darkened hearth. For the fireplace and chimney above.

A tight squeeze, but wide—wide enough for me.

I didn't hesitate as I grabbed onto the ledge and hauled myself up, arms buckling. Immortal strength—it got me only so far, and I'd become so weak, so malnourished.

I had *let them* make me weak. Bent to it like some wild horse broken to the bit.

The soot-stained bricks were loose, uneven. Perfect for climbing.

Faster—I had to go faster.

But my shoulders scraped against the brick, and it *reeked* in here, like carrion and burned hair, and there was an oily sheen on the stone, like cooked fat—

The Weaver's screaming was cut short as I was halfway up her chimney, sunlight and trees almost visible, every breath a near-sob.

I reached for the next brick, fingernails breaking as I hauled myself up so violently that my arms barked in protest against the squeezing of the stone around me, and—

And I was stuck.

Stuck, as the Weaver hissed from within her house, "What little mouse is climbing about in my chimney?"

I had just enough room to look down as the Weaver's rotted face appeared below.

She put that milk-white hand on the ledge, and I realized how little room there was between us.

My head emptied out.

I pushed against the grip of the chimney, but couldn't budge.

I was going to die here. I was going to be dragged down by those beautiful hands and ripped apart and eaten. Maybe while I was still alive, she'd set that hideous mouth on my flesh and gnaw and tear and bite and—

Black panic crushed in, and I was again trapped under a nearby mountain, in a muddy trench, the Middengard Wyrm barreling for me. I'd barely escaped, barely—

I couldn't breathe, couldn't breathe, couldn't breathe—

The Weaver's nails scratched against the brick as she took a step up.

No, no, no, no, no—

I kicked and kicked against the bricks.

"Did you think you could steal and flee, thief?"

I would have preferred the Middengard Wyrm. Would have preferred those massive, sharp teeth to her jagged stumps—

Stop.

The word came out of the darkness of my mind.

And the voice was my own.

Stop, it said—*I* said.

Breathe.

Think.

The Weaver came closer, brick crumbling under her hands. She'd climb up like a spider—like I was a fly in her web—

Stop.

And that word quieted everything.

I mouthed it.

Stop, stop, stop.

Think.

I had survived the Wyrm—survived Amarantha. And I had been granted gifts. Considerable gifts.

Like strength.

I *was* strong.

I slammed a hand against the chimney wall, as low as I could get. The Weaver hissed at the debris that rained down. I smashed my fist again, rallying that strength.

I was not a pet, not a doll, not an animal.

I was a survivor, and I was strong.

I would not be weak, or helpless again. I would not, *could not* be broken. Tamed.

I pounded my fist into the bricks over and over, and the Weaver paused.

Paused long enough for the brick I'd loosened to slide free into my waiting palm.

And for me to hurl it at her hideous, horrible face as hard as I could.

Bone crunched and she roared, black blood spraying. But I rammed my shoulders into the sides of the chimney, skin tearing beneath my leather. I kept going, going, going, until I was stone breaking stone, until nothing and no one held me back and I was scaling the chimney.

I didn't dare stop, not as I reached the lip and hauled myself out, tumbling onto the thatched roof. Which was not thatched with hay at all.

But hair.

And with all that fat lining the chimney—all that fat now gleaming on my skin . . . the hair clung to me. In clumps and strands and tufts. Bile rose, but the front door banged open—a shriek following it.

No—not that way. Not to the ground.

Up, up, up.

A tree branch hung low and close by, and I scrambled across that heinous roof, trying not to think about who and what I was stepping on, what clung to my skin, my clothes. A heartbeat later, I'd jumped onto the waiting branch, scrambling into the leaves and moss as the Weaver screamed, "*WHERE ARE YOU?*"

But I was running through the tree—running toward another one nearby. I leaped from branch to branch, bare hands tearing on the wood. Where was Rhysand?

Farther and farther I fled, her screams chasing me, though they grew ever-distant.

Where are you, where are you, where are you—

And then, lounging on a branch in a tree before me, one arm draped over the edge, Rhysand drawled, "What the hell did you *do*?"

I skidded to a stop, breathing raw. I thought my lungs might actually be bleeding.

"*You*," I hissed.

But he raised a finger to his lips and winnowed to me—grabbing my waist with one hand and cupping the back of my neck with his other as he spirited us away—

To Velaris. To just above the House of Wind.

We free-fell, and I didn't have breath to scream as his wings appeared, spreading wide, and he curved us into a steady glide . . . right through the open windows of what had to be a war room. Cassian was there—in the middle of arguing with Amren about something.

Both froze as we landed on the red floor.

There was a mirror on the wall behind them, and I glimpsed myself long enough to know why they were gaping.

My face was scratched and bloody, and I was covered in dirt and grease—*boiled fat*—and mortar dust, the hair stuck to me, and I smelled—

"You smell like barbecue," Amren said, cringing a bit.

Cassian loosened the hand he'd wrapped around the fighting knife at his thigh.

I was still panting, still trying to gobble down breath. The hair clinging to me scratched and tickled, and—

"You kill her?" Cassian said.

"No," Rhys answered for me, loosely folding his wings. "But given how much the Weaver was screaming, I'm dying to know what Feyre darling did."

Grease—I had the grease and hair of *people* on me—

I vomited all over the floor.

Cassian swore, but Amren waved a hand and it was instantly gone—along with the mess on me. But I could feel the ghost of it there, the remnants of people, the mortar of those bricks . . .

"She . . . detected me somehow," I managed to say, slumping against the large black table and wiping my mouth against the shoulder of my leathers. "And locked the doors and windows. So I had to climb out through the chimney. I got stuck," I added as Cassian's brows rose, "and when she tried to climb up, I threw a brick at her face."

Silence.

Amren looked to Rhysand. "And where were you?"

"Waiting, far enough away that she couldn't detect me."

I snarled at him, "I could have used some help."

"You survived," he said. "And found a way to help yourself." From the hard glimmer in his eye, I knew he was aware of the panic that had almost gotten me killed, either through mental shields I'd forgotten to raise or whatever anomaly in our bond. He'd been aware of it—and let me endure it.

Because it *had* almost gotten me killed, and I'd be no use to him if it happened when it mattered—with the Book. Exactly like he'd said.

"That's what this was also about," I spat. "Not just this *stupid ring*," I reached into my pocket, slamming the ring down on the table, "or my *abilities*, but if I can master my panic."

Cassian swore again, his eyes on that ring.

Amren shook her head, sheet of dark hair swaying. "Brutal, but effective."

Rhys only said, "Now you know. That you can use your abilities to hunt our objects, and thus track the Book at the Summer Court, *and* master yourself."

"You're a prick, Rhysand," Cassian said quietly.

Rhys merely tucked his wings in with a graceful snap. "You'd do the same."

Cassian shrugged, as if to say fine, he would.

I looked at my hands, my nails bloody and cracked. And I said to Cassian, "I want you to teach me—how to fight. To get strong. If the offer to train still stands."

Cassian's brows rose, and he didn't bother looking to Rhys for approval. "You'll be calling *me* a prick pretty damn fast if we train. And I don't know anything about training humans—how breakable your bodies are. Were, I mean," he added with a wince. "We'll figure it out."

"I don't want my only option to be running," I said.

"Running," Amren cut in, "kept you alive today."

I ignored her. "I want to know how to fight my way out. I don't want to have to wait on anyone to rescue me." I faced Rhys, crossing my arms. "Well? Have I proved myself?"

But he merely picked up the ring and gave me a nod of thanks. "It was my mother's ring." As if that were all the explanation and answers owed.

"How'd you lose it?" I demanded.

"I didn't. My mother gave it to me as a keepsake, then took it back when I reached maturity—and gave it to the Weaver for safekeeping."

"Why?"

"So I wouldn't waste it."

Nonsense and idiocy and—I wanted a bath. I wanted *quiet* and a bath. The need for those things hit me strong enough that my knees buckled.

I'd barely looked at Rhys before he grabbed my hand, flared his wings, and had us soaring back through the windows. We free-fell for five thunderous, wild heartbeats before he winnowed to my bedroom in the town house. A hot bath was already running. I staggered to it, exhaustion hitting me like a physical blow, when Rhys said, "And what about training your other . . . gifts?"

Through the rising steam from the tub, I said, "I think you and I would shred each other to bits."

"Oh, we most definitely will." He leaned against the bathing room threshold. "But it wouldn't be fun otherwise. Consider *our* training now officially part of your work requirements with me." A jerk of the chin. "Go ahead—try to get past my shields."

I knew which ones he was talking about. "I'm tired. The bath will go cold."

"I promise it'll be just as hot in a few moments. Or, if you mastered your gifts, you might be able to take care of that yourself."

I frowned. But took a step toward him, then another—making him yield a step, two, into the bedroom. The phantom grease and hair clung to me, reminded me what he'd done—

I held his stare, those violet eyes twinkling.

"You feel it, don't you," he said over the burbling and chittering garden birds. "Your power, stalking under your skin, purring in your ear."

"So what if I do?"

A shrug. "I'm surprised Ianthe didn't carve you up on an altar to see what that power looks like inside you."

"What, precisely, is your issue with her?"

"I find the High Priestesses to be a perversion of what they once were—once promised to be. Ianthe among the worst of them."

A knot twisted in my stomach. "Why do you say that?"

"Get past my shields and I'll *show* you."

So that explained the turn in conversation. A taunt. Bait.

Holding his stare . . . I let myself fall for it. I let myself imagine that line between us—a bit of braided light . . . And there was his mental shield at the other end of the bond. Black and solid and impenetrable. No way in. However I'd slipped through before . . . I had no idea. "I've had enough tests for the day."

Rhys crossed the two feet between us. "The High Priestesses have burrowed into a few of the courts—Dawn, Day, and Winter, mostly. They've entrenched themselves so thoroughly that their spies are everywhere, their followers near-fanatic with devotion. And yet, during those fifty years, they escaped. They remained hidden. I would not be surprised if Ianthe sought to establish a foothold in the Spring Court."

"You mean to tell me they're all black-hearted villains?"

"No. Some, yes. Some are compassionate and selfless and wise. But there are some who are merely self-righteous . . . Though those are the ones that always seem the most dangerous to me."

"And Ianthe?"

A knowing sparkle in his eyes.

He really wouldn't tell me. He'd dangle it before me like a piece of meat—

I lunged. Blindly, wildly, but I sent my power lashing down that line between us.

And yelped as it slammed against his inner shields, the reverberations echoing in me as surely as if I'd hit something with my body.

Rhys chuckled, and I saw fire. "Admirable—sloppy, but an admirable effort."

Panting a bit, I seethed.

But he said, "Just for trying . . . ," and took my hand in his. The bond went taut, that thing under my skin pulsing, and—

There was dark, and the colossal sense of *him* on the other side of his mental barricade of black adamant. That shield went on forever, the product of half a millennia of being hunted, attacked, hated. I brushed a mental hand against that wall.

Like a mountain cat arching into a touch, it seemed to purr—and then relaxed its guard.

His mind opened for me. An antechamber, at least. A single space he'd carved out, to allow me to see—

A bedroom carved from obsidian; a mammoth bed of ebony sheets, large enough to accommodate wings.

And on it, sprawled in nothing but her skin, lay Ianthe.

I reeled back, realizing it was a memory, and Ianthe was in *his* bed, in *his* court beneath that mountain, her full breasts peaked against the chill—

"There is more," Rhys's voice said from far away as I struggled to pull out. But my mind slammed into the shield—the other side of it. He'd trapped me in here—

"You kept me waiting," Ianthe sulked.

The sensation of hard, carved wood digging into my back—Rhysand's back—as he leaned against the bedroom door. "Get out."

Ianthe gave a little pout, bending her knee and shifting her legs wider, baring herself to him. "I see the way you look at me, High Lord."

"You see what you want to see," he—we—said. The door opened beside him. "Get out."

A coy tilt of her lips. "I heard you like to play games." Her slender hand drifted low, trailing past her belly button. "I think you'll find me a diverting playmate."

Icy wrath crept through me—him—as he debated the merits of splattering her on the walls, and how much of an inconvenience it'd cause. She'd hounded him relentlessly—stalked the other males, too. Azriel had left last night because of it. And Mor was about one more comment away from snapping her neck.

"I thought your allegiance lay with other courts." His voice was so cold. The voice of the High Lord.

"My allegiance lies with the future of Prythian, with the true power in this land." Her fingers slid between her legs—and halted. Her gasp cleaved the room as he sent a tendril of power blasting for her, pinning that arm to the bed—away from herself. "Do you know what a union

between us could do for Prythian, for the world?" she said, eyes devouring him still.

"You mean yourself."

"Our offspring could rule Prythian."

Cruel amusement danced through him. "So you want my crown—and for me to play stud?"

She tried to writhe her body, but his power held her. "I don't see anyone else worthy of the position."

She'd be a problem—now, and later. He knew it. Kill her now, end the threat before it began, face the wrath of the other High Priestesses, or . . . see what happened. "Get out of my bed. Get out of my room. And get out of my court."

He released his power's grip to allow her to do so.

Ianthe's eyes darkened, and she slithered to her feet, not bothering with her clothes, draped over his favorite chair. Each step toward him had her generous breasts bobbing. She stopped barely a foot away. "You have no idea what I can make you feel, High Lord."

She reached a hand for him, right between his legs.

His power lashed around her fingers before she could grab him.

He crunched the power down, twisting.

Ianthe screamed. She tried backing away, but his power froze her in place—so much power, so easily controlled, roiling around her, contemplating ending her existence like an asp surveying a mouse.

Rhys leaned close to breathe into her ear, "Don't ever touch me. Don't ever touch another male in my court." His power snapped bones and tendons, and she screamed again. "Your hand will heal," he said, stepping back. "The next time you touch me or anyone in my lands, you will find that the rest of you will not fare so well."

Tears of agony ran down her face—the effect wasted by the hatred lighting her eyes. "You will regret this," she hissed.

He laughed softly, a lover's laugh, and a flicker of power had her thrown onto her ass in the hallway. Her clothes followed a heartbeat later. Then the door slammed.

Like a pair of scissors through a taut ribbon, the memory was severed, the shield behind me fell, and I stumbled back, blinking.

"Rule one," Rhys told me, his eyes glazed with the rage of that memory, "don't go into someone's mind unless you hold the way open. A daemati might leave their minds spread wide for you—and then shut you inside, turn you into their willing slave."

A chill went down my spine at the thought. But what he'd shown me . . .

"Rule two," he said, his face hard as stone, "when—"

"When was that," I blurted. I knew him well enough not to doubt its truth. "When did that happen between you?"

The ice remained in his eyes. "A hundred years ago. At the Court of Nightmares. I allowed her to visit after she'd begged for years, insisting she wanted to build ties between the Night Court and the priestesses. I'd heard rumors about her nature, but she was young and untried, and I hoped that perhaps a new High Priestess might indeed be the change her order needed. It turned out that she was already well trained by some of her less-benevolent sisters."

I swallowed hard, my heart thundering. "She—she didn't act that way at . . ."

Lucien.

Lucien had hated her. Had made vague, vicious allusions to not liking her, to being approached by her—

I was going to throw up. Had she . . . had she pursued him like that? Had he . . . had he been forced to say yes because of her position?

And if I went back to the Spring Court one day . . . How would I ever convince Tamlin to dismiss her? What if, now that I was gone, she was—

"Rule two," Rhys finally went on, "be prepared to see things you might not like."

Only fifty years later, Amarantha had come. And done exactly to Rhys what he'd wanted to kill Ianthe for. He'd let it happen to him. To keep them safe. To keep Azriel and Cassian from the nightmares that would haunt him forever, from enduring any more pain than what they'd suffered as children . . .

I lifted my head to ask him more. But Rhys had vanished.

Alone, I peeled off my clothes, struggling with the buckles and straps he'd put on me—when had it been? An hour or two ago?

It felt as if a lifetime had passed. And I was now a certified Book-tracker, it seemed.

Better than a party-planning wife for breeding little High Lords. What Ianthe had wanted to make me—to serve whatever agenda she had.

The bath was indeed hot, as he'd promised. And I mulled over what he'd shown me, seeing that hand again and again reach between his legs, the ownership and arrogance in that gesture—

I shut out the memory, the bath water suddenly cold.

CHAPTER 22

Word still hadn't come from the Summer Court the following morning, so Rhysand made good on his decision to bring us to the mortal realm.

"What does one wear, exactly, in the human lands?" Mor said from where she sprawled across the foot of my bed. For someone who claimed to have been out drinking and dancing until the Mother knew when, she appeared unfairly perky. Cassian and Azriel, grumbling and wincing over breakfast, had looked like they'd been run over by wagons. Repeatedly. Some small part of me wondered what it would be like to go out with them—to see what Velaris might offer at night.

I rifled through the clothes in my armoire. "Layers," I said. "They . . . cover everything up. The décolletage might be a little daring depending on the event, but . . . everything else gets hidden beneath skirts and petticoats and nonsense."

"Sounds like the women are used to not having to run—or fight. I don't remember it being that way five hundred years ago."

I paused on an ensemble of turquoise with accents of gold—rich, bright, regal. "Even with the wall, the threat of faeries remained, so . . . surely practical clothes would have been necessary to run, to fight any that crept through. I wonder what changed." I pulled out the top and pants for her approval.

Mor merely nodded—no commentary like Ianthe might have provided, no beatific *intervention*.

I shoved away the thought, and the memory of what she'd tried to do to Rhys, and went on, "Nowadays, most women wed, bear children, and then plan their children's marriages. Some of the poor might work in the fields, and a rare few are mercenaries or hired soldiers, but . . . the wealthier they are, the more restricted their freedoms and roles become. You'd think that money would buy you the ability to do whatever you pleased."

"Some of the High Fae," Mor said, pulling at an embroidered thread in my blanket, "are the same."

I slipped behind the dressing screen to untie the robe I'd donned moments before she'd entered to keep me company while I prepared for our journey today.

"In the Court of Nightmares," she went on, that voice falling soft and a bit cold once more, "females are . . . prized. Our virginity is guarded, then sold off to the highest bidder—whatever male will be of the most advantage to our families."

I kept dressing, if only to give myself something to do while the horror of what I began to suspect slithered through my bones and blood.

"I was born stronger than anyone in my family. Even the males. And I couldn't hide it, because they could smell it—the same way you can smell a High Lord's Heir before he comes to power. The power leaves a mark, an . . . echo. When I was twelve, before I bled, I prayed it meant no male would take me as a wife, that I would escape what my elder cousins had endured: loveless, sometimes brutal, marriages."

I tugged my blouse over my head, and buttoned the velvet cuffs at my wrists before adjusting the sheer, turquoise sleeves into place.

"But then I began bleeding a few days after I turned seventeen. And the moment my first blood came, my power awoke in full force, and even that gods-damned mountain trembled around us. But instead of being horrified, every single ruling family in the Hewn City saw me as a prize mare. Saw that power and wanted it bred into their bloodline, over and over again."

"What about your parents?" I managed to say, slipping my feet into the midnight-blue shoes. It'd be the end of winter in the mortal lands—most shoes would be useless. Actually, my current ensemble would be useless, but only for the moments I'd be outside—bundled up.

"My family was beside themselves with glee. They could have their pick of an alliance with any of the other ruling families. My pleas for choice in the matter went unheard."

She got out, I reminded myself. Mor got out, and now lived with people who cared for her, who loved her.

"The rest of the story," Mor said as I emerged, "is long, and awful, and I'll tell you some other time. I came in here to say I'm not going with you—to the mortal realm."

"Because of how they treat women?"

Her rich brown eyes were bright, but calm. "When the queens come, I will be there. I wish to see if I recognize any of my long-dead friends in their faces. But . . . I don't think I would be able to . . . behave with any others."

"Did Rhys tell you not to go?" I said tightly.

"No," she said, snorting. "He tried to convince me to come, actually. He said I was being ridiculous. But Cassian . . . he gets it. The two of us wore him down last night."

My brows rose a bit. Why they'd gone out and gotten drunk, no doubt. To ply their High Lord with alcohol.

Mor shrugged at the unasked question in my eyes. "Cassian helped Rhys get me out. Before either had the real rank to do so. For Rhys, getting caught would have been a mild punishment, perhaps a bit of social shunning. But Cassian . . . he risked everything to make sure I stayed out of that court. And he laughs about it, but he believes he's a low-born bastard, not worthy of his rank or life here. He has no idea that he's worth more than any other male I met in that court—and outside of it. Him and Azriel, that is."

Yes—Azriel, who kept a step away, whose shadows trailed him and seemed to fade in her presence. I opened my mouth to ask about her history with him, but the clock chimed ten. Time to go.

My hair had been arranged before breakfast in a braided coronet atop my head, a small diadem of gold—flecked with lapis lazuli—set before it. Matching earrings dangled low enough to brush the sides of my neck, and I picked up the twisting gold bracelets that had been left out on the dresser, sliding one onto either wrist.

Mor made no comment—and I knew that if I had worn nothing but my undergarments, she would have told me to own every inch of it. I turned to her. "I'd like my sisters to meet you. Maybe not today. But if you ever feel like it . . ."

She cocked her head.

I rubbed the back of my bare neck. "I want them to hear your story. And know that there is a special strength . . . " As I spoke I realized I needed to hear it, know it, too. "A special strength in enduring such dark trials and hardships . . . And still remaining warm, and kind. Still willing to trust—and reach out."

Mor's mouth tightened and she blinked a few times.

I went for the door, but paused with my hand on the knob. "I'm sorry if I was not as welcoming to you as you were to me when I arrived at the Night Court. I was . . . I'm trying to learn how to adjust."

A pathetic, inarticulate way of explaining how ruined I'd become.

But Mor hopped off the bed, opened the door for me, and said, "There are good days and hard days for me—even now. Don't let the hard days win."

Today, it seemed, would indeed be yet another hard day.

With Rhys, Cassian, and Azriel ready to go—Amren and Mor remaining in Velaris to run the city and plan our inevitable trip to Hybern—I was left with only one choice: who to fly with.

Rhys would winnow us off the coast, right to the invisible line where the wall bisected our world. There was a tear in its magic about half a mile offshore—which we'd fly through.

But standing in that hallway, all of them in their fighting leathers and me bundled in a heavy, fur-lined cloak, I took one look at Rhys and felt those hands on my thighs again. Felt how it'd been to look inside his mind, felt his cold rage, felt him . . . defend himself, his people, his friends, using the power and masks in his arsenal. He'd seen and endured such . . . such unspeakable things, and yet . . . his hands on my thighs had been gentle, the touch like—

I didn't let myself finish the thought as I said, "I'll fly with Azriel."

Rhys and Cassian looked as if I'd declared I wanted to parade through Velaris in nothing but my skin, but the shadowsinger merely bowed his head and said, "Of course." And that, thankfully, was that.

Rhys winnowed in Cassian first, returning a heartbeat later for me and Azriel.

The spymaster had waited in silence. I tried not to look too uncomfortable as he scooped me into his arms, those shadows that whispered to him stroking my neck, my cheek. Rhys was frowning a bit, and I just gave him a sharp look and said, "Don't let the wind ruin my hair."

He snorted, gripped Azriel's arm, and we all vanished into a dark wind.

Stars and blackness, Azriel's scarred hands clenching tightly around me, my arms entwined around his neck, bracing, waiting, counting—

Then blinding sunlight, roaring wind, a plunge down, down—

Then we tilted, shooting straight. Azriel's body was warm and hard, though those brutalized hands were considerate as he gripped me. No shadows trailed us, as if he'd left them in Velaris.

Below, ahead, behind, the vast, blue sea stretched. Above, fortresses of clouds plodded along, and to my left . . . A dark smudge on the horizon. Land.

Spring Court land.

I wondered if Tamlin was on the western sea border. He'd once hinted about trouble there. Could he sense me, sense us, now?

I didn't let myself think about it. Not as I *felt* the wall.

As a human, it had been nothing but an invisible shield.

As a faerie . . . I couldn't see it, but I could hear it crackling with power—the tang of it coating my tongue.

"It's abhorrent, isn't it," Azriel said, his low voice nearly swallowed up by the wind.

"I can see why you—*we* were deterred for all these centuries," I admitted. Every heartbeat had us racing closer to that gargantuan, nauseating sense of power.

"You'll get used to it—the wording," he said. Clinging to him so tightly, I couldn't see his face. I watched the light shift inside the sapphire Siphon instead, as if it were the great eye of some half-slumbering beast from a frozen wasteland.

"I don't really know where I fit in anymore," I admitted, perhaps only because the wind was screeching around us and Rhys had already winnowed ahead to where Cassian's dark form flew—beyond the wall.

"I've been alive almost five and a half centuries, and I'm not sure of that, either," Azriel said.

I tried to pull back to read the beautiful, icy face, but he tightened his grip, a silent warning to brace myself.

How Azriel knew where the cleft was, I had no idea. It all looked the same to me: invisible, open sky.

But I felt the wall as we swept through. Felt it lunge for me, as if enraged we'd slipped past, felt the power flare and try to close that gap but failing—

Then we were out.

The wind was biting, the temperature so cold it snatched the breath from me. That bitter wind seemed somehow less alive than the spring air we'd left behind.

Azriel banked, veering toward the coastline, where Rhys and Cassian were now sweeping over the land. I shivered in my fur-lined cloak, clinging to Azriel's warmth.

We cleared a sandy beach at the base of white cliffs, and flat, snowy land dotted with winter-ravaged forests spread beyond them.

The human lands.

My home.

CHAPTER 23

It had been a year since I had stalked through that labyrinth of snow and ice and killed a faerie with hate in my heart.

My family's emerald-roofed estate was as lovely at the end of winter as it had been in the summer. A different sort of beauty, though—the pale marble seemed warm against the stark snow piled high across the land, and bits of evergreen and holly adorned the windows, the archways, and the lampposts. The only bit of decoration, of celebration, humans bothered with. Not when they'd banned and condemned every holiday after the War, all a reminder of their immortal overseers.

Three months with Amarantha had destroyed me. I couldn't begin to imagine what millennia with High Fae like her might do—the scars it'd leave on a culture, a people.

My people—or so they had once been.

Hood up, fingers tucked into the fur-lined pockets of my cloak, I stood before the double doors of the house, listening to the clear ringing of the bell I'd pulled a heartbeat before.

Behind me, hidden by Rhys's glamours, my three companions waited, unseen.

I'd told them it would be best if I spoke to my family first. Alone.

I shivered, craving the moderate winter of Velaris, wondering how it could be so temperate in the far north, but . . . everything in Prythian was strange. Perhaps when the wall hadn't existed, when magic had flowed freely between realms, the seasonal differences hadn't been so vast.

The door opened, and a merry-faced, round housekeeper—Mrs. Laurent, I recalled—squinted at me. "May I help . . . " The words trailed off as she noticed my face.

With the hood on, my ears and crown were hidden, but that glow, that preternatural stillness . . . She didn't open the door wider.

"I'm here to see my family," I choked out.

"Your—your father is away on business, but your sisters . . . " She didn't move.

She knew. She could tell there was something different, something *off*—

Her eyes darted around me. No carriage, no horse.

No footprints through the snow.

Her face blanched, and I cursed myself for not thinking of it—

"Mrs. Laurent?"

Something in my chest broke at Elain's voice from the hall behind her.

At the sweetness and youth and kindness, untouched by Prythian, unaware of what I'd done, become—

I backed away a step. I couldn't do this. Couldn't bring this upon them.

Then Elain's face appeared over Mrs. Laurent's round shoulder.

Beautiful—she'd always been the most beautiful of us. Soft and lovely, like a summer dawn.

Elain was exactly as I'd remembered her, the way I'd made myself remember her in those dungeons, when I told myself that if I failed, if Amarantha crossed the wall, she'd be next. The way she'd be next if the King of Hybern shattered the wall, if I didn't get the Book of Breathings.

Elain's golden-brown hair was half up, her pale skin creamy and flushed with color, and her eyes, like molten chocolate, were wide as they took me in.

They filled with tears and silently overran, spilling down those lovely cheeks.

Mrs. Laurent didn't yield an inch. She'd shut this door in my face the moment I so much as breathed wrong.

Elain lifted a slender hand to her mouth as her body shook with a sob.

"Elain," I said hoarsely.

Footsteps on the sweeping stairs behind them, then—

"Mrs. Laurent, draw up some tea and bring it to the drawing room."

The housekeeper looked to the stairs, then to Elain, then to me.

A phantom in the snow.

The woman merely gave me a look that promised death if I harmed my sisters as she turned into the house, leaving me before Elain, still quietly crying.

But I took a step over the threshold and looked up the staircase.

To where Nesta stood, a hand braced on the rail, staring as if I were a ghost.

The house was beautiful, but there was something untouched about it. Something new, compared to the age and worn love of Rhys's homes in Velaris.

And seated before the carved marble sitting room hearth, my hood on, hands outstretched toward the roaring fire, I felt . . . felt like they had let in a wolf.

A wraith.

I had become too big for these rooms, for this fragile mortal life, too stained and wild and . . . powerful. And I was about to bring that permanently into their lives as well.

Where Rhys, Cassian, and Azriel were, I didn't know. Perhaps they stood as shadows in the corner, watching. Perhaps they'd remained outside in the snow. I wouldn't put it past Cassian and Azriel to be now flying the grounds, inspecting the layout, making wider circles until they reached the village, my ramshackle old cottage, or maybe even the forest itself.

Nesta looked the same. But older. Not in her face, which was as grave and stunning as before, but . . . in her eyes, in the way she carried herself.

Seated across from me on a small sofa, my sisters stared—and waited.

I said, "Where is Father?" It felt like the only safe thing to say.

"In Neva," Nesta said, naming one of the largest cities on the continent. "Trading with some merchants from the other half of the world. And attending a summit about the threat above the wall. A threat I wonder if you've come back to warn us about."

No words of relief, of love—never from her.

Elain lifted her teacup. "Whatever the reason, Feyre, we are happy to see you. Alive. We thought you were—"

I pulled my hood back before she could go on.

Elain's teacup rattled in its saucer as she noticed my ears. My longer, slender hands—the face that was undeniably Fae.

"I *was* dead," I said roughly. "I was dead, and then I was reborn—remade."

Elain set her shivering teacup onto the low-lying table between us. Amber liquid splashed over the side, pooling in the saucer.

And as she moved, Nesta angled herself—ever so slightly. Between me and Elain.

It was Nesta's gaze I held as I said, "I need you to listen."

They were both wide-eyed.

But they did.

I told them my story. In as much detail as I could endure, I told them of Under the Mountain. Of my trials. And Amarantha. I told them about death. And rebirth.

Explaining the last few months, however, was harder.

So I kept it brief.

But I explained what needed to happen here—the threat Hybern posed. I explained what this house needed to be, what we needed to be, and what I needed from them.

And when I finished, they remained wide-eyed. Silent.

It was Elain who at last said, "You—you want other High Fae to come . . . *here*. And . . . and the Queens of the Realm."

I nodded slowly.

"Find somewhere else," Nesta said.

I turned to her, already pleading, bracing for a fight.

"Find somewhere else," Nesta said again, straight-backed. "I don't want them in my house. Or near Elain."

"Nesta, please," I breathed. "There is nowhere else; nowhere I can go without someone hunting me, crucifying me—"

"And what of us? When the people around here learn we're Fae sympathizers? Are we any better than the Children of the Blessed, then? Any standing, any influence we have—gone. And Elain's wedding—"

"Wedding," I blurted.

I hadn't noticed the pearl-and-diamond ring on her finger, the dark metal band glinting in the firelight.

Elain's face was pale, though, as she looked at it.

"In five months," Nesta said. "She's marrying a lord's son. And his father has devoted his life to hunting down *your kind* when they cross the wall."

Your kind.

"So there will be no meeting here," Nesta said, shoulders stiff. "There will be no Fae in this house."

"Do you include me in that declaration?" I said quietly.

Nesta's silence was answer enough.

But Elain said, "Nesta."

Slowly, my eldest sister looked at her.

"Nesta," Elain said again, twisting her hands. "If . . . if we do not help Feyre, there won't *be* a wedding. Even Lord Nolan's battlements and all his men, couldn't save me from . . . from them." Nesta didn't so much as flinch. Elain pushed, "We keep it secret—we send the servants away. With the spring approaching, they'll be glad to go home. And if Feyre needs to be in and out for meetings, she'll send word ahead, and we'll clear them out. Make up excuses to send them on holidays. Father won't be back until the summer, anyway. No one will know." She put a hand on Nesta's knee, the purple of my sister's gown nearly swallowing up the ivory hand. "Feyre gave and gave—for years. Let us now help her. Help . . . others."

My throat was tight, and my eyes burned.

Nesta studied the dark ring on Elain's finger, the way she still seemed to cradle it. A lady—that's what Elain would become. What she was risking for this.

I met Nesta's gaze. "There is no other way."

Her chin lifted slightly. "We'll send the servants away tomorrow."

"Today," I pushed. "We don't have any time to lose. Order them to leave now."

"I'll do it," Elain said, taking a deep breath and squaring her shoulders. She didn't wait for either of us before she strode out, graceful as a doe.

Alone with Nesta, I said, "Is he good—the lord's son she's to marry?"

"She thinks he is. She loves him like he is."

"And what do you think?"

Nesta's eyes—my eyes, our mother's eyes—met mine. "His father built a wall of stone around their estate so high even the trees can't reach over it. I think it looks like a prison."

"Have you said anything to her?"

"No. The son, Graysen, is kind enough. As smitten with Elain as she is with him. It's the father I don't like. He sees the money she has to offer their estate—and his crusade against the Fae. But the man is old. He'll die soon enough."

"Hopefully."

A shrug. Then Nesta asked, "Your High Lord . . . You went through all that"—she waved a hand at me, my ears, my body—"and it still did not end well?"

I was heavy in my veins again. "That lord built a wall to keep the Fae out. My High Lord wanted to keep me caged in."

"Why? He let you come back here all those months ago."

"To save me—protect me. And I think . . . I think what happened to him, to us, Under the Mountain broke him." Perhaps more than it had broken me. "The drive to protect at all costs, even my own well-being . . . I think he wanted to stifle it, but he couldn't. He couldn't let go of it." There was . . . there was much I still had to do, I realized. To settle things. Settle myself.

"And now you are at a new court."

Not quite a question, but I said, "Would you like to meet them?"

CHAPTER 24

It took hours for Elain to work her charm on the staff to swiftly pack their bags and leave, each with a purse of money to hasten the process. Mrs. Laurent, though the last to depart, promised to keep what she'd seen to herself.

I didn't know where Rhys, Cassian, and Azriel had been waiting, but when Mrs. Laurent had hauled herself into the carriage crammed with the last of the staff, heading down to the village to catch transportation to wherever they all had family, there was a knock on the door.

The light was already fading, and the world outside was thick with shades of blue and white and gray, stained golden as I opened the front door and found them waiting.

Nesta and Elain were in the large dining room—the most open space in the house.

Looking at Rhys, Cassian, and Azriel, I knew I'd been right to select it as the meeting spot.

They were enormous—wild and rough and ancient.

Rhys's brows lifted. "You'd think they'd been told plague had befallen the house."

I pulled the door open wide enough to let them in, then quickly shut it against the bitter cold. "My sister Elain can convince anyone to do anything with a few smiles."

Cassian let out a low whistle as he turned in place, surveying the grand entry hall, the ornate furniture, the paintings. All of it paid for by Tamlin—initially. He'd taken such care of my family, yet his own . . . I didn't want to think about his family, murdered by a rival court for whatever reason no one had ever explained to me. Not now that I was living amongst them—

He'd been good—there was a part of Tamlin that was good—

Yes. He'd given me everything I needed to become myself, to feel safe. And when he got what he wanted . . . He'd stopped. Had tried, but not really. He'd let himself remain blind to what I needed after Amarantha.

"Your father must be a fine merchant," Cassian said. "I've seen castles with less wealth."

I found Rhys studying me, a silent question written across his face. I answered, "My father is away on business—and attending a meeting in Neva about the threat of Prythian."

"Prythian?" Cassian said, twisting toward us. "Not Hybern?"

"It's possible my sisters were mistaken—your lands are foreign to them. They merely said 'above the wall.' I assumed they thought it was Prythian."

Azriel came forward on feet as silent as a cat's. "If humans are aware of the threat, rallying against it, then that might give us an advantage when contacting the queens."

Rhys was still watching me, as if he could see the weight that had pressed into me since arriving here. The last time I'd been in this house, I'd been a woman in love—such frantic, desperate love that I went back into Prythian, I went Under the Mountain, as a mere human. As fragile as my sisters now seemed to me.

"Come," Rhys said, offering me a subtle, understanding nod before motioning to lead the way. "Let's make this introduction."

✢

My sisters were standing by the window, the light of the chandeliers coaxing the gold in their hair to glisten. So beautiful, and young, and alive—but when would that change? How would it be to speak to them when I remained this way while their skin had grown paper-thin and wrinkled, their backs curved with the weight of years, their white hands speckled?

I would be barely into my immortal existence when theirs was wiped out like a candle before a cold breath.

But I could give them a few good years—safe years—until then.

I crossed the room, the three males a step behind, the wooden floors as shining and polished as a mirror beneath us. I had removed my cloak now that the servants were gone, and it was to me—not the Illyrians—that my sisters first looked. At the Fae clothes, the crown, the jewelry.

A stranger—this part of me was now a stranger to them.

Then they took in the winged males—or two of them. Rhys's wings had vanished, his leathers replaced with his fine black jacket and pants.

My sisters both stiffened at Cassian and Azriel, at those mighty wings tucked in tight to powerful bodies, at the weapons, and then at the devastatingly beautiful faces of all three males.

Elain, to her credit, did not faint.

And Nesta, to hers, did not hiss at them. She just took a not-so-subtle step in front of Elain, and ducked her fisted hand behind her simple, elegant amethyst gown. The movement did not go unnoticed by my companions.

I halted a good four feet away, giving my sisters breathing space in a room that had suddenly been deprived of all air. I said to the males, "My sisters, Nesta and Elain Archeron."

I had not thought of my family name, had not used it, for years and years. Because even when I had sacrificed and hunted for them, I had not wanted my father's name—not when he sat before that little fire and let us starve. Let me walk into the woods alone. I'd stopped using it the day I'd killed that rabbit, and felt its blood stain my hands, the same way the blood of those faeries had marred it years later like an invisible tattoo.

My sisters did not curtsy. Their hearts wildly pounded, even Nesta's, and the tang of their terror coated my tongue—

"Cassian," I said, inclining my head to the left. Then I shifted to the right, grateful those shadows were nowhere to be found as I said, "Azriel." I half turned. "And Rhysand, High Lord of the Night Court."

Rhys had dimmed it, too, I realized. The night rippling off him, the otherworldly grace and thrum of power. But looking in those star-flecked violet eyes, no one would ever mistake him for anything but extraordinary.

He bowed to my sisters. "Thank you for your hospitality—and generosity," he said with a warm smile. But there was something strained in it.

Elain tried to return the smile but failed.

And Nesta just looked at the three of them, then at me, and said, "The cook left dinner on the table. We should eat before it goes cold." She didn't wait for my agreement before striding off—right to the head of the polished cherry table.

Elain rasped, "Nice to meet you," before hustling after her, the silk skirts of her cobalt dress whispering over the parquet floor.

Cassian was grimacing as we trailed them, Rhys's brows were raised, and Azriel looked more inclined to blend into the nearest shadow and avoid this conversation all together.

Nesta was waiting at the head of the table, a queen ready to hold court. Elain trembled in the upholstered, carved wood chair to her left.

I did them all a favor and took the one to Nesta's right. Cassian claimed the spot beside Elain, who clenched her fork as if she might wield it against him, and Rhys slid into the seat beside me, Azriel on his other side. A faint smile bloomed upon Azriel's mouth as he noticed Elain's fingers white-knuckled on that fork, but he kept silent, focusing instead, as Cassian was subtly trying to do, on adjusting his wings around a human chair. Cauldron damn me. I should have remembered. Though I doubted either would appreciate it if I now brought in two stools.

I sighed through my nose and yanked the lids off the various dishes and casseroles. Poached salmon with dill and lemon from the hothouse, whipped potatoes, roast chicken with beets and turnips from the root cellar, and some casserole of egg, game meat, and leeks. Seasonal food—whatever they had left at the end of the winter.

I scooped food onto my plate, the sounds of my sisters and companions doing the same filling the silence. I took a bite and fought my cringe.

Once, this food would have been rich and flavorful.

Now it was ash in my mouth.

Rhys was digging into his chicken without hesitation. Cassian and Azriel ate as if they hadn't had a meal in months. Perhaps being warriors, fighting in wars, had given them the ability to see food as strength—and put taste aside.

I found Nesta watching me. "Is there something wrong with our food?" she said flatly.

I made myself take another bite, each movement of my jaw an effort. "No." I swallowed and gulped down a healthy drink of water.

"So you can't eat normal food anymore—or are you too good for it?" A question and a challenge.

Rhys's fork clanked on his plate. Elain made a small, distressed noise.

And though Nesta had let me use this house, though she'd tried to cross the wall for me and we'd worked out a tentative truce, the *tone*, the disgust and disapproval . . .

I laid my hand flat on the table. "I can eat, drink, fuck, and fight just as well as I did before. Better, even."

Cassian choked on his water. Azriel shifted on his seat, angling to spring between us if need be.

Nesta let out a low laugh.

But I could taste fire in my mouth, hear it roaring in my veins, and—

A blind, solid *tug* on the bond, cooling darkness sweeping into me, my temper, my senses, calming that fire—

I scrambled to throw my mental shields up. But they were intact.

Rhys didn't so much as blink at me before he said evenly to Nesta, "If you ever come to Prythian, you will discover why your food tastes so different."

Nesta looked down her nose at him. "I have little interest in ever setting foot in your land, so I'll have to take your word on it."

"Nesta, please," Elain murmured.

Cassian was sizing up Nesta, a gleam in his eyes that I could only interpret as a warrior finding himself faced with a new, interesting opponent.

Then, Mother above, Nesta shifted her attention to Cassian, noticing that gleam—what it meant. She snarled softly, "What are you looking at?"

Cassian's brows rose—little amusement to be found now. "Someone who let her youngest sister risk her life every day in the woods while she did nothing. Someone who let a fourteen-year-old child go out into that forest, so close to the wall." My face began heating, and I opened my mouth. To say what, I didn't know. "Your sister died—*died* to save my people. She is willing to do so again to protect you from war. So don't expect me to sit here with my mouth shut while you sneer at her for a choice she did not get to make—and insult *my* people in the process."

Nesta didn't bat an eyelash as she studied the handsome features, the muscled torso. Then turned to me. Dismissing him entirely.

Cassian's face went almost feral. A wolf who had been circling a doe . . . only to find a mountain cat wearing its hide instead.

Elain's voice wobbled as she noted the same thing and quickly said to him, "It . . . it is very hard, you understand, to . . . accept it." I realized the dark metal of her ring . . . it was iron. Even though I had told them about iron being useless, there it was. The gift from her Fae-hating soon-to-be-husband's family. Elain cast pleading eyes on Rhys, then Azriel, such mortal fear coating her features, her scent. "We are raised this way. We hear stories of your kind crossing the wall to hurt us. Our own neighbor, Clare Beddor, was taken, her family murdered . . ."

A naked body spiked to a wall. Broken. Dead. Nailed there for months.

Rhys was staring at his plate. Unmoving. Unblinking.

He had given Amarantha Clare's name—given it, despite knowing I'd lied to him about it.

Elain said, "It's all very disorienting."

"I can imagine," Azriel said. Cassian flashed him a glare. But Azriel's attention was on my sister, a polite, bland smile on his face. Her shoulders loosened a bit. I wondered if Rhys's spymaster often got his information through stone-cold manners as much as stealth and shadows.

Elain sat a little higher as she said to Cassian, "And as for Feyre's hunting during those years, it was not Nesta's neglect alone that is to blame. We were scared, and had received no training, and everything had been taken, and we failed her. Both of us."

Nesta said nothing, her back rigid.

Rhys gave me a warning look. I gripped Nesta's arm, drawing her attention to me. "Can we just . . . start over?"

I could almost taste her pride roiling in her veins, barking to not back down.

Cassian, damn him, gave her a taunting grin.

But Nesta merely hissed, "Fine." And went back to eating.

Cassian watched every bite she took, every bob of her throat as she swallowed.

I forced myself to clean my plate, aware of Nesta's own attention on *my* eating.

Elain said to Azriel, perhaps the only two civilized ones here, "Can you truly fly?"

He set down his fork, blinking. I might have even called him self-conscious. He said, "Yes. Cassian and I hail from a race of faeries called Illyrians. We're born hearing the song of the wind."

"That's very beautiful," she said. "Is it not—frightening, though? To fly so high?"

"It is sometimes," Azriel said. Cassian tore his relentless attention from Nesta long enough to nod his agreement. "If you are caught in a storm, if the current drops away. But we are trained so thoroughly that the fear is gone before we're out of swaddling." And yet, Azriel had not been trained until long after that. *You get used to the wording*, he'd told me earlier. How often did he have to remind himself to use such words? Did "we" and "our" and "us" taste as foreign on his tongue as they did on mine?

"You look like High Fae," Nesta cut in, her voice like a honed blade. "But you are not?"

"Only the High Fae who look like *them*," Cassian drawled, waving a hand to me and Rhys, "are High Fae. Everyone else, any other differences, mark you as what they like to call 'lesser' faeries."

Rhysand at last said, "It's become a term used for ease, but masks a long, bloody history of injustices. Many lesser faeries resent the term—and wish for us all to be called one thing."

"Rightly so," Cassian said, drinking from his water.

Nesta surveyed me. "But you were not High Fae—not to begin. So what do they call you?" I couldn't tell if it was a jab or not.

Rhys said, "Feyre is whoever she chooses to be."

Nesta now examined us all, raising her eyes to that crown. But she said, "Write your letter to the queens tonight. Tomorrow, Elain and I will go to the village to dispatch it. If the queens do come here," she added, casting a frozen glare at Cassian, "I'd suggest bracing yourselves for prejudices far deeper than ours. And contemplating how you plan to get us *all* out of this mess should things go sour."

"We'll take that into account," Rhys said smoothly.

Nesta went on, utterly unimpressed by any of us, "I assume you'll want to stay the night."

Rhys glanced at me in silent question. We could easily leave, the males finding the way home in the dark, but . . . Too soon, perhaps, the world would go to hell. I said, "If it's not too much trouble, then yes. We'll leave after breakfast tomorrow."

Nesta didn't smile, but Elain beamed. "Good. I think there are a few bedrooms ready—"

"We'll need two," Rhys interrupted quietly. "Next to each other, with two beds each."

I narrowed my brows at him.

Rhys explained to me, "Magic is different across the wall. So our shields, our senses, might not work right. I'm taking no chances. Especially in a house with a woman betrothed to a man who gave her an iron engagement ring."

Elain flushed a bit. "The—the bedrooms that have two beds aren't next to each other," she murmured.

I sighed. "We'll move things around. It's fine. This one," I added with a glare in Rhys's direction, "is only cranky because he's old and it's past his bedtime."

Rhys chuckled, Cassian's wrath slipping enough that he grinned, and Elain, noticing Azriel's ease as proof that things weren't indeed about to go badly, offered one of her own as well.

Nesta just rose to her feet, a slim pillar of steel, and said to no one in particular, "If we're done eating, then this meal is over."

And that was that.

✠

Rhys wrote the letter for me, Cassian and Azriel chiming in with corrections, and it took us until midnight before we had a draft we all thought sounded impressive, welcoming, and threatening enough.

My sisters cleaned the dishes while we worked, and had excused themselves to bed hours before, mentioning where to find our rooms.

Cassian and Azriel were to share one, Rhys and I the other.

I frowned at the large guest bedroom as Rhys shut the door behind us. The bed was large enough for two, but I wasn't sharing it. I whirled to him, "I'm not—"

Wood thumped on carpet, and a small bed appeared by the door. Rhys plopped onto it, tugging off his boots. "Nesta is a delight, by the way."

"She's . . . her own creature," I said. It was perhaps the kindest thing I could say about her.

"It's been a few centuries since someone got under Cassian's skin that easily. Too bad they're both inclined to kill the other."

Part of me shuddered at the havoc the two would wreak if they decided to stop fighting.

"And Elain," Rhys said, sighing as he removed his other boot, "should not be marrying that lord's son, not for about a dozen reasons, the least of which being the fact that you won't be invited to the wedding. Though maybe that's a good thing."

I hissed. "That's not funny."

"At least you won't have to send a gift, either. I doubt her father-in-law would deign to accept it."

"You have a lot of nerve mocking my sisters when your own friends have equally as much melodrama." His brows lifted in silent question. I snorted. "Oh, so you haven't noticed the way Azriel looks at Mor? Or how she sometimes watches *him*, defends him? And how both of them do *such* a good job letting Cassian be a buffer between them most of the time?"

Rhys leveled a look at me. "I'd suggest keeping those observations to yourself."

"You think I'm some busybody gossip? My life is miserable enough as it is—why would I want to spread that misery to those around me as well?"

"Is it miserable? Your life, I mean." A careful question.

"I don't know. Everything is happening so quickly that I don't know what to feel." It was more honest than I'd been in a while.

"Hmmm. Perhaps once we return home, I should give you the day off."

"How considerate of you, *my lord*."

He snorted, unbuttoning his jacket. I realized I stood in all my finery—with nothing to wear to sleep.

A snap of Rhys's fingers, and my nightclothes—and some flimsy underthings—appeared on the bed. "I couldn't decide which scrap of lace I wanted you to wear, so I brought you a few to choose from."

"Pig," I barked, snatching the clothes and heading to the adjoining bathing room.

The room was toasty when I emerged, Rhys in the bed he'd summoned from wherever, all light gone save for the murmuring embers in the hearth. Even the sheets were warm as I slid between them.

"Thank you for warming the bed," I said into the dimness.

His back was to me, but I heard him clearly as he said, "Amarantha never once thanked me for that."

Any warmth leeched away. "She didn't suffer enough."

Not even close, for what she had done. To me, to him, to Clare, to so many others.

Rhys didn't answer. Instead he said, "I didn't think I could get through that dinner."

"What do you mean?" He'd been rather . . . calm. Contained.

"Your sisters mean well, or one of them does. But seeing them, sitting at that table . . . I hadn't realized it would hit me as strongly. How young you were. How they didn't protect you."

"I managed just fine."

"We owe them our gratitude for letting us use this house," he said quietly, "but it will be a long while yet before I can look at your sisters without wanting to roar at them."

"A part of me feels the same way," I admitted, nestling down into the blankets. "But if I hadn't gone into those woods, if they hadn't let me go out there alone . . . You would still be enslaved. And perhaps Amarantha would now be readying her forces to wipe out these lands."

Silence. Then, "I am paying you a wage, you know. For all of this."

"You don't need to." Even if . . . even if I had no money of my own.

"Every member of my court receives one. There's already a bank account in Velaris for you, where your wages will be deposited. And you have lines of credit at most stores. So if you don't have enough on you when you're shopping, you can have the bill sent to the House."

"I—you didn't have to do that." I swallowed hard. "And how much, exactly, am I getting paid each month?"

"The same amount the others receive." No doubt a generous—likely *too* generous—salary. But he suddenly asked, "When is your birthday?"

"Do I even need to count them anymore?" He merely waited. I sighed. "It's the Winter Solstice."

He paused. "That was months ago."

"Mmmhmm."

"You didn't . . . I don't remember seeing you celebrate it."

Through the bond, through my unshielded, mess of a mind. "I didn't tell anyone. I didn't want a party when there was already all that celebrating going on. Birthdays seem meaningless now, anyway."

He was quiet for a long minute. "You were truly born on the Winter Solstice?"

"Is that so hard to believe? My mother claimed I was so withdrawn and strange because I was born on the longest night of the year. She tried one year to have my birthday on another day, but forgot to do it the next time—there was probably a more advantageous party she had to plan."

"Now I know where Nesta gets it. Honestly, it's a shame we can't stay longer—if only to see who'll be left standing: her or Cassian."

"My money's on Nesta."

A soft chuckle that snaked along my bones—a reminder that he'd once bet on me. Had been the only one Under the Mountain who had put money on me defeating the Middengard Wyrm. He said, "So's mine."

CHAPTER 25

Standing beneath the latticework of snow-heavy trees, I took in the slumbering forest and wondered if the birds had gone quiet because of my presence. Or that of the High Lord beside me.

"Freezing my ass off first thing in the morning isn't how I intended to spend our day off," Rhysand said, frowning at the wood. "I should take you to the Illyrian Steppes when we return—the forest there is far more interesting. And warmer."

"I have no idea where those are." Snow crunched under the boots Rhys had summoned when I declared I wanted to train with him. And not physically, but—with the powers I had. Whatever they were. "You showed me a blank map that one time, remember?"

"Precautions."

"Am I ever going to see a proper one, or will I be left to guess about where everything is?"

"You're in a lovely mood today," Rhys said, and lifted a hand in the air between us. A folded map appeared, which he took his sweet time opening. "Lest you think I don't trust you, Feyre darling . . . " He pointed to just south of the Northern Isles. "These are the Steppes. Four days that way on foot," he dragged a finger upward and into the mountains along the isles, "will take you into Illyrian territory."

I took in the map, noted the peninsula jutting out about halfway up the western coast of the Night Court and the name marked there. *Velaris*. He'd once shown me a blank one—when I had belonged to Tamlin and been little more than a spy and prisoner. Because he'd known I'd tell Tamlin about the cities, their locations.

That Ianthe might learn about it, too.

I pushed back against that weight in my chest, my gut.

"Here," Rhys said, pocketing the map and gesturing to the forest around us. "We'll train here. We're far enough now."

Far enough from the house, from anyone else, to avoid detection. Or casualties.

Rhys held out a hand, and a thick, stumpy candle appeared in his palm. He set it on the snowy ground. "Light it, douse it with water, and dry the wick."

I knew he meant without my hands.

"I can't do a single one of those things," I said. "What about physical shielding?" At least I'd been able to do *some* of that.

"That's for another time. Today, I suggest you start trying some *other* facet of your power. What about shape-shifting?"

I glared at him. "Fire, water, and air it is." Bastard—insufferable bastard.

He didn't push the matter, thankfully—didn't ask *why* shape-shifting might be the one power I'd never bother to pull apart and master. Perhaps for the same reason I didn't particularly want to ask about one key piece of his history, didn't want to know if Azriel and Cassian had helped when the Spring Court's ruling family had been killed.

I looked Rhys over from head to toe: the Illyrian warrior garb, the sword over his shoulder, the wings, and that general sense of overwhelming power that always radiated from him. "Maybe you should . . . go."

"Why? You seemed so insistent that *I* train you."

"I can't concentrate with you around," I admitted. "And go . . . far. I can feel you from a room away."

A suggestive curve shaped his lips.

I rolled my eyes. "Why don't you just hide in one of those pocket-realms for a bit?"

"It doesn't work like that. There's no air there." I gave him a look to say he should definitely do it then, and he laughed. "Fine. Practice all you want in privacy." He jerked his chin at my tattoo. "Give a shout down the bond if you get anything accomplished before breakfast."

I frowned at the eye in my palm. "What—literally shout at the tattoo?"

"You could try rubbing it on certain body parts and I might come faster."

He vanished into nothing before I could hurl the candle at him.

Alone in the frost-gilded forest, I replayed his words and a quiet chuckle rasped out of me.

I wondered if I should have tested out the bow and arrows I'd been given before asking him to leave. I hadn't yet tried out the Illyrian bow—hadn't shot anything in months, actually.

I stared at the candle. Nothing happened.

An hour passed.

I thought of everything that enraged me, sickened me; thought of Ianthe and her entitlement, her demands. Not even a wisp of smoke emerged.

When my eyes were on the verge of bleeding, I took a break to scrounge through the pack I'd brought. I found fresh bread, a magically warmed canister of stew, and a note from Rhysand that said:

I'm bored. Any sparks yet?

Not surprisingly, a pen clattered in the bottom of the bag.

I grabbed the pen and scribbled my response atop the canister before watching the letter vanish right out of my palm: *No, you snoop. Don't you have important things to do?*

The letter flitted back a moment later.

I'm watching Cassian and Nesta get into it again over their tea. Something you subjected me to when you kicked me off training. I thought this was our day off.

I snorted and wrote back, *Poor baby High Lord. Life is so hard.*

Paper vanished, then reappeared, his scribble now near the top of the paper, the only bit of clear space left. *Life is better when you're around. And look at how lovely your handwriting is.*

I could almost feel him waiting on the other side, in the sunny breakfast room, half paying attention to my eldest sister and the Illyrian warrior's sparring. A faint smile curved my lips. *You're a shameless flirt,* I wrote back.

The page vanished. I watched my open palm, waiting for it to return.

And I was so focused on it that I didn't notice anyone was behind me until the hand covered my mouth and yanked me clean off my feet.

I thrashed, biting and clawing, shrieking as whoever it was hauled me up.

I tried to shove away, snow churning around us like dust on a road, but the arms that gripped me were immovable, like bands of iron and—

A rasping voice sounded in my ear, "Stop, or I snap your neck."

I knew that voice. It prowled through my nightmares.

The Attor.

CHAPTER 26

The Attor had vanished in the moments after Amarantha died, suspected to have fled for the King of Hybern. And if it was here, in the mortal lands—

I went pliant in its arms, buying a wisp of time to scan for something, anything to use against it.

"Good," it hissed in my ear. "Now tell me—"

Night exploded around us.

The Attor screamed—*screamed*—as that darkness swallowed us, and I was wrenched from its spindly, hard arms, its nails slicing into my leather. I collided face-first with packed, icy snow.

I rolled, flipping back, whirling to get my feet under me—

The light returned as I rose into a crouch, knife angled.

And there was Rhysand, binding the Attor to a snow-shrouded oak with nothing but twisting bands of night. Like the ones that had crushed Ianthe's hand. Rhysand's own hands were in his pockets, his face cold and beautiful as death. "I'd been wondering where you slithered off to."

The Attor panted as it struggled against the bonds.

Rhysand merely sent two spears of night shooting into its wings.

The Attor shrieked as those spears met flesh—and sank deep into the bark behind it.

"Answer my questions, and you can crawl back to your master," Rhys said, as if he were inquiring about the weather.

"Whore," the Attor spat. Silvery blood leaked from its wings, hissing as it hit the snow.

Rhys smiled. "You forget that I rather enjoy these things." He lifted a finger.

The Attor screamed, "*No!*" Rhys's finger paused. "I was sent," it panted, "to get her."

"Why?" Rhys asked with that casual, terrifying calm.

"That was my order. I am not to question. The king wants her."

My blood went as cold as the woods around us.

"Why?" Rhys said again. The Attor began screaming—this time beneath the force of a power I could not see. I flinched.

"*Don't know, don't know, don't know.*" I believed it.

"Where is the king currently?"

"Hybern."

"Army?"

"Coming soon."

"How large?"

"Endless. We have allies in every territory, all waiting."

Rhys cocked his head as if contemplating what to ask next. But he straightened, and Azriel slammed into the snow, sending it flying like water from a puddle. He'd flown in so silently, I hadn't even heard the beat of his wings. Cassian must have stayed at the house to defend my sisters.

There was no kindness on Azriel's face as the snow settled—the immovable mask of the High Lord's shadowsinger.

The Attor began trembling, and I almost felt bad for it as Azriel stalked for him. Almost—but didn't. Not when these woods were so close to the chateau. To my sisters.

Rhys came to my side as Azriel reached the Attor. "The next time you try to take her," Rhys said to the Attor, "I kill first; ask questions later."

Azriel caught his eye. Rhys nodded. The Siphons atop his scarred hands flickered like rippling blue fire as he reached for the Attor. Before the Attor could scream, it and the spymaster vanished.

I didn't want to think about where they'd go, what Azriel would do. I hadn't even known Azriel possessed the ability to winnow, or whatever power he'd channeled through his Siphons. He'd let Rhys winnow us both in the other day—unless the power was too draining to be used so lightly.

"Will he kill him?" I said, my puffs of breath uneven.

"No." I shivered at the raw power glazing his taut body. "We'll use him to send a message to Hybern that if they want to hunt the members of my court, they'll have to do better than that."

I started—at the claim he'd made of me, and at the words. "You knew—you knew he was hunting me?"

"I was curious who wanted to snatch you the first moment you were alone."

I didn't know where to start. So Tamlin was right—about my safety. To some degree. It didn't excuse anything. "So you never planned to stay with me while I trained. You used me as *bait*—"

"Yes, and I'd do it again. You were safe the entire time."

"*You should have told me!*"

"Maybe next time."

"*There will be no next time!*" I slammed a hand into his chest, and he staggered back a step from the strength of the blow. I blinked. I'd forgotten—forgotten that strength in my panic. Just like with the Weaver. I'd forgotten how strong I was.

"Yes, you did," Rhysand snarled, reading the surprise on my face, that icy calm shattering. "You forgot that strength, and that you can burn and become darkness, and grow claws. You *forgot. You stopped fighting.*"

He didn't just mean the Attor. Or the Weaver.

And the rage rose up in me in such a mighty wave that I had no thought in my head but wrath: at myself, what I'd been forced to do, what had been done to me, to him.

"So what if I did?" I hissed, and shoved him again. "So *what* if I did?"

I went to shove him again, but Rhys winnowed away a few feet.

I stormed for him, snow crunching underfoot. "It's not easy." The rage ran me over, obliterated me. I lifted my arms to slam my palms into his chest—

And he vanished again.

He appeared behind me, so close that his breath tickled my ear as he said, "You have no idea how *not* easy it is."

I whirled, grappling for him. He vanished before I could strike him, pound him.

Rhys appeared across the clearing, chuckling. "Try harder."

I couldn't fold myself into darkness and pockets. And if I could—if I could turn myself into smoke, into air and night and stars, I'd use it to appear right in front of him and smack that smile off his face.

I moved, even if it was futile, even as he rippled into darkness, and I hated him for it—for the wings and ability to move like mist on the wind. He appeared a step away, and I pounced, hands out—*talons* out—

And slammed into a tree.

He laughed as I bounced back, teeth singing, talons barking as they shredded through wood. But I was already lunging as he vanished, lunging like I could disappear into the folds of the world as well, track him across eternity—

And so I did.

Time slowed and curled, and I could see the darkness of him turn to smoke and veer, as if it were running for another spot in the clearing. I hurtled for that spot, even as I felt my own lightness, folding my very self into wind and shadow and dust, the looseness of it radiating out of me, all while I aimed for where he was headed—

Rhysand appeared, a solid figure in my world of smoke and stars.

And his eyes were wide, his mouth split in a grin of wicked delight, as I winnowed in front of him and tackled him into the snow.

CHAPTER 27

I panted, sprawled on top of Rhys in the snow while he laughed hoarsely. "*Don't*," I snarled into his face, "*ever*," I pushed his rock-hard shoulders, talons curving at my fingertips, "*use me as bait again*."

He stopped laughing.

I pushed harder, those nails digging in through his leather. "You said I could be a weapon—teach me to become one. *Don't* use me like a pawn. And if being one is part of my *work* for you, then I'm done. *Done*."

Despite the snow, his body was warm beneath me, and I wasn't sure I'd realized just how much bigger he was until our bodies were flush—too close. Much, much too close.

Rhys cocked his head, loosening a chunk of snow clinging to his hair. "Fair enough."

I shoved off him, snow crunching as I backed away. My talons were gone.

He hoisted himself up onto his elbows. "Do it again. Show me how you did it."

"No." The candle he'd brought now lay in pieces, half-buried under the snow. "I want to go back to the chateau." I was cold, and tired, and he'd . . .

His face turned grave. "I'm sorry."

I wondered how often he said those two words. I didn't care.

I waited while he uncoiled to his feet, brushing the snow off him, and held out a hand.

It wasn't just an offer.

You forgot, he'd said. I had.

"Why does the King of Hybern want me? Because he knows I can nullify the Cauldron's power with the Book?"

Darkness flickered, the only sign of the temper Rhysand had once again leashed. "That's what I'm going to find out."

You stopped fighting.

"I'm sorry," he repeated, hand still outstretched. "Let's eat breakfast, then go home."

"Velaris isn't my home."

I could have sworn hurt flashed in his eyes before he spirited us back to my family's house.

CHAPTER 28

My sisters ate breakfast with Rhys and me, Azriel gone to wherever he'd taken the Attor. Cassian had flown off to join him the moment we returned. He'd given Nesta a mocking bow, and she'd given him a vulgar gesture I hadn't realized she knew how to make.

Cassian had merely laughed, his eyes snaking over Nesta's ice-blue gown with a predatory intent that, given her hiss of rage, he knew would set her spitting. Then he was gone, leaving my sister on the broad doorstep, her brown-gold hair ruffled by the chill wind stirred by his mighty wings.

We brought my sisters to the village to mail our letter, Rhys glamouring us so we were invisible while they went into the little shop to post them. After we returned home, our good-byes were quick. I knew Rhys wanted to return to Velaris—if only to learn what the Attor was up to.

I'd said as much to Rhys while he flew us through the wall, into the warmth of Prythian, then winnowed us to Velaris.

Morning mist still twined through the city and the mountains around it. The chill also remained—but not nearly as unforgiving as the cold of the mortal world. Rhys left me in the foyer, huffing hot air into my frozen palms, without so much as a good-bye.

Hungry again, I found Nuala and Cerridwen, and I gobbled down cheese-and-chive scones while thinking through what I'd seen, what I'd done.

Not an hour later, Rhys found me in the living room, my feet propped on the couch before the fire, a book in my lap, a cup of rose tea steaming on the low table before me. I stood as he entered, scanning him for any sign of injury. Something tight in my chest eased when I found nothing amiss.

"It's done," he said, dragging a hand through his blue-black hair. "We learned what we needed to." I braced myself to be shut out, to be told it'd be taken care of, but Rhys added, "It's up to you, Feyre, to decide how much of our methods you want to know about. What you can handle. What we did to the Attor wasn't pretty."

"I want to know everything," I said. "Take me there."

"The Attor isn't in Velaris. He was in the Hewn City, in the Court of Nightmares—where it took Azriel less than an hour to break him." I waited for more, and as if deciding I wasn't about to crumple, Rhys stalked closer, until less than a foot of the ornate red carpet lay between us. His boots, usually impeccably polished . . . that was silver blood speckled on them. Only when I met his gaze did he say, "I'll show you."

I knew what he meant, and steadied myself, blocking out the murmuring fire and the boots and the lingering cold around my heart.

Immediately, I was in that antechamber of his mind—a pocket of memory he'd carved for me.

Darkness flowed through me, soft and seductive, echoing up from an abyss of power so great it had no end and no beginning.

"Tell me how you tracked her," Azriel said in the quiet voice that had broken countless enemies.

I—Rhys—leaned against the far wall of the holding cell, arms crossed. Azriel crouched before where the Attor was chained to a chair in the center of the room. A few levels above, the Court of Nightmares reveled on, unaware their High Lord had come.

I'd have to pay them a visit soon. Remind them who held their leash.

Soon. But not today. Not when Feyre had winnowed.

And she was still pissed as hell at me.

Rightly so, if I was being honest. But Azriel had learned that a small enemy force had infiltrated the North two days ago, and my suspicions were confirmed. Either to get at Tamlin or at me, they wanted her. Maybe for their own experimenting.

The Attor let out a low laugh. "I received word from the king that's where you were. I don't know how he knew. I got the order, flew to the wall as fast as I could."

Azriel's knife was out, balanced on a knee. Truth-Teller—the name stamped in silver Illyrian runes on the scabbard. He'd already learned that the Attor and a few others had been stationed on the outskirts of the Illyrian territory. I was half tempted to dump the Attor in one of the war-camps and see what the Illyrians did to it.

The Attor's eyes shifted toward me, glowing with a hatred I'd become well accustomed to. "Good luck trying to keep her, High Lord."

Azriel said, "Why?"

People often made the mistake of assuming Cassian was the wilder one; the one who couldn't be tamed. But Cassian was all hot temper—temper that could be used to forge and weld. There was an icy rage in Azriel I had never been able to thaw. In the centuries I'd known him, he'd said little about his life, those years in his father's keep, locked in darkness. Perhaps the shadow-singer gift had come to him then, perhaps he'd taught himself the language of shadow and wind and stone. His half-brothers hadn't been forthcoming, either. I knew because I'd met them, asked them, and had shattered their legs when they'd spat on Azriel instead.

They'd walked again—eventually.

The Attor said, "Do you think it is not common knowledge that you took her from Tamlin?"

I knew that already. That had been Azriel's task these days: monitor the situation with the Spring Court, and prepare for our own attack on Hybern.

But Tamlin had shut down his borders—sealed them so tightly that even flying overhead at night was impossible. And any ears and eyes Azriel had once possessed in the court had gone deaf and blind.

"The king could help you keep her—consider sparing you, if you worked with him . . ."

As the Attor spoke, I rummaged through its mind, each thought more vile and hideous than the next. It didn't even know I'd slipped inside, but—there: images of the army that had been built, the twin to the one I'd fought against five centuries ago; of Hybern's shores full of ships, readying for an assault; of the king, lounging on his throne in his crumbling castle. No sign of Jurian sulking about or the Cauldron. Not a whisper of the Book being on their minds. Everything the Attor had confessed was true. And it had no more value.

Az looked over his shoulder. The Attor had given him everything. Now it was just babbling to buy time.

I pushed off the wall. "Break its legs, shred its wings, and dump it off the coast of Hybern. See if it survives." The Attor began thrashing, begging. I paused by the door and said to it, "I remember every moment of it. Be grateful I'm letting you live. For now."

I hadn't let myself see the memories from Under the Mountain: of me, of the others . . . of what it had done to that human girl I'd given Amarantha in Feyre's place. I didn't let myself see what it had been like to beat Feyre—to torment and torture her.

I might have splattered him on the walls. And I needed him to send a message more than I needed my own vengeance.

The Attor was already screaming beneath Truth-Teller's honed edge when I left the cell.

Then it was done. I staggered back, spooling myself into my body.

Tamlin had closed his borders. "What *situation* with the Spring Court?"

"None. As of right now. But you know how far Tamlin can be driven to . . . protect what he thinks is his."

The image of paint sliding down the ruined study wall flashed in my mind.

"I should have sent Mor that day," Rhys said with quiet menace.

I snapped up my mental shields. I didn't want to talk about it. "Thank you for telling me," I said, and took my book and tea up to my room.

"Feyre," he said. I didn't stop. "I am sorry—about deceiving you earlier."

And this, letting me into his mind . . . a peace offering. "I need to write a letter."

✠

The letter was quick, simple. But each word was a battle.

Not because of my former illiteracy. No, I could now read and write just fine.

It was because of the message that Rhys, standing in the foyer, now read:

I left of my own free will.

I am cared for and safe. I am grateful for all that you did for me, all that you gave.

Please don't come looking for me. I'm not coming back.

He swiftly folded it in two and it vanished. "Are you sure?"

Perhaps it would help with whatever *situation* was going on at the Spring Court. I glanced to the windows beyond him. The mist wreathing the city had wandered off, revealing a bright, cloudless sky. And somehow, my head felt clearer than it had in days—months.

A city lay out there, that I had barely observed or cared about.

I wanted it—life, people. I wanted to see it, feel its rush through my blood. No boundaries, no limits to what I might encounter or do.

"I am no one's pet," I said. Rhys's face was contemplative, and I wondered if he remembered that he'd told me the same thing once, when I was too lost in my own guilt and despair to understand. "What next?"

"For what it's worth, I did actually want to give you a day to rest—"

"Don't coddle me."

"I'm not. And I'd hardly call our encounter this morning *rest*. But you will forgive me if I make assessments based on your current physical condition."

"I'll be the person who decides that. What about the Book of Breathings?"

"Once Azriel returns from dealing with the Attor, he's to put his other skill set to use and infiltrate the mortal queens' courts to learn where they're keeping it—and what their plans might be. And as for the half in Prythian . . . We'll go to the Summer Court within a few days, if my request to visit is approved. High Lords visiting other courts makes everyone jumpy. We'll deal with the Book then."

He shut his mouth, no doubt waiting for me to trudge upstairs, to brood and sleep.

Enough—I'd had enough of sleeping.

I said, "You told me that this city was better seen at night. Are you all talk, or will you ever bother to show me?"

A low laugh as he looked me over. I didn't recoil from his gaze.

When his eyes found mine again, his mouth twisted in a smile so few saw. Real amusement—perhaps a bit of happiness edged with relief. The male behind the High Lord's mask. "Dinner," he said. "Tonight. Let's find out if *you*, Feyre darling, are all talk—or if you'll allow a Lord of Night to take you out on the town."

Amren came to my room before dinner. Apparently, we were *all* going out tonight.

Downstairs, Cassian and Mor were sniping at each other about whether Cassian could fly faster short-distance than Mor could winnow to the same spot. I assumed Azriel was nearby, seeking sanctuary in the shadows. Hopefully, he'd gotten some rest after dealing with the Attor—and would rest a bit more before heading into the mortal realm to spy on those queens.

Amren, at least, knocked this time before entering. Nuala and Cerridwen, who had finished setting combs of mother-of-pearl into my hair, took one look at the delicate female and vanished into puffs of smoke.

"Skittish things," Amren said, her red lips cutting a cruel line. "Wraiths always are."

"Wraiths?" I twisted in the seat before the vanity. "I thought they were High Fae."

"Half," Amren said, surveying my turquoise, cobalt, and white clothes. "Wraiths are nothing but shadow and mist, able to walk through walls, stone—you name it. I don't even want to know how those two were conceived. High Fae will stick their cocks anywhere."

I choked on what could have been a laugh or a cough. "They make good spies."

"Why do you think they're now whispering in Azriel's ear that I'm in here?"

"I thought they answered to Rhys."

"They answer to both, but they were trained by Azriel first."

"Are they spying on me?"

"No." She frowned at a loose thread in her rain cloud–colored shirt. Her chin-length dark hair swayed as she lifted her head. "Rhys has told them time and again not to, but I don't think Azriel will ever trust me fully. So they're reporting on my movements. And with good reason."

"Why?"

"Why not? I'd be disappointed if Rhysand's spymaster didn't keep tabs on me. Even go against orders to do so."

"Rhys doesn't punish him for disobeying?"

Those silver eyes glowed. "The Court of Dreams is founded on three things: to defend, to honor, and to cherish. Were you expecting brute strength and obedience? Many of Rhysand's top officials have little to no power. He values loyalty, cunning, compassion. And Azriel, despite his disobedience, is acting to defend his court, his people. So, no. Rhysand does not punish that. There are rules, but they are flexible."

"What about the Tithe?"

"What Tithe?"

I stood from the little bench. "The Tithe—taxes, whatever. Twice a year."

"There are taxes on city dwellers, but there is no Tithe." She clicked her tongue. "But the High Lord of Spring enacts one."

I didn't want to think about it entirely, not yet—not with that letter now on its way to him, if not already delivered. So I reached for the small box on the vanity and pulled out her amulet. "Here." I handed over the gold-and-jewel-encrusted thing. "Thank you."

Amren's brows rose as I dropped it into her waiting palm. "You gave it back."

"I didn't realize it was a test."

She set it back into the case. "Keep it. There's no magic to it."

I blinked. "You lied—"

She shrugged, heading for the door. "I found it at the bottom of my jewelry box. You needed something to believe you could get out of the Prison again."

"But Rhys kept looking at it—"

"Because *he* gave it to me two hundred years ago. He was probably surprised to see it again, and wondered why I'd given it to you. Likely *worried* why I might have given it to you."

I clenched my teeth, but Amren was already breezing through the door with a cheerful, "You're welcome."

CHAPTER 29

Despite the chill night, every shop was open as we walked through the city. Musicians played in the little squares, and the Palace of Thread and Jewels was packed with shoppers and performers, High Fae and lesser faeries alike. But we continued past, down to the river itself, the water so smooth that the stars and lights blended on its dark surface like a living ribbon of eternity.

The five of them were unhurried as we strolled across one of the wide marble bridges spanning the Sidra, often moving forward or dropping back to chat with one another. From the ornate lanterns that lined either side of the bridge, faelight cast golden shadows on the wings of the three males, gilding the talons at the apex of each.

The conversation ranged from the people they knew, matches and teams for sports I'd never heard of (apparently, Amren was a vicious, obsessive supporter of one), new shops, music they'd heard, clubs they favored . . . Not a mention of Hybern or the threats we faced—no doubt from secrecy, but I had a feeling it was also because tonight, this time together . . . they did not want that terrible, hideous presence intruding. As if they were all just ordinary citizens—even Rhys. As if they weren't the most powerful people in this court, maybe in all of Prythian. And no one, absolutely no one, on the street balked or paled or ran.

Awed, perhaps a little intimidated, but . . . no fear. It was so unusual that I kept silent, merely observing them—their world. The normalcy that they each fought so hard to preserve. That I had once raged against, resented.

But there was no place like this in the world. Not so serene. So loved by its people and its rulers.

The other side of the city was even more crowded, with patrons in finery out to attend the many theaters we passed. I'd never seen a theater before—never seen a play, or a concert, or a symphony. In our ramshackle village, we'd gotten mummers and minstrels at best—herds of beggars yowling on makeshift instruments at worst.

We strolled along the riverside walkway, past shops and cafés, music spilling from them. And I thought—even as I hung back from the others, my gloved hands stuffed into the pockets of my heavy blue overcoat—that the sounds of it all might have been the most beautiful thing I'd ever heard: the people, and the river, and the music; the clank of silverware on plates; the scrape of chairs being pulled out and pushed in; the shouts of vendors selling their wares as they ambled past.

How much had I missed in these months of despair and numbness?

But no longer. The lifeblood of Velaris thrummed through me, and in rare moments of quiet, I could have sworn I heard the clash of the sea, clawing at the distant cliffs.

Eventually, we entered a small restaurant beside the river, built into the lower level of a two-story building, the whole space bedecked in greens and golds and barely big enough to fit all of us. And three sets of Illyrian wings.

But the owner knew them, and kissed them each on the cheek, even Rhysand. Well, except for Amren, whom the owner bowed to before she hustled back into her kitchen and bade us sit at the large table that was half in, half out of the open storefront. The starry night was crisp, the wind rustling the potted palms placed with loving care along the riverside walkway railing. No doubt spelled to keep from dying in the winter—just as the warmth of the restaurant kept the chill from disturbing us or any of those dining in the open air at the river's edge.

Then the food platters began pouring out, along with the wine and the conversation, and we dined under the stars beside the river. I'd never had such food—warm and rich and savory and spicy. Like it filled not only my stomach, but that lingering hole in my chest, too.

The owner—a slim, dark-skinned female with lovely brown eyes—was standing behind my chair, chatting with Rhys about the latest shipment of spices that had come to the Palaces. "The traders were saying the prices might rise, High Lord, especially if rumors about Hybern awakening are correct."

Down the table, I felt the others' attention slide to us, even as they kept talking.

Rhys leaned back in his seat, swirling his goblet of wine. "We'll find a way to keep the prices from skyrocketing."

"Don't trouble yourself, of course," the owner said, wringing her fingers a bit. "It's just . . . so lovely to have such spices available again—now that . . . that things are better."

Rhys gave her a gentle smile, the one that made him seem younger. "I wouldn't be troubling myself—not when I like your cooking so much."

The owner beamed, flushing, and looked to where I'd half twisted in my seat to watch her. "Is it to your liking?"

The happiness on her face, the satisfaction that only a day of hard work doing something you love could bring, hit me like a stone.

I—I remembered feeling that way. After painting from morning until night. Once, that was all I had wanted for myself. I looked to the dishes, then back at her, and said, "I've lived in the mortal realm, and lived in other courts, but I've never had food like this. Food that makes me . . . feel awake."

It sounded about as stupid as it felt coming out, but I couldn't think of another way to say it. But the owner nodded like she understood and squeezed my shoulder. "Then I'll bring you a special dessert," she said, and strode into her kitchen.

I turned back to my plate, but found Rhysand's eyes on me. His face was softer, more contemplative than I'd ever seen it, his mouth slightly open.

I lifted my brows. *What?*

He gave me a cocky grin and leaned in to hear the story Mor was telling about—

I forgot what she was talking about as the owner emerged with a metal goblet full of dark liquid and placed it before Amren.

Rhys's Second hadn't touched her plate, but pushed the food around like she might actually be trying to be polite. When she saw the goblet laid before her, she flicked her brows up. "You didn't have to do that."

The owner shrugged her slim shoulders. "It's fresh and hot, and we needed the beast for tomorrow's roast, anyway."

I had a horrible feeling I knew what was inside.

Amren swirled the goblet, the dark liquid lapping at the sides like wine, then sipped from it. "You spiced it nicely." Blood gleamed on her teeth.

The owner bowed. "No one leaves my place hungry," she said before walking away.

Indeed, I almost asked Mor to roll me out of the restaurant by the time we were done and Rhys had paid the tab, despite the owner's protests. My muscles were barking thanks to my earlier *training* in the mortal forest, and at some point during the meal, every part of me I'd used while tackling Rhys into the snow had started to ache.

Mor rubbed her stomach in lazy circles as we paused beside the river.

"I want to go dancing. I won't be able to fall asleep when I'm this full. Rita's is right up the street."

Dancing. My body groaned in protest and I glanced about for an ally to shoot down this ridiculous idea.

But Azriel—*Azriel* said, his eyes wholly on Mor, "I'm in."

"Of course you are," Cassian grumbled, frowning at him. "Don't you have to be off at dawn?"

Mor's frown now mirrored Cassian's—as if she realized where and what he'd be doing tomorrow. She said to Azriel, "We don't have to—"

"I want to," Azriel said, holding her gaze long enough that Mor dropped it, twisted toward Cassian, and said, "Will you deign to join us, or do you have plans to ogle your muscles in the mirror?"

Cassian snorted, looping his elbow through hers and leading her up the street. "I'll go—for the drinks, you ass. No dancing."

"Thank the Mother. You nearly shattered my foot the last time you tried."

It was an effort not to stare at Azriel as he watched them head up the steep street, arm in arm and bickering with every step. The shadows gathered around his shoulders, like they were indeed whispering to him, shielding him, perhaps. His broad chest expanded with a deep breath that sent them skittering, and then he set into an easy, graceful stroll after them. If Azriel was going with them, then any excuse I might make *not* to—

I turned pleading eyes to Amren, but she'd vanished.

"She's getting more blood in the back to take home with her," Rhys said in my ear, and I nearly jumped out of my skin. His chuckle was warm against my neck. "And then she'll be going right to her apartment to gorge herself."

I tried not to shudder as I faced him. "Why blood?"

"It doesn't seem polite to ask."

I frowned up at him. "Are *you* going dancing?"

He peered over my shoulder at his friends, who had almost scaled the steep street, some people pausing to greet them. "I'd rather walk home," Rhys said at last. "It's been a long day."

Mor turned back at the top of the hill, her purple clothes floating around her in the winter wind, and raised a dark gold brow. Rhys shook his head, and she waved, followed by short waves from Azriel and Cassian, who'd dropped back to talk with his brother-in-arms.

Rhys gestured forward. "Shall we? Or are you too cold?"

Consuming blood with Amren in the back of the restaurant sounded more appealing, but I shook my head and fell into step beside him as we walked along the river toward the bridge.

I drank in the city as greedily as Amren had gobbled down the spiced blood, and I almost stumbled as I spied the glimmer of color across the water.

The Rainbow of Velaris glowed like a fistful of jewels, as if the paint they used on their houses came alive in the moonlight.

"This is my favorite view in the city," Rhys said, stopping at the metal railing along the river walkway and gazing toward the artists' quarter. "It was my sister's favorite, too. My father used to have to drag her kicking and screaming out of Velaris, she loved it so much."

I fumbled for the right response to the quiet sorrow in those words. But like a useless fool, I merely asked, "Then why are both your houses on the other side of the river?" I leaned against the railing, watching the reflections of the Rainbow wobble on the river surface like bright fishes struggling in the current.

"Because I wanted a quiet street—so I could visit this clamor whenever I wished and then have a home to retreat to."

"You could have just reordered the city."

"Why the hell would I change one thing about this place?"

"Isn't that what High Lords do?" My breath clouded in front of me in the brisk night. "Whatever they please?"

He studied my face. "There are a great many things that I wish to do, and don't get to."

I hadn't realized how close we were standing. "So when you buy jewelry for Amren, is it to keep yourself in her good graces or because you're—together?"

Rhys barked a laugh. "When I was young and stupid, I once invited her to my bed. She laughed herself hoarse. The jewelry is just because I enjoy buying it for a friend who works hard for me, and has my back when I need it. Staying in her good graces is an added bonus."

None of it surprised me. "And you didn't marry anyone."

"So many questions tonight." I stared at him until he sighed. "I've had lovers, but I never felt tempted to invite one of them to share a life with me. And I honestly think that if I'd asked, they all would have said no."

"I would have thought they'd be fighting each other to win your hand." Like Ianthe.

"Marrying me means a life with a target on your back—and if there were offspring, then a life of knowing they'd be hunted from the moment they were conceived. Everyone knows what happened to my family—and my people know that beyond our borders, we are hated."

I still didn't know the full story, but I asked, "Why? Why are you hated? Why keep the truth of this place secret? It's a shame no one knows about it—what good you do here."

"There was a time when the Night Court *was* a Court of Nightmares and was ruled from the Hewn City. Long ago. But an ancient High Lord had a different vision, and rather than allowing the world to see his territory vulnerable at a time of change, he sealed the borders and staged a coup, eliminating the worst of the courtiers and predators, building Velaris for the dreamers, establishing trade and peace."

His eyes blazed, as if he could peer all the way back in time to see it. With those remarkable gifts of his, it wouldn't surprise me.

"To preserve it," Rhys continued, "he kept it a secret, and so did his offspring, and their offspring. There are many spells on the city itself—laid by him, and his Heirs, that make those who trade here unable to spill our secrets, and grant them adept skills at lying in order to keep the origin of their goods, their ships, hidden from the rest of the world. Rumor has it that ancient High Lord cast his very life's blood upon the stones and river to keep that spell eternal.

"But along the way, despite his best intentions, darkness grew again—not as bad as it had once been . . . But bad enough that there is a permanent divide within my court. We allow the world to see the other half, to fear them—so that they might never guess this place thrives here. And we allow the Court of Nightmares to continue, blind to Velaris's existence, because we know that without them, there are some courts and kingdoms that might strike us. And invade our borders to discover the many, many secrets we've kept from the other High Lords and courts these millennia."

"So truly none of the others know? In the other courts?"

"Not a soul. You will not find it on a single map, or mentioned in any book beyond those written here. Perhaps it is our loss to be so contained and isolated, but . . . " He gestured to the city around us. "My people do not seem to be suffering much for it."

Indeed, they did not. Thanks to Rhys—and his Inner Circle. "Are you worried about Az going to the mortal lands tomorrow?"

He tapped a finger against the rail. "Of course I am. But Azriel has infiltrated places far more harrowing than a few mortal courts. He'd find my worrying insulting."

"Does he mind what he does? Not the spying, I mean. What he did to the Attor today."

Rhys loosed a breath. "It's hard to tell with him—and he'd never tell me. I've witnessed Cassian rip apart opponents and then puke his guts up once the carnage stopped, sometimes even mourn them. But Azriel . . . Cassian tries, I try—but I think the only person who ever gets him to admit to any sort of feeling is Mor. And that's only when she's pestered him to the point where even his infinite patience has run out."

I smiled a bit. "But he and Mor—they never . . . ?"

"That's between them—and Cassian. I'm not stupid or arrogant enough to get in the middle of it." Which I would certainly be if I shoved my nose in their business.

We walked in silence across the packed bridge to the other side of the river. My muscles quivered at the steep hills between us and the town house.

I was about to beg Rhys to fly me home when I caught the strands of music pouring from a group of performers outside a restaurant.

My hands slackened at my sides. A reduced version of the symphony I'd heard in a chill dungeon, when I had been so lost to terror and despair that I had hallucinated—hallucinated as this music poured into my cell . . . and kept me from shattering.

And once more, the beauty of it hit me, the layering and swaying, the joy and peace.

They had never played a piece like it Under the Mountain—never this sort of music. And I'd never heard music in my cell save for that one time.

"You," I breathed, not taking my eyes from the musicians playing so skillfully that even the diners had set down their forks in the cafés nearby. "You sent that music into my cell. Why?"

Rhysand's voice was hoarse. "Because you were breaking. And I couldn't find another way to save you."

The music swelled and built. I'd seen a palace in the sky when I'd hallucinated—a place between sunset and dawn . . . a house of moonstone pillars. "I saw the Night Court."

He glanced sidelong at me. "I didn't send those images to you."

I didn't care. "Thank you. For everything—for what you did. Then . . . and now."

"Even after the Weaver? After this morning with my trap for the Attor?"

My nostrils flared. "You ruin everything."

Rhys grinned, and I didn't notice if people were staring as he slid an arm under my legs, and shot us both into the sky.

I could learn to love it, I realized. The flying.

I was reading in bed, listening to the merry chatter of the toasty birch fire across the room, when I turned the page of my book and a piece of paper fell out.

I took one look at the cream stationery and the handwriting and sat up straight.

On it, Rhysand had written,

I might be a shameless flirt, but at least I don't have a horrible temper. You should come tend to my wounds from our squabble in the snow. I'm bruised all over thanks to you.

Something clicked against the nightstand, and a pen rolled across the polished mahogany. Hissing, I snatched it up and scribbled:

Go lick your wounds and leave me be.

The paper vanished.

It was gone for a while—far longer than it should have taken to write the few words that appeared on the paper when it returned.

I'd much rather you licked my wounds for me.

My heart pounded, faster and faster, and a strange sort of rush went through my veins as I read the sentence again and again. A challenge.

I clamped my lips shut to keep from smiling as I wrote,

Lick you where, exactly?

The paper vanished before I'd even completed the final mark.

His reply was a long time coming. Then,

Wherever you want to lick me, Feyre.

I'd like to start with "Everywhere," but I can choose, if necessary.

I wrote back,

Let's hope my licking is better than yours. I remember how horrible you were at it Under the Mountain.

Lie. He'd licked away my tears when I'd been a moment away from shattering.

He'd done it to keep me distracted—keep me angry. Because anger was better than feeling nothing; because anger and hatred were the long-lasting fuel in the endless dark of my despair. The same way that music had kept me from breaking.

Lucien had come to patch me up a few times, but no one risked quite so much in keeping me not only alive, but as mentally intact as I could be considering the circumstances. Just as he'd been doing these past few weeks—taunting and teasing me to keep the hollowness at bay. Just as he was doing now.

I was under duress, his next note read. *If you want, I'd be more than happy to prove you wrong. I've been told I'm very, very good at licking.*

I clenched my knees together and wrote back, *Good night.*

A heartbeat later, his note said, *Try not to moan too loudly when you dream about me. I need my beauty rest.*

I got up, chucked the letter in the burbling fire, and gave it a vulgar gesture.

I could have sworn laughter rumbled down the hall.

I didn't dream about Rhys.

I dreamed about the Attor, its claws on me, gripping me as I was punched. I dreamed about its hissing laughter and foul stench.

But I slept through the night. And did not wake once.

CHAPTER 30

Cassian might have been cocky grins and vulgarity most of the time, but in the sparring ring in a rock-carved courtyard atop the House of Wind the next afternoon, he was a stone-cold killer.

And when those lethal instincts were turned on me . . .

Beneath the fighting leathers, even with the brisk temperature, my skin was slick with sweat. Each breath ravaged my throat, and my arms trembled so badly that any time I so much as tried to use my fingers, my pinkie would start shaking uncontrollably.

I was watching it wobble of its own accord when Cassian closed the gap between us, gripped my hand, and said, "This is because you're hitting on the wrong knuckles. Top two—pointer and middle finger—that's where the punches should connect. Hitting here," he said, tapping a callused finger on the already-bruised bit of skin in the vee between my pinkie and ring finger, "will do more damage to you than to your opponent. You're lucky the Attor didn't want to get into a fistfight."

We'd been going at it for an hour now, walking through the basic steps of hand-to-hand combat. And it turned out that I might have been good at hunting, at archery, but using my left side? Pathetic. I was as uncoordinated as a newborn fawn attempting to walk. Punching *and* stepping with the left side of my body at once had been nearly impossible, and I'd stumbled into Cassian more often than I'd hit him. The right punches—those were easy.

"Get a drink," he said. "Then we're working on your core. No point in learning to punch if you can't even hold your stance."

I frowned toward the sound of clashing blades in the open sparring ring across from us.

Azriel, surprisingly, had returned from the mortal realm by lunch. Mor had intercepted him first, but I'd gotten a secondhand report from Rhys that he'd found some sort of barrier around the queens' palace, and had needed to return to assess what might be done about it.

Assess—and brood, it seemed, since Azriel had barely managed a polite hello to me before launching into sparring with Rhysand, his face grim and tight. They'd been at it now for an hour straight, their slender blades like flashes of quicksilver as they moved around and around. I wondered if it was as much for practice as it was for Rhys to help his spymaster work off his frustration.

At some point since I'd last looked, despite the sunny winter day, they'd removed their leather jackets and shirts.

Their tan, muscled arms were both covered in the same manner of tattoos that adorned my own hand and forearm, the ink flowing across their shoulders and over their sculpted pectoral muscles. Between their wings, a line of them ran down the column of their spine, right beneath where they typically strapped their blades.

"We get the tattoos when we're initiated as Illyrian warriors—for luck and glory on the battlefield," Cassian said, following my stare. I doubted Cassian was drinking in the rest of the image, though: the stomach muscles gleaming with sweat in the bright sun, the bunching of their powerful thighs, the rippling strength in their backs, surrounding those mighty, beautiful wings.

Death on swift wings.

The title came out of nowhere, and for a moment, I saw the painting I'd create: the darkness of those wings, faintly illuminated with lines of red and gold by the radiant winter sun, the glare off their blades, the harshness of the tattoos against the beauty of their faces—

I blinked, and the image was gone, like a cloud of hot breath on a cold night.

Cassian jerked his chin toward his brothers. "Rhys is out of shape and won't admit it, but Azriel is too polite to beat him into the dirt."

Rhys looked anything but out of shape. Cauldron boil me, what the hell did they *eat* to look like that?

My knees wobbled a bit as I strode to the stool where Cassian had brought a pitcher of water and two glasses. I poured one for myself, my pinkie trembling uncontrollably again.

My tattoo, I realized, had been made with Illyrian markings. Perhaps Rhys's own way of wishing me luck and glory while facing Amarantha.

Luck and glory. I wouldn't mind a little of either of those things these days.

Cassian filled a glass for himself and clinked it against mine, so at odds from the brutal taskmaster who, moments ago, had me walking through punches, hitting his sparring pads, and trying not to crumple on the ground to beg for death. So at odds from the male who had gone head to head with my sister, unable to resist matching himself against Nesta's spirit of steel and flame.

"So," Cassian said, gulping down the water. Behind us, Rhys and Azriel clashed, separated, and clashed again. "When are you going to talk about how you wrote a letter to Tamlin, telling him you've left for good?"

The question hit me so viciously that I sniped, "How about when you talk about how you tease and taunt Mor to hide whatever it is you feel for her?" Because I had no doubt that he was well aware of the role he played in their little tangled web.

The beat of crunching steps and clashing blades behind us stumbled—then resumed.

Cassian let out a startled, rough laugh. "Old news."

"I have a feeling that's what she probably says about you."

"Get back in the ring," Cassian said, setting down his empty glass. "No core exercises. Just fists. You want to mouth off, then back it up."

But the question he'd asked swarmed in my skull. *You've left for good; you've left for good; you've left for good.*

I had—I'd meant it. But without knowing what he thought, if he'd even care that much . . . No, I knew he'd care. He'd probably trashed the manor in his rage.

If my mere mention of him suffocating me had caused him to destroy his study, then this . . . I had been frightened by those fits of pure rage, cowed by them. And it had been love—I had loved him so deeply, so greatly, but . . .

"Rhys told you?" I said.

Cassian had the wisdom to look a bit nervous at the expression on my face. "He informed Azriel, who is . . . monitoring things and needs to know. Az told me."

"I assume it was while you were out drinking and dancing." I drained the last of my water and walked back into the ring.

"Hey," Cassian said, catching my arm. His hazel eyes were more green than brown today. "I'm sorry. I didn't mean to hit a nerve. Az only told me because I told him *I* needed to know for my own forces; to know what to expect. None of us . . . we don't think it's a joke. What you did was a hard call. A really damn hard call. It was just my shitty way of trying to see if you needed to talk about it. I'm sorry," he repeated, letting go.

The stumbling words, the earnestness in his eyes . . . I nodded as I resumed my place. "All right."

Though Rhysand kept at it with Azriel, I could have sworn his eyes were on me—had been on me from the moment Cassian had asked me that question.

Cassian shoved his hands into the sparring pads and held them up. "Thirty one-two punches; then forty; then fifty." I winced at him over his gloves as I wrapped my hands. "You didn't answer my question," he said with a tentative smile—one I doubted his soldiers or Illyrian brethren ever saw.

It had been love, and I'd meant it—the happiness, the lust, the peace . . . I'd felt all of those things. Once.

I positioned my legs at twelve and five and lifted my hands up toward my face.

But maybe those things had blinded me, too.

Maybe they'd been a blanket over my eyes about the temper. The need for control, the need to protect that ran so deep he'd locked me up. Like a prisoner.

"I'm fine," I said, stepping and jabbing with my left side. Fluid—smooth like silk, as if my immortal body at last aligned.

My fist slammed into Cassian's sparring pad, snatching back as fast as a snake's bite as I struck with my right, shoulder and foot twisting.

"One," Cassian counted. Again, I struck, one-two. "Two. And fine is good—fine is great."

Again, again, again.

We both knew "fine" was a lie.

I had done everything—*everything* for that love. I had ripped myself to shreds, I had killed innocents and debased myself, and he had *sat* beside Amarantha on that throne. And he couldn't do anything, hadn't risked it—hadn't risked being caught until there was one night left, and all he'd wanted to do wasn't free me, but fuck me, and—

Again, again, again. One-two; one-two; one-two—

And when Amarantha had broken me, when she had snapped my bones and made my blood boil in its veins, he'd just knelt and begged her. He hadn't tried to kill her, hadn't crawled for me. Yes, he'd fought for me—but I'd fought harder for him.

Again, again, again, each pound of my fists on the sparring pads a question and an answer.

And he had the nerve once his powers were back to shove me into a cage. The *nerve* to say I was no longer useful; I was to be cloistered for *his* peace of mind. He'd given me everything I needed to become myself, to feel safe, and when he got what he wanted—when he got his power back, his lands back . . . he stopped trying. He was still good, still Tamlin, but he was just . . . wrong.

And then I was sobbing through my clenched teeth, the tears washing away that infected wound, and I didn't care that Cassian was there, or Rhys or Azriel.

The clashing steel stopped.

And then my fists connected with bare skin, and I realized I'd punched through the sparring pads—no, *burned* through them, and—

And I stopped, too.

The wrappings around my hands were now mere smudges of soot. Cassian's upraised palms remained before me—ready to take the blow, if I needed to make it. "I'm all right," he said quietly. Gently.

And maybe I was exhausted and broken, but I breathed, "I killed them."

I hadn't said the words aloud since it had happened.

Cassian's lips tightened. "I know." Not condemnation, not praise. But grim understanding.

My hands slackened as another shuddering sob worked its way through me. "It should have been me."

And there it was.

Standing there under the cloudless sky, the winter sun beating on my head, nothing around me save for rock, no shadows in which to hide, nothing to cling to . . . There it was.

Then darkness swept in, soothing, gentle darkness—no, shade—and a sweat-slick male body halted before me. Gentle fingers lifted my chin until I looked up . . . at Rhysand's face.

His wings had wrapped around us, cocooned us, the sunlight casting the membrane in gold and red. Beyond us, outside, in another world, maybe, the sounds of steel on steel—Cassian and Azriel sparring—began.

"You will feel that way every day for the rest of your life," Rhysand said. This close, I could smell the sweat on him, the sea-and-citrus scent beneath it. His eyes were soft. I tried to look away, but he held my chin firm. "And I know this because I have felt that way every day since my mother and sister were slaughtered and I had to bury them myself, and even retribution didn't fix it." He wiped away the tears on one cheek, then another. "You can either let it wreck you, let it get you killed like it nearly did with the Weaver, or you can learn to live with it."

For a long moment, I just stared at the open, calm face—maybe his true face, the one beneath all the masks he wore to keep his people safe. "I'm sorry—about your family," I rasped.

"I'm sorry I didn't find a way to spare you from what happened Under the Mountain," Rhys said with equal quiet. "From dying. From *wanting* to die." I began to shake my head, but he said, "I have two kinds of nightmares: the ones where I'm again Amarantha's whore or my friends are . . . And the ones where I hear your neck snap and see the light leave your eyes."

I had no answer to that—to the tenor in his rich, deep voice. So I examined the tattoos on his chest and arms, the glow of his tan skin, so golden now that he was no longer caged inside that mountain.

I stopped my perusal when I got to the vee of muscles that flowed beneath the waist of his leather pants. Instead, I flexed my hand in front of me, my skin warm from the heat that had burned through those pads.

"Ah," he said, wings sweeping back as he folded them gracefully behind him. "That."

I squinted at the flood of sunlight. "Autumn Court, right?"

He took my hand, examining it, the skin already bruised from sparring. "Right. A gift from its High Lord, Beron."

Lucien's father. Lucien—I wondered what he made of all this. If he missed me. If Ianthe continued to . . . prey on him.

Still sparring, Cassian and Azriel were trying their best not to look like they were eavesdropping.

"I'm not well versed in the complexities of the other High Lords' elemental gifts," Rhys said, "but we can figure it out—day by day, if need be."

"If you're the most powerful High Lord in history . . . does that mean the drop I got from you holds more sway over the others?" Why I'd been able to break into his head that one time?

"Give it a try." He jerked his chin toward me. "See if you can summon darkness. I won't ask you to try to winnow," he added with a grin.

"I don't know how I did it to begin with."

"Will it into being."

I gave him a flat stare.

He shrugged. "Try thinking of me—how good-looking I am. How talented—"

"How arrogant."

"That, too." He crossed his arms over his bare chest, the movement making the muscles in his stomach flicker.

"Put a shirt on while you're at it," I quipped.

A feline smile. "Does it make you uncomfortable?"

"I'm surprised there aren't more mirrors in this house, since you seem to love looking at yourself so much."

Azriel launched into a coughing fit. Cassian just turned away, a hand clamped over his mouth.

Rhys's lips twitched. "There's the Feyre I adore."

I scowled, but closed my eyes and tried to look inward—toward any dark corner of myself I could find. There were too many.

Far too many.

And right now—right now they each contained that letter I'd written yesterday.

A good-bye.

For my own sanity, my *own* safety . . .

"There are different kinds of darkness," Rhys said. I kept my eyes shut. “There is the darkness that frightens, the darkness that soothes, the darkness that is restful.” I pictured each. “There is the darkness of lovers, and the darkness of assassins. It becomes what the bearer wishes it to be, needs it to be. It is not wholly bad or good.”

I only saw the darkness of that dungeon cell; the darkness of the Bone Carver’s lair.

Cassian swore, but Azriel murmured a soft challenge that had their blades striking again.

“Open your eyes.” I did.

And found darkness all around me. Not from me—but from Rhys. As if the sparring ring had been wiped away, as if the world had yet to begin.

Quiet.

Soft.

Peaceful.

Lights began twinkling—little stars, blooming irises of blue and purple and white. I reached out a hand toward one, and starlight danced on my fingertips. Far away, in another world perhaps, Azriel and Cassian sparred in the dark, no doubt using it as a training exercise.

I shifted the star between my fingers like a coin on the hand of a magician. Here in the soothing, sparkling dark, a steady breath filled my lungs.

I couldn’t remember the last time I’d done such a thing. Breathed easily.

Then the darkness splintered and vanished, swifter than smoke on a wind. I found myself blinking back the blinding sun, arm still out, Rhysand still before me.

Still without a shirt.

He said, “We can work on it later. For now.” He sniffed. “Go take a bath.”

I gave him a particularly vulgar gesture—and asked Cassian to fly me home instead.

CHAPTER 31

"Don't dance so much on your toes," Cassian said to me four days later, as we spent the unusually warm afternoon in the sparring ring. "Feet planted, daggers up. Eyes on mine. If you were on a battlefield, you would have been dead with that maneuver."

Amren snorted, picking at her nails while she lounged in a chaise. "She heard you the first ten times you said it, Cassian."

"Keep talking, Amren, and I'll drag you into the ring and see how much practice you've actually been doing."

Amren just continued cleaning her nails—with a tiny bone, I realized. "Touch me, Cassian, and I'll remove your favorite part. Small as it might be."

He let out a low chuckle. Standing between them in the sparring ring atop the House of Wind, a dagger in each hand, sweat sliding down my body, I wondered if I should find a way to slip out. Perhaps winnow—though I hadn't been able to do it again since that morning in the mortal realm, despite my quiet efforts in the privacy of my own bedroom.

Four days of this—training with him, working with Rhys afterward on trying to summon flame or darkness. Unsurprisingly, I made more progress with the former.

Word had not yet arrived from the Summer Court. Or from the Spring Court, regarding my letter. I hadn't decided if that was a good thing. Azriel continued his attempt to infiltrate the human queens' courts, his network of spies now seeking a foothold to get inside. That he hadn't managed to do so yet had made him quieter than usual—colder.

Amren's silver eyes flicked up from her nails. "Good. You can play with her."

"Play with who?" said Mor, stepping from the stairwell shadows.

Cassian's nostrils flared. "Where'd you go the other night?" he asked Mor without so much as a nod of greeting. "I didn't see you leave Rita's." Their usual dance hall for drinking and revelry.

They'd dragged me out two nights ago—and I'd spent most of the time sitting in their booth, nursing my wine, talking over the music with Azriel, who had arrived content to brood, but reluctantly joined me in observing Rhys holding court at the bar. Females and males watched Rhysand throughout the hall—and the shadowsinger and I made a game of betting on who, exactly, would work up the nerve to invite the High Lord home.

Unsurprisingly, Az won every round. But at least he was smiling by the end of the night—to Mor's delight when she'd stumbled back to our table to chug another drink before prancing onto the dance floor again.

Rhys didn't accept any offers that came his way, no matter how beautiful they were, no matter how they smiled and laughed. And his refusals were polite—firm, but polite.

Had he been with anyone since Amarantha? Did he *want* another person in his bed after Amarantha? Even the wine hadn't given me the nerve to ask Azriel about it.

Mor, it seemed, went to Rita's more than anyone else—practically lived there, actually. She shrugged at Cassian's demand and another chaise like Amren's appeared. "I just went . . . out," she said, plopping down.

"With whom?" Cassian pushed.

"Last I was aware," Mor said, leaning back in the chair, "I didn't take orders from you, Cassian. Or report to you. So where I was, and who I was with, is none of your damn concern."

"You didn't tell Azriel, either."

I paused, weighing those words, Cassian's stiff shoulders. Yes, there was some tension between him and Mor that resulted in that bickering, but . . . perhaps . . . perhaps Cassian accepted the role of buffer not to keep them apart, but to keep the shadowsinger from hurt. From being *old news*, as I'd called him.

Cassian finally remembered I'd been standing in front of him, noted the look of understanding on my face, and gave me a warning one in return. Fair enough.

I shrugged and took a moment to set down the daggers and catch my breath. For a heartbeat, I wished Nesta were there, if only to see *them* go head to head. We hadn't heard from my sisters—or the mortal queens. I wondered when we'd send another letter or try another route.

"Why, exactly," Cassian said to Amren and Mor, not even bothering to try to sound pleasant, "are you two *ladies* here?"

Mor closed her eyes as she tipped back her head, sunning her golden face with the same irreverence that Cassian perhaps sought to shield Azriel from—and Mor herself perhaps tried to shield Azriel from as well. "Rhys is coming in a few moments to give us some news, apparently. Didn't Amren tell you?"

"I forgot," Amren said, still picking at her nails. "I was having too much fun watching Feyre evade Cassian's tried-and-true techniques to get people to do what he wants."

Cassian's brows rose. "You've been here for an *hour*."

"Oops," Amren said.

Cassian threw up his hands. "Get off your ass and give me twenty lunges—"

A vicious, unearthly snarl cut him off.

But Rhys strolled out of the stairwell, and I couldn't decide if I should be relieved or disappointed that Cassian versus Amren was put to a sudden stop.

He was in his fine clothes, not fighting leathers, his wings nowhere in sight. Rhys looked at them, at me, the daggers I'd left in the dirt, and then said, "Sorry to interrupt while things were getting interesting."

"Fortunately for Cassian's balls," Amren said, nestling back in her chaise, "you arrived at the right time."

Cassian snarled halfheartedly at her.

Rhys laughed, and said to none of us in particular, "Ready to go on a summer holiday?"

Mor said, "The Summer Court invited you?"

"Of course they did. Feyre, Amren, and I are going tomorrow."

Only the three of us? Cassian seemed to have the same thought, his wings rustling as he crossed his arms and faced Rhys. "The Summer Court is full of hotheaded fools and arrogant pricks," he warned. "I should join you."

"You'd fit right in," Amren crooned. "Too bad you still aren't going."

Cassian pointed a finger at her. "Watch it, Amren."

She bared her teeth in a wicked smile. "Believe me, I'd prefer not to go, either."

I clamped my lips shut to keep from smiling or grimacing, I didn't know.

Rhys rubbed his temples. "Cassian, considering the fact that the last time you visited, it didn't end well—"

"I wrecked *one* building—"

"*And*," Rhys cut him off. "Considering the fact that they are utterly terrified of sweet Amren, *she* is the wiser choice."

I didn't know if there was anyone alive who *wasn't* utterly terrified of her.

"It could easily be a trap," Cassian pushed. "Who's to say the delay in replying wasn't because they're contacting our enemies to ambush you?"

"That is *also* why Amren is coming," Rhys said simply.

Amren was frowning—bored and annoyed.

Rhys said too casually, "There is also a great deal of treasure to be found in the Summer Court. If the Book is hidden, Amren, you might find other objects to your liking."

"Shit," Cassian said, throwing up his hands again. "Really, Rhys? It's bad enough we're stealing from them, but robbing them blind—"

"Rhysand *does* have a point," Amren said. "Their High Lord is young and untested. I doubt he's had much time to catalog his inherited hoard since he was appointed Under the Mountain. I doubt he'll know anything is missing. Very well, Rhysand—I'm in."

No better than a firedrake guarding its trove indeed. Mor gave me a secret, subtle look that conveyed the same thing, and I swallowed a chuckle.

Cassian started to object again, but Rhys said quietly, "I will need you—not Amren—in the human realm. The Summer Court has banned you for eternity, and though your presence would be a good distraction while Feyre does what she has to, it could lead to more trouble than it's worth."

I stiffened. What I had to do—meaning track down that Book of Breathings and steal it. Feyre Cursebreaker . . . and thief.

"Just cool your heels, Cassian," Amren said, eyes a bit glazed—as she no doubt imagined the treasure she might steal from the Summer Court. "We'll be fine without your swaggering and growling at everyone. Their High Lord owes Rhys a favor for saving his life Under the Mountain—and keeping his secrets."

Cassian's wings twitched, but Mor chimed in, "And the High Lord also probably wants to figure out where we stand in regard to any upcoming conflict."

Cassian's wings settled again. He jerked his chin at me. "Feyre, though. It's one thing to have her here—even when everyone knows it. It's another to bring her to a different court, and introduce her as a member of our own."

The message it'd send to Tamlin. If my letter wasn't enough.

But Rhys was done. He inclined his head to Amren and strolled for the open archway. Cassian lurched a step, but Mor lifted a hand. "Leave it," she murmured. Cassian glared, but obeyed.

I took that as a chance to follow after Rhys, the warm darkness inside the House of Wind blinding me. My Fae eyes adjusted swiftly, but for the first few steps down the narrow hallway, I trailed after Rhys on memory alone.

"Any more traps I should know about before we go tomorrow?" I said to his back.

Rhys looked over a shoulder, pausing atop the stair landing. "Here I was, thinking your notes the other night indicated you'd forgiven me."

I took in that half grin, the chest I might have suggested I'd lick and had avoided looking at for the past four days, and halted a healthy distance away. "One would think a High Lord would have more important things to do than pass notes back and forth at night."

"I do have more important things to do," he purred. "But I find myself unable to resist the temptation. The same way you can't resist watching me whenever we're out. So territorial."

My mouth went a bit dry. But—flirting with him, fighting with him . . . It was easy. Fun.

Maybe I deserved both of those things.

So I closed the distance between us, smoothly stepped past him, and said, "*You* haven't been able to keep away from me since Calanmai, it seems."

Something rippled in his eyes that I couldn't place, but he flicked my nose—hard enough that I hissed and batted his hand away.

"I can't wait to see what that sharp tongue of yours can do at the Summer Court," he said, gaze fixed on my mouth, and vanished into shadow.

CHAPTER 32

In the end, only Amren and I joined Rhys, Cassian having failed to sway his High Lord, Azriel still off overseeing his network of spies and investigating the human realm, and Mor tasked with guarding Velaris. Rhys would winnow us directly into Adriata, the castle-city of the Summer Court—and there we would stay, for however long it took me to detect and then steal the first half of the Book.

As Rhys's newest pet, I would be granted tours of the city and the High Lord's personal residence. If we were lucky, none of them would realize that Rhys's lapdog was actually a bloodhound.

And it was a very, very good disguise.

Rhys and Amren stood in the town house foyer the next day, the rich morning sunlight streaming through the windows and pooling on the ornate carpet. Amren wore her usual shades of gray—her loose pants cut to just beneath her navel, the billowing top cropped to show the barest slice of skin along her midriff. Alluring as a calm sea under a cloudy sky.

Rhys was in head-to-toe black accented with silver thread—no wings. The cool, cultured male I'd first met. His favorite mask.

For my own, I'd selected a flowing lilac dress, its skirts floating on a phantom wind beneath the silver-and-pearl-crusted belt at my waist. Matching night-blooming silver flowers had been embroidered to climb from the hem to brush my thighs, and a few more twined down the folds at my shoulders. The perfect gown to combat the warmth of the Summer Court.

It swished and sighed as I descended the last two stairs into the foyer. Rhys surveyed me with a long, unreadable sweep from my silver-slippered feet to my half-up hair. Nuala had curled the strands that had been left down—soft, supple curls that brought out the gold in my hair.

Rhys simply said, "Good. Let's go."

My mouth popped open, but Amren explained with a broad, feline smile, "He's pissy this morning."

"Why?" I asked, watching Amren take Rhys's hand, her delicate fingers dwarfed by his. He held out the other to me.

"Because," Rhys answered for her, "I stayed out late with Cassian and Azriel, and they took me for all I was worth in cards."

"Sore loser?" I gripped his hand. His calluses scraped against my own—the only reminder of the trained warrior beneath the clothes and veneer.

"I am when my brothers tag-team me," he grumbled. He offered no warning before we vanished on a midnight wind, and then—

Then I was squinting at the glaring sun off a turquoise sea, just as I was trying to reorder my body around the dry, suffocating heat, even with the cooling breeze off the water.

I blinked a few times—and that was as much reaction as I let myself show as I yanked my hand from Rhys's grip.

We seemed to be standing on a landing platform at the base of a tan stone palace, the building itself perched atop a mountain-island in the heart of a half-moon bay. The city spread around and below us, toward that sparkling sea—the buildings all from that stone, or glimmering white material that might have been coral or pearl. Gulls flapped over the many turrets and spires, no clouds above them, nothing on the breeze with them but salty air and the clatter of the city below.

Various bridges connected the bustling island to the larger landmass that circled it on three sides, one of them currently raising itself so a many-masted ship could cruise through. Indeed, there were more ships than I could count—some merchant vessels, some fishing ones, and some, it seemed, ferrying people from the island-city to the mainland, whose sloping shores were crammed full of more buildings, more people.

More people like the half dozen before us, framed by a pair of sea glass doors that opened into the palace itself. On our little balcony, there was no option to escape—no path out but winnowing away . . . or going through those doors. Or, I supposed, the plunge awaiting us to the red roofs of the fine houses a hundred feet below.

"Welcome to Adriata," said the tall male in the center of the group.

And I knew him—remembered him.

Not from memory. I'd already remembered that the handsome High Lord of Summer had rich brown skin, white hair, and eyes of crushing, turquoise blue. I'd already remembered he'd been forced to watch as his courtier's mind was invaded and then his life snuffed out by Rhysand. As Rhysand lied to Amarantha about what he'd learned, and spared the male from a fate perhaps worse than death.

No—I now remembered the High Lord of Summer in a way I couldn't quite explain, like some fragment of me knew it had come from him, from here. Like some piece of me said, *I remember, I remember, I remember. We are one and the same, you and I.*

Rhys merely drawled, "Good to see you again, Tarquin."

The five other people behind the High Lord of Summer swapped frowns of varying severity. Like their lord, their skin was dark, their hair in shades of white or silver, as if they had lived under the bright sun their entire lives. Their eyes, however, were of every color. And they now shifted between me and Amren.

Rhys slid one hand into a pocket and gestured with the other to

Amren. "Amren, I think you know. Though you haven't met her since your . . . promotion." Cool, calculating grace, edged with steel.

Tarquin gave Amren the briefest of nods. "Welcome back to the city, lady."

Amren didn't nod, or bow, or so much as curtsy. She looked over Tarquin, tall and muscled, his clothes of sea-green and blue and gold, and said, "At least you are far more handsome than your cousin. He was an eyesore." A female behind Tarquin outright glared. Amren's red lips stretched wide. "Condolences, of course," she added with as much sincerity as a snake.

Wicked, cruel—that's what Amren and Rhys were . . . what *I* was to be to these people.

Rhys gestured to me. "I don't believe you two were ever formally introduced Under the Mountain. Tarquin, Feyre. Feyre, Tarquin." No titles here—either to unnerve them or because Rhys found them a waste of breath.

Tarquin's eyes—such stunning, crystal blue—fixed on me.

I remember you, I remember you, I remember you.

The High Lord did not smile.

I kept my face neutral, vaguely bored.

His gaze drifted to my chest, the bare skin revealed by the sweeping vee of my gown, as if he could see where that spark of life, his power, had gone.

Rhys followed that gaze. "Her breasts *are* rather spectacular, aren't they? Delicious as ripe apples."

I fought the urge to scowl, and instead slid my attention to him, as indolently as he'd looked at me, at the others. "Here I was, thinking you had a fascination with my mouth."

Delighted surprise lit Rhys's eyes, there and gone in a heartbeat.

We both looked back to our hosts, still stone-faced and stiff-backed.

Tarquin seemed to weigh the air between my companions and me, then said carefully, "You have a tale to tell, it seems."

"We have many tales to tell," Rhys said, jerking his chin toward the glass doors behind them. "So why not get comfortable?"

The female a half-step behind Tarquin inched closer. "We have refreshments prepared."

Tarquin seemed to remember her and put a hand on her slim shoulder. "Cresseida—Princess of Adriata."

The ruler of his capital—or wife? There was no ring on either of their fingers, and I didn't recognize her from Under the Mountain. Her long, silver hair blew across her pretty face in the briny breeze, and I didn't mistake the light in her brown eyes for anything but razor-sharp cunning. "A pleasure," she murmured huskily to me. "And an honor."

My breakfast turned to lead in my gut, but I didn't let her see what the groveling did to me; let her realize it was ammunition. Instead I gave her my best imitation of Rhysand's shrug. "The honor's mine, princess."

The others were hastily introduced: three advisers who oversaw the city, the court, and the trade. And then a broad-shouldered, handsome male named Varian, Cresseida's younger brother, captain of Tarquin's guard, and Prince of Adriata. His attention was fixed wholly on Amren—as if he knew where the biggest threat lay. And would be happy to kill her, if given the chance.

In the brief time I'd known her, Amren had never looked more delighted.

We were led into a palace crafted of shell-flecked walkways and walls, countless windows looking out to the bay and mainland or the open sea beyond. Sea glass chandeliers swayed on the warm breeze over gurgling streams and fountains of fresh water. High fae—servants and courtiers—hurried across and around them, most brown-skinned and clad in loose, light clothing, all far too preoccupied with their own matters to take note or interest in our presence. No lesser faeries crossed our path—not one.

I kept a step behind Rhysand as he walked at Tarquin's side, that mighty power of his leashed and dimmed, the others flowing behind us. Amren remained within reach, and I wondered if she was also to be my bodyguard. Tarquin and Rhys had been talking lightly, both already sounding bored, of the approaching Nynsar—of the native flowers that both courts would display for the minor, brief holiday.

Calanmai wouldn't be too long after that.

My stomach twisted. If Tamlin was intent on upholding tradition, if I was no longer with him . . . I didn't let myself get that far down the road. It wouldn't be fair. To me—to him.

"We have four main cities in my territory," Tarquin said to me, looking over his muscled shoulder. "We spend the last month of winter and first spring months in Adriata—it's finest at this time of year."

Indeed, I supposed that with endless summer, there was no limit to how one might enjoy one's time. In the country, by the sea, in a city under the stars . . . I nodded. "It's very beautiful."

Tarquin stared at me long enough that Rhys said, "The repairs have been going well, I take it."

That hauled Tarquin's attention back. "Mostly. There remains much to be done. The back half of the castle is a wreck. But, as you can see, we've finished most of the inside. We focused on the city first—and those repairs are ongoing."

Amarantha had sacked the city? Rhys said, "I hope no valuables were lost during its occupation."

"Not the most important things, thank the Mother," Tarquin said.

Behind me, Cresseida tensed. The three advisers peeled off to attend to other duties, murmuring farewell—with wary looks in Tarquin's direction. As if this might very well be the first time he'd needed to play host and *they* were watching their High Lord's every move.

He gave them a smile that didn't reach his eyes, and said nothing more as he led us into a vaulted room of white oak and green glass—overlooking the mouth of the bay and the sea that stretched on forever.

I had never seen water so vibrant. Green and cobalt and midnight. And for a heartbeat, a palette of paint flashed in my mind, along with the blue and yellow and white and black I might need to paint it . . .

"This is my favorite view," Tarquin said beside me, and I realized I'd gone to the wide windows while the others had seated themselves around the mother-of-pearl table. A handful of servants were heaping fruits, leafy greens, and steamed shellfish onto their plates.

"You must be very proud," I said, "to have such stunning lands."

Tarquin's eyes—so like the sea beyond us—slid to me. "How do they compare to the ones you have seen?" Such a carefully crafted question.

I said dully, "Everything in Prythian is lovely, when compared to the mortal realm."

"And is being immortal lovelier than being human?"

I could feel everyone's attention on us, even as Rhys engaged Cresseida and Varian in bland, edged discussion about the status of their fish markets. So I looked the High Lord of Summer up and down, as he had examined me, brazenly and without a shred of politeness, and then said, "You tell me."

Tarquin's eyes crinkled. "You are a pearl. Though I knew that the day you threw that bone at Amarantha and splattered mud on her favorite dress."

I shut out the memories, the blind terror of that first trial.

What did he make of that tug between us—did he realize it was his own power, or think it was a bond of its own, some sort of strange allure?

And if I had to steal from him . . . perhaps that meant getting closer. "I do not remember you being quite so handsome Under the Mountain. The sunlight and sea suit you."

A lesser male might have preened. But Tarquin knew better—knew that I had been with Tamlin, and was now with Rhys, and had now been brought here. Perhaps he thought me no better than Ianthe. "How, exactly, do you fit within Rhysand's court?"

A direct question, after such roundabout ones—to no doubt get me on uneven footing.

It almost worked—I nearly admitted, "*I don't know*," but Rhys said from the table, as if he'd heard every word, "Feyre is a member of my Inner Circle. And is my Emissary to the Mortal Lands."

Cresseida, seated beside him, said, "Do you have much contact with the mortal realm?"

I took that as an invitation to sit—and get away from the too-heavy stare of Tarquin. A seat had been left open for me at Amren's side, across from Rhys.

The High Lord of the Night Court sniffed at his wine—white, sparkling—and I wondered if he was trying to piss them off by implying they'd poisoned it as he said, "I prefer to be prepared for every potential situation. And, given that Hybern seems set on making themselves a nuisance, striking up a conversation with the humans might be in our best interest."

Varian drew his focus away from Amren long enough to say roughly, "So it's been confirmed, then? Hybern is readying for war."

"They're done readying," Rhys drawled, at last sipping from his wine. Amren didn't touch her plate, though she pushed things around as she always did. I wondered what—who—she'd eat while here. Varian seemed like a good guess. "War is imminent."

"Yes, you mentioned that in your letter," Tarquin said, claiming the seat at the head of the table between Rhys and Amren. A bold move, to situate himself between two such powerful beings. Arrogance—or an attempt at friendship? Tarquin's gaze again drifted to me before focusing on Rhys. "And you know that against Hybern, we will fight. We lost enough good people Under the Mountain. I have no interest in being slaves again. But if you are here to ask me to fight in another war, Rhysand—"

"That is not a possibility," Rhys smoothly cut in, "and had not even entered my mind."

My glimmer of confusion must have shown, because Cresseida crooned to me, "High Lords have gone to war for less, you know. Doing it over such an *unusual* female would be nothing unexpected."

Which was likely why they had accepted this invitation, favor or no. To feel us out.

If—if Tamlin went to war to get me back. No. No, that wouldn't be an option.

I'd written to him, told him to stay away. And he wasn't foolish enough to start a war he could not win. Not when he wouldn't be fighting other High Fae, but Illyrian warriors, led by Cassian and Azriel. It would be slaughter.

So I said, bored and flat and dull, "Try not to look too excited, princess. The High Lord of Spring has no plans to go to war with the Night Court."

"And are you in contact with Tamlin, then?" A saccharine smile.

My next words were quiet, slow, and I decided I did not mind stealing from them, not one bit. "There are things that are public knowledge, and things that are not. My relationship with him is well known. Its current standing, however, is none of your concern. Or anyone else's. But I do know Tamlin, and I know that there will be no internal war between courts—at least not over me, or *my* decisions."

"What a relief, then," Cresseida said, sipping from her white wine before cracking a large crab claw, pink and white and orange. "To know we are not harboring a stolen bride—and that we need not bother returning her to her master, as the law demands. And as any wise person might do, to keep trouble from their doorstep."

Amren had gone utterly still.

"I left of my own free will," I said. "And no one is my master."

Cresseida shrugged. "Think that all you want, lady, but the law is the law. You are—were his bride. Swearing fealty to another High Lord does not change that. So it is a very good thing that he respects your decisions. Otherwise, all it would take would be one letter from him to Tarquin, requesting your return, and we would have to obey. Or risk war ourselves."

Rhysand sighed. "You are always a joy, Cresseida."

Varian said, "Careful, High Lord. My sister speaks the truth."

Tarquin laid a hand on the pale table. "Rhysand is our guest—his courtiers are our guests. And we will treat them as such. We will treat them, Cresseida, as we treat people who saved our necks when all it would have taken was one word from them for us to be very, very dead."

Tarquin studied me and Rhysand—whose face was gloriously disinterested. The High Lord of Summer shook his head and said to Rhys, "We have more to discuss later, you and I. Tonight, I'm throwing a party for you all on my pleasure barge in the bay. After that, you're free to roam in this city wherever you wish. You will forgive its princess if she is protective of her people. Rebuilding these months has been long and hard. We do not wish to do it again any time soon."

Cresseida's eyes grew dark, haunted.

"Cresseida made many sacrifices on behalf of her people," Tarquin offered gently—to me. "Do not take her caution personally."

"We all made sacrifices," Rhysand said, the icy boredom now shifting into something razor-sharp. "And you now sit at this table with your family because of the ones Feyre made. So you will forgive *me*, Tarquin, if I tell your princess that if she sends word to Tamlin, or if any of your people try to bring her to him, their lives will be forfeit."

Even the sea breeze died.

"Do not threaten me in my own home, Rhysand," Tarquin said. "My gratitude goes only so far."

"It's not a threat," Rhys countered, the crab claws on his plate cracking open beneath invisible hands. "It's a promise."

They all looked at me, waiting for any response.

So I lifted my glass of wine, looked them each in the eye, holding Tarquin's gaze the longest, and said, "No wonder immortality never gets dull."

Tarquin chuckled—and I wondered if his loosed breath was one of profound relief.

And through that bond between us, I felt Rhysand's flicker of approval.

CHAPTER 33

We were given a suite of connecting rooms, all centered on a large, lavish lounge that was open to the sea and city below. My bedroom was appointed in seafoam and softest blue with pops of gold—like the gilded clamshell atop my pale wood dresser. I had just set it down when the white door behind me clicked open and Rhys slid in.

He leaned against the door once he shut it, the top of his black tunic unbuttoned to reveal the upper whorls of the tattoo spanning his chest.

"The problem, I've realized, will be that I like Tarquin," he said by way of greeting. "I even like Cresseida. Varian, I could live without, but I bet a few weeks with Cassian and Azriel, and he'd be thick as thieves with them and I'd have to learn to like him. Or he'd be wrapped around Amren's finger, and I'd have to leave him alone entirely or risk her wrath."

"And?" I took up a spot against the dresser, where clothes that I had not packed but were clearly of Night Court origin had been already waiting for me.

The space of the room—the large bed, the windows, the sunlight—filled the silence between us.

"And," Rhys said, "I want you to find a way to do what you have to do without making enemies of them."

"So you're telling me don't get caught."

A nod. Then, "Do you like that Tarquin can't stop looking at you? I can't tell if it's because he wants you, or because he knows you have his power and wants to see how much."

"Can't it be both?"

"Of course. But having a High Lord lusting after you is a dangerous game."

"First you taunt me with Cassian, now Tarquin? Can't you find other ways to annoy me?"

Rhys prowled closer, and I steadied myself for his scent, his warmth, the impact of his power. He braced a hand on either side of me, gripping the dresser. I refused to shrink away. "You have one task here, Feyre. One task that no one can know about. So do anything you have to in order to accomplish it. But get that book. And do not get caught."

I wasn't some simpering fool. I knew the risks. And that *tone*, that *look* he always gave me . . . "*Anything*?" His brows rose. I breathed, "If I fucked him for it, what would you do?"

His pupils flared, and his gaze dropped to my mouth. The wood dresser groaned beneath his hands. "You say such atrocious things." I waited, my heart an uneven beat. He at last met my eyes again. "You are always free to do what you want, with whomever you want. So if you want to ride him, go ahead."

"Maybe I will." Though a part of me wanted to retort, *Liar*.

"Fine." His breath caressed my mouth.

"Fine," I said, aware of every inch between us, the distance smaller and smaller, the challenge heightening with each second neither of us moved.

"Do not," he said softly, his eyes like stars, "jeopardize this mission."

"I know the cost." The sheer power of him enveloped me, shaking me awake.

The salt and the sea and the breeze tugged on me, sang to me.

And as if Rhys heard them, too, he inclined his head toward the unlit candle on the dresser. "Light it."

I debated arguing, but looked at the candle, summoning fire, summoning that hot anger he managed to rile—

The candle was knocked off the dresser by a violent splash of water, as if someone had chucked a bucketful.

I gaped at the water drenching the dresser, its dripping on the marble floor the only sound.

Rhys, hands still braced on either side of me, laughed quietly. "Can't you ever follow orders?"

But whatever it was—being here, close to Tarquin and his power . . . I could feel that water answering me. Feel it coating the floor, feel the sea churning and idling in the bay, taste the salt on the breeze. I held Rhys's gaze.

No one was my master—but I might be master of everything, if I wished. If I dared.

Like a strange rain, the water rose from the floor as I willed it to become like those stars Rhys had summoned in his blanket of darkness. I willed the droplets to separate until they hung around us, catching the light and sparkling like crystals on a chandelier.

Rhys broke my stare to study them. "I suggest," he murmured, "you not show Tarquin that little trick in the bedroom."

I sent each and every one of those droplets shooting for the High Lord's face.

Too fast, too swiftly for him to shield. Some of them sprayed me as they ricocheted off him.

Both of us now soaking, Rhys gaped a bit—then smiled. "Good work," he said, at last pushing off the dresser. He didn't bother to wipe away the water gleaming on his skin. "Keep practicing."

But I said, "Will he go to war? Over me?"

He knew who I meant. The hot temper that had been on Rhys's face moments before turned to lethal calm. "I don't know."

"I—I would go back. If it came to that, Rhysand. I'd go back, rather than make you fight."

He slid a still-wet hand into his pocket. "Would you *want* to go back? Would going to war on your behalf make you love him again? Would that be a grand gesture to win you?"

I swallowed hard. "I'm tired of death. I wouldn't want to see anyone else die—least of all for me."

"That doesn't answer my question."

"No. I wouldn't want to go back. But I would. Pain and killing wouldn't win me."

Rhys stared at me for a moment longer, his face unreadable, before he strode to the door. He stopped with his fingers on the sea urchin–shaped handle. "He locked you up because he knew—the bastard knew what a treasure you are. That you are worth more than land or gold or jewels. He knew, and wanted to keep you all to himself."

The words hit me, even as they soothed some jagged piece in my soul. "He did—does love me, Rhysand."

"The issue isn't whether he loved you, it's how much. Too much. Love can be a poison."

And then he was gone.

The bay was calm enough—perhaps willed to flatness by its lord and master—that the pleasure barge hardly rocked throughout the hours we dined and drank aboard it.

Crafted of richest wood and gold, the enormous boat was amply sized for the hundred or so High Fae trying their best not to observe every movement Rhys, Amren, and I made.

The main deck was full of low tables and couches for eating and relaxing, and on the upper level, beneath a canopy of tiles set with mother-of-pearl, our long table had been set. Tarquin was summer incarnate in turquoise and gold, bits of emerald shining at his buttons and fingers. A crown of sapphire and white gold fashioned like cresting waves sat atop his seafoam-colored hair—so exquisite that I often caught myself staring at it.

As I was now, when he turned to where I sat on his right and noticed my stare.

"You'd think with our skilled jewelers, they could make a crown a bit more comfortable. This one digs in horribly."

A pleasant enough attempt at conversation, when I'd stayed quiet throughout the first hour, instead watching the island-city, the water, the mainland—casting a net of awareness, of blind power, toward it, to see if anything answered. If the Book slumbered somewhere out there.

Nothing had answered my silent call. So I figured it was as good a time as any as I said, "How did you keep it out of her hands?"

Saying Amarantha's name here, amongst such happy, celebrating people, felt like inviting in a rain cloud.

Seated at his left, deep in conversation with Cresseida, Rhys didn't so much as look over at me. Indeed, he'd barely spoken to me earlier, not even noting my clothes.

Unusual, given that even *I* had been pleased with how I looked, and had again selected it for myself: my hair unbound and swept off my face with a headband of braided rose gold, my sleeveless, dusk-pink chiffon gown—tight in the chest and waist—the near-twin to the purple one I'd worn that morning. Feminine, soft, pretty. I hadn't felt like those things in a long, long while. Hadn't wanted to.

But here, being those things wouldn't earn me a ticket to a life of party planning. Here, I could be soft and lovely at sunset, and awaken in the morning to slide into Illyrian fighting leathers.

Tarquin said, "We managed to smuggle out most of our treasure when the territory fell. Nostrus—my predecessor—was my cousin. I served as prince of another city. So I got the order to hide the trove in the dead of night, fast as we could."

Amarantha had killed Nostrus when he'd rebelled—and executed his entire family for spite. Tarquin must have been one of the few surviving members, if the power had passed to him.

"I didn't know the Summer Court valued treasure so much," I said.

Tarquin huffed a laugh. "The earliest High Lords did. We do now out of tradition, mostly."

I said carefully, casually, "So is it gold and jewels you value, then?"

"Among other things."

I sipped my wine to buy time to think of a way to ask without raising suspicions. But maybe being direct about it would be better. "Are outsiders allowed to see the collection? My father was a merchant—I spent most of my childhood in his office, helping him with his goods. It would be interesting to compare mortal riches to those made by Fae hands."

Rhys kept talking to Cresseida, not even a hint of approval or amusement going through our bond.

Tarquin cocked his head, the jewels in his crown glinting. "Of course. Tomorrow—after lunch, perhaps?"

He wasn't stupid, and he might have been aware of the game, but . . . the offer was genuine. I smiled a bit, nodding. I looked toward the crowd milling about on the deck below, the lantern-lit water beyond, even as I felt Tarquin's gaze linger.

He said, "What was it like? The mortal world?"

I picked at the strawberry salad on my plate. "I only saw a very small slice of it. My father was called the Prince of Merchants—but I was too young to be taken on his voyages to other parts of the mortal world. When I was eleven, he lost our fortune on a shipment to Bharat. We spent the next eight years in poverty, in a backwater village near the wall. So I can't speak for the entirety of the mortal world when I say that what I saw there was . . . hard. Brutal. Here, class lines are far more blurred, it seems. There, it's defined by money. Either you have it and you don't share it, or you are left to starve and fight for your survival.

My father . . . He regained his wealth once I went to Prythian." My heart tightened, then dropped into my stomach. "And the very people who had been content to let us starve were once again our friends. I would rather face every creature in Prythian than the monsters on the other side of the wall. Without magic, without power, money has become the only thing that matters."

Tarquin's lips were pursed, but his eyes were considering. "Would you spare them if war came?"

Such a dangerous, loaded question. I wouldn't tell him what we were doing over the wall—not until Rhys had indicated we should.

"My sisters dwell with my father on his estate. For them, I would fight. But for those sycophants and peacocks . . . I would not mind to see their order disrupted." Like the hate-mongering family of Elain's betrothed.

Tarquin said very quietly, "There are some in Prythian who would think the same of the courts."

"What—get rid of the High Lords?"

"Perhaps. But mostly eliminate the inherent privileges of High Fae over the lesser faeries. Even the terms imply a level of unfairness. Maybe it is more like the human realm than you realize, not as blurred as it might seem. In some courts, the lowest of High Fae servants has more rights than the wealthiest of lesser faeries."

I became aware that we were not the only people on the barge, at this table. And that we were surrounded by High Fae with animal-keen hearing. "Do you agree with them? That it should change?"

"I am a young High Lord," he said. "Barely eighty years old." So he'd been thirty when Amarantha took over. "Perhaps others might call me inexperienced or foolish, but I have seen those cruelties firsthand, and known many good lesser faeries who suffered for merely being born on the wrong side of power. Even within my own residences, the confines of tradition pressure me to enforce the rules of my predecessors: the lesser faeries are neither to be seen nor heard as they work. I would like to one day see a Prythian in which they have a voice, both in my home and in the world beyond it."

I scanned him for any deceit, manipulation. I found none.

Steal from him—I *would* steal from him. But what if I asked instead? Would he give it to me, or would the traditions of his ancestors run too deep?

"Tell me what that look means," Tarquin said, bracing his muscled arms on the gold tablecloth.

I said baldly, "I'm thinking it would be very easy to love you. And easier to call you my friend."

He smiled at me—broad and without restraint. "I would not object to either."

Easy—very easy to fall in love with a kind, considerate male.

But I glanced over at Cresseida, who was now almost in Rhysand's lap. And Rhysand was smiling like a cat, one finger tracing circles on the back of her hand while she bit her lip and beamed. I faced Tarquin, my brows high in silent question.

He made a face and shook his head.

I hoped they went to her room.

Because if I had to listen to Rhys bed her . . . I didn't let myself finish the thought.

Tarquin mused, "It has been many years since I saw her look like that."

My cheeks heated—shame. Shame for what? Wanting to throttle her for no good reason? Rhysand teased and taunted me—he never . . . seduced me, with those long, intent stares, the half smiles that were pure Illyrian arrogance.

I supposed I'd been granted that gift once—and had used it up and fought for it and broken it. And I supposed that Rhysand, for all he had sacrificed and done . . . He deserved it as much as Cresseida.

Even if . . . even if for a moment, I wanted it.

I wanted to feel like that again.

And . . . I was lonely.

I had been lonely, I realized, for a very, very long time.

Rhys leaned in to hear something Cresseida was saying, her lips brushing his ear, her hand now entwining with his.

And it wasn't sorrow, or despair, or terror that hit me, but . . . unhappiness. Such bleak, sharp unhappiness that I got to my feet.

Rhys's eyes shifted toward me, at last remembering I existed, and there was nothing on his face—no hint that he felt any of what I did through our bond. I didn't care if I had no shield, if my thoughts were wide open and he read them like a book. He didn't seem to care, either. He went back to chuckling at whatever Cresseida was telling him, sliding closer.

Tarquin had risen to his feet, scanning me and Rhys.

I was unhappy—not just broken. But unhappy.

An emotion, I realized. It was an emotion, rather than the unending emptiness or survival-driven terror.

"I need some fresh air," I said, even though we were in the open. But with the golden lights, the people up and down the table . . . I needed to find a spot on this barge where I could be alone, just for a moment, mission or no.

"Would you like me to join you?"

I looked at the High Lord of Summer. I hadn't lied. It would be easy to fall in love with a male like him. But I wasn't entirely sure that even with the hardships he'd encountered Under the Mountain, Tarquin could understand the darkness that might always be in me. Not only from Amarantha, but from years spent being hungry, and desperate.

That I might always be a little bit vicious or restless. That I might crave peace, but never a cage of comfort.

"I'm fine, thank you," I said, and headed for the sweeping staircase that led down onto the stern of the ship—brightly lit, but quieter than the main areas at the prow. Rhys didn't so much as look in my direction as I walked away. Good riddance.

I was halfway down the wood steps when I spotted Amren and Varian—both leaning against adjacent pillars, both drinking wine, both ignoring each other. Even as they spoke to no one else.

Perhaps that was another reason why she'd come: to distract Tarquin's watchdog.

I reached the main deck, found a spot by the wooden railing that was a bit more shadowed than the rest, and leaned against it. Magic propelled the boat—no oars, no sails. So we moved through the bay, silent and smooth, hardly a ripple in our wake.

I didn't realize I'd been waiting for him until the barge docked at the base of the island-city, and I'd somehow spent the entire final hour alone.

When I filed onto land with the rest of the crowd, Amren, Varian, and Tarquin were waiting for me at the docks, all a bit stiff-backed.

Rhysand and Cresseida were nowhere to be seen.

CHAPTER 34

Mercifully, there was no sound from his closed bedroom. And no sounds came out of it during that night, when I jolted awake from a nightmare of being turned over a spit, and couldn't remember where I was.

Moonlight danced on the sea beyond my open windows, and there was silence—such silence.

A weapon. I was a weapon to find that book, to stop the king from breaking the wall, to stop whatever he had planned for Jurian and the war that might destroy my world. That might destroy this place—and a High Lord who might very well overturn the order of things.

For a heartbeat, I missed Velaris, missed the lights and the music and the Rainbow. I missed the cozy warmth of the town house to welcome me in from the crisp winter, missed . . . what it had been like to be a part of their little unit.

Maybe wrapping his wings around me, writing me notes, had been Rhys's way of ensuring his weapon didn't break beyond repair.

That was fine—fair enough. We owed each other nothing beyond our promises to work and fight together.

He could still be my friend. Companion—whatever this thing was between us. His taking someone to his bed didn't change those things.

It'd just been a relief to think that for a moment, he might have been as lonely as me.

✠

I didn't have the nerve to come out of my room for breakfast, to see if Rhys had returned.

To see whom he came to breakfast with.

I had nothing else to do, I told myself as I lay in bed, until my lunch-time visit with Tarquin. So I stayed there until the servants came in, apologized for disturbing me, and started to leave. I stopped them, saying I'd bathe while they cleaned the room. They were polite—if nervous—and merely nodded as I did as I'd claimed.

I took my time in the bath. And behind the locked door, I let that kernel of Tarquin's power come out, first making the water rise from the tub, then shaping little animals and creatures out of it.

It was about as close to transformation as I'd let myself go. Contemplating how I might give myself animalistic features only made me shaky, sick. I could ignore it, ignore that occasional scrape of claws in my blood for a while yet.

I was on to water-butterflies flitting through the room when I realized I'd been in the tub long enough that the bath had gone cold.

Like the night before, Nuala walked through the walls from wherever *she* was staying in the palace, and dressed me, somehow attuned to when I'd be ready. Cerridwen, she told me, had drawn the short stick and was seeing to Amren. I didn't have the nerve to ask about Rhys, either.

Nuala selected seafoam green accented with rose gold, curling and then braiding back my hair in a thick, loose plait glimmering with bits of pearl. Whether Nuala knew why I was there, what I'd be doing, she didn't say. But she took extra care of my face, brightening my lips with raspberry pink, dusting my cheeks with the faintest blush. I might have looked innocent, charming—were it not for my gray-blue eyes. More hollow than they'd been last night, when I'd admired myself in the mirror.

I'd seen enough of the palace to navigate to where Tarquin had said to meet before we bid good night. The main hall was situated on a level about halfway up—the perfect meeting place for those who dwelled in the spires above and those who worked unseen and unheard below.

This level held all the various council rooms, ballrooms, dining rooms, and whatever other rooms might be needed for visitors, events, gatherings. Access to the residential levels from which I'd come was guarded by four soldiers at each stairwell—all of whom watched me carefully as I waited against a seashell pillar for their High Lord. I wondered if he could sense that I'd been playing with his power in the bathtub, that the piece of him he'd yielded was now here and answering to me.

Tarquin emerged from one of the adjacent rooms as the clock struck two—followed by my own companions.

Rhysand's gaze swept over me, noting the clothes that were obviously in honor of my host and his people. Noting the way I did not meet his eyes, or Cresseida's, as I looked solely at Tarquin and Amren beside him—Varian now striding off to the soldiers at the stairs—and gave them both a bland, close-lipped smile.

"You're looking well today," Tarquin said, inclining his head.

Nuala, it seemed, was a spectacularly good spy. Tarquin's pewter tunic was accented with the same shade of seafoam green as my clothes. We might as well have been a matching set. I supposed with my brown-gold hair and pale skin, I was his mirror opposite.

I could feel Rhys still assessing me.

I shut him out. Maybe I'd send a water-dog barking after him later—let it bite him in the ass.

"I hope I'm not interrupting," I said to Amren.

Amren shrugged her slim shoulders, clad in flagstone gray today. "We were finishing up a rather lively debate about armadas and who might be in charge of a unified front. Did you know," she said, "that before they became so big and powerful, Tarquin and Varian led Nostrus's fleet?"

Varian, several feet away, stiffened, but did not turn.

I met Tarquin's eye. "You didn't mention you were a sailor." It was an effort to sound intrigued, like I had nothing at all bothering me.

Tarquin rubbed his neck. "I had planned to tell you during our tour." He held out an arm. "Shall we?"

Not one word—I had not uttered one word to Rhysand. And I wasn't about to start as I looped my arm through Tarquin's, and said to none of them in particular, "See you later."

Something brushed against my mental shield, a rumble of something dark—powerful.

Perhaps a warning to be careful.

Though it felt an awful lot like the dark, flickering emotion that had haunted me—so much like it that I stepped a bit closer to Tarquin. And then I gave the High Lord of Summer a pretty, mindless smile that I had not given to *anyone* in a long, long time.

That brush of emotion went silent on the other side of my shields.

Good.

✢

Tarquin brought me to a hall of jewels and treasure so vast that I gawked for a good minute. A minute that I used to scan the shelves for any twinkle of feeling—anything that *felt* like the male at my side, like the power I'd summoned in the bathtub.

"And this is—this is just *one* of the troves?" The room had been carved deep beneath the castle, behind a heavy lead door that had only opened when Tarquin placed his hand on it. I didn't dare get close enough to the lock to see if it might work under my touch—*his* feigned signature.

A fox in the chicken coop. That's what I was.

Tarquin loosed a chuckle. "My ancestors were greedy bastards."

I shook my head, striding to the shelves built into the wall. Solid stone—no way to break in, unless I tunneled through the mountain itself. Or if someone winnowed me. Though there were likely wards similar to those on the town house and the House of Wind.

Boxes overflowed with jewels and pearls and uncut gems, gold heaped in trunks so high it spilled onto the cobblestone floor. Suits of ornate armor stood guard against one wall; dresses woven of cobwebs and starlight leaned against another. There were swords and daggers of every sort. But no books. Not one.

"Do you know the history behind each piece?"

"Some," he said. "I haven't had much time to learn about it all."

Good—maybe he wouldn't know about the Book, wouldn't miss it.

I turned in a circle. "What's the most valuable thing in here?"

"Thinking of stealing?"

I choked on a laugh. "Wouldn't asking that question make me a lousy thief?"

Lying, two-faced wretch—that's what asking *that* question made me.

Tarquin studied me. "I'd say I'm looking at the most valuable thing in here."

I didn't fake the blush. "You're—very kind."

His smile was soft. As if his position had not yet broken the compassion in him. I hoped it never did. "Honestly, I don't know what's the most valuable thing. These are all priceless heirlooms of my house."

I walked up to a shelf, scanning. A necklace of rubies was splayed on a velvet pillow—each of them the size of a robin's egg. It'd take a tremendous female to wear that necklace, to dominate the gems and not the other way around.

On another shelf, a necklace of pearls. Then sapphires.

And on another . . . a necklace of black diamonds.

Each of the dark stones was a mystery—and an answer. Each of them slumbered.

Tarquin came up behind me, peering over my shoulder at what had snagged my interest. His gaze drifted to my face. "Take it."

"What?" I whirled to him.

He rubbed the back of his neck. "As a thank-you. For Under the Mountain."

Ask it now—ask him for the Book instead.

But that would require trust, and . . . kind as he was, he was a High Lord.

He pulled the box from its resting spot and shut the lid before handing it to me. "You were the first person who didn't laugh at my idea to break down class barriers. Even Cresseida snickered when I told her. If you won't accept the necklace for saving us, then take it for that."

"It is a good idea, Tarquin. Appreciating it doesn't mean you have to reward me."

He shook his head. "Just take it."

It would insult him if I refused—so I closed my hands around the box.

Tarquin said, "It will suit you in the Night Court."

"Perhaps I'll stay here and help you revolutionize the world."

His mouth twisted to the side. "I could use an ally in the North."

Was that why he had brought me? Why he'd given me the gift? I hadn't realized how alone we were down here, that I was beneath ground, in a place that could be easily sealed—

"You have nothing to fear from me," he said, and I wondered if my scent was that readable. "But I meant it—you have . . . sway with Rhysand. And he is notoriously difficult to deal with. He gets what he wants, has plans he does not tell anyone about until after he's completed them, and does not apologize for any of it. Be his emissary to the human realm—but also be ours. You've seen my city. I have three others like it. Amarantha wrecked them almost immediately after she took over. All my people want now is peace, and safety, and to never have to look over their shoulders again. Other High Lords have told me about Rhys—and warned me about him. But he spared me Under the Mountain. Brutius was my cousin, and we had forces gathering in all of our cities to storm Under the Mountain. They caught him sneaking out through the tunnels to meet with them. Rhys saw that in Brutius's mind—I know he did. And yet he lied to her face, and defied her when she gave the order to turn him into a living ghost. Maybe it was for his own schemes, but I know it was a mercy. He knows that I am young—and inexperienced, and he spared me." Tarquin shook his head, mostly at himself. "Sometimes, I think Rhysand . . . I think he might have been her whore to spare us all from her full attention."

I would betray nothing of what I knew. But I suspected he could see it in my eyes—the sorrow at the thought.

"I know I'm supposed to look at you," Tarquin said, "and see that he's made you into a pet, into a monster. But I see the kindness in you. And I think that reflects more on him than anything. I think it shows that you and he might have many secrets—"

"Stop," I blurted. "Just—stop. You know I can't tell you anything. And I can't promise you anything. Rhysand is High Lord. I only serve in his court."

Tarquin glanced at the ground. "Forgive me if I've been forward. I'm still learning how to play the games of these courts—to my advisers' chagrin."

"I hope you never learn how to play the games of these courts."

Tarquin held my gaze, face wary, but a bit bleak. "Then allow me to ask you a blunt question. Is it true you left Tamlin because he locked you up in his house?"

I tried to block out the memory, the terror and agony of my heart breaking apart. But I nodded.

"And is it true that you were saved from confinement by the Night Court?"

I nodded again.

Tarquin said, "The Spring Court is my southern neighbor. I have tenuous ties with them. But unless asked, I will not mention that you were here."

Thief, liar, manipulator. I didn't deserve his alliance.

But I bowed my head in thanks. "Any other treasure troves to show me?"

"Are gold and jewels not impressive enough? What of your merchant's eye?"

I tapped the box. "Oh, I got what I wanted. Now I'm curious to see how much your alliance is worth."

Tarquin laughed, the sound bouncing off the stone and wealth around us. "I didn't feel like going to my meetings this afternoon, anyway."

"What a reckless, wild young High Lord."

Tarquin linked elbows with me again, patting my arm as he led me from the chamber. "You know, I think it might be very easy to love you, too, Feyre. Easier to be your friend."

I made myself look away shyly as he sealed the door shut behind us, placing a palm flat on the space above the handle. I listened to the click of locks sliding into place.

He took me to other rooms beneath his palace, some full of jewels, others weapons, others clothes from eras long since past. He showed me one full of books, and my heart leaped—but there was nothing in there. Nothing but leather and dust and quiet. No trickle of power that felt like the male beside me—no hint of the book I needed.

Tarquin brought me to one last room, full of crates and stacks covered in sheets. And as I beheld all the artwork looming beyond the open door I said, "I think I've seen enough for today."

He asked no questions as he resealed the chamber and escorted me back to the busy, sunny upper levels.

There had to be other places where it might be stored. Unless it was in another city.

I had to find it. Soon. There was only so long Rhys and Amren could draw out their political debates before we had to go home. I just prayed I'd find it fast enough—and not hate myself any more than I currently did.

+

Rhysand was lounging on my bed as if he owned it.

I took one look at the hands crossed behind his head, the long legs draped over the edge of the mattress, and ground my teeth. "What do you want?" I shut the door loud enough to emphasize the bite in my words.

"Flirting and giggling with Tarquin did you no good, I take it?"

I chucked the box onto the bed beside him. "You tell me."

The smile faltered as he sat up, flipping open the lid. "This isn't the Book."

"No, but it's a beautiful gift."

"You want me to buy you jewelry, Feyre, then say the word. Though given your wardrobe, I thought you were aware that it was *all* bought for you."

I hadn't realized, but I said, "Tarquin is a good male—a good High Lord. You should just *ask* him for the damned Book."

Rhys snapped shut the lid. "So he plies you with jewels and pours honey in your ear, and now you feel bad?"

"He wants your alliance—desperately. He wants to trust you, rely on you."

"Well, Cresseida is under the impression that her cousin is rather ambitious, so I'd be careful to read between his words."

"Oh? Did she tell you that before, during, or after you took her to bed?"

Rhys stood in a graceful, slow movement. "Is that why you wouldn't look at me? Because you think I fucked her for information?"

"Information or your own pleasure, I don't care."

He came around the bed, and I stood my ground, even as he stopped with hardly a hand's breadth between us. "Jealous, Feyre?"

"If I'm jealous, then you're jealous about Tarquin and his honey pouring."

Rhysand's teeth flashed. "Do you think I particularly like having to flirt with a lonely female to get information about her court, her High Lord? Do you think I feel good about myself, doing that? Do you think I enjoy doing it just so you have the space to ply Tarquin with your smiles and pretty eyes, so we can get the Book and go home?"

"You seemed to enjoy yourself plenty last night."

His snarl was soft—vicious. "I didn't take her to bed. She wanted to, but I didn't so much as kiss her. I took her out for a drink in the city, let her talk about her life, her pressures, and brought her back to her room, and went no farther than the door. I waited for you at breakfast, but you slept in. Or avoided me, apparently. And I tried to catch your eye this afternoon, but you were *so good* at shutting me out completely."

"Is that what got under your skin? That I shut you out, or that it was so easy for Tarquin to get in?"

"What got under my skin," Rhys said, his breathing a bit uneven, "is that you *smiled* at him."

The rest of the world faded to mist as the words sank in. "You are jealous."

He shook his head, stalking to the little table against the far wall and knocking back a glass of amber liquid. He braced his hands on the table, the powerful muscles of his back quivering beneath his shirt as the shadow of those wings struggled to take form.

"I heard what you told him," he said. "That you thought it would be easy to fall in love with him. You meant it, too."

"So?" It was the only thing I could think of to say.

"I was jealous—of that. That I'm not . . . that sort of person. For anyone. The Summer Court has always been neutral; they only showed backbone during those years Under the Mountain. I spared Tarquin's life because I'd heard how he wanted to even out the playing field between High Fae and lesser faeries. I've been trying to do that for years. Unsuccessfully, but . . . I spared him for that alone. And Tarquin, with his neutral court . . . he will never have to worry about someone walking away because the threat against their life, their children's lives, will always be there. So, yes, I was jealous of him—because it will always be easy for him. And he will never know what it is to look up at the night sky and wish."

The Court of Dreams.

The people who knew that there was a price, and one worth paying, for that dream. The bastard-born warriors, the Illyrian half-breed, the monster trapped in a beautiful body, the dreamer born into a court of nightmares . . . And the huntress with an artist's soul.

And perhaps because it was the most vulnerable thing he'd said to me, perhaps it was the burning in my eyes, but I walked to where he stood over the little bar. I didn't look at him as I took the decanter of amber liquid and poured myself a knuckle's length, then refilled his.

But I met his stare as I clinked my glass against his, the crystal ringing clear and bright over the crashing sea far below, and said, "To the people who look at the stars and wish, Rhys."

He picked up his glass, his gaze so piercing that I wondered why I had bothered blushing at all for Tarquin.

Rhys clinked his glass against mine. "To the stars who listen—and the dreams that are answered."

CHAPTER 35

Two days passed. Every moment of it was a balancing act of truth and lies. Rhys saw to it that I was not invited to the meetings he and Amren held to distract my kind host, granting me time to scour the city for any hint of the Book.

But not too eagerly; not too intently. I could not look too intrigued as I wandered the streets and docks, could not ask too many leading questions of the people I encountered about the treasures and legends of Adriata. Even when I awoke at dawn, I made myself wait until a reasonable hour before setting out into the city, made myself take an extended bath to secretly practice that water-magic. And while crafting water-animals grew tedious after an hour . . . it came to me easily. Perhaps because of my proximity to Tarquin, perhaps because of whatever affinity for water was already in my blood, my soul—though I certainly was in no position to ask.

Once breakfast had finally been served and consumed, I made sure to look a bit bored and aimless when I finally strode through the shining halls of the palace on my way out into the awakening city.

Hardly anyone recognized me as I casually examined shops and houses and bridges for any glimmer of a spell that *felt* like Tarquin, though I doubted they had reason to. It had been the High Fae—the nobility—that had been kept Under the Mountain. These people had been left here . . . to be tormented.

Scars littered the buildings, the streets, from what had been done in retaliation for their rebellion: burn marks, gouged bits of stone, entire buildings turned to rubble. The back of the castle, as Tarquin had claimed, was indeed in the middle of being repaired. Three turrets were half shattered, the tan stone charred and crumbling. No sign of the Book. Workers toiled there—and throughout the city—to fix those broken areas.

Just as the people I saw—High Fae and faeries with scales and gills and long, spindly webbed fingers—all seemed to be slowly healing. There were scars and missing limbs on more than I could count. But in their eyes . . . in their eyes, light gleamed.

I had saved them, too.

Freed them from whatever horrors had occurred during those five decades.

I had done a terrible thing to save them . . . but I had saved them.

And it would never be enough to atone, but . . . I did not feel quite so heavy, despite not finding a glimmer of the Book's presence, when I returned to the palace atop the hill on the third night to await Rhysand's report on the day's meetings—and learn if he'd managed to discover anything, too.

As I strode up the steps of the palace, cursing myself for remaining so out of shape even with Cassian's lessons, I spied Amren perched on the ledge of a turret balcony, cleaning her nails.

Varian leaned against the threshold of another tower balcony within jumping range—and I wondered if he was debating if he could clear the distance fast enough to push her off.

A cat playing with a dog—that's what it was. Amren was practically washing herself, silently daring him to get close enough to sniff. I doubted Varian would like her claws.

Unless that was why he hounded her day and night.

I shook my head, continuing up the steps—watching as the tide swept out.

The sunset-stained sky caught on the water and tidal muck. A little night breeze whispered past, and I leaned into it, letting it cool the sweat on me. There had once been a time when I'd dreaded the end of summer, had prayed it would hold out for as long as possible. Now the thought of endless warmth and sun made me . . . bored. Restless.

I was about to turn back to the stairs when I beheld the bit of land that had been revealed near the tidal causeway. The small building.

No wonder I hadn't seen it, as I'd never been up this high in the day when the tide was out . . . And during the rest of the day, from the muck and seaweed now gleaming on it, it would have been utterly covered.

Even now, it was half submerged. But I couldn't tear my eyes from it.

Like it was a little piece of home, wet and miserable-looking as it was, and I need only hurry along the muddy causeway between the quieter part of the city and the mainland—fast, fast, fast, so I might catch it before it vanished beneath the waves again.

But the site was too visible, and from the distance, I couldn't definitively tell if it *was* the Book contained within.

We'd have to be absolutely certain before we went in—to warrant the risks in searching. Absolutely certain.

I wished I didn't, but I realized I already had a plan for that, too.

We dined with Tarquin, Cresseida, and Varian in their family dining room—a sure sign that the High Lord did indeed want that alliance, ambition or no.

Varian was studying Amren as if he was trying to solve a riddle she'd posed to him, and she paid him no heed whatsoever as she debated with

Cresseida about the various translations of some ancient text. I'd been leading up to my question, telling Tarquin of the things I'd seen in his city that day—the fresh fish I'd bought for myself on the docks.

"You ate it right there," Tarquin said, lifting his brows.

Rhys had propped his head on a fist as I said, "They fried it with the other fishermen's lunches. Didn't charge me extra for it."

Tarquin let out an impressed laugh. "I can't say I've ever done that—sailor or no."

"You should," I said, meaning every word. "It was delicious."

I'd worn the necklace he'd given me, and Nuala and I planned my clothes around it. We'd decided on gray—a soft, dove shade—to show off the glittering black. I had worn nothing else—no earrings, no bracelets, no rings. Tarquin had seemed pleased by it, even though Varian had choked when he beheld me in an heirloom of his household. Cresseida, surprisingly, had told me it suited me and it didn't fit in here, anyway. A backhanded compliment—but praise enough.

"Well, maybe I'll go tomorrow. If you'll join me."

I grinned at Tarquin—aware of every one I offered him, now that Rhys had mentioned it. Beyond his giving me brief, nightly updates on their lack of progress with discovering anything about the Book, we hadn't really spoken since that evening I'd filled his glass—though it had been because of our own full days, not awkwardness.

"I'd like that," I said. "Perhaps we could go for a walk in the morning down the causeway when the tide is out. There's that little building along the way—it looks fascinating."

Cresseida stopped speaking, but I went on, sipping from my wine. "I figure since I've seen most of the city now, I could see it on my way to visit some of the mainland, too."

Tarquin's glance at Cresseida was all the confirmation I needed.

That stone building indeed guarded what we sought.

"It's a temple ruin," Tarquin said blandly—the lie smooth as silk. "Just mud and seaweed at this point. We've been meaning to repair it for years."

"Maybe we'll take the bridge then. I've had enough of mud for a while."

Remember that I saved you, that I fought the Middengard Wyrm—forget the threat . . .

Tarquin's eyes held mine—for a moment too long.

In the span of a blink, I hurled my silent, hidden power toward him, a spear aimed toward his mind, those wary eyes.

There was a shield in place—a shield of sea glass and coral and the undulating sea.

I became that sea, became the whisper of waves against stone, the glimmer of sunlight on a gull's white wings. I became *him*—became that mental shield.

And then I was through it, a clear, dark tether showing me the way back should I need it. I let instinct, no doubt granted from Rhys, guide me forward. To what I needed to see.

Tarquin's thoughts hit me like pebbles. *Why does she ask about the temple? Of all the things to bring up . . .* Around me, they continued eating. *I* continued eating. I willed my own face, in a different body, a different world, to smile pleasantly.

Why did they want to come here so badly? Why ask about my trove?

Like lapping waves, I sent my thoughts washing over his.

She is harmless. She is kind, and sad, and broken. You saw her with your people—you saw how she treated them. How she treats you. Amarantha did not break that kindness.

I poured my thoughts into him, tinting them with brine and the cries of terns—wrapping them in the essence that was Tarquin, the essence he'd given to me.

Take her to the mainland tomorrow. That'll keep her from asking about the temple. She saved Prythian. She is your friend.

My thoughts settled in him like a stone dropped into a pool. And as the wariness faded in his eyes, I knew my work was done.

I hauled myself back, back, back, slipping through that ocean-and-pearl wall, reeling inward until my body was a cage around me.

Tarquin smiled. "We'll meet after breakfast. Unless Rhysand wants me for more meetings." Neither Cresseida nor Varian so much as glanced at him. Had Rhys taken care of their own suspicions?

Lightning shot through my blood, even as my blood chilled to realize what I'd done—

Rhys waved a lazy hand. "By all means, Tarquin, spend the day with my lady."

My lady. I ignored the two words. But I shut out my own marveling at what I'd accomplished, the slow-building horror at the invisible violation Tarquin would never know about.

I leaned forward, bracing my bare forearms on the cool wood table. "Tell me what there is to see on the mainland," I asked Tarquin, and steered him away from the temple on the tidal causeway.

✢

Rhys and Amren waited until the household lights dimmed before coming into my room.

I'd been sitting in bed, counting down the minutes, forming my plan. None of the guest rooms looked out on the causeway—as if they wanted no one to notice it.

Rhys arrived first, leaning against the closed door. "What a fast learner you are. It takes most daemati years to master that sort of infiltration."

My nails bit into my palms. "You knew—that I did it?" Speaking the words aloud felt too much, too . . . real.

A shallow nod. "And what expert work you did, using the essence of *him* to trick his shields, to get past them . . . Clever lady."

"He'll never forgive me," I breathed.

"He'll never know." Rhys angled his head, silky dark hair sliding over his brow. "You get used to it. The sense that you're crossing a boundary, that you're violating them. For what it's worth, I didn't particularly enjoy convincing Varian and Cresseida to find other matters more interesting."

I dropped my gaze to the pale marble floor.

"If you hadn't taken care of Tarquin," he went on, "the odds are we'd be knee-deep in shit right now."

"It was my fault, anyway—I was the one who asked about the temple. I was only cleaning up my own mess." I shook my head. "It doesn't feel right."

"It never does. Or it shouldn't. Far too many daemati lose that sense. But here—tonight . . . the benefits outweighed the costs."

"Is that also what you told yourself when you went into my mind? What was the benefit then?"

Rhys pushed off the door, crossing to where I sat on the bed. "There are parts of your mind I left undisturbed, things that belong solely to you, and always will. And as for the rest . . . " His jaw clenched. "You scared the shit out of me for a long while, Feyre. Checking in that way . . . I couldn't very well stroll into the Spring Court and ask how you were doing, could I?" Light footsteps sounded in the hall—Amren. Rhys held my gaze though as he said, "I'll explain the rest some other time."

The door opened. "It seems like a stupid place to hide a book," Amren said by way of greeting as she entered, plopping onto the bed.

"And the last place one would look," Rhys said, prowling away from me to take a seat on the vanity stool before the window. "They could spell it easily enough against wet and decay. A place only visible for brief moments throughout the day—when the land around it is exposed for all to see? You could not ask for a better place. We have the eyes of thousands watching us."

"So how do we get in?" I said.

"It's likely warded against winnowing," Rhys said, bracing his forearms on his thighs. "I won't risk tripping any alarms by trying. So we go in at night, the old-fashioned way. I can carry you both, then keep watch," he added when I lifted my brows.

"Such gallantry," Amren said, "to do the easy part, then leave us helpless females to dig through mud and seaweed."

"Someone needs to be circling high enough to see anyone approaching—or sounding the alarm. And masking you from sight."

I frowned. "The locks respond to his touch; let's hope they respond to mine."

Amren said, "When do we move?"

"Tomorrow night," I said. "We note the guard's rotations tonight at low tide—figure out where the watchers are. Who we might need to take out before we make our move."

"You think like an Illyrian," Rhys murmured.

"I believe that's supposed to be a compliment," Amren confided.

Rhys snorted, and shadows gathered around him as he loosened his grip on his power. "Nuala and Cerridwen are already on the move inside the castle. I'll take to the skies. The two of you should go for a midnight walk—considering how hot it is." Then he was gone with a rustle of invisible wings and a warm, dark breeze.

Amren's lips were bloodred in the moonlight. I knew who would have the task of taking out any spying eyes—and wind up with a meal. My mouth dried out a bit. "Care for a stroll?"

CHAPTER 36

The following day was torture. Slow, unending, hot-as-hell torture.

Feigning interest in the mainland as I walked with Tarquin, met his people, smiled at them, grew harder as the sun meandered across the sky, then finally began inching toward the sea. Liar, thief, deceiver—that's what they'd call me soon.

I hoped they'd know—that Tarquin would know—that we'd done it for their sake.

Supreme arrogance, perhaps, to think that way, but . . . it was true. Given how quickly Tarquin and Cresseida had glanced at each other, guided me away from that temple . . . I'd bet that they wouldn't have handed over that book. For whatever reasons of their own, they wanted it.

Maybe this new world of Tarquin's could only be built on trust . . . But he wouldn't get a chance to build it if it was all wiped away beneath the King of Hybern's armies.

That's what I told myself over and over as we walked through his city—as I endured the greetings of his people. Perhaps not as joyous as those in Velaris, but . . . a tentative hard-won warmth. People who had endured the worst and tried now to move beyond it.

As I should be moving beyond my own darkness.

When the sun was at last sliding into the horizon, I confessed to Tarquin that I was tired and hungry—and, being kind and accommodating, he took me back, buying me a baked fish pie on the way home. He'd even eaten a fried fish at the docks that afternoon.

Dinner was worse.

We'd be gone before breakfast—but they didn't know that. Rhys mentioned returning to the Night Court tomorrow afternoon, so perhaps an early departure wouldn't be so suspicious. He'd leave a note about urgent business, thanking Tarquin for his hospitality, and then we'd vanish home—to Velaris. If it went according to plan.

We'd learned where the guards were stationed, how their rotations operated, and where their posts were on the mainland, too.

And when Tarquin kissed my cheek good night, saying he wished that it was not my last evening and perhaps he would see about visiting the Night Court soon . . . I almost fell to my knees to beg his forgiveness.

Rhysand's hand on my back was a solid warning to keep it together—even as his face held nothing but that cool amusement.

I went to my room. And found Illyrian fighting leathers waiting for me. Along with that belt of Illyrian knives.

So I dressed for battle once again.

✠

Rhys flew us in close to low tide, dropping us off before taking to the skies, where he'd circle, monitoring the guards on the island and mainland, while we hunted.

The muck reeked, squelching and squeezing us with every step from the narrow causeway road to the little temple ruin. Barnacles, seaweed, and limpets clung to the dark gray stones—and every step into the sole interior chamber had that *thing* in my chest saying *where are you, where are you, where are you?*

Rhys and Amren had checked for wards around the site—but found none. Odd, but fortunate. Thanks to the open doorway, we didn't dare risk a light, but with the cracks in the stone overhead, the moonlight provided enough illumination.

Knee-deep in muck, the tidal water slinking out over the stones, Amren and I surveyed the chamber, barely more than forty feet wide.

"I can feel it," I breathed. "Like a clawed hand running down my spine." Indeed, my skin tingled, hair standing on end beneath my warm leathers. "It's—sleeping."

"No wonder they hid it beneath stone and mud and sea," Amren muttered, the muck squelching as she turned in place.

I shivered, the Illyrian knives on me now feeling as useful as toothpicks, and again turned in place. "I don't feel anything in the walls. But it's here."

Indeed, we both looked down at the same moment and cringed.

"We should have brought a shovel," she said.

"No time to get one." The tide was fully out now. Every minute counted. Not just for the returning water—but the sunrise that was not too far off.

Every step an effort through the firm grip of the mud, I honed in on that feeling, that call. I stopped in the center of the room—dead center. *Here, here, here,* it whispered.

I leaned down, shuddering at the icy muck, at the bits of shell and debris that scraped my bare hands as I began hauling it away. "Hurry."

Amren hissed, but stooped to claw at the heavy, dense mud. Crabs and skittering things tickled my fingers. I refused to think about them.

So we dug, and dug, until we were covered in salty mud that burned our countless little cuts as we panted at a stone floor. And a lead door.

Amren swore. "Lead to keep its full force in, to preserve it. They used to line the sarcophagi of the great rulers with it—because they thought they'd one day awaken."

"If the King of Hybern goes unchecked with that Cauldron, they might very well."

Amren shuddered, and pointed. "The door is sealed."

I wiped my hand on the only clean part of me—my neck—and used the other to scrape away the last bit of mud from the round door. Every brush against the lead sent pangs of cold through me. But there—a carved whorl in the center of the door. "This has been here for a very long time," I murmured.

Amren nodded. "I would not be surprised if, despite the imprint of the High Lord's power, Tarquin and his predecessors had never set foot here—if the blood-spell to ward this place instantly transferred to them once they assumed power."

"Why covet the Book, then?"

"Wouldn't you want to lock away an object of terrible power? So no one could use it for evil—or their own gain? Or perhaps they locked it away for their own bargaining chip if it ever became necessary. I had no idea why they, of all courts, was granted the half of the Book in the first place."

I shook my head and laid my hand flat on the whorl in the lead.

A jolt went through me like lightning, and I grunted, bearing down on the door.

My fingers froze to it, as if the power were leeching my essence, drinking as Amren drank, and I felt it hesitate, question—

I am Tarquin. I am summer; I am warmth; I am sea and sky and planted field.

I became every smile he'd given me, became the crystalline blue of his eyes, the brown of his skin. I felt my own skin shift, felt my bones stretch and change. Until I *was* him, and it was a set of male hands I now possessed, now pushed against the door. Until the essence of me became what I had tasted in that inner, mental shield of his—sea and sun and brine. I did not give myself a moment to think of what power I might have just used. Did not allow any part of me that *wasn't* Tarquin to shine through.

I am your master, and you will let me pass.

The lock pulled harder and harder, and I could barely breathe—

Then a click and groan.

I shifted back into my own skin, and scrambled into the piled mud right as the door sank and swung away, tucking beneath the stones to reveal a spiral staircase drifting into a primordial gloom. And on a wet, salty breeze from below came the tendrils of power.

Across the open stair, Amren's face had gone paler than usual, her silver eyes glowing bright. "I never saw the Cauldron," she said, "but it must be terrible indeed if even a grain of its power feels . . . like this."

Indeed, that power was filling the chamber, my head, my lungs—smothering and drowning and seducing—

"Quickly," I said, and a small ball of faelight shot down the curve of the stairs, illuminating gray, worn steps slick with slime.

I drew my hunting knife and descended, one hand braced on the freezing stone wall to keep from slipping.

I made it one rotation down, Amren close behind, before faelight danced on waist-deep, putrid water. I scanned the passage at the foot of the stairs. "There's a hall, and a chamber beyond that. All clear."

"Then hurry the hell up," Amren said.

Bracing myself, I stepped into the dark water, biting down my yelp at the near-freezing temperature, the oiliness of it. Amren gagged, the water nearly up to her chest.

"This place no doubt fills up swiftly once the tide comes back in," she observed as we sloshed through the water, frowning at the many drainage holes in the walls.

We went only slow enough for her to detect any sort of ward or trap, but—there was none. Nothing at all. Though who would ever come down here, to such a place?

Fools—desperate fools, that's who.

The long stone hall ended in a second lead door. Behind it, that power coiled, overlaying Tarquin's imprint. "It's in there."

"Obviously."

I scowled at her, both of us shivering. The cold was deep enough that I wondered if I might have already been dead in my human body. Or well on my way to it.

I laid my palm flat on the door. The sucking and questioning and draining were worse this time. So much worse, and I had to brace my tattooed hand on the door to keep from falling to my knees and crying out as it ransacked me.

I am summer, I am summer, I am summer.

I didn't shift into Tarquin this time—didn't need to. A click and groan, and the lead door rolled into the wall, water merging and splashing as I stumbled back into Amren's waiting arms. "Nasty, nasty lock," she hissed, shuddering not just from the water.

My head was spinning. Another lock and I might very well pass out.

But the faelight bobbed into the chamber beyond us, and we both halted.

The water had not merged with another source—but rather halted against an invisible threshold. The dry chamber beyond was empty save for a round dais and pedestal.

And a small, lead box atop it.

Amren waved a tentative hand over the air where the water just—stopped. Then, satisfied there were no waiting wards or tricks, she stepped beyond, dripping onto the gray stones as she stood in the chamber, wincing a bit, and beckoned.

Wading as fast as I could, I followed her, half falling onto the floor as my body adjusted to sudden air. I turned—and sure enough, the water was a black wall, as if there were a pane of glass keeping it in place.

"Let's be quick about it," she said, and I didn't disagree.

We both carefully surveyed the chamber: floors, walls, ceilings. No signs of hidden mechanisms or triggers.

Though no larger than an ordinary book, the lead box seemed to gobble up the faelight—and inside it, whispering . . . The seal of Tarquin's power, and the Book.

And now I heard, clear as if Amren herself whispered it:

Who are you—what are you? Come closer—let me smell you, let me see you . . .

We paused on opposite sides of the pedestal, the faelight hovering over the lid. "No wards," Amren said, her voice barely more than the scrape of her boots on the stone. "No spells. You have to remove it—carry it out." The thought of touching that box, getting close to that thing inside it— "The tide is coming back in," Amren added, surveying the ceiling.

"That soon?"

"Perhaps the sea knows. Perhaps the sea is the High Lord's servant."

And if we were caught down here when the water came in—

I did not think my little water-animals would help. Panic writhed in my gut, but I pushed it away and steeled myself, lifting my chin.

The box would be heavy—and cold.

Who are you, who are you, who are you—

I flexed my fingers and cracked my neck. *I am summer; I am sea and sun and green things.*

"Come on, come on," Amren murmured. Above, water trickled over the stones.

Who are you, who are you, who are you—

I am Tarquin; I am High Lord; I am your master.

The box quieted. As if that were answer enough.

I snatched the box off the pedestal, the metal biting into my hands, the power an oily smear through my blood.

An ancient, cruel voice hissed:

Liar.

And the door slammed shut.

CHAPTER 37

"*NO!*" Amren screamed, at the door in an instant, her fist a radiant forge as she slammed it into the lead—once, twice.

And above—the rush and gargle of water tumbling downstairs, filling the chamber—

No, no, no—

I reached the door, sliding the box into the wide inside pocket of my leather jacket while Amren's blazing palm flattened against the door, burning, heating the metal, swirls and whorls radiating out through it as if they were a language all her own, and then—

The door burst open.

Only for a flood to come crashing in.

I grappled for the threshold, but missed as the water slammed me back, sweeping me under the dark, icy surface. The cold stole the breath from my lungs. Find the floor, find the floor—

My feet connected and I pushed up, gulping down air, scanning the dim chamber for Amren. She was clutching the threshold, eyes on me, hand out—glowing bright.

The water already flowed up to my breasts, and I rushed to her, fighting the onslaught flooding the chamber, willing that new strength into my body, my arms—

The water became easier, as if that kernel of power soothed its current, its wrath, but Amren was now climbing up the threshold. "You have it?" she shouted over the roaring water.

I nodded, and I realized her outstretched hand wasn't for me—but for the door she'd forced back into the wall. Holding it away until I could get out.

I shoved through the archway, Amren slipping around the threshold—just as the door rolled shut again, so violently that I wondered at the power she'd used to push it back.

The only downside was that the water in the hall now had much less space to fill.

"Go," she said, but I didn't wait for her approval before I grabbed her, hooking her feet around my stomach as I hoisted her onto my back.

"Just—do what you have to," I gritted out, neck craned above the rising water. Not too much farther to the stairs—the stairs that were now a cascade. Where the hell was Rhysand?

But Amren held out a palm in front of us, and the water buckled and trembled. Not a clear path, but a break in the current. I directed that kernel of Tarquin's power—*my* power now—toward it. The water calmed further, straining to obey my command.

I ran, gripping her thighs probably hard enough to bruise. Step by step, water now raging down, now at my jaw, now at my mouth—

But I hit the stairs, almost slipping on the slick step, and Amren's gasp stopped me cold.

Not a gasp of shock, but a gasp for air as a wall of water poured down the stairs. As if a mighty wave had swept over the entire site. Even my own mastery over the element could do nothing against it.

I had enough time to gulp down air, to grab Amren's legs and brace myself—

And watch as that door atop the stairs slid shut, sealing us in a watery tomb.

I was dead. I knew I was dead, and there was no way out of it.

I had consumed my last breath, and I would be aware for every second until my lungs gave out and my body betrayed me and I swallowed that fatal mouthful of water.

Amren beat at my hands until I let go, until I swam after her, trying to calm my panicking heart, my lungs, trying to convince them to make each second count as Amren reached the door and slammed her palm into it. Symbols flared—again and again. But the door held.

I reached her, shoving my body into the door, over and over, and the lead dented beneath my shoulders. Then I had talons, talons not claws, and I was slicing and punching at the metal—

My lungs were on fire. My lungs were seizing—

Amren pounded on the door, that bit of faelight guttering, as if it were counting down her heartbeats—

I had to take a breath, had to open my mouth and take a breath, had to ease the burning—

Then the door was ripped away.

And the faelight remained bright enough for me to see the three beautiful, ethereal faces hissing through fish's teeth as their spindly webbed fingers snatched us out of the stairs, and into their frogskin arms.

Water-wraiths.

But I couldn't stand it.

And as those spiny hands grabbed my arm, I opened my mouth, water shoving in, cutting off thought and sound and breath. My body seized, those talons vanishing—

Debris and seaweed and water shot past me, and I had the vague sense of being hurtled through the water, so fast the water burned beneath my eyelids.

And then hot air—air, air, air, but my lungs were full of water as—

A fist slammed into my stomach and I vomited water across the waves. I gulped down air, blinking at the bruised purple and blushing pink of the morning sky.

A sputter and gasp not too far from me, and I treaded water as I turned in the bay to see Amren vomiting as well—but alive.

And in the waves between us, onyx hair plastered to their strange heads like helmets, the water-wraiths floated, staring with dark, large eyes.

The sun was rising beyond them—the city encircling us stirring.

The one in the center said, "Our sister's debt is paid."

And then they were gone.

Amren was already swimming for the distant mainland shore.

Praying they didn't come back and make a meal of us, I hurried after her, trying to keep my movements small to avoid detection.

We both reached a quiet, sandy cove and collapsed.

✠

A shadow blocked out the sun, and a boot toed my calf. "What," said Rhysand, still in battle-black, "are you two doing?"

I opened my eyes to find Amren hoisting herself up on her elbows. "Where the *hell* were you?" she demanded.

"You two set off every damned trigger in the place. I was hunting down each guard who went to sound the alarm." My throat was ravaged—and sand tickled my cheeks, my bare hands. "I thought you had it covered," he said to her.

Amren hissed, "That *place*, or that damned book, nearly nullified my powers. We almost drowned."

His gaze shot to me. "I didn't feel it through the bond—"

"It probably nullified that, too, you stupid bastard," Amren snapped.

His eyes flickered. "Did you get it?" Not at all concerned that we were half-drowned and had very nearly been dead.

I touched my jacket—the heavy metal lump within.

"Good," Rhys said, and I looked behind him at the sudden urgency in his tone.

Sure enough, in the castle across the bay, people were darting about.

"I missed some guards," he gritted out, grabbed both our arms, and we vanished.

The dark wind was cold and roaring, and I had barely enough strength to cling to him.

It gave out entirely, along with Amren's, as we landed in the town house foyer—and we both collapsed to the wood floor, spraying sand and water on the carpet.

Cassian shouted from the dining room behind us, "What the hell?"

I glared up at Rhysand, who merely stepped toward the breakfast table. "I'm waiting for an explanation, too," he merely said to wide-eyed Cassian, Azriel, and Mor.

But I turned to Amren, who was still hissing on the floor. Her red-rimmed eyes narrowed. "How?"

"During the Tithe, the water-wraith emissary said they had no gold, no food to pay. They were starving." Every word ached, and I thought I might vomit again. He'd deserve it, if I puked all over the carpet. Though he'd probably take it from my wages. "So I gave her some of my jewelry to pay her dues. She swore that she and her sisters would never forget the kindness."

"Can someone explain, please?" Mor called from the room beyond.

We remained on the floor as Amren began quietly laughing, her small body shaking.

"What?" I demanded.

"Only an immortal with a mortal heart would have given one of those horrible beasts the money. It's so . . . " Amren laughed again, her dark hair plastered with sand and seaweed. For a moment, she even looked human. "Whatever luck you live by, girl . . . thank the Cauldron for it."

The others were all watching, but I felt a chuckle whisper out of me.

Followed by a laugh, as rasping and raw as my lungs. But a real laugh, perhaps edged by hysteria—and profound relief.

We looked at each other, and laughed again.

"Ladies," Rhysand purred—a silent order.

I groaned as I got to my feet, sand falling everywhere, and offered a hand to Amren to rise. Her grip was firm, but her quicksilver eyes were surprisingly tender as she squeezed it before snapping her fingers.

We were both instantly clean and warm, our clothes dry. Save for a wet patch around my breast—where that box waited.

My companions were solemn-faced as I approached and reached inside that pocket. The metal bit into my fingers, so cold it burned.

I dropped it onto the table.

It thudded, and they all recoiled, swearing.

Rhys crooked a finger at me. "One last task, Feyre. Unlock it, please."

My knees were buckling—my head spinning and mouth bone-dry and full of salt and grit, but . . . I wanted to be rid of it.

So I slid into a chair, tugging that hateful box to me, and placed a hand on top.

Hello, liar, it purred.

"Hello," I said softly.

Will you read me?

"No."

The others didn't say a word—though I felt their confusion shimmering in the room. Only Rhys and Amren watched me closely.

Open, I said silently.

Say please.

"Please," I said.

The box—the Book—was silent. Then it said, *Like calls to like.*

"Open," I gritted out.

Unmade and Made; Made and Unmade—that is the cycle. Like calls to like.

I pushed my hand harder, so tired I didn't care about the thoughts tumbling out, the bits and pieces that were a part of and not part of me: heat and water and ice and light and shadow.

Cursebreaker, it called to me, and the box clicked open.

I sagged back in my chair, grateful for the roaring fire in the nearby fireplace.

Cassian's hazel eyes were dark. "I never want to hear that voice again."

"Well, you will," Rhysand said blandly, lifting the lid. "Because you're coming with us to see those mortal queens as soon as they deign to visit."

I was too tired to think about that—about what we had left to do. I peered into the box.

It was not a book—not with paper and leather.

It had been formed of dark metal plates bound on three rings of gold, silver, and bronze, each word carved with painstaking precision, in an alphabet I could not recognize. Yes, it indeed turned out my reading lessons were unnecessary.

Rhys left it inside the box as we all peered in—then recoiled.

Only Amren remained staring at it. The blood drained from her face entirely.

"What language is that?" Mor asked.

I thought Amren's hands might have been shaking, but she shoved them into her pockets. "It is no language of this world."

Only Rhys was unfazed by the shock on her face. As if he'd suspected what the language might be. Why he had picked her to be a part of this hunt.

"What is it, then?" Azriel asked.

She stared and stared at the Book—as if it were a ghost, as if it were a miracle—and said, "It is the Leshon Hakodesh. The Holy Tongue." Those quicksilver eyes shifted to Rhysand, and I realized she'd understood, too, why she'd gone.

Rhysand said, "I heard a legend that it was written in a tongue of mighty beings who feared the Cauldron's power and made the Book to combat it. Mighty beings who were here . . . and then vanished. You are the only one who can uncode it."

It was Mor who warned, "Don't play those sorts of games, Rhysand."

But he shook his head. "Not a game. It was a gamble that Amren would be able to read it—and a lucky one."

Amren's nostrils flared delicately, and for a moment, I wondered if she might throttle him for not telling her his suspicions, that the Book might indeed be more than the key to our own salvation.

Rhys smiled at her in a way that said he'd be willing to let her try.

Even Cassian slid a hand toward his fighting knife.

But then Rhysand said, "I thought, too, that the Book might also contain the spell to free you—and send you home. If they were the ones who wrote it in the first place."

Amren's throat bobbed—slightly.

Cassian said, "Shit."

Rhys went on, "I did not tell you my suspicions, because I did not want to get your hopes up. But if the legends about the language were indeed right . . . Perhaps you might find what you've been looking for, Amren."

"I need the other piece before I can begin decoding it." Her voice was raw.

"Hopefully our request to the mortal queens will be answered soon," he said, frowning at the sand and water staining the foyer. "And hopefully the next encounter will go better than this one."

Her mouth tightened, yet her eyes were blazing bright. "Thank you."

Ten thousand years in exile—alone.

Mor sighed—a loud, dramatic sound no doubt meant to break the heavy silence—and complained about wanting the full story of what happened.

But Azriel said, "Even if the book can nullify the Cauldron . . . there's Jurian to contend with."

We all looked at him. "That's the piece that doesn't fit," Azriel clarified, tapping a scarred finger on the table. "Why resurrect him in the first place? And how does the king keep him bound? What does the king have over Jurian to keep him loyal?"

"I'd considered that," Rhys said, taking a seat across from me at the table, right between his two brothers. Of course he had considered it. Rhys shrugged. "Jurian was . . . obsessive in his pursuits of things. He died with many of those goals left unfinished."

Mor's face paled a bit. "If he suspects Miryam is alive—"

"Odds are, Jurian believes Miryam is gone," Rhys said. "And who better to raise his former lover than a king with a Cauldron able to resurrect the dead?"

"Would Jurian ally with Hybern just because he thinks Miryam is dead and wants her back?" Cassian said, bracing his arms on the table.

"He'd do it to get revenge on Drakon for winning her heart," Rhys said. He shook his head. "We'll discuss this later." And I made a note to ask him who these people were, what their history was—to ask Rhys why he'd never hinted Under the Mountain that he *knew* the man behind the eye on Amarantha's ring. After I'd had a bath. And water. And a nap.

But they all looked to me and Amren again—still waiting for the story. Brushing a few grains of sand off, I let Amren launch into the tale, each word more unbelievable than the last.

Across the table, I lifted my gaze from my clothes and found Rhys's eyes already on me.

I inclined my head slightly, and lowered my shield only long enough to say down the bond: *To the dreams that are answered.*

A heartbeat later, a sensual caress trailed along my mental shields—a polite request. I let it drop, let him in, and his voice filled my head. *To the huntresses who remember to reach back for those less fortunate—and water-wraiths who swim very, very fast.*

CHAPTER 38

Amren took the Book to wherever it was she lived in Velaris, leaving the five of us to eat. While Rhys told them of our visit to the Summer Court, I managed to scarf down breakfast before the exhaustion of staying up all night, unlocking those doors, and very nearly dying hit me. When I awoke, the house was empty, the afternoon sunlight warm and golden, and the day so unusually warm and lovely that I brought a book down to the small garden in the back.

The sun eventually shifted, shading the garden to the point of frigidness again. Not quite willing to give up the sun yet, I trudged the three levels to the rooftop patio to watch it set.

Of course—*of course*—Rhysand was already lounging in one of the white-painted iron chairs, an arm slung over the back while his other hand idly gripped a glass of some sort of liquor, a crystal decanter full of it set on the table before him.

His wings were draped behind him on the tile floor, and I wondered if he was also taking advantage of the unusually mild day to sun them as I cleared my throat.

"I know you're there," he said without turning from the view of the Sidra and the red-gold sea beyond.

I scowled. "If you want to be alone, I can go."

He jerked his chin toward the empty seat at the iron table. Not a glowing invitation, but . . . I sat down.

There was a wood box beside the decanter—and I might have thought it was something for whatever he was drinking had I not noticed the dagger fashioned of mother-of-pearl in the lid.

Had I not sworn I could smell the sea and heat and soil that was Tarquin. "What is that?"

Rhys drained his glass, held up a hand—the decanter floating to him on a phantom wind—and poured himself another knuckle's length before he spoke.

"I debated it for a good while, you know," he said, staring out at his city. "Whether I should just ask Tarquin for the Book. But I thought that he might very well say no, then sell the information to the highest bidder. I thought he might say yes, and it'd still wind up with too many people knowing our plans and the potential for that information to get out. And at the end of the day, I needed the *why* of our mission to remain secret for as long as possible." He drank again, and dragged a hand through his blue-black hair. "I didn't like stealing from him. I didn't like hurting his guards. I didn't like vanishing without a word, when, ambition or no, he did truly want an alliance. Maybe even friendship. No other High Lords have ever bothered—or dared. But I think Tarquin wanted to be my friend."

I glanced between him and the box and repeated, "What is that?"

"Open it."

I gingerly flipped back the lid.

Inside, nestled on a bed of white velvet, three rubies glimmered, each the size of a chicken egg. Each so pure and richly colored that they seemed crafted of—

"Blood rubies," he said.

I pulled back the fingers that had been inching toward the stones.

"In the Summer Court, when a grave insult has been committed, they send a blood ruby to the offender. An official declaration that there is a price on their head—that they are now hunted, and will soon be dead. The box arrived at the Court of Nightmares an hour ago."

Mother above. "I take it one of these has my name on it. And yours. And Amren's."

The lid flipped shut on a dark wind. "I made a mistake," he said. I opened my mouth, but he went on, "I should have wiped the minds of the guards and let them continue on. Instead, I knocked them out. It's been a while since I had to do any sort of physical . . . defending like that, and I was so focused on my Illyrian training that I forgot the other arsenal at my disposal. They probably awoke and went right to him."

"He would have noticed the Book was missing soon enough."

"We could have denied that we stole it and chalked it up to coincidence." He drained his glass. "I made a mistake."

"It's not the end of the world if you do that every now and then."

"You've been told you are now public enemy number one of the Summer Court and you're fine with it?"

"No. But I don't blame you."

He loosed a breath, staring out at his city as the warmth of the day succumbed to winter's bite once more. It didn't matter to him.

"Perhaps you could return the Book once we've neutralized the Cauldron—apologize."

Rhys snorted. "No. Amren will get that book for as long as she needs it."

"Then make it up to him in some way. Clearly, *you* wanted to be his friend as much as he wanted to be yours. You wouldn't be so upset otherwise."

"I'm not upset. I'm pissed off."

"Semantics."

He gave me a half smile. "Feuds like the one we just started can last centuries—millennia. If that's the cost of stopping this war, helping Amren . . . I'll pay it."

He'd pay with everything he had, I realized. Any hopes for himself, his own happiness.

"Do the others know—about the blood rubies?"

"Azriel was the one who brought them to me. I'm debating how I'll tell Amren."

"Why?"

Darkness filled those remarkable eyes. "Because her answer would be to go to Adriata and wipe the city off the map."

I shuddered.

"Exactly," he said.

I stared out at Velaris with him, listening to the sounds of the day wrapping up—and the night unfolding. Adriata felt rudimentary by comparison.

"I understand," I said, rubbing some warmth into my now-chilled hands, "why you did what you had to in order to protect this city." Imagining the destruction that had been wreaked upon Adriata here in Velaris made my blood run cold. His eyes slid to me, wary and dull. I swallowed. "And I understand why you will do anything to keep it safe during the times ahead."

"And your point is?"

A bad day—this was a bad day, I realized, for him. I didn't scowl at the bite in his words. "Get through this war, Rhysand, and then worry about Tarquin and the blood rubies. Nullify the Cauldron, stop the king from shattering the wall and enslaving the human realm again, and then we'll figure out the rest after."

"You sound as if you plan to stay here for a while." A bland, but edged question.

"I can find my own lodging, if that's what you're referring to. Maybe I'll use that generous paycheck to get myself something lavish."

Come on. Wink at me. Play with me. Just—stop looking like that.

He only said, "Spare your paycheck. Your name has already been added to the list of those approved to use my household credit. Buy whatever you wish. Buy yourself a whole damn house if you want."

I ground my teeth, and maybe it was panic or desperation, but I said sweetly, "I saw a pretty shop across the Sidra the other day. It sold what looked to be lots of lacy little things. Am I allowed to buy that on your credit, too, or does that come out of my personal funds?"

Those violet eyes again drifted to me. "I'm not in the mood."

There was no humor, no mischief. I could go warm myself by a fire inside, but . . .

He had stayed. And fought for me.

Week after week, he'd fought for me, even when I had no reaction, even when I had barely been able to speak or bring myself to care if I lived or died or ate or starved. I couldn't leave him to his own dark thoughts, his own guilt. He'd shouldered them alone long enough.

So I held his gaze. "I never knew Illyrians were such morose drunks."

"I'm not drunk—I'm drinking," he said, his teeth flashing a bit.

"Again, semantics." I leaned back in my seat, wishing I'd brought my coat. "Maybe you should have slept with Cresseida after all—so you could both be sad and lonely together."

"So you're entitled to have as many bad days as you want, but I can't get a few hours?"

"Oh, take however long you want to mope. I was going to invite you to come shopping with me for said lacy little unmentionables, but . . . sit up here forever, if you have to."

He didn't respond.

I went on, "Maybe I'll send a few to Tarquin—with an offer to wear them for him if he forgives us. Maybe he'll take those blood rubies right back."

His mouth barely, barely tugged up at the corners. "He'd see that as a taunt."

"I gave him a few smiles and he handed over a family heirloom. I bet he'd give me the keys to his territory if I showed up wearing those undergarments."

"Someone thinks mighty highly of herself."

"Why shouldn't I? You seem to have difficulty *not* staring at me day and night."

There it was—a kernel of truth and a question.

"Am I supposed to deny," he drawled, but something sparked in those eyes, "that I find you attractive?"

"You've never said it."

"I've told you many times, and quite frequently, how attractive I find you."

I shrugged, even as I thought of all those times—when I'd dismissed them as teasing compliments, nothing more. "Well, maybe you should do a better job of it."

The gleam in his eyes turned into something predatory. A thrill went through me as he braced his powerful arms on the table and purred, "Is that a challenge, Feyre?"

I held that predator's gaze—the gaze of the most powerful male in Prythian. "*Is* it?"

His pupils flared. Gone was the quiet sadness, the isolated guilt. Only that lethal focus—on me. On my mouth. On the bob of my throat as I tried to keep my breathing even. He said, slow and soft, "Why don't we go down to that store right now, Feyre, so you can try on those lacy little things—so I can help you pick which one to send to Tarquin."

My toes curled inside my fleece-lined slippers. Such a dangerous line we walked together. The ice-kissed night wind rustled our hair.

But Rhys's gaze cut skyward—and a heartbeat later, Azriel shot from the clouds like a spear of darkness.

I wasn't sure whether I should be relieved or not, but I left before Azriel could land, giving the High Lord and his spymaster some privacy.

As soon as I entered the dimness of the stairwell, the heat rushed from me, leaving a sick, cold feeling in my stomach.

There was flirting, and then there was . . . this.

I had loved Tamlin. Loved him so much I had not minded destroying myself for it—for him. And then everything had happened, and now I was here, and . . . and I might have very well gone to that pretty shop with Rhysand.

I could almost see what would have happened:

The shop ladies would have been polite—a bit nervous—and given us privacy as Rhys sat on the settee in the back of the shop while I went behind the curtained-off chamber to try on the red lace set I'd eyed thrice now. And when I emerged, mustering up more bravado than I felt, Rhys would have looked me up and down. Twice.

And he would have kept staring at me as he informed the shop ladies that the store was closed and they should all come back tomorrow, and we'd leave the tab on the counter.

I would have stood there, naked save for scraps of red lace, while we listened to the quick, discreet sounds of them closing up and leaving.

And he would have looked at me the entire time—at my breasts, visible through the lace; at the plane of my stomach, now finally looking less starved and taut. At the sweep of my hips and thighs—between them. Then he would have met my gaze again, and crooked a finger with a single murmured, "Come here."

And I would have walked to him, aware of every step, as I at last stopped in front of where he sat. Between his legs.

His hands would have slid to my waist, the calluses scraping my skin. Then he'd have tugged me a bit closer before leaning in to brush a kiss to my navel, his tongue—

I swore as I slammed into the post of the stairwell landing.

And I blinked—blinked as the world returned and I realized . . .

I glared at the eye tattooed in my hand and hissed both with my tongue and that silent voice within the bond itself, "*Prick.*"

In the back of my mind, a sensual male voice chuckled with midnight laughter.

My face burning, cursing him for the vision he'd slipped past my mental shields, I reinforced them as I entered my room. And took a very, very cold bath.

I ate with Mor that night beside the crackling fire in the town house dining room, Rhys and the others off somewhere, and when she finally asked why I kept scowling every time Rhysand's name was mentioned, I told her about the vision he'd sent into my mind. She'd laughed until wine came out of her nose, and when I scowled at *her*, she told me I should be proud: when Rhys was prepared to brood, it took nothing short of a miracle to get him out of it.

I tried to ignore the slight sense of triumph—even as I climbed into bed.

I was just starting to drift off, well past two in the morning thanks to chatting with Mor on the couch in the living room for hours and hours about all the great and terrible places she'd seen, when the house let out a groan.

Like the wood itself was being warped, the house began to moan and shudder—the colored glass lights in my room tinkling.

I jolted upright, twisting to the open window. Clear skies, nothing—

Nothing but the darkness leaking into my room from the hall door.

I knew that darkness. A kernel of it lived in me.

It rushed in from the cracks of the door like a flood. The house shuddered again.

I vaulted from bed, yanked the door open, and darkness swept past me on a phantom wind, full of stars and flapping wings and—pain.

So much pain, and despair, and guilt and fear.

I hurtled into the hall, utterly blind in the impenetrable dark. But there was a thread between us, and I followed it—to where I knew his room was. I fumbled for the handle, then—

More night and stars and wind poured out, my hair whipping around me, and I lifted an arm to shield my face as I edged into the room. "Rhysand."

No response. But I could feel him there—feel that lifeline between us.

I followed it until my shins banged into what had to be his bed. "*Rhysand*," I said over the wind and dark. The house shook, the floorboards clattering under my feet. I patted the bed, feeling sheets and blankets and down, and then—

Then a hard, taut male body. But the bed was enormous, and I couldn't get a grip on him. "*Rhysand!*"

Around and around the darkness swirled, the beginning and end of the world.

I scrambled onto the bed, lunging for him, feeling what was his arm, then his stomach, then his shoulders. His skin was freezing as I gripped his shoulders and shouted his name.

No response, and I slid a hand up his neck, to his mouth—to make sure he was still breathing, that this wasn't his power floating away from him—

Icy breath hit my palm. And, bracing myself, I rose up on my knees, aiming blindly, and slapped him.

My palm stung—but he didn't move. I hit him again, *pulling* on that bond between us, shouting his name down it like it was a tunnel, banging on that wall of ebony adamant within his mind, roaring at it.

A crack in the dark.

And then his hands were on me, flipping me, pinning me with expert skill to the mattress, a taloned hand at my throat.

I went still. "Rhysand." I breathed. *Rhys*, I said through the bond, putting a hand against that inner shield.

The dark shuddered.

I threw my own power out—black to black, soothing his darkness, the rough edges, willing it to calm, to soften. My darkness sang his own a lullaby, a song my wet nurse had hummed when my mother had shoved me into her arms to go back to attending parties.

"It was a dream," I said. His hand was so cold. "It was a dream."

Again, the dark paused. I sent my own veils of night brushing up against it, running star-flecked hands down it.

And for a heartbeat, the inky blackness cleared enough that I saw his face above me: drawn, lips pale, violet eyes wide—scanning.

"Feyre," I said. "I'm Feyre." His breathing was jagged, uneven. I gripped the wrist that held my throat—held, but didn't hurt. "You were dreaming."

I willed that darkness inside myself to echo it, to sing those raging fears to sleep, to brush up against that ebony wall within his mind, gentle and soft . . .

Then, like snow shaken from a tree, his darkness fell away, taking mine with it.

Moonlight poured in—and the sounds of the city.

His room was similar to mine, the bed so big it must have been built to accommodate wings, but all tastefully, comfortably appointed. And he was naked above me—utterly naked. I didn't dare look lower than the tattooed panes of his chest.

"Feyre," he said, his voice hoarse. As if he'd been screaming.

"Yes," I said. He studied my face—the taloned hand at my throat. And released me immediately.

I lay there, staring up at where he now knelt on the bed, rubbing his hands over his face. My traitorous eyes indeed dared to look lower than his chest—but my attention snagged on the twin tattoos on each of his knees: a towering mountain crowned by three stars. Beautiful—but brutal, somehow.

"You were having a nightmare," I said, easing into a sitting position. Like some dam had been cracked open inside me, I glanced at my hand—and willed it to vanish into shadow. It did.

Half a thought scattered the darkness again.

His hands, however, still ended in long, black talons—and his feet . . . they ended in claws, too. The wings were out, slumped down behind him. And I wondered how close he'd been to fully shifting into that beast he'd once told me he hated.

He lowered his hands, talons fading into fingers. "I'm sorry."

"That's why you're staying here, not at the House. You don't want the others seeing this."

"I normally keep it contained to my room. I'm sorry it woke you."

I fisted my hands in my lap to keep from touching him. "How often does it happen?"

Rhys's violet eyes met mine, and I knew the answer before he said, "As often as you."

I swallowed hard. "What did you dream of tonight?"

He shook his head, looking toward the window—to where snow had dusted the nearby rooftops. "There are memories from Under the Mountain, Feyre, that are best left unshared. Even with you."

He'd shared enough horrific things with me that they had to be . . . beyond nightmares, then. But I put a hand on his elbow, naked body and all. "When you want to talk, let me know. I won't tell the others."

I made to slither off the bed, but he grabbed my hand, keeping it against his arm. "Thank you."

I studied the hand, the ravaged face. Such pain lingered there—and exhaustion. The face he never let anyone see.

I pushed up onto my knees and kissed his cheek, his skin warm and soft beneath my mouth. It was over before it started, but—but how many nights had I wanted someone to do the same for me?

His eyes were a bit wide as I pulled away, and he didn't stop me as I eased off the bed. I was almost out the door when I turned back to him.

Rhys still knelt, wings drooping across the white sheets, head bowed, his tattoos stark against his golden skin. A dark, fallen prince.

The painting flashed into my mind.

Flashed—and stayed there, glimmering, before it faded.

But it remained, shining faintly, in that hole inside my chest.

The hole that was slowly starting to heal over.

CHAPTER 39

"Do you think you can decode it once we get the other half?" I said to Amren, lingering by the front door of her apartment the next afternoon.

She owned the top floor of a three-story building, the sloped ceiling ending on either side in a massive window. One looked out on the Sidra; the other on a tree-lined city square. The entire apartment consisted of one giant room: the faded oak floors were covered in equally worn carpets, furniture was scattered about as if she constantly moved it for whatever purpose.

Only her bed, a large, four-poster monstrosity canopied in gossamer, seemed set in a permanent place against the wall. There was no kitchen—only a long table and a hearth burning hot enough to make the room near-stifling. The dusting of snow from the night before had vanished in the dry winter sun by midmorning, the temperature crisp but mild enough that the walk here had been invigorating.

Seated on the floor before a low-lying table scattered with papers, Amren looked up from the gleaming metal of the book. Her face was paler than usual, her lips wan. "It's been a long while since I used this language—I want to master it again before tackling the Book. Hopefully by then, those haughty queens will have given us their share."

"And how long will relearning the language take?"

"Didn't His Darkness fill you in?" She went back to the Book.

I strode for the long wooden table and set the package I'd brought on the scratched surface. A few pints of hot blood—straight from the butcher. I'd nearly run here to keep them from going cold. "No," I said, taking out the containers. "He didn't." Rhys had already been gone by breakfast, though one of his notes had been on a bedside table.

Thank you—for last night, was all it had said. No pen to write a response.

But I'd hunted down one anyway, and had written back, *What do the tattooed stars and mountain on your knees mean?*

The paper had vanished a heartbeat later. When it hadn't returned, I'd dressed and gone to breakfast. I was halfway through my eggs and toast when the paper appeared beside my plate, neatly folded.

That I will bow before no one and nothing but my crown.

This time, a pen had appeared. I'd merely written back, *So dramatic.* And through our bond, on the other side of my mental shields, I could have sworn I heard his laugh.

Smiling at the memory, I unscrewed the lid on the first jar, the tang of blood filling my nostrils. Amren sniffed, then whipped her head to the glass pints. "You—oh, I like you."

"It's lamb, if that makes a difference. Do you want me to heat it up?"

She rushed from the Book, and I just watched as she clutched the jar in both hands and gulped it down like water.

Well, at least I wouldn't have to bother finding a pot in this place.

Amren drank half in one go. A trickle of blood ran down her chin, and she let it drip onto her gray shirt—rumpled in a way I'd never seen. Smacking her lips, she set the jar on the table with a great sigh. Blood gleamed on her teeth. "Thank you."

"Do you have a favorite?"

She jerked her bloody chin, then wiped it with a napkin as she realized she'd made a mess. "Lamb has always been my favorite. Horrible as it is."

"Not—human?"

She made a face. "Watery, and often tastes like what they last ate. And since most humans have piss-poor palates, it's too much of a gamble. But lamb . . . I'll take goat, too. The blood's purer. Richer. Reminds me of—another time. And place."

"Interesting," I said, and meant it. I wondered what world, exactly, she meant.

She drained the rest, color already blooming on her face, and placed the jar in the small sink along the wall.

"I thought you'd live somewhere more . . . ornate," I admitted.

Indeed, all her fine clothes were hanging on racks near the bed, her jewelry scattered on a few armoires and tables. There was enough of the latter to provide an emperor's ransom.

She shrugged, plopping down beside the Book once more. "I tried that once. It bored me. And I didn't like having servants. Too nosy. I've lived in palaces and cottages and in the mountains and on the beach, but I somehow like this apartment by the river the best." She frowned at the skylights that dotted the ceiling. "It also means I never have to host parties or guests. Both of which I abhor."

I chuckled. "Then I'll keep my visit short."

She let out an amused huff, crossing her legs beneath her. "Why *are* you here?"

"Cassian said you'd been holed up in here night and day since we got back, and I thought you might be hungry. And—I had nothing else to do."

"Cassian is a busybody."

"He cares about you. All of you. You're the only family he has." They were *all* the only family they each had.

"Ach," she said, studying a piece of paper. But it seemed to please her nonetheless. A gleam of color caught my attention on the floor near her.

She was using her blood ruby as a paperweight.

"Rhys convinced you not to destroy Adriata for the blood ruby?"

Amren's eyes flicked up, full of storms and violent seas. "He did no such thing. *That* convinced me not to destroy Adriata." She pointed to her dresser.

Sprawled across the top like a snake lay a familiar necklace of diamonds and rubies. I'd seen it before—in Tarquin's trove. "How . . . what?"

Amren smiled to herself. "Varian sent it to me. To soften Tarquin's declaration of our blood feud."

I'd thought the rubies would need to be worn by a mighty female—and could think of no mightier female than the one before me. "Did you and Varian . . . ?"

"Tempting, but no. The prick can't decide if he hates or wants me."

"Why can't it be both?"

A low chuckle. "Indeed."

Thus began weeks of waiting. Waiting for Amren to relearn a language spoken by no other in our world. Waiting for the mortal queens to answer our request to meet.

Azriel continued his attempt to infiltrate their courts—still to no avail. I heard about it mostly from Mor, who always knew when he'd return to the House of Wind, and always made a point to be there the moment he touched down.

She told me little of the specifics—even less about how the frustration of *not* being able to get his spies *or* himself into those courts took a toll on him. The standards to which he held himself, she confided in me, bordered on sadistic.

Getting Azriel to take *any* time for himself that didn't involve work or training was nearly impossible. And when I pointed out that he *did* go to Rita's with her whenever she asked, Mor simply informed me that it had taken her *four centuries* to get him to do that. I sometimes wondered what went on up at the House of Wind while Rhys and I stayed at the town house.

I only really visited in the mornings, when I filled the first half of my day training with Cassian—who, along with Mor, had decided to point out what foods I should be eating to gain back the weight I'd lost, to become strong and swift again. And as the days passed, I went from physical defense to learning to wield an Illyrian blade, the weapon so fine, I'd nearly taken Cassian's arm off.

But I was learning to use it—slowly. Painfully. I'd had one break from Cassian's brutal training—just one morning, when he'd flown to the human realm to see if my sisters had heard from the queens and deliver *another* letter from Rhys to be sent to them.

I assumed seeing Nesta went about as poorly as could be imagined, because my lesson the following morning was longer and harder than it'd been in previous days. I'd asked what, exactly, Nesta had said to him to get under his skin so easily. But Cassian had only snarled and told me to mind my own business, and that my family was full of bossy, know-it-all females.

Part of me had wondered if Cassian and Varian might need to compare notes.

Most afternoons . . . if Rhys was around, I'd train with him. Mind to mind, power to power. We slowly worked through the gifts I'd been given—flame and water, ice and darkness. There were others, we knew, that had gone undiscovered, undelved. Winnowing still remained impossible. I hadn't been able to do it since that snowy morning with the Attor.

It'd take time, Rhys told me each day, when I'd inevitably snap at him—time, to learn and master each one.

He infused each lesson with information about the High Lords whose power I'd stolen: about Beron, the cruel and vain High Lord of the Autumn Court; about Kallias, the quiet and cunning High Lord of Winter; about Helion Spell-Cleaver, the High Lord of Day, whose one thousand libraries had been personally looted by Amarantha, and whose clever people excelled at spell work and archived the knowledge of Prythian.

Knowing *who* my power had come from, Rhys said, was as important as learning the nature of the power itself. We never spoke of shape-shifting—of the talons I could sometimes summon. The threads that went along with us looking at that gift were too tangled, the unspoken history too violent and bloody.

So I learned the other courts' politics and histories, and learned their masters' powers, until my waking and sleeping hours were spent with flame singeing my mouth and hoarfrost cracking between my fingers. And each night, exhausted from a day of training my body and powers, I tumbled into a heavy sleep, laced with jasmine-scented darkness.

Even my nightmares were too tired to hound me.

On the days when Rhys was called elsewhere, to deal with the inner workings of his own court, to remind them who ruled them or mete out judgment, to prepare for our inevitable visit to Hybern, I would read, or sit with Amren while she worked on the Book, or stroll through Velaris with Mor. The latter was perhaps my favorite, and the female certainly excelled at finding ways to spend money. I'd peeked only once at the account Rhys had set up for me—just once, and realized he was grossly, *grossly* overpaying me.

I tried not to be disappointed on those afternoons that he was gone, tried not to admit that I'd begun looking forward to it—mastering my powers, and . . . bantering with him. But even when he was gone, he would talk to me, in the notes that had become our own strange secret.

One day, he'd written to me from Cesere, a small city in the northeast where he was meeting with the few surviving priestesses to discuss rebuilding after their temple had been wrecked by Hybern's forces. None of the priestesses were like Ianthe, he'd promised.

Tell me about the painting.

I'd written back from my seat in the garden, the fountain finally revived with the return of milder weather, *There's not much to say.*

Tell me about it anyway.

It had taken me a while to craft the response, to think through that little hole in me and what it had once meant and felt like. But then I said, *There was a time when all I wanted was enough money to keep me and my family fed so that I could spend my days painting. That was all I wanted. Ever.*

A pause. Then he'd written, *And now?*

Now, I'd replied, *I don't know what I want. I can't paint anymore.*

Why?

Because that part of me is empty. Though maybe that night I'd seen him kneeling in the bed . . . maybe that had changed a bit. I had contemplated the next sentence, then written, *Did you always want to be High Lord?*

A lengthy pause again. *Yes. And no. I saw how my father ruled and knew from a young age that I did not want to be like him. So I decided to be a different sort of High Lord; I wanted to protect my people, change the perceptions of the Illyrians, and eliminate the corruption that plagued the land.*

For a moment, I hadn't been able to stop myself from comparing: Tamlin hadn't wanted to be High Lord. He resented being High Lord—and maybe . . . maybe that was part of why the court had become what it was. But Rhysand, with a vision, with the will and desire and passion to do it . . . He'd built something.

And then gone to the mat to defend it.

It was what he'd seen in Tarquin, why those blood rubies had hit him so hard. Another High Lord with vision—a radical vision for the future of Prythian.

So I wrote back, *At least you make up for your shameless flirting by being one hell of a High Lord.*

He'd returned that evening, smirking like a cat, and had merely said "One hell of a High Lord?" by way of greeting.

I'd sent a bucket's worth of water splashing into his face.

Rhys hadn't bothered to shield against it. And instead shook his wet hair like a dog, spraying me until I yelped and darted away. His laughter had chased me up the stairs.

Winter was slowly loosening its grip when I awoke one morning and found another letter from Rhys beside my bed. No pen.

No training with your second-favorite Illyrian this morning. The queens finally deigned to write back. They're coming to your family's estate tomorrow.

I didn't have time for nerves. We left after dinner, soaring into the thawing human lands under cover of darkness, the brisk wind screaming as Rhys held me tightly.

+

My sisters were ready the following morning, both dressed in finery fit for any queen, Fae or mortal.

I supposed I was, too.

I wore a white gown of chiffon and silk, cut in typical Night Court fashion to reveal my skin, the gold accents on the dress glittering in the midmorning light streaming through the sitting room windows. My father, thankfully, would remain on the continent for another two months—due to whatever vital trade he'd been seeking across the kingdoms.

Near the fireplace, I stood beside Rhys, who was clad in his usual black, his wings gone, his face a calm mask. Only the dark crown atop his head—the metal shaped like raven's feathers—was different. The crown that was the sibling to my gold diadem.

Cassian and Azriel monitored everything from the far wall, no weapons in sight.

But their Siphons gleamed, and I wondered what manner of weapon, exactly, they could craft with it, if the need demanded it. For that had been one of the demands the queens had issued for this meeting: no weapons. No matter that the Illyrian warriors themselves were weapons enough.

Mor, in a red gown similar to mine, frowned at the clock atop the white mantel, her foot tapping on the ornate carpet. Despite my wishes for her to get to know my sisters, Nesta and Elain had been so tense and pale when we'd arrived that I'd immediately decided now was not the time for such an encounter.

One day—one day, I'd bring them all together. If we didn't die in this war first. If these queens chose to help us.

Eleven o'clock struck.

There had been two other demands.

The meeting was to begin at eleven. No earlier. No later.

And they had wanted the exact geographical location of the house. The layout and size of each room. Where the furniture was. Where the windows and doors were. What room, likely, we would greet them in.

Azriel had provided it all, with my sisters' help.

The chiming of the clock atop the mantel was the only sound.

And I realized, as it finished its last strike, that the third demand wasn't just for security.

No, as a wind brushed through the room, and five figures appeared, flanked by two guards apiece, I realized it was because the queens could winnow.

CHAPTER 40

The mortal queens were a mixture of age, coloring, height, and temperament. The eldest of them, clad in an embroidered wool dress of deepest blue, was brown-skinned, her eyes sharp and cold, and unbent despite the heavy wrinkles carved into her face.

The two who appeared middle-aged were opposites: one dark, one light; one sweet-faced, one hewn from granite; one smiling and one frowning. They even wore gowns of black and white—and seemed to move in question and answer to each other. I wondered what their kingdoms were like, what relations they had. If the matching silver rings they each wore bound them in other ways.

And the youngest two queens . . . One was perhaps a few years older than me, black-haired and black-eyed, careful cunning oozing from every pore as she surveyed us.

And the final queen, the one who spoke first, was the most beautiful—the only beautiful one of them. These were women who, despite their finery, did not care if they were young or old, fat or thin, short or tall. Those things were secondary; those things were a sleight of hand.

But this one, this beautiful queen, perhaps no older than thirty . . .

Her riotously curly hair was as golden as Mor's, her eyes of purest amber. Even her brown, freckled skin seemed dusted with gold. Her body was supple where she'd probably learned men found it distracting, lithe where it showed grace. A lion in human flesh.

"Well met," Rhysand said, remaining still as their stone-faced guards scanned us, the room. As the queens now took our measure.

The sitting room was enormous enough that one nod from the golden queen had the guards peeling off to hold positions by the walls, the doors. My sisters, silent before the bay window, shuffled aside to make room.

Rhys stepped forward. The queens all sucked in a little breath, as if bracing themselves. Their guards casually, perhaps foolishly, rested a hand on the hilt of their broadswords—so large and clunky compared to Illyrian blades. As if they stood a chance—against any of us. Myself included, I realized with a bit of a start.

But it was Cassian and Azriel who would play the role of mere guards today—distractions.

But Rhys bowed his head slightly and said to the assembled queens, "We are grateful you accepted our invitation." He lifted a brow. "Where is the sixth?"

The ancient queen, her blue gown heavy and rich, merely said, "She is unwell, and could not make the journey." She surveyed me. "You are the emissary."

My back stiffened. Beneath her gaze, my crown felt like a joke, like a bauble, but— "Yes," I said. "I am Feyre."

A cutting glance toward Rhysand. "And you are the High Lord who wrote us such an interesting letter after your first few were dispatched."

I didn't dare look at him. He'd sent many letters through my sisters by now.

You didn't ask what was inside them, he said mind to mind with me, laughter dancing along the bond. I'd left my mental shields down—just in case we needed to silently communicate.

"I am," Rhysand said with a hint of a nod. "And this is my cousin, Morrigan."

Mor stalked toward us, her crimson gown floating on a phantom wind. The golden queen sized her up with each step, each breath. A threat—for beauty and power and dominance. Mor bowed at my side. "It has been a long time since I met with a mortal queen."

The black-clad queen placed a moon-white hand on her lower bodice. "Morrigan—*the* Morrigan from the War."

They all paused as if in surprise. And a bit of awe and fear.

Mor bowed again. "Please—sit." She gestured to the chairs we'd laid out a comfortable distance from each other, all far enough apart that the guards could flank their queens as they saw fit.

Almost as one, the queens sat. Their guards, however, remained at their posts around the room.

The golden-haired queen smoothed her voluminous skirts and said, "I assume those are our hosts." A cutting look at my sisters.

Nesta had gone straight-backed, but Elain bobbed a curtsy, flushing rose pink.

"My sisters," I clarified.

Amber eyes slid to me. To my crown. Then Rhys's. "An emissary wears a golden crown. Is that a tradition in Prythian?"

"No," Rhysand said smoothly, "but she certainly looks good enough in one that I can't resist."

The golden queen didn't smile as she mused, "A human turned into a High Fae . . . and who is now standing beside a High Lord at the place of honor. Interesting."

I kept my shoulders back, chin high. Cassian had been teaching me these weeks about how to feel out an opponent—what were her words but the opening movements in another sort of battle?

The eldest declared to Rhys, "You have an hour of our time. Make it count."

"How is it that you can winnow?" Mor asked from her seat beside me.

The golden queen now gave a smile—a small, mocking one—and replied, "It is our secret, and our gift from your kind."

Fine. Rhys looked to me, and I swallowed as I inched forward on my seat. "War is coming. We called you here to warn you—and to beg a boon."

There would be no tricks, no stealing, no seduction. Rhys could not even risk looking inside their heads for fear of triggering the inherent wards around the Book and destroying it.

"We know war is coming," the oldest said, her voice like crackling leaves. "We have been preparing for it for many years."

It seemed the three others were positioned as observers while the eldest and the golden-haired one led the charge.

I said as calmly and clearly as I could, "The humans in this territory seem unaware of the larger threat. We've seen no signs of preparation." Indeed, Azriel had gleaned as much these weeks, to my dismay.

"This territory," the golden one explained coolly, "is a slip of land compared to the vastness of the continent. It is not in our interests to defend it. It would be a waste of resources."

No. *No*, that—

Rhys drawled, "Surely the loss of even one innocent life would be abhorrent."

The eldest queen folded her withered hands in her lap. "Yes. To lose one life is always a horror. But war is war. If we must sacrifice this tiny territory to save the majority, then we shall do it."

I didn't dare look at my sisters. Look at this house, that might very well be turned to rubble. I rasped, "There are good people here."

The golden queen sweetly parried with, "Then let the High Fae of Prythian defend them."

Silence.

And it was Nesta who hissed from behind us, "We have servants here. With families. There are *children* in these lands. And you mean to leave us all in the hands of the Fae?"

The eldest one's face softened. "It is no easy choice, girl—"

"It is the choice of *cowards*," Nesta snapped.

I interrupted before Nesta could dig us a deeper grave, "For all that your kind hate ours . . . You'd leave the Fae to defend your people?"

"Shouldn't they?" the golden one asked, sending that cascade of curls sliding over a shoulder as she angled her head to the side. "Shouldn't they defend against a threat of their own making?" A snort. "Should Fae blood not be spilled for their crimes over the years?"

"Neither side is innocent," Rhys countered calmly. "But we might protect those who are. Together."

"Oh?" said the eldest, her wrinkles seeming to harden, deepen. "The High Lord of the Night Court asks us to join with him, save lives with him. To fight for peace. And what of the lives you have taken during your long, hideous existence? What of the High Lord who walks with darkness in his wake, and shatters minds as he sees fit?" A crow's laugh. "We have heard of you, even on the continent, Rhysand. We have heard what the Night Court does, what you do to your enemies. *Peace?* For a male who melts minds and tortures for sport, I did not think you knew the word."

Wrath began simmering in my blood; embers crackled in my ears. But I cooled that fire I'd slowly been stoking these past weeks and tried, "If you will not send forces here to defend your people, then the artifact we requested—"

"Our half of the Book, child," the crone cut me off, "does not leave our sacred palace. It has not left those white walls since the day it was gifted as part of the Treaty. It will never leave those walls, not while we stand against the terrors in the North."

"Please," was all I said.

Silence again.

"Please," I repeated. Emissary—I was their emissary, and Rhys had chosen me for this. To be the voice of both worlds. "I was turned into *this*—into a faerie—because one of the commanders from Hybern *killed* me."

Through our bond, I could have sworn I felt Rhys flinch.

"For fifty years," I pushed on, "she terrorized Prythian, and when I defeated her, when I freed its people, she *killed* me. And before she did, I witnessed the horrors that she unleashed on human and faerie alike. One of them—just *one* of them was able to cause such destruction and suffering. Imagine what an army like her might do. And now their king plans to use a weapon to shatter the wall, to destroy *all* of you. The war will be swift, and brutal. And you will not win. *We* will not win. Survivors will be slaves, and their children's children will be slaves. Please . . . Please, give us the other half of the Book."

The eldest queen swapped a glance with the golden one before saying gently, placatingly, "You are young, child. You have much to learn about the ways of the world—"

"Do not," Rhys said with deadly quiet, "condescend to her." The eldest queen—who was but a child to *him*, to his centuries of existence—had the good sense to look nervous at that tone. Rhys's eyes were glazed, his face as unforgiving as his voice as he went on, "Do not insult Feyre for speaking with her heart, with compassion for those who cannot defend themselves, when you speak from only selfishness and cowardice."

The eldest stiffened. "For the greater good—"

"Many atrocities," Rhys purred, "have been done in the name of the greater good."

No small part of me was impressed that she held his gaze. She said simply, "The Book will remain with us. We will weather this storm—"

"That's enough," Mor interrupted.

She got to her feet.

And Mor looked each and every one of those queens in the eye as she said, "I am the Morrigan. You know me. What I am. You know that my gift is truth. So you will hear my words now, and know them as truth—as your ancestors once did."

Not a word.

Mor gestured behind her—to me. "Do you think it is any simple coincidence that a human has been made immortal again, at the very moment when our old enemy resurfaces? I fought side by side with Miryam in the War, fought beside her as Jurian's ambition and bloodlust drove him mad, and drove them apart. Drove him to torture Clythia to death, then battle Amarantha until his own." She took a sharp breath, and I could have sworn Azriel inched closer at the sound. But Mor blazed on, "I marched back into the Black Land with Miryam to free the slaves left in that burning sand, the slavery she had herself escaped. The slaves Miryam had promised to return to free. I marched with her—my friend. Along with Prince Drakon's legion. Miryam was my *friend*, as Feyre is now. And your ancestors, those queens who signed that Treaty . . . They were my friends, too. And when I look at you . . . " She bared her teeth. "I see *nothing* of those women in you. When I look at you, I know that your ancestors would be *ashamed*.

"You laugh at the idea of peace? That we can have it between our peoples?" Mor's voice cracked, and again Azriel subtly shifted nearer to her, though his face revealed nothing. "There is an island in a forgotten, stormy part of the sea. A vast, lush island, shielded from time and spying eyes. And on that island, Miryam and Drakon still live. With their children. With *both* of their peoples. Fae and human and those in between. Side by side. For five hundred years, they have prospered on that island, letting the world believe them dead—"

"Mor," Rhys said—a quiet reprimand.

A secret, I realized, that perhaps had remained hidden for five centuries.

A secret that had fueled the dreams of Rhysand, of his court.

A land where two dreamers had found peace between their peoples.

Where there was no wall. No iron wards. No ash arrows.

The golden queen and ancient queen looked to each other again.

The ancient one's eyes were bright as she declared, "Give us proof. If you are not the High Lord that rumor claims, give us one shred of proof that you are as you say—a male of peace."

There was one way. Only one way to show them, prove it to them.

Velaris.

My very bones cried out at the thought of revealing that gem to these . . . spiders.

Rhys rose in a fluid motion. The queens did the same. His voice was like a moonless night as he said, "You desire proof?" I held my breath, praying . . . praying he wouldn't tell them. He shrugged, the silver thread in his jacket catching the sunlight. "I shall get it for you. Await my word, and return when we summon you."

"We are summoned by no one, human or faerie," the golden queen simpered.

Perhaps that was why they'd taken so long to reply. To play some power game.

"Then come at your leisure," Rhys said, with enough of a bite that the queens' guards stepped forward. Cassian only grinned at them—and the wisest among them instantly paled.

Rhys barely inclined his head as he added, "Perhaps then you'll comprehend how vital the Book is to *both* our efforts."

"We will consider it once we have your *proof*." The ancient one nearly spat the word. Some part of me reminded myself that she was old, and royal, and smacking that sneer off her face would *not* be in our best interests. "That book has been ours to protect for five hundred years. We will not hand it over without due consideration."

The guards flanked them—as if the words had been some predetermined signal. The golden queen smirked at me, and said, "Good luck."

Then they were gone. The sitting room was suddenly too big, too quiet.

And it was Elain—*Elain*—who sighed and murmured, "I hope they all burn in hell."

CHAPTER 41

We were mostly silent during the flight and winnowing to Velaris. Amren was already waiting in the town house, her clothes rumpled, face unnervingly pale. I made a note to get her more blood immediately.

But rather than gather in the dining or sitting room, Rhys strolled down the hall, hands in his pockets, past the kitchen, and out into the courtyard garden in the back.

The rest of us lingered in the foyer, staring after him—the silence radiating from him. Like the calm before a storm.

"It went well, I take it," Amren said. Cassian gave her a look, and trailed after his friend.

The sun and arid day had warmed the garden, bits of green now poking their heads out here and there in the countless beds and pots. Rhys sat on the rim of the fountain, forearms braced on his knees, staring at the moss-flecked flagstone between his feet.

We all found our seats in the white-painted iron chairs throughout. If only humans could see them: faeries, sitting on iron. They'd throw away those ridiculous baubles and jewelry. Perhaps even Elain would receive an engagement ring that hadn't been forged with hate and fear.

"If you're out here to brood, Rhys," Amren said from her perch on a little bench, "then just say so and let me go back to my work."

Violet eyes lifted to hers. Cold, humorless. "The humans wish for proof of our good intentions. That we can be trusted."

Amren's attention cut to me. "Feyre was not enough?"

I tried not to let the words sting. No, I had not been enough; perhaps I'd even failed in my role as emissary—

"She is more than enough," Rhys said with that deadly calm, and I wondered if I'd sent my own pathetic thoughts down the bond. I snapped my shield up once more. "They're fools. Worse—frightened fools." He studied the ground again, as if the dried moss and stone made up some pattern no one but him could see.

Cassian said, "We could . . . depose them. Get newer, smarter queens on their thrones. Who might be willing to bargain."

Rhys shook his head. "One, it'd take too long. We don't have that time." I thought of the past few wasted weeks, how hard Azriel had tried to get into those courts. If even his shadows and spies could not breach their inner workings, then I doubted an assassin would. The confirming shake of the head Azriel gave Cassian said as much. "Two," Rhys continued, "who knows if that would somehow impact the magic of their half of the Book. It must be given freely. It's possible the magic is strong enough to see our scheming." He sucked on his teeth. "We are stuck with them."

"We could try again," Mor said. "Let me speak to them, let me go to their palace—"

"No," Azriel said. Mor raised her brows, and a faint color stained Azriel's tan face. But his features were set, his hazel eyes solid. "You're not setting foot in that human realm."

"I fought in the War, you will do well to remember—"

"No," Azriel said again, refusing to break her stare. His shifting wings rasped against the back of his chair. "They would string you up and make an example of you."

"They'd have to catch me first."

"That palace is a death trap for our kind," Azriel countered, his voice low and rough. "Built by Fae hands to protect the humans from us. You set foot inside it, Mor, and you won't walk out again. Why do you think we've had such trouble getting a foothold in there?"

"If going into their territory isn't an option," I cut in before Mor could say whatever the temper limning her features hissed at her to retort and surely wound the shadowsinger more than she intended, "and deceit or any mental manipulation might make the magic wreck the Book . . . What proof can be offered?" Rhys lifted his head. "Who is—who is this Miryam? Who was she to Jurian, and who was that prince you spoke of—Drakon? Perhaps we . . . perhaps they could be used as proof. If only to vouch for you."

The heat died from Mor's eyes as she shifted a foot against the moss and flagstone.

But Rhys interlocked his fingers in the space between his knees before he said, "Five hundred years ago, in the years leading up to the War, there was a Fae kingdom in the southern part of the continent. It was a realm of sand surrounding a lush river delta. The Black Land. There was no crueler place to be born a human—for no humans were born free. They were all of them slaves, forced to build great temples and palaces for the High Fae who ruled. There was no escape; no chance of having their freedom purchased. And the queen of the Black Land . . . " Memory stirred in his face.

"She made Amarantha seem as sweet as Elain," Mor explained with soft venom.

"Miryam," Rhys continued, "was a half-Fae female born of a human mother. And as her mother was a slave, as the conception was . . . against her mother's will, so, too, was Miryam born in shackles, and deemed human—denied any rights to her Fae heritage."

"Tell the full story another time," Amren cut in. "The gist of it, girl," she said to me, "is that Miryam was given as a wedding gift by the queen to her betrothed, a foreign Fae prince named Drakon. He was horrified, and let Miryam escape. Fearing the queen's wrath, she fled through the desert, across the sea, into more desert . . . and was found by Jurian. She fell in with his rebel armies, became his lover, and was a healer amongst the warriors. Until a devastating battle found her tending to Jurian's new Fae allies—including Prince Drakon. Turns out, Miryam had opened his eyes to the monster he planned to wed. He'd broken the engagement, allied his armies with the humans, and had been looking for the beautiful slave-girl for three years. Jurian had no idea that his new ally coveted his lover. He was too focused on winning the War, on destroying Amarantha in the North. As his obsession took over, he was blind to witnessing Miryam and Drakon falling in love behind his back."

"It wasn't behind his back," Mor snapped. "Miryam ended it with Jurian before she ever laid a finger on Drakon."

Amren shrugged. "Long story short, girl, when Jurian was slaughtered by Amarantha, and during the long centuries after, she told him what had happened to his lover. That she'd betrayed him for a Fae male. Everyone believed Miryam and Drakon perished while liberating her people from the Black Land at the end of the War—even Amarantha."

"And they didn't," I said. Rhys and Mor nodded. "It was all a way to escape, wasn't it? To start over somewhere else, with both their peoples?" Another set of nods. "So why not show the queens that? You started to tell them—"

"Because," Rhys cut in, "in addition to it not proving a thing about *my* character, which seemed to be their biggest gripe, it would be a grave betrayal of our friends. Their only wish was to remain hidden—to live in peace with their peoples. They fought and bled and suffered enough for it. I will not bring them into this conflict."

"Drakon's aerial army," Cassian mused, "was as good as ours. We might need to call upon him by the end."

Rhys merely shook his head. Conversation over. And perhaps he was right: revealing Drakon and Miryam's peaceful existence explained nothing about his own intentions. About his own merits and character.

"So, what do we offer them instead?" I asked. "What do we show them?"

Rhys's face was bleak. "We show them Velaris."

"What?" Mor barked. But Amren shushed her.

"You can't mean to bring them here," I said.

"Of course not. The risks are too great, entertaining them for even a night would likely result in bloodshed." Rhys said. "So I plan to merely show them."

"They'll dismiss it as mind tricks," Azriel countered.

"No," Rhys said, getting to his feet. "I mean to *show* them—playing by their own rules."

Amren clicked her nails against each other. "What do you mean, High Lord?"

But Rhys only said to Mor, "Send word to your father. We're going to pay him and my other court a visit."

My blood iced over. The Court of Nightmares.

There was an orb, it turned out, that had belonged to Mor's family for millennia: the Veritas. It was rife with the truth-magic she'd claimed to possess—that many in her bloodline also bore. And the Veritas was one of their most valued and guarded talismans.

Rhys wasted no time planning. We'd go to the Court of Nightmares within the Hewn City tomorrow afternoon, winnowing near the massive mountain it was built within, and then flying the rest of the way.

Mor, Cassian, and I were mere distractions to make Rhys's sudden visit less suspicious—while Azriel stole the orb from Mor's father's chambers.

The orb was known amongst the humans, had been wielded by them in the War, Rhys told me over a quiet dinner that night. The queens would know it. And would know it was absolute truth, not illusion or a trick, when we used it to show them—like peering into a living painting—that this city and its good people existed.

The others had suggested other places within his territory to prove he wasn't some warmongering sadist, but none had the same impact as Velaris, Rhys claimed. For his people, for the *world*, he'd offer the queens this slice of truth.

After dinner, I wandered into the streets, and found myself eventually standing at the edge of the Rainbow, the night in full swing, patrons and artists and everyday citizens bustling from shop to shop, peering in the galleries, buying supplies.

Compared to the sparkling lights and bright colors of the little hill sloping down to the river ahead, the streets behind me were shadowed, sleeping.

I'd been here nearly two months and hadn't worked up the courage to walk through the artists' quarter.

But this place . . . Rhys would risk this beautiful city, these lovely people, all for a shot at peace. Perhaps the guilt of leaving it protected while the rest of Prythian had suffered drove him; perhaps offering up Velaris on a silver platter was his own attempt to ease the weight. I rubbed at my chest, an ache building in there.

I took a step toward the quarter—and halted.

Maybe I should have asked Mor to come. But she'd left after dinner, pale-faced and jumpy, ignoring Cassian's attempt to speak with her. Azriel had taken to the clouds to contact his spies. He'd quietly promised the pacing Cassian to find Mor when he was done.

And Rhys . . . He had enough going on. And he hadn't objected when I stated I was going for a walk. He hadn't even warned me to be careful. If it was trust, or absolute faith in the safety of his city, or just that he knew how badly I'd react if he tried to tell me not to go or warn me, I didn't know.

I shook my head, clearing my thoughts as I again stared down the main street of the Rainbow.

I'd felt flickers these past few weeks in that hole inside my chest—flickers of images, but nothing solid. Nothing roaring with life and demand. Not in the way it had that night, seeing him kneel on that bed, naked and tattooed and winged.

It'd be stupid to venture into the quarter, anyway, when it might very well be ruined in any upcoming conflict. It'd be stupid to fall in love with it, when it might be torn from me.

So, like a coward, I turned and went home.

Rhys was waiting in the foyer, leaning against the post of the stair banister. His face was grim.

I halted in the middle of the entry carpet. "What's wrong?"

His wings were nowhere to be seen, not even the shadow of them. "I'm debating asking you to stay tomorrow."

I crossed my arms. "I thought I was going." *Don't lock me up in this house, don't shove me aside—*

He ran a hand through his hair. "What I have to be tomorrow, who I have to become, is not . . . it's not something I want you to see. How I will treat you, treat others . . ."

"The mask of the High Lord," I said quietly.

"Yes." He took a seat on the bottom step of the stairs.

I remained in the center of the foyer as I asked carefully, "Why don't you want me to see that?"

"Because you've only started to look at me like I'm not a monster, and I can't stomach the idea of anything you see tomorrow, being beneath that mountain, putting you back into that place where I found you."

Beneath that mountain—underground. Yes, I'd forgotten that. Forgotten I'd see the court that Amarantha had modeled her own after, that I'd be trapped beneath the earth . . .

But with Cassian, and Azriel, and Mor. With . . . him.

I waited for the panic, the cold sweat. Neither came. "Let me help. In whatever way I can."

Bleakness shaded the starlight in those eyes. "The role you will have to play is not a pleasant one."

"I trust you." I sat beside him on the stairs, close enough that the heat of his body warmed the chill night air clinging to my overcoat. "Why did Mor look so disturbed when she left?"

His throat bobbed. I could tell it was rage, and pain, that kept him from telling me outright—not mistrust. After a moment, he said, "I was there, in the Hewn City, the day her father declared she was to be sold in marriage to Eris, eldest son of the High Lord of the Autumn Court." Lucien's brother. "Eris had a reputation for cruelty, and Mor . . . begged me not to let it happen. For all her power, all her wildness, she had no voice, no rights with those people. And my father didn't particularly care if his cousins used their offspring as breeding stock."

"What happened?" I breathed.

"I brought Mor to the Illyrian camp for a few days. And she saw Cassian, and decided she'd do the one thing that would ruin her value to these people. I didn't know until after, and . . . it was a mess. With Cassian, with her, with our families. And it's another long story, but the short of it is that Eris refused to marry her. Said she'd been sullied by a bastard-born lesser faerie, and he'd now sooner fuck a sow. Her family . . . they . . . " I'd never seen him at such a loss for words. Rhys cleared his throat. "When they were done, they dumped her on the Autumn Court border, with a note nailed to her body that said she was Eris's problem."

Nailed—*nailed* to her.

Rhys said with soft wrath, "Eris left her for dead in the middle of their woods. Azriel found her a day later. It was all I could do to keep him from going to either court and slaughtering them all."

I thought of that merry face, the flippant laughter, the female that did not care who approved. Perhaps because she had seen the ugliest her kind had to offer. And had survived.

And I understood—why Rhys could not endure Nesta for more

than a few moments, why he could not let go of that anger where her failings were concerned, even if I had.

Beron's fire began crackling in my veins. *My* fire, not his. Not his son's, either.

I took Rhys's hand, and his thumb brushed against the back of my palm. I tried not to think about the ease of that stroke as I said in a hard, calm voice I barely recognized, "Tell me what I need to do tomorrow."

CHAPTER 42

I was not frightened.

Not of the role that Rhys had asked me to play today. Not of the roaring wind as we winnowed into a familiar, snow-capped mountain range refusing to yield to spring's awakening kiss. Not of the punishing drop as Rhys flew us between the peaks and valleys, swift and sleek. Cassian and Azriel flanked us; Mor would meet us at the gates to the mountain base.

Rhys's face was drawn, his shoulders tense as I gripped them. I knew what to expect, but . . . even after he'd told me what he needed me to do, even after I had agreed, he'd been . . . aloof. Haunted.

Worried for me, I realized.

And just because of that worry, just to get that tightness off his face, even for these few minutes before we faced his unholy realm beneath that mountain, I said over the wind, "Amren and Mor told me that the span of an Illyrian male's wings says a lot about the size of . . . other parts."

His eyes shot to mine, then to pine-tree-coated slopes below. "Did they now."

I shrugged in his arms, trying not to think about the naked body that night all those weeks ago—though I hadn't glimpsed much. "They also said Azriel's wings are the biggest."

Mischief danced in those violet eyes, washing away the cold distance, the strain. The spymaster was a black blur against the pale blue sky. "When we return home, let's get out the measuring stick, shall we?"

I pinched the rock-hard muscle of his forearm. Rhys flashed me a wicked grin before he tilted down—

Mountains and snow and trees and sun and utter free fall through wisps of cloud—

A breathless scream came out of me as we plummeted. Throwing my arms around his neck was instinct. His low laugh tickled my nape. "You're willing to brave my brand of darkness and put up one of your own, willing to go to a watery grave and take on the Weaver, but a little free fall makes you scream?"

"I'll leave you to rot the next time you have a nightmare," I hissed, my eyes still shut and body locked as he snapped out his wings to ease us into a steady glide.

"No, you won't," he crooned. "You liked seeing me naked too much."

"Prick."

His laugh rumbled against me. Eyes closed, the wind roaring like a wild animal, I adjusted my position, gripping him tighter. My knuckles brushed one of his wings—smooth and cool like silk, but hard as stone with it stretched taut.

Fascinating. I blindly reached again . . . and dared to run a fingertip along some inner edge.

Rhysand shuddered, a soft groan slipping past my ear. "That," he said tightly, "is very sensitive."

I snatched my finger back, pulling away far enough to see his face. With the wind, I had to squint, and my braided hair ripped this way and that, but—he was entirely focused on the mountains around us. "Does it tickle?"

He flicked his gaze to me, then to the snow and pine that went on forever. "It feels like this," he said, and leaned in so close that his lips brushed the shell of my ear as he sent a gentle breath into it. My back arched on instinct, my chin tipping up at the caress of that breath.

"Oh," I managed to say. I felt him smile against my ear and pull away.

"If you want an Illyrian male's attention, you'd be better off grabbing him by the balls. We're trained to protect our wings at all costs. Some males attack first, ask questions later, if their wings are touched without invitation."

"And during sex?" The question blurted out.

Rhys's face was nothing but feline amusement as he monitored the mountains. "During sex, an Illyrian male can find completion just by having someone touch his wings in the right spot."

My blood thrummed. Dangerous territory; more lethal than the drop below. "Have *you* found that to be true?"

His eyes stripped me bare. "I've never allowed anyone to see or touch my wings during sex. It makes you vulnerable in a way that I'm not . . . comfortable with."

"Too bad," I said, staring out too casually toward the mighty mountain that now appeared on the horizon, towering over the others. And capped, I noted, with that glimmering palace of moonstone.

"Why?" he asked warily.

I shrugged, fighting the upward tugging of my lips. "Because I bet you could get into some interesting positions with those wings."

Rhys loosed a barking laugh, and his nose grazed my ear. I felt him open his mouth to whisper something, but—

Something dark and fast and sleek shot for us, and he plunged down and away, swearing.

But another one, and another, kept coming.

Not just ordinary arrows, I realized as Rhys veered, snatching one out of the air. Others bounced harmlessly off a shield he blasted up.

He studied the wood in his palm and dropped it with a hiss. Ash arrows. To kill faeries.

And now that I was one . . .

Faster than the wind, faster than death, Rhys shot for the ground. Flew, not winnowed, because he wanted to know where our enemies were, didn't want to lose them. The wind bit my face, screeched in my ears, ripped at my hair with brutal claws.

Azriel and Cassian were already hurtling for us. Shields of translucent blue and red encircled them—sending those arrows bouncing off. Their Siphons at work.

The arrows shot from the pine forest coating the mountains, then vanished.

Rhys slammed into the ground, snow flying in his wake, and fury like I hadn't seen since that day in Amarantha's court twisted his features. I could feel it thrumming against me, roiling through the clearing we now stood in.

Azriel and Cassian were there in an instant, their colored shields shrinking back into their Siphons. The three of them forces of nature in the pine forest, Rhysand didn't even look at me as he ordered Cassian, "Take her to the palace, and stay there until I'm back. Az, you're with me."

Cassian reached for me, but I stepped away. "No."

"What?" Rhys snarled, the word near-guttural.

"Take me with you," I said. I didn't want to go to that moonstone palace to pace and wait and wring my fingers.

Cassian and Azriel, wisely, kept their mouths shut. And Rhys, Mother bless him, only tucked in his wings and crossed his arms—waiting to hear my reasons.

"I've seen ash arrows," I said a bit breathlessly. "I might recognize where they were made. And if they came from the hand of another High Lord . . . I can detect that, too." If they'd come from Tarquin . . . "And I can track just as well on the ground as any of you." Except for Azriel, maybe. "So you and Cassian take the skies," I said, still waiting for the rejection, the order to lock me up. "And I'll hunt on the ground with Azriel."

The wrath radiating through the snowy clearing ebbed into frozen, too-calm rage. But Rhys said, "Cassian—I want aerial patrols on the sea borders, stationed in two-mile rings, all the way out toward Hybern. I want foot soldiers in the mountain passes along the southern border; make sure those warning fires are ready on every peak. We're not going to rely on magic." He turned to Azriel. "When you're done, warn your spies that they might be compromised, and prepare to get them out. And put fresh ones in. We keep this contained. We don't tell anyone inside that court what happened. If anyone mentions it, say it was a training exercise."

Because we couldn't afford to let that weakness show, even amongst his subjects.

His eyes at last found mine. "We've got an hour until we're expected at court. Make it count."

✠

We searched, but the missed arrows had been snatched up by our attackers—and even the shadows and wind told Azriel nothing, as if our enemy had been hidden from them as well.

But that was twice now that they'd known where Rhys and I would be.

Mor found Azriel and me after twenty minutes, wanting to know what the hell had happened. We'd explained—and she'd winnowed away, to spin whatever excuse would keep her horrible family from suspecting anything was amiss.

But at the end of the hour, we hadn't found a single track. And we could delay our meeting no longer.

The Court of Nightmares lay behind a mammoth set of doors carved into the mountain itself. And from the base, the mountain rose so high I couldn't see the palace I had once stayed in atop it. Only snow, and rock, and birds circling above. There was no one outside—no village, no signs of life. Nothing to indicate a whole city of people dwelled within.

But I did not let my curiosity or any lingering trepidation show as Mor and I entered. Rhys, Cassian, and Azriel would arrive minutes later.

There were sentries at the stone gates, clothed not in black, as I might have suspected, but in gray and white—armor meant to blend into the mountain face. Mor didn't so much as look at them as she led me silently inside the mountain-city.

My body clenched as soon as the darkness, the scent of rock and fire and roasting meat, hit me. I had been here before, suffered here—

Not Under the Mountain. This was not Under the Mountain.

Indeed, Amarantha's court had been the work of a child.

The Court of Nightmares was the work of a god.

While Under the Mountain had been a series of halls and rooms and levels, this . . . this was truly a city.

The walkway that Mor led us down was an avenue, and around us, rising high into gloom, were buildings and spires, homes and bridges. A metropolis carved from the dark stone of the mountain itself, no inch of it left unmarked or without some lovely, hideous artwork etched into it. Figures danced and fornicated; begged and reveled. Pillars were carved to look like curving vines of night-blooming flowers. Water ran throughout in little streams and rivers tapped from the heart of the mountain itself.

The Hewn City. A place of such terrible beauty that it was an effort to keep the wonder and dread off my face. Music was already playing somewhere, and our hosts still did not come out to greet us. The people we passed—only High Fae—were clothed in finery, their faces deathly pale and cold. Not one stopped us, not one smiled or bowed.

Mor ignored them all. Neither of us had said one word. Rhys had told me not to—that the walls had ears here.

Mor led me down the avenue toward another set of stone gates, thrown open at the base of what looked to be a castle *within* the mountain. The official seat of the High Lord of the Night Court.

Great, scaled black beasts were carved into those gates, all coiled together in a nest of claws and fangs, sleeping and fighting, some locked in an endless cycle of devouring each other. Between them flowed vines of jasmine and moonflowers. I could have sworn the beasts seemed to writhe in the silvery glow of the bobbing faelights throughout the mountain-city. The Gates of Eternity—that's what I'd call the painting that flickered in my mind.

Mor continued through them, a flash of color and life in this strange, cold place.

She wore deepest red, the gossamer and gauze of her sleeveless gown clinging to her breasts and hips, while carefully placed shafts left much of her stomach and back exposed. Her hair was down in rippling waves, and cuffs of solid gold glinted around her wrists. A queen—a queen who bowed to no one, a queen who had faced them all down and triumphed. A queen who owned her body, her life, her destiny, and never apologized for it.

My clothes, which she had taken a moment in the pine wood to shift me into, were of a similar ilk, nearly identical to those I had been forced to wear Under the Mountain. Two shafts of fabric that hardly covered my breasts flowed to below my navel, where a belt across my hips joined them into one long shaft that draped between my legs and barely covered my backside.

But unlike the chiffon and bright colors I had worn then, this one was fashioned of black, glittering fabric that sparkled with every swish of my hips.

Mor had fashioned my hair onto a crown atop my head—right behind the black diadem that had been set before it, accented with flecks of diamond that made it glisten like the night sky. She'd darkened and lengthened my eyelashes, sweeping out an elegant, vicious line of kohl at the outer corner of each. My lips she'd painted bloodred.

Into the castle beneath the mountain we strode. There were more people here, milling about the endless halls, watching our every breath. Some looked like Mor, with their gold hair and beautiful faces. They even hissed at her.

Mor smirked at them. Part of me wished she'd rip their throats out instead.

We at last came to a throne room of polished ebony. More of the serpents from the front gates were carved here—this time, wrapped around the countless columns supporting the onyx ceiling. It was so high up that gloom hid its finer details, but I knew more had been carved there, too. Great beasts to monitor the manipulations and scheming within this room. The throne itself had been fashioned out of a few of them, a head snaking around either side of the back—as if they watched over the High Lord's shoulder.

A crowd had gathered—and for a moment, I was again in Amarantha's throne room, so similar was the atmosphere, the malice. So similar was the dais at the other end.

A golden-haired, beautiful man stepped into our path toward that ebony throne, and Mor smoothly halted. I knew he was her father without him saying a word.

He was clothed in black, a silver circlet atop his head. His brown eyes were like old soil as he said to her, "Where is he?"

No greeting, no formality. He ignored me wholly.

Mor shrugged. "He arrives when he wishes to." She continued on.

Her father looked at me then. And I willed my face into a mask like hers. Disinterested. Aloof.

Her father surveyed my face, my body—and where I thought he'd sneer and ogle . . . there was nothing. No emotion. Just heartless cold.

I followed Mor before disgust wrecked my own icy mask.

Banquet tables against the black walls were covered with fat, succulent fruits and wreaths of golden bread, interrupted with roast meats, kegs of cider and ale, and pies and tarts and little cakes of every size and variety.

It might have made my mouth water . . . Were it not for the High Fae in their finery. Were it not for the fact that no one touched the food—the power and wealth lying in letting it go to waste.

Mor went right up to the obsidian dais, and I halted at the foot of the steps as she took up a place beside the throne and said to the crowd in a voice that was clear and cruel and cunning, "Your High Lord approaches. He is in a foul mood, so I suggest being on your best behavior—unless you wish to be the evening entertainment."

And before the crowd could begin murmuring, I felt it. Felt—him.

The very rock beneath my feet seemed to tremble—a pulsing, steady beat.

His footsteps. As if the mountain shuddered at each touch.

Everyone in that room went still as death. As if petrified that their very breathing would draw the attention of the predator now strolling toward us.

Mor's shoulders were back, her chin high—feral, wanton pride at her master's arrival.

Remembering my role, I kept my own chin lowered, watching beneath my brows.

First Cassian and Azriel appeared in the doorway. The High Lord's general and shadowsinger—and the most powerful Illyrians in history.

They were not the males I had come to know.

Clad in battle-black that hugged their muscled forms, their armor was intricate, scaled—their shoulders impossibly broader, their faces a portrait of unfeeling brutality. They reminded me, somehow, of the ebony beasts carved into the pillars they passed.

More Siphons, I realized, glimmered in addition to the ones atop each of their hands. A Siphon in the center of their chest. One on either shoulder. One on either knee.

For a moment, my knees quaked, and I understood what the camp-lords had feared in them. If one Siphon was what most Illyrians needed to handle their killing power . . . Cassian and Azriel had seven each. *Seven.*

The courtiers had the good sense to back away a step as Cassian and Azriel strolled through the crowd, toward the dais. Their wings gleamed, the talons at the apex sharp enough to pierce air—like they'd honed them.

Cassian's focus had gone right to Mor, Azriel indulging in all of a glance before scanning the people around them. Most shirked from the spymaster's eyes—though they trembled as they beheld Truth-Teller at his side, the Illyrian blade peeking above his left shoulder.

Azriel, his face a mask of beautiful death, silently promised them all endless, unyielding torment, even the shadows shuddering in his wake. I knew why; knew for whom he'd gladly do it.

They had tried to sell a seventeen-year-old girl into marriage with a sadist—and then brutalized her in ways I couldn't, wouldn't, let myself consider. And these people now lived in utter terror of the three companions who stood at the dais.

Good. They should be afraid of them.

Afraid of me.

And then Rhysand appeared.

He had released the damper on his power, on who he was. His power filled the throne room, the castle, the mountain. The world. It had no end and no beginning.

No wings. No weapons. No sign of the warrior. Nothing but the elegant, cruel High Lord the world believed him to be. His hands were in his pockets, his black tunic seeming to gobble up the light. And on his head sat a crown of stars.

No sign of the male who had been drinking on the roof; no sign of the fallen prince kneeling on his bed. The full impact of him threatened to sweep me away.

Here—here was the most powerful High Lord ever born.

The face of dreams and nightmares.

Rhys's eyes met mine briefly from across the room as he strolled between the pillars. To the throne that was his by blood and sacrifice and might. My own blood sang at the power that thrummed from him, at the sheer beauty of him.

Mor stepped off the dais, dropping to one knee in a smooth bow. Cassian and Azriel followed suit.

So did everyone in that room.

Including me.

The ebony floor was so polished I could see my red-painted lips in it; see my own expressionless face. The room was so silent I could hear each of Rhys's footsteps toward us.

"Well, well," he said to no one in particular. "Looks like you're all on time for once."

Raising his head as he continued kneeling, Cassian gave Rhys a half grin—the High Lord's commander incarnate, eager to do his bloodletting.

Rhys's boots stopped in my line of sight.

His fingers were icy on my chin as he lifted my face.

The entire room, still on the floor, watched. But this was the role he needed me to play. To be a distraction and novelty. Rhys's lips curved upward. "Welcome to my home, Feyre Cursebreaker."

I lowered my eyes, my kohl-thick lashes tickling my cheek. He clicked his tongue, his grip on my chin tightening. Everyone noticed the push of his fingers, the predatory angle of his head as he said, "Come with me."

A tug on my chin, and I rose to my feet. Rhys dragged his eyes over me and I wondered if it wasn't entirely for show as they glazed a bit.

He led me the few steps onto the dais—to the throne. He sat, smiling faintly at his monstrous court. He owned every inch of the throne. These people.

And with a tug on my waist, he perched me on his lap.

The High Lord's whore. Who I'd become Under the Mountain—who the world expected me to be. The dangerous new pet that Mor's father would now seek to feel out.

Rhys's hand slid along my bare waist, the other running down my exposed thigh. Cold—his hands were so cold I almost yelped.

He must have felt the silent flinch. A heartbeat later, his hands had warmed. His thumb, curving around the inside of my thigh, gave a slow, long stroke as if to say *Sorry*.

Rhys indeed leaned in to bring his mouth near my ear, well aware his subjects had not yet risen from the floor. As if they had once done so before they were bidden, long ago, and had learned the consequences. Rhysand whispered to me, his other hand now stroking the bare skin of my ribs in lazy, indolent circles, "Try not to let it go to your head."

I knew they could all hear it. So did he.

I stared at their bowed heads, my heart hammering, but said with midnight smoothness, "What?"

Rhys's breath caressed my ear, the twin to the breath he'd brushed against it merely an hour ago in the skies. "That every male in here is contemplating what they'd be willing to give up in order to get that pretty, red mouth of yours on them."

I waited for the blush, the shyness, to creep in.

But I *was* beautiful. I was strong.

I had survived—triumphed. As Mor had survived in this horrible, poisoned house . . .

So I smiled a bit, the first smile of my new mask. Let them see that pretty, red mouth, and my white, straight teeth.

His hand slid higher up my thigh, the proprietary touch of a male who knew he owned someone body and soul. He'd apologized in advance for it—for this game, these roles we'd have to play.

But I leaned into that touch, leaned back into his hard, warm body. I was pressed so closely against him that I could feel the deep rumble of his voice as he at last said to his court, "Rise."

As one, they did. I smirked at some of them, gloriously bored and infinitely amused.

Rhys brushed a knuckle along the inside of my knee, and every nerve in my body narrowed to that touch.

"Go play," he said to them all.

They obeyed, the crowd dispersing, music striking up from a distant corner.

"Keir," Rhys said, his voice cutting through the room like lightning on a stormy night.

It was all he needed to summon Mor's father to the foot of the dais. Keir bowed again, his face lined with icy resentment as he took in Rhys, then me—glancing once at Mor and the Illyrians. Cassian gave Keir a slow nod that told him he remembered—and would never forget—what the Steward of the Hewn City had done to his own daughter.

But it was from Azriel that Keir cringed. From the sight of Truth-Teller.

One day, I realized, Azriel would use that blade on Mor's father. And take a long, long while to carve him up.

"Report," Rhys said, stroking a knuckle down my ribs. He gave a dismissive nod to Cassian, Mor, and Azriel, and the trio faded away into the crowd. Within a heartbeat, Azriel had vanished into shadows and was gone. Keir didn't even turn.

Before Rhys, Keir was nothing more than a sullen child. Yet I knew Mor's father was older. Far older. The Steward clung to power, it seemed.

Rhys *was* power.

"Greetings, milord," Keir said, his deep voice polished smooth. "And greetings to your . . . guest."

Rhys's hand flattened on my thigh as he angled his head to look at me. "She is lovely, isn't she?"

"Indeed," Keir said, lowering his eyes. "There is little to report, milord. All has been quiet since your last visit."

"No one for me to punish?" A cat playing with his food.

"Unless you'd like for me to select someone here, no, milord."

Rhys clicked his tongue. "Pity." He again surveyed me, then leaned to tug my earlobe with his teeth.

And damn me to hell, but I leaned farther back as his teeth pressed down at the same moment his thumb drifted high on the side of my thigh, sweeping across sensitive skin in a long, luxurious touch. My body went loose and tight, and my breathing . . . Cauldron damn me again, the scent of him, the citrus and the sea, the power roiling off him . . . my breathing hitched a bit.

I knew he noticed; knew he felt that shift in me.

His fingers stilled on my leg.

Keir began mentioning people I didn't know in the court, bland reports on marriages and alliances, blood-feuds, and Rhys let him talk.

His thumb stroked again—this time joined with his pointer finger.

A dull roaring was filling my ears, drowning out everything but that touch on the inside of my leg. The music was throbbing, ancient, wild, and people ground against each other to it.

His eyes on the Steward, Rhys made vague nods every now and then. While his fingers continued their slow, steady stroking on my thighs, rising higher with every pass.

People were watching. Even as they drank and ate, even as some danced in small circles, people were watching. I was sitting in his lap, his own personal plaything, his every touch visible to them . . . and yet it might as well have been only the two of us.

Keir listed the expenses and costs of running the court, and Rhys gave another vague nod. This time, his nose brushed the spot between my neck and shoulder, followed by a passing graze of his mouth.

My breasts tightened, becoming full and heavy, aching—aching like what was now pooling in my core. Heat filled my face, my blood.

But Keir said at last, as if his own self-control slipped the leash, "I had heard the rumors, and I didn't quite believe them." His gaze settled on me, on my breasts, peaked through the folds of my dress, of my legs, spread wider than they'd been minutes before, and Rhys's hand in dangerous territory. "But it seems true: Tamlin's pet is now owned by another master."

"You should see how I make her beg," Rhys murmured, nudging my neck with his nose.

Keir clasped his hands behind his back. "I assume you brought her to make a statement."

"You know everything I do is a statement."

"Of course. This one, it seems, you enjoy putting in cobwebs and crowns."

Rhys's hand paused, and I sat straighter at the tone, the disgust. And I said to Keir in a voice that belonged to another woman, "Perhaps I'll put a leash on *you*."

Rhys's approval tapped against my mental shield, the hand at my ribs now making lazy circles. "She does enjoy playing," he mused onto my shoulder. He jerked his chin toward the Steward. "Get her some wine."

Pure command. No politeness.

Keir stiffened, but strode off.

Rhys didn't dare break from his mask, but the light kiss he pressed beneath my ear told me enough. Apology and gratitude—and more apologies. He didn't like this any more than I did. And yet to get what we needed, to buy Azriel time . . . He'd do it. And so would I.

I wondered, then, with his hands beneath my breasts and between my legs, what Rhys *wouldn't* give of himself. Wondered if . . . if perhaps the arrogance and swagger . . . if they masked a male who perhaps thought he wasn't worth very much at all.

A new song began, like dripping honey—and edged into a swift-moving wind, punctuated with driving, relentless drums.

I twisted, studying his face. There was nothing warm in his eyes, nothing of the friend I'd made. I opened my shield enough to let him in.

What? His voice floated into my mind.

I reached down the bond between us, caressing that wall of ebony adamant. A small sliver cracked—just for me. And I said into it, *You are good, Rhys. You are kind. This mask does not scare me. I see you beneath it.*

His hands tightened on me, and his eyes held mine as he leaned forward to brush his mouth against my cheek. It was answer enough—and . . . an unleashing.

I leaned a bit more against him, my legs widening ever so slightly. *Why'd you stop?* I said into his mind, into him.

A near-silent growl reverberated against me. He stroked my ribs again, in time to the beat of the music, his thumb rising nearly high enough to graze the underside of my breasts.

I let my head drop back against his shoulder.

I let go of the part of me that heard their words—*whore, whore, whore*—

Let go of the part that said those words alongside them—*traitor, liar, whore*—

And I just *became.*

I became the music, and the drums, and the wild, dark thing in the High Lord's arms.

His eyes were wholly glazed—and not with power or rage. Something red-hot and edged with glittering darkness exploded in my mind.

I dragged a hand down his thigh, feeling the hidden warrior's strength there. Dragged it back up again in a long, idle stroke, needing to touch him, feel him.

I was going to catch fire and burn. I was going to start burning right here—

Easy, he said with wicked amusement through the open sliver in my shield. *If you become a living candle, poor Keir will throw a hissy fit. And then you'd ruin the party for everyone.*

Because the fire would let them all know I wasn't normal—and no doubt Keir would inform his almost-allies in the Autumn Court. Or one of these other monsters would.

Rhys shifted his hips, rubbing against me with enough pressure that for a second, I didn't care about Keir, or the Autumn Court, or what Azriel might be doing right now to steal the orb.

I had been so cold, so lonely, for so long, and my body cried out at the contact, at the joy of being touched and held and *alive.*

The hand that had been on my waist slid across my abdomen, hooking into the low-slung belt there. I rested my head between his shoulder and neck, staring at the crowd as they stared at me, savoring every place where Rhys and I connected and wanting *more more more*.

At last, when my blood had begun to boil, when Rhys skimmed the underside of my breast with his knuckle, I looked to where I knew Keir was standing, watching us, my wine forgotten in his hand.

We both did.

The Steward was staring unabashedly as he leaned against the wall. Unsure whether to interrupt. Half terrified to. *We* were his distraction. *We* were the sleight of hand while Az stole the orb.

I knew Rhys was still holding Keir's gaze as the tip of his tongue slid up my neck.

I arched my back, eyes heavy-lidded, breathing uneven. I'd burn and burn and burn—

I think he's so disgusted that he might have given me the orb just to get out of here, Rhys said in my mind, that other hand drifting dangerously south. But there was such a growing ache there, and I wore nothing beneath that would conceal the damning evidence if he slid his hand a fraction higher.

You and I put on a good show, I said back. The person who said that, husky and sultry—I'd never heard that voice come out of me before. Even in my mind.

His hand slid to my upper thigh, fingers curving in.

I ground against him, trying to shift those hands away from what he'd learn—

To find him hard against my backside.

Every thought eddied from my head. Only a thrill of power remained as I writhed along that impressive length. Rhys let out a low, rough laugh.

Keir just watched and watched and watched. Rigid. Horrified. Stuck here, until Rhys released him—and not thinking twice about why. Or where the spymaster had gone.

So I turned around again, meeting Rhysand's now-blazing eyes, and then licked up the column of his throat. Wind and sea and citrus and sweat. It almost undid me.

I faced forward, and Rhys dragged his mouth along the back of my neck, right over my spine, just as I shifted against the hardness pushing into me, insistent and dominating. Precisely as his hand slid a bit too high on my inner thigh.

I felt the predatory focus go right to the slickness he'd felt there. Proof of my traitorous body. His arms tightened around me, and my face burned—perhaps a bit from shame, but—

Rhys sensed my focus, my fire slip. *It's fine,* he said, but that mental voice sounded breathless. *It means nothing. It's just your body reacting—*

Because you're so irresistible? My attempt to deflect sounded strained, even in my mind.

But he laughed, probably for my benefit.

We'd danced around and teased and taunted each other for months. And maybe it was my body's reaction, maybe it was *his* body's reaction, but the taste of him threatened to destroy me, consume me, and—

Another male. I'd had another male's hands all over me, when Tamlin and I were barely—

Fighting my nausea, I pasted a sleepy, lust-fogged smile on my face. Right as Azriel returned and gave Rhys a subtle nod. He'd gotten the orb.

Mor slid up to the spymaster, running a proprietary hand over his shoulders, his chest, as she circled to look into his face. Az's scar-mottled hand wrapped around her bare waist—squeezing once. The confirmation she also needed.

She offered him a little grin that would no doubt spread rumors, and sauntered into the crowd again. Dazzling, distracting, leaving them thinking Az had been here the whole time, leaving them pondering if she'd extend Azriel an invitation to her bed.

Azriel just stared after Mor, distant and bored. I wondered if he was as much of a mess inside as I was.

Rhys crooked a finger to Keir, who, scowling a bit in his daughter's direction, stumbled forward with my wine. He'd barely reached the dais before Rhys's power took it from him, floating the goblet to us.

Rhys set it on the ground beside the throne, a stupid task he'd thought up for the Steward to remind him of his powerlessness, that this throne was not his.

"Should I test it for poison?" Rhys drawled even as he said into my mind, *Cassian's waiting. Go.*

Rhys had the same, sex-addled expression on his perfect face—but his eyes . . . I couldn't read the shadows in his eyes.

Maybe—maybe for all our teasing, after Amarantha, he didn't *want* to be touched by a woman like that. Didn't even enjoy being wanted like that.

I had been tortured and tormented, but his horrors had gone to another level.

"No, milord," Keir groveled. "I would never dare harm you." Another distraction, this conversation. I took that as my cue to stride to Cassian, who was snarling by a pillar at anyone who came too close.

I felt the eyes of the court slide to me, felt them all sniff delicately at what was so clearly written over my body. But as I passed Keir, even with the High Lord at my back, he hissed almost too quietly to hear, "You'll get what's coming to you, whore."

Night exploded into the room.

People cried out. And when the darkness cleared, Keir was on his knees.

Rhys still lounged on the throne. His face a mask of frozen rage.

The music stopped. Mor appeared at the edge of the crowd—her own features set in smug satisfaction. Even as Azriel approached her side, standing too close to be casual.

"Apologize," Rhys said. My heart thundered at the pure command, the utter wrath.

Keir's neck muscles strained, and sweat broke out on his lip.

"I said," Rhys intoned with such horrible calm, "apologize."

The Steward groaned. And when another heartbeat passed—

Bone cracked. Keir screamed.

And I watched—I watched as his arm fractured into not two, not three, but *four* different pieces, the skin going taut and loose in all the wrong spots—

Another crack. His elbow disintegrated. My stomach churned.

Keir began sobbing, the tears half from rage, judging by the hatred in his eyes as he looked at me, then Rhys. But his lips formed the words, *I'm sorry*.

The bones of his other arm splintered, and it was an effort not to cringe.

Rhys smiled as Keir screamed again and said to the room, "Should I kill him for it?"

No one answered.

Rhys chuckled. He said to his Steward, "When you wake up, you're not to see a healer. If I hear that you do . . . " Another crack—Keir's pinkie finger went saggy. The male shrieked. The heat that had boiled my blood turned to ice. "If I hear that you do, I'll carve you into pieces and bury them where no one can stand a chance of putting you together again."

Keir's eyes widened in true terror now. Then, as if an invisible hand had struck the consciousness from him, he collapsed to the floor.

Rhys said to no one in particular, "Dump him in his room."

Two males who looked like they could be Mor's cousins or brothers rushed forward, gathering up the Steward. Mor watched them, sneering faintly—though her skin was pale.

He'd wake up. That's what Rhys had said.

I made myself keep walking as Rhys summoned another courtier to give him reports on whatever trivial matters.

But my attention remained on the throne behind me, even as I slipped beside Cassian, daring the court to approach, to play with me. None did.

And for the long hour afterward, my focus half remained on the High Lord whose hands and mouth and body had suddenly made me feel awake—burning. It didn't make me forget, didn't make me obliterate hurts or grievances, it just made me . . . alive. Made me feel as if I'd been asleep for a year, slumbering inside a glass coffin, and he had just shattered through it and shaken me to consciousness.

The High Lord whose power had not scared me. Whose wrath did not wreck me.

And now—now I didn't know where that put me.

Knee-deep in trouble seemed like a good place to start.

CHAPTER 43

The wind roared around Rhys and me as he winnowed from the skies above his court. But Velaris didn't greet us.

Rather, we were standing by a moonlit mountain lake ringed in pine trees, high above the world. We'd left the court as we'd come in—with swagger and menace. Where Cassian, Azriel, and Mor had gone with the orb, I had no idea.

Alone at the edge of the lake, Rhys said hoarsely, "I'm sorry."

I blinked. "What do you possibly have to be sorry for?"

His hands were shaking—as if in the aftermath of that fury at what Keir had called me, what he'd threatened. Perhaps he'd brought us here before heading home in order to have some privacy before his friends could interrupt. "I shouldn't have let you go. Let you see that part of us. Of me." I'd never seen him so raw, so . . . stumbling.

"I'm fine." I didn't know what to make of what had been done. Both between us and to Keir. But it had been my choice. To play that role, to wear these clothes. To let him touch me. But . . . I said slowly, "We knew what tonight would require of us. Please—please don't start . . . protecting me. Not like that." He knew what I meant. He'd protected me

Under the Mountain, but that primal, male rage he'd just shown Keir . . . A shattered study splattered in paint flashed through my memory.

Rhys rasped, "I will never—*never* lock you up, force you to stay behind. But when he threatened you tonight, when he called you . . ." Whore. That's what they'd called *him*. For fifty years, they'd hissed it. I'd listened to Lucien spit the words in his face. Rhys released a jagged breath. "It's hard to shut down my instincts."

Instincts. Just like . . . like someone *else* had instincts to protect, to hide me away. "Then you should have prepared yourself better," I snapped. "You seemed to be going along *just fine* with it, until Keir said—"

"I will *kill* anyone who harms you," Rhys snarled. "I will *kill* them, and take a damn long time doing it." He panted. "Go ahead. Hate me—despise me for it."

"You are my *friend*," I said, and my voice broke on the word. I hated the tears that slipped down my face. I didn't even know why I was crying. Perhaps for the fact that it had felt real on that throne with him, even for a moment, and . . . and it likely hadn't been. Not for him. "You're my friend—and I understand that you're High Lord. I understand that you will defend your true court, and punish threats against it. But I can't . . . I don't want you to stop telling me things, inviting me to do things, because of the threats against me."

Darkness rippled, and wings tore from his back. "I am not him," Rhys breathed. "I will *never* be him, act like him. He locked you up and let you wither, and die."

"He tried—"

"Stop comparing. *Stop* comparing me to him."

The words cut me short. I blinked.

"You think I don't know how stories get written—how *this* story will be written?" Rhys put his hands on his chest, his face more open, more anguished than I'd seen it. "I am the dark lord, who stole away the bride of spring. I am a demon, and a nightmare, and I will meet a bad end. He is the golden prince—the hero who will get to keep you as his reward for not dying of stupidity and arrogance."

The things I love have a tendency to be taken from me. He'd admitted that to me Under the Mountain.

But his words were kindling to my temper, to whatever pit of fear was yawning open inside of me. "And what about my story?" I hissed. "What about *my* reward? What about what *I* want?"

"What is it that you want, Feyre?"

I had no answer. I didn't know. Not anymore.

"What is it that you *want*, Feyre?"

I stayed silent.

His laugh was bitter, soft. "I thought so. Perhaps you should take some time to figure that out one of these days."

"Perhaps I don't know what I want, but at least I don't hide what I am behind a mask," I seethed. "At least I let them see who I am, broken bits and all. Yes—it's to save your people. But what about the other masks, Rhys? What about letting your friends see your real face? But maybe it's easier not to. Because what if you did let someone in? And what if they saw *everything*, and still walked away? Who could blame them—who would want to bother with that sort of mess?"

He flinched.

The most powerful High Lord in history flinched. And I knew I'd hit hard—and deep.

Too hard. Too deep.

"Rhys," I said.

"Let's go home."

The word hung between us, and I wondered if he'd take it back—even as I waited for my own mouth to bark that it wasn't home. But the thought of the clear, crisp blue skies of Velaris at sunset, the sparkle of the city lights . . .

Before I could say yes, he grabbed my hand, not meeting my stare, and winnowed us away.

The wind was hollow as it roared around us, the darkness cold and foreign.

Cassian, Azriel, and Mor were indeed waiting at the town house. I bid them good night while they ambushed Rhysand for answers about what Keir had said to provoke him.

I was still in my dress—which felt vulgar in the light of Velaris—but found myself heading into the garden, as if the moonlight and chill might cleanse my mind.

Though, if I was being honest . . . I was waiting for him. What I'd said . . .

I had been awful. He'd told me those secrets, those vulnerabilities in confidence. And I'd thrown them in his face.

Because I knew it'd hurt him. And I knew I hadn't been talking about him, not really.

Minutes passed, the night still cool enough to remind me that spring had not fully dawned, and I shivered, rubbing my arms as the moon drifted. I listened to the fountain, and the city music . . . he didn't come. I wasn't sure what I'd even tell him.

I knew he and Tamlin were different. Knew that Rhysand's protective anger tonight had been justified, that I would have had a similar reaction. I'd been bloodthirsty at the barest details of Mor's suffering, had wanted to *punish* them for it.

I had known the risks. I had known I'd be sitting in his lap, touching him, using him. I'd been using him for a while now. And maybe I should tell him I didn't . . . I didn't want or expect anything from him.

Maybe Rhysand needed to flirt with me, taunt me, as much for a distraction and sense of normalcy as I did.

And maybe I'd said what I had to him because . . . because I'd realized that I might very well be the person who wouldn't let anyone in.

And tonight, when he'd recoiled after he'd seen how he affected me . . . It had crumpled something in my chest.

I had been jealous—of Cresseida. I had been so profoundly unhappy on that barge because I'd wanted to be the one he smiled at like that.

And I knew it was wrong, but . . . I did not think Rhys would call me a whore if I wanted it—wanted . . . *him*. No matter how soon it was after Tamlin.

Neither would his friends. Not when they had been called the same and worse.

And learned to live—and love—beyond it. Despite it.

So maybe it was time to tell Rhys that. To explain that I didn't want to pretend. I didn't want to write it off as a joke, or a plan, or a distraction.

And it'd be hard, and I was scared and might be difficult to deal with, but . . . I was willing to try—with him. To try to . . . be something. Together. Whether it was purely sex, or more, or something between or beyond them, I didn't know. We'd find out.

I was healed—or healing—enough to want to try.

If he was willing to try, too.

If he didn't walk away when I voiced what I wanted: him.

Not the High Lord, not the most powerful male in Prythian's history.

Just . . . him. The person who had sent music into that cell; who had picked up that knife in Amarantha's throne room to fight for me when no one else dared, and who had kept fighting for me every day since, refusing to let me crumble and disappear into nothing.

So I waited for him in the chilled, moonlit garden.

But he didn't come.

Rhys wasn't at breakfast. Or lunch. He wasn't in the town house at all.

I'd even written him a note on the last piece of paper we'd used.

I want to talk to you.

I'd waited thirty minutes for the paper to vanish.

But it'd stayed in my palm—until I threw it in the fire.

I was pissed enough that I stalked into the streets, barely remarking that the day was balmy, sunny, that the very air now seemed laced with citrus and wildflowers and new grass. Now that we had the orb, he'd no doubt be in touch with the queens. Who would no doubt waste our time, just to remind us they were important; that they, too, had power.

Part of me wished Rhys could crush their bones the way he'd done with Keir's the night before.

I headed for Amren's apartment across the river, needing the walk to clear my head.

Winter had indeed yielded to spring. By the time I was halfway there, my overcoat was slung over my arm, and my body was slick with sweat beneath my heavy cream sweater.

I found Amren the same way I'd seen her the last time: hunched over the Book, papers strewn around her. I set the blood on the counter.

She said without looking up, "Ah. The reason why Rhys bit my head off this morning."

I leaned against the counter, frowning. "Where's he gone off to?"

"To hunt whoever attacked you yesterday."

If they had ash arrows in their arsenal . . . I tried to soothe the worry that bit deep. "Do you think it was the Summer Court?" The blood ruby still sat on the floor, still used as a paperweight against the river breeze blowing in from the open windows. Varian's necklace was now beside her bed. As if she fell asleep looking at it.

"Maybe," Amren said, dragging a finger along a line of text. She must be truly absorbed to not even bother with the blood. I debated leaving her to it. But she went on, "Regardless, it seems that our enemies have a track on Rhys's magic. Which means they're able to find him when he winnows anywhere or if he uses his powers." She at last looked up. "You lot are leaving Velaris in two days. Rhys wants you stationed at one of the Illyrian war-camps—where you'll fly down to the human lands once the queens send word."

"Why not today?"

Amren said, "Because Starfall is tomorrow night—the first we've had together in fifty years. Rhys is expected to be here, amongst his people."

"What's Starfall?"

Amren's eyes twinkled. "Outside of these borders, the rest of the world celebrates tomorrow as Nynsar—the Day of Seeds and Flowers." I almost flinched at that. I hadn't realized just how much time had passed since I'd come here. "But Starfall," Amren said, "only at the Night Court can you witness it—only within this territory is Starfall celebrated in lieu of the Nynsar revelry. The rest, and the why of it, you'll find out. It's better left as a surprise."

Well, that explained why people had seemed to already be preparing for a celebration of sorts: High Fae and faeries hustling home with arms full of vibrant wildflower bouquets and streamers and food. The streets were being swept and washed, storefronts patched up with quick, skilled hands.

I asked, "Will we come back here once we leave?"

She returned to the Book. "Not for a while."

Something in my chest started sinking. To an immortal, a while must be . . . a long, long time.

I took that as an invitation to leave, and headed for the door in the back of the loft. But Amren said, "When Rhys came back, after Amarantha, he was a ghost. He pretended he wasn't, but he was. You made him come alive again."

Words stalled, and I didn't want to think about it, not when whatever good I'd done—whatever good we'd done for *each other*—might have been wiped away by what I'd said to him.

So I said, "He is lucky to have all of you."

"No," she said softly—more gently than I'd ever heard. "*We* are lucky to have him, Feyre." I turned from the door. "I have known many High Lords," Amren continued, studying her paper. "Cruel ones, cunning ones, weak ones, powerful ones. But never one that dreamed. Not as he does."

"Dreams of what?" I breathed.

"Of peace. Of freedom. Of a world united, a world thriving. Of something better—for all of us."

"He thinks he'll be remembered as the villain in the story."

She snorted.

"But I forgot to tell him," I said quietly, opening the door, "that the villain is usually the person who locks up the maiden and throws away the key."

"Oh?"

I shrugged. "He was the one who let me out."

If you've moved elsewhere, I wrote after getting home from Amren's apartment, *you could have at least given me the keys to this house. I keep leaving the door unlocked when I go out. It's getting to be too tempting for the neighborhood burglars.*

No response. The letter didn't even vanish.

I tried after breakfast the next day—the morning of Starfall. *Cassian says you're sulking in the House of Wind. What un-High-Lord-like behavior. What of my training?*

Again, no reply.

My guilt and—and whatever else it was—started to shift. I could barely keep from shredding the paper as I wrote my third one after lunch.

Is this punishment? Or do people in your Inner Circle not get second chances if they piss you off? You're a hateful coward.

I was climbing out of the bath, the city abuzz with preparations for the festivities at sundown, when I looked at the desk where I'd left the letter.

And watched it vanish.

Nuala and Cerridwen arrived to help me dress, and I tried not to stare at the desk as I waited—waited and waited for the response.

It didn't come.

CHAPTER 44

But despite the letter, despite the mess between us, as I gaped at the mirror an hour later, I couldn't quite believe what stared back.

I had been so relieved these past few weeks to be sleeping at all that I'd forgotten to be grateful that I was keeping down my food.

The fullness had come back to my face, my body. What should have taken weeks longer as a human had been hurried along by the miracle of my immortal blood. And the dress . . .

I'd never worn anything like it, and doubted I'd ever wear anything like it again.

Crafted of tiny blue gems so pale they were almost white, it clung to every curve and hollow before draping to the floor and pooling like liquid starlight. The long sleeves were tight, capped at the wrists with cuffs of pure diamond. The neckline grazed my collarbones, the modesty of it undone by how the gown hugged areas I supposed a female might enjoy showing off. My hair had been swept off my face with two combs of silver and diamond, then left to drape down my back. And I thought, as I stood alone in my bedroom, that I might have looked like a fallen star.

Rhysand was nowhere to be found when I worked up the courage to go to the rooftop garden. The beading on the dress clinked and hissed against the floors as I walked through the nearly dark house, all the lights softened or extinguished.

In fact, the whole city had blown out its lights.

A winged, muscled figure stood atop the roof, and my heart stumbled.

But then he turned, just as the scent hit me. And something in my chest sank a bit as Cassian let out a low whistle. "I should have let Nuala and Cerridwen dress me."

I didn't know whether to smile or wince. "You look rather good despite it." He did. He was out of his fighting clothes and armor, sporting a black tunic cut to show off that warrior's body. His black hair had been brushed and smoothed, and even his wings looked cleaner.

Cassian held his arms out. His Siphons remained—a metal, fingerless gauntlet that stretched beneath the tailored sleeves of his jacket. "Ready?"

He'd kept me company the past two days, training me each morning. While he'd shown me more particulars on how to use an Illyrian blade—mostly how to disembowel someone with it—we'd chatted about everything: our equally miserable lives as children, hunting, food . . . Everything, that is, except for the subject of Rhysand.

Cassian had mentioned only once that Rhys was up at the House, and I supposed my expression had told him enough about not wanting to hear anything else. He grinned at me now. "With all those gems and beads, you might be too heavy to carry. I hope you've been practicing your winnowing in case I drop you."

"Funny." I allowed him to scoop me into his arms before we shot into the sky. Winnowing might still evade me, but I wished I had wings, I realized. Great, powerful wings so I might fly as they did; so I might see the world and all it had to offer.

Below us, every lingering light winked out. There was no moon; no music flitted through the streets. Silence—as if waiting for something.

Cassian soared through the quiet dark to where the House of Wind loomed. I could make out crowds gathered on the many balconies and patios only from the faint gleam of starlight on their hair, then the clink of their glasses and low chatter as we neared.

Cassian set me down on the crowded patio off the dining room, only a few revelers bothering to look at us. Dim bowls of faelight inside the House illuminated spreads of food and endless rows of green bottles of sparkling wine atop the tables. Cassian was gone and returned before I missed him, pressing a glass of the latter into my hand. No sign of Rhysand.

Maybe he'd avoid me the entire party.

Someone called Cassian's name from down the patio, and he clapped me on the shoulder before striding off. A tall male, his face in shadow, clasped forearms with Cassian, his white teeth gleaming in the darkness. Azriel stood with the stranger already, his wings tucked in tight to keep revelers from knocking into them. He, Cassian, and Mor had all been quiet today—understandably so. I scanned for signs of my other—

Friends.

The word sounded in my head. Was that what they were?

Amren was nowhere in sight, but I spotted a golden head at the same moment she spied me, and Mor breezed to my side. She wore a gown of pure white, little more than a slip of silk that showed off her generous curves. Indeed, a glance over her shoulder revealed Azriel staring blatantly at the back view of it, Cassian and the stranger already too deep in conversation to notice what had drawn the spymaster's attention. For a moment, the ravenous hunger on Azriel's face made my stomach tighten.

I'd remembered feeling like that. Remembered how it felt to yield to it. How I'd come close to doing that the other night.

Mor said, "It won't be long now."

"Until *what?*" No one had told me what to expect, as they hadn't wanted to ruin the *surprise* of Starfall.

"Until the fun."

I surveyed the party around us—"This isn't the fun?"

Mor lifted an eyebrow. "None of us really care about this part. Once it starts, you'll see." She took a sip of her sparkling wine. "That's some dress. You're lucky Amren is hiding in her little attic, or she'd probably steal it right off you. The vain drake."

"She won't take time off from decoding?"

"Yes, and no. Something about Starfall disturbs her, she claims. Who knows? She probably does it to be contrary."

Even as she spoke, her words were distant—her face a bit tight. I said quietly, "Are you . . . ready for tomorrow?" Tomorrow, when we'd leave Velaris to keep anyone from noticing our movements in this area. Mor, Azriel had told me tightly over breakfast that morning, would return to the Court of Nightmares. To check in on her father's . . . recovery.

Probably not the best place to discuss our plans, but Mor shrugged. "I don't have any choice but to be ready. I'll come with you to the camp, then go my way afterward."

"Cassian will be happy about that," I said. Even if Azriel was the one trying his best *not* to stare at her.

Mor snorted. "Maybe."

I lifted a brow. "So you two . . . ?"

Another shrug. "Once. Well, not even. I was seventeen, he wasn't even a year older."

When everything had happened.

But there was no darkness on her face as she sighed. "Cauldron, that was a long time ago. I visited Rhys for two weeks when he was training in the war-camp, and Cassian, Azriel, and I became friends. One night, Rhys and his mother had to go back to the Night Court, and Azriel went with them, so Cassian and I were left alone. And that night, one thing led to another, and . . . I wanted Cassian to be the one who did it. I wanted to choose." A third shrug. I wondered if Azriel had wished to be the one she chose instead. If he'd ever admitted to it to Mor—or Rhys.

If he resented that he'd been away that night, that Mor hadn't considered him.

"Rhys came back the next morning, and when he learned what had happened . . . " She laughed under her breath. "We try not to talk about the Incident. He and Cassian . . . I've never seen them fight like that. Hopefully I never will again. I know Rhys wasn't pissed about my virginity, but rather the danger that losing it had put me in. *Azriel* was even angrier about it—though he let Rhys do the walloping. They knew what my family would do for *debasing* myself with a bastard-born lesser faerie." She brushed a hand over her abdomen, as if she could feel that nail they'd spiked through it. "They were right."

"So you and Cassian," I said, wanting to move on from it, that darkness, "you were never together again after that?"

"No," Mor said, laughing quietly. "I was desperate, reckless that night. I'd picked him not just for his kindness, but also because I wanted my first time to be with one of the legendary Illyrian warriors. I wanted to lie with the greatest of Illyrian warriors, actually. And I'd taken one look at Cassian and known. After I got what I wanted, after . . . everything, I didn't like that it caused a rift with him and Rhys, or even him and Az, so . . . never again."

"And you were never with anyone after it?" Not the cold, beautiful shadowsinger who tried so hard not to watch her with longing on his face?

"I've had lovers," Mor clarified, "but . . . I get bored. And Cassian has had them, too, so don't get that unrequited-love, moony-woo-woo look. He just wants what he can't have, and it's irritated him for centuries that I walked away and never looked back."

"Oh, it drives him insane," Rhys said from behind me, and I jumped. But the High Lord was circling me. I crossed my arms as he paused and smirked. "You look like a woman again."

"You really know how to compliment females, cousin," Mor said, and patted him on the shoulder as she spotted an acquaintance and went to say hello.

I tried not to look at Rhys, who was in a black jacket, casually unbuttoned at the top so that the white shirt beneath—also unbuttoned at the neck—showed the tattoos on his chest peeking through. Tried not to look—and failed.

"Do you plan to ignore me some more?" I said coolly.

"I'm here now, aren't I? I wouldn't want you to call me a hateful coward again."

I opened my mouth, but felt all the wrong words start to come out. So I shut it and looked for Azriel or Cassian or anyone who might talk to me. Going up to a stranger was starting to sound appealing when Rhys said a bit hoarsely, "I wasn't punishing you. I just . . . I needed time."

I didn't want to have this conversation here—with so many people listening. So I gestured to the party and said, "Will you please tell me what this . . . gathering is about?"

Rhysand stepped up behind me, snorting as he said into my ear, "Look up."

Indeed, as I did so, the crowd hushed.

"No speech for your guests?" I murmured. Easy—I just wanted it to be easy between us again.

"Tonight's not about me, though my presence is appreciated and noted," he said. "Tonight's about that."

As he pointed . . .

A star vaulted across the sky, brighter and closer than any I'd seen before. The crowd and city below cheered, raising their glasses as it passed right overhead, and only when it had disappeared over the curve of the horizon did they drink deeply.

I leaned back a step into Rhys—and quickly stepped away, out of his heat and power and scent. We'd done enough damage in a similar position at the Court of Nightmares.

Another star crossed the sky, twirling and twisting over itself, as if it were reveling in its own sparkling beauty. It was chased by another, and another, until a brigade of them were unleashed from the edge of the horizon, like a thousand archers had loosed them from mighty bows.

The stars cascaded over us, filling the world with white and blue light. They were like living fireworks, and my breath lodged in my throat as the stars kept on falling and falling.

I'd never seen anything so beautiful.

And when the sky was full with them, when the stars raced and danced and flowed across the world, the music began.

Wherever they were, people began dancing, swaying and twirling, some grabbing hands and spinning, spinning, spinning to the drums, the strings, the glittering harps. Not like the grinding and thrusting of the Court of Nightmares, but—joyous, peaceful dancing. For the love of sound and movement and life.

I lingered with Rhysand at the edge of it, caught between watching the people dancing on the patio, hands upraised, and the stars streaming past, closer and closer until I swore I could have touched them if I'd leaned out.

And there were Mor and Azriel—and Cassian. The three of them dancing together, Mor's head tipped back to the sky, arms up, the starlight gleaming on the pure white of her gown. Dancing as if it might be her last time, flowing between Azriel and Cassian like the three of them were one unit, one being.

I looked behind me to find Rhys watching them, his face soft. Sad.

Separated for fifty years, and reunited—only to be cleaved apart so soon to fight again for their freedom.

Rhys caught my gaze and said, "Come. There's a better view. Quieter." He held a hand out to me.

That sorrow, that weight, lingered in his eyes. And I couldn't bear to see it—just as I couldn't bear to see my three friends dancing together as if it was the last time they'd ever do it.

Rhys led me to a small private balcony jutting from the upper level of the House of Wind. On the patios below, the music still played, the people still danced, the stars wheeling by, close and swift.

He let go as I took a seat on the balcony rail. I immediately decided against it as I beheld the drop, and backed away a healthy step.

Rhys chuckled. "If you fell, you know I'd bother to save you before you hit the ground."

"But not until I was close to death?"

"Maybe."

I leaned a hand against the rail, peering at the stars whizzing past. "As punishment for what I said to you?"

"I said some horrible things, too," he murmured.

"I didn't mean it," I blurted. "I meant it more about myself than you. And I'm sorry."

He watched the stars for a moment before he replied. "You were right, though. I stayed away because you were right. Though I'm glad to hear my absence felt like a punishment."

I snorted, but was grateful for the humor—for the way he'd always been able to amuse me. "Any news with the orb or the queens?"

"Nothing yet. We're waiting for them to deign to reply."

We were silent again, and I studied the stars. "They're not—they're not stars at all."

"No." Rhys came up beside me at the rail. "Our ancestors thought they were, but . . . They're just spirits, on a yearly migration to somewhere. Why they pick this day to appear here, no one knows."

I felt his eyes upon me, and tore my gaze from the shooting stars. Light and shadow passed over his face. The cheers and music of the city far, far below were barely audible over the crowd gathered at the House.

"There must be hundreds of them," I managed to say, dragging my stare back to the stars whizzing past.

"Thousands," he said. "They'll keep coming until dawn. Or, I hope they will. There were less and less of them the last time I witnessed Starfall."

Before Amarantha had locked him away.

"What's happening to them?" I looked in time to see him shrug. Something twanged in my chest.

"I wish I knew. But they keep coming back despite it."

"Why?"

"Why does anything cling to something? Maybe they love wherever they're going so much that it's worth it. Maybe they'll keep coming back, until there's only one star left. Maybe that one star will make the trip forever, out of the hope that someday—if it keeps coming back often enough—another star will find it again."

I frowned at the wine in my hand. "That's . . . a very sad thought."

"Indeed." Rhys rested his forearms on the balcony edge, close enough for my fingers to touch if I dared.

A calm, full silence enveloped us. Too many words—I still had too many words in me.

I don't know how much time passed, but it must have been a while, because when he spoke again, I jolted. "Every year that I was Under the Mountain and Starfall came around, Amarantha made sure that I . . . serviced her. The entire night. Starfall is no secret, even to outsiders—even the Court of Nightmares crawls out of the Hewn City to look up at the sky. So she knew . . . She knew what it meant to me."

I stopped hearing the celebrations around us. "I'm sorry." It was all I could offer.

"I got through it by reminding myself that my friends were safe; that Velaris was safe. Nothing else mattered, so long as I had that. She could use my body however she wanted. I didn't care."

"So why aren't you down there with them?" I asked, even as I tucked the horror of what had been done to him into my heart.

"They don't know—what she did to me on Starfall. I don't want it to ruin their night."

"I don't think it would. They'd be happy if you let them shoulder the burden."

"The same way you rely on others to help with your own troubles?"

We stared at each other, close enough to share breath.

And maybe all those words bottled up in me . . . Maybe I didn't need them right now.

My fingers grazed his. Warm and sturdy—patient, as if waiting to see what else I might do. Maybe it was the wine, but I stroked a finger down his.

And as I turned to him more fully, something blinding and tinkling slammed into my face.

I reeled back, crying out as I bent over, shielding my face against the light that I could still see against my shut eyes.

Rhys let out a startled laugh.

A *laugh*.

And when I realized that my eyes hadn't been singed out of their sockets, I whirled on him. "I could have been blinded!" I hissed, shoving him. He took a look at my face and burst out laughing again. Real laughter, open and delighted and lovely.

I wiped at my face, and when I pulled my hands down, I gaped. Pale green light—like drops of paint—glowed in flecks on my hand.

Splattered star-spirit. I didn't know if I should be horrified or amused. Or disgusted.

When I went to rub it off, Rhys caught my hands. "Don't," he said, still laughing. "It looks like your freckles are glowing."

My nostrils flared, and I went to shove him again, not caring if my new strength knocked him off the balcony. He could summon wings; he could deal with it.

He sidestepped me, veering toward the balcony rail, but not fast enough to avoid the careening star that collided with the side of his face.

He leaped back with a curse. I laughed, the sound rasping out of me. Not a chuckle or snort, but a cackling laugh.

And I laughed again, and again, as he lowered his hands from his eyes.

The entire left side of his face had been hit.

Like heavenly war paint, that's what it looked like. I could see why he didn't want me to wipe mine away.

Rhys was examining his hands, covered in the dust, and I stepped toward him, peering at the way it glowed and glittered.

He went still as death as I took one of his hands in my own and traced a star shape on the top of his palm, playing with the glimmer and shadows, until it looked like one of the stars that had hit us.

His fingers tightened on mine, and I looked up. He was smiling at me. And looked so un-High-Lord-like with the glowing dust on the side of his face that I grinned back.

I hadn't even realized what I'd done until his own smile faded, and his mouth parted slightly.

"Smile again," he whispered.

I hadn't smiled for him. Ever. Or laughed. Under the Mountain, I had never grinned, never chuckled. And afterward . . .

And this male before me . . . my friend . . .

For all that he had done, I had never given him either. Even when I had just . . . I had just painted something. On him. For him.

I'd—painted again.

So I smiled at him, broad and without restraint.

"You're exquisite," he breathed.

The air was too tight, too close between our bodies, between our joined hands. But I said, "You owe me two thoughts—back from when I first came here. Tell me what you're thinking."

Rhys rubbed his neck. "You want to know why I didn't speak or see you? Because I was so convinced you'd throw me out on my ass. I just . . . " He dragged a hand through his hair, and huffed a laugh. "I figured hiding was a better alternative."

"Who would have thought the High Lord of the Night Court could be afraid of an illiterate human?" I purred. He grinned, nudging me with an elbow. "That's one," I pushed. "Tell me another thought."

His eyes fell on my mouth. "I'm wishing I could take back that kiss Under the Mountain."

I sometimes forgot that kiss, when he'd done it to keep Amarantha from knowing that Tamlin and I had been in the forgotten hall, tangled up together. Rhysand's kiss had been brutal, demanding, and yet . . . "Why?"

His gaze settled on the hand I'd painted instead, as if it were easier to face. "Because I didn't make it pleasant for you, and I was jealous and pissed off, and I knew you hated me."

Dangerous territory, I warned myself.

No. Honesty, that's what it was. Honesty, and trust. I'd never had that with anyone.

Rhys looked up, meeting my gaze. And whatever was on my face—I think it might have been mirrored on his: the hunger and longing and surprise.

I swallowed hard, traced another line of stardust along the inside of his powerful wrist. I didn't think he was breathing. "Do you—do you want to dance with me?" I whispered.

He was silent for long enough that I lifted my head to scan his face. But his eyes were bright—silver-lined. "You want to dance?" he rasped, his fingers curling around mine.

I pointed with my chin toward the celebration below. "Down there—with them." Where the music beckoned, where *life* beckoned. Where he should spend the night with his friends, and where I wanted to spend it with them, too. Even with the strangers in attendance.

I did not mind stepping out of the shadows, did not mind even *being* in the shadows to begin with, so long as he was with me. My friend through so many dangers—who had fought for me when no one else would, even myself.

"Of course I'll dance with you," Rhys said, his voice still raw. "All night, if you wish."

"Even if I step on your toes?"

"Even then."

He leaned in, brushing his mouth against my heated cheek. I closed my eyes at the whisper of a kiss, at the hunger that ravaged me in its wake, that might ravage Prythian. And all around us, as if the world itself were indeed falling apart, stars rained down.

Bits of stardust glowed on his lips as he pulled away, as I stared up at him, breathless, while he smiled. The smile the world would likely never see, the smile he'd given up for the sake of his people, his lands. He said softly, "I am . . . very glad I met you, Feyre."

I blinked away the burning in my eyes. "Come on," I said, tugging on his hand. "Let's go join the dance."

CHAPTER 45

The Illyrian war-camp deep in the northern mountains was freezing. Apparently, spring was still little more than a whisper in the region.

Mor winnowed us all in, Rhysand and Cassian flanking us.

We had danced. All of us together. And I had never seen Rhys so happy, laughing with Azriel, drinking with Mor, bickering with Cassian. I'd danced with each of them, and when the night had shifted toward dawn and the music became soft and honeyed, I had let Rhys take me in his arms and dance with me, slowly, until the other guests had left, until Mor was asleep on a settee in the dining room, until the gold disc of the sun gilded Velaris.

He'd flown me back to the town house through the pink and purple and gray of the dawn, both of us silent, and had kissed my brow once before walking down the hall to his own room.

I didn't lie to myself about why I waited for thirty minutes to see if my door would open. Or to at least hear a knock. But nothing.

We were bleary-eyed but polite at the lunch table hours later, Mor and Cassian unusually quiet, talking mostly to Amren and Azriel, who had come to bid us farewell. Amren would continue working on the Book until we received the second half—if we received it; the shadow-singer was heading out to gather information and manage his spies stationed at the other courts and attempting to break into the human one. I managed to speak to them, but most of my energy went into *not* looking at Rhysand, or thinking about the feeling of his body pressed to mine as we'd danced for hours, that brush of his mouth on my skin.

I'd barely been able to fall asleep because of it.

Traitor. Even if I'd left Tamlin, I was a traitor. I'd been gone for two months—just two. In faerie terms, it was probably considered less than a day.

Tamlin had given me so much, done so many kind things for me and my family. And here I was, wanting another male, even as I hated Tamlin for what he'd done, how he'd failed me. *Traitor.*

The word continued echoing in my head as I stood at Mor's side, Rhys and Cassian a few steps ahead, and peered out at the wind-blown camp. Mor had barely given Azriel more than a brief embrace before bidding him good-bye. And for all the world, the spymaster looked like he didn't care—until he gave me a swift, warning look. I was still torn between amusement and outrage at the assumption I'd stick my nose into *his* business. Indeed.

Built near the top of a forested mountain, the Illyrian camp was all bare rock and mud, interrupted only by crude, easy-to-pack tents centered around large fire pits. Near the tree line, a dozen permanent buildings had been erected of the gray mountain stone. Smoke puffed from their chimneys against the brisk cloudy morning, occasionally swirled by the passing wings overhead.

So many winged males soaring past on their way to other camps or in training.

Indeed, on the opposite end of the camp, in a rocky area that ended in a sheer plunge off the mountain, were the sparring and training rings. Racks of weapons were left out to the elements; in the chalk-painted rings males of all ages now trained with sticks and swords and shields and spears. Fast, lethal, brutal. No complaints, no shouts of pain.

There was no warmth here, no joy. Even the houses at the other end of the camp had no personal touches, as if they were used only for shelter or storage.

And this was where Rhys, Azriel, and Cassian had grown up—where Cassian had been cast out to survive on his own. It was so cold that even bundled in my fur-lined leather, I was shivering. I couldn't imagine a child going without adequate clothing—or shelter—for a night, much less eight years.

Mor's face was pale, tight. "I hate this place," she said under her breath, the heat of it clouding the air in front of us. "It should be burned to the ground."

Cassian and Rhys were silent as a tall, broad-shouldered older male approached, flanked by five other Illyrian warriors, wings all tucked in, hands within casual reach of their weapons.

No matter that Rhys could rip their minds apart without lifting a finger.

They each wore Siphons of varying colors on the backs of their hands, the stones smaller than Azriel and Cassian's. And only one. Not like the seven apiece that my two friends wore to manage their tremendous power.

The male in front said, "Another camp inspection? Your dog," he jerked his chin at Cassian, "was here just the other week. The girls are training."

Cassian crossed his arms. "I don't see them in the ring."

"They do chores first," the male said, shoulders pushing back and wings flaring slightly, "then when they've finished, they get to train."

A low snarl slipped past Mor's mouth, and the male turned our way. He stiffened. Mor flashed him a wicked smile. "Hello, Lord Devlon."

The leader of the camp, then.

He gave her a dismissive once-over and looked back to Rhys. Cassian's warning growl rumbled in my stomach.

Rhys said at last, "Pleasant as it always is to see you, Devlon, there are two matters at hand: First, the girls, as you were clearly told by Cassian, are to train *before* chores, not after. Get them out on the pitch. Now." I shuddered at the pure command in that tone. He continued, "Second, we'll be staying here for the time being. Clear out my mother's old house. No need for a housekeeper. We'll look after ourselves."

"The house is occupied by my top warriors."

"Then un-occupy it," Rhysand said simply. "And have them clean it before they do."

The voice of the High Lord of the Night Court—who delighted in pain, and made his enemies tremble.

Devlon sniffed at me. I poured every bit of cranky exhaustion into holding his narrowed gaze. "Another like that . . . creature you bring here? I thought she was the only one of her ilk."

"Amren," Rhys drawled, "sends her regards. And as for *this* one . . . " I tried not to flinch away from meeting his stare. "She's mine," he said quietly, but viciously enough that Devlon and his warriors nearby heard. "And if any of you lay a hand on her, you lose that hand. And then you lose your head." I tried not to shiver, as Cassian and Mor showed no reaction at all. "And once Feyre is done killing you," Rhys smirked, "then I'll grind your bones to dust."

I almost laughed. But the warriors were now assessing the threat Rhys had established me as—and coming up short with answers. I gave them all a small smile, anyway, one I'd seen Amren make a hundred times. Let them wonder what I could do if provoked.

"We're heading out," Rhys said to Cassian and Mor, not even bothering to dismiss Devlon before walking toward the tree line. "We'll be back at nightfall." He gave his cousin a look. "Try to stay out of trouble, please. Devlon hates us the least of the war-lords and I don't feel like finding another camp."

Mother above, the others must be . . . unpleasant, if Devlon was the mildest of them.

Mor winked at us both. "I'll try."

Rhys just shook his head and said to Cassian, "Check on the forces, then make sure those girls are practicing like they should be. If Devlon or the others object, do what you have to."

Cassian grinned in a way that showed he'd be more than happy to do exactly that. He was the High Lord's general . . . and yet Devlon called him a dog. I didn't want to imagine what it had been like for Cassian without that title growing up.

Then finally Rhys looked at me again, his eyes shuttered. "Let's go."

"You heard from my sisters?"

A shake of the head. "No. Azriel is checking today if they received a response. You and I . . . " The wind rustled his hair as he smirked. "We're going to train."

"Where?"

He gestured to the sweeping land beyond—to the forested steppes he'd once mentioned. "Away from any potential casualties." He offered his hand as his wings flared, his body preparing for flight.

But all I heard were those two words he'd said, echoing against the steady beat of *traitor, traitor*:

She's mine.

Being in Rhys's arms again, against his body, was a test of stubbornness. For both of us. To see who'd speak about it first.

We'd been flying over the most beautiful mountains I'd ever seen—snowy and flecked with pines—heading toward rolling steppes beyond them when I said, "You're training female Illyrian warriors?"

"Trying to." Rhys gazed across the brutal landscape. "I banned wing-clipping a long, long time ago, but . . . at the more zealous camps, deep within the mountains, they do it. And when Amarantha took over, even the milder camps started doing it again. To keep their women safe, they claimed. For the past hundred years, Cassian has been trying to build an aerial fighting unit amongst the females, trying to prove that they have a place on the battlefield. So far, he's managed to train a few dedicated warriors, but the males make life so miserable that many of them left. And for the girls in training . . . " A hiss of breath. "It's a long road. But Devlon is one of the few who even lets the girls train without a tantrum."

"I'd hardly call disobeying orders 'without a tantrum.' "

"Some camps issued decrees that if a female was caught training, she was to be deemed unmarriageable. I can't fight against things like that, not without slaughtering the leaders of each camp and personally raising each and every one of their offspring."

"And yet your mother loved them—and you three wear their tattoos."

"I got the tattoos in part for my mother, in part to honor my brothers, who fought every day of their lives for the right to wear them."

"Why do you let Devlon speak to Cassian like that?"

"Because I know when to pick my fights with Devlon, and I know Cassian would be pissed if I stepped in to crush Devlon's mind like a grape when he could handle it himself."

A whisper of cold went through me. "Have you thought about doing it?"

"I did just now. But most camp-lords never would have given the three of us a shot at the Blood Rite. Devlon let a half-breed and two bastards take it—and did not deny us our victory."

Pines dusted with fresh snow blurred beneath us.

"What's the Blood Rite?"

"So many questions today." I squeezed his shoulder hard enough to hurt, and he chuckled. "You go unarmed into the mountains, magic banned, no Siphons, wings bound, with no supplies or clothes beyond what you have on you. You, and every other Illyrian male who wants to move from novice to true warrior. A few hundred head into the mountains at the start of the week—not all come out at the end."

The frost-kissed landscape rolled on forever, unyielding as the warriors who ruled over it. "Do you—kill each other?"

"Most try to. For food and clothes, for vengeance, for glory between feuding clans. Devlon allowed us to take the Rite—but also made sure Cassian, Azriel, and I were dumped in different locations."

"What happened?"

"We found each other. Killed our way across the mountains to get to each other. Turns out, a good number of Illyrian males wanted to prove they were stronger, smarter than us. Turns out they were wrong."

I dared a look at his face. For a heartbeat, I could see it: blood-splattered, savage, fighting and slaughtering to get to his friends, to protect and save them.

Rhys set us down in a clearing, the pine trees towering so high they seemed to caress the underside of the heavy, gray clouds passing on the swift wind.

"So, you're not using magic—but I am?" I said, taking a few steps from him.

"Our enemy is keyed in on my powers. You, however, remain invisible." He waved his hand. "Let's see what all your practicing has amounted to."

I didn't feel like it. I just said, "When—when did you meet Tamlin?"

I knew what Rhysand's father had done. I hadn't let myself think too much about it.

About how he'd killed Tamlin's father and brothers. And mother.

But now, after last night, after the Court of Nightmares . . . I had to know.

Rhys's face was a mask of patience. "Show me something impressive, and I'll tell you. Magic—for answers."

"I know what sort of game you're playing—" I cut myself off at the hint of a smirk. "Very well."

I held out my hand before me, palm cupped, and willed silence into my veins, my mind.

Silence and calm and weight, like being underwater.

In my hand, a butterfly of water flapped and danced.

Rhys smiled a bit, but the amusement died as he said, "Tamlin was younger than me—born when the War started. But after the War, when he'd matured, we got to know each other at various court functions. He . . . " Rhys clenched his jaw. "He seemed decent for a High Lord's son. Better than Beron's brood at the Autumn Court. Tamlin's brothers were equally as bad, though. Worse. And they knew Tamlin would take the title one day. And to a half-breed Illyrian who'd had to prove himself, defend his power, I saw what Tamlin went through . . . I befriended him. Sought him out whenever I was able to get away from the war-camps or court. Maybe it was pity, but . . . I taught him some Illyrian techniques."

"Did anyone know?"

He raised his brows—giving a pointed look to my hand.

I scowled at him and summoned songbirds of water, letting them flap around the clearing as they'd flown around my bathing room at the Summer Court.

"Cassian and Azriel knew," Rhys went on. "My family knew. And disapproved." His eyes were chips of ice. "But Tamlin's father was threatened by it. By me. And because he was weaker than both me and Tamlin, he wanted to prove to the world that he wasn't. My mother and sister were to travel to the Illyrian war-camp to see me. I was supposed to meet them halfway, but I was busy training a new unit and decided to stay."

My stomach turned over and over and over, and I wished I had something to lean against as Rhys said, "Tamlin's father, brothers, and Tamlin himself set out into the Illyrian wilderness, having heard from Tamlin—*from me*—where my mother and sister would be, that I had plans to see them. I was supposed to be there. I wasn't. And they slaughtered my mother and sister anyway."

I began shaking my head, eyes burning. I didn't know what I was trying to deny, or erase, or condemn.

"It should have been me," he said, and I understood—understood what he'd said that day I'd wept before Cassian in the training pit.

"They put their heads in boxes and sent them down the river—to the nearest camp. Tamlin's father kept their wings as trophies. I'm surprised you didn't see them pinned in the study."

I was going to vomit; I was going to fall to my knees and weep.

But Rhys looked at the menagerie of water-animals I'd crafted and said, "What else?"

Perhaps it was the cold, perhaps it was his story, but hoarfrost cracked in my veins, and the wild song of a winter wind howled in my heart. I felt it then—how easy it would be to jump between them, *join* them together, my powers.

Each one of my animals halted mid-air . . . and froze into perfectly carved bits of ice.

One by one, they dropped to the earth. And shattered.

They were one. They had come from the same, dark origin, the same eternal well of power. Once, long ago—before language was invented and the world was new.

Rhys merely continued, "When I heard, when my father heard . . . I wasn't wholly truthful to you when I told you Under the Mountain that my father killed Tamlin's father and brothers. I went with him. Helped him. We winnowed to the edge of the Spring Court that night, then went the rest of the way on foot—to the manor. I slew Tamlin's brothers on sight. I held their minds, and rendered them helpless while I cut them into pieces, then melted their brains inside their skulls. And when I got to the High Lord's bedroom—he was dead. And my father . . . my father had killed Tamlin's mother as well."

I couldn't stop shaking my head.

"My father had promised not to touch her. That we weren't the kind of males who would do that. But he lied to me, and he did it, anyway. And then he went for Tamlin's room."

I couldn't breathe—couldn't breathe as Rhys said, "I tried to stop him. He didn't listen. He was going to kill him, too. And I couldn't . . . After all the death, I was done. I didn't care that Tamlin had been there, had allowed them to kill my mother and sister, that he'd come to kill me because he didn't want to risk standing against them. I was done with death. So I stopped my father before the door. He tried to go through me. Tamlin opened the door, saw us—smelled the blood already leaking into the hallway. And I didn't even get to say a word before Tamlin killed my father in one blow.

"I felt the power shift to me, even as I saw it shift to him. And we just looked at each other, as we were both suddenly crowned High Lord—and then I ran."

He'd murdered Rhysand's family. The High Lord I'd loved—he'd murdered his friend's family, and when I'd asked how *his* family died, he'd merely told me a rival court had done it. *Rhysand* had done it, and—

"He didn't tell you any of that."

"I—I'm sorry," I breathed, my voice hoarse.

"What do you possibly have to be sorry for?"

"I didn't know. I didn't know that he'd done that—"

And Rhys thought I'd been comparing him—comparing *him* against Tamlin, as if I held him to be some paragon . . .

"Why did you stop?" he said, motioning to the ice shards on the pine-needle carpet.

The people he'd loved most—gone. Slaughtered in cold blood. Slaughtered by *Tamlin*.

The clearing exploded in flame.

The pine needles vanished, the trees groaned, and even Rhys swore as fire swept through the clearing, my heart, and devoured everything in its path.

No wonder he'd made Tamlin beg that day I'd been formally introduced to him. No wonder he'd relished every chance to taunt Tamlin. Maybe my presence here was just to—

No. I knew that wasn't true. I knew my being here had nothing to do with what was between him and Tamlin, though he no doubt enjoyed interrupting our wedding day. Saved me from that wedding day, actually.

"Feyre," Rhys said as the fire died.

But there it was—crackling inside my veins. Crackling beside veins of ice, and water.

And darkness.

Embers flared around us, floating in the air, and I sent out a breath of soothing dark, a breath of ice and water, as if it were a wind—a wind at dawn, sweeping clean the world.

The power did not belong to the High Lords. Not any longer.

It belonged to me—as I belonged *only* to me, as my future was *mine* to decide, to forge.

Once I discovered and mastered what the others had given me, I could weave them together—into something new, something of every court and none of them.

Flame hissed as it was extinguished so thoroughly that no smoke remained.

But I met Rhys's stare, his eyes a bit wide as he watched me work. I rasped, "Why didn't you tell me sooner?"

The sight of him in his Illyrian fighting gear, wings spread across the entire width of the clearing, his blade peeking over his shoulder . . .

There, in that hole in my chest—I saw the image there. At first interpretation, he'd look terrifying, vengeance and wrath incarnate. But if you came closer . . . the painting would show the beauty on his face, the wings flared not to hurt, but to carry me from danger, to shield me.

"I didn't want you to think I was trying to turn you against him," he said.

The painting—I could see it; *feel* it. I wanted to paint it.

I wanted to paint.

I didn't wait for him to stretch out his hand before I went to him. And looking up into his face I said, "I want to paint you."

He gently lifted me into his arms. "Nude would be best," he said in my ear.

CHAPTER 46

I was so cold I might never be warm again. Even during winter in the mortal realm, I'd managed to find some kernel of heat, but after nearly emptying my cache of magic that afternoon, even the roaring hearth fire couldn't thaw the chill around my bones. Did spring *ever* come to this blasted place?

"They pick these locations," Cassian said across from me as we dined on mutton stew around the table tucked into the corner of the front of the stone house. "Just to ensure the strongest among us survive."

"Horrible people," Mor grumbled into her earthenware bowl. "I don't blame Az for never wanting to come here."

"I take it training the girls went well," Rhys drawled from beside me, his thigh so close its warmth brushed my own.

Cassian drained his mug of ale. "I got one of them to confess they hadn't received a lesson in ten days. They'd all been too busy with 'chores,' apparently."

"No born fighters in this lot?"

"Three, actually," Mor said. "Three out of ten isn't bad at all. The others, I'd be happy if they just learned to defend themselves. But those three . . . They've got the instinct—the claws. It's their stupid families that want them clipped and breeding."

I rose from the table, taking my bowl to the sink tucked into the wall. The house was simple, but still bigger and in better condition than our old cottage. The front room served as kitchen, living area, and dining room, with three doors in the back: one for the cramped bathing room, one for the storage room, and one being a back door, because no true Illyrian, according to Rhys, ever made a home with only one exit.

"When do you head for the Hewn City tomorrow?" Cassian said to her—quietly enough that I knew it was probably time to head upstairs.

Mor scraped the bottom of her bowl. Apparently, Cassian had made the stew—it hadn't been half-bad. "After breakfast. Before. I don't know. Maybe in the afternoon, when they're all just waking up."

Rhys was a step behind me, bowl in hand, and motioned to leave my dirty dish in the sink. He inclined his head toward the steep, narrow stairs at the back of the house. They were wide enough to fit only one Illyrian warrior—another safety measure—and I glanced at the table one last time before disappearing upstairs.

Mor and Cassian both stared at their empty bowls of food, softly talking for once.

Every step upward, I could feel Rhys at my back, the heat of him, the ebb and flow of his power. And in this small space, the scent of him washed over me, beckoned to me.

Upstairs was dark, illuminated by the small window at the end of the hall, and the moonlight streaming in through a thin gap in the pines around us. There were only two doors up here, and Rhys pointed to one of them. "You and Mor can share tonight—just tell her to shut up if she babbles too much." I wouldn't, though. If she needed to talk, to distract herself and be ready for what was to come tomorrow, I'd listen until dawn.

He put a hand on his own doorknob, but I leaned against the wood of my door.

It'd be so easy to take the three steps to cross the hall.

To run my hands over that chest, trace those beautiful lips with my own.

I swallowed as he turned to me.

I didn't want to think what it meant, what I was doing. What this was—whatever it was—between us.

Because things between us had never been normal, not from the very first moment we'd met on Calanmai. I'd been unable to easily walk away from him then, when I'd thought he was deadly, dangerous. But now . . .

Traitor, traitor, traitor—

He opened his mouth, but I had already slipped inside my room and shut the door.

Freezing rain trickled through the pine boughs as I stalked through the mists in my Illyrian fighting leathers, armed with a bow, quiver, and knives, shivering like a wet dog.

Rhys was a few hundred feet behind, carrying our packs. We'd flown deep into the forest steppes, far enough that we'd have to spend the night out here. Far enough that no one and nothing might see another "glorious explosion of flame and temper," as Rhys had put it. Azriel hadn't brought word from my sisters of the queens' status, so we had time to spare. Though Rhys certainly hadn't looked like it when he informed me that morning. But at least we wouldn't have to camp out here. Rhys had promised there was some sort of wayfarer's inn nearby.

I turned toward where Rhys trailed behind me, spotting his massive wings first. Mor had set off before I'd even been awake, and Cassian had been pissy and on edge during breakfast . . . So much so that I'd been glad to leave as soon as I'd finished my porridge. And felt slightly bad for the Illyrians who had to deal with him that day.

Rhys paused once he caught up, and even with the trees and rain between us, I could see his brows lift in silent question of why I'd paused. We hadn't spoken of Starfall or the Court of Nightmares—and last night, as I twisted and turned in the tiny bed, I'd decided: fun and distraction. It didn't need to be complicated. Keeping things purely physical . . . well, it didn't feel like as much of a betrayal.

I lifted a hand, signaling Rhys to stay where he was. After yesterday, I didn't want him too close, lest I burn him. Or worse. He sketched a dramatic bow, and I rolled my eyes as I stalked to the stream ahead, contemplating where I might indeed try to play with Beron's fire. *My* fire.

Every step away, I could feel Rhys's stare devouring me. Or maybe that was through the bond, brushing against my mental shields—flashes of hunger so insatiable that it was an effort to focus on the task ahead and not on the feeling of what his hands had been like, stroking my thighs, pushing me against him.

I could have sworn I felt a trickle of amusement on the other side of my mental shield, too. I hissed and made a vulgar gesture over my shoulder, even as I let my shield drop, just a bit.

That amusement turned into full delight—and then a lick of pleasure that went straight down my spine. Lower.

My face heated, and a twig cracked under my boot, as loud as lightning. I gritted my teeth. The ground sloped toward a gray, gushing stream, fast enough that it had to be fed by the towering snow-blasted mountains in the distance.

Good—this spot was good. An extra supply of water to drown any flames that might escape, plenty of open space. The wind blew away from me, tugging my scent southward, deeper into the forest as I opened my mouth to tell Rhys to stay back.

With that wind, and the roaring stream, it was no surprise that I didn't hear them until they had surrounded me.

"Feyre."

I whirled, arrow nocked and aimed at the source of the voice—

Four Spring Court sentinels stalked from the trees behind me like wraiths, armed to the teeth and wide-eyed. Two, I knew: Bron and Hart.

And between them stood Lucien.

CHAPTER 47

If I wanted to escape, I could either face the stream or face them. But Lucien . . .

His red hair was tied back, and there wasn't a hint of finery on him: just armored leather, swords, knives . . . His metal eye roamed over me, his golden skin pale. "We've been hunting for you for over two months," he breathed, now scanning the woods, the stream, the sky.

Rhys. Cauldron save me. Rhys was too far back, and—

"How did you find me?" My steady, cold voice wasn't one I recognized. But—*hunting* for me. As if I were indeed prey.

If Tamlin was here . . . My blood went icier than the freezing rain now sluicing down my face, into my clothes.

"Someone tipped us off you'd been out here, but it was luck that we caught your scent on the wind, and—" Lucien took a step toward me.

I stepped back. Only three feet between me and the stream.

Lucien's eye widened slightly. "We need to get out of here. Tamlin's been—he hasn't been himself. I'll take you right to—"

"No," I breathed.

The word rasped through the rain, the stream, the pine forest.

The four sentinels glanced between each other, then to the arrow I kept aimed.

Lucien took me in again.

And I could see what he was now gleaning: the Illyrian fighting leathers. The color and fullness that had returned to my face, my body.

And the silent steel of my eyes.

"Feyre," he said, holding out a hand. "Let's go home."

I didn't move. "That stopped being my home the day you let him lock me up inside of it."

Lucien's mouth tightened. "It was a mistake. We *all* made mistakes. He's sorry—more sorry than you realize. So am I." He stepped toward me, and I backed up another few inches.

Not much space remained between me and the gushing waters below.

Cassian's training crashed into me, as if all the lessons he'd been drilling into me each morning were a net that caught me as I free-fell into my rising panic. Once Lucien touched me, he'd winnow us out. Not far—he wasn't that powerful—but he was fast. He'd jump miles away, then farther, and farther, until Rhys couldn't reach me. He *knew* Rhys was here.

"Feyre," Lucien pleaded, and dared another step, his hand outraised.

My arrow angled toward him, my bowstring groaning.

I'd never realized that while Lucien had been trained as a warrior, Cassian, Azriel, Mor, and Rhys were Warriors. Cassian could wipe Lucien off the face of the earth in a single blow.

"Put the arrow down," Lucien murmured, like he was soothing a wild animal.

Behind him, the four sentinels closed in. Herding me.

The High Lord's pet and possession.

"Don't," I breathed. "Touch. Me."

"You don't understand the mess we're in, Feyre. We—*I* need you home. Now."

I didn't want to hear it. Peering at the stream below, I calculated my odds.

The look cost me. Lucien lunged, hand out. One touch, that was all it'd take—

I was not the High Lord's pet any longer.

And maybe the world should learn that I did indeed have fangs.

Lucien's finger grazed the sleeve of my leather jacket.

And I became smoke and ash and night.

The world stilled and bent, and there was Lucien, lunging so slowly for what was now blank space as I stepped around him, as I hurtled for the trees behind the sentinels.

I stopped, and time resumed its natural flow. Lucien staggered, catching himself before he went over the cliff—and whirled, eye wide to discover me now standing behind his sentinels. Bron and Hart flinched and backed away. From me.

And from Rhysand at my side.

Lucien froze. I made my face a mirror of ice; the unfeeling twin to the cruel amusement on Rhysand's features as he picked at a fleck of lint on his dark tunic.

Dark, elegant clothes—no wings, no fighting leathers.

The unruffled, fine clothes . . . Another weapon. To hide just how skilled and powerful he was; to hide where he came from and what he loved. A weapon worth the cost of the magic he'd used to hide it—even if it put us at risk of being tracked.

"Little Lucien," Rhys purred. "Didn't the Lady of the Autumn Court ever tell you that when a woman says no, she means it?"

"Prick," Lucien snarled, storming past his sentinels, but not daring to touch his weapons. "You filthy, whoring prick."

I loosed a growl.

Lucien's eyes sliced to me and he said with quiet horror, "What have you done, Feyre?"

"Don't come looking for me again," I said with equal softness.

"He'll never stop looking for you; never stop waiting for you to come home."

The words hit me in the gut—like they were meant to. It must have shown in my face because Lucien pressed, "What did he do to you? Did he take your mind and—"

"Enough," Rhys said, angling his head with that casual grace. "Feyre and I are busy. Go back to your lands before I send your heads as a reminder to my old friend about what happens when Spring Court flunkies set foot in my territory."

The freezing rain slid down the neck of my clothes, down my back. Lucien's face was deathly pale. "You made your point, Feyre—now come home."

"I'm not a child playing games," I said through my teeth. That's how they'd seen me: in need of coddling, explaining, defending . . .

"Careful, Lucien," Rhysand drawled. "Or Feyre darling will send you back in pieces, too."

"We are not your enemies, Feyre," Lucien pleaded. "Things got bad, Ianthe got out of hand, but it doesn't mean you give up—"

"You gave up," I breathed.

I felt even Rhys go still.

"*You* gave up on me," I said a bit more loudly. "You were my friend. And you picked *him*—picked obeying him, even when you saw what his orders and his rules did to me. Even when you saw me wasting away *day by day*."

"You have *no idea* how volatile those first few months were," Lucien snapped. "We *needed* to present a unified, obedient front, and I was supposed to be the example to which all others in our court were held."

"You *saw* what was happening to me. But you were too afraid of him to truly do anything about it."

It was fear. Lucien had pushed Tamlin, but to a point. He'd always yielded at the end.

"I begged you," I said, the words sharp and breathless. "I begged you so many times to help me, to get me out of the house, even for an hour. And you left me alone, or shoved me into a room with Ianthe, or told me to stick it out."

Lucien said too quietly, "And I suppose the Night Court is so much better?"

I remembered—remembered what I was supposed to know, to have experienced. What Lucien and the others could never know, not even if it meant forfeiting my own life.

And I would. To keep Velaris safe, to keep Mor and Amren and Cassian and Azriel and . . . *Rhys* safe.

I said to Lucien, low and quiet and as vicious as the talons that formed at the tips of my fingers, as vicious as the wondrous weight between my shoulder blades, "When you spend so long trapped in darkness, Lucien, you find that the darkness begins to stare back."

A pulse of surprise, of wicked delight against my mental shields, at the dark, membranous wings I knew were now poking over my shoulders. Every icy kiss of rain sent jolts of cold through me. Sensitive—so sensitive, these Illryian wings.

Lucien backed up a step. "What did you do to yourself?"

I gave him a little smile. "The human girl you knew died Under the Mountain. I have no interest in spending immortality as a High Lord's pet."

Lucien started shaking his head. "Feyre—"

"Tell Tamlin," I said, choking on his name, on the thought of what he'd done to Rhys, to his family, "if he sends anyone else into these lands, I will hunt each and every one of you down. And I will demonstrate exactly what the darkness taught me."

There was something like genuine pain on his face.

I didn't care. I just watched him, unyielding and cold and dark. The creature I might one day have become if I had stayed at the Spring Court, if I had remained broken for decades, centuries . . . until I learned to quietly direct those shards of pain outward, learned to savor the pain of others.

Lucien nodded to his sentinels. Bron and Hart, wide-eyed and shaking, vanished with the other two.

Lucien lingered for a moment, nothing but air and rain between us. He said softly to Rhysand, "You're dead. You, and your entire cursed court."

Then he was gone. I stared at the empty space where he'd been, waiting, waiting, not letting that expression off my face until a warm, strong finger traced a line down the edge of my right wing.

It felt like—like having my ear breathed into.

I shuddered, arching as a gasp came out of me.

And then Rhys was in front of me, scanning my face, the wings behind me. "How?"

"Shape-shifting," I managed to say, watching the rain slide down his golden-tan face. And it was distracting enough that the talons, the wings, the rippling darkness faded, and I was left light and cold in my own skin.

Shape-shifting . . . at the sight of part of the history, the male I had not really let myself remember. Shape-shifting—a gift from Tamlin that I had not wanted, or needed . . . until now.

Rhys's eyes softened. "That was a very convincing performance."

"I gave him what he wanted to see," I murmured. "We should find another spot."

He nodded, and his tunic and pants vanished, replaced by those familiar fighting leathers, the wings, the sword. My warrior—

Not *my* anything.

"Are you all right?" he said as he scooped me into his arms to fly us to another location.

I nestled into his warmth, savoring it. "The fact that it was so easy, that I felt so little, upsets me more than the encounter itself."

Perhaps that had been my problem all along. Why I hadn't dared take that final step at Starfall. I was guilty that I *didn't* feel awful, not truly. Not for wanting him.

A few mighty flaps had us soaring up through the trees and sailing low over the forest, rain slicing into my face.

"I knew things were bad," Rhysand said with quiet rage, barely audible over the freezing bite of the wind and rain, "but I thought Lucien, at least, would have stepped in."

"I thought so, too," I said, my voice smaller than I intended.

He squeezed me gently, and I blinked at him through the rain. For once, his eyes were on me, not the landscape below. "You look good with wings," he said, and kissed my brow.

Even the rain stopped feeling so cold.

CHAPTER 48

Apparently, the nearby "inn" was little more than a raucous tavern with a few rooms for rent—usually by the hour. And, as it was, there were no vacancies. Save for a tiny, *tiny* room in what had once been part of the attic.

Rhys didn't want anyone knowing who, exactly, was amongst the High Fae, faeries, Illyrians, and whoever else was packed in the inn below. Even I barely recognized him as he—without magic, without anything but adjusting his posture—muted that sense of otherworldly power until he was nothing but a common, very good-looking Illyrian warrior, pissy about having to take the last available room, so high up that there was only a narrow staircase leading to it: no hall, no other rooms. If I needed to use the bathing room, I'd have to venture to the level below, which . . . given the smells and sounds of the half dozen rooms on that level, I made a point to use quickly on our way up and then vow not to visit again until morning.

A day of playing with water and fire and ice and darkness in the freezing rain had wrecked me so thoroughly that no one looked my way, not even the drunkest and loneliest of patrons in the town's tavern. The small town was barely that: a collection of an inn, an outfitter's store, supply store, and a brothel. All geared toward the hunters, warriors, and travelers passing through this part of the forest either on their way to the Illyrian lands or out of them. Or just for the faeries who dwelled here, solitary and glad to be that way. Too small and too remote for Amarantha or her cronies to have ever bothered with.

Honestly, I didn't care where we were, so long as it was dry and warm. Rhys opened the door to our attic room and stood aside to let me pass.

Well, at least it was one of those things.

The ceiling was so slanted that to get to the other side of the bed, I'd have to crawl across the mattress; the room so cramped it was nearly impossible to walk around the bed to the tiny armoire shoved against the other wall. I could sit on the bed and open the armoire easily.

The bed.

"I asked for two," Rhys said, hands already up.

His breath clouded in front of him. Not even a fireplace. And not enough space to even demand he sleep on the floor. I didn't trust my mastery over flame to attempt warming the room. I'd likely burn this whole filthy place to the ground.

"If you can't risk using magic, then we'll have to warm each other," I said, and instantly regretted it. "Body heat," I clarified. And, just to wipe that look off his face I added, "My sisters and I had to share a bed—I'm used to it."

"I'll try to keep my hands to myself."

My mouth went a bit dry. "I'm hungry."

He stopped smiling at that. "I'll go down and get us food while you change." I lifted a brow. He said, "Remarkable as my own abilities are to blend in, my face is recognizable. I'd rather not be down there long enough to be noticed." Indeed, he fished a cloak from his pack and slid it on, the panels fitting over his wings—which he wouldn't risk vanishing again. He'd used power earlier in the day—small enough, he said, that it might not be noticed, but we wouldn't be returning to that part of the forest anytime soon.

He tugged on the hood, and I savored the shadows and menace and wings.

Death on swift wings. That's what I'd call the painting.

He said softly, "I love it when you look at me like that."

The purr in his voice heated my blood. "Like what?"

"Like my power isn't something to run from. Like you see me."

And to a male who had grown up knowing he was the most powerful High Lord in Prythian's history, that he could shred minds if he wasn't careful, that he was alone—alone in his power, in his burden, but that fear was his mightiest weapon against the threats to his people . . . I'd hit home when we'd fought after the Court of Nightmares.

"I was afraid of you at first."

His white teeth flashed in the shadows of his hood. "No, you weren't. Nervous, maybe, but never afraid. I've felt the genuine terror of enough people to know the difference. Maybe that's why I couldn't keep away."

When? Before I could ask, he walked downstairs, shutting the door behind him.

My half-frozen clothes were a misery to peel off as they clung to my rain-swollen skin, and I knocked into the slanted ceiling, nearby walls, and slammed my knee into the brass bedpost as I changed. The room was so cold I had to get undressed in segments: replacing a freezing shirt for a dry one, pants for fleece-lined leggings, sodden socks for thick, hand-knit lovelies that went up to my calves. When I'd tucked myself into an oversized sweater that smelled faintly of Rhys, I sat cross-legged on the bed and waited.

The bed wasn't small, but certainly not large enough for me to pretend I wouldn't be sleeping next to him. Especially with the wings.

The rain tinkled on the roof mere inches away, a steady beat to the thoughts that now pulsed in my head.

The Cauldron knew what Lucien was reporting to Tamlin, likely at this very moment, if not hours ago.

I'd sent that note to Tamlin . . . and he'd chosen to ignore it. Just as he'd ignored or rejected nearly all of my requests, acted out of his deluded sense of what *he* believed was right for my well-being and safety. And Lucien had been prepared to take me against my will.

Fae males were territorial, dominant, arrogant—but the ones in the Spring Court . . . something had festered in their training. Because I knew—deep in my bones—that Cassian might push and test my limits, but the moment I said no, he'd back off. And I knew that if . . . that if I had been wasting away and Rhys had done nothing to stop it, Cassian or Azriel would have pulled me out. They would have taken me somewhere—wherever I needed to be—and dealt with Rhys later.

But Rhys . . . Rhys would never have *not* seen what was happening to me; would never have been so misguided and arrogant and self-absorbed. He'd known what Ianthe was from the moment he met her. And he'd understood what it was like to be a prisoner, and helpless, and to struggle—every day—with the horrors of both.

I had loved the High Lord who had shown me the comforts and wonders of Prythian; I had loved the High Lord who let me have the time and food and safety to paint. Maybe a small part of me might always care for him, but . . . Amarantha had broken us both. Or broken me so that who he was and what I now was no longer fit.

And I could let that go. I could accept that. Maybe it would be hard for a while, but . . . maybe it'd get better.

Rhys's feet were near-silent, given away only by the slight groan of the stairs. I rose to open the door before he could knock, and found him standing there, tray in his hands. Two stacks of covered dishes sat on it, along with two glasses and a bottle of wine, and—

"Tell me that's stew I smell." I breathed in, stepping aside and shutting the door while he set the tray on the bed. Right—not even room for a table up here.

"Rabbit stew, if the cook's to be believed."

"I could have lived without hearing that," I said, and Rhys grinned. That smile tugged on something low in my gut, and I looked away, sitting down beside the food, careful not to jostle the tray. I opened the lid of the top dishes: two bowls of stew. "What's the other one beneath?"

"Meat pie. I didn't dare ask what kind of meat." I shot him a glare, but he was already edging around the bed to the armoire, his pack in hand. "Go ahead and eat," he said, "I'm changing first."

Indeed, he was soaked—and had to be freezing and sore.

"You should have changed before going downstairs." I picked up the spoon and swirled the stew, sighing at the warm tendrils of steam that rose to kiss my chilled face.

The rasp and slurp of wet clothes being shucked off filled the room. I tried not to think about that bare, golden chest, the tattoos. The hard muscles. "You were the one training all day. Getting you a hot meal was the least I could do."

I took a sip. Bland, but edible and, most importantly, *hot*. I ate in silence, listening to the rustle of his clothes being donned, trying to think of ice baths, of infected wounds, of toe fungus—anything but his naked body, so close . . . and the bed I was sitting on. I poured myself a glass of wine—then filled his.

At last, Rhys squeezed between the bed and jutting corner of the wall, his wings tucked in close. He wore loose, thin pants, and a tight-fitting shirt of what looked to be softest cotton. "How do you get it over the wings?" I asked while he dug into his own stew.

"The back is made of slats that close with hidden buttons . . . But in normal circumstances, I just use magic to seal it shut."

"It seems like you have a great deal of magic constantly in use at once."

A shrug. "It helps me work off the strain of my power. The magic needs release—draining—or else it'll build up and drive me insane.

That's why we call the Illyrian stones Siphons—they help them channel the power, empty it when necessary."

"Actually insane?" I set aside the empty stew bowl and removed the lid from the meat pie.

"Actually insane. Or so I was warned. I can feel it, though—the pull of it, if I go too long without releasing it."

"That's horrible."

Another shrug. "Everything has its cost, Feyre. If the price of being strong enough to shield my people is that I have to struggle with that same power, then I don't mind. Amren taught me enough about controlling it. Enough that I owe a great deal to her. Including the current shield around my city while we're here."

Everyone around him had some use, some mighty skill. And yet there I was . . . nothing more than a strange hybrid. More trouble than I was worth.

"You're not," he said.

"Don't read my thoughts."

"I can't help what you sometimes shout down the bond. And besides, everything is usually written on your face, if you know where to look. Which made your performance today so much more impressive."

He set aside his stew just as I finished devouring my meat pie, and I slid back on the bed to the pillows, cupping my glass of wine between my chilled hands. I watched him eat while I drank. "Did you think I would go with him?"

He paused mid-bite, then lowered his fork. "I heard every word between you. I knew you could take care of yourself, and yet . . . " He went back to his pie, swallowing a bite before continuing. "And yet I found myself deciding that if you took his hand, I would find a way to live with it. It would be your choice."

I sipped from my wine. "And if he had grabbed me?"

There was nothing but uncompromising will in his eyes. "Then I would have torn apart the world to get you back."

A shiver went down my spine, and I couldn't look away from him. "I would have fired at him," I breathed, "if he had tried to hurt you."

I hadn't even admitted that to myself.

His eyes flickered. "I know."

He finished eating, placed the empty tray in the corner, and faced me on the bed, refilling my glass before tending to his. He was so tall he had to stoop to keep from hitting his head on the slanted ceiling.

"One thought in exchange for another," I said. "No training involved, please."

A chuckle rasped out of him, and he drained his glass, setting it on the tray.

He watched me take a long drink from mine. "I'm thinking," he said, following the flick of my tongue over my bottom lip, "that I look at you and feel like I'm dying. Like I can't breathe. I'm thinking that I want you so badly I can't concentrate half the time I'm around you, and this room is too small for me to properly bed you. Especially with the wings."

My heart stumbled a beat. I didn't know what to do with my arms, my legs, my face. I gulped down the rest of my wine and discarded the glass beside the bed, steeling my spine as I said, "I'm thinking that I can't stop thinking about you. And that it's been that way for a long while. Even before I left the Spring Court. And maybe that makes me a traitorous, lying piece of trash, but—"

"It doesn't," he said, his face solemn.

But it did. I'd wanted to see Rhysand during those weeks between visits. And hadn't cared when Tamlin stopped visiting my bedroom. Tamlin had given up on me, but I'd also given up on him. And I was a lying piece of trash for it.

I murmured, "We should go to sleep."

The patter of the rain was the only sound for a long moment before he said, "All right."

I crawled over the bed to the side tucked almost against the slanted ceiling and shimmied beneath the quilt. Cool, crisp sheets wrapped around me like an icy hand. But my shiver was from something else entirely as the mattress shifted, the blanket moved, and then the two candles beside the bed went out.

Darkness hit me at the same moment the warmth from his body did. It was an effort not to nudge toward it. Neither one of us moved, though.

I stared into the dark, listening to that icy rain, trying to steal the warmth from him.

"You're shivering so hard the bed is shaking," he said.

"My hair is wet," I said. It wasn't a lie.

Rhys was silent, then the mattress groaned, sinking directly behind me as his warmth poured over me. "No expectations," he said. "Just body heat." I scowled at the laughter in his voice.

But his broad hands slid under and over me: one flattening against my stomach and tugging me against the hard warmth of him, the other sliding under my ribs and arms to band around my chest, pressing his front into me. He tangled his legs with mine, and then a heavier, warmer darkness settled over us, smelling of citrus and the sea.

I lifted a hand toward that darkness, and met with a soft, silky material—his wing, cocooning and warming me. I traced my finger along it, and he shuddered, his arms tightening around me.

"Your finger . . . is very cold," he gritted out, the words hot on my neck.

I tried not to smile, even as I tilted my neck a bit more, hoping the heat of his breath might caress it again. I dragged my finger along his wing, the nail scraping gently against the smooth surface. Rhys tensed, his hand splaying across my stomach.

"You cruel, wicked thing," he purred, his nose grazing the exposed bit of neck I'd arched beneath him. "Didn't anyone ever teach you manners?"

"I never knew Illyrians were such sensitive babies," I said, sliding another finger down the inside of his wing.

Something hard pushed against my behind. Heat flooded me, and

I went taut and loose all at once. I stroked his wing again, two fingers now, and he twitched against my backside in time with the caress.

The fingers he'd spread over my stomach began to make idle, lazy strokes. He swirled one around my navel, and I inched imperceptibly closer, grinding up against him, arching a bit more to give that other hand access to my breasts.

"Greedy," he murmured, his lips hovering over my neck. "First you terrorize me with your cold hands, now you want . . . what is it you want, Feyre?"

More, more, more, I almost begged him as his fingers traveled down the slope of my breasts, while his other hand continued its idle stroking along my stomach, my abdomen, slowly—so slowly—heading toward the low band of my pants and the building ache beneath it.

Rhysand's teeth scraped against my neck in a lazy caress. "What is it you want, Feyre?" He nipped at my earlobe.

I cried out just a little, arching fully against him, as if I could get that hand to slip exactly to where I wanted it. I knew what he wanted me to say. I wouldn't give him the satisfaction of it. Not yet.

So I said, "I want a distraction." It was breathless. "I want—fun."

His body again tensed behind mine.

And I wondered if he somehow didn't see it for the lie it was; if he thought . . . if he thought that was all I indeed wanted.

But his hands resumed their roaming. "Then allow me the pleasure of distracting you."

He slipped a hand beneath the top of my sweater, diving clean under my shirt. Skin to skin, the calluses of his hands made me groan as they scraped the top of my breast and circled around my peaked nipple. "I love these," he breathed onto my neck, his hand sliding to my other breast. "You have no idea how much I love these."

I groaned as he caressed a knuckle against my nipple, and I bowed into the touch, silently begging him. He was hard as granite behind me, and I ground against him, eliciting a soft, wicked hiss from him. "Stop that," he snarled onto my skin. "You'll ruin *my* fun."

I would do no such thing. I began twisting, reaching for him, needing to just *feel* him, but he clicked his tongue and pushed himself harder against me, until there was no room for my hand to even slide in.

"I want to touch you first," he said, his voice so guttural I barely recognized it. "Just—let me touch you." He palmed my breast for emphasis.

It was enough of a broken plea that I paused, yielding as his other hand again trailed lazy lines on my stomach.

I can't breathe when I look at you.

Let me touch you.

Because I was jealous, and pissed off . . .

She's mine.

I shut out the thoughts, the bits and pieces he'd given me.

Rhys slid his finger along the band of my pants again, a cat playing with its dinner.

Again.

Again.

"Please," I managed to say.

He smiled against my neck. "There are those missing manners." His hand at last trailed beneath my pants. The first brush of him against me dragged a groan from deep in my throat.

He snarled in satisfaction at the wetness he found waiting for him, and his thumb circled that spot at the apex of my thighs, teasing, brushing up against it, but never quite—

His other hand gently squeezed my breast at the same moment his thumb pushed down exactly where I wanted. I bucked my hips, my head fully back against his shoulder now, panting as his thumb flicked—

I cried out, and he laughed, low and soft. "Like that?"

A moan was my only reply. *More more more.*

His fingers slid down, slow and brazen, straight through the core of me, and every point in my body, my mind, my soul, narrowed to the feeling of his fingers poised there like he had all the time in the world.

Bastard. "*Please*," I said again, and ground my ass against him for emphasis.

He hissed at the contact and slid a finger inside me. He swore. "Feyre—"

But I'd already started to move on him, and he swore again in a long exhale. His lips pressed into my neck, kissing up, up toward my ear.

I let out a moan so loud it drowned out the rain as he slid in a second finger, filling me so much I couldn't think around it, couldn't breathe. "That's it," he murmured, his lips tracing my ear.

I was sick of my neck and ear getting such attention. I twisted as much as I could, and found him staring at me, at the hand down the front of my pants, watching me move on him.

He was still staring at me when I captured his mouth with my own, biting on his lower lip.

Rhys groaned, plunging his fingers in deeper. Harder.

I didn't care—I didn't care one bit about what I was and who I was and where I'd been as I yielded fully to him, opening my mouth. His tongue swept in, moving in a way that I knew exactly what he'd do if he got between my legs.

His fingers plunged in and out, slow and hard, and my very existence narrowed to the feel of them, to the tightness in me ratcheting up with every deep stroke, every echoing thrust of his tongue in my mouth.

"You have no idea how much I—" He cut himself off, and groaned again. "*Feyre*."

The sound of my name on his lips was my undoing. Release barreled down my spine, and I cried out, only to have his lips cover mine, as if he could devour the sound. His tongue flicked the roof of my mouth while I shuddered around him, clenching tight. He swore again, breathing hard, fingers stroking me through the last throes of it, until I was limp and trembling in his arms.

I couldn't breathe hard enough, fast enough, as Rhys withdrew his fingers, pulling back so I could meet his stare. He said, "I wanted to do that when I felt how drenched you were at the Court of Nightmares. I wanted to have you right there in the middle of everyone. But mostly I just wanted to do this." His eyes held mine as he brought those fingers to his mouth and sucked on them.

On the taste of me.

I was going to eat him alive. I slid a hand up to his chest to pin him down, but he gripped my wrist. "When you lick me," he said roughly, "I want to be alone—far away from everyone. Because when you lick me, Feyre," he said, pressing nipping kisses to my jaw, my neck, "I'm going to let myself roar loud enough to bring down a mountain."

I was instantly liquid again, and he laughed under his breath. "And when I lick *you*," he said, sliding his arms around me and tucking me in tight to him, "I want you splayed out on a table like my own personal feast."

I whimpered.

"I've had a long, long time to think about how and where I want you," Rhys said onto the skin of my neck, his fingers sliding under the band of my pants, but stopping just beneath. Their home for the evening. "I have no intention of doing it all in one night. Or in a room where I can't even fuck you against the wall."

I shuddered. He remained long and hard against me. I had to feel him, had to get that considerable length inside of me—

"Sleep," he said. He might as well have commanded me to breathe underwater.

But he began stroking my body again—not to arouse, but to soothe—long, luxurious strokes down my stomach, my sides.

Sleep found me faster than I'd thought.

And maybe it was the wine, or the aftermath of the pleasure he'd wrung from me, but I didn't have a single nightmare.

CHAPTER 49

I awoke, warm and rested and calm.

Safe.

Sunlight streamed through the filthy window, illuminating the reds and golds in the wall of wing before me—where it had been all night, shielding me from the cold.

Rhysand's arms were banded around me, his breathing deep and even. And I knew it was just as rare for him to sleep that soundly, peacefully.

What we'd done last night . . .

Carefully, I twisted to face him, his arms tightening slightly, as if to keep me from vanishing with the morning mist.

His eyes were open when I nestled my head against his arm. Within the shelter of his wing, we watched each other.

And I realized I might very well be content to do exactly that forever.

I said quietly, "Why did you make that bargain with me? Why demand a week from me every month?"

His violet eyes shuttered.

And I didn't dare admit what I expected, but it was not, "Because I wanted to make a statement to Amarantha; because I wanted to piss off Tamlin, and I needed to keep you alive in a way that wouldn't be seen as merciful."

"Oh."

His mouth tightened. "You know—you know there is nothing I wouldn't do for my people, for my family."

And I'd been a pawn in that game.

His wing folded back, and I blinked at the watery light. "Bath or no bath?" he said.

I cringed at the memory of the grimy, reeking bathing room a level below. Using it to see to my needs would be bad enough. "I'd rather bathe in a stream," I said, pushing past the sinking in my gut.

Rhys let out a low laugh and rolled out of bed. "Then let's get out of here."

For a heartbeat, I wondered if I'd dreamed up everything that had happened the night before. From the slight, pleasant soreness between my legs, I knew I hadn't, but . . .

Maybe it'd be easier to pretend that nothing had happened.

The alternative might be more than I could endure.

We flew for most of the day, far and wide, close to where the forested steppes rose up to meet the Illyrian Mountains. We didn't speak of the night before—we barely spoke at all.

Another clearing. Another day of playing with my power. Summoning wings, winnowing, fire and ice and water and—now wind. The wind and breezes that rippled across the sweeping valleys and wheat fields of the Day Court, then whipped up the snow capping their highest peaks.

I could feel the words rising in him as the hours passed. I'd catch him watching me whenever I paused for a break—catch him opening up his mouth . . . and then shutting it.

It rained at one point, and then turned colder and colder with the cloud cover. We had yet to stay in the woods past dark, and I wondered what sort of creatures might prowl through them.

The sun was indeed sinking by the time Rhys gathered me in his arms and took to the skies.

There was only the wind, and his warmth, and the boom of his powerful wings.

I ventured, "What is it?"

His attention remained on the dark pines sweeping past. "There is one more story I need to tell you."

I waited. He didn't continue.

I put my hand against his cheek, the first intimate touch we'd had all day. His skin was chilled, his eyes bleak as they slid to me. "I don't walk away—not from you," I swore quietly.

His gaze softened. "Feyre—"

Rhys roared in pain, arching against me.

I felt the impact—felt blinding pain through the bond that ripped through my own mental shields, felt the shudder of the dozen places the arrows struck him as they shot from bows hidden beneath the forest canopy.

And then we were falling.

Rhys gripped me, and his magic twisted around us in a dark wind, readying to winnow us out—and failed.

Failed, because those were ash arrows through him. Through his wings. They'd tracked us—yesterday, the little magic he'd used with Lucien, they'd somehow *tracked* it and found us even so far away—

More arrows—

Rhys flung out his power. Too late.

Arrows shredded his wings. Struck his legs.

And I think I was screaming. Not for fear as we plummeted, but for him—for the blood and the greenish sheen on those arrows. Not just ash, but poison—

A dark wind—his power—slammed into me, and then I was being

thrown far and wide as he sent me tumbling beyond the arrows' range, tumbling through the air—

Rhys's roar of wrath shook the forest, the mountains beyond. Birds rose up in waves, taking to the skies, fleeing that bellow.

I slammed into the dense canopy, my body barking in agony as I shattered through wood and pine and leaf. Down and down—

Focus focus focus

I flung out a wave of that hard air that had once shielded me from Tamlin's temper. Threw it out beneath me like a net.

I collided with an invisible wall so solid I thought my right arm might snap.

But—I stopped falling through the branches.

Thirty feet below, the ground was nearly impossible to see in the growing darkness.

I did not trust that shield to hold my weight for long.

I scrambled across it, trying not to look down, and leaped the last few feet onto a wide pine bough. Hurtling over the wood, I reached the trunk and clung to it, panting, reordering my mind around the pain, the steadiness of being on ground.

I listened—for Rhys, for his wings, for his next roar. Nothing.

No sign of the archers who he'd been falling to meet. Who he'd thrown me far, far away from. Trembling, I dug my nails into the bark as I listened for him.

Ash arrows. Poisoned ash arrows.

The forest grew ever darker, the trees seeming to wither into skeletal husks. Even the birds hushed themselves.

I stared at my palm—at the eye inked there—and sent a blind thought through it, down that bond. *Where are you? Tell me and I'll come to you. I'll find you.*

There was no wall of onyx adamant at the end of the bond. Only endless shadow.

Things—great, enormous things—were rustling in the forest.

Rhysand. No response.

The last of the light slipped away.

Rhysand, please.

No sound. And the bond between us . . . silent. I'd always felt it protecting me, seducing me, laughing at me on the other side of my shields. And now . . . it had vanished.

A guttural howl rippled from the distance, like rocks scraping against each other.

Every hair on my body rose. We never stayed out here past sunset.

I took steadying breaths, nocking one of my few remaining arrows into my bow.

On the ground, something sleek and dark slithered past, the leaves crunching under what looked to be enormous paws tipped in needle-like claws.

Something began screaming. High, panicked screeches. As if it were being torn apart. Not Rhys—something else.

I began shaking again, the tip of my arrow gleaming as it shuddered with me.

Where are you where are you where are you

Let me find you let me find you let me find you

I unstrung my bow. Any bit of light might give me away.

Darkness was my ally; darkness might shield me.

It had been anger the first time I'd winnowed—and anger the second time I'd done it.

Rhys was hurt. They had *hurt* him. Targeted him. And now . . . Now . . .

It was not hot anger that poured through me.

But something ancient, and frozen, and so vicious that it honed my focus into razor-sharpness.

And if I wanted to track him, if I wanted to get to the spot I'd last seen him . . . I'd become a figment of darkness, too.

I was running down the branch just as something crashed through the brush nearby, snarling and hissing. But I folded myself into smoke and starlight, and winnowed from the edge of my branch and into the tree across from me. The creature below loosed a cry, but I paid it no heed.

I was night; I was wind.

Tree to tree, I winnowed, so fast the beasts roaming the forest floor barely registered my presence. And if I could grow claws and wings . . . I could change my eyes, too.

I'd hunted at dusk often enough to see how animal eyes worked, how they glowed.

Cool command had my own eyes widening, shifting—a temporary blindness as I winnowed between trees again, running down a wide branch and winnowing through the air for the next—

I landed, and the night forest became bright. And the things prowling on the forest floor below . . . I didn't look at them.

No, I kept my attention on winnowing through the trees until I was on the outskirts of the spot where we'd been attacked, all the while tugging on that bond, searching for that familiar wall on the other side of it. Then—

An arrow was stuck in the branches high above me. I winnowed onto the broad bough.

And when I yanked out that length of ash wood, when I felt my immortal body quail in its presence, a low snarl slipped out of me.

I hadn't been able to count how many arrows Rhys had taken. How many he'd shielded me from, using his own body.

I shoved the arrow into my quiver, and continued on, circling the area until I spotted another—down by the pine-needle carpet.

I thought frost might have gleamed in my wake as I winnowed in the direction the arrow would have been shot, finding another, and another. I kept them all.

Until I discovered the place where the pine branches were broken and shattered. Finally I smelled Rhys, and the trees around me glimmered with ice as I spied his blood splattered on the branches, the ground.

And ash arrows all around the site.

As if an ambush had been waiting, and unleashed a hail of hundreds, too fast for him to detect or avoid. Especially if he'd been distracted with me. Distracted all day.

I winnowed in bursts through the site, careful not to stay on the ground too long lest the creatures roaming nearby scent me.

He'd fallen hard, the tracks told me. And they'd had to drag him away. Quickly.

They'd tried to hide the blood trail, but even without his mind speaking to me, I could find that scent anywhere. I *would* find that scent anywhere.

They might have been good at concealing their tracks, but I was better.

I continued my hunt, an ash arrow now nocked into my bow as I read the signs.

Two dozen at least had taken him away, though more had been there for the initial assault. The others had winnowed out, leaving limited numbers to haul him toward the mountains—toward whoever might be waiting.

They were moving swiftly. Deeper and deeper into the woods, toward the slumbering giants of the Illyrian Mountains. His blood had flowed all the way.

Alive, it told me. He was alive—though if the wounds weren't clotting . . . The ash arrows were doing their work.

I'd brought down one of Tamlin's sentinels with a single well-placed ash arrow. I tried not to think about what a barrage of them could do. His roar of pain echoed in my ears.

And through that merciless, unyielding rage, I decided that if Rhys was not alive, if he was harmed beyond repair . . . I didn't care who they were and why they had done it.

They were all dead.

Tracks veered from the main group—scouts probably sent to find a spot for the night. I slowed my winnowing, carefully tracing their steps now. Two groups had split, as if trying to hide where they'd gone. Rhys's scent clung to both.

They'd taken his clothes, then. Because they'd known I'd track them, seen me with him. They'd known I'd come for him. A trap—it was likely a trap.

I paused at the top branches of a tree overlooking where the two groups had cleaved, scanning the ground. One headed deeper into the mountains. One headed along them.

Mountains were Illyrian territory—mountains would run the risk of being discovered by a patrol. They'd assume that's where *I* would doubt they would be stupid enough to go. They'd assume I'd think they'd keep to the unguarded, unpatrolled forest.

I weighed my options, smelling the two paths.

They hadn't counted on the small, second scent that clung there, entwined with his.

And I didn't let myself think about it as I winnowed toward the mountain tracks, outracing the wind. I didn't let myself think about the fact that *my* scent was on Rhys, clinging to him after last night. He'd changed his clothes that morning—but the smell on his body . . . Without taking a bath, I was all over him.

So I winnowed toward him, toward *me*. And when the narrow cave appeared at the foot of a mountain, the faintest glimmer of light escaping from its mouth . . . I halted.

A whip cracked.

And every word, every thought and feeling, went out of me. Another whip—and another.

I slung my bow over my shoulder and pulled out a second ash arrow. It was quick work to bind the two arrows together, so that a tip gleamed on either end—and to do the same for two more. And when I was done, when I looked at the twin makeshift daggers in either hand, when that whip sounded again . . . I winnowed into the cave.

They'd picked one with a narrow entrance that opened into a wide, curving tunnel, setting up their little camp around the bend to avoid detection.

The scouts at the front—two High Fae males with unmarked armor who I didn't recognize—didn't notice as I went past.

Two other scouts patrolled just inside the cave mouth, watching those at the front. I was there and vanished before they could spot me. I rounded the corner, time slipping and bending, and my night-dark eyes burned at the light. I changed them, winnowing between one blink and the next, past the other two guards.

And when I beheld the four others in that cave, beheld the tiny fire they'd built and what they'd already done to him . . . I pushed against the bond between us—almost sobbing as I felt that adamant wall . . . But there was nothing behind it. Only silence.

They'd found strange chains of bluish stone to spread his arms, suspending him from either wall of the cave. His body sagged from them, his back a ravaged slab of meat. And his wings . . .

They'd left the ash arrows through his wings. Seven of them.

His back to me, only the sight of the blood running down his skin told me he was alive.

And it was enough—it was enough that I detonated.

I winnowed to the two guards holding twin whips.

The others around them shouted as I dragged my ash arrows across their throats, deep and vicious, just like I'd done countless times while hunting. One, two—then they were on the ground, whips limp. Before the guards could attack, I winnowed again to the ones nearest.

Blood sprayed.

Winnow, strike; winnow, strike.

Those wings—those beautiful, powerful wings—

The guards at the mouth of the cave had come rushing in.

They were the last to die.

And the blood on my hands felt different from what it had been like Under the Mountain. This blood . . . I savored. Blood for blood. Blood for every drop they'd spilled of his.

Silence fell in the cave as their final shouts finished echoing, and I winnowed in front of Rhys, shoving the bloody ash daggers into my belt. I gripped his face. Pale—too pale.

But his eyes opened to slits and he groaned.

I didn't say anything as I lunged for the chains holding him, trying not to notice the bloody handprints I'd left on him. The chains were like ice—worse than ice. They felt *wrong*. I pushed past the pain and strangeness of them, and the weakness that barreled down my spine, and unlatched him.

His knees slammed into the rock so hard I winced, but I rushed to the other arm, still upraised. Blood flowed down his back, his front, pooling in the dips between his muscles.

"Rhys," I breathed. I almost dropped to my own knees as I felt a flicker of *him* behind his mental shields, as if the pain and exhaustion had reduced it to window-thinness. His wings, peppered with those arrows, remained spread—so painfully taut that I winced. "Rhys—we need to winnow home."

His eyes opened again, and he gasped, "Can't."

Whatever poison was on those arrows, then his magic, his strength . . .

But we couldn't stay here, not when the other group was nearby. So I said, "Hold on," and gripped his hand before I threw us into night and smoke.

Winnowing was so heavy, as if all the weight of him, all that power, dragged me back. It was like wading through mud, but I focused on the forest, on a moss-shrouded cave I'd seen earlier that day while slaking my thirst, tucked into the side of the riverbank. I'd peeked into it, and nothing but leaves had been within. At least it was safe, if not a bit damp. Better than being in the open—and it was our only option.

Every mile was an effort. But I kept my grip on his hand, terrified that if I let go, I'd leave him somewhere I might never be able to find, and—

And then we were there, in that cave, and he grunted in agony as we slammed into the wet, cold stone floor.

"Rhys," I pleaded, stumbling in the dark—such impenetrable dark, and with those creatures around us, I didn't risk a fire—

But he was so cold, and still bleeding.

I willed my eyes to shift again, and my throat tightened at the damage. The lashings across his back kept dribbling blood, but the wings . . . "I have to get these arrows out."

He grunted again, hands braced on the floor. And the sight of him like that, unable to even make a sly comment or half smile . . .

I went up to his wing. "This is going to hurt." I clenched my jaw as I studied the way they'd pierced the beautiful membrane. I'd have to snap the arrows in two and slide each end out.

No—not snapping. I'd have to cut it—slowly, carefully, smoothly, to keep any shards and rough bits from causing further damage. Who knew what an ash splinter might do if it got stuck in there?

"Do it," he panted, his voice hoarse.

There were seven arrows in total: three in this wing, four in the other. They'd removed the ones from his legs, for whatever reason—the wounds already half-clotted.

Blood dripped on the floor.

I took the knife from where it was strapped to my thigh, studied the entry wound, and gently gripped the shaft. He hissed. I paused.

"Do it," Rhys repeated, his knuckles white as he fisted his hands on the ground.

I set the small bit of serrated edge against the arrow and began sawing as gently as I could. The blood-soaked muscles of his back shifted and tensed, and his breathing turned sharp, uneven. Too slow—I was going too slowly.

But any faster and it might hurt him more, might damage the sensitive wing.

"Did you know," I said over the sound of my sawing, "that one summer, when I was seventeen, Elain bought me some paint? We'd had just enough to spend on extra things, and she bought me and Nesta presents. She didn't have enough for a full set, but bought me red and blue and yellow. I used them to the last drop, stretching them as much as I could, and painted little decorations in our cottage."

His breath heaved out of him, and I finally sawed through the shaft. I didn't let him know what I was doing before I yanked out the arrowhead in a smooth pull.

He swore, body locking up, and blood gushed out—then stopped.

I almost loosed a sigh of relief. I set to work on the next arrow.

"I painted the table, the cabinets, the doorway . . . And we had this old, black dresser in our room—one drawer for each of us. We didn't have much clothing to put in there, anyway." I got through the second arrow faster, and he braced himself as I tugged it out. Blood flowed, then clotted. I started on the third. "I painted flowers for Elain on her drawer," I said, sawing and sawing. "Little roses and begonias and irises. And for Nesta . . . " The arrow clattered to the ground and I ripped out the other end.

I watched the blood flow and stop—watched him slowly lower the wing to the ground, his body trembling.

"Nesta," I said, starting on the other wing, "I painted flames for her. She was always angry, always burning. I think she and Amren would be fast friends. I think she would like Velaris, despite herself. And I think Elain—Elain would like it, too. Though she'd probably cling to Azriel, just to have some peace and quiet."

I smiled at the thought—at how handsome they would be together. If the warrior ever stopped quietly loving Mor. I doubted it. Azriel would likely love Mor until he was a whisper of darkness between the stars.

I finished the fourth arrow and started on the fifth.

Rhys's voice was raw as he said to the floor, "What did you paint for yourself?"

I drew out the fifth, moving to the sixth before saying, "I painted the night sky."

He stilled. I went on, "I painted stars and the moon and clouds and just endless, dark sky." I finished the sixth, and was well on my way sawing through the seventh before I said, "I never knew why. I rarely went outside at night—usually, I was so tired from hunting that I just wanted to sleep. But I wonder . . . " I pulled out the seventh and final arrow. "I wonder if some part of me knew what was waiting for me. That I would never be a gentle grower of things, or someone who burned like fire—but that I would be quiet and enduring and as faceted as the night. That I would have beauty, for those who knew where to look, and if people didn't bother to look, but to only fear it . . . Then I didn't particularly care for them, anyway. I wonder if, even in my despair and hopelessness, I was never truly alone. I wonder if I was looking for this place—looking for you all."

The blood stopped flowing, and his other wing lowered to the ground. Slowly, the lashes on his back began to clot. I walked around to where he was bowed over the floor, hands braced on the rock, and knelt.

His head lifted. Pain-filled eyes, bloodless lips. "You saved me," he rasped.

"You can explain who they were later."

"Ambush," Rhys said anyway, his eyes scanning my face for signs of hurt. "Hybern soldiers with ancient chains from the king himself, to nullify my power. They must have traced the magic I used yesterday . . . I'm sorry." The words tumbled out of him. I brushed back his dark hair. That was why I hadn't been able to use the bond, to speak mind to mind.

"Rest," I said, and moved to retrieve the blanket from my pack. It'd have to do. He gripped my wrist before I could rise. His eyelids lowered. Consciousness ripped from him—too fast. Much too fast and too heavy.

"I was looking for you, too," Rhys murmured.

And passed out.

CHAPTER 50

I slept beside him, offering what warmth I could, monitoring the cave entrance the entirety of the night. The beasts in the forest prowled past in an endless parade, and only in the gray light before dawn did their snarls and hissing fade.

Rhys was unconscious as watery sunlight painted the stone walls, his skin clammy. I checked his wounds and found them barely healed, an oily sheen oozing from them.

And when I put a hand on his brow, I swore at the heat.

Poison had coated those arrows. And that poison remained in his body.

The Illyrian camp was so distant that my own powers, feeble from the night before, wouldn't get us far.

But if they had those horrible chains to nullify his powers, had ash arrows to bring him down, then that poison . . .

An hour passed. He didn't get better. No, his golden skin was pale—paling. His breaths were shallow. "Rhys," I said softly.

He didn't move. I tried shaking him. If he could tell me what the poison was, maybe I could try to find something to help him . . . He did not awaken.

Around midday, panic gripped me in a tight fist.

I didn't know anything about poisons or remedies. And out here, so far from anyone . . . Would Cassian track us down in time? Would Mor winnow in? I tried to rouse Rhys over and over.

The poison had dragged him down deep. I would not risk waiting for help to arrive.

I would not risk him.

So I bundled him in as many layers as I could spare, yet took my cloak, kissed his brow, and left.

We were only a few hundred yards from where I'd been hunting the night before, and as I emerged from the cave, I tried not to look at the tracks of the beasts who had passed through, right above us. Enormous, horrible tracks.

What I was to hunt would be worse.

We were already near running water—so I made my trap close by, building my snare with hands that I refused to let shake.

I placed the cloak—mostly new, rich, lovely—in the center of my snare. And I waited.

An hour. Two.

I was about to start bargaining with the Cauldron, with the Mother, when a creeping, familiar silence fell over the wood.

Rippling toward me, the birds stopped chirping, the wind stopped sighing in the pines.

And when a crack sounded through the forest, followed by a screech that hollowed out my ears, I nocked an arrow into my bow and set off to see the Suriel.

It was as horrific as I remembered:

Tattered robes barely concealing a body made of not skin, but what looked to be solid, worn bone. Its lipless mouth held too-large teeth, and its fingers—long, spindly—clicked against each other while it weighed the fine cloak I'd laid in the center of my snare, as if the cloth had been blown in on a wind.

"Feyre Cursebreaker," it said, turning toward me, in a voice that was both one and many.

I lowered my bow. "I have need of you."

Time—I was running out of time. I could feel it, that urgency begging me to hurry through the bond.

"What fascinating changes a year has wrought on you—on the world," it said.

A year. Yes, it had been over a year now since I'd first crossed the wall.

"I have questions," I said.

It smiled, each of those stained, too-large brown teeth visible. "You have two questions."

An answer and an order.

I didn't waste time; not with Rhys, not when this wood might be full of enemies hunting for us.

"What poison was used on those arrows?"

"Bloodbane," it said.

I didn't know that poison—had never heard of it.

"Where do I find the cure?"

The Suriel clicked its bone fingers against each other, as if the answer lay inside the sound. "In the forest."

I hissed, my brows flattening. "Please—please don't be cryptic. *What* is the cure?"

The Suriel cocked its head, the bone gleaming in the light. "Your blood. Give him your blood, Cursebreaker. It is rich with the healing gift of the High Lord of the Dawn. It shall spare him from the bloodbane's wrath."

"That's it?" I pushed. "*How much* blood?"

"A few mouthfuls will do." A hollow, dry wind—not at all like the misty, cold veils that usually drifted past—brushed my face. "I helped you before. I have helped you now. And you will free me before I lose my patience, Cursebreaker."

Some primal, lingering human part of me trembled as I took in the snare around its legs, pinning it to the ground. Perhaps this time, the Suriel had let itself be caught. And knew how to free itself—had learned it the moment I'd spared it from the naga.

A test—of honor. And a favor. For the arrow I'd shot to save it last year.

But I nocked an ash arrow into my bow, cringing at the sheen of poison coating it. "Thank you for your help," I said, bracing myself for flight should it charge at me.

The Suriel's stained teeth clacked against each other. "If you wish to speed your mate's healing, in addition to your blood, a pink-flowered weed sprouts by the river. Make him chew it."

I fired my arrow at the snare before I finished hearing its words.

The trap sprang free. And the word clicked through me.

Mate.

"What did you say?"

The Suriel rose to its full height, towering over me even from across the clearing. I had not realized that despite the bone, it was muscled—powerful.

"If you wish to . . . " The Suriel paused, and grinned, showing nearly all of those brown, thick teeth. "You did not know, then."

"Say it," I gritted out.

"The High Lord of the Night Court is your mate."

I wasn't entirely sure I was breathing.

"Interesting," the Suriel said.

Mate.

Mate.

Mate.

Rhysand was my mate.

Not lover, not husband, but more than that. A bond so deep, so permanent that it was honored over all others. Rare, cherished.

Not Tamlin's mate.

Rhysand's.

I was jealous, and pissed off . . .

You're mine.

The words slipped out of me, low and twisted, "Does he know?"

The Suriel clenched the robes of its new cloak in its bone-fingers. "Yes."

"For a long while?"

"Yes. Since—"

"No. He can tell me—I want to hear it from his lips."

The Suriel cocked its head. "You are—you are feeling too much, too fast. I cannot read it."

"How can I possibly be his mate?" Mates were equals—matched, at least in some ways.

"He is the most powerful High Lord to ever walk this earth. You are . . . new. You are made of all seven High Lords. Unlike anything. Are you two not similar in that? Are you not matched?"

Mate. And he knew—he'd *known*.

I glanced toward the river, as if I could see all the way to the cave, to where Rhysand slept.

When I looked back at the Suriel, it was gone.

✠

I found the pink weed, and ripped it out of the ground as I stalked back to the cave.

Mercifully, Rhys was half-awake, the layers I'd thrown on him now scattered across the blanket, and he gave me a strained smile as I entered.

I chucked the weed at him, showering his bare chest with soil. "Chew on that."

He blinked blearily at me.

Mate.

But he obeyed, frowning at the plant before he plucked off a few leaves and started chewing. He grimaced as he swallowed. I tore off my jacket, shoved up my sleeve, and strode to him. He'd known, and kept it from me.

Had the others known? Had they guessed?

He'd—he'd promised not to lie, not to keep things from me.

And this—this *most important thing in my immortal existence* . . .

I drew a dagger across my forearm, the cut long and deep, and dropped to my knees before him. I didn't feel the pain. "Drink this. *Now.*"

Rhys blinked again, brows raising, but I didn't give him the chance to object before I gripped the back of his head, lifted my arm to his mouth, and shoved him against my skin.

He paused as my blood touched his lips. Then his mouth opened wider, his tongue brushing my arm as he sucked in my blood. One mouthful. Two. Three.

I yanked back my arm, the wound already healing, and shoved down my sleeve.

"You don't get to ask questions," I said, and he looked up at me, exhaustion and pain lining his face, my blood shining on his lips. Part of me hated the words, for acting like this while he was wounded, but I didn't care. "You only get to answer them. And nothing more."

Wariness flooded his eyes, but he nodded, biting off another mouthful of the weed and chewing.

I stared down at him, the half-Illyrian warrior who was my soul-bonded partner.

"How long have you known that I'm your mate?"

Rhys stilled. The entire world stilled.

He swallowed. "Feyre."

"How long have you known that I'm your mate?"

"You . . . You ensnared the Suriel?" How he'd pieced it together, I didn't give a shit.

"I said you don't get to ask questions."

I thought something like panic might have flashed over his features. He chewed again on the plant—as if it instantly helped, as if he knew that he wanted to be at his full strength to face this, face me. Color was already blooming on his cheeks, perhaps from whatever healing was in my blood.

"I suspected for a while," Rhys said, swallowing once more. "I knew for certain when Amarantha was killing you. And when we stood on the balcony Under the Mountain—right after we were freed, I *felt* it snap into place between us. I think when you were Made, it . . . it heightened the smell of the bond. I looked at you then and the strength of it hit me like a blow."

He'd gone wide-eyed, had stumbled back as if shocked—terrified. And had vanished.

That had been over half a year ago.

My blood pounded in my ears. "When were you going to tell me?"

"Feyre."

"*When were you going to tell me?*"

"I don't know. I wanted to yesterday. Or whenever you'd noticed that it wasn't just a bargain between us. I hoped you might realize when I took you to bed, and—"

"Do the others know?"

"Amren and Mor do. Azriel and Cassian suspect."

My face burned. They knew—they— "Why didn't you tell me?"

"You were in love with him; you were going to marry him. And then you . . . you were enduring everything and it didn't feel right to tell you."

"I deserved to know."

"The other night you told me you wanted a distraction, you wanted *fun*. Not a mating bond. And not to someone like me—a mess." So the words I'd spat after the Court of Nightmares had haunted him.

"You promised—you promised no secrets, no games. You *promised*."

Something in my chest was caving in on itself. Some part of me I'd thought long gone.

"I know I did," Rhys said, the glow returning to his face. "You think

I didn't want to tell you? You think I liked hearing you wanted me only for amusement and release? You think it didn't drive me out of my mind so completely that those bastards shot me out of the sky because I was too busy wondering if I should just tell you, or wait—or maybe take whatever pieces that you offered me and be happy with it? Or that maybe I should let you go so you don't have a lifetime of assassins and High Lords hunting you down for being with me?"

"I don't want to hear this. I don't want to hear you explain how you assumed that you knew best, that I couldn't handle it—"

"I didn't do that—"

"I don't want to hear you tell me that you decided I was to be kept in the dark while your friends knew, while *you all* decided what was right for me—"

"Feyre—"

"Take me back to the Illyrian camp. Now."

He was panting in great, rattling gulps. "Please."

But I stormed to him and grabbed his hand. "*Take me back now.*"

And I saw the pain and sorrow in his eyes. Saw it and didn't care, not as that thing in my chest was twisting and breaking. Not as my heart—my *heart*—ached, so viciously that I realized it'd somehow been repaired in these past few months. Repaired by him.

And now it hurt.

Rhys saw all that and more on my face, and I saw nothing but agony in his as he rallied his strength and, grunting in pain, winnowed us into the Illyrian camp.

CHAPTER 51

We slammed into freezing mud right outside the little stone house.

I think he'd meant to winnow us into it, but his powers had given out. Across the yard, I spied Cassian—and Mor—at the window of the house, eating breakfast. Their eyes went wide, and then they were rushing for the door.

"Feyre," Rhys groaned, bare arms buckling as he tried to rise.

I left him lying in the mud and stormed toward the house.

The door flung open, and Cassian and Mor were sprinting for us, scanning every inch of our bodies. Cassian realized I was in one piece and hurtled for Rhys, who was struggling to rise, mud covering his bare skin, but Mor—Mor saw my face.

I went up to her, cold and hollow. "I want you to take me somewhere far away," I said. "Right now." I needed to get away—needed to think, to have space and quiet and calm.

Mor looked between us, biting her lip.

"Please," I said, and my voice broke on the word.

Behind me, Rhys moaned my name again.

Mor scanned my face once more, and gripped my hand.

We vanished into wind and night.

Brightness assaulted me, and I gobbled up my surroundings: mountains and snow all around, fresh and gleaming in the midday light, so clean against the dirt on me.

We were high up on the peaks, and about a hundred yards away, a log cabin stood tucked between two upper fangs of the mountains, shielding it from the wind. The house was dark—there was nothing around it for as far as I could see.

"The house is warded, so no one can winnow in. No one can get beyond this point, actually, without our family's permission." Mor stepped ahead, snow crunching under her boots. Without the wind, the day was mild enough to remind me that spring had dawned in the world, though I'd bet it would be freezing once the sun vanished. I trailed after her, something zinging against my skin. "You're—allowed in," Mor said.

"Because I'm his mate?"

She kept wading through the knee-high snow. "Did you guess, or did he tell you?"

"The Suriel told me. After I went to hunt it for information on how to heal him."

She swore. "Is he—is he all right?"

"He'll live," I said. She didn't ask any other questions. And I wasn't feeling generous enough to supply further information. We reached the door to the cabin, which she unlocked with a wave of her hand.

A main, wood-paneled room consisting of a kitchen to the right, a living area with a leather sofa covered in furs to the left; a small hall in the back that led to two bedrooms and a shared bathing room, and nothing else.

"We got sent up here for 'reflection' when we were younger," Mor said. "Rhys used to smuggle in books and booze for me."

I cringed at the sound of his name. "It's perfect," I said tightly. Mor waved a hand, and a fire sprang to life in the hearth, heat flooding the room. Food landed on the counters of the kitchen, and something in the pipes groaned. "No need for firewood," she said. "It'll burn until you leave." She lifted a brow as if to ask when that would be.

I looked away. "Please don't tell him where I am."

"He'll try to find you."

"Tell him I don't want to be found. Not for a while."

Mor bit her lip. "It's not my business—"

"Then don't say anything."

She did, anyway. "He wanted to tell you. And it killed him not to. But . . . I've never seen him so happy as he is when he's with you. And I don't think that has anything to do with you being his mate."

"I don't care." She fell silent, and I could feel the words she wanted to say building up. So I said, "Thank you for bringing me here." A polite dismissal.

Mor bowed her head. "I'll check back in three days. There are clothes in the bedrooms, and all the hot water you want. The house is spelled to take care of you—merely wish or speak for things, and it'll be done."

I only wanted solitude and quiet, but . . . a hot bath sounded like a nice way to start.

She left the cottage before I could say anything else.

Alone, no one around for miles, I stood in the silent cabin and stared at nothing.

PART THREE

THE HOUSE OF MIST

CHAPTER 52

There was a deep, sunken tub in the floor of the mountain cabin—large enough to accommodate Illyrian wings. I filled it with water near-scalding, not caring how the magic of this house operated, only that it worked. Hissing and wincing, I climbed in.

Three days without a bath and I could have wept at the warmth and cleanliness of it.

No matter that I'd once gone weeks without one—not when drawing hot water for it in my family's cottage had been more trouble than it was worth. Not when we didn't even have a bathtub and it required buckets and buckets to get clean.

I washed with dark soap that smelled of smoke and pine, and when I was done, I sat there, watching the steam slither amongst the few candles.

Mate.

The word chased me from the bath sooner than I wanted, and hounded me as I pulled on the clothes I'd found in a drawer of the bedroom: dark leggings, a large, cream-colored sweater that hung to mid-thigh, and thick socks. My stomach grumbled, and I realized I hadn't eaten since the day before, because—

Because he'd been injured, and I'd gone out of my mind—absolutely insane—when he'd been taken from me, shot out of the sky like a bird.

I'd acted on instinct, on a drive to protect him that had come from so deep in me . . .

So deep in me—

I found a container of soup on the wood counter that Mor must have brought in, and scrounged up a cast iron pot to heat it. Fresh, crusty bread sat near the stove, and I ate half of it while waiting for the soup to warm.

He'd suspected it before I'd even freed us from Amarantha.

My wedding day . . . Had he interrupted to spare me from a horrible mistake or for his own ends? Because I was his mate, and letting me bind myself to someone else was unacceptable?

I ate my dinner in silence, with only the murmuring fire for company.

And beneath the barrage of my thoughts, a throb of relief.

My relationship with Tamlin had been doomed from the start. I had left—only to find my mate. To go to my mate.

If I were looking to spare us both from embarrassment, from rumor, only that—only that I had found my true mate—would do the trick.

I was not a lying piece of traitorous filth. Not even close. Even if Rhys . . . Rhys had known I was his mate.

While I'd shared a bed with Tamlin. For months and months. He'd known I was sharing a bed with him, and hadn't let it show. Or maybe he didn't care.

Maybe he didn't want the bond. Had hoped it'd vanish.

I'd owed nothing to Rhys then—had nothing to apologize for.

But he'd known I'd react badly. That it'd hurt me more than help me.

And what if I had known?

What if I *had* known that Rhys was my mate while I'd loved Tamlin?

It didn't excuse his not telling me. Didn't excuse the recent weeks, when I'd hated myself so much for wanting him so badly—when he should have told me. But . . . I understood.

I washed the dishes, swept the crumbs off the small dining table between the kitchen and living area, and climbed into one of the beds.

Just last night, I'd been curled beside him, counting his breaths to make sure he didn't stop making them. The night before, I'd been in his arms, his fingers between my legs, his tongue in my mouth. And now . . . though the cabin was warm, the sheets were cold. The bed was large—empty.

Through the small glass window, the snow-blasted land around me glowed blue in the moonlight. The wind was a hollow moan, brushing great, sparkling drifts of snow past the cabin.

I wondered if Mor had told him where I was.

Wondered if he'd indeed come looking for me.

Mate.

My mate.

Sunlight on snow awoke me, and I squinted at the brightness, cursing myself for not closing the curtains. It took me a moment to remember where I was; why I was in this isolated cabin, deep in the mountains of—I didn't know what mountains these were.

Rhys had once mentioned a favorite retreat that Mor and Amren had burned to cinders in a fight. I wondered if this was it; if it had been rebuilt. Everything was comfortable, worn, but in relatively good shape.

Mor and Amren had known.

I couldn't decide if I hated them for it.

No doubt, Rhys had ordered them to keep quiet, and they'd respected his wishes, but . . .

I made the bed, fixed breakfast, washed the dishes, and then stood in the center of the main living space.

I'd run away.

Precisely how Rhys expected me to run—how I'd told him anyone in their right mind *would* run from him. Like a coward, like a fool, I'd left him injured in the freezing mud.

I'd walked away from him—a day after I'd told him he was the only thing I'd never walk away from.

I'd demanded honesty, and at the first true test, I hadn't even let him give it to me. I hadn't granted him the consideration of hearing him out.

You see me.

Well, I'd refused to see him. Maybe I'd refused to see what was right in front of me.

I'd walked away.

And maybe . . . maybe I shouldn't have.

Boredom hit me halfway through the day.

Supreme, unrelenting boredom, thanks to being trapped inside while the snow slowly melted under the mild spring day, listening to it drip-drip-dripping off the roof.

It made me nosy—and once I'd finished going through the drawers and closets of both bedrooms (clothes, old bits of ribbon, knives and weapons tucked between as if one of them had chucked them in and just forgotten), the kitchen cabinets (food, preserved goods, pots and pans, a stained cookbook), and the living area (blankets, some books, more weapons hidden *everywhere*), I ventured into the supply closet.

For a High Lord's retreat, the cabin was . . . not common, because everything had been made and appointed with care, but . . . casual. As if this were the sole place where they might all come, and pile into beds and on the couch, and not be anyone but themselves, taking turns with who cooked that night and who hunted and who cleaned and—

A family.

It felt like a family—the one I'd never quite had, had never dared really hope for. Had stopped expecting when I'd grown used to the space and formality of living in a manor. To being a symbol for a broken people, a High Priestess's golden idol and puppet.

I opened the storeroom door, a blast of cold greeting me, but candles sputtered to life, thanks to the magic that kept the place hospitable. Shelves free of dust (another magical perk, no doubt) gleamed with more food stores. Books, sporting equipment, packs and ropes and, big surprise, more weapons. I sorted through it all, these remnants of adventures past and future, and almost missed them as I walked past.

Half a dozen cans of paint.

Paper, and a few canvases. Brushes, old and flecked with paint from lazy hands.

There were other art supplies—pastels and watercolors, what looked to be charcoal for sketching, but . . . I stared at the paint, the brushes.

Which of them had tried to paint while stuck here—or enjoying a holiday with them all?

I told myself my hands were trembling with the cold as I reached for the paint and pried open the lid.

Still fresh. Probably from the magic preserving this place.

I peered into the dark, gleaming interior of the can I'd opened: blue.

And then I started gathering supplies.

I painted all day.

And when the sun vanished, I painted all through the night.

The moon had set by the time I washed my hands and face and neck and stumbled into bed, not even bothering to undress before unconsciousness swept me away.

I was up, brush in hand, before the spring sun could resume its work thawing the mountains around me.

I paused only long enough to eat. The sun was setting again, exhausted from the dent it'd made in the layer of snow outside, when a knock sounded on the front door.

Splattered in paint—the cream-colored sweater utterly wrecked—I froze.

Another knock, light, but insistent. Then—"Please don't be dead."

I didn't know whether it was relief or disappointment that sank in my chest as I opened the door and found Mor huffing hot air into her cupped hands.

She looked at the paint on my skin, in my hair. At the brush in my hand.

And then at what I had done.

Mor stepped in from the brisk spring night and let out a low whistle as she shut the door. "Well, you've certainly been busy."

Indeed.

I'd painted nearly every surface in the main room.

And not with just broad swaths of color, but with decorations—little images. Some were basic: clusters of icicles drooping down the sides of the threshold. They melted into the first shoots of spring, then burst into full blooms of summer, before brightening and deepening into fall leaves. I'd painted a ring of flowers round the card table by the window; leaves and crackling flames around the dining table.

But in between the intricate decorations, I'd painted them. Bits and pieces of Mor, and Cassian, and Azriel, and Amren . . . and Rhys.

Mor went up to the large hearth, where I'd painted the mantel in black shimmering with veins of gold and red. Up close, it was a solid, pretty bit of paint. But from the couch . . . "Illyrian wings," she said. "Ugh, they'll never stop gloating about it."

But she went to the window, which I'd framed in tumbling strands of gold and brass and bronze. Mor fingered her hair, cocking her head. "Nice," she said, surveying the room again.

Her eyes fell on the open threshold to the bedroom hallway, and she grimaced. "Why," she said, "are Amren's eyes there?"

Indeed, right above the door, in the center of the archway, I'd painted a pair of glowing silver eyes. "Because she's always watching."

Mor snorted. "That simply won't do. Paint my eyes next to hers. So the males of this family will know we're *both* watching them the next time they come up here to get drunk for a week straight."

"They do that?"

"They used to." *Before Amarantha.* "Every autumn, the three of them would lock themselves in this house for five days and drink and drink and hunt and hunt, and they'd come back to Velaris looking halfway to death but grinning like fools. It warms my heart to know that from now on, they'll have to do it with me and Amren staring at them."

A smile tugged on my lips. "Who does this paint belong to?"

"Amren," Mor said, rolling her eyes. "We were all here one summer, and she wanted to teach herself to paint. She did it for about two days before she got bored and decided to start hunting poor creatures instead."

A quiet chuckle rasped out of me. I strode to the table, which I'd used as my main surface for blending and organizing paints. And maybe I was a coward, but I kept my back to her as I said, "Any news from my sisters?"

Mor started rifling through the cabinets, either to look for food or assess what I needed. She said over a shoulder, "No. Not yet."

"Is he . . . hurt?" I'd left him in the freezing mud, injured and working the poison out of his system. I'd tried not to dwell on it while I'd painted.

"Still recovering, but fine. Pissed at me, of course, but he can shove it."

I combined Mor's yellow gold with the red I'd used for the Illyrian wings, and blended until vibrant orange emerged. "Thank you—for not telling him I was here."

A shrug. Food began popping onto the counter: fresh bread, fruit, containers of something that I could smell from across the kitchen and made me nearly groan with hunger. "You should talk to him, though. Make him stew over it, of course, but . . . hear him out." She didn't look at me as she spoke. "Rhys always has his reasons, and he might be arrogant as all hell, but he's usually right about his instincts. He makes mistakes, but . . . You should hear him out."

I'd already decided that I would, but I said, "How was your visit to the Court of Nightmares?"

She paused, her face going uncharacteristically pale. "Fine. It's always a delight to see my parents. As you might guess."

"Is your father healing?" I added the cobalt of Azriel's Siphons to the orange and mixed until a rich brown appeared.

A small, grim smile. "Slowly. I might have snapped some more bones when I visited. My mother has since banished me from their private quarters. Such a shame."

Some feral part of me beamed in savage delight at that. "A pity indeed," I said. I added a bit of frost white to lighten the brown, checked it against the gaze she slid to me, and grabbed a stool to stand on as I began painting the threshold. "Rhys really makes you do this often? Endure visiting them?"

Mor leaned against the counter. "Rhys gave me permission the day he became High Lord to kill them all whenever I pleased. I attend these meetings, go to the Court of Nightmares, to . . . remind them of that sometimes. And to keep communication between our two courts flowing, however strained it might be. If I were to march in there tomorrow and slaughter my parents, he wouldn't blink. Perhaps be inconvenienced by it, but . . . he would be pleased."

I focused on the speck of caramel brown I painted beside Amren's eyes. "I'm sorry—for all that you endured."

"Thank you," she said, coming over to watch me. "Visiting them always leaves me raw."

"Cassian seemed concerned." Another prying question.

She shrugged. "Cassian, I think, would also savor the opportunity to shred that entire court to pieces. Starting with my parents. Maybe I'll let him do it one year as a present. Him and Azriel both. It'd make a perfect solstice gift."

I asked perhaps a bit too casually. "You told me about the time with Cassian, but did you and Azriel ever . . . ?"

A sharp laugh. "No. Azriel? After that time with Cassian, I swore off any of Rhys's friends. Azriel's got no shortage of lovers, though, don't worry. He's better at keeping them secret than we are, but . . . he has them."

"So if he were ever interested would you . . . ?"

"The issue, actually, wouldn't be me. It'd be him. I could peel off my clothes right in front of him and he wouldn't move an inch. He might have defied and proved those Illyrian pricks wrong at every turn, but it won't matter if Rhys makes him Prince of Velaris—he'll see himself as a bastard-born nobody, and not good enough for anyone. Especially me."

"But . . . *are* you interested?"

"Why are you asking such things?" Her voice became tight, sharp. More wary than I'd ever heard.

"I'm still trying to figure out how you all work together."

A snort, that wariness gone. I tried not to look too relieved. "We have five centuries of tangled history for you to sort through. Good luck."

Indeed. I finished her eyes—honey brown to Amren's quicksilver. But almost in answer, Mor declared, "Paint Azriel's. Next to mine. And Cassian's next to Amren's."

I lifted my brows.

Mor gave me an innocent smile. "So we can all watch over you."

I just shook my head and hopped off the stool to start figuring out how to paint hazel eyes.

Mor said quietly, "Is it so bad—to be his mate? To be a part of our court, our family, tangled history and all?"

I blended the paint in the small dish, the colors swirling together like so many entwined lives. "No," I breathed. "No, it's not."

And I had my answer.

CHAPTER 53

Mor stayed overnight, even going so far as to paint some rudimentary stick figures on the wall beside the storeroom door. Three females with absurdly long, flowing hair that all resembled hers; and three winged males, who she somehow managed to make look puffed up on their own sense of importance. I laughed every time I saw it.

She left after breakfast, having to walk out to where the no-winnowing shield ended, and I waved to her distant, shivering figure before she vanished into nothing.

I stared across the glittering white expanse, thawed enough that bald patches peppered it—revealing bits of winter-white grass reaching toward the blue sky and mountains. I knew summer had to eventually reach even this melting dreamland, for I'd found fishing poles and sporting equipment that suggested warm-weather usage, but it was hard to imagine snow and ice becoming soft grass and wildflowers.

Brief as a glimmering spindrift, I saw myself there: running through the meadow that slumbered beneath the thin crust of snow, splashing through the little streams already littering the floor, feasting on fat summer berries as the sun set over the mountains . . .

And then I would go home to Velaris, where I would finally walk through the artists' quarter, and enter those shops and galleries and learn what they knew, and maybe—maybe one day—I would open my own shop. Not to sell my work, but to teach others.

Maybe teach the others who were like me: broken in places and trying to fight it—trying to learn who they were around the dark and pain. And I would go home at the end of every day exhausted but content—fulfilled.

Happy.

I'd go home every day to the town house, to my friends, chock full of stories of their own days, and we'd sit around that table and eat together.

And Rhysand . . .

Rhysand . . .

He would be there. He'd give me the money to open my own shop; and because I wouldn't charge anyone, I'd sell my paintings to pay him back. Because I would pay him back, mate or no.

And he'd be here during the summer, flying over the meadow, chasing me across the little streams and up the sloped, grassy mountainside. He would sit with me under the stars, feeding me fat summer berries. And he would be at that table in the town house, roaring with laughter—never again cold and cruel and solemn. Never again anyone's slave or whore.

And at night . . . At night we'd go upstairs together, and he would whisper stories of his adventures, and I'd whisper about my day, and . . .

And there it was.

A future.

The future I saw for myself, bright as the sunrise over the Sidra.

A direction, and a goal, and an invitation to see what else immortality might offer me. It did not seem so listless, so empty, anymore.

And I would fight until my last breath to attain it—to defend it.

So I knew what I had to do.

✠

Five days passed, and I painted every room in the cottage. Mor had winnowed in extra paint before she'd left, along with more food than I could possibly eat.

But after five days, I was sick of my own thoughts for company—sick of waiting, sick of the thawing, dripping snow.

Thankfully, Mor returned that night, banging on the door, thunderous and impatient.

I'd taken a bath an hour before, scrubbing off paint in places I hadn't even known it was possible to smear it, and my hair was still drying as I flung open the door to the blast of cool air.

But Mor wasn't leaning against the threshold.

CHAPTER 54

I stared at Rhys.

He stared at me.

His cheeks were tinged pink with cold, his dark hair ruffled, and he honestly looked *freezing* as he stood there, wings tucked in tight.

And I knew that one word from me, and he'd go flying off into the crisp night. That if I shut the door, he'd go and not push it.

His nostrils flared, scenting the paint behind me, but he didn't break his stare. Waiting.

Mate.

My—mate.

This beautiful, strong, selfless male . . . Who had sacrificed and wrecked himself for his family, his people, and didn't feel it was enough, that *he* wasn't enough for anyone . . . Azriel thought he didn't deserve someone like Mor. And I wondered if Rhys . . . if he somehow felt the same about me. I stepped aside, holding the door open for him.

I could have sworn I felt a pulse of knee-wobbling relief through the bond.

But Rhys took in the painting I'd done, gobbling down the bright colors that now made the cottage come alive, and said, "You painted us."

"I hope you don't mind."

He studied the threshold to the bedroom hallway. "Azriel, Mor, Amren, and Cassian," he said, marking the eyes I'd painted. "You do know that one of them is going to paint a moustache under the eyes of whoever pisses them off that day."

I clamped my lips to keep the smile in. "Oh, Mor already promised to do that."

"And what about my eyes?"

I swallowed. All right, then. No dancing around it.

My heart was pounding so wildly I knew he could hear it. "I was afraid to paint them."

Rhys faced me fully. "Why?"

No more games, no more banter. "At first, because I was so mad at you for not telling me. Then because I was worried I'd like them too much and find that you . . . didn't feel the same. Then because I was scared that if I painted them, I'd start wishing you were here so much that I'd just stare at them all day. And it seemed like a pathetic way to spend my time."

A twitch of his lips. "Indeed."

I glanced at the shut door. "You flew here."

He nodded. "Mor wouldn't tell me where you'd gone, and there are only so many places that are as secure as this one. Since I didn't want our Hybern friends tracking me to you, I had to do it the old-fashioned way. It took . . . a while."

"You're—better?"

"Healed completely. Quickly, considering the bloodbane. Thanks to you."

I avoided his stare, turning for the kitchen. "You must be hungry. I'll heat something up."

Rhys straightened. "You'd—make me food?"

"Heat," I said. "I can't cook."

It didn't seem to make a difference. But whatever it was, the act of offering him food . . . I dumped some cold soup into a pan and lit the burner. "I don't know the rules," I said, my back to him. "So you need to explain them to me."

He lingered in the center of the cabin, watching my every move. He said hoarsely, "It's an . . . important moment when a female offers her mate food. It goes back to whatever beasts we were a long, long time ago. But it still matters. The first time matters. Some mated pairs will make an occasion of it—throwing a party just so the female can formally offer her mate food . . . That's usually done amongst the wealthy. But it means that the female . . . accepts the bond."

I stared into the soup. "Tell me the story—tell me everything."

He understood my offer: tell me while I cooked, and I'd decide at the end whether or not to offer him that food.

A chair scraped against the wood floor as he sat at the table. For a moment, there was only silence, interrupted by the clack of my spoon against the pot.

Then Rhys said, "I was captured during the War. By Amarantha's army."

I paused my stirring, my gut twisting.

"Cassian and Azriel were in different legions, so they had no idea that my forces and I had been taken prisoner. And that Amarantha's captains held us for weeks, torturing and slaughtering my warriors. They put ash bolts through my wings, and they had those same chains from the other night to keep me down. Those chains are one of Hybern's greatest assets—stone delved from deep in their land, capable of nullifying a High Fae's powers. Even mine. So they chained me up between two trees, beating me when they felt like it, trying to get me to tell them where the Night Court forces were, using my warriors—their deaths and pain—to break me.

"Only I didn't break," he said roughly, "and they were too dumb to know that I was an Illyrian, and all they had to do to get me to yield would have been to try to cut off my wings. And maybe it was luck, but they never did. And Amarantha . . . She didn't care that I was there. I was yet another High Lord's son, and Jurian had just slaughtered her sister. All she cared about was getting to him—*killing* him. She had no idea that every second, every breath, I plotted her death. I was willing to make it my last stand: to kill her at any cost, even if it meant shredding my wings to break free. I'd watched the guards and learned her schedule, so I knew where she'd be. I set a day, and a time. And I was ready—I was so damned ready to make an end of it, and wait for Cassian and Azriel and Mor on the other side. There was nothing but my rage, and my relief that my friends weren't there. But the day before I was to kill Amarantha, to make my final stand and meet my end, she and Jurian faced each other on the battlefield."

He paused, swallowing.

"I was chained in the mud, forced to watch as they battled. To watch as Jurian took my killing blow. Only—she slaughtered him. I watched her rip out his eye, then rip off his finger, and when he was prone, I watched her drag him back to the camp. Then I listened to her slowly, over days and days, tear him apart. His screaming was endless. She was so focused on torturing him that she didn't detect my father's arrival. In the panic, she killed Jurian rather than see him liberated, and fled. So my father rescued me—and told his men, told Azriel, to leave the ash spikes in my wings as punishment for getting caught. I was so injured that the healers informed me if I tried to fight before my wings healed, I'd never fly again. So I was forced to return home to recover—while the final battles were waged.

"They made the Treaty, and the wall was built. We'd long ago freed our slaves in the Night Court. We didn't trust the humans to keep our secrets, not when they bred so quickly and frequently that my forefathers couldn't hold all their minds at once. But our world was changed nonetheless. We were all changed by the War. Cassian and Azriel came back different; I came back different. We came here—to this cabin. I was still so injured that they carried me here between them.

We were here when the messages arrived about the final terms of the Treaty.

"They stayed with me when I roared at the stars that Amarantha, for all she had done, for every crime committed, would go unpunished. That the King of Hybern would go unpunished. Too much killing had occurred on either side for everyone to be brought to justice, they said. Even my father gave me an order to let it go—to build toward a future of co-existence. But I never forgave what Amarantha had done to my warriors. And I never forgot it, either. Tamlin's father—he was her friend. And when my father slaughtered him, I was so damn smug that perhaps she'd feel an inkling of what I'd felt when she murdered my soldiers."

My hands were shaking as I stirred the soup. I'd never known . . . never thought . . .

"When Amarantha returned to these shores centuries later, I still wanted to kill her. The worst part was, she didn't even know who I was. Didn't even remember that I was the High Lord's son that she'd held captive. To her, I was merely the son of the man who had killed her friend—I was just the High Lord of the Night Court. The other High Lords were convinced she wanted peace and trade. Only Tamlin mistrusted her. I hated him, but he'd known Amarantha personally—and if he didn't trust her . . . I knew she hadn't changed.

"So I planned to kill her. I told no one. Not even Amren. I'd let Amarantha think I was interested in trade, in alliance. I decided I'd go to the party thrown Under the Mountain for all the courts to celebrate our trade agreement with Hybern . . . And when she was drunk, I'd slip into her mind, make her reveal every lie and crime she'd committed, and then I'd turn her brain to liquid before anyone could react. I was prepared to go to war for it."

I turned, leaning against the counter. Rhys was looking at his hands, as if the story were a book he could read between them.

"But she thought faster—acted faster. She had been trained against my particular skill set, and had extensive mental shields. I was so busy working to tunnel through them that I didn't think about the drink in my hand. I hadn't wanted Cassian or Azriel or anyone else there that night to witness what I was to do—so no one bothered to sniff my drink.

"And as I felt my powers being ripped away by that spell she'd put on it at the toast, I flung them out one last time, wiping Velaris, the wards, all that was good, from the minds of the Court of Nightmares—the only ones I'd allowed to come with me. I threw the shield around Velaris, binding it to my friends so that they had to remain or risk that protection collapsing, and used the last dregs to tell them mind to mind what was happening, and to stay away. Within a few seconds, my power belonged wholly to Amarantha."

His eyes lifted to mine. Haunted, bleak.

"She slaughtered half the Court of Nightmares right then and there. To prove to me that she could. As vengeance for Tamlin's father. And I knew . . . I knew in that moment there was nothing I wouldn't do to keep her from looking at my court again. From looking too long at who I was and what I loved. So I told myself that it was a new war, a different sort of battle. And that night, when she kept turning her attention to me, I knew what she wanted. I knew it wasn't about fucking me so much as it was about getting revenge at my father's ghost. But if that was what she wanted, then that was what she would get. I made her beg, and scream, and used my lingering powers to make it so good for her that she wanted more. Craved more."

I gripped the counter to keep from sliding to the ground.

"Then she cursed Tamlin. And my other great enemy became the one loophole that might free us all. Every night that I spent with Amarantha, I knew that she was half wondering if I'd try to kill her. I couldn't use my powers to harm her, and she had shielded herself against physical attacks. But for fifty years—whenever I was inside her, I'd think about killing her. She had no idea. None. Because I was so good at my job that she thought I enjoyed it, too. So she began to trust me—more than the others. Especially when I proved what I could do to her enemies. But I was glad to do it. I hated myself, but I was glad to do it. After a decade, I stopped expecting to see my friends or my people again. I forgot what their faces looked like. And I stopped hoping."

Silver gleamed in his eyes, and he blinked it away. "Three years ago," he said quietly, "I began to have these . . . dreams. At first, they were glimpses, as if I were staring through someone else's eyes. A crackling hearth in a dark home. A bale of hay in a barn. A warren of rabbits. The images were foggy, like looking through cloudy glass. They were brief—a flash here and there, every few months. I thought nothing of them, until one of the images was of a hand . . . This beautiful, human hand. Holding a brush. Painting—flowers on a table."

My heart stopped beating.

"And that time, I pushed a thought back. Of the night sky—of the image that brought me joy when I needed it most. Open night sky, stars, and the moon. I didn't know if it was received, but I tried, anyway."

I wasn't sure I was breathing.

"Those dreams—the flashes of that person, that woman . . . I treasured them. They were a reminder that there was some peace out there in the world, some light. That there was a place, and a person, who had enough safety to paint flowers on a table. They went on for years, until . . . a year ago. I was sleeping next to Amarantha, and I jolted awake from this dream . . . this dream that was clearer and brighter, like that fog had been wiped away. She—you were dreaming. I was in your dream, watching as you had a nightmare about some woman slitting your throat, while you were chased by the Bogge . . . I couldn't reach you, speak to you. But you were seeing our kind. And I realized that the fog had probably been the wall, and that you . . . you were now in Prythian.

"I saw you through your dreams—and I hoarded the images, sorting through them over and over again, trying to place where you were, who you were. But you had such horrible nightmares, and the creatures belonged to all courts. I'd wake up with your scent in my nose, and it would haunt me all day, every step. But then one night, you dreamed of standing amongst green hills, seeing unlit bonfires for Calanmai."

There was such silence in my head.

"I knew there was only one celebration that large; I knew those hills—and I knew you'd probably be there. So I told Amarantha . . . " Rhys swallowed. "I told her that I wanted to go to the Spring Court for the celebration, to spy on Tamlin and see if anyone showed up wishing to conspire with him. We were so close to the deadline for the curse that she was paranoid—restless. She told me to bring back traitors. I promised her I would."

His eyes lifted to mine again.

"I got there, and I could smell you. So I tracked that scent, and . . . And there you were. Human—utterly human, and being dragged away by those piece-of-shit picts, who wanted to . . . " He shook his head. "I debated slaughtering them then and there, but then they shoved you, and I just . . . moved. I started speaking without knowing what I was saying, only that you were there, and I was touching you, and . . . " He loosed a shuddering breath.

There you are. I've been looking for you.

His first words to me—not a lie at all, not a threat to keep those faeries away.

Thank you for finding her for me.

I had the vague feeling of the world slipping out from under my feet like sand washing away from the shore.

"You looked at me," Rhys said, "and I knew you had no idea who I was. That I might have seen your dreams, but you hadn't seen mine. And you were just . . . human. You were so young, and breakable, and had no interest in me whatsoever, and I knew that if I stayed too long, someone would see and report back, and she'd find you. So I started walking away, thinking you'd be glad to get rid of me. But then you called after me, like you couldn't let go of me just yet, whether you knew it or not. And I knew . . . I knew we were on dangerous ground, somehow. I knew that I could never speak to you, or see you, or think of you again.

"I didn't want to know why you were in Prythian; I didn't even want to know your name. Because seeing you in my dreams had been one thing, but in person . . . Right then, deep down, I think I knew what you were. And I didn't let myself admit it, because if there was the slightest chance that you were my mate . . . They would have done such unspeakable things to you, Feyre.

"So I let you walk away. I told myself after you were gone that maybe . . . maybe the Cauldron had been kind, and not cruel, for letting me see you. Just once. A gift for what I was enduring. And when you were gone, I found those three picts. I broke into their minds, reshaping their lives, their histories, and dragged them before Amarantha. I made them confess to conspiring to find other rebels that night. I made them lie and claim that they hated her. I watched her carve them up while they were still alive, protesting their innocence. I enjoyed it—because I knew what they had wanted to do to you. And knew that it would have paled in comparison to what Amarantha would have done if she'd found you."

I wrapped a hand around my throat. *I had my reasons to be out then*, he'd once said to me Under the Mountain. *Do not think, Feyre, that it did not cost me*.

Rhys kept staring at the table as he said, "I didn't know. That you were with Tamlin. That you were staying at the Spring Court. Amarantha sent me that day after the Summer Solstice because I'd been so successful on Calanmai. I was prepared to mock him, maybe pick a fight. But then I got into that room, and the scent was familiar, but hidden . . . And then I saw the plate, and felt the glamour, and . . . There you were. Living in my second-most enemy's house. Dining with him. Reeking of his scent. Looking at him like . . . Like you loved him."

The whites of his knuckles showed.

"And I decided that I had to scare Tamlin. I had to scare you, and Lucien, but mostly Tamlin. Because I saw how he looked at you, too. So what I did that day . . . " His lips were pale, tight. "I broke into your mind and held it enough that you felt it, that it terrified you, hurt you. I made Tamlin beg—as Amarantha had made me beg, to show him how powerless he was to save you. And I prayed my performance was enough to get him to send you away. Back to the human realm, away from Amarantha. Because she was going to find you. If you broke that curse, she was going to find you and kill you.

"But I was so selfish—I was so stupidly selfish that I couldn't walk away without knowing your name. And you were looking at me like I was a monster, so I told myself it didn't matter, anyway. But you lied when I asked. I knew you did. I had your mind in my hands, and you had the defiance and foresight to lie to my face. So I walked away from you again. I vomited my guts up as soon as I left."

My lips wobbled, and I pressed them together.

"I checked back once. To ensure you were gone. I went with them the day they sacked the manor—to make my performance complete. I told Amarantha the name of that girl, thinking you'd invented it. I had no idea . . . I had no idea she'd send her cronies to retrieve Clare. But if I admitted my lie . . . " He swallowed hard. "I broke into Clare's head when they brought her Under the Mountain. I took away her pain, and told her to scream when expected to. So they . . . they did those things to her, and I tried to make it right, but . . . After a week, I couldn't let them do it. Hurt her like that anymore. So while they tortured her, I slipped into her mind again and ended it. She didn't feel any pain. She felt none of what they did to her, even at the end. But . . . But I still see her. And my men. And the others that I killed for Amarantha."

Two tears slid down his cheeks, swift and cold.

He didn't wipe them away as he said, "I thought it was done after that. With Clare's death, Amarantha believed you were dead. So you were safe, and far away, and my people were safe, and Tamlin had lost, so . . . it was done. We were done. But then . . . I was in the back of the throne room that day the Attor brought you in. And I have never known such horror, Feyre, as I did when I watched you make that bargain. Irrational, stupid terror—I didn't know you. I didn't even know your name. But I thought of those painter's hands, the flowers I'd seen you create. And how she'd delight in breaking your fingers apart. I had to stand and watch as the Attor and its cronies beat you. I had to watch the disgust and hatred on your face as you looked at me, watched me threaten to shatter Lucien's mind. And then—then I learned your name. Hearing you say it . . . it was like an answer to a question I'd been asking for five hundred years.

"I decided, then and there, that I was going to fight. And I would fight dirty, and kill and torture and manipulate, but I was going to fight. If there was a shot of freeing us from Amarantha, you were it. I thought . . . I thought the Cauldron had been sending me these dreams to tell me that you would be the one to save us. Save my people.

"So I watched your first trial. Pretending—always pretending to be that person you hated. When you were hurt so badly against the Wyrm . . . I found my way in with you. A way to defy Amarantha, to spread the seeds of hope to those who knew how to read the message, and a way to keep you alive without seeming too suspicious. And a way to get back at Tamlin . . . To use him against Amarantha, yes, but . . . To get back at him for my mother and sister, and for . . . having you. When we made that bargain, you were so hateful that I knew I'd done my job well.

"So we endured it. I made you dress like that so Amarantha wouldn't suspect, and made you drink the wine so you would not remember the nightly horrors in that mountain. And that last night, when I found you two in the hall . . . I was jealous. I was jealous of him, and pissed off that he'd used that one shot of being unnoticed not to get you out, but to be with you, and . . . Amarantha saw that jealousy. She saw me kissing you to hide the evidence, but she saw why. For the first time, she saw why. So that night, after I left you, I had to . . . service her. She kept me there longer than usual, trying to squeeze the answers out of me. But I gave her what she wanted to hear: that you were nothing, that you were human garbage, that I'd use and discard you. Afterward . . . I wanted to see you. One last time. Alone. I thought about telling you everything—but who I'd become, who you thought I was . . . I didn't dare shatter that deception.

"But your final trial came, and . . . When she started torturing you, something snapped in a way I couldn't explain, only that seeing you bleeding and screaming undid me. It broke me at last. And I knew as I picked up that knife to kill her . . . I knew right then what you were. I knew that you were my mate, and you were in love with another male, and had destroyed yourself to save him, and that . . . that I didn't care. If you were going to die, I was going to die with you. I couldn't stop thinking it over and over as you screamed, as I tried to kill her: you were my mate, my mate, my mate.

"But then she snapped your neck."

Tears rolled down his face.

"And I felt you die," he whispered.

Tears were sliding down my own cheeks.

"And this beautiful, wonderful thing that had come into my life, this gift from the Cauldron . . . It was gone. In my desperation, I clung to that bond. Not the bargain—the bargain was nothing, the bargain was like a cobweb. But I grabbed that bond between us and I *tugged*, I willed you to hold on, to stay with me, because if we could get free . . . If we could get free, then all seven of us were there. We could bring you back. And I didn't care if I had to slice into all of their minds to do it. I'd *make* them save you." His hands were shaking. "You'd freed us with your last breath, and my power—I wrapped my power around the bond. The mating bond. I could feel you flickering there, holding on."

Home. Home had been at the end of the bond, I'd told the Bone Carver. Not Tamlin, not the Spring Court, but . . . Rhysand.

"So Amarantha died, and I spoke to the High Lords mind to mind, convincing them to come forward, to offer that spark of power. None of them disagreed. I think they were too stunned to think of saying no.

And . . . I again had to watch as Tamlin held you. Kissed you. I wanted to go home, to Velaris, but I had to stay, to make sure things were set in motion, that you were all right. So I waited as long as I could, then I sent a tug through the bond. Then you came to find me.

"I almost told you then, but . . . You were so sad. And tired. And for once, you looked at me like . . . like I was worth something. So I promised myself that the next time I saw you, I'd free you of the bargain. Because I was selfish, and knew that if I let go right then, he'd lock you up and I'd never get to see you again. When I went to leave you . . . I think transforming you into Fae made the bond lock into place permanently. I'd known it existed, but it *hit* me then—hit me so strong that I panicked. I knew if I stayed a second longer, I'd damn the consequences and take you with me. And you'd hate me forever.

"I landed at the Night Court, right as Mor was waiting for me, and I was so frantic, so . . . unhinged, that I told her everything. I hadn't seen her in fifty years, and my first words to her were, 'She's my mate.' And for three months . . . for three months I tried to convince myself that you were better off without me. I tried to convince myself that everything I'd done had made you hate me. But I felt you through the bond, through your open mental shields. I felt your pain, and sadness, and loneliness. I felt you struggling to escape the darkness of Amarantha the same way I was. I heard you were going to marry him, and I told myself you were happy. I should let you be happy, even if it killed me. Even if you were my mate, you'd earned that happiness.

"The day of your wedding, I'd planned to get rip-roaring drunk with Cassian, who had no idea why, but . . . But then I felt you again. I felt your panic, and despair, and heard you beg someone—anyone—to save you. I lost it. I winnowed to the wedding, and barely remembered who I was supposed to be, the part I was supposed to play. All I could see was you, in your stupid wedding dress—so thin. So, so thin, and pale. And I wanted to kill him for it, but I had to get you out. Had to call in that bargain, just once, to get you away, to see if you were all right."

Rhys looked up at me, eyes desolate. "It killed me, Feyre, to send you back. To see you waste away, month by month. It killed me to know he was sharing your bed. Not just because you were my mate, but because I . . . " He glanced down, then up at me again. "I knew . . . I knew I was in love with you that moment I picked up the knife to kill Amarantha.

"When you finally came here . . . I decided I wouldn't tell you. Any of it. I wouldn't let you out of the bargain, because your hatred was better than facing the two alternatives: that you felt nothing for me, or that you . . . you might feel something similar, and if I let myself love you, you would be taken from me. The way my family was—the way my friends were. So I didn't tell you. I watched as you faded away. Until that day . . . that day he locked you up.

"I would have killed him if he'd been there. But I broke some very, very fundamental rules in taking you away. Amren said if I got you to admit that we were mates, it would keep any trouble from our door, but . . . I couldn't force the bond on you. I couldn't try to seduce you into accepting the bond, either. Even if it gave Tamlin license to wage war on me. You had been through so much already. I didn't want you to think that everything I did was to win you, just to keep my lands safe. But I couldn't . . . I couldn't stop being around you, and loving you, and wanting you. I still can't stay away."

He leaned back, loosing a long breath.

Slowly, I turned around, to where the soup was now boiling, and ladled it into a bowl.

He watched every step I took to the table, the steaming bowl in my hands.

I stopped before him, staring down.

And I said, "You love me?"

Rhys nodded.

And I wondered if love was too weak a word for what he felt, what he'd done for me. For what I felt for him.

I set the bowl down before him. "Then eat."

CHAPTER 55

I watched him consume every spoonful, his eyes darting between where I stood and the soup.

When he was done, he set down his spoon.

"Aren't you going to say anything?" he said at last.

"I was going to tell you what I'd decided the moment I saw you on the threshold."

Rhys twisted in his seat toward me. "And now?"

Aware of every breath, every movement, I sat in his lap. His hands gently braced my hips as I studied his face. "And now I want you to know, Rhysand, that I love you. I want you to know . . . " His lips trembled, and I brushed away the tear that escaped down his cheek. "I want you to know," I whispered, "that I am broken and healing, but every piece of my heart belongs to you. And I am honored—*honored* to be your mate."

His arms wrapped around me and he pressed his forehead to my shoulder, his body shaking. I stroked a hand through his silken hair.

"I love you," I said again. I hadn't dared say the words in my head. "And I'd endure every second of it over again so I could find you. And if war comes, we'll face it. Together. I won't let them take me from you. And I won't let them take you from me, either."

Rhys looked up, his face gleaming with tears. He went still as I leaned in, kissing away one tear. Then the other. As he had once kissed away mine.

When my lips were wet and salty with them, I pulled back far enough to see his eyes. "You're mine," I breathed.

His body shuddered with what might have been a sob, but his lips found my own.

It was gentle—soft. The kiss he might have given me if we'd been granted time and peace to meet across our two separate worlds. To court each other. I slid my arms around his shoulders, opening my mouth to him, and his tongue slipped in, caressing my own. Mate—my mate.

He hardened against me, and I groaned into his mouth.

The sound snapped whatever leash he'd had on himself, and Rhysand scooped me up in a smooth movement before laying me flat on the table—amongst and on top of all the paints.

He deepened the kiss, and I wrapped my legs around his back, hooking him closer. He tore his lips from my mouth to my neck, where he dragged his teeth and tongue down my skin as his hands slid under my sweater and went up, up, to cup my breasts. I arched into the touch, and lifted my arms as he peeled away my sweater in one easy motion.

Rhys pulled back to survey me, my body naked from the waist up. Paint soaked into my hair, my arms. But all I could think of was his mouth as it lowered to my breast and sucked, his tongue flicking against my nipple.

I plunged my fingers into his hair, and he braced a hand beside my head—smack atop a palette of paint. He let out a low laugh, and I watched, breathless, as he took that hand and traced a circle around my breast, then lower, until he painted a downward arrow beneath my belly button.

"Lest you forget where this is going to end," he said.

I snarled at him, a silent order, and he laughed again, his mouth finding my other breast. He ground his hips against me, teasing—teasing me so horribly that I had to touch him, had to just feel *more* of him. There was paint all over my hands, my arms, but I didn't care as I grabbed at his clothes. He shifted enough to let me remove them, weapons and leather thudding to the ground, revealing that beautiful tattooed body, the powerful muscles and wings now peeking above them.

My mate—my mate.

His mouth crashed into mine, his bare skin so warm against my own, and I gripped his face, smearing paint there, too. Smearing it in his hair, until great streaks of blue and red and green ran through it. His hands found my waist, and I bucked my hips off the table to help him remove my socks, my leggings.

Rhys pulled back again, and I let out a bark of protest—that choked off into a gasp as he gripped my thighs and yanked me to the edge of the table, through paints and brushes and cups of water, hooked my legs over his shoulders to rest on either side of those beautiful wings, and knelt before me.

Knelt on those stars and mountains inked on his knees. He would bow for no one and nothing—

But his mate. His equal.

The first lick of Rhysand's tongue set me on fire.

I want you splayed out on the table like my own personal feast.

He growled his approval at my moan, my taste, and unleashed himself on me entirely.

A hand pinning my hips to the table, he worked me in great sweeping strokes. And when his tongue slid inside me, I reached up to grip the edge of the table, to grip the edge of the world that I was very near to falling off.

He licked and kissed his way to the apex of my thighs, just as his fingers replaced where his mouth had been, pumping inside me as he sucked, his teeth scraping ever so slightly—

I bowed off the table as my climax shattered through me, splintering my consciousness into a million pieces. He kept licking me, fingers still moving. "Rhys," I rasped.

Now. I wanted him now.

But he remained kneeling, feasting on me, that hand pinning me to the table.

I went over the edge again. And only when I was trembling, half sobbing, limp with pleasure, did Rhys rise from the floor.

He looked me over, naked, covered in paint, his own face and body smeared with it, and give me a slow, satisfied male smile. "You're *mine*," he snarled, and hefted me up into his arms.

I wanted the wall—I wanted him to just take me against the wall, but he carried me into the room I'd been using and set me down on the bed with heartbreaking gentleness.

Wholly naked, I watched as he unbuttoned his pants, and the considerable length of him sprang free. My mouth went dry at the sight of it. I wanted him, wanted every glorious inch of him in me, wanted to claw at him until our souls were forged together.

He didn't say anything as he came over me, wings tucked in tight. He'd never gone to bed with a female while his wings were out. But I was his mate. He would yield only for me.

And I wanted to touch him.

I leaned up, reaching over his shoulder to caress the powerful curve of his wing.

Rhys shuddered, and I watched his cock twitch.

"Play later," he ground out.

Indeed.

His mouth found mine, the kiss open and deep, a clash of tongues and teeth. He lay me down on the pillows, and I locked my legs around his back, careful of the wings.

Though I stopped caring as he nudged at my entrance. And paused.

"*Play later*," I snarled into his mouth.

Rhys laughed in a way that skittered along my bones, and slid in. And in. And in.

I could hardly breathe, hardly think beyond where our bodies were joined. He stilled inside me, letting me adjust, and I opened my eyes to find him staring down at me. "Say it again," he murmured.

I knew what he meant.

"You're mine," I breathed.

Rhys pulled out slightly and thrust back in slow. So torturously slow.

"You're mine," I gasped out.

Again, he pulled out, then thrust in.

"You're mine."

Again—faster, deeper this time.

I felt it then, the bond between us, like an unbreakable chain, like an undimmable ray of light.

With each pounding stroke, the bond glowed clearer and brighter and stronger. "You're mine," I whispered, dragging my hands through his hair, down his back, across his wings.

My friend through many dangers.

My lover who had healed my broken and weary soul.

My mate who had waited for me against all hope, despite all odds.

I moved my hips in time with his. He kissed me over and over, and both of our faces turned damp. Every inch of me burned and tightened, and my control slipped entirely as he whispered, "I love you."

Release tore through my body, and he pounded into me, hard and fast, drawing out my pleasure until I felt and saw and smelled that bond between us, until our scents *merged*, and I was his and he was mine, and we were the beginning and middle and end. We were a song that had been sung from the very first ember of light in the world.

Rhys roared as he came, slamming in to the hilt. Outside, the mountains trembled, the remaining snow rushing from them in a cascade of glittering white, only to be swallowed up by the waiting night below.

Silence fell, interrupted only by our panting breaths.

I took his paint-smeared face between my own colorful hands and made him look at me.

His eyes were radiant like the stars I'd painted once, long ago.

And I smiled at Rhys as I let that mating bond shine clear and luminous between us.

I don't know how long we lay there, lazily touching each other, as if we might indeed have all the time in the world.

"I think I fell in love with you," Rhys murmured, stroking a finger down my arm, "the moment I realized you were cleaving those bones to make a trap for the Middengard Wyrm. Or maybe the moment you flipped me off for mocking you. It reminded me so much of Cassian. For the first time in decades, I wanted to *laugh.*"

"You fell in love with me," I said flatly, "because I reminded you of your friend?"

He flicked my nose. "I fell in love with you, smartass, because you were one of us—because you weren't afraid of me, and you decided to end your spectacular victory by throwing that piece of bone at Amarantha like a javelin. I felt Cassian's spirit beside me in that moment, and could have sworn I heard him say, '*If you don't marry her, you stupid prick, I will.*' "

I huffed a laugh, sliding my paint-covered hand over his tattooed chest. Paint—right.

We were both covered in it. So was the bed.

Rhys followed my eyes and gave me a grin that was positively wicked. "How convenient that the bathtub is large enough for two."

My blood heated, and I rose from the bed only to have him move faster—scooping me up in his arms. He was splattered with paint, his hair crusted with it, and his poor, beautiful wings . . . Those were my handprints on them. Naked, he carried me into the bath, where the water was already running, the magic of this cabin acting on our behalf.

He strode down the steps into the water, his hiss of pleasure a brush of air against my ear. And I might have moaned a little myself when the hot water hit me as he sat us both down in the tub.

A basket of soaps and oils appeared along the stone rim, and I pushed off him to sink further beneath the surface. The steam wafted between us, and Rhys picked up a bar of that pine tar–smelling soap and handed it to me, then passed a washrag. "Someone, it seems, got my wings dirty."

My face heated, but my gut tightened. Illyrian males and their wings—so sensitive.

I twirled my finger to motion him to turn around. He obeyed, spreading those magnificent wings enough for me to find the paint stains. Carefully, so carefully, I soaped up the washcloth and began wiping the red and blue and purple away.

The candlelight danced over his countless, faint scars—nearly invisible save for harder bits of membrane. He shuddered with each pass, hands braced on the lip of the tub. I peeked over his shoulder to see the evidence of that sensitivity, and said, "At least the rumors about wingspan correlating with the size of other parts were right."

His back muscles tensed as he choked out a laugh. "Such a dirty, wicked mouth."

I thought of all the places I wanted to put that mouth and blushed a bit.

"I think I was falling in love with you for a while," I said, the words barely audible over the trickle of water as I washed his beautiful wings. "But I knew on Starfall. Or came close to knowing and was so scared of it that I didn't want to look closer. I was a coward."

"You had perfectly good reasons to avoid it."

"No, I didn't. Maybe—thanks to Tamlin, yes. But it had nothing to do with you, Rhys. *Nothing* to do with you. I was never afraid of the consequences of being with you. Even if every assassin in the world hunts us . . . It's worth it. *You* are worth it."

His head dipped a bit. And he said hoarsely, "Thank you."

My heart broke for him then—for the years he'd spent thinking the opposite. I kissed his bare neck, and he reached back to drag a finger down my cheek.

I finished the wings and gripped his shoulder to turn him to face me. "What now?" Wordlessly, he took the soap from my hands and turned me, rubbing down my back, scrubbing lightly with the cloth.

"It's up to you," Rhys said. "We can go back to Velaris and have the bond verified by a priestess—no one like Ianthe, I promise—and be declared officially Mated. We could have a small party to celebrate—dinner with our . . . cohorts. Unless you'd rather have a large party, though I think you and I are in agreement about our aversion for them." His strong hands kneaded muscles that were tight and aching in my back, and I groaned. "We could also go before a priestess and be declared husband and wife as well as mates, if you want a more human thing to call me."

"What will *you* call me?"

"Mate," he said. "Though also calling you my wife sounds mighty appealing, too." His thumbs massaged the column of my spine. "Or if you want to wait, we can do none of those things. We're mated, whether it's shouted across the world or not. There's no rush to decide."

I turned. "I was asking about Jurian, the king, the queens, and the Cauldron, but I'm glad to know I have so many options where our relationship stands. And that you'll do whatever I want. I must have you wrapped completely around my finger."

His eyes danced with feline amusement. "Cruel, beautiful thing."

I snorted. The idea that he found me beautiful at all—

"You are," he said. "You're the most beautiful thing I've ever seen. I thought that from the first moment I saw you on Calanmai."

And it was stupid, stupid for beauty to mean anything at all, but . . . My eyes burned.

"Which is good," he added, "because you thought *I* was the most beautiful male you'd ever seen. So it makes us even."

I scowled, and he laughed, hands sliding to grip my waist and tug me to him. He sat down on the built-in bench of the tub, and I straddled him, idly stroking his muscled arms.

"Tomorrow," Rhys said, features becoming grave. "We're leaving tomorrow for your family's estate. The queens sent word. They return in three days."

I started. "You're telling me this *now*?"

"I got sidetracked," he said, his eyes twinkling.

And the light in those eyes, the quiet joy . . . They knocked the breath from me. A future—we would have a future together. *I* would have a future. A *life*.

His smile faded into something awed, something . . . reverent, and I reached out to cup his face in my hands—

To find my skin glowing.

Faintly, as if some inner light shone beneath my skin, leaking out into the world. Warm and white light, like the sun—like a star. Those wonder-filled eyes met mine, and Rhys ran a finger down my arm. "Well, at least now I can gloat that I literally make my mate glow with happiness."

I laughed, and the glow flared a little brighter. He leaned in, kissing me softly, and I melted for him, wrapping my arms around his neck. He was rock-hard against me, pushing against where I sat poised right above him. All it would take would be one smooth motion and he'd be inside me—

But Rhys stood from the water, both of us dripping wet, and I hooked my legs around him as he walked us back into the bedroom. The sheets had been changed by the domestic magic of the house, and they were warm and smooth against my naked body as he set me down and stared at me. Shining—I was shining bright and pure as a star. "Day Court?" I asked.

"I don't care," he said roughly, and removed the glamour from himself.

It was a small magic, he'd once told me, to keep the damper on who he was, what his power looked like.

As the full majesty of him was unleashed, he filled the room, the world, my soul, with glittering ebony power. Stars and wind and shadows; peace and dreams and the honed edge of nightmares. Darkness rippled from him like tendrils of steam as he reached out a hand and laid it flat against the glowing skin of my stomach.

That hand of night splayed, the light leaking through the wafting shadows, and I hoisted myself up on my elbows to kiss him.

Smoke and mist and dew.

I moaned at the taste of him, and he opened his mouth for me, letting me brush my tongue against his, scrape it against his teeth. Everything he was had been laid before me—one final question.

I wanted it all.

I gripped his shoulders, guiding him onto the bed. And when he lay flat on his back, I saw the flash of protest at the pinned wings. But I crooned, "Illyrian baby," and ran my hands down his muscled abdomen—farther. He stopped objecting.

He was enormous in my hand—so hard, yet so silken that I just ran a finger down him in wonder. He hissed, cock twitching as I brushed my thumb over the tip. I smirked as I did it again.

He reached for me, but I froze him with a look. "My turn," I told him.

Rhys gave me a lazy, male smile before he settled back, tucking a hand behind his head. Waiting.

Cocky bastard.

So I leaned down and put my mouth on him.

He jerked at the contact with a barked, "*Shit*," and I laughed around him, even as I took him deeper into my mouth.

His hands were now fisted in the sheets, white-knuckled as I slid my tongue over him, grazing slightly with my teeth. His groan was fire to my blood.

Honestly, I was surprised he waited the full minute before interrupting me.

Pouncing was a better word for what Rhys did.

One second, he was in my mouth, my tongue flicking over the broad head of him; the next, his hands were on my waist and I was being flipped onto my front. He nudged my legs apart with his knees, spreading me as he gripped my hips, tugging them up, up before he sheathed himself deep in me with a single stroke.

I moaned into the pillow at every glorious inch of him, rising onto my forearms as my fingers grappled into the sheets.

Rhys pulled out and plunged back in, eternity exploding around me in that instant, and I thought I might break apart from not being able to get enough of him.

"Look at you," he murmured as he moved in me, and kissed the length of my spine.

I managed to rise up enough to see where we were joined—to see the sunlight shimmer off me against the rippling night of him, merging and blending, enriching. And the sight of it wrecked me so thoroughly that I climaxed with his name on my lips.

Rhys hauled me up against him, one hand cupping my breast as the other rolled and stroked that bundle of nerves between my legs, and I couldn't tell where one climax ended and the second began as he thrust in again, and again, his lips on my neck, on my ear.

I could die from this, I decided. From wanting him, from the pleasure of being with him.

He twisted us, pulling out only long enough to lie on his back and haul me over him.

There was a glimmer in the darkness—a flash of lingering pain, a scar. And I understood why he wanted me like this, wanted to end it like this, with me astride him.

It broke my heart. I leaned forward to kiss him, softly, tenderly.

As our mouths met, I slid onto him, the fit so much deeper, and he murmured my name into my mouth. I kissed him again and again, and rode him gently. Later—there would be other times to go hard and fast. But right now . . . I wouldn't think of why this position was one he wanted to end in, to have me banish the stained dark with the light.

But I would glow—for him, I'd glow. For my own future, I'd glow.

So I sat up, hands braced on his broad chest, and unleashed that light in me, letting it drive out the darkness of what had been done to him, my mate, my friend.

Rhys barked my name, thrusting his hips up. Stars wheeled as he slammed deep.

I think the light pouring out of me might have been starlight, or maybe my own vision fractured as release barreled into me again and Rhys found his, gasping my name over and over as he spilled himself in me.

When we were done, I remained atop him, fingertips digging into his chest, and marveled at him. At us.

He tugged on my wet hair. "We'll have to find a way to put a damper on that light."

"I can keep the shadows hidden easily enough."

"Ah, but you only lose control of those when you're pissed. And since I have every intention of making you as happy as a person can be . . . I have a feeling we'll need to learn to control that wondrous glow."

"Always thinking; always calculating."

Rhys kissed the corner of my mouth. "You have no idea how many things I've thought up when it comes to you."

"I remember mention of a wall."

His laugh was a sensual promise. "Next time, Feyre, I'll fuck you against the wall."

"Hard enough to make the pictures fall off."

Rhys barked a laugh. "Show me again what you can do with that wicked mouth."

I obliged him.

It was wrong to compare, because I knew probably every High Lord could keep a woman from sleeping all night, but Rhysand was . . . ravenous. I got perhaps an hour total of sleep that night, though I supposed I was to equally share the blame.

I couldn't stop, couldn't get enough of the taste of him in my mouth, the feel of him inside of me. More, more, more—until I thought I might burst out of my skin from pleasure.

"It's normal," Rhys said around a mouthful of bread as we sat at the table for breakfast. We'd barely made it into the kitchen. He'd taken one step out of bed, giving me a full view of his glorious wings, muscled back, and that beautiful backside, and I'd leaped on him. We'd tumbled to the floor and he'd shredded the pretty little area rug beneath his talons as I rode him.

"What's normal?" I said. I could barely look at him without wanting to combust.

"The . . . frenzy," he said carefully, as if fearful the wrong word might send us both hurtling for each other before we could get sustenance into our bodies. "When a couple accepts the mating bond, it's . . . overwhelming. Again, harkening back to the beasts we once were. Probably something about ensuring the female was impregnated." My heart paused at that. "Some couples don't leave the house for a week. Males get so volatile that it can be dangerous for them to be in public, anyway. I've seen males of reason and education shatter a room because another male looked too long in their mate's direction, too soon after they'd been mated."

I hissed out a breath. Another shattered room flashed in my memory.

Rhys said softly, knowing what haunted me, "I'd like to believe I have more restraint than the average male, but . . . Be patient with me, Feyre, if I'm a little on edge."

That he'd admit that much . . . "You don't want to leave this house."

"I want to stay in that bedroom and fuck you until we're both hoarse."

That fast, I was ready for him, aching for him, but—but we had to go. Queens. Cauldron. Jurian. War. "About—pregnancy," I said.

And might as well have thrown a bucket of ice over both of us.

"We didn't—I'm not taking a tonic. I haven't been, I mean."

He set down his bread. "Do you want to start taking it again?"

If I did, if I started today, it'd negate what we'd done last night, but . . . "If I am a High Lord's mate, I'm expected to bear you offspring, aren't I? So perhaps I shouldn't."

"You are not expected to bear me *anything*," he snarled. "Children are rare, yes. So rare, and so precious. But I don't want you to have them unless you want to—unless we *both* want to. And right now, with this war coming, with Hybern . . . I'll admit that I'm terrified at the thought of my mate being pregnant with so many enemies around us. I'm terrified of what *I* might do if you're pregnant and threatened. Or harmed."

Something tight in my chest eased, even as a chill went down my back as I considered that power, that rage I'd seen at the Night Court, unleashed upon the earth. "Then I'll start taking it today, once we get back."

I rose from the table on shaky knees and headed for the bedroom. I had to bathe—I was covered in him, my mouth tasted of him, despite breakfast. Rhys said softly from behind me, "I would be happy beyond reason, though, if you one day did honor me with children. To share that with you."

I turned back to him. "I want to live first," I said. "With you. I want to see things and have adventures. I want to learn what it is to be immortal, to be your mate, to be part of your family. I want to be . . . ready for them. And I selfishly want to have you all to myself for a while."

His smile was gentle, sweet. "You take all the time you need. And if I get you all to myself for the rest of eternity, then I won't mind that at all."

I made it to the edge of the bath before Rhys caught me, carried me into the water, and made love to me, slow and deep, amid the billowing steam.

CHAPTER 56

Rhys winnowed us to the Illyrian camp. We wouldn't be staying long enough to be at risk—and with ten thousand Illyrian warriors surrounding us on the various peaks, Rhys doubted anyone would be stupid enough to attack.

We'd just appeared in the mud outside the little house when Cassian drawled from behind us, "Well, it's about time."

The savage, wild snarl that ripped out of Rhys was like nothing I'd heard, and I gripped his arm as he whirled on Cassian.

Cassian looked at him and laughed.

But the Illyrian warriors in the camp began shooting into the sky, hauling women and children with them.

"Hard ride?" Cassian tied back his dark hair with a worn strap of leather.

Preternatural quiet now leaked from Rhys where the snarl had erupted a moment before. And rather than see him turn the camp to rubble I said, "When he bashes your teeth in, Cassian, don't come crying to me."

Cassian crossed his arms. "Mating bond chafing a bit, Rhys?"

Rhys said nothing.

Cassian snickered. "Feyre doesn't look too tired. Maybe she could give me a ride—"

Rhys exploded.

Wings and muscles and snapping teeth, and they were rolling through the mud, fists flying, and—

And Cassian had known exactly what he was saying and doing, I realized as he kicked Rhys off him, as Rhys didn't touch that power that could have flattened these mountains.

He'd seen the edge in Rhys's eyes and known he had to dull it before we could go any further.

Rhys had known, too. Which was why we'd winnowed here first—and not Velaris.

They were a sight to behold, two Illyrian males fighting in the mud and stones, panting and spitting blood. None of the other Illyrians dared land.

Nor would they, I realized, until Rhys had worked off his temper—or left the camp entirely. If the average male needed a week to adjust . . . What was required of Rhysand? A month? Two? A year?

Cassian laughed as Rhys slammed a fist into his face, blood spraying. Cassian slung one right back at him, and I cringed as Rhys's head knocked to the side. I'd seen Rhys fight before, controlled and elegant, and I'd seen him mad, but never so . . . feral.

"They'll be at it for a while," Mor said, leaning against the threshold of the house. She held open the door. "Welcome to the family, Feyre."

And I thought those might have been the most beautiful words I'd ever heard.

Rhys and Cassian spent an hour pummeling each other into exhaustion, and when they trudged back into the house, bloody and filthy, one look at my mate was all it took for me to crave the smell and feel of him.

Cassian and Mor instantly found somewhere else to be, and Rhys didn't bother taking my clothes all the way off before he bent me over the kitchen table and made me moan his name loud enough for the Illyrians still circling high above to hear.

But when we finished, the tightness in his shoulders and the tension coiled in his eyes had vanished . . . And a knock on the door from Cassian had Rhys handing me a damp washcloth to clean myself. A moment later, the four of us had winnowed to the music and light of Velaris.

To home.

✣

The sun had barely set as Rhys and I walked hand in hand into the dining room of the House of Wind, and found Mor, Azriel, Amren, and Cassian already seated. Waiting for us.

As one, they stood.

As one, they looked at me.

And as one, they bowed.

It was Amren who said, "We will serve and protect."

They each placed a hand over their heart.

Waiting—for my reply.

Rhys hadn't warned me, and I wondered if the words were supposed to come from my heart, spoken without agenda or guile. So I voiced them.

"Thank you," I said, willing my voice to be steady. "But I'd rather you were my friends before the serving and protecting."

Mor said with a wink, "We are. But we will serve and protect."

My face warmed, and I smiled at them. My—family.

"Now that we've settled that," Rhys drawled from behind me, "can we please eat? I'm famished." Amren opened her mouth with a wry smile, but he added, "Do *not* say what you were going to say, Amren." Rhys gave Cassian a sharp look. Both of them were still bruised—but healing fast. "Unless you want to have it out on the roof."

Amren clicked her tongue and instead jerked her chin at me. "I heard you grew fangs in the forest and killed some Hybern beasts. Good for you, girl."

"She saved his sorry ass is more like it," Mor said, filling her glass of wine. "Poor little Rhys got himself in a bind."

I held out my own glass for Mor to fill. "He does need unusual amounts of coddling."

Azriel choked on his wine, and I met his gaze—warm for once. Soft, even. I felt Rhys tense beside me and quickly looked away from the spymaster.

A glance at the guilt in Rhys's eyes told me he was sorry. And fighting it. So strange, the High Fae with their mating and primal instincts. So at odds with their ancient traditions and learning.

We left for the mortal lands soon after dinner. Mor carried the orb; Cassian carried her, Azriel flying close, and Rhys . . . Rhys held me tightly, his arms strong and unyielding around me. We were silent as we soared over the dark water.

As we went to show the queens the secret they'd all suffered so much, for so long, to keep.

CHAPTER 57

Spring had at last dawned on the human world, crocuses and daffodils poking their heads out of the thawed earth.

Only the eldest and the golden-haired queens came this time.

They were escorted by just as many guards, however.

I once again wore my flowing, ivory gown and crown of gold feathers, once again beside Rhysand as the queens and their sentries winnowed into the sitting room.

But now Rhys and I stood hand in hand—unflinching, a song without end or beginning.

The eldest queen slid her cunning eyes over us, our hands, our crowns, and merely sat without our bidding, adjusting the skirts of her emerald gown around her. The golden queen remained standing for a moment longer, her shining, curly head angling slightly. Her red lips twitched upward as she claimed the seat beside her companion.

Rhys did not so much as lower his head to them as he said, "We appreciate you taking the time to see us again."

The younger queen merely gave a little nod, her amber gaze leaping over to our friends behind us: Cassian and Azriel on either side of the bay of windows where Elain and Nesta stood in their finery, Elain's garden in bloom behind them. Nesta's shoulders were already locked. Elain bit her lip.

Mor stood on Rhys's other side, this time in blue-green that reminded me of the Sidra's calm waters, the onyx box containing the Veritas in her tan hands.

The ancient queen, surveying us all with narrowed eyes, let out a huff. "After being so gravely insulted the last time . . . " A simmering glare thrown at Nesta. My sister leveled a look of pure, unyielding flame right back at her. The old woman clicked her tongue. "We debated for many days whether we should return. As you can see, three of us found the insult to be unforgivable."

Liar. To blame it on Nesta, to try to sow discord between us for what Nesta had tried to defend . . . I said with surprising calm, "If that is the worst insult any of you have ever received in your lives, I'd say you're all in for quite a shock when war comes."

The younger one's lips twitched again, amber eyes alight—a lion incarnate. She purred to me, "So he won your heart after all, Cursebreaker."

I held her stare as Rhys and I both sat in our chairs, Mor sliding into one beside him. "I do not think," I said, "that it was mere coincidence that the Cauldron let us find each other on the eve of war returning between our two peoples."

"The Cauldron? And two peoples?" The golden one toyed with a ruby ring on her finger. "*Our* people do not invoke a Cauldron; *our* people do not have magic. The way I see it, there is *your* people—and ours. *You* are little better than those Children of the Blessed." She lifted a groomed brow. "What *does* happen to them when they cross the wall?" She angled her head at Rhys, at Cassian and Azriel. "Are they prey? Or are they used and discarded, and left to grow old and infirm while you remain young forever? Such a pity . . . so unfair that you, Cursebreaker, received what all those fools no doubt begged for. Immortality, eternal youth . . . What would Lord Rhysand have done if you had aged while he did not?"

Rhys said evenly, "Is there a point to your questions, other than to hear yourself talk?"

A low chuckle, and she turned to the ancient queen, her yellow dress rustling with the movement. The old woman simply extended a wrinkled hand to the box in Mor's slender fingers. "Is that the proof we asked for?"

Don't do it, my heart began bleating. *Don't show them.*

Before Mor could so much as nod, I said, "Is my love for the High Lord not proof enough of our good intentions? Does my sisters' presence here not speak to you? There is an iron engagement ring upon my sister's finger—and yet she stands with us."

Elain seemed to be fighting the urge to tuck her hand behind the skirts of her pale pink and blue dress, but stayed tall while the queens surveyed her.

"I would say that it is proof of her idiocy," the golden one sneered, "to be engaged to a Fae-hating man . . . and to risk the match by associating with you."

"Do not," Nesta hissed with quiet venom, "judge what you know *nothing* about."

The golden one folded her hands in her lap. "The viper speaks again." She raised her brows at me. "Surely the wise move would have been to have her sit this meeting out."

"She offers up her house and risks her social standing for us to have these meetings," I said. "She has the right to hear what is spoken in them. To stand as a representative of the people of these lands. They both do."

The crone interrupted the younger before she could reply, and again waved that wrinkled hand at Mor. "Show us, then. Prove us wrong."

Rhys gave Mor a subtle nod. No—no, it wasn't right. Not to show them, not to reveal the treasure that was Velaris, that was my home . . .

War is sacrifice, Rhys said into my mind, through the small sliver I now kept open for him. *If we do not gamble Velaris, we risk losing Prythian—and more.*

Mor opened the lid of the black box.

The silver orb inside glimmered like a star under glass. "This is the

Veritas," Mor said in a voice that was young and old. "The gift of my first ancestor to our bloodline. Only a few times in the history of Prythian have we used it—have we unleashed its truth upon the world."

She lifted the orb from its velvet nest. It was no larger than a ripe apple, and fit within her cupped palms as if her entire body, her entire being, had been molded for it.

"Truth is deadly. Truth is freedom. Truth can break and mend and bind. The Veritas holds in it the truth of the world. I am the Morrigan," she said, her eyes not wholly of this earth. The hair on my arms rose. "You know I speak truth."

She set the Veritas onto the carpet between us. Both queens leaned in.

But it was Rhys who said, "You desire proof of our goodness, our intentions, so that you may trust the Book in our hands?" The Veritas began pulsing, a web of light spreading with each throb. "There is a place within my lands. A city of peace. And art. And prosperity. As I doubt you or your guards will dare pass through the wall, then I will show it to you—show you the truth of these words, show you this place within the orb itself."

Mor stretched out a hand, and a pale cloud swirled from the orb, merging with its light as it drifted past our ankles.

The queens flinched, the guards edging forward with hands on their weapons. But the clouds continued roiling as the truth of it, of Velaris, leaked from the orb, from whatever it dragged up from Mor, from Rhys. From the truth of the world.

And in the gray gloom, a picture appeared.

It was Velaris, as seen from above—as seen by Rhys, flying in. A speck in the coast, but as he dropped down, the city and the river became clearer, vibrant.

Then the image banked and swerved, as if Rhys had flown through his city just this morning. It shot past boats and piers, past the homes and streets and theaters. Past the Rainbow of Velaris, so colorful and lovely in the new spring sun. People, happy and thoughtful, kind and welcoming, waved to him. Moment after moment, images of the Palaces, of the restaurants, of the House of Wind. All of it—all of that secret, wondrous city. My home.

And I could have sworn that there was love in that image. I could not explain how the Veritas conveyed it, but the colors . . . I understood the colors, and the light, what they conveyed, what the orb somehow picked up from whatever link it had to Rhys's memories.

The illusion faded, color and light and cloud sucked back into the orb.

"That is Velaris," Rhys said. "For five thousand years, we have kept it a secret from outsiders. And now you know. That is what I protect with the rumors, the whispers, the fear. Why I fought for your people in the War—only to begin my own supposed reign of terror once I ascended my throne, and ensured everyone heard the legends about it. But if the cost of protecting my city and people is the contempt of the world, then so be it."

The two queens were gaping at the carpet as if they could still see the city there. Mor cleared her throat. The golden one, as if Mor had barked, started and dropped an ornate lace handkerchief on the ground. She leaned to pick it up, cheeks a bit red.

But the crone raised her eyes to us. "Your trust is . . . appreciated."

We waited.

Both of their faces turned grave, unmoved. And I was glad I was sitting as the eldest added at last, "We will consider."

"There is no time to consider," Mor countered. "Every day lost is another day that Hybern gets closer to shattering the wall."

"We will discuss amongst our companions, and inform you at our leisure."

"Do you not understand the risks you take in doing so?" Rhys said, no hint of condescension. Only—only perhaps shock. "You need this alliance as much as we do."

The ancient queen shrugged her frail shoulders. "Did you think we would be moved by your letter, your plea?" She jerked her chin to the guard closest, and he reached into his armor to pull out a folded letter. The old woman read, "*I write to you not as a High Lord, but as a male in love with a woman who was once human. I write to you to beg you to act quickly. To save her people—to help save my own. I write to you so one day we might know true peace. So I might one day be able to live in a world where the woman I love may visit her family without fear of hatred and reprisal. A better world.*" She set down the letter.

Rhys had written that letter weeks ago . . . before we'd mated. Not a demand for the queens to meet—but a love letter. I reached across the space between us and took his hand, squeezing gently. Rhys's fingers tightened around my own.

But then the ancient one said, "Who is to say that this is not all some grand manipulation?"

"What?" Mor blurted.

The golden queen nodded her agreement and dared say to Mor, "A great many things have changed since the War. Since your so-called friendships with our ancestors. Perhaps you are not who you say you are. Perhaps the High Lord has crept into our minds to make us believe you are the Morrigan."

Rhys was silent—we all were. Until Nesta said too softly, "This is the talk of madwomen. Of arrogant, stupid *fools*."

Elain grabbed for Nesta's hand to silence her. But Nesta stalked forward a step, face white with rage. "Give them the Book."

The queens blinked, stiffening.

My sister snapped, "*Give them the Book.*"

And the eldest queen hissed, "*No.*"

The word clanged through me.

But Nesta went on, flinging out an arm to encompass us, the room, the world, "There are innocent people here. In these lands. If you will not risk your necks against the forces that threaten us, then grant those people a fighting chance. Give my sister the Book."

The crone sighed sharply through her nose. "An evacuation may be possible—"

"You would need ten thousand ships," Nesta said, her voice breaking. "You would need an armada. I have calculated the numbers. And if you are readying for war, you will not send your ships to us. We are stranded here."

The crone gripped the polished arms of her chair as she leaned forward a bit. "Then I suggest asking one of your winged males to carry you across the sea, girl."

Nesta's throat bobbed. "Please." I didn't think I'd ever heard that word from her mouth. "Please—do not leave us to face this alone."

The eldest queen remained unmoved. I had no words in my head.

We had shown them . . . we had . . . we had done everything. Even Rhys was silent, his face unreadable.

But then Cassian crossed to Nesta, the guards stiffening as the Illyrian moved through them as if they were stalks of wheat in a field.

He studied Nesta for a long moment. She was still glaring at the queens, her eyes lined with tears—*tears* of rage and despair, from that fire that burned her so violently from within. When she finally noticed Cassian, she looked up at him.

His voice was rough as he said, "Five hundred years ago, I fought on battlefields not far from this house. I fought beside human and faerie alike, bled beside them. I will stand on that battlefield again, Nesta Archeron, to protect this house—your people. I can think of no better way to end my existence than to defend those who need it most."

I watched a tear slide down Nesta's cheek. And I watched as Cassian reached up a hand to wipe it away.

She did not flinch from his touch.

I didn't know why, but I looked at Mor.

Her eyes were wide. Not with jealousy, or irritation, but . . . something perhaps like awe.

Nesta swallowed and at last turned away from Cassian. He stared at my sister a moment longer before facing the queens.

Without signal, the two women rose.

Mor demanded, on her feet as well, "Is it a sum you're after? Name your price, then."

The golden queen snorted as their guards closed in around them. "We have all the riches we need. We will now return to our palace to deliberate with our sisters."

"You're already going to say no," Mor pushed.

The golden queen smirked. "Perhaps." She took the crone's withered hand.

The ancient queen lifted her chin. "We appreciate the gesture of your trust."

Then they were gone.

Mor swore. And I looked at Rhys, my own heart breaking, about to demand why he hadn't pushed, why he hadn't said more—

But his eyes were on the chair where the golden queen had been seated.

Beneath it, somehow hidden by her voluminous skirts while she'd sat, was a box.

A box . . . that she must have removed from wherever she was hiding it when she'd leaned down to pick up her handkerchief.

Rhys had known it. Had stopped speaking to get them out as fast as possible.

How and where she'd smuggled in that lead box was the least of my concerns.

Not as the voice of the second and final piece of the Book filled the room, sang to me.

Life and death and rebirth

Sun and moon and dark

Rot and bloom and bones

Hello, sweet thing. Hello, lady of night, princess of decay. Hello, fanged beast and trembling fawn. Love me, touch me, sing me.

Madness. Where the first half had been cold cunning, this box . . . this was chaos, and disorder, and lawlessness, joy and despair.

Rhys smoothly picked it up and set it on the golden queen's chair. He did not need my power to open it—because no High Lord's spells had been keyed to it.

Rhys flipped back the lid. A note lay atop the golden metal of the book.

I read your letter. About the woman you love. I believe you. And I believe in peace.

I believe in a better world.

If anyone asks, you stole this during the meeting.

Do not trust the others. The sixth queen was not ill.

That was it.

Rhys picked up the Book of Breathings.

Light and dark and gray and light and dark and gray—

He said to my two sisters, Cassian sticking close to Nesta, "It is your choice, ladies, whether you wish to remain here, or come with us. You have heard the situation at hand. You have done the math about an evacuation." A nod of approval as he met Nesta's gray-blue stare. "Should you choose to remain, a unit of my soldiers will be here within the hour to guard this place. Should you wish to come live with us in that city we just showed them, I'd suggest packing now."

Nesta looked to Elain, still silent and wide-eyed. The tea she'd prepared—the finest, most exotic tea money could buy—sat undisturbed on the table.

Elain thumbed the iron ring on her finger.

"It is your choice," Nesta said with unusual gentleness. For her, Nesta would go to Prythian.

Elain swallowed, a doe caught in a snare. "I—I can't. I . . ."

But my mate nodded—kindly. With understanding. "The sentries will be here, and remain unseen and unfelt. They will look after themselves. Should you change your minds, one will be waiting in this room every day at noon and at midnight for you to speak. My home is your home. Its doors are always open to you."

Nesta looked between Rhys and Cassian, then to me. Despair still paled her face, but . . . she bowed her head. And said to me, "That was why you painted stars on your drawer."

CHAPTER 58

We immediately returned to Velaris, not trusting the queens to go long without noticing the Book's absence, especially if the vague mention of the sixth alluded to further foul play amongst them.

Amren had the second half within minutes, not even bothering to ask about the meeting before she vanished into the dining room of the town house and shut the doors behind her. So we waited.

And waited.

✠

Two days passed.

Amren still hadn't cracked the code.

Rhys and Mor left in the early afternoon to visit the Court of Nightmares—to return the Veritas to Keir without his knowing, and ensure that the Steward was indeed readying his forces. Cassian had reports that the Illyrian legions were now camped across the mountains, waiting for the order to fly out to wherever our first battle might be.

There would be one, I realized. Even if we nullified the Cauldron using the Book, even if *I* was able to stop that Cauldron and the king from using it to shatter the wall and the world, he had armies gathered. Perhaps we'd take the fight to him once the Cauldron was disabled.

There was no word from my sisters, no report from Azriel's soldiers that they'd changed their minds. My father, I remembered, was still trading in the continent for the Mother knew what goods. Another variable in this.

And there was no word from the queens. It was of them that I most frequently thought. Of the two-faced, golden-eyed queen with not just a lion's coloring . . . but a lion's heart, too.

I hoped I saw her again.

With Rhys and Mor gone, Cassian and Azriel came to stay at the town house as they continued to plan our inevitable visit to Hybern. After that first dinner, when Cassian had broken out one of Rhys's *very* old bottles of wine so we could celebrate my mating in style, I'd realized they'd come to stay for company, to dine with me, and . . . the Illyrians had taken it upon themselves to look after me.

Rhys said as much that night when I'd written him a letter and watched it vanish. Apparently, he didn't mind his enemies knowing he was at the Court of Nightmares. If Hybern's forces tracked him there . . . good luck to them.

I'd written to Rhys, *How do I tell Cassian and Azriel I don't need them here to protect me? Company is fine, but I don't need sentries.*

He'd written back, *You* don't *tell them. You set boundaries if they cross a line, but you are their friend—and my mate. They will protect you on instinct. If you kick their asses out of the house, they'll just sit on the roof.*

I scribbled, *You Illyrian males are insufferable.*

Rhys had just said, *Good thing we make up for it with impressive wingspans.*

Even with him across the territory, my blood had heated, my toes curling. I'd barely been able to hold the pen long enough to write, *I'm missing that impressive wingspan in my bed. Inside me.*

He'd replied, *Of course you are.*

I'd hissed, jotting down, *Prick.*

I'd almost felt his laughter down the bond—our mating bond. Rhys wrote back, *When I return, we're going to that shop across the Sidra and you're going to try on all those lacy little underthings for me.*

I fell asleep thinking about it, wishing my hand was his, praying he'd finish at the Court of Nightmares and return to me soon. Spring was bursting all across the hills and peaks around Velaris. I wanted to sail over the yellow and purple blooms with him.

The next afternoon, Rhys was still gone, Amren was still buried in the book, Azriel off on a patrol of the city and nearby shoreline, and Cassian and I were—of all things—just finishing up an early afternoon performance of some ancient, revered Fae symphony. The amphitheater was on the other side of the Sidra, and though he'd offered to fly me, I'd wanted to walk. Even if my muscles were barking in protest after his brutal lesson that morning.

The music had been lovely—strange, but lovely, written at a time, Cassian had told me, when humans had not even walked the earth. He found the music puzzling, off-kilter, but . . . I'd been entranced.

Walking back across one of the main bridges spanning the river, we remained in companionable silence. We'd dropped off more blood for Amren—who said thank you and get the hell out—and were now headed toward the Palace of Thread and Jewels, where I wanted to buy both of my sisters presents for helping us. Cassian had promised to send them down with the next scout dispatched to retrieve the latest report. I wondered if he'd send anything to Nesta while he was at it.

I paused at the center of the marble bridge, Cassian halting beside me as I peered down at the blue-green water idling past. I could feel the threads of the current far below, the strains of salt and fresh water twining together, the swaying weeds coating the mussel-flecked floor, the tickling of small, skittering creatures over rock and mud. Could Tarquin sense such things? Did he sleep in his island-palace on the sea and swim through the dreams of fishes?

Cassian braced his forearms on the broad stone railing, his red Siphons like living pools of flame.

I said, perhaps because I was a busybody who liked to stick my nose in other people's affairs, "It meant a great deal to me—what you promised my sister the other day."

Cassian shrugged, his wings rustling. "I'd do it for anyone."

"It meant a lot to her, too." Hazel eyes narrowed slightly. But I casually watched the river. "Nesta is different from most people," I explained. "She comes across as rigid and vicious, but I think it's a wall. A shield—like the ones Rhys has in his mind."

"Against what?"

"Feeling. I think Nesta feels everything—sees too much; sees and feels it all. And she burns with it. Keeping that wall up helps from being overwhelmed, from caring too greatly."

"She barely seems to care about anyone other than Elain."

I met his stare, scanning that handsome, tan face. "She will never be like Mor," I said. "She will never love freely and gift it to everyone who crosses her path. But the few she does care for . . . I think Nesta would shred the world apart for them. Shred herself apart for them. She and I have our . . . issues. But Elain . . . " My mouth quirked to the side. "She will never forget, Cassian, that you offered to defend Elain. Defend her people. As long as she lives, she will remember that kindness."

He straightened, rapping his knuckles against the smooth marble. "Why are you telling me this?"

"I just—thought you should know. For whenever you see her again and she pisses you off. Which I'm certain will happen. But know that deep down, she is grateful, and perhaps does not possess the ability to say so. Yet the feeling—the heart—is there."

I paused, debating pushing him, but the river flowing beneath us shifted.

Not a physical shifting. But . . . a tremor in the current, in the bedrock, in the skittering things crawling on it. Like ink dropped in water.

Cassian instantly went on alert as I scanned the river, the banks on either side.

"What the hell is that?" he murmured. He tapped the Siphon on each hand with a finger.

I gaped as scaled black armor began unfolding and slithering up his wrists, his arms, replacing the tunic that had been there. Layer after layer, coating him like a second skin, flowing up to his shoulders. The additional Siphons appeared, and more armor spread across his neck, his shoulders, down his chest and waist. I blinked, and it had covered his legs—then his feet.

The sky was cloudless, the streets full of chatter and life.

Cassian kept scanning, a slow rotation over Velaris.

The river beneath me remained steady, but I could feel it roiling, as if trying to flee from— "From the sea," I breathed. Cassian's gaze shot straight ahead, to the river before us, to the towering cliffs in the distance that marked the raging waves where it met the ocean.

And there, on the horizon, a smear of black. Swift-moving—spreading wider as it grew closer.

"Tell me those are birds," I said. My power flooded my veins, and I curled my fingers into fists, willing it to calm, to steady—

"There's no Illyrian patrol that's supposed to know about this place . . . ," he said, as if it were an answer. His gaze cut to me. "We're going back to the town house right now."

The smear of black separated, fracturing into countless figures. Too big for birds. Far too big. I said, "You have to sound the alarm—"

But people were. Some were pointing, some were shouting.

Cassian reached for me, but I jumped back. Ice danced at my fingertips, wind howled in my blood. I'd pick them off one by one— "Get Azriel and Amren—"

They'd reached the sea cliffs. Countless, long-limbed flying creatures, some bearing soldiers in their arms . . . An invading host. "Cassian."

But an Illyrian blade had appeared in Cassian's hand, twin to the one across his back. A fighting knife now shone in the other. He held them both out to me. "Get back to the town house—right now."

I most certainly would not go. If they were flying, I could use my power to my advantage: freeze their wings, burn them, break them. Even if there were so many, even if—

So fast, as if they were carried on a fell wind, the force reached the outer edges of the city. And unleashed arrows upon the shrieking people rushing for cover in the streets. I grabbed his outstretched weapons, the cool metal hilts hissing beneath my forge-hot palms.

Cassian lifted his hand into the air. Red light exploded from his Siphon, blasting up and away—forming a hard wall in the sky above the city, directly in the path of that oncoming force.

He ground his teeth, grunting as the winged legion slammed into his shield. As if he felt every impact.

The translucent red shield shoved out farther, knocking them back—

We both watched in mute horror as the creatures lunged for the shield, arms out—

They were not just any manner of faerie. Any rising magic in me sputtered and went out at the sight of them.

They were all like the Attor.

All long-limbed, gray-skinned, with serpentine snouts and razor-sharp teeth. And as the legion of its ilk punched through Cassian's shield as if it were a cobweb, I beheld on their spindly gray arms gauntlets of that bluish stone I'd seen on Rhys, glimmering in the sun.

Stone that broke and repelled magic. Straight from the unholy trove of the King of Hybern.

One after one after one, they punched through his shield.

Cassian sent another wall barreling for them. Some of the creatures peeled away and launched themselves upon the outskirts of the city, vulnerable outside of his shield. The heat that had been building in my palms faded to clammy sweat.

People were shrieking, fleeing. And I knew his shields would not hold—

"*GO!*" Cassian roared. I lurched into motion, knowing he likely lingered because I stayed, that he needed Azriel and Amren and—

High above us, three of them slammed into the dome of the red shield. Clawing at it, ripping through layer after layer with those stone gauntlets.

That's what had delayed the king these months: gathering his arsenal. Weapons to fight magic, to fight High Fae who would rely on it—

A hole ripped open, and Cassian threw me to the ground, shoving me against the marble railing, his wings spreading wide over me, his legs as solid as the bands of carved rock at my back—

Screams on the bridge, hissing laughter, and then—

A wet, crunching thud.

"Shit," Cassian said. "*Shit*—"

He moved a step, and I lunged from under him to see what it was, who it was—

Blood shone on the white marble bridge, sparkling like rubies in the sun.

There, on one of those towering, elegant lampposts flanking the bridge . . .

Her body was bent, her back arched on the impact, as if she were in the throes of passion.

Her golden hair had been shorn to the skull. Her golden eyes had been plucked out.

She was twitching where she had been impaled on the post, the metal pole straight through her slim torso, gore clinging to the metal above her.

Someone on the bridge vomited, then kept running.

But I could not break my stare from the golden queen. Or from the Attor, who swept through the hole it had made and alighted atop the blood-soaked lamppost.

"Regards," it hissed, "of the mortal queens. And Jurian." Then the Attor leaped into flight, fast and sleek—heading right for the theater district we'd left.

Cassian had pressed me back down against the bridge—and he surged toward the Attor. He halted, remembering me, but I rasped, "*Go.*"

"Run home. *Now.*"

That was the final order—and his good-bye as he shot into the sky after the Attor, who had already disappeared into the screaming streets.

Around me, hole after hole was punched through that red shield, those winged creatures pouring in, dumping the Hybern soldiers they had carried across the sea.

Soldiers of every shape and size—lesser faeries.

The golden queen's gaping mouth was opening and closing like a fish on land. Save her, help her—

My blood. I could—

I took a step. Her body slumped.

And from wherever in me that power originated, I felt her death whisper past.

The screams, the beating wings, the whoosh and thud of arrows erupted in the sudden silence.

I ran. I ran for my side of the Sidra, for the town house. I didn't trust myself to winnow—could barely think around the panic barking through my head. I had minutes, perhaps, before they hit my street. Minutes to get there and bring as many inside with me as I could. The house was warded. No one would get in, not even these things.

Faeries were rushing past, racing for shelter, for friends and family. I hit the end of the bridge, the steep hills rising up—

Hybern soldiers were already atop the hill, at the two Palaces, laughing at the screams, the pleading as they broke into buildings, dragging people out. Blood dribbled down the cobblestones in little rivers.

They had done this. Those queens had . . . had given this city of art and music and food over to these . . . monsters. The king must have used the Cauldron to break its wards.

A thunderous *boom* rocked the other side of the city, and I went down at the impact, blades flying, hands ripping open on the cobblestones. I whirled toward the river, scrambling up, lunging for my weapons.

Cassian and Azriel were both in the skies now. And where they flew, those winged creatures died. Arrows of red and blue light shot from them, and those shields—

Twin shields of red and blue merged, sizzling, and slammed into the rest of the aerial forces. Flesh and wings tore, bone melted—

Until hands encased in stone tumbled from the sky. Only hands. Clattering on rooftops, splashing into the river. All that was left of them—what two Illyrian warriors had worked their way around.

But there were countless more who had already landed. Too many. Roofs were wrenched apart, doors shattered, screaming rising and then silenced—

This was not an attack to sack the city. It was an extermination.

And rising up before me, merely a few blocks down, the Rainbow of Velaris was bathed in blood.

The Attor and his ilk had converged there.

As if the queens had told him where to strike; where in Velaris would be the most defenseless. The beating heart of the city.

Fire was rippling, black smoke staining the sky—

Where was Rhys, where was my mate—

Across the river, thunder boomed again.

And it was not Cassian, or Azriel, who held the other side of the river. But Amren.

Her slim hands had only to point, and soldiers would fall—fall as if their own wings failed them. They slammed into the streets, thrashing, choking, clawing, shrieking, just as the people of Velaris had shrieked.

I whipped my head to the Rainbow a few blocks away—left unprotected. Defenseless.

The street before me was clear, the lone safe passage through hell.

A female screamed inside the artists' quarter. And I knew my path.

I flipped my Illyrian blade in my hand and winnowed into the burning and bloody Rainbow.

This was my home. These were my people.

If I died defending them, defending that small place in the world where art thrived . . .

Then so be it.

And I became darkness, and shadow, and wind.

I winnowed into the edge of the Rainbow as the first of the Hybern soldiers rounded its farthest corner, spilling onto the river avenue, shredding the cafés where I had lounged and laughed. They did not see me until I was upon them.

Until my Illyrian blade cleaved through their heads, one after another.

Six went down in my wake, and as I halted at the foot of the Rainbow, staring up into the fire and blood and death . . . Too many. Too many soldiers.

I'd never make it, never kill them all—

But there was a young female, green-skinned and lithe, an ancient, rusted bit of pipe raised above her shoulder. Standing her ground in front of her storefront—a gallery. People crouched inside the shop were sobbing.

Before them, laughing at the faerie, at her raised scrap of metal, circled five winged soldiers. Playing with her, taunting her.

Still she held the line. Still her face did not crumple. Paintings and pottery were shattered around her. And more soldiers were landing, spilling down, butchering—

Across the river, thunder boomed—Amren or Cassian or Azriel, I didn't know.

The river.

Three soldiers spotted me from up the hill. Raced for me.

But I ran faster, back for the river at the foot of the hill, for the singing Sidra.

I hit the edge of the quay, the water already stained with blood, and slammed my foot down in a mighty stomp.

And as if in answer, the Sidra rose.

I yielded to that thrumming power inside my bones and blood and breath. I became the Sidra, ancient and deep. And I bent it to my will.

I lifted my blades, willing the river higher, shaping it, forging it.

Those Hybern soldiers stopped dead in their tracks as I turned toward them.

And wolves of water broke from behind me.

The soldiers whirled, fleeing.

But my wolves were faster. *I* was faster as I ran with them, in the heart of the pack.

Wolf after wolf roared out of the Sidra, as colossal as the one I had once killed, pouring into the streets, racing upward.

I made it five steps before the pack was upon the soldiers taunting the shop owner.

I made it seven steps before the wolves brought them down, water shoving down their throats, drowning them—

I reached the soldiers, and my blade sang as I severed their choking heads from their bodies.

The shopkeeper was sobbing as she recognized me, her rusted bar still raised. But she nodded—only once.

I ran again, losing myself amongst my water-wolves. Some of the soldiers were taking to the sky, flapping upward, backtracking.

So my wolves grew wings, and talons, and became falcons and hawks and eagles.

They slammed into their bodies, their armor, drenching them. The airborne soldiers, realizing they hadn't been drowned, halted their flight and laughed—sneering.

I lifted a hand skyward, and clenched my fingers into a fist.

The water soaking them, their wings, their armor, their faces . . . It turned to ice.

Ice that was so cold it had existed before light, before the sun had warmed the earth. Ice of a land cloaked in winter, ice from the parts of me that felt no mercy, no sympathy for what these creatures had done and were doing to my people.

Frozen solid, dozens of the winged soldiers fell to the earth as one. And shattered upon the cobblestones.

My wolves raged around me, tearing and drowning and hunting. And those that fled them, those that took to the skies—they froze and shattered; froze and shattered. Until the streets were laden with ice and gore and broken bits of wing and stone.

Until the screaming of my people stopped, and the screams of the soldiers became a song in my blood. One of the soldiers rose up above the brightly painted buildings . . . I knew him.

The Attor was flapping, frantic, blood of the innocent coating his gray skin, his stone gauntlets. I sent an eagle of water shooting for him, but he was quicker, nimble.

He evaded my eagle, and my hawk, and my falcon, soaring high, clawing his way through the air. Away from me, my power—from Cassian and Azriel, holding the river and the majority of the city, away from Amren, using whatever dark power she possessed to send so many droves of them crashing down without visible injury.

None of my friends saw the Attor sailing up, sailing free.

It would fly back to Hybern—to the king. It had chosen to come here, to lead them. For spite. And I had no doubt that the golden, lioness-queen had suffered at its hands. As Clare had.

Where are you?

Rhys's voice sounded distantly in my head, through the sliver in my shield.

WHERE ARE YOU?

The Attor was getting away. With each heartbeat, it flew higher and higher—

WHERE—

I sheathed the Illyrian blade and fighting knife through my belt and scrambled to pick up the arrows that had fallen on the street. Shot at my people. Ash arrows, coated in familiar greenish poison. Bloodbane.

I'm exactly where I need to be, I said to Rhys.

And then I winnowed into the sky.

CHAPTER 59

I winnowed to a nearby rooftop, an ash arrow clenched in either hand, scanning where the Attor was high above, flapping—

FEYRE.

I slammed a mental shield of adamant up against that voice; against him.

Not now. Not this moment.

I could vaguely feel him pounding against that shield. Roaring at it. But even he could not get in.

The Attor was *mine*.

In the distance, rushing toward me, toward Velaris, a mighty darkness devoured the world. Soldiers in its path did not emerge again.

My mate. Death incarnate. Night triumphant.

I spotted the Attor again, veering toward the sea, toward Hybern, still over the city.

I winnowed, throwing my awareness toward it like a net, spearing mind to mind, using the tether like a rope, leading me through time and distance and wind—

I latched onto the oily smear of its malice, pinpointing my being, my focus onto the core of it. A beacon of corruption and filth.

When I emerged from wind and shadow, I was right atop the Attor.

It shrieked, wings curving as I slammed into it. As I plunged those poisoned ash arrows through each wing. Right through the main muscle.

The Attor arched in pain, its forked tongue cleaving the air between us. The city was a blur below, the Sidra a mere stream from the height.

In the span of a heartbeat, I wrapped myself around the Attor. I became a living flame that burned everywhere I touched, became unbreakable as the adamant wall inside my mind.

Shrieking, the Attor thrashed against me—but its wings, with those arrows, with my grip . . .

Free fall.

Down into the world. Into blood and pain. The wind tore at us.

The Attor could not break free of my flaming grasp. Or from my poisoned arrows skewering its wings. Laming him. Its burning skin stung my nose.

As we fell, my dagger found its way into my hand.

The darkness consuming the horizon shot closer—as if spotting me.

Not yet.

Not yet.

I angled my dagger over the Attor's bony, elongated rib cage. "This is for Rhys," I hissed in its pointed ear.

The reverberation of steel on bone barked into my hand.

Silvery blood warmed my fingers. The Attor screamed.

I yanked out my dagger, blood flying up, splattering my face.

"This is for Clare."

I plunged my blade in again, twisting.

Buildings took form. The Sidra ran red, but the sky was empty—free of soldiers. So were the streets.

The Attor was screaming and hissing, cursing and begging, as I ripped free the blade.

I could make out people; make out their shapes. The ground swelled up to meet us. The Attor was bucking so violently it was all I could do to keep it in my forge-hot grip. Burning skin ripped away, carried above us.

"And this," I breathed, leaning close to say the words into its ear, into its rotted soul. I slid my dagger in a third time, relishing the splintering of bones and flesh. "This is for *me*."

I could count the cobblestones. See Death beckoning with open arms.

I kept my mouth beside its ear, close as a lover, as our reflection in a pool of blood became clear. "I'll see you in hell," I whispered, and left my blade in its side.

Wind rippled the blood upon the cobblestones mere inches away.

And I winnowed out, leaving the Attor behind.

I heard the crack and splatter, even as I sifted through the world, propelled by my own power and the velocity of my plummet. I emerged a few feet away—my body taking longer than my mind to catch up.

My feet and legs gave out, and I rocked back into the wall of a pink-painted building behind me. So hard the plaster dented and cracked against my spine, my shoulders.

I panted, trembling. And on the street ahead—what lay broken and oozing on the cobblestones . . . The Attor's wings were a twisted ruin. Beyond that, scraps of armor, splintered bone, and burned flesh were all that remained.

That wave of darkness, Rhysand's power, at last hit my side of the river.

No one cried out at the star-flecked cascade of night that cut off all light.

I thought I heard vague grunting and scraping—as if it had sought out hidden soldiers lingering in the Rainbow, but then . . .

The wave vanished. Sunlight.

A crunch of boots before me, the beat and whisper of mighty wings.

A hand on my face, tilting up my chin as I stared and stared at the splattered ruin of the Attor. Violet eyes met mine.

Rhys. Rhys was here.

And . . . and I had . . .

He leaned forward, his brow sweat-coated, his breathing uneven. He gently pressed a kiss to my mouth.

To remind us both. Who we were, what we were. My icy heart thawed, the fire in my gut was soothed by a tendril of dark, and the water trickled out of my veins and back into the Sidra.

Rhys pulled back, his thumb stroking my cheek. People were weeping. Keening.

But no more screams of terror. No more bloodshed and destruction.

My mate murmured, "Feyre Cursebreaker, the Defender of the Rainbow."

I slid my arms around his waist and sobbed.

And even as his city wailed, the High Lord of the Night Court held me until I could at last face this blood-drenched new world.

CHAPTER 60

"Velaris is secure," Rhys said in the black hours of the night. "The wards the Cauldron took out have been remade."

We had not stopped to rest until now. For hours we'd worked, along with the rest of the city, to heal, to patch up, to hunt down answers any way we could. And now we were all again gathered, the clock chiming three in the morning.

I didn't know how Rhys was standing as he leaned against the mantel in the sitting room. I was near-limp on the couch beside Mor, both of us coated in dirt and blood. Like the rest of them.

Sprawled in an armchair built for Illyrian wings, Cassian's face was battered and healing slowly enough that I knew he'd drained his power during those long minutes when he'd defended the city alone. But his hazel eyes still glowed with the embers of rage.

Amren was hardly better off. The tiny female's gray clothes hung mostly in strips, her skin beneath pale as snow. Half-asleep on the couch across from mine, she leaned against Azriel, who kept casting alarmed glances at her, even as his own wounds leaked a bit. Atop his scarred hands, Azriel's blue Siphons were dull, muted. Utterly empty.

As I had helped the survivors in the Rainbow tend to their wounded, count their dead, and begin repairs, Rhys had checked in every now and then while he'd rebuilt the wards with whatever power lingered in his arsenal. During one of our brief breaks, he'd told me what Amren had done on her side of the river.

With her dark power, she had spun illusions straight into the soldiers' minds. They believed they had fallen into the Sidra and were drowning; they believed they were flying a thousand feet above and had dived, fast and swift, for the city—only to find the street mere feet away, and the crunch of their skulls. The crueler ones, the wickedest ones, she had unleashed their own nightmares upon them—until they died from terror, their hearts giving out.

Some had fallen into the river, drinking their own spreading blood as they drowned. Some had disappeared wholly.

"Velaris might be secure," Cassian replied, not even bothering to lift his head from where it rested against the back of the chair, "but for how long? Hybern knows about this place, thanks to those wyrm-queens. Who else will they sell the information to? How long until the other courts come sniffing? Or Hybern uses that Cauldron again to take down our defenses?"

Rhys closed his eyes, his shoulders tight. I could already see the weight pushing down on that dark head.

I hated to add to that burden, but I said, "If we all go to Hybern to destroy the Cauldron . . . who will defend the city?"

Silence. Rhys's throat bobbed.

Amren said, "I'll stay." Cassian opened his mouth to object, but Rhys slowly looked at his Second. Amren held his gaze as she added, "If Rhys must go to Hybern, then I am the only one of you who might hold the city until help arrives. Today was a surprise. A bad one. When you leave, we will be better prepared. The new wards we built today will not fall so easily."

Mor loosed a sigh. "So what do we do now?"

Amren simply said, "We sleep. We eat."

And it was Azriel who added, his voice raw with the aftermath of battle-rage, "And then we retaliate."

Rhys did not come to bed.

And when I emerged from the bath, the water clouded with dirt and blood, he was nowhere to be found.

But I felt for the bond between us and trudged upstairs, my stiff legs barking in pain. He was sitting on the roof—in the dark. His great wings were spread behind him, draped over the tiles.

I slid into his lap, looping my arms around his neck.

He stared at the city around us. "So few lights. So few lights left tonight."

I did not look. I only traced the lines of his face, then brushed my thumb over his mouth. "It is not your fault," I said quietly.

His eyes shifted to mine, barely visible in the dark. "Isn't it? I handed this city over to them. I said I would be willing to risk it, but . . . I don't know who I hate more: the king, those queens, or myself."

I brushed the hair out of his face. He gripped my hand, halting my fingers. "You shut me out," he breathed. "You—shielded against me. Completely. I couldn't find a way in."

"I'm sorry."

Rhys let out a bitter laugh. "Sorry? Be impressed. That shield . . . What you did to the Attor . . . " He shook his head. "You could have been killed."

"Are you going to scold me for it?"

His brows furrowed. Then he buried his face in my shoulder. "How could I scold you for defending my people? I want to throttle you, yes, for not going back to the town house, but . . . You chose to fight for them. For Velaris." He kissed my neck. "I don't deserve you."

My heart strained. He meant it—truly felt that way. I stroked his hair again. And I said to him, the words the only sounds in the silent, dark city, "We deserve each other. And we deserve to be happy."

Rhys shuddered against me. And when his lips found mine, I let him lay me down upon the roof tiles and make love to me under the stars.

Amren cracked the code the next afternoon. The news was not good.

"To nullify the Cauldron's power," she said by way of greeting as we crowded around the dining table in the town house, having rushed in from the repairs we'd all been making on very little sleep, "you must touch the Cauldron—and speak these words." She had written them all down for me on a piece of paper.

"You know this for certain?" Rhys said. He was still bleak-eyed from the attack, from healing and helping his people all day.

Amren hissed. "I'm trying not to be insulted, Rhysand."

Mor elbowed her way between them, staring at the two assembled pieces of the Book of Breathings. "What happens if we put both halves together?"

"Don't put them together," Amren simply said.

With either piece laid out, their voices blended and sang and hissed—evil and good and madness; dark and light and chaos.

"You put the pieces together," she clarified when Rhys gave her a questioning look, "and the blast of power will be felt in every corner and hole in the earth. You won't just attract the King of Hybern. You'll draw enemies far older and more wretched. Things that have long been asleep—and should remain so."

I cringed a bit. Rhys put a hand on my back.

"Then we move in now," Cassian said. His face had healed, but he limped a bit from an injury I couldn't see beneath his fighting leathers. He jerked his chin to Rhys. "Since you can't winnow without being tracked, Mor and Az will winnow us all in, Feyre breaks the Cauldron, and we get out. We'll be there and gone before anyone notices and the King of Hybern will have a new piece of cookware."

I swallowed. "It could be anywhere in his castle."

"We know where it is," Cassian countered.

I blinked. Azriel said to me, "We've been able to narrow it down to the lower levels." Through his spying, their planning for this *trip* all these months. "Every inch of the castle and surrounding lands is heavily guarded, but not impossible to get through. We've worked out the timing of it—for a small group of us to get in and out, quick and silent, and be gone before they know what's happening."

Mor said to him, "*But* the King of Hybern could notice Rhys's presence the moment he arrives. And if Feyre needs time to nullify the Cauldron, and we don't know *how* much time, that's a risky variable."

Cassian said, "We've considered that. So you and Rhys will winnow us in off the coast; we fly in while he stays." They'd have to winnow me, I realized, since I still had not yet mastered doing it over long distances. At least, not with many stops in between. "As for the spell," Cassian continued, "it's a risk we'll have to take."

Silence fell as they waited for Rhys's answer. My mate scanned my face, eyes wide.

Azriel pushed, "It's a solid plan. The king doesn't know our scents. We wreck the Cauldron and vanish before he notices . . . It'll be a graver insult than the bloodier, direct route we'd been considering, Rhys. We beat them yesterday, so when we go into that castle . . . " Vengeance indeed danced in that normally placid face. "We'll leave a few reminders that we won the last damn war for a reason."

Cassian nodded grimly. Even Mor smiled a bit.

"Are you asking me," Rhys finally said, far too calmly, "to *stay outside* while my mate goes into his stronghold?"

"Yes," Azriel said with equal calm, Cassian shifting himself slightly between them. "If Feyre can't nullify the Cauldron easily or quickly, we steal it—send the pieces back to the bastard when we're done breaking it apart. Either way, Feyre calls you through the bond when we're done—you and Mor winnow us out. They won't be able to track you fast enough if you only come to retrieve us."

Rhysand dropped onto the couch beside me at last, loosing a breath. His eyes slid to me. "If you want to go, then you go, Feyre."

If I hadn't been already in love with him, I might have loved him for that—for not insisting I stay, even if it drove his instincts mad, for not locking me away in the aftermath of what had happened yesterday.

And I realized—I realized how badly I'd been treated before, if my standards had become so low. If the freedom I'd been granted felt like a privilege and not an inherent right.

Rhys's eyes darkened, and I knew he read what I thought, felt. "You might be my mate," he said, "but you remain your own person. You decide your fate—your choices. Not me. You chose yesterday. You choose every day. Forever."

And maybe he only understood because he, too, had been helpless and without choices, had been forced to do such horrible things, and locked up. I threaded my fingers through his and squeezed. Together—together we'd find our peace, our future. Together we'd fight for it.

"Let's go to Hybern," I said.

I was halfway up the stairs an hour later when I realized that I still had no idea what room to go to. I'd gone to my bedroom since we'd returned from the cabin, but . . . what of his?

With Tamlin, he'd kept his own rooms and slept in mine. And I supposed—I supposed it'd be the same.

I was almost to my bedroom door when Rhysand drawled from behind me, "We can use your room if you like, but . . . " He was leaning against his open bedroom door. "Either your room or mine—but we're sharing one from now on. Just tell me whether I should move my clothes or yours. If that's all right with you."

"Don't you—you don't want your own space?"

"No," he said baldly. "Unless you do. I need you protecting me from our enemies with your water-wolves."

I snorted. He'd made me tell him that part of my tale over and over. I jerked my chin toward his bedroom. "Your bed is bigger."

And that was that.

I walked in to find my clothes already there, a second armoire now beside his. I stared at the massive bed, then at all the open space around us.

Rhys shut the door and went to a small box on the desk—then silently handed it to me.

My heart thundered as I opened the lid. The star sapphire gleamed in the candlelight, as if it were one of the Starfall spirits trapped in stone. "Your mother's ring?"

"My mother gave me that ring to remind me she was always with me, even during the worst of my training. And when I reached my majority, she took it away. It was an heirloom of her family—had been handed down from female to female over many, many years. My sister wasn't yet born, so she wouldn't have known to give it to her, but . . . My mother gave it to the Weaver. And then she told me that if I were to marry or mate, then the female would either have to be smart or strong enough to get it back. And if the female wasn't either of those things, then she wouldn't survive the marriage. I promised my mother that any potential bride or mate would have the test . . . And so it sat there for centuries."

My face heated. "You said this was something of value—"

"It is. To me, and my family."

"So my trip to the Weaver—"

"It was vital that we learn if you could detect those objects. But . . . I picked the object out of pure selfishness."

"So I won my wedding ring without even being asked if I wanted to marry you."

"Perhaps."

I cocked my head. "Do—do you want me to wear it?"

"Only if you want to."

"When we go to Hybern . . . Let's say things go badly. Will anyone be able to tell that we're mated? Could they use that against you?"

Rage flickered in his eyes. "If they see us together and can scent us both, they'll know."

"And if I show up alone, wearing a Night Court wedding ring—"

He snarled softly.

I closed the box, leaving the ring inside. "After we nullify the Cauldron, I want to do it all. Get the bond declared, get married, throw a stupid party and invite everyone in Velaris—all of it."

Rhys took the box from my hands and set it down on the nightstand before herding me toward the bed. "And if I wanted to go one step beyond that?"

"I'm listening," I purred as he laid me on the sheets.

CHAPTER 61

I'd never worn so much steel. Blades had been strapped all over me, hidden in my boots, my inside pockets. And then there was the Illyrian blade down my back.

Just a few hours ago, I'd known such overwhelming happiness after such horror and sorrow. Just a few hours ago, I'd been in his arms while he made love to me.

And now Rhysand, my mate and High Lord and partner, stood beside me in the foyer, Mor and Azriel and Cassian armed and ready in their scale-like armor, all of us too quiet.

Amren said, "The King of Hybern is old, Rhys—very old. Do not linger."

A voice near my chest whispered, *Hello lovely, wicked liar.*

The two halves of the Book of Breathings, each part tucked into a different pocket. In one of them, the spell I was to say had been written out clearly. I hadn't dared speak it, though I had read it a dozen times.

"We'll be in and out before you miss us," Rhysand said. "Guard Velaris well."

Amren studied my gloved hands and weapons. "That Cauldron," she said, "makes the Book seem harmless. If the spell fails, or if you cannot move it, then *leave*." I nodded. She surveyed us all again. "Fly well." I supposed that was as much concern as she'd show.

We turned to Mor—whose arms were out, waiting for me. Cassian and Rhys would winnow with Azriel, my mate dropped off a few miles from the coast before the Illyrians found Mor and me seconds later.

I moved toward her, but Rhys stepped in front of me, his face tense. I rose up on my toes and kissed him. "I'll be fine—we'll all be fine." His eyes held mine through the kiss, and when I broke away, his gaze went right to Cassian.

Cassian bowed. "With my life, High Lord. I'll protect her with my life."

Rhys looked to Azriel. He nodded, bowing, and said, "With both of our lives."

It was satisfactory enough to my mate—who at last looked at Mor.

She nodded once, but said, "I know my orders."

I wondered what those might be—why I hadn't been told—but she gripped my hand.

Before I could say good-bye to Amren, we were gone.

✢

Gone—and plunging through open air, toward a night-dark sea—

A warm body slammed into mine, catching me before I could panic and perhaps winnow myself somewhere. "Easy," Cassian said, banking right. I looked below to see Mor still plummeting, then winnow again into nothing.

No sign or glimmer of Rhys's presence near or behind us. A few yards ahead, Azriel was a swift shadow over the black water. Toward the landmass we were now approaching.

Hybern.

No lights burned on it. But it felt . . . old. As if it were a spider that had been waiting in its web for a long, long time.

"I've been here twice," Cassian murmured. "Both times, I was counting down the minutes until I could leave."

I could see why. A wall of bone-white cliffs arose, their tops flat and grassy, leading away to a terrain of sloping, barren hills. And an overwhelming sense of nothingness.

Amarantha had slaughtered all her slaves rather than free them. She had been a commander here—one of many. If that force that had attacked Velaris was a vanguard . . . I swallowed, flexing my hands beneath my gloves.

"That's his castle ahead," Cassian said through clenched teeth, swerving.

Around a bend in the coast, built into the cliffs and perched above the sea, was a lean, crumbling castle of white stone.

Not imperious marble, not elegant limestone, but . . . off-white. Bone-colored. Perhaps a dozen spires clawed at the night sky. A few lights flickered in the windows and balconies. No one outside—no patrol. "Where is everyone?"

"Guard shift." They'd planned this around it. "There's a small sea door at the bottom. Mor will be waiting for us there—it's the closest entrance to the lower levels."

"I'm assuming she can't winnow us in."

"Too many wards to risk the time it'd cost for her to break through them. Rhys might be able to. But we'll meet him at the door on the way out."

My mouth went a bit dry. Over my heart, the Book said, *Home—take me home.*

And indeed I could feel it. With every foot we flew in, faster and faster, dipping down so the spray from the ocean chilled me to my bones, I could feel it.

Ancient—cruel. Without allegiance to anyone but itself.

The Cauldron. They needn't have bothered learning where it was held inside this castle. I had no doubt I'd be drawn right to it. I shuddered.

"Easy," Cassian said again. We swept in toward the base of the cliffs to the sea door before a platform. Mor was waiting, sword out, the door open.

Cassian loosed a breath, but Azriel reached her first, landing swiftly and silently, and immediately prowled into the castle to scout the hall ahead.

Mor waited for us—her eyes on Cassian as we landed. They didn't speak, but their glance was too long to be anything but casual. I wondered what their training, their honed senses, detected.

The passage ahead was dark, silent. Azriel appeared a heartbeat later. "Guards are down." There was blood on his knife—an ash knife. Az's cold eyes met mine. "Hurry."

I didn't need to focus to track the Cauldron to its hiding place. It tugged on my every breath, hauling me to its dark embrace.

Any time we reached a crossroads, Cassian and Azriel would branch out, usually returning with bloodied blades, faces grim, silently warning me to hurry.

They'd been working these weeks, through whatever sources Azriel had, to get this encounter down to an exact schedule. If I needed more time than they'd allotted, if the Cauldron couldn't be moved . . . it might all be for nothing. But not these deaths. No, those I did not mind at all.

These people—these people had hurt Rhys. They'd brought *tools* with them to incapacitate him. They had sent that legion to wreck and butcher my city.

I descended through an ancient dungeon, the stones dark and stained. Mor kept at my side, constantly monitoring. The last line of defense.

If Cassian and Azriel were hurt, I realized, she was to make sure I got out by whatever means. Then return.

But there was no one in the dungeon—not that I encountered, once the Illyrians were done with them. They had executed this masterfully. We found another stairwell, leading down, down, down—

I pointed, nausea roiling. "There. It's down there."

Cassian took the stairs, Illyrian blade stained with dark blood.

Neither Mor nor Azriel seemed to breathe until Cassian's low whistle bounced off the stairwell stones from below.

Mor put a hand on my back, and we descended into the dark.

Home, the Book of Breathings sighed. *Home*.

Cassian was standing in a round chamber beneath the castle—a ball of faelight floating above his shoulder.

And in the center of the room, atop a small dais, sat the Cauldron.

CHAPTER 62

The Cauldron was absence and presence. Darkness and . . . whatever the darkness had come from.

But not life. Not joy or light or hope.

It was perhaps the size of a bathtub, forged of dark iron, its three legs—those three legs the king had ransacked those temples to find—crafted like creeping branches covered in thorns.

I had never seen something so hideous—and alluring.

Mor's face had drained of color. "Hurry," she said to me. "We've got a few minutes."

Azriel scanned the room, the stairs we'd strode down, the Cauldron, its legs. I made to approach the dais, but he extended an arm into my path. "Listen."

So we did.

Not words. But a throbbing.

Like blood pulsed through the room. Like the Cauldron had a heartbeat.

Like calls to like. I moved toward it. Mor was at my back, but didn't stop me as I stepped up onto the dais.

Inside the Cauldron was nothing but inky, swirling black.

Perhaps the entire universe had come from it.

Azriel and Cassian tensed as I laid a hand on the lip. Pain—pain and ecstasy and power and weakness flowed into me. Everything that was and wasn't, fire and ice, light and dark, deluge and drought.

The map for creation.

Reeling back into myself, I readied to read that spell.

The paper trembled as I pulled it from my pocket. As my fingers brushed the half of the Book inside.

Sweet-tongued liar, lady of many faces—

One hand on half of the Book of Breathings, the other on the Cauldron, I took a step outside myself, a jolt passing through my blood as if I were no more than a lightning rod.

Yes, you see now, princess of carrion—you see what you must do . . .

"Feyre," Mor murmured in warning.

But my mouth was foreign, my lips might as well have been as far away as Velaris while the Cauldron and the Book flowed through me, communing.

The other one, the Book hissed. *Bring the other one . . . let us be joined, let us be free.*

I slid the Book from my pocket, tucking it into the crook of my arm as I tugged the second half free. *Lovely girl, beautiful bird—so sweet, so generous . . .*

Together together together

"Feyre." Mor's voice cut through the song of both halves.

Amren had been wrong. Separate, their power was cleaved—not enough to take on the abyss of the Cauldron's might. But together . . . Yes, together, the spell would work when I spoke it.

Whole, I would become not a conduit between them, but rather their master. There was no moving the Cauldron—it had to be now.

Realizing what I was about to do, Mor lunged for me with a curse.

Too slow.

I laid the second half of the Book atop the other.

A silent ripple of power hollowed out my ears, buckled my bones.

Then nothing.

From far away, Mor said, "We can't risk—"

"Give her a minute," Cassian cut her off.

I was the Book and the Cauldron and sound and silence.

I was a living river through which one flowed into the other, eddying and ebbing, over and over, a tide with no end or beginning.

The spell—the words—

I looked to the paper in my hand, but my eyes did not see, my lips did not move.

I was not a tool, not a pawn. I would not be a conduit, not be the lackey of these *things*—

I'd memorized the spell. I would say it, breathe it, think it—

From the pit of my memory the first word formed. I slogged toward it, reaching for that one word, that one word that would be a tether back into myself, into who I was—

Strong hands tugged me back, wrenching me away.

Murky light and moldy stone poured into me, the room spinning as I gasped down breath, finding Azriel shaking me, eyes so wide I could see the white around them. What had happened, what—

Steps sounded above. Azriel instantly shoved me behind him, bloodied blade lifting.

The movement cleared my head enough to feel something wet and warm trickle down my lip and chin. Blood—my nose had been bleeding.

But those steps grew louder, and my friends had their weapons angled as a handsome brown-haired male swaggered down the steps. Human—his ears were round. But his eyes . . .

I knew the color of those eyes. I'd stared at one, encased in crystal, for three months.

"Stupid fool," he said to me.

"Jurian," I breathed.

CHAPTER 63

I gauged the distance between my friends and Jurian, weighed my sword against the twin ones crossed over his back. Cassian took a step toward the descending warrior and snarled, "*You.*"

Jurian snickered. "Worked your way up the ranks, did you? Congratulations."

I felt him sweep toward us. Like a ripple of night and wrath, Rhys appeared at my side. The Book was instantly gone, his movement so slick as he took it from me and tucked it into his own jacket that I barely registered it had happened.

But the moment that metal left my hands . . . Mother above, what had happened? I'd failed, failed so completely, been so pathetically overwhelmed by it—

"You look good, Jurian," Rhys said, strolling to Cassian's side—casually positioning himself between me and the ancient warrior. "For a corpse."

"Last time I saw you," Jurian sneered, "you were warming Amarantha's sheets."

"So you remember," Rhysand mused, even as my rage flared. "Interesting."

Jurian's eyes sliced to Mor. "Where is Miryam?"

"She's dead," Mor said flatly. The lie that had been told for five hundred years. "She and Drakon drowned in the Erythrian Sea." The impassive face of the princess of nightmares.

"Liar," Jurian crooned. "You were always such a liar, Morrigan."

Azriel growled, the sound unlike any I'd heard from him before.

Jurian ignored him, chest starting to heave. "*Where did you take Miryam?*"

"Away from you," Mor breathed. "I took her to Prince Drakon. They were mated and married that night you slaughtered Clythia. And she never thought of you again."

Wrath twisted his tan face. Jurian—hero of the human legions . . . who along the way had turned himself into a monster as awful as those he'd fought.

Rhys reached back to grab my hand. We'd seen enough. I gripped the rim of the Cauldron again, willing it to obey, to come with us. I braced for the wind and darkness.

Only they didn't come.

Mor gripped Cassian and Azriel's hands—and stayed still.

Jurian smiled.

Rhysand drawled, hand tightening in mine, "New trick?"

Jurian shrugged. "I was sent to distract you—while he worked his spell." His smile turned lupine. "You won't leave this castle unless he allows you to. Or in pieces."

My blood ran cold. Cassian and Azriel crouched into fighting stances, but Rhys cocked his head. I felt his dark power rise and rise, as if he'd splatter Jurian then and there.

But nothing happened. Not even a brush of night-flecked wind.

"Then there's that," Jurian said. "Didn't you remember? Perhaps you forgot. It was a good thing I was there, awake for every moment, Rhysand. She stole *his* book of spells—to take your powers."

Inside me, like a key clicking in a lock, that molten core of power just . . . halted. Whatever tether to it between my mind and soul was snipped—no, squeezed so tight by some invisible hand that nothing could flow.

I reached for Rhys's mind, for the bond—

I slammed into a hard wall. Not of adamant, but of foreign, unfeeling stone.

"He made sure," Jurian went on as I banged against that internal wall, tried to summon my own gifts to no avail, "that particular book was returned to him. She didn't know how to use half of the nastier spells. Do you know what it is like to be unable to sleep, to drink or eat or breathe or *feel* for five hundred years? Do you understand what it is like to be constantly awake, forced to watch everything she did?"

It had made him insane—tortured his soul until he went insane. That's what the sharp gleam was in his eyes.

"It couldn't have been so bad," Rhys said, even as I knew he was unleashing every ounce of will on that spell that contained us, bound us, "if you're now working for her master."

A flash of too-white teeth. "Your suffering will be long, and thorough."

"Sounds delightful," Rhys said, now turning us from the room. A silent shout to *run*.

But someone appeared atop the stairs.

I knew him—in my bones. The shoulder-length black hair, the ruddy skin, the clothes that edged more toward practicality than finery. He was of surprisingly average height, but muscled like a young man.

But his face—which looked perhaps like a human man in his forties . . . Blandly handsome. To hide the depthless, hateful black eyes that burned there.

The King of Hybern said, "The trap was so easy, I'm honestly a bit disappointed you didn't see it coming."

Faster than any of us could see, Jurian fired a hidden ash bolt through Azriel's chest.

Mor screamed.

We had no choice but to go with the king.

The ash bolt was coated in bloodbane that the King of Hybern claimed flowed where he willed it. If we fought, if we did not come with him upstairs, the poison would shoot to his heart. And with our magic locked down, without the ability to winnow . . .

If I could somehow get to Azriel, give him a mouthful of my blood . . . But it'd take too long, require too many moving parts.

Cassian and Rhys hauled Azriel between them, his blood splattering on the floor behind us as we went up the twisting stairways of the king's castle.

I tried not to step in it as Mor and I followed behind, Jurian at our backs. Mor was shaking—trying hard not to, but shaking as she stared at the protruding end of that arrow, visible between the gap in Azriel's wings.

None of us dared strike the King of Hybern where he stalked ahead, leading the way. He'd taken the Cauldron with him, vanishing it with a snap of his fingers and a wry look at me.

We knew the king wasn't bluffing. It'd take one move on their part for Azriel to die.

The guards were out now. And courtiers. High Fae and creatures—I didn't know where they fit in—who smiled like we were their next meal. Their eyes were all dead. Empty.

No furniture, no art. As if this castle were the skeleton of some mighty creature.

The throne room doors were open, and I balked. A throne room—*the* throne room that had honed Amarantha's penchant for public displays of cruelty. Faelights slithered along the bone-white walls, the windows looking out to the crashing sea far below.

The king mounted a dais carved of a single block of dark emerald—his throne assembled from the bones of . . . I felt the blood drain from my face. Human bones. Brown and smooth with age.

We stopped before it, Jurian leering at our backs. The throne room doors shut.

The king said to no one in particular, "Now that I've upheld my end of the bargain, I expect you to uphold yours." From the shadows near a side door, two figures emerged.

I began shaking my head as if I could unsee it as Lucien and Tamlin stepped into the light.

CHAPTER 64

Rhysand went still as death. Cassian snarled. Hanging between them, Azriel tried and failed to lift his head.

But I was staring at Tamlin—at that face I had loved and hated so deeply—as he halted a good twenty feet away from us.

He wore his bandolier of knives—Illyrian hunting-blades, I realized.

His golden hair was cut shorter, his face more gaunt than I'd last seen it. And his green eyes . . . Wide as they scanned me from head to toe. Wide as they took in my fighting leathers, the Illyrian sword and knives, the way I stood within my group of friends—my family.

He'd been working with the King of Hybern. "No," I breathed.

But Tamlin dared one more step closer, staring at me as if I were a ghost. Lucien, metal eye whirring, stopped him with a hand on his shoulder.

"No," I said again, this time louder.

"What was the cost," Rhysand said softly from my side. I clawed and tore at the wall separating our minds; heaved and pulled against that fist stifling my magic.

Tamlin ignored him, looking at the king at last. "You have my word."

The king smiled.

I took a step toward Tamlin. "*What have you done?*"

The King of Hybern said from his throne, "We made a bargain. I give you over, and he agrees to let my forces enter Prythian through his territory. And then use it as a base as we remove that ridiculous wall."

I shook my head. Lucien refused to meet the pleading stare I threw his way.

"You're insane," Cassian hissed.

Tamlin held out a hand. "Feyre." An order—like I was no better than a summoned dog.

I made no movement. I had to get free; had to get that damn power free—

"You," the king said, pointing a thick finger at me, "are a very difficult female to get ahold of. Of course, we've also agreed that you'll work for me once you've been returned home to your husband, but . . . Is it husband-to-be, or husband? I can't remember."

Lucien glanced between us all, face paling. "Tamlin," he murmured.

But Tamlin didn't lower the hand stretched toward me. "I'm taking you home."

I backed up a step—toward where Rhysand still held Azriel with Cassian.

"There's that other bit, too. The other thing I wanted," the king went on. "Well, Jurian wanted. Two birds with one stone, really. The High Lord of Night dead—and to learn who his friends were. It drove Jurian quite mad, honestly, that you never revealed it during those fifty years. So now you know, Jurian. And now you can do what you please with them."

Around me, my friends were tense—taut. Even Azriel was subtly moving a bloody, scarred hand closer to his blades. His blood pooled at the edge of my boots.

I said steadily, clearly, to Tamlin, "I'm not going anywhere with you."

"You'll say differently, my dear," the king countered, "when I complete the final part of my bargain."

Horror coiled in my gut.

The king jerked his chin at my left arm. "Break that bond between you two."

"Please," I whispered.

"How else is Tamlin to have his bride? He can't very well have a wife who runs off to another male once a month."

Rhys remained silent, though his grip tightened on Azriel. Observing—weighing, sorting through the lock on his power. The thought of that silence between our souls being permanent . . .

My voice cracked as I said to Tamlin, still at the opposite end of the crude half circle we'd formed before the dais, "Don't. Don't let him. I told you—I *told you* that I was fine. That I left—"

"You weren't well," Tamlin snarled. "He *used* that bond to manipulate you. Why do you think I was gone so often? I was looking for a way to get you *free*. And you *left*."

"I left because I was going to *die* in that house!"

The King of Hybern clicked his tongue. "Not what you expected, is it?"

Tamlin growled at him, but again held out his hand toward me. "Come home with me. Now."

"No."

"Feyre." An unflinching command.

Rhys was barely breathing—barely moving.

And I realized . . . realized it was to keep his scent from becoming apparent. Our scent. Our mating bond.

Jurian's sword was already out—and he was looking at Mor as if he was going to kill her first. Azriel's blood-drained face twisted with rage as he noticed that stare. Cassian, still holding him upright, took them all in, assessing, readying himself to fight, to defend.

I stopped beating at the fist on my power. Stroked it gently—lovingly.

I am Fae and not-Fae, all and none, I told the spell that gripped me. *You do not hold me. I am as you are—real and not, little more than gathered wisps of power. You do not hold me.*

"I'll come with you," I said softly to Tamlin, to Lucien, shifting on his feet, "if you leave them alone. Let them go."

You do not hold me.

Tamlin's face contorted with wrath. "They're monsters. They're—" He didn't finish as he stalked across the floor to grab me. To drag me out of here, then no doubt winnow away.

You do not hold me.

The fist gripping my power relaxed. Vanished.

Tamlin lunged for me over the few feet that remained. So fast—too fast—

I became mist and shadow.

I winnowed beyond his reach. The king let out a low laugh as Tamlin stumbled.

And went sprawling as Rhysand's fist connected with his face.

Panting, I retreated right into Rhysand's arms as one looped around my waist, as Azriel's blood on him soaked into my back. Behind us, Mor leaped in to fill the space Rhys had vacated, slinging Azriel's arm over her shoulders.

But that wall of hideous stone remained in my mind, and still blocked Rhys's own power.

Tamlin rose, wiping the blood now trickling from his nose as he backed to where Lucien held his position with a hand on his sword.

But just as Tamlin neared his Emissary, he staggered a step. His face went white with rage.

And I knew Tamlin understood a moment before the king laughed. "I don't believe it. Your bride left you only to find her mate. The Mother has a warped sense of humor, it seems. And what a talent—tell me, girl: how did you unravel that spell?"

I ignored him. But the hatred in Tamlin's eyes made my knees buckle. "I'm sorry," I said, and meant it.

Tamlin's eyes were on Rhysand, his face near-feral. "*You,*" he snarled, the sound more animal than Fae. "*What did you do to her?*"

Behind us, the doors opened and soldiers poured in. Some looked like the Attor. Some looked worse. More and more, filling up the room, the exits, armor and weapons clanking.

Mor and Cassian, Azriel sagging and heavy-lidded between them, scanned each soldier and weapon, sizing up our best odds of escape. I left them to it as Rhys and I faced Tamlin.

"I'm not going with you," I spat at Tamlin. "And even if I did . . . You spineless, *stupid* fool for selling us out to *him*! Do you know what he wants to do with that Cauldron?"

"Oh, I'm going to do many, many things with it," the king said.

And the Cauldron appeared again between us.

"Starting now."

Kill him kill him kill him

I could not tell if the voice was mine or the Cauldron's. I didn't care. I unleashed myself.

Talons and wings and shadows were instantly around me, surrounded by water and fire—

Then they vanished, stifled as that invisible hand gripped my power again, so hard I gasped.

"Ah," the king said to me, clicking his tongue, "that. Look at you. A child of all seven courts—like and unlike all. How the Cauldron purrs in your presence. Did you plan to use it? Destroy it? With that book, you could do anything you wished."

I didn't say anything. The king shrugged. "You'll tell me soon enough."

"I made no bargain with you."

"No, but your master did, so you will obey."

Molten rage poured into me. I hissed at Tamlin, "If you bring me from here, if you take me from my mate, I will *destroy* you. I will destroy your court, and everything you hold dear."

Tamlin's lips thinned. But he said simply, "You don't know what you're talking about."

Lucien cringed.

The king jerked his chin to the guards by the side door through which Tamlin and Lucien had appeared. "No—she doesn't." The doors opened again. "There will be no destroying," the king went on as people—as *women* walked through those doors.

Four women. Four humans. The four remaining queens.

"Because," the king said, the queens' guards falling into rank behind them, hauling something in the core of their formation, "you will find, Feyre Archeron, that it is in your best interest to behave."

The four queens sneered at us with hate in their eyes. Hate.

And parted to let their personal guards through.

Fear like I had never known entered my heart as the men dragged my sisters, gagged and bound, before the King of Hybern.

CHAPTER 65

This was some new hell. Some new level of nightmare. I even went so far as to try to wake myself up.

But there they were—in their nightgowns, the silk and lace dirty, torn.

Elain was quietly sobbing, the gag soaked with her tears. Nesta, hair disheveled as if she'd fought like a wildcat, was panting as she took us in. Took in the Cauldron.

"You made a very big mistake," the king said to Rhysand, my mate's arms banded around me, "the day you went after the Book. I had no need of it. I was content to let it lie hidden. But the moment your forces started sniffing around . . . I decided who better than to be my liaison to the human realm than my newly reborn friend, Jurian? He'd just finished all those months of recovering from the process, and longed to see what his former home had become, so he was more than happy to visit the continent for an extended visit."

Indeed the queens smiled at him—bowed their heads. Rhys's arms tightened in silent warning.

"The brave, cunning Jurian, who suffered so badly at the end of the

War—now my ally. Here to help me convince these queens to aid in my cause. For a price of his own, of course, but it has no bearing here. And wiser to work with me, my men, than to allow you monsters in the Night Court to rule and attack. Jurian was right to warn their Majesties that you'd try to take the Book—that you would feed them lies of love and goodness, when *he* had seen what the High Lord of the Night Court was capable of. The hero of the human forces, reborn as a gesture to the human world of my good faith. I do not wish to invade the continent—but to work with them. My powers ensconced their court from *prying* eyes, just to show them the benefits." A smirk at Azriel, who could hardly lift his head to snarl back. "Such impressive attempts to infiltrate their sacred palace, Shadowsinger—and utter proof to their Majesties, of course, that your court is not as benevolent as you seem."

"Liar," I hissed, and whirled on the queens, daring only a step away from Rhys. "They are *liars*, and if you do not let my sisters go, I will *slaughter*—"

"Do you hear the threats, the language they use in the Night Court?" the king said to the mortal queens, their guards now around us in a half circle. "Slaughter, ultimatums . . . They wish to end life. I desire to give it."

The eldest queen said to him, refusing to acknowledge me, my words, "Then show us—prove this gift you mentioned."

Rhysand tugged me back against him. He said quietly to the queen, "You're a fool."

The king cut in, "Is she? Why submit to old age and ailments when what I offer is so much better?" He waved a hand toward me. "Eternal youth. Do you deny the benefits? A mortal queen becomes one who might reign forever. Of course, there are risks—the transition can be . . . difficult. But a strong-willed individual could survive."

The youngest queen, the dark-haired one, smiled slightly. Arrogant youth—and bitter old age. Only the two others, the ones who wore white and black, seemed to hesitate, stepping closer to each other—and their towering guards.

The ancient queen lifted her chin, "Show us. Demonstrate it can be done, that it is safe." She had spoken of eternal youth that day, had spat in my face about it. Two-faced *bitch*.

The king nodded. "Why did you think I asked my dear friend Ianthe to see who Feyre Archeron would appreciate having with her for eternity?" Even as horror filled my ears with roaring silence, I glanced at the queens, the question no doubt written on my face. The king explained, "Oh, I asked them first. They deemed it too . . . uncouth to betray two young, misguided women. Ianthe had no such qualms. Consider it my wedding present for you both," he added to Tamlin.

But Tamlin's face tightened. "What?"

The king cocked his head, savoring every word. "I think the High Priestess was waiting until your return to tell you, but didn't you ever ask *why* she believed I might be able to break the bargain? Why she had so many musings on the idea? So many millennia have the High Priestesses been forced to their knees for the High Lords. And during those years she dwelled in that foreign court . . . such an open mind, she has. Once we met, once I painted for her a portrait of a Prythian free of High Lords, where the High Priestesses might rule with grace and wisdom . . . She didn't take much convincing."

I was going to vomit. Tamlin, to his credit, looked like he might, too.

Lucien's face had slackened. "She sold out—she sold out Feyre's family. To you."

I had told Ianthe everything about my sisters. She had asked. Asked who they were, where they lived. And I had been so stupid, so broken . . . I had fed her every detail.

"Sold out?" The king snorted. "Or saved from the shackles of mortal death? Ianthe suggested they were both strong-willed women, like their sister. No doubt they'll survive. And prove to our queens it *can* be done. If one has the strength."

My heart stopped. "*Don't you—*

The king cut me off, "I would suggest bracing yourselves."

And then hell exploded in the hall.

Power, white and unending and hideous, barreled into us.

All I knew was Rhysand's body covering mine as we were all thrown to the floor, the shout of pain as he took the brunt of the king's power.

Cassian twisted, wings flaring wide as he shielded Azriel.

His wings—his wings—

Cassian's scream as his wings shredded under talons of pure magic was the most horrific sound I'd ever heard. Mor surged for him, but too late.

Rhys was moving in an instant, as if he'd lunge for the king, but power hit us again, and again. Rhys slammed to his knees.

My sisters were shrieking over their gags. But Elain's cry—a warning. A warning to—

To my right, now exposed, Tamlin ran for me. To grab me at last.

I hurled a knife at him—as hard as I could.

He had to dive to miss it. And he backed away at the second one I had ready, gaping at me, at Rhys, as if he could indeed see the mating bond between us.

But I whirled as soldiers pressed in, cutting us off. Whirled, and saw Cassian and Azriel on the ground, Jurian laughing softly at the blood gushing from Cassian's ravaged wings—

Shreds of them remained.

I scrambled for him. My blood. It might be enough, be—

Mor, on her knees beside Cassian, hurtled for the king with a cry of pure wrath.

He sent a punch of power to her. She dodged, a knife angled in her hand, and—

Azriel cried out in pain.

She froze. Stopped a foot from the throne. Her knife clattered to the floor.

The king rose. "What a mighty queen you are," he breathed.

And Mor backed away. Step by step.

"What a prize," the king said, that black gaze devouring her.

Azriel's head lifted from where he was sprawled in his own blood, eyes full of rage and pain as he snarled at the king, "*Don't you touch her.*"

Mor looked at Azriel—and there was real fear there. Fear—and something else. She didn't stop moving until she again kneeled beside him and pressed a hand to his wound. Azriel hissed—but covered her bloody fingers with his own.

Rhys positioned himself between me and the king as I dropped to my knees before Cassian. I ripped at the leather covering my forearm—

"Put the prettier one in first," the king said, Mor already forgotten.

I twisted—only to have the king's guards grab me from behind. Rhys was instantly there, but Azriel shouted, back arching as the king's poison worked its way in.

"Please refrain," the king said, "from getting any stupid ideas, Rhysand." He smiled at me. "If any of you interfere, the shadowsinger dies. Pity about the other brute's wings." He gave my sisters a mockery of a bow. "Ladies, eternity awaits. Prove to their Majesties the Cauldron is safe for . . . strong-willed individuals."

I shook my head, unable to breathe, to think a way out of it—

Elain was shaking, sobbing, as she was hauled forward. Toward the Cauldron.

Nesta began thrashing against the men that held her.

Tamlin said, "Stop."

The king did no such thing.

Lucien, beside Tamlin, again put a hand on his sword. "Stop this."

Nesta was bellowing at the guards, at the king, as Elain yielded step after step toward that Cauldron. As the king waved his hand, and liquid filled it to the brim. *No, no*—

The queens only watched, stone-faced. And Rhys and Mor, separated from me by those guards, did not dare to even shift a muscle.

Tamlin spat at the king, "This is not part of our deal. *Stop this now.*"

"I don't care," the king said simply.

Tamlin launched himself at the throne, as if he'd rip him to shreds.

That white-hot magic slammed into him, shoving him to the ground. Leashing him.

Tamlin strained against the collar of light on his neck, around his wrists. His golden power flared—to no avail. I tore at the fist still gripping my own, sliced at it, over and over—

Lucien staggered a step forward as Elain was gripped between two guards and hoisted up. She began kicking then, weeping while her feet slammed into the sides of the Cauldron as if she'd push off it, as if she'd knock it down—

"*That is enough.*" Lucien surged for Elain, for the Cauldron.

And the king's power leashed him, too. On the ground beside Tamlin, his single eye wide, Lucien had the good sense to look horrified as he glanced between Elain and the High Lord.

"Please," I begged the king, who motioned Elain to be shoved into the water. "Please, I will do anything, I will give you anything." I shot to my feet, stepping away from where Cassian lay prostrate, and looked to the queens. "Please—you do not need proof, I am proof that it works. Jurian is proof it is safe."

The ancient queen said, "You are a thief, and a liar. You conspired with our sister. Your punishment should be the same as hers. Consider this a gift instead."

Elain's foot hit the water, and she screamed—screamed in terror that hit me so deep I began sobbing. "Please," I said to none of them.

Nesta was still fighting, still roaring through her gag.

Elain, who Nesta would have killed and whored and stolen for. Elain, who had been gentle and sweet. Elain, who was to marry a lord's son who hated faeries . . .

The guards shoved my sister into the Cauldron in a single movement.

My cry hadn't finished sounding before Elain's head went under.

She did not come up.

Nesta's screaming was the only sound. Cassian blindly lurched toward it—toward her, moaning in pain.

The King of Hybern bowed slightly to the queens. "Behold."

Rhys, a wall of guards still cleaving us, curled his fingers into a fist. But he did not move, as Mor and I did not dare move, not with Azriel's life dangling in the king's grasp.

And as if it had been tipped by invisible hands, the Cauldron turned on its side.

More water than seemed possible dumped out in a cascade. Black, smoke-coated water.

And Elain, as if she'd been thrown by a wave, washed onto the stones facedown.

Her legs were so pale—so delicate. I couldn't remember the last time I'd seen them bare.

The queens pushed forward. Alive, she had to be *alive*, had to have wanted to live—

Elain sucked in a breath, her fine-boned back rising, her wet nightgown nearly sheer.

And as she rose from the ground onto her elbows, the gag in place, as she twisted to look at me—

Nesta began roaring again.

Pale skin started to glow. Her face had somehow become more beautiful—infinitely beautiful, and her ears . . . Elain's ears were now pointed beneath her sodden hair.

The queens gasped. And for a moment, all I could think of was my father. What he would do, what he would say, when his most beloved daughter looked at him with a Fae face.

"So we can survive," the dark-haired youngest breathed, eyes bright.

I fell to my knees, the guards not bothering to grab me as I sobbed. What he'd done, what he'd done—

"The hellcat now, if you'll be so kind," the King of Hybern said.

I whipped my head to Nesta as she went silent. The Cauldron righted itself.

Cassian again stirred, slumping on the floor—but his hand twitched. Toward Nesta.

Elain was still shivering on the wet stones, her nightgown shoved up to her thighs, her small breasts fully visible beneath the soaked fabric. Guards snickered.

Lucien snarled at the king over the bite of the magic at his throat, "*Don't just leave her on the damned floor*—"

There was a flare of light, and a scrape, and then Lucien was stalking toward Elain, freed of his restraints. Tamlin remained leashed on the ground, a gag of white, iridescent magic in his mouth now. But his eyes were on Lucien as—

As Lucien took off his jacket, kneeling before Elain. She cringed away from the coat, from him—

The guards hauled Nesta toward the Cauldron.

There were different kinds of torture, I realized.

There was the torture that I had endured, that Rhys had endured.

And then there was this.

The torture that Rhys had worked so hard those fifty years to avoid; the nightmares that haunted him. To be unable to move, to fight . . . while our loved ones were broken. My eyes met with those of my mate. Agony rippled in that violet stare—rage and guilt and utter agony. The mirror to my own.

Nesta fought every step of the way.

She did not make it easy for them. She clawed and kicked and bucked.

And it was not enough.

And we were not enough to save her.

I watched as she was hoisted up. Elain remained shuddering on the ground, Lucien's coat draped around her. She did not look at the Cauldron behind her, not as Nesta's thrashing feet slammed into the water.

Cassian stirred again, his shredded wings twitching and spraying blood, his muscles quivering. At Nesta's shouts, her raging, his eyes fluttered open, glazed and unseeing, an answer to some call in his blood, a promise he'd made her. But pain knocked him under again.

Nesta was shoved into the water up to her shoulders. She bucked even as the water sprayed. She clawed and screamed her rage, her defiance.

"*Put her under*," the king hissed.

The guards, straining, shoved her slender shoulders. Her brown-gold head.

And as they pushed her head down, she thrashed one last time, freeing her long, pale arm.

Teeth bared, Nesta pointed one finger at the King of Hybern.

One finger, a curse and a damning.

A promise.

And as Nesta's head was forced under the water, as that hand was violently shoved down, the King of Hybern had the good sense to look somewhat unnerved.

Dark water lapped for a moment. The surface went flat.

I vomited on the floor.

The guards at last let Rhysand kneel beside me in the growing pool of Cassian's blood—let him tuck me into him as the Cauldron again tilted.

Water poured forth, Lucien hoisting Elain in his arms and out of the way. The bonds on Tamlin vanished, along with the gag. He was instantly on his feet, snarling at the king. Even the fist on my mind lightened to a mere caress. As if he knew he'd won.

I didn't care. Not as Nesta was sprawled upon the stones.

I knew that she was different.

From however Elain had been Made . . . Nesta was different.

Even before she took her first breath, I felt it.

As if the Cauldron in making her . . . had been forced to give more than it wanted. As if Nesta had fought even after she went under, and had decided that if she was to be dragged into hell, she was taking that Cauldron with her.

As if that finger she'd pointed was now a death-promise to the King of Hybern.

Nesta took a breath. And when I beheld my sister, with her somehow magnified beauty, her ears . . . When Nesta looked to me . . .

Rage. Power. Cunning.

Then it was gone, horror and shock crumpling her face, but she didn't pause, didn't halt. She was free—she was loose.

She was on her feet, tripping over her slightly longer, leaner limbs, ripping the gag from her mouth—

Nesta slammed into Lucien, grabbing Elain from his arms, and screamed at him as he fell back, "*Get off her!*"

Elain's feet slipped against the floor, but Nesta gripped her upright, running her hands over Elain's face, her shoulders, her hair— "*Elain, Elain, Elain*," she sobbed.

Cassian again stirred—trying to rise, to answer Nesta's voice as she held my sister and cried her name again and again.

But Elain was staring over Nesta's shoulder.

At Lucien—whose face she had finally taken in.

Dark brown eyes met one eye of russet and one of metal.

Nesta was still weeping, still raging, still inspecting Elain—

Lucien's hands slackened at his sides.

His voice broke as he whispered to Elain, "You're my mate."

CHAPTER 66

I didn't let Lucien's declaration sink in.

Nesta, however, whirled on him. "She is *no such thing*," she said, and shoved him again.

Lucien didn't move an inch. His face was pale as death as he stared at Elain. My sister said nothing, the iron ring glinting dully on her finger.

The King of Hybern murmured, "Interesting. So very interesting." He turned to the queens. "See? I showed you not once, but twice that it is safe. Who should like to be Made first? Perhaps you'll get a handsome Fae lord as your mate, too."

The youngest queen stepped forward, her eyes indeed darting between all the Fae men assembled. As if they were hers for the picking.

The king chuckled. "Very well, then."

Hate flooded me, so violent I had no control over it, no song in my heart but its war-cry. I was going to kill them. I was going to kill *all* of them—

"If you're so willing to hand out bargains," Rhys suddenly said, rising to his feet and tugging me with him, "perhaps I'll make one with you."

"Oh?"

Rhys shrugged.

No. No more bargains—no more sacrifices. No more giving himself away piece by piece.

No more.

And if the king refused, if there was nothing to do but watch my friends die . . .

I could not accept it. I could not endure it—not that.

And for Rhys, for the family I'd found . . . They had not needed me—not really. Only to nullify the Cauldron.

I had failed them. Just as I had failed my sisters, whose lives I'd now shattered . . .

I thought of that ring waiting for me at home. I thought of the ring on Elain's finger, from a man who would now likely hunt her down and kill her. If Lucien let her leave at all.

I thought of all the things I wanted to paint—and never would.

But for them—for my family both of blood and my own choosing, for my mate . . . The idea that hit me did not seem so frightening.

And so I was not afraid.

I dropped to my knees in a spasm, gripping my head as I gnashed my teeth and sobbed, sobbed and panted, pulling at my hair—

The fist of that spell didn't have time to seize me again as I exploded past it.

Rhys reached for me, but I unleashed my power, a flash of that white, pure light, all that could escape with the damper from the king's spell. A flash of the light that was only for Rhys, only because of Rhys. I hoped he understood.

It erupted through the room, the gathered force hissing and dropping back.

Even Rhys had frozen—the king and queens openmouthed. My sisters and Lucien had whirled, too.

But there, deep within Day's light . . . I gleaned it. A purifying, clear power. Cursebreaker—spellbreaker. The light wiped through every physical trapping, showing me the snarls of spells and glamours, showing me the way through . . . I burned brighter, looking, looking—

Buried inside the bone-walls of the castle, the wards were woven strong.

I sent that blinding light flaring once more—a distraction and sleight of hand as I severed the wards at their ancient arteries.

Now I only had to play my part.

The light faded, and I was curled on the floor, head in my hands.

Silence. Silence as they all gawked at me.

Even Jurian had stopped gloating from where he now leaned against the wall.

But my eyes were only on Tamlin as I lowered my hands, gulping down air, and blinked. I looked at the host and the blood and the Night Court, and then finally back at him as I breathed, "Tamlin?"

He didn't move an inch. Beyond him, the king gaped at me. Whether he knew I'd ripped his wards wide open, whether he knew it was intentional, was not my concern—not yet.

I blinked again, as if clearing my head. "Tamlin?" I peered at my hands, the blood, and when I beheld Rhys, when I saw my grim-faced friends, and my drenched, immortal sisters—

There was nothing but shock and confusion on Rhys's face as I scrambled back from him.

Away from them. Toward Tamlin. "Tamlin," I managed to say again. Lucien's eye widened as he stepped between me and Elain. I whirled on the King of Hybern. "Where—" I again faced Rhysand. "What did you do to me," I breathed, low and guttural. Backing toward Tamlin. "*What did you do?*"

Get them out. Get my sisters out.

Play—please play along. Please—

There was no sound, no shield, no glimmer of feeling in our bond. The king's power had blocked it out too thoroughly. There was nothing I could do against it, Cursebreaker or no.

But Rhys slid his hands into his pockets as he purred, "How did you get free?"

"What?" Jurian seethed, pushing off the wall and storming toward us.

But I turned toward Tamlin and ignored the features and smell and clothes that were all wrong. He watched me warily. "Don't let him take me again, don't let him—don't—" I couldn't keep the sobs from shuddering out, not as the full force of what I was doing hit me.

"Feyre," Tamlin said softly. And I knew I had won.

I sobbed harder.

Get my sisters out, I begged Rhys through the silent bond. *I ripped the wards open for you—all of you. Get them out.*

"Don't let him take me," I sobbed again. "I don't want to go back."

And when I looked at Mor, at the tears streaming down her face as she helped Cassian get upright, I knew she realized what I meant. But the tears vanished—became sorrow for Cassian as she turned a hateful, horrified face to Rhysand and spat, "What did you do to that girl?"

Rhys cocked his head. "How did you do it, Feyre?" There was so much blood on him. One last game—this was one last game we were to play together.

I shook my head. The queens had fallen back, their guards forming a wall between us.

Tamlin watched me carefully. So did Lucien.

So I turned to the king. He was smiling. Like he knew.

But I said, "Break the bond."

Rhysand went still as death.

I stormed to the king, knees barking as I dropped to the floor before his throne. "Break the bond. The bargain, the—the mating bond. He—he made me do it, made me swear it—"

"No," Rhysand said.

I ignored him, even as my heart broke, even as I knew that he hadn't meant to say it— "Do it," I begged the king, even as I silently prayed he wouldn't notice his ruined wards, the door I'd left wide open. "I know you can. Just—free me. Free me from it."

"*No*," Rhysand said.

But Tamlin was staring between us. And I looked at him, the High Lord I had once loved, and I breathed, "No more. No more death—no more killing." I sobbed through my clenched teeth. Made myself look at my sisters. "*No more.* Take me *home* and let them go. Tell him it's part of the bargain and let them go. But no more—please."

Cassian slowly, every movement pained, stirred enough to look over a shredded wing at me. And in his pain-glazed eyes, I saw it—the understanding.

The Court of Dreams. I had belonged to a court of dreams. And dreamers.

And for their dreams . . . for what they had worked for, sacrificed for . . . I could do it.

Get my sisters out, I said to Rhys one last time, sending it into that stone wall between us.

I looked to Tamlin. "No more." Those green eyes met mine—and the sorrow and tenderness in them was the most hideous thing I'd ever seen. "Take me home."

Tamlin said flatly to the king, "Let them go, break her bond, and let's be done with it. Her sisters come with us. You've already crossed too many lines."

Jurian began objecting, but the king said, "Very well."

"No," was all Rhys said again.

Tamlin snarled at him, "I don't give a *shit* if she's your mate. I don't give a shit if you think you're entitled to her. She is *mine*—and one day, I am going to repay every bit of pain she felt, every bit of suffering and despair. One day, perhaps when she decides she wants to end you, I'll be happy to oblige her."

Walk away—just go. Take my sisters with you.

Rhys was only staring at me. "Don't."

But I backed away—until I hit Tamlin's chest, until his hands, warm and heavy, landed on my shoulders. "Do it," he said to the king.

"No," Rhys said again, his voice breaking.

But the king pointed at me. And I screamed.

Tamlin gripped my arms as I screamed and screamed at the pain that tore through my chest, my left arm.

Rhysand was on the ground, roaring, and I thought he might have said my name, might have bellowed it as I thrashed and sobbed. I was being shredded, I was dying, I was dying—

No. No, I didn't want it, I didn't want to—

A crack sounded in my ears.

And the world cleaved in two as the bond snapped.

CHAPTER 67

I fainted.

When I opened my eyes, mere seconds had passed. Mor was now hauling away Rhys, who was panting on the floor, eyes wild, fingers clenching and unclenching—

Tamlin yanked off the glove on my left hand.

Pure, bare skin greeted him. No tattoo.

I was sobbing and sobbing, and his arms came around me. Every inch of them felt wrong. I nearly gagged on his scent.

Mor let go of Rhysand's jacket collar, and he crawled—*crawled* back toward Azriel and Cassian, their blood splashing on his hands, on his neck, as he hauled himself through it. His rasping breaths sliced into me, my soul—

The king merely waved a hand at him. "You are free to go, Rhysand. Your friend's poison is gone. The wings on the other, I'm afraid, are a bit of a mess."

Don't fight it—don't say anything, I begged him as Rhys reached his brothers. *Take my sisters. The wards are down.*

Silence.

So I looked—just once—at Rhysand, and Cassian, and Mor, and Azriel.

They were already looking at me. Faces bloody and cold and enraged. But beneath them . . . I knew it was love beneath them. They understood the tears that rolled down my face as I silently said good-bye.

Then Mor, swift as an adder, winnowed to Lucien. To my sisters. To show Rhys, I realized, what I'd done, the hole I'd blasted for them to escape—

She slammed Lucien away with a palm to the chest, and his roar shook the halls as Mor grabbed my sisters by the arm and vanished.

Lucien's bellow was still sounding as Rhys lunged, gripping Azriel and Cassian, and did not even turn toward me as they winnowed out.

The king shot to his feet, spewing his wrath at his guards, at Jurian, for not grabbing my sisters. Demanding to know what had happened to the castle wards—

I barely heard him. There was only silence in my head. Such silence where there had once been dark laughter and wicked amusement. A wind-blasted wasteland.

Lucien was shaking his head, panting, and whirled to us. "*Get her back*," he snarled at Tamlin over the ranting of the king. A mate—a mate already going wild to defend what was his.

Tamlin ignored him. So I did, too. I could barely stand, but I faced the king as he slumped into his throne, gripping the arms so tightly the whites of his knuckles showed. "Thank you," I breathed, a hand on my chest—the skin so pale, so white. "Thank you."

He merely said to the gathered queens, now a healthy distance away, "Begin."

The queens looked at each other, then their wide-eyed guards, and snaked toward the Cauldron, their smiles growing. Wolves circling prey. One of them sniped at another for pushing her—the king murmured something to them all that I didn't bother to hear.

Jurian stalked over to Lucien amid the rising squabble, laughing under his breath. "Do you know what Illyrian bastards do to pretty females? You won't have a mate left—at least not one that's useful to you in any way."

Lucien's answering growl was nothing short of feral.

I spat at Jurian's feet. "You can go to hell, you hideous prick."

Tamlin's hands tightened on my shoulders. Lucien spun toward me, and that metal eye whirred and narrowed. Centuries of cultivated reason clicked into place.

I was not panicking at my sisters being taken.

I said quietly, "We will get her back."

But Lucien was watching me warily. Too warily.

I said to Tamlin, "Take me home."

But the king cut in over the bickering of the queens, "Where is it."

I preferred the amused, arrogant voice to the flat, brutal one that sliced through the hall.

"You—*you* were to wield the Book of Breathings," the king said. "I could feel it in here, with . . ."

The entire castle shuddered as he realized I had not been holding it in my jacket.

I just said to him, "Your mistake."

His nostrils flared. Even the sea far below seemed to recoil in terror at the wrath that whitened his ruddy face. But he blinked and it was gone. He said tightly to Tamlin, "When the Book is retrieved, I expect your presence here."

Power, smelling of lilac and cedar and the first bits of green, swirled around me. Readying us to winnow away—through the wards they had no inkling I'd smashed apart.

So I said to the king, and Jurian, and the queens assembled, already at the lip of the Cauldron and hissing over who would go in first, "I will light your pyres myself for what you did to my sisters."

Then we were gone.

CHAPTER 68

Rhysand

I slammed into the floor of the town house, and Amren was instantly there, hands on Cassian's wings, swearing at the damage. Then at the hole in Azriel's chest.

Even her healing couldn't fix both. No, we'd need a real healer for each of them, and fast, because if Cassian lost those wings . . . I knew he'd prefer death. Any Illyrian would.

"Where is she?" Amren demanded.

Where is she where is she where is she

"Get the Book out of here," I said, dumping the pieces onto the ground. I hated the touch of them, their madness and despair and joy. Amren ignored the order.

Mor hadn't appeared—dropping off or hiding Nesta and Elain wherever she deemed safest.

"Where is she?" Amren said again, pressing a hand to Cassian's ravaged back. I knew she didn't mean Mor.

As if my thoughts had summoned her, my cousin appeared—panting, haggard. She dropped to the floor before Azriel, her blood-caked hands shaking as she ripped the arrow free of his chest, blood showering the carpet. She shoved her fingers over the wound, light flaring as her power knit bone and flesh and vein together.

"*Where is she?*" Amren snapped one more time.

I couldn't bring myself to say the words.

So Mor said them for me as she knelt over Azriel, both of my brothers mercifully unconscious. "Tamlin offered passage through his lands and our heads on platters to the king in exchange for trapping Feyre, breaking her bond, and getting to bring her back to the Spring Court. But Ianthe betrayed Tamlin—told the king where to find Feyre's sisters. So the king had Feyre's sisters brought with the queens—to prove he could make them immortal. He put them in the Cauldron. We could do nothing as they were turned. He had us by the balls."

Those quicksilver eyes shot to me. "Rhysand."

I managed to say, "We were out of options, and Feyre knew it. So she pretended to free herself from the control Tamlin thought I'd kept on her mind. Pretended that she . . . hated us. And told him she'd go home—but only if the killing stopped. If we went free."

"And the bond," Amren breathed, Cassian's blood shining on her hands as she slowed its dribbling.

Mor said, "She asked the king to break the bond. He obliged."

I thought I might be dying—thought my chest might actually be cleaved in two.

"That's impossible," Amren said. "That sort of bond cannot be broken."

"The king said he could do it."

"The king is a fool," Amren barked. "That sort of bond *cannot* be broken."

"No, it can't," I said.

They both looked at me.

I cleared my head, my shattering heart—breaking for what my mate had done, sacrificed for me and my family. For her sisters. Because she hadn't thought . . . hadn't thought she was essential. Even after all she had done. "The king broke the bargain between us. Hard to do, but he couldn't tell that it wasn't the mating bond."

Mor started. "Does—does Feyre know—"

"Yes," I breathed. "And now my mate is in our enemy's hands."

"Go get her," Amren hissed. "*Right now*."

"*No*," I said, and hated the word.

They gaped at me, and I wanted to roar at the sight of the blood coating them, at my unconscious and suffering brothers on the carpet before them.

But I managed to say to my cousin, "Weren't you listening to what Feyre said to him? She promised to destroy him—from within."

Mor's face paled, her magic flaring on Azriel's chest. "She's going into that house to take him down. To take them all down."

I nodded. "She is now a spy—with a direct line to me. What the King of Hybern does, where he goes, what his plans are, she will know. And report back."

For between us, faint and soft, hidden so none might find it . . . between us lay a whisper of color, and joy, of light and shadow—a whisper of *her*. Our bond.

"She's your mate," Amren bit at me. "Not your spy. *Go get her*."

"She is my mate. And my spy," I said too quietly. "And she is the High Lady of the Night Court."

"What?" Mor whispered.

I caressed a mental finger down that bond now hidden deep, deep within us, and said, "If they had removed her other glove, they would have seen a second tattoo on her right arm. The twin to the other. Inked last night, when we crept out, found a priestess, and I swore her in as my High Lady."

"Not—not consort," Amren blurted, blinking. I hadn't seen her surprised in . . . centuries.

"Not consort, not wife. Feyre is High Lady of the Night Court." My equal in every way; she would wear my crown, sit on a throne beside mine. Never sidelined, never designated to breeding and parties and child-rearing. My queen.

As if in answer, a glimmer of love shuddered down the bond. I clamped down on the relief that threatened to shatter any calm I feigned having.

"You mean to tell me," Mor breathed, "that my High Lady is now surrounded by enemies?" A lethal sort of calm crept over her tear-stained face.

"I mean to tell you," I said, watching the blood clot on Cassian's wings with Amren's tending. Beneath Mor's own hands, Azriel's bleeding at last eased. Enough to keep them alive until the healer got here. "I mean to tell you," I said again, my power building and rubbing itself against my skin, my bones, desperate to be unleashed upon the world, "that your High Lady made a sacrifice for her court—and we will move when the time is right."

Perhaps Lucien being Elain's mate would help—somehow. I'd find a way.

And then I'd assist my mate in ripping the Spring Court, Ianthe, those mortal queens, and the King of Hybern to shreds. Slowly.

"Until then?" Amren demanded. "What of the Cauldron—of the Book?"

"Until then," I said, staring toward the door as if I might see her walk through it, laughing and vibrant and beautiful, "we go to war."

CHAPTER 69

Feyre

Tamlin landed us in the gravel of the front drive.

I had forgotten how quiet it was here.

How small. Empty.

Spring bloomed—the air gentle and scented with roses.

Still lovely. But there were the front doors he'd sealed me behind. There was the window I'd banged on, trying to get out. A pretty, rose-covered prison.

But I smiled, head throbbing, and said through my tears, "I thought I'd never see it again."

Tamlin was just staring at me, as if not quite believing it. "I thought you would never, either."

And you sold us out—sold out every innocent in this land for that. All so you could have me back.

Love—love was a balm as much as it was a poison.

But it was love that burned in my chest. Right alongside the bond that the King of Hybern hadn't so much as touched, because he hadn't known how deep and far he'd have to delve to cleave it. To cleave me and Rhysand apart.

It had hurt—hurt like hell to have the bargain between us ended—and Rhys had done his job perfectly, his horror flawless. We had always been so good at playing together.

I had not doubted him, had not said anything but *Yes* when he'd taken me down to the temple the night before, and I'd sworn my vows. To him, to Velaris, to the Night Court.

And now . . . a gentle, loving stroke down that bond, concealed beneath that wasteland where the bargain had been. I sent a glimmer of feeling back down the line, wishing I could touch him, hold him, laugh with him.

But I kept those thoughts clear from my face. Kept anything but quiet relief from it as I leaned into Tamlin, sighing. "It feels—feels as if some of it was a dream, or a nightmare. But . . . But I remembered you. And when I saw you there today, I started clawing at it, fighting, because I knew it might be my only chance, and—"

"How did you break free of his control," Lucien said flatly from behind us.

Tamlin gave him a warning growl.

I'd forgotten he was there. My sister's mate. The Mother, I decided, did have a sense of humor. "I wanted it—I don't know how. I just wanted to break free of him, so I did."

We stared each other down, but Tamlin brushed a thumb over my shoulder. "Are—are you hurt?"

I tried not to bristle. I knew what he meant. That he thought Rhysand would do anything like that to anyone— "I—I don't know," I stammered. "I don't . . . I don't remember those things."

Lucien's metal eye narrowed, as if he could sense the lie.

But I looked up at Tamlin, and brushed my hand over his mouth. My bare, empty skin. "You're real," I said. "You freed me."

It was an effort not to turn my hands into claws and rip out his eyes. Traitor—liar. Murderer.

"You freed yourself," Tamlin breathed. He gestured to the house.

"Rest—and then we'll talk. I . . . need to find Ianthe. And make some things very, very clear."

"I—I want to be a part of it this time," I said, halting when he tried to herd me back into that beautiful prison. "No more . . . No more shutting me out. No more guards. Please. I have so much to tell you about them—bits and pieces, but . . . I can help. We can get my sisters back. Let me help."

Help lead you in the wrong direction. Help bring you and your court to your knees, and take down Jurian and those conniving, traitorous queens. And then tear Ianthe into tiny, tiny pieces and bury them in a pit no one can find.

Tamlin scanned my face, and finally nodded. "We'll start over. Do things differently. When you were gone, I realized . . . I'd been wrong. So wrong, Feyre. And I'm sorry."

Too late. Too damned late. But I rested my head on his arm as he slipped it around me and led me toward the house. "It doesn't matter. I'm home now."

"Forever," he promised.

"Forever," I parroted, glancing behind—to where Lucien stood in the gravel drive.

His gaze on me. Face hard. As if he'd seen through every lie.

As if he knew of the second tattoo beneath my glove, and the glamour I now kept on it.

As if he knew that they had let a fox into a chicken coop—and he could do nothing.

Not unless he never wanted to see his mate—Elain—again.

I gave Lucien a sweet, sleepy smile. So our game began.

We hit the sweeping marble stairs to the front doors of the manor.

And so Tamlin unwittingly led the High Lady of the Night Court into the heart of his territory.

ACKNOWLEDGMENTS

Thank you to the following people who make my life blessed beyond all measure:

To my husband, Josh: You got me through this year. (Through many years before it, but this one in particular.) I don't have the words to describe how much I love you, and how grateful I am for all that you do. For the countless meals you cooked so I didn't have to stop writing; for the hundreds of dishes you washed afterward so I could run back into my office and keep working; for the hours of dog-walking, especially those early mornings, just so I could get some sleep . . . This book is now a *real* book because of you. Thank you for carrying me when I was too weary, for wiping away my tears when my heart was heavy, and for coming with me on so many adventures around the world.

To Annie, who can't read this, but who deserves credit, anyway: Every second with you is a gift. Thank you for making a fairly solitary job not the slightest bit lonely—and for the laughter and joy and love you've brought into my life. Love you, baby pup.

To Susan Dennard, my Threadsister and *anam cara*: Pretty sure I'm a broken record at this point, but *thank you* for being a friend worth waiting for, and for the fun, truly epic times we've had together. To Alex Bracken, Erin Bowman, Lauren Billings, Christina Hobbs, Victoria Aveyard, Jennifer L. Armentrout, Gena Showalter, and Claire Legrand: I'm so lucky to call you guys my friends. I adore you all.

To my agent, Tamar Rydzinski: What would I do without you? You've been my rock, my guiding star, and my fairy godmother from the very beginning. Seven books later, I still don't have the words to express my gratitude. To my editor, Cat Onder: Working with you on these books has been a highlight of my career. Thank you for your wisdom, your kindness, and your editorial brilliance.

To my phenomenal teams at Bloomsbury worldwide and CAA—Cindy Loh, Cristina Gilbert, Jon Cassir, Kathleen Farrar, Nigel Newton, Rebecca McNally, Natalie Hamilton, Sonia Palmisano, Emma Hopkin, Ian Lamb, Emma Bradshaw, Lizzy Mason, Courtney Griffin, Erica Barmash, Emily Ritter, Grace Whooley, Eshani Agrawal, Nick Thomas, Alice Grigg, Elise Burns, Jenny Collins, Linette Kim, Beth Eller, Diane Aronson, Emily Klopfer, Melissa Kavonic, Donna Mark, John Candell, Nicholas Church, Adiba Oemar, Hermione Lawton, Kelly de Groot, and the entire foreign rights team—it's an honor to know and work with you. Thank you for making my dreams come true. To Cassie Homer: Thank you for *everything*. You are an absolute delight.

To my family (especially my parents): I love you to the moon and back.

To Louisse Ang, Nicola Wilksinson, Elena Yip, Sasha Alsberg, Vilma Gonzalez, Damaris Cardinali, Alexa Santiago, Rachel Domingo, Jamie Miller, Alice Fanchiang, and the Maas Thirteen: your generosity, friendship, and support mean the world to me.

And, lastly, to my readers: You guys are the greatest. The actual greatest. None of this would have been possible without *you*. Thank you from the very bottom of my heart for all that you do for me and my books.

FEYRE'S STORY CONTINUES IN . . .

READ ON FOR A SNEAK PEEK AT THE NEXT BOOK IN THIS ELECTRIFYING SERIES.

The painting was a lie.

A bright, pretty lie, bursting with pale pink blooms and fat beams of sunshine.

I'd begun it yesterday, an idle study of the rose garden lurking beyond the open windows of the studio. Through the tangle of thorns and satiny leaves, the brighter green of the hills rolled away into the distance.

Incessant, unrelenting spring.

If I'd painted this glimpse into the court the way my gut had urged me, it would have been flesh-shredding thorns, flowers that choked off the sunlight for any plants smaller than them, and rolling hills stained red.

But each brushstroke on the wide canvas was calculated; each dab and swirl of blending colors meant to portray not just idyllic spring, but a sunny disposition as well. Not too happy, but gladly, finally healing from horrors I carefully divulged.

I supposed that in the past weeks, I had crafted my demeanor as intricately as one of these paintings. I supposed that if I had also chosen to show myself as I truly wished, I would have been adorned with flesh-shredding talons, and hands that choked the life out of those now in my company. I would have left the gilded halls stained red.

But not yet.

Not yet, I told myself with every brushstroke, with every move I'd made these weeks. Swift revenge helped no one and nothing but my own, roiling rage.

Even if every time I spoke to them, I heard Elain's sobbing as she was forced into the Cauldron. Even if every time I looked at them, I saw Nesta fling that finger at the King of Hybern in a death-promise. Even if every time I scented them, my nostrils were again full of the tang of Cassian's blood as it pooled on the dark stones of that bone-castle.

The paintbrush snapped between my fingers.

I'd cleaved it in two, the pale handle damaged beyond repair.

Cursing under my breath, I glanced to the windows, the doors. This place was too full of watching eyes to risk throwing it in the rubbish bin.

I cast my mind around me like a net, trawling for any others near enough to witness, to be spying. I found none.

I held my hands before me, one half of the brush in each palm.

For a moment, I let myself see past the glamour that concealed the tattoo on my right hand and forearm. The markings of my true heart. My true title.

High Lady of the Night Court.

Half a thought had the broken paintbrush going up in flames.

The fire did not burn me, even as it devoured wood and brush and paint.

When it was nothing but smoke and ash, I invited in a wind that swept them from my palms and out the open windows.

For good measure, I summoned a breeze from the garden to snake through the room, wiping away any lingering tendril of smoke, filling it with the musty, suffocating smell of roses.

Perhaps when my task here was done, I'd burn this manor to the ground, too. Starting with those roses.

Two approaching presences tapped against the back of my mind, and I snatched up another brush, dipping it in the closest swirl of paint, and lowered the invisible, dark snares I'd erected around this room to alert me of any visitors.

I was working on the way the sunlight illuminated the delicate veins in a rose petal, trying not to think of how I'd once seen it do the same to Illyrian wings, when the doors opened.

I made a good show of appearing lost in my work, hunching my shoulders a bit, angling my head. And made an even better show of slowly looking over my shoulder, as if the struggle to part myself from the painting was a true effort.

But the battle was the smile I forced to my mouth. To my eyes—the real tell of a smile's genuine nature. I'd practiced in the mirror. Over and over.

So my eyes easily crinkled as I gave a subdued yet happy smile to Tamlin.

To Lucien.

"Sorry to interrupt," Tamlin said, scanning my face for any sign of the shadows I remembered to occasionally fall prey to, the ones I wielded to keep him at bay when the sun sank beyond those foothills. "But I thought you might want to get ready for the meeting."

I made myself swallow. Lower the paintbrush. No more than the nervous, unsure girl I'd been long ago. "Is—you talked it over with Ianthe? She's truly coming?"

I hadn't seen her yet. The High Priestess who had betrayed my sisters to Hybern, betrayed *us* to Hybern.

And even if Rhysand's murky, swift reports through the mating bond had soothed some of my dread and terror . . . She was responsible for it. What had happened weeks ago.

It was Lucien who answered, studying my painting as if it held the proof I knew he was searching for. "Yes. She . . . had her reasons. She is willing to explain them to you."

Perhaps along with her reasons for laying her hands on whatever males she pleased, whether they wished her to or not. For doing it to Rhys, and Lucien.

I wondered what Lucien truly made of it. And the fact that the collateral in her friendship with Hybern had wound up being *his* mate. Elain.

We had not spoken of Elain save for once, the day after I'd returned.

Despite what Jurian implied regarding how my sisters will be treated by Rhysand, I had told him, *despite what the Night Court is like*, *they won't hurt Elain or Nesta like that—not yet. Rhysand has more creative ways to harm them.*

Lucien still seemed to doubt it.

But then again, I had also implied, in my own "gaps" of memory, that perhaps I had not received the same creativity or courtesy.

That they believed it so easily, that they thought Rhysand would ever force someone . . . I added the insult to the long, long list of things to repay them for.

I set down the brush and pulled off the paint-flecked smock, carefully laying it on the stool I'd been perched on for two hours now.

"I'll go change," I murmured, flicking my loose braid over a shoulder.

Tamlin nodded, monitoring my every movement as I neared them. "The painting looks beautiful."

"It's nowhere near done," I said, dredging up that girl who had shunned praise and compliments, who had wanted to go unnoticed. "It's still a mess."

Frankly, it was some of my best work, even if its soullessness was only apparent to me.

"I think we all are," Tamlin offered with a tentative smile.

I reined in the urge to roll my eyes, and returned his smile, brushing my hand over his shoulder as I passed.

Lucien was waiting outside my new bedroom when I emerged ten minutes later.

It had taken me two days to stop going to the old one—to turn right at the top of the stairs and not left. But there was nothing in that old bedroom.

I'd looked into it once, the day after I returned.

Shattered furniture; shredded bedding; clothes strewn about as if he'd gone looking for me inside the armoire. No one, it seemed, had been allowed in to clean.

But it was the vines—the thorns—that had made it unlivable. My old bedroom had been overrun with them. They'd curved and slithered over the walls, entwined themselves amongst the debris. As if they'd crawled off the trellises beneath my windows, as if a hundred years had passed and not months.

That bedroom was now a tomb.

I gathered the soft pink skirts of my gauzy dress in a hand and shut the bedroom door behind me. Lucien remained leaning against the door across from mine.

His room.

I didn't doubt he'd ensured I now stayed across from him. Didn't doubt that the metal eye he possessed was always turned toward my own chambers, even while he slept.

"I'm surprised you're so calm, given your promises in Hybern," Lucien said by way of greeting.

The promise I'd made to kill the human queens, the King of Hybern, Jurian, and Ianthe for what they'd done to my sisters. To my friends.

"You yourself said Ianthe had her reasons. Furious as I might be, I can hear her out."

I had not told Lucien of what I knew regarding her true nature. It would mean explaining that Rhys had thrown her out of his own home, that Rhys had done it to defend himself and the members of his court, and it would raise too many questions, undermine too many carefully crafted lies that had kept him and his court—*my* court—safe.

Though I wondered if, after Velaris, it was even necessary. Our enemies knew of the city, knew it was a place of good and peace. And had tried to destroy it at the first opportunity.

The guilt for the attack on Velaris after Rhys had revealed it to those human queens would haunt my mate for the rest of our immortal lives.

"She's going to spin a story that you'll want to hear," Lucien warned.

I shrugged, heading down the carpeted, empty hall. "I can decide for myself. Though it sounds like you've already chosen not to believe her."

He fell into step beside me. "She dragged two innocent women into this."

"She was working to ensure Hybern's alliance held strong."

Lucien halted me with a hand around my elbow.

I allowed it because *not* allowing it, winnowing the way I'd done in the woods those months ago, or using an Illyrian defensive maneuver to knock him on his ass, would ruin my ruse. "You're smarter than that."

I studied the broad, tan hand wrapped around my elbow. Then I met one eye of russet and one of whirring gold.

Lucien breathed, "Where is he keeping her?"

I knew who he meant.

I shook my head. "I don't know. Rhysand has a hundred places where they could be, but I doubt he'd use any of them to hide Elain, knowing that I'm aware of them."

"Tell me anyway. List all of them."

"You'll die the moment you set foot in his territory."

"I survived well enough when I found you."

"You couldn't see that he had me in thrall. You let him take me back." Lie, lie, lie.

But the hurt and guilt I expected weren't there. Lucien slowly released his grip. "I need to find her."

"You don't even know Elain. The mating bond is just a physical reaction overriding your good sense."

"Is that what it did to you and Rhys?"

A quiet, dangerous question. But I made fear enter my eyes, let myself drag up memories of the Weaver, the Carver, the Middengard Wyrm so that old terror drenched my scent. "I don't want to talk about that," I said, my voice a rasping wobble.

A clock chimed on the main level. I sent a silent prayer of thanks to the Mother and launched into a quick walk. "We'll be late."

Lucien only nodded. But I felt his gaze on my back, fixed right on my spine, as I headed downstairs. To see Ianthe.

And at last decide how I was going to shred her into pieces.

The High Priestess looked exactly as I remembered, both in those memories Rhys had shown me and in my own daydreamings of using the talons hidden beneath my nails to carve out her eyes, then her tongue, then open up her throat.

My rage had become a living thing inside my chest, an echoing heartbeat that soothed me to sleep and stirred me to waking. I quieted it as I stared at Ianthe across the formal dining table, Tamlin and Lucien flanking me.

She still wore the pale hood and silver circlet set with its limpid blue stone.

Like a Siphon—the jewel in its center reminded me of Azriel's and Cassian's Siphons. And I wondered if, like the Illyrian warriors', the jewel somehow helped shape an unwieldy gift of magic into something more refined, deadlier. She had never removed it—but then again, I had never seen Ianthe summon any greater power than igniting a ball of faelight in a room.

The High Priestess lowered her teal eyes to the dark wood table, the hood casting shadows on her perfect face. "I wish to begin by saying how truly sorry I am. I acted out of a desire to . . . to grant what I believed you perhaps yearned for but did not dare voice, while also keeping our allies in Hybern satisfied with our allegiance."

Pretty, poisoned lies. But finding her true motive . . . I'd been waiting these weeks for this meeting. Had spent these weeks pretending to convalesce, pretending to *heal* from the horrors I'd survived at Rhysand's hands.

"Why would I ever wish for my sisters to endure that?" My voice came out trembling, cold.

Ianthe lifted her head, scanning my unsure, if not a bit aloof, face. "So you could be with them forever. And if Lucien had discovered that Elain was his mate beforehand, it would have been . . . devastating to realize he'd only have a few decades."

The sound of Elain's name on her lips sent a snarl rumbling up my throat. But I leashed it, falling into that mask of pained quiet, the newest in my arsenal.

Lucien answered, "If you expect our gratitude, you'll be waiting a while, Ianthe."

Tamlin shot him a warning look—both at the words and the tone. Perhaps Lucien would kill Ianthe before I had the chance, just for the horror she'd put his mate through that day.

"No," Ianthe breathed, eyes wide, the perfect picture of remorse and guilt. "No, I don't expect gratitude in the least. Or forgiveness. But understanding . . . This is my home, too." She lifted a slender hand clad in silver rings and bracelets to encompass the room, the manor. "We have all had to make alliances we didn't believe we'd ever forge—perhaps unsavory ones, yes, but . . . Hybern's force is too great to stop. It now can only be weathered like any other storm." A glance toward Tamlin. "We have worked so hard to prepare ourselves for Hybern's inevitable arrival—all these months. I made a grave mistake, and I will always regret any pain I caused, but let us continue this good work together. Let us find a way to ensure our lands and people survive."

"At the cost of how many others?" Lucien demanded.

Again, that warning look from Tamlin. But Lucien ignored him.

"What I saw in Hybern," Lucien said, gripping the arms of his chair hard enough that the carved wood groaned. "Any promises he made of peace and immunity . . ." He halted, as if remembering that Ianthe might very well feed this back to the king. He loosened his grip on the chair, his long fingers flexing before settling on the arms again. "We have to be careful."

"We will be," Tamlin promised. "But we've already agreed to certain conditions. Sacrifices. If we break apart now . . . even with Hybern as our ally, we have to present a solid front. Together."

He still trusted her. Still thought that Ianthe had merely made a bad call. Had no idea what lurked beneath the beauty, the clothes, and the pious incantations.

But then again, that same blindness kept him from realizing what prowled beneath my skin as well. Ianthe bowed her head again. "I will endeavor to be worthy of my friends."

Lucien seemed to be trying very, very hard not to roll his eyes.

But Tamlin said, "We'll all try."

That was his new favorite word: *try*.

I only swallowed, making sure he heard it, and nodded slowly, keeping my eyes on Ianthe. "Don't ever do anything like that again."

A fool's command—one she'd expected me to make, from the quickness with which she nodded. Lucien leaned back in his seat, refusing to say anything else.

"Lucien is right, though," I blurted, the portrait of concern. "What of the people in this court during this conflict?" I frowned at Tamlin. "They were brutalized by Amarantha—I'm not sure how well they will endure living beside Hybern. They have suffered enough."

Tamlin's jaw tightened. "Hybern has promised that our people shall remain untouched and undisturbed." *Our* people. I nearly scowled—even as I nodded again in understanding. "It was a part of our . . . bargain." When he'd sold out all of Prythian, sold out everything decent and good in himself, to *retrieve* me. "Our people will be safe when Hybern arrives. Though I've sent out word that families should . . . relocate to the eastern part of the territory. For the time being."

Good. At least he'd considered those potential casualties—at least he cared that much about his people, understood what sorts of sick games Hybern liked to play and that he might swear one thing but mean another. If he was already moving those most at risk during this conflict out of the way . . . It made my work here all the easier. And east—a bit of information I tucked away. If east was safe, then the west . . . Hybern would indeed be coming from that direction. Arriving there.

Tamlin blew out a breath. "That brings me to the other reason behind this meeting."

I braced myself, schooling my face into bland curiosity, as he declared, "The first delegation from Hybern arrives tomorrow." Lucien's golden skin paled. Tamlin added, "Jurian will be here by noon."

I'd barely heard a whisper of Jurian these past weeks—hadn't seen the resurrected human commander since that night in Hybern.

Jurian had been reborn through the Cauldron using the hideous remnants of him that Amarantha had hoarded as trophies for five hundred years, his soul trapped and aware within his own magically preserved eye. He was mad—had gone mad long before the King of Hybern had resurrected him to lead the human queens down a path of ignorant submission.

Tamlin and Lucien had to know. Had to have seen that gleam in Jurian's eyes.

But . . . they also did not seem to entirely mind that the King of Hybern possessed the Cauldron—that it was capable of cleaving this world apart. Starting with the wall. The only thing standing between the gathering, lethal Fae armies and the vulnerable human lands below.

No, that threat certainly didn't seem to keep Lucien or Tamlin awake at night. Or from inviting these monsters into their home.

Tamlin had promised upon my return that I was to be included in the planning, in every meeting. And he was true to his word when he explained that Jurian would arrive with two other commanders from Hybern, and I would be present for it. They indeed wished to survey the wall, to test for the perfect spot to rend it once the Cauldron had recovered its strength.

Turning my sisters into Fae, apparently, had drained it.

My smugness at the fact was short-lived.

My first task: learn where they planned to strike, and how long the Cauldron required to return to its full capacity. And then smuggle that information to Rhysand and the others.

I took extra care dressing the next day, after sleeping fitfully thanks to a dinner with a guilt-ridden Ianthe, who went to excessive lengths to kiss my ass and Lucien's. The priestess apparently wished to wait until the Hybern commanders were settled before making her appearance. She'd cooed about wanting to ensure they had the chance to get to know us before she intruded, but one look at Lucien told me that he and I, for once, agreed: she had likely planned some sort of grand entrance.

It made little difference to me—to my plans.

Plans that I sent down the mating bond the next morning, words and images tumbling along a night-filled corridor.

I did not dare risk using the bond too often. I had communicated with Rhysand only once since I'd arrived. Just once, in the hours after I'd walked into my old bedroom and spied the thorns that had conquered it.

It had been like shouting across a great distance, like speaking underwater. *I am safe and well*, I'd fired down the bond. *I'll tell you what I know soon.* I'd waited, letting the words travel into the dark. Then I'd asked, *Are they alive? Hurt?*

I didn't remember the bond between us being so hard to hear, even when I'd dwelled on this estate and he'd used it to see if I was still breathing, to make sure my despair hadn't swallowed me whole.

But Rhysand's response had come a minute later. *I love you. They are alive. They are healing.*